THE
INCENDIARY'S
TRAIL

THE INCENDIARY'S TRAIL

JAMES MCCREET

Macmillan New Writing

First published 2009 by Macmillan New Writing
an imprint of Pan Macmillan Ltd
Pan Macmillan, 20 New Wharf Road, London N1 9RR
Basingstoke and Oxford
Associated companies throughout the world
www.panmacmillan.com

ISBN 978-0-230-73627-6

A CIP catalogue record for this book is available from
the British Library.

Typeset by InType Libra, London
Printed and bound in the UK by CPI Mackays, Chatham ME5 8TD

For my wife Moniczka

Kocham cie

If every man who receives a cheque for a story which owes its springs to Poe were to pay tithe to a monument for the master, he would have a pyramid as big as that of Cheops.

— Sir Arthur Conan Doyle

ONE

'*Murder! Murder! Mur-der!*'

A ragged-looking boy ran shouting from the darkness towards the larger gaslit streets of Lambeth.

And silence again filled the nameless alley from which he had emerged. Its cobbles were greasy with night rain and its gutters stopped with soil. A weak halo of moisture hung about the bare flame of the gaslight at its entrance, though the open door of the house was in shadow. Close by, the river breathed mud.

No sign of interest yet stirred. Any common fight or drunken disagreement might yield its cry of 'Murder!' It was an area where such things were common enough. Only a fool, or a drunk, attended cries of murder before dawn in this place.

Or a policeman. The sound of boots clattered from the main street, echoing among dank brickwork and sagging timbers: Police Constable Cullen, a burly six-footer holding his bullseye lamp before him as he ran behind the boy back towards the house. They approached the low lodging house and paused, panting, at the door.

Here, the boy drew back, unwilling to proceed further

into the house. If he shivered, it was horror rather than cold that animated his frame, fear rather than hunger that swirled in his stomach. The policeman touched his slender shoulder.

'All right, lad. You stay here and direct the other officers when they come. You can do that, can't you? Good lad.'

The boy wrapped his arms around himself and looked to the main street. PC Cullen held up his lamp and entered.

The cramped hallway smelled of damp and the previous evening's meat and potatoes. The kitchen to his left was empty, its grate just ashes at this hour and the plates still on the table, unwashed. Muffled sobs, low voices and the shuffle of feet came from an upstairs room.

There were no gaslights in this squalid tenement – only candles and oil. The beam of the constable's lamp cast a flickering light up the narrow, uncarpeted staircase. He coughed loudly to announce his presence.

'Police! I am coming up the stairs.'

A thin, reedy wail started in the room above: an inhuman sound made only by the desperate, the insane and beasts. It raised the very hairs on PC Cullen's neck and crawled with icy fingers up his scalp into his stovepipe hat. He patted the truncheon at his hip to be sure of its presence. Then he drew it.

Footfalls skittered hollowly like rats in the wall. From the top of the stairs, he saw a hallway and an open door. Within, he could see a single oil lamp standing on a table by a peeling wall. A dull painting of fields and farm workers hung askew on the wall. The place was clearly little more than a cheap lodging house – albeit a curiously uncrowded one.

Whispers emanated from the room and sent fresh shivers across PC Cullen's back. His knuckles whitened on the truncheon.

2

'I am entering!'

He stepped into the room with his lamp held high and flashed its beam rapidly about him. Immediately, he became aware of a group of people standing in the shadows against the far wall: perhaps half a dozen of them. Their static nature and collective breathing unnerved him. He turned his lamp full upon them and beheld . . . a vision that dealt a hammer blow to his heart.

'*O! O!* What is this infernal place? L— protect me!'

The beam from his lamp jerked crazily across their faces: a spectacle he had never before witnessed – a tableau of horror that defied reality but which could not be denied. He backed towards the door, fumbling for his rattle as his eyes again beheld what they would not believe. The faces – if one could call them such – were now directed as one at another spot to his side. He turned swiftly with the lamp, expecting an assault.

'*O! O!* In the name of G—! O! G— protect me!'

As the seated figure fell under the beam of the lamp, the walls seemed to crowd in upon him. There, in the stark and emotionless eye of the light, was not a human thing but a hideous waxwork. The blood, however – it's unmistakable metallic tang and its dull glistening – was real enough He turned and banged furiously down the stairs into the street, where he set the rattle going with all the energy he could muster, calling out:

'Murder! Murder! Murder!'

Still shaking, he began muttering to himself and rubbing his eyes, as those benighted residents of Bethlem Hospital are wont to do:

'I have never seen . . . O! It is burned on my brain even when I close my eyes!'

A clatter of boots was heard at the corner and two other police officers approached the grim alley with truncheons drawn. Breathing heavily, the taller one spoke:

'What is it, Cully? A murder? You look as pale as—'

Cullen removed his hat and wiped his face with a handkerchief. He rested a supporting hand against the doorframe. His colleagues looked from one to the other with foreboding: John Cullen was not known for his sensitive nature. When he spoke, it was with a constricted throat.

'Corbett – go . . . go to the watch house and fetch the surgeon. Tell the inspector . . . tell him there's been a murder in this dwelling. PC Hamilton – we must guard this place until reinforcements arrive. There is going to be a sensation about this one and no mistake. O! I feel quite—'

And here the doughty PC Cullen vomited. If it were not for the extreme nature of what he had witnessed, he might have been reprimanded for such behaviour while on duty. He would not be the last to react thus.

By now, lights were appearing at windows, curtains were twitching and the first weak streaks of dawn were struggling through an overcast sky, barred by the manufacturer's chimneys. Smoke started to billow brown and yellow from houses as the city began to wake, though the miserable streets remained dark.

Not a soul could be seen, but the news was already spreading. The young boy who had first heralded the crime was gone. Husbands spoke to wives, mothers to children, neighbours to neighbours. And as the early workers ventured out into the metropolis with crusts of bread in their pockets and hot tea in their bellies, they spoke to their workmates. People were coming – first from the surrounding streets, then from surrounding districts. They came hungry for news, that currency of conversation.

By the time Sergeant George Williamson of the Detective Force and Police Surgeon McLeod had arrived, there was a handful of people being prevented from entering by PCs Cullen and Hamilton. Constable Cullen, who knew of Mr Williamson only by rumour and reputation, recognized him immediately.

The detective's pockmarked face bespoke a near fatal acquaintance with smallpox that lent a perpetual scowl to his features, while his legs were bowed slightly from his years of walking out in all weathers as a beat policeman. Even in his stovepipe, he was visibly at the lower height limitation for the force and, in his civilian clothes, he might have been an artisan of some kind – a watchmaker, perhaps, or a skilled tailor who could take the measure of a man with a glance. To him, an eighth of an inch was as critical as a yard. He was a hero to many constables.

PC Cullen spoke with care: 'Nobody has entered or left since I arrived, sir. I believe this is the only door. There is a dead, er . . . woman upstairs and a number of, er, people in the room. They are—'

'Has the property been searched, PC Cullen? Have you made a search of the surrounding area for a weapon? Have you questioned the people upstairs or the local residents for what was heard or seen about the time of the crime?'

'No, sir . . . I have been standing guard here.'

'Well, see to it, PC Cullen! Enquire of these people what they may have witnessed and search the streets for any likely weapon or evidence of a crime. The murderer could very well be one of these people standing here, couldn't he? Or she.'

At this revelation, a murmur went up from the people standing about the alleyway. They moved apart and looked at each other with new suspicion.

'Yes, sir!'

'Now – let us see the scene of the crime.'

Mr Williamson held up his lamp (noting immediately that the door lock was damaged) and entered, closely followed by Dr McLeod. They had seen murders enough to walk without fear up the narrow staircase to that room above. As he ascended, the detective directed his lamp at the treads for signs of blood or anything dropped by the fleeing murderer – if indeed he had fled. It was difficult to see anything but the coarsest detail in the gloom and a man could easily hide himself in the shadows.

They turned into the open room at the top and Mr Williamson shone his lamp at the people still cowering against one wall. They were seemingly unmoved since PC Cullen's entrance. Four years on the beat and two more as a detective had not prepared him for what he saw.

The first face to appear in the lamplight was up in the roof timbers. The man must have been seven or eight feet tall and possessed of shoulders like an ox. A huge prow of a chin projected from his face as he stared dumbly at the lamp and his arms hung limply by his side. But for his immensity, he could have been a child, admonished and sent to stand in the corner.

Next to the giant was a man of average height and build, but without a face – or rather it was a horribly disfigured face which appeared to have folded in on itself, sucking his features into a fleshy cleft and twisting his mouth into a gash of awkwardly protruding teeth. His tiny black eyes darted nervously about him and his hands reached up – too late –

to cover his shame. A fervid tongue licked rapidly at the contorted lips.

Beside this man was a woman of gigantic bulk sitting in a huge chair that must have been made for her. Rolls of pudding-like fat supported her head where a neck should have been and her arms sprouted from her vast body like two enormous air-filled bladders. They twitched obscenely like the fins of a large fish out of water. By her leg, some kind of dog cowered. But . . . no, this was no dog. It was a child of about seven whose entire countenance was covered in hair, right to the very eyeballs. Incisors glistened between her lips as she flinched away from the light and whimpered in a canine fashion.

Still another appeared to be a child attired in the garb of an adult: a tiny suit and waistcoat complete with a minuscule top hat. He (if it was a he) looked frankly back at the detective, seemingly unashamed and unabashed.

Detective Williamson stood rigid. His province was the law, but it seemed that here the very laws of Nature had been violated. Dr McLeod, who knew professionally of such things, was at once repelled and fascinated by the spectacle.

'A freak show, Williamson! We have stumbled on the residents of a freak show. I believe I have read of it in *the Times*: "Dr Zwigoff's Anatomical Wonders", they call it. It's been at Vauxhall Gardens the last fortnight. But where is the . . . O! Good L—!'

The bullseye lamp settled on the figure of a seated young woman – a girl, really – the corpse.

Girl . . . or girls? Two red-haired heads presented themselves; two slender necks descended to one body with two arms and two legs. But only the left throat bore a gaping wound that had emptied a body's worth of blood over the front of her dress, soaking it to an almost uniform black in the light of the police lamp. McLeod approached the body with some trepidation.

'Well, I have not seen the likes of *this* since the London visit of the Siamese twins, Chang and Eng,' he said with the forced jocularity used by a surgeon instructing a tremulous student. 'A real rarity, Williamson: two spinal columns, joining . . .'

But the detective was barely listening. He looked ill at ease. Though confident amongst pickpockets and magsmen, bullies, procurers and drunks, nothing here was familiar to him. It was a world he had never ventured into – one of many worlds within the world of London. Still, there was a procedure to be followed.

'Is she dead, doctor?'

McLeod reached out to feel for a pulse, hesitating briefly before choosing the unharmed neck. He held his lamp to the wound.

'Hmm. Dead. A single strike, probably with a razor. Made with extreme force. It has severed the artery, of course. The body is still warm. The killer cannot have gone far, Mr Williamson. Perhaps your men will catch him hereabouts if they are sharp. And if he is not already here among us.'

The detective looked from the body to the other people in the room. Though fearful in aspect, they were unthreatening. Indeed, he reflected, they had more to fear from the world than it from them. Now they huddled together against the wall like rats before a dog. He addressed them:

'You have nothing to fear, unless you are part of this grisly crime. I will conceal you from the crowds and protect you from their gaze. And I will question each of you in turn. Who is the master here? Where is Dr Zwigoff?'

Fearful faces looked back at him. From among their number, the tiny figure emerged: a strangely proportioned homunculus no bigger than a child, but with all the facial attributes of a man. When he spoke, it was with a high, rasping voice:

'Henry Coggins is our protector, sir. He styles himself Dr Zwigoff, but he is no doctor that I know of. He is out drinking, sir. He often returns at dawn.'

'Does he? Well, I will be speaking to him also if he returns and proves able to converse. We will remove the body and begin questioning directly. But first, I believe we would all appreciate a cup of hot tea. Dr McLeod, we must move everyone out of this room to preserve it intact. We will adjourn to the kitchen.'

Outside, the handful of people had grown. Others had heard the stories, which had now achieved levels of horror barely credible even to those who wanted to believe. They spoke not only of a murder, but of many-headed monsters and giants, demons and wolf-children – things all too easily believed by those superstitious folk from the country or those raised on the myths of the city. They muttered the latest 'knowledge':

'It is the secret progeny of a priest and a nun, hidden from human sight!'

'It is a warning from Heaven against our Sin – the Apocalypse is near.'

'It is Spring-Heeled Jack, returned with others of his kind!'

The clamour for news was a hunger among them. Here, on their very doorstep, the most outrageous crime of the decade (of the century, even) had been committed: the brutal, bloody murder of a human abomination – one of many such creatures lurking in a den of hideous natural accidents.

They could not know then, of course, as they puffed on their clay pipes and shuffled their feet for warmth, that it was merely the first in a chain of events that would shock and fascinate the city as never before, setting it alight like one of those periodical conflagrations that reduce all to ashes. It was the spark to an inferno that would be fanned uncontrollably by the winds of rumour, speculation and print – a story as famous as the city that bore it.

TWO

London: the greatest city on earth, the beginning and end to numberless journeys, and the setting for infinite stories – the modern Babylon.

Should the provincial or rural reader cast an eye over the metropolis from the heights of St Paul's, he would see more factory chimneys than spires, more ships' masts than chimneys. Moored there at St Katharine's, there at the East and West Indias, there at the old London docks and the Thames Pool are the ships of the world, those copper-sheathed brigs and cutters, those packets, colliers, schooners and barks listed daily in that great organ, *the Times*. Here is the *Spartan* of St Domingo, the *Eagle* of St John's, the *United Kingdom* of Honduras, and the *Jane May* bound directly for the Barbadoes.

In those thick-walled warehouses and cellars is stored the produce of the globe: spices of India, tobacco of Virginia, rum and sugar from the Indies. In musty vaults lay rows of bottles, bales of tea, boxes of pungent horn and hides, bolts of silk and bags of cotton. The songs of sailors ring out as barrels roll and tackle takes the strain of multitudinous cargoes. Negroes, Chinese, and coffee-skinned Arabs haul on ropes or wait for the tide to carry them away to sea.

From his vantage of St Paul's, the visiting reader would hear the city speak: the infernal, interminable rattle of wheels and hooves on roads, the street seller's yells, the hammering and digging of ceaseless construction on new streets, new sewers, new railway lines and warehouses. And above this entire clamour, the noise of the people themselves: a million and more souls inhabiting the streets and clogging the bridges. The solicitors, tidewaiters, fellmongers, patterers, coal-whippers, watermen, milliners, lightermen, costermongers, beggars and police. Not only English, but Italians with their greased hair and earrings; robed Hindoos of India; magdalenes of Spain, Belgium and France – a veritable glossolalia rising from those busy thoroughfares.

Let us descend there from our observation point, pinch our noses and enter the same air: thick with smoke, pungent with equine effluvia and scented with the city's industries. The vagaries of the wind evoke the unspeakable tannery, the yeasty brewery, the foundry, the distillery and, of course, the river, whose muddy swell has fattened London since Hadrian's time and before.

This multiplying behemoth consumes all who approach it, reaching ever outwards with exploratory tentacles of streets, encircling villages and turning green to grey. Unsleeping, it regenerates from its very detritus: picked clean by ragpickers, mudlarks, pure-finders and dredgers – all of whom comb the streets and rivers to make anew what was discarded.

Who can know the city? Who can map it? They may try, but it challenges comprehension and encompassment like the Paradox of Zeno. It is divided by the river into Middlesex and Surrey, north and south, then cut further, into quarters, by the affluent west and working east. The parishes come next, partitioning the streets by church and parochial finance; then the wards and police divisions, the Ragged School boundaries and the contracts allocating dust collection. Even the Thames itself is chopped and segmented by the bridges from west to east.

One may map the many streets, but not see them. Yes, we know broad Oxford-street and Regents-street with their bustle, clatter and advertising. We know the quiet and arboreal avenues of the west where carriages ride on straw and the fine people dress in silks for the Season. But the shoulder-wide alleys and foetid yards of the rookeries are invisible to almost all. For who would wander voluntarily into the shadows of St Giles or Bermondsey? Not even the police are willing to enter some uncharted cellars and courts of those *terrae incognitae*.

To cartographers and statisticians, such areas might well be blanks. The rookeries of London are cities within a city, a country within this country – but one barely touched by modernity, learning or religion. There, in their own world, they survive in wretched poverty and filth. Unlit streets of overflowing gutters and ramshackle tenements are home to multiple families, shoeless and dressed in rags. Not for these people the latest advances in science and the arts; they find their amusement at the dogfight, the penny gaff and the gin palace. No great future monuments for these people – merely the gaol, the river, transportation, the gallows and the grave.

And it is here among the rank odours of the manufactories and beside the slime-slick river steps that crime breeds like a contagion. Here are the coiners, cracksmen, pickpockets, bullies and prigs. Here are the marine stores and pawnbrokers where gentlemen's watches and ladies hand-kerchiefs find new homes. You will not see earnest tables in *the Times* documenting the fluctuations of 'business' in *these* markets, but crime is the epidemic feared by all of its readers . . . feared *and* craved.

For who attracts the attention of the newspaper and the broadsheets hawked in the street? Who is it that appears in the peep-shows, back-shows and dumb-shows? Who is the subject of the patterer that stands and recounts stories to the crowds? One may often read of Queen Victoria and Prince Albert, or venerate Lord Nelson and Mr Peel, but true renown is reserved for the names of Courvoisier, Greenacre, Rush and Mr Daniel Good:

Murderers!

Nothing galvanizes the metropolis like a murder. They are discussed earnestly in the clubs in the west, editorialized in the newspapers and recounted breathlessly on the omnibus. Though ignorant of world affairs, scripture, law or even their own written language, the common populace knows every detail of the latest murder – even more, perhaps, than the detectives who hunt the killers. Every detail, every splash, stab and gruesome fact is brought to light with equal shock and guilty pleasure. And until the bloody hand is discovered in their midst, while death hides in every unknown face, the people live in prolonged hiatus.

Then capture brings rapture. The visitor to London on the day of execution would think himself at Greenwich or Smithfield fairs rather than in front of Newgate prison. No coronation or victory brings such crowds as people flood to finally cast their eyes upon the face of the murderer of their imaginations. Only by seeing his death can the story be put to rest – at least in the present, for his fame will last for generations in print.

Like the miasma of cholera, the news of this recent crime spread by word of mouth: 'Have you heard? . . . A terrible murder in Lambeth . . . A horrible, inhuman act . . . monsters living together in an unholy coven . . . black magic and witchcraft here in the very heart of London.'

Naturally, the 'news' was embellished. Having not seen it for themselves, they pictured the scene in the peep-show theatres of their mind, fed on a legacy of shocking murders past. This one, as every one before it, was undoubtedly the worst, the most brutal, the most morally debased and bloody. Indeed, it had to be – for otherwise it would attract barely any attention at all in this city where murder is commonplace.

So this is London: a city divided and hidden, but with no discernible borders. It is both Jerusalem and Gomorrah. Charity bodies may catalogue and writers may research, but its secrets remain hidden. They arrive from the country and change their names; they are born and die unrecorded and nameless. The protean metropolis has many faces and disguises. Is that well-dressed fellow a gentleman shopping, or a professional pickpocket about his work? This woman descending from her carriage in black silks is beyond reproach as she tenders her counterfeit notes. Look closely at that leprous beggar . . . and discern that his 'sores' are manufactured from soap and vinegar.

The very mechanisms we use to know a man are here made nonsense. A change of clothes or accent, a letter of trust or a £100 banknote and the criminal is re-made a swell. Lord Russell no doubt had the utmost trust in the references of his valet Courvoisier, until the Frenchman killed him.

Might not every chambermaid, cook and butler hold a knife within the walls of one's home? Might not every pawn-broker be a blackmailer, every drinking partner a confidence trickster and every night-lurker an incendiary?

We may tabulate the minutest change in the wool trade, or the markets of Birmingham and Manchester. We hold the globe in the palm of our hands as we read of China, France and the United States. But who is to illuminate the shadows that hide our fear? Who can make visible the invisible and venture where no other dare go? Who?

I.

Some call me a 'penny-a-liner': a newspaperman. Others are less kind, preferring the epithets of scamp, blackguard, rapscallion or drunk. I am a writer, though they call me a fabulist and accuse me of mixing fiction and fact. They impugn even my style and the 'verbosity' of my copy. They do not know – and cannot comprehend – that the man on the street wants to *see* his story, wants to feel its cold fingers up his back and hear its footsteps echoing down dark streets.

In the newspapers, my pen is concise. In the broadsheets it is exclamatory. In my stories it becomes the very city itself. Who else can sniff out the facts as I can? Who else is at home in the public house, the dockyard, the watch house and the gaol cell? Only I can reveal the city to those who would see it, pulling aside the veils of smoke and darkness to light the anonymous courts. I seek out and find even those secrets that are not written in official ledgers. Everybody speaks, and I am there to listen. In this modern Hades, I am the Sybil to Virgil, the Virgil to Dante Alighieri. I follow the story wherever it may go, and I tell it.

This one has begun, and I am mindful of returning to it.

THREE

———•———

Daylight had finally come to illuminate that melancholy alley in Lambeth, though it still seemed in mourning. Leaden clouds hovered almost as low as the chimneys, clouds that were darkened further by the thick pall of smoke that had already begun to pour forth from a million hearths. The people gathered outside the lodging house had swelled, encouraged into an excitable state by rumour, and by the sensation that the accidental revelation of the body had caused.

Dr McLeod had had the unfortunate bicephaloid covered in a sheet and removed on a stretcher to his mortuary. As it was being transported from the house, however, the onlookers had surged forward to see the horror. In the *mêlée*, a curious hand had pulled away the sheet to reveal the two heads hanging limp, the blood-soaked dress and the gaping wound. They recoiled with a collective gasp, then rushed in anew to see what they dare not see.

Reinforcements had been sent for and now a line of 'bluebottles' stood guard before the house. Among them, only PC Cullen had seen the horror within, and the other constables deferred to him as he rallied them against the crowd:

'Move along there, Hamilton . . . Keep them away from that window, PC Birch! . . . Everybody move back now – *we are trying to conduct an investigation!*'

Inside, Detective Williamson had moved everyone to the downstairs kitchen to leave the murder scene as it was when the crime had been committed. The plain kitchen table was designated the interrogation space and the witnesses were called in turn as the detective was ready for them. He would have preferred to keep each testimony private, but the circumstances forbade it. A fire had been lit and more lamps brought to cast light on the proceeding . . . and what a scene was presented there.

With the hirsute child whimpering like a real dog, the vast woman had been manhandled down the stairs by the giant man and sturdy PC Cullen. She was now settled by the fire, stroking the child's head soothingly. The giant man had folded himself on to a chair, his knees higher than table height, and struck a quite ridiculous figure with his enormous hands about a mug of tea. Everything in his sphere was of childlike proportions, and indeed his very expression was one of great mental simplicity. Though possessed of the strength to crush a man's scull in his palm, he would evidently not harm a flower, unless by the clumsiness of his form. Meanwhile, the man with the twisted face sat slightly apart from the group and wore a cap low to conceal as much of his countenance as possible. He stared into the flames with an unfathomable emotion. Both he and the giant had claimed to have been asleep in the other room at the time of the murder, woken only by the cries following it.

Among the motley group, the most articulate thus far was the pygmy-like man who had first spoken to Williamson. His name was Mr Hardy, though he appeared theatrically under the *soubriquet* of 'Goliath'. Despite his diminutive nature, he was in every other respect like a man, albeit with a queer sense of compression natural to his size. He gave his testimony in a curious falsetto as the detective made notes:

'We retired to bed, as is our habit, at around midnight – the ladies in the one room and the gentlemen in the other. We are appearing at Vauxhall Gardens as you know, and it is quite exhausting to be the object of curious stares and exclamations. One never becomes accustomed to it, detective.

'Mr Coggins, our protector (as he likes to call himself), went out almost as soon as we had returned here in our covered carriage from Vauxhall. As I told you, it is his custom when we are in the city to be out all night at the public houses and gin palaces.'

Here, the detective raised a hand to pause the testimony and made a note. Then he went on: 'Excuse me – why was the lady with two . . . the lady—?'

'Her name was Eliza-Beth.'

'Thank you. Why was Eliza-Beth sitting while everyone else was asleep?'

'I believe she was writing a letter. She had received a letter the night before last and she may have been replying to it. At all accounts, she was sitting at the table in the early hours of Sunday when the killer struck.'

'There is no letter on the table now.'

'Perhaps the killer took it. I am not a policeman; I can only report what I believe to be true, detective.'

'And I thank you for it, Mr Hardy. Do you know of anyone here whom Eliza-Beth confided in, perhaps about the contents of the letter she received? Or where that letter might be now?'

'I know she kept the letter beside her bosom. She did not trust Mr Coggins with any of her possessions. As for a confidant, she shared secrets only with Eugenia, our "bearded lady".' The diminutive man indicated the huge woman.

'But she has no beard,' remarked Williamson.

'Indeed. But Mr Coggins likes her to wear a theatrical beard, her natural bulk being judged an insufficient "wonder" on its own account. The audience is more prone to believe the beard when they behold her size, or so Mr Coggins holds.'

'I perceive that you have no great respect for your protector.'

'He is an unspeakable man, but you see how we are. What life could we have on our own accounts? We are objects of derision, curiosity and abhorrence. We may not find any public employment or even walk in the street as others can. This is the only way we can live: among our own kind. What little dignity we possess together is superior to any we would earn alone.'

Detective Williamson nodded to himself sombrely and, as he wrote, raised a hand to touch the disfigurement of his own face. Mr Hardy noted the unconscious gesture with knowing smile.

'I thank you, sir, for your testimony,' said Mr Williamson. 'I will question Mr Coggins thoroughly when he returns, you can be sure. Now I must speak to the large lady here.'

'Eugenia. A poor pun, as I am sure you appreciate.'

'I'm sorry, I do not . . .'

'"Eugenia" comes from the Greek. It means "well born".'

'Oh, I see. Well . . . I thank you once more.'

With this, the detective turned the page in his notebook, made a new heading and carried his chair across to Eugenia,

'The Bearded Lady'. She filled her purpose-made chair as if poured into it and later set, like liquid pork fat. Upon closer inspection, her eyes – swollen and red from crying – peered like two gems from the soft upholstery of her face, and her whole frame was perpetually agitated, like gelatin, with a wheezy breathing. She fondled the head of the dog-child by her side with her pink and dimpled hand.

'Tell me, madam,' began the detective, 'did you see the murderer?'

'I was awoken by his cries, Constable.'

'"Sergeant", if you please. I am Detective Sergeant Williamson.'

'Oh, forgive me, m'lud. One policeman is as good as another to me.'

He waved away the observation impatiently. 'What was the nature of the cries you heard?'

'Well, I was sleeping in my chair. It is difficult to move me to a bed each night, as you might imagine, and, besides, I have grown accustomed to this chair of mine, which was manufactured especially for me by a renowned coach-maker of Long-acre. As strong as a carriage it is, and made of—'

'To the matter of the answer, please.'

'Oh, of course. I heard, "Oh, G—! A monster!" – then a scrabbling of footsteps. When I raised my head, I saw nothing. Nor did I hear the shoes of the man on the wooden stairs. He must have been eager to leave, I can tell you. I directly saw poor, poor Eliza twitching in her chair and raising hands to her neck . . . and . . . O! It was *her* shoes beating the floor in terror! And Beth was shrieking, "O! O! We are killed!"'

The immense lady descended once more into sobbing

and raised a sodden handkerchief to her eyes, dabbing it into each soft dimple of flesh.

Mr Williamson looked through his notes. 'Excuse me – who is Beth? I have no record . . .'

'Why, Beth is the other girl who was killed.'

'There was another murder here?'

Eugenia looked at the detective as if he were a fool. 'Eliza had her throat cut. Beth, her "sister", died as a consequence, for they shared the same heart, according to the doctors who frequently come to examine us. Poor Beth was killed as surely as Eliza, and that evil man has the burden of *two* murders on his head.'

'Oh, I see.' He made a note. 'And then what happened?'

'Well, of course, I could not easily get out of my chair to come to her aid, so I let forth a tremendous hue and cry. I have been a singer in my time and have a good pair of lungs. I almost brought down the rafters, I can tell you. That was when Mr Hardy was awakened and rushed to our room – too late, I fear. Her . . . her fingers were still clutching at her neck as the last drops of blood leaked from her body. Oh, I can see it now!'

'Did Beth offer any final words?'

'No, m'lud. She was past words.'

'Did anyone think to run out after the murderer?'

'Which one of us would venture on to the streets without causing a sensation? No, Mr Hardy woke the boy downstairs. We sent him to find a policeman. You know the rest.'

'There is a great deal I do not know, madam. Why, for instance, was nobody woken by the street-door lock being broken? Were not the others woken by the cries of the killer, or of Beth?'

'Well, I can't say, Commissioner. Maybe you are accustomed to sleeping in the isolation of your own bedroom, but when one lives only in boarding houses around the country, or in carriages and barns, one is able to sleep at the drop of a hat. It would take a locomotive to wake some of us here. As for the lock, I cannot say.'

Mr Williamson elected to overlook the promotion conferred on him by the lady, but made a further note in his book.

'What of the letter she received lately? Did Eliza-Beth intimate its contents to you?'

'She did indeed, but swore me to everlasting secrecy.'

'A woman is dead, madam. The secret you are bound to keep has passed with her to an everlasting realm and may hold the key to apprehending her murderer. Search your soul and ask if she would allow you to tell under the circumstances.'

'I gave my word I would never tell.'

'I understand. But I must warn you that I have no objection to having you transported through the public streets to the gaol where I will have you held until you reveal the facts that may catch a murderer.'

'You are a cruel man, detective. And with I so terribly upset by the murder . . .' The lady folded her ample arms across a voluminous chest, though the fingertips did not quite touch.

'I am a policeman in pursuit of a criminal. I will do all I can to protect you and your group – but I will not be obstructed in my duty. You have nobody's propriety to protect now that Eliza-Beth is deceased. Speak frankly.'

Mr Hardy, who had been following the whole conversation from the fireside, spoke up:

'Tell the detective what you know, Eugenia. Eliza-Beth would wish it.'

The dog-child nuzzled at her knee and Eugenia lowered a hand to fondle the child's ears. Then the lady's tear-moistened eyes raised heavenwards, as if in communication with the newly departed soul.

'Very well. Eliza-Beth had received a letter concerning her parentage. You may not realize, m'lud, that many of us here have no knowledge of our origins. At our birth, our aspect was such that our own parents rejected us, leaving us at the church or the hospital or the ash-heap. We are raised with-out the bonds of love – only the curious stare of the crowd. Eliza – poor, misguided girl – believed that her parents would one day return for her.'

'And the letter was from her parents?'

'From her mother. She said that she had followed Eliza-Beth's history since her birth and had never once stopped thinking of her. Doubtless she had come to see the show at Vauxhall and determined finally to approach her daughter after all these years. No date was given, but Eliza-Beth was in an ecstasy of joy at the prospect of once again meeting her mother.'

'Was there a return address?'

'I did not see the letter. Eliza-Beth kept it close to her heart at all times lest somebody take her one valuable pos-session. Rather, her second valuable possession.'

'Her *second* possession?'

'Why, yes. She wore a locket about her neck in which she treasured two locks of hair: one from her father and one from her mother – or so she believed and maintained. It was gold, but its value would have been equal to her had it been fashioned from lead.'

'I saw no locket about Eliza's neck.'

'They took it in turns to wear it, so jealous were they of its significance.'

'Neither was Beth wearing a locket.'

'Then the murderer took it, or it is lost in the house, for Eliza-Beth was never without it and would not yield it except in death. Even Mr Coggins was unable to get his hands on it, much as he tried.'

'I understand that Eliza-Beth was writing a letter when she was killed. Do you know how she was planning to send this letter if she had no return address?'

'I do not know. Perhaps she did have an address, or perhaps someone was going to collect it; we have many visiters here. Indeed, it was a visiter who delivered it here. Perhaps she was writing it merely for her own fancy.'

'Who delivered the letter?'

'I did not see the gentleman. He brought it to the street door and gave the boy a penny to bring it upstairs.'

'And where is this boy now?'

'If he is not downstairs at this moment, I have no idea.'

'Hmm. You spoke of visiters. What visiters do you have in this place?'

At this moment, however, the questioning was interrupted by the return of Mr Henry Coggins. A commotion was heard from outside the door and the baritone of PC Cullen insisting, 'No admittance here!' A scuffle of feet was heard, and the repeated phrase, 'This is my abode! *Let me through!*'

'I apprehend that Mr Coggins is returned,' muttered Mr Hardy. A flutter of reaction went through the group. Then the man himself burst into the room, hatless.

He was a diminutive figure whose immediate identifying

characteristic was the preposterous blond peruke that sat askew on his head, perhaps knocked that way by the scuffle outside. He was perspiring freely and clearly still under the influence of alcohol, swaying slightly. Sergeant Williamson's first thought was that the face resembled something one might see on a butcher's block – and a particularly cheap and disreputable butcher at that.

'What in d— is happening here?' yelled the bewigged fellow. 'Hardy! What is this b— circus? Hardy, where are you? I can't see you. Step out from where you are, man – you're no bigger than a cat for G—'s sake! Must I look under the tables?'

'I will thank you to remember, when you speak so, that ladies are present,' remonstrated Mr Williamson in an even voice as Mr Coggins stared wildly about him for his tiny employee.

The bleary eyes of the self-styled 'Dr Zwigoff' settled upon the now standing Detective Williamson. He reached up to the hat he had evidently lost while on his debauches and instead set the peruke level with an air of authority. His clothing – a suit that must once have been expensive when made for its original owner – was in a state of disruption and he reeked of pipe smoke and gin.

'And who in the name of C— might you be, sitting at my kitchen table as if you owned it and telling me how to speak to my own employees? I have a mind to knock you down, sir.'

Mr Hardy jumped down from the chair he was occupying by the fire:

'This is Sergeant Williamson of the Detective Force, Mr Coggins. He is here about the murder of Eliza-Beth. He has been ques—'

'*Murder?* Did you say murder, Mr Hardy?'

Williamson raised his voice: '*Mr Coggins*. The lady called Eliza-Beth has been murdered here this night and lies at the mortuary as we speak. I have been waiting for you to return so that I might—'

'Eliza-Beth dead? It's not possible.'

'I understand that you are shocked at this loss, but—'

'"Loss", you say? You understand it right! Of all my "anatomical curiosities", she was the biggest draw among the crowds, not to mention private showings. I shall be ruined! Do you realize how rare such a specimen is, constable? *Ruined*, I say!'

'I am not a constable. I am Detective Sergeant George Williamson and I hold the power to have you taken directly to the nearest watch house and incarcerated for drunkenness and unreasonable behaviour if I so choose. At the moment, however, I would like you to accompany me upstairs so I might speak with you away from these good people. I perceive that they are ill at ease in your company.'

'Ill at ease? Why, you d— scoundrel! They positively revere me, I'll have you know. And if I wasn't feeling so unsteady on my feet on account of the early hour, I would knock you down.'

What followed was brief and efficacious. PC Cullen was requested to enter the house and escort Mr Coggins upstairs, which journey was occasioned by some accidental violence to his person on account of falling a number of times against the constable's fist. He thus found himself somewhat more sober and attentive when forced into a chair in his own room for the interview with Mr Williamson. The peruke had again been disturbed from its customary situation, though he was insensible to it.

'Now, Mr Coggins. I will be brief because I see you are emotional after your night out. I know that you have been absent since around ten o'clock last evening, so you are not a suspect. At least, not yet. The lady Eugenia told me that you have a number of visiters at this house. Who are they and why do they come?'

Perceiving that his testimony was of some worth to the detective, Mr Coggins adopted a coyness not native to his character: 'Well, Mr Williamson. There are a number of people who visit, but I cannot recall directly who they were.'

'Perhaps your memory might be aided by a trip to the gaol, escorted by PC Cullen. I assumed that you have already formed a close acquaintance.'

'He's a bully, that man. Hmm. Well, if you insist on this course of questioning . . . We generally receive the same kind of people when we are in London. The doctors are great ones for measuring and sketching, of course. You wouldn't believe how many of them have offered me money for the skeleton of Eliza-Beth on her eventual passing – not that I would consider such a thing, you understand.'

'Have any doctors visited since you have been appearing at Vauxhall Gardens?'

'Just one. A strange cove, he was, too. He didn't make sketches like they usually do. But he gave me a card that said he was a doctor of Harley-street. I have the card about the place somewhere if you don't believe me.'

'What do you mean that he was a "strange cove"?'

'Well, I have met a good many doctors and they are all alike. This man was certainly educated and he knew a lot of medical words like "skeleton" and suchlike. But there was something I just couldn't place. He wore a scarf to prevent him breathing mephitic air, he said. Still, he paid what was due . . . Oh, you needn't look at me that way – I can't live on air alone.'

'I will ask to see that card.' The detective made a note. 'Who else has visited?'

'We had a writer fellow who said he was preparing a book on the "underworld" of London. The "underworld" if you like! Do I seem like the underworld to you, detective?'

'I could not say. What did this writer want to research?'

'Oh, he asked my employees about their origins, where they were born and if they recalled their parents. He wrote it all down in a strange hand – Greek perhaps. He had a terrible chest on him, poor fellow – the consumption I suspect. And he took great interest in me and my business. We travel all across these isles and my name is well known across the land, as "Dr Zwigoff" of course. It is my little conceit – it sounds more theatrical than "Coggins", you understand.'

'Quite. Did the writer also leave a card?'

'He did, and paid, too. More than the clergyman, at any account. He gave me nothing.'

'The clergyman?'

'Oh yes! An odd one, he was. "Apocalypse" this and "Revelation" that – a veritable walking scripture! He didn't want to talk to the ladies and gentlemen, only to look at them. I couldn't tell if he was incensed or ecstatic as he condemned us all. He called me – what was it? – the "Devil's minion" or some such nonsense. Quite coddled in the head, as my grandmother used to say. There was a real smell of fire and brimstone about him! He left no card, but I recall his name: Reverend Josiah Archer. I'm told he preaches on street corners.'

'I believe I know of him. Does this conclude the series of visiters?'

'No, there was another – though I must insist that my revelation of her name remains a strict secret between us because she is well known about the Haymarket.'

'I am a sergeant of the Detective Force, Mr Coggins – not a fellow you might happen to meet in a public house. We are not making conversation but conducting a murder investigation.'

'Does this mean I am not to receive my customary fee for an interview?'

'Indeed it does. I may, however, be inclined to offer you your freedom.'

'I see how it goes with you, Detective. Well – the lady in question was none other than Mary Chatterton, she of the Night Rooms at Haymarket. She was here just two nights ago.'

'You surprise me, Mr Coggins. I understand the other visiters' motives, but why would Mary Chatterton visit this house?'

'I admit I was also surprised. She said she had seen the show at Vauxhall and felt a great pity for the performers. She spoke to Eliza-Beth and to Eugenia particularly. She was once a great beauty was Miss Chatterton: quite the courtesan. I've heard that the nights at her suppers can be quite "warm", as they say. Not that I know of such things personally, you understand.'

'Naturally. Did any of the visiters pass a letter to Eliza-Beth?'

'Ah-ha! The letter! You are a sharp one, Mr Williamson! I was very curious about that letter. It was delivered the same night that Mary came, only much later. I saw Eliza-Beth reading it just the other day and tried my best to get a look at it, but she kept it tightly in her bodice. I couldn't even get it while she was sleeping . . . not that I tried. But even if I had wanted to—'

'Who delivered it?'

'That I cannot tell you. I asked her about it, but she was a secretive one . . . or I should say two. In truth, she was two people: Eliza the quiet one and Beth the natural performer. I have seen one of them sleeping while the other spoke. In my job, you see some curious things, detective, I can tell you. Have you seen the dog-child? I paid a pretty penny for her. Lord knows where she comes from – she cannot speak a word of any human tongue. She just barks like a dog. Still, the public love her! You should see the shock when they behold her!'

'Tell me something, Mr Coggins. Do you feel no guilt about your work?'

'Guilt? Why? I am the protector of these poor people. I give them a home and a retreat from the prying eyes of the public. Without me they would surely be dead.'

'And do you share the profits of your show with them?'

'I feed them and clothe them. I provide their accommodation and transport.'

'Hmm. Well, I think have finished with you for the moment. I will need to spend some more time at the scene of the murder when I conclude my questioning downstairs. I have had the door to the room securely fastened and you may not enter.'

'I am paying the rent for this property—'

'You will not enter until my investigation is complete.'

'But—'

At that moment, the voice of Mr Hardy echoed up the staircase:

'Sergeant Williamson! I think we have unearthed a clue.'

The detective left Mr Coggins looking quite ill in his chair and descended to find Mr Hardy and Eugenia apparently conversing with the dog-child. At least, the child was making a variety of canine noises: panting, barking, whimpering and growling. Even in her present company, she was a singular specimen: completely covered in fine hair but for her eyes and the palms of her hands.

Mr Hardy turned to Williamson: 'The little girl says she saw the murderer!'

'How do you know this if the child cannot speak?'

'True, she cannot speak, but she can communicate and we have learned to understand many of her utterances. Eugenia particularly has been able to fashion a mode of language with her. It seems she was watching and saw everything as the man entered the room. He walked quietly and held some manner of weapon. He approached Eliza-Beth and apparently became transfixed by her appearance. He recoiled, cried out, and then leaped forward to strike her.'

'You have understood all of this from the child's bestial noises?'

Eugenia spoke: 'We have raised her and know her almost like a daughter.'

'Has she provided a description of the man? Can she illustrate him, perhaps?'

A piece of paper, a steel pen and some ink were produced from Mr Coggin's room (as he complained of the cost) and the child was encouraged to sketch the murderer. Throughout the process, Eugenia cajoled details in her quasi-canine tongue and pointed to various aspects of the depiction. Not for the first time that day, Mr Williamson wondered at the oddness of the situation he found himself in.

Though extremely rudimentary, the result gave some

impression of the man in question. He wore knee breeches and flat-soled shoes, a cloth cap, a waistcoat and a jacket. About his neck was a stock. It could have been a labouring man of almost any profession. Only the shoes were anomalous: Williamson would have expected boots to complement the working-man's *ensemble*.

'What is this line on his face here, from the forehead down to the chin?' asked the detective.

Eugenia grunted to the child in a strangulated yet vaguely interrogative fashion and indicated the line. The little girl then raised a tiny, hairy finger to Williamson's own pox-scarred face. Despite himself, he blushed.

'A scar? He has a scar down his face?'

The facts were checked and the child concurred: the killer had a scar crossing downwards over the left eye. Under the circumstances, the detective was fortunate to have elicited so much information from the girl – if it could be trusted. Anything subtler would surely be more difficult to procure.

Williamson was musing thus on the facts of the case when PC Cullen escorted a panting constable into the room: a messenger.

'Sir – I am come directly from Giltspur-street and am directed to tell you to report there immediately. A carriage is waiting.'

'I am in the midst of an investigation here, constable. The blood is still fresh and I must look over the crime scene once more now that it is light. I will come to Giltspur-street in my own time. I can assure you of that.'

'Please, sir, I was sent here by Superintendent Wilberforce and Inspector Newsome. They are waiting there now and told me that you should return with me as matter of exceptional priority.'

'Their exact words, I assume.'

'Yes, sir. I wrote it down.'

'Hmm. This is highly inconvenient. Constable Cullen – I am placing you in charge here. You are to prevent anyone from entering the room upstairs, with force if necessary. Direct the constables outside to begin arresting the gathered people if they do not disperse. The situation is becoming ridiculous. Tell them also to say nothing to the journalists who will inevitably descend. See that the description of the killer is distributed to all watch houses. Someone is sure to know that face. And also send out word that the wandering clergyman is to visit me at this address today. I will return as soon as I may.'

'Yes, sir! And Mr Coggins? I fear he will make trouble.'

'You are empowered to make more for him than he makes for you.'

'Yes, sir!'

And with that, the detective put on his hat and walked out to the carriage.

FOUR

Standing at the very core of penal London, Giltspur-street Compter presents a rusticated Portland stone *façade*. Close by, one will find the Old Bailey, the infamous Newgate gaol (termed 'the Stone Jug' by its familiars) and the now closed Fleet prison. To the criminal classes, these are streets to be avoided – except perhaps on the day of an execution, when the distracted crowds present an opportunity too good to be missed.

The innocent man rides past in his carriage or cab; ladies stroll by arm in arm; children clutching coins hotly in their palms run past on their way to the bakers for a treasured meat pie. Do such people give a thought to the faceless hundreds confined behind the anonymous walls? The drunk, the destitute, the violent and the condemned are accommodated there: out of sight, but indisputably present – out of common society, yet still invisibly within it.

Shall we, in fancy, leave the light and bustle of the street to ascend the steps and pass through the stone arch into the dim interior of the compter on that day? Therein, the cold scent of imprisoning stone was all about; the echo of bolts and the voices of the confined replaced the intercourse of the free. Escorted by a burly turnkey, Mr Merrill, we pass through heavy doors to the song of the lock and approach a solitary cell in which a singular prisoner was being remanded. Exceptionally, he was in the company of two of the highest-ranking officers of the Metropolitan Police's Detective Force.

Inspector Albert Newsome was a lightly built man with thick eyebrows and a mass of curly red hair. One of the first policemen to join in 1829, he had dedicated years to maintaining order on the streets and been a natural choice for the highest ranks of the new Detective Force. If he had the reputation of being something of a ruffian – and he did – it was perhaps because he had progressed through the university of the broken bottle and the shouted expletive rather than Oxford or Cambridge.

Alongside him stood Superintendent Sir Henry Wilberforce, an old soldier and perhaps the tallest man on the force at six feet five inches. His hair was a steel grey and his eyes a penetrating icy blue. He *had* been to Oxford and carried his patrician gaze with the rigidity of the military. Together they were attempting to interrogate the man sitting cross-legged on the horsehair mattress before them.

'Your situation is quite hopeless,' continued Mr Wilberforce. 'If only you would speak to us, we might find some amelioration in the crimes of which you stand accused.

'Or perhaps you are eager to spend a prolonged period in this rude cell as we search out more evidence against you?' added Mr Newsome. 'I'm sure that the Lord Mayor would be happy to send you off to Australia. I hear that men are dying of influenza in the Woolwich hulk *Justitia* as we speak, and I feel sure there's a hammock for one such as you.'

At this, the prisoner evinced no trace of emotion. Since the interview had begun, he had given away nothing more than a slight stiffening about the jaw. Everything about him was an enigma as extraordinary as the details of his capture. As to that, I defer to page seven of *the Times*, dated three days previously, and written by no lesser a person than myself (on account of their regular court correspondent being violently waylaid by a robber the night before).

MANSION-HOUSE. – Yesterday a man who would not speak to give his name was brought before the LORD MAYOR charged with both robbery and falsely and fraudulently personating a police constable. Mr Humphreys appeared for the prosecution.

The LORD MAYOR, when the prisoner was brought to the bar, remonstrated with him for his refusal to speak and warned him that this would inevitably go against him. The arresting constable, Pc. Jackson, was then called.

The LORD MAYOR. – Constable, since the prisoner will not speak, will you provide the peculiar details of your arrest?

Pc. Jackson. – Sir, I was conducting my beat and saw the prisoner behaving oddly as I passed an alleyway shortly before dawn. Specifically, he was bending to retrieve a package from the ground. My suspicions aroused, I asked him to halt, but he became agitated and made to run. I set my rattle going and ran to apprehend him. He struggled fearfully before I could affix my handcuffs.

The LORD MAYOR. – And what was the package in question?

Pc Jackson. – A full set of cracksman's tools of very fine quality: wedges, a jemmy, prisers, an American cutter, a rimer and the like – unmarked by a manufacturer but most likely made in Sheffield. And all wrapped in lint so as to make no noise. I also saw that the prisoner appeared to be wearing the uniform of a constable.

The LORD MAYOR. – Appeared to be? Are you uncertain of a constable's appearance, constable?

Here the public in attendance laughed and the Pc. became flustered.

Pc. Jackson. – No, sir. He was wearing a black tail-coat, but the lining was the blue of a police uniform. On closer inspection, I saw that the lining also contained eight buttons identical to those on a police tunic and that the inner collar was numbered as a police tunic with a Stepney division code: 156K. What with his blue trousers and hat, he had only to reverse the jacket and become to all appearances a police constable.

Upon further questioning from the LORD MAYOR, Pc. Jackson revealed that the prisoner was also wearing a pair of specially constructed shoes with cork soles of the kind sometimes worn by cracksmen.

The LORD MAYOR. – Did the prisoner have in his possession any valuables?

Pc. Jackson. – A diamond, sir. It was about his neck on a steel chain, like a watch chain. Concerning his deception, he also had a dagger concealed within his tail-coat, and a number of cards, all with different names, professions and addresses.

The constable here stood down and the LORD MAYOR addressed the prisoner.

The LORD MAYOR. – Prisoner, all of the evidence – including your impertinent silence – points to your being a thief. I will have you remanded at Giltspur-street compter until further inquiries can ascertain the ownership of that diamond, of any recent robberies in the environs of the arrest and of the veracity of the addresses on those cards. To the charge of personating a police constable, I fine you five pounds or one month in gaol if you are unable to pay.

Thus remanded, the unnamed man now faced the two senior officers with inexplicable calmness. Demonstrating an irregular amount of curiosity in the prisoner, they had made an acute physical examination of his person and discovered yet more oddities.

He was of police regulation height (five feet nine inches) and of a lithe yet muscular build. Across his back was a horrifying series of old scars that bespoke a severe flogging, while his ankles and wrists showed similar scarring. His left shoulder bore a curious and intricate tattoo of the kind often displayed by sailors who have navigated the islands of the South Seas. Of his face, the most striking features were his pale-grey eyes – like wood smoke – and a slightly crooked nose that had evidently been broken. His age might have been guessed at thirty.

His clothing, *viz.* the stolen uniform, had been (well) tailored to fit him, though no identifying mark could be found therein. His pockets were empty but for articles discovered on his arrest. Though he had not spoken since being admitted to the cell, the gaolers were of the opinion that he was an intelligent man, English by birth and well aware (though unafraid) of his situation. How they could tell this, they could not express – it was merely the intuition of the turnkey.

For the two interrogating officers, the situation was a perplexing one. They had nothing with which to identify the man: no name in his hat or clothes, no documents or known acquaintances, and no recognition on the part of local constables (who could normally be relied upon to know every face on their beat). The calling cards he had been captured with had all proved to be false names, unheard of at the addresses specified. His very clothing – that usual indicator of social position and profession – was chimerical, being fraudulent in every respect. It was, in essence, a disguise. Without hearing his voice, they could not even be sure of his nationality. How else does one know a man? Take away his voice and his usual appearance; take away his habitual location and his profession; take away the spider's web of relationships that situates him in the city and the story of his past . . . and what is left? You have a man who might have been dropped from the sky or washed up on the shore. Is such a man a man at all? One might as well gaze upon the unformed Genesiac clay.

Among the warders of Giltspur, however, there was a more pressing topic of conversation than the prisoner's identity. Why had two such important men elected to leave Whitehall to interview personally a mere thief? The reason had its origins in a meeting that had taken place two months previously in a room at 4, Whitehall Place – Division A of the Metropolitan Police and known more colloquially as Scotland Yard.

At the head of the plain wooden table was Commissioner of Police Sir Richard Mayne. Superintendent Wilberforce was to his left, and Inspector Newsome sat to his right. The polished wood surface was bereft of paper or writing implements. Though the windows were closed, the carriage traffic of Whitehall and the sound of river steamers could be heard occasionally above the crackle of the fire.

Sir Richard took in the other gentlemen with his piercing

barrister's gaze. He presented an imposing aspect with his dark side-whiskers, his pale skin and his long, thin nose, this man who stood alongside Commissioner Sir Charles Warren as guardian of the Metropolitan Police and of the very Law itself. His voice – bearing the merest trace of an Irish brogue – carried the clarity and authority of one whose opinions are sought by ministers and judges:

'Gentlemen, I have arranged this meeting at your request. Also at your request, I have agreed that no record of it shall take place, that it shall be remembered only by our individual memories and go with us, unspoken, to the grave. At the same time, I must express my severest reservations at the practice. Now, you may proceed.'

The other two gentlemen looked from one to the other for who would speak first. Inspector Newsome nodded slightly and began.

'Thank you, Sir Richard. I will try to state my case without preamble, for the proposal at hand is mine, although it has found sympathy with Superintendent Wilberforce. In short, the Detective Force is proving highly effective, though quite recent in establishment. Our freedom to investigate across police districts, and our civilian attire, has helped greatly in the pursuit of crime. And yet . . .'

He paused and spread his hands across the polished tabletop, casting a glance at Wilberforce. The older man caught the look and pursed his lips at what he had to say:

'Sir Richard, I am certain you have seen the recent press reports about crime and the police. They are saying that crime – especially of the fatal kind, of murder – is an epidemic raging out of control, that it is infecting the body of our city entirely untroubled by the authorities. They point to a list of recent unsolved murders whose perpetrators walk free among us even now: the boy Brill at Ruislip, Eliza Davies the barmaid of Frederick-street, Richard Westwood of Princes-street, and Eliza Grimwood of Waterloo-road. And let us not forget the recent case of Sarah M'Farlane, who named her murderer to constables at the scene. They knew of the man, the Frenchman Dalmas, and yet he remained at liberty until *voluntarily* turning himself in some time later! We are being humiliated, sir.'

Sir Richard looked unblinkingly at each man:

'I have read such things. But I remind you of the great progress the Metropolitan Police has made since it was established by Mr Peel. Now we have the respect of much of the populace and I believe crime has been reduced greatly. The newspapers can be hysterical. Need I remind you of Mr Peel's fifth tenet of policing: that we encourage cooperation and trust from the public by our impartiality rather than by pandering to their whims and "scandals"? Is that what you wish?'

Again, the two lower-ranking officers exchanged looks, neither wanting to enter into an argument with their superior, yet both convinced of its necessity. Inspector Newsome ventured:

'Certainly not, sir. But I have identified a number of areas requiring attention. For instance, a man may become a policeman on the grounds of height and on the production of proofs of good character—'

'I know the regulations, Mr Newsome.'

'Yes, sir. But height and character are no evidence of analytical intelligence, as we saw with the case of Daniel Good and with Miss M'Farlane. Those constables could do little more than follow the rules they had been given, without applying individual thought to the situation.'

'And that is why we established your Detective Force,' answered Sir Richard. 'With men of higher acumen, who are given the freedom to investigate serious cases as they see fit.'

Here, Inspector Wilberforce cleared his throat preparatory to speaking:

'With respect, sir. The men of the Detective Force are a fine body, but they have weaknesses. Recruited from the regular constables as they are, their faces are often known to every inhabitant of their district, which rather nullifies their civilian attire. Furthermore, a beat policeman acquires a particular gait during his years on the street. Any criminal can identify it, even when they do not know the detective by sight.'

'Indeed,' added Mr Newsome, keen to keep up the momentum. 'You will have seen the recent figures showing unarguably that the criminal sees us more clearly than we see him. The majority of crimes are committed during the "relief", when the beat officer returns to the watch house to be relieved. Our own regulations and practices are used against us.'

'And, if I may add more,' interjected Mr Wilberforce, 'our men are forbidden to associate with known criminals and are dissuaded from entering a public house unless in pursuit of a specific crime. Even then, if he is not in uniform, he must reveal his true identity when challenged. Such regulations only hinder our men in their duty.'

Sir Richard stared at the surface of the table for a long moment, his cool demeanour betrayed by blazing eyes. Questioning the Metropolitan Police was analogous to questioning his judgement. He spoke without raising his eyes from the table:

'Gentlemen, the policeman – whether detectives or not –

must by necessity be honest, temperate, sober and industrious. We all know the terrible legacy left to us by those early constables who were corrupt and violent drunks. No policeman under my authority will be associating with criminals – only observing them and locking them away. Our detectives are to observe and gather information for the *prevention* of crime. You know this.'

'And we most emphatically agree, sir,' added Mr Wilberforce. 'We have seen already that disguise and deception can lead to accusations of entrapment from the judiciary. I am thinking of the case of those two constables in plain clothes who ordered drinks from a bar keeping unlicensed Sunday hours.'

Sir Richard's hand came down on the table. 'My patience is being tried. First you disagree; then you agree. Why are we sitting here in conference? We concur that no policeman will associate with nor descend to the status of a thief.'

'But might not a thief rise to the status of a policeman?'

The question was put by Mr Newsome, with the solicitude of a man who holds a lucifer match to a volatile substance. A thunderous silence descended over the room and the fire crackled as if impelled by Sir Richard's resultant countenance. His voice took a hard edge:

'Are you suggesting, Inspector Newsome, that we recruit thieves to become police constables? If so, I must question your sanity. It is a mockery of everything for which we stand.'

Mr Wilberforce held up a hand to stay Mr Newsome's next utterance, and made his own:

'Not thieves, sir, but one thief – or rather one kind of thief. And not to be a policeman, but merely to aid a detective in his investigations. If you would permit me, I would like to make my case before you cast out our suggestion entirely.'

The police commissioner let forth a long sigh and waved a dismissive hand. 'Proceed. But understand that my scepticism is insurmountable. I listen only out of respect for your previous military achievements, Mr Wilberforce.'

'Thank you, sir. I will be brief. Let me introduce the figure of the cracksman, whom you undoubtedly know. He is a prince among criminals: often educated, often dressed like a gentleman – occasionally an actual gentleman. Not for him the insensate robbery or violent act. He plans his robberies many weeks in advance; he is patient and judicious; he is intelligent and careful. He is very seldom caught, unless stumbled on in the commission of his crime, for he is not a man to boast in public houses or sell his acquisitions through pawnbrokers. Indeed, he knows that sobriety and anonymity are the keys to his continued freedom. Other criminals know of him by reputation, but not by sight.'

'If I may add something,' ventured Mr Newsome, 'the cracksman is to the criminal world as the detective is to the world of policing. Both parties possess many of the same essential attributes – except honesty. Moreover, there is no corner of the city that is closed to the cracksman; no regulations bind him in the pursuit of his goal and he knows the criminal classes better than any policeman. Better still, he is virtually invisible. He is limited by none of the restrictions that bind our detectives, though he may possess their skills. Were he an honest man, he might be the greatest detective alive.'

The inspector concluded boldly and caught Mr Wilberforce's approving gaze. They believed they had made a good case and raised many of the issues discussed privately prior to this extraordinary conference. Silence reigned in the room as Sir Richard contemplated what he had heard. A street hawker shouting his wares was heard indistinctly through the window.

Sir Richard stood as if to end the meeting. The other men also stood.

'But he is not honest, gentlemen. In the eyes of the law – and of myself – he is a criminal like any other criminal, no better or worse than the petty thief or the vulgar bully. To have such a man working for the police would taint us for decades to come. And even if I did give my consent to this frankly ridiculous scheme, how would you propose to coerce such a figure as the cracksman to give up his profitable life of crime to work with his sworn enemy the police? Have you considered this?'

'Yes, sir,' answered Mr Newsome. 'Although I admit it would not be easy. First, we would have to catch such a man. We would then have to hold a punishment over his head to compel him to act in our interests. It may also be neces-sary . . . necessary to offer the possibility of a pardon in payment for his services.'

'Aha! Now I know you are joking with me, Mr New-some! Catch the elusive cracksman in the commission of his crime, hold him in gaol and then offer him work with the Detective Force in return for a pardon? Excellent! A reward for his crime! Maybe you would like to present other crim-inals with similar gifts?'

Superintendent Wilberforce interceded: 'We understand, sir, that this is an extraordinary proposal. We would not consider using such a man except in extraordinary circum-stances, and then only once. It would not become a regular practice – merely an experiment.'

'You are right, Mr Wilberforce,' retorted Sir Richard. 'It would not and will not. I have listened to your ideas and I am not impressed. I have worked tirelessly to see the Metropolitan Police become the shining beacon of propriety it is today and I will not countenance criminals within our ranks. I trust the matter is now concluded. Gentlemen – I have work to attend to.'

And with this, the commissioner left the room colder than when he had entered it. The two remaining men returned to their seats in defeat, but not entirely surprised by the conclusion.

'Fear not,' said Mr Wilberforce. 'There will be another case like that of Daniel Good or Miss M'Farlane. We are at the mercy of the newspapers when such things occur. Though he may aver otherwise, Sir Richard is highly sensitive to public opinion and he may have to make a choice: further humiliation or a bending of the regulations.'

'I hope you are right. Our hands are currently as securely manacled as those we arrest. I abhor the criminal as much as any policeman, but if I can use him to solve a greater crime, I will do so.'

'Then we must wait and – dare I say it? – hope for an occasion to approach Commissioner Mayne again.'

'And to apprehend a cracksman at work.'

'That, I believe, is the greater challenge.'

Having left their mysterious prisoner to consider their words, Superintendent Wilberforce and Inspector Newsome now sat in a secluded room at Giltspur-street Compter. The old soldier Wilberforce, lighting a briarwood pipe, displayed a more excited demeanour than was his habit as they prepared to play their accustomed game.

'He is quite an enigma, is he not, Mr Newsome? What do you adduce from the evidence at hand?'

'Well, the tattoo suggests he's a seaman, or associates among them. This might point to an address off Ratcliff Highway or about the docks. Similarly, the flogging scars bespeak the discipline of a ship, and the dagger is something the sailor is seldom without.'

'Hmm. I concur he may *once* have been a sailor, but nothing about his clothes or gait suggests that he is one still. And the dagger is not typical of a sailor's knife – it is more like the thin-bladed knives carried by some Italians or Corsicans. In addition, there is an intelligence to his face that one does not see among the seafaring class. Do you know much of phrenology?'

'No, I am sceptical of it, but there is undoubtedly some native wit in his countenance. One would expect little less from an experienced cracksman.'

'If he *is* a cracksman.'

'We have the tools, Mr Wilberforce. Why else would he be carrying such a package? And then there is the diamond – a large and exceptionally high-quality specimen.'

'That, as you well know, is the weakest point of the evidence against him. The diamond was suspended about his neck on a steel chain that had clearly been fastened there. It was not possible to pull it over his head. And the diamond itself was suspended inside a steel capsule on the chain, the strength and quality of which being such that we had difficulty cutting it free. All of which leads me to conclude that the necklace and capsule was made for strength alone – not show. In short, I believe it belongs to him.'

'What you say is true, Mr Wilberforce, but this in turn

raises the question of why a man would carry a large diamond about his neck inside a steel capsule.'

'For the purposes of bribery, of course. When the cracksman is caught away from his base, he is lost. He necessarily trusts no one and may even eschew the company of women in order to protect his anonymity. What does he do when trapped and cornered like a fox? He uses his one bargaining piece: the valuable diamond that cannot be pulled from his neck by force. The only way to obtain it is to lead the cracksman to his freedom.'

'Or to decapitate him, which would not discommode a number of criminals I have known. Nevertheless, you make a good argument and I admit it is a quite brilliant piece of forethought on the part of the prisoner, if our reasoning is correct.'

'Indeed, most everything about him shows remarkable ingenuity, from the cork-soled shoes to the reversible tailcoat. Tell me, was the number on his collar a genuine one?'

'Yes, I have checked it. It belongs to PC Wiseman of Stepney Division. He lost his jacket in a fight with a Negro man a number of weeks ago – a most unusual event, in fact. The constable was accosted while on his beat and knocked unconscious. He woke to find his head supported on a rag and his tailcoat missing. Not a word was exchanged during the brief assault.'

'Curious.' Mr Wilberforce puffed at his pipe, which had already filled the room with its fragrant smoke. 'What do you make, then, of his silence? Could it be that he is mute?'

'I think not. It is the masterstroke of his strategy. We know nothing about him, and can discern nothing. He knows this and is certainly hiding something from us. Of course, we could arrange for some of the turnkeys here to persuade him to speak, but I suspect he has experienced worse treatment and would not break his silence until almost dead. The scars about his wrists and ankles would suggest a period of worse incarceration.'

The two men contemplated the facts in silence for a moment. The sound of a fight erupted from somewhere within the prison walls and echoed along endless passages to where they were sitting. Outside, the great city of London was about its criminal activities: cutting purses, picking pockets, burgling houses, counterfeiting and plotting. Somewhere, a murderer was lurking.

'Is he the man we are looking for, Mr Newsome?'

'He may be. The question is if he can be turned to our purposes. It may require some deception on our part.'

'Of what are you thinking?'

'Most likely he knows nothing of PC Wiseman. If our prisoner *is* implicated somehow in the theft of the uniform – or even if he is not – we could tell him that the PC in question is dead. He is in possession of the "dead man's" uniform and a dagger. On this evidence alone he could hang, especially if he persists in his silence.'

'It is a cruel deception.'

'We already have him for burglary. I feel sure there is a resident within range of the arrest who will readily admit to having lost a large diamond. Thus, transportation is likely a further bargaining wedge. As with those tools of his safe-breaking trade, we may apply them to the tiny fissures of his resolve and crack the cracksman.'

'I am sure you are correct, though there is no call for the services of such a man at present. Sir Richard would not permit it for the whimsy of our experiment.'

'The time will come, and if we engineer it correctly, our man will be waiting still.'

A knock at the door interrupted that thought as it drifted with the tobacco smoke. A turnkey entered.

'Gentlemen – Sergeant Williamson is arrived.'

FIVE

And as Sergeant Williamson laid forth the details of the crime to his superiors, its perpetrator was walking the streets a free man, dressed exactly as the dog-child had portrayed. He could have been a costermonger or a dock-labourer if the hour had been different. In fact, he was that species of sub-criminal known as a 'bully': the man who, in concert with a base street girl, plays the role of the outraged 'husband' to extort money from her client – or simply clubs the unfortunate fellow insensible for his watch and wallet. Accordingly, he was known as 'Bully' Bradford.

His face, red and broken-veined with excessive drink, was that of the common labouring man: a blank slate, animated only with slyness and suggestion. No knowledge but that of the lower social strata showed in his muddy eyes, and no kindness that could not be priced. As many of his ilk, he was short and stocky – born for a lifetime of hauling cargoes.

Walking now with his hands in his pockets, he looked behind him at every other step and navigated a zigzag course through alleys and across courts familiar only to one who had grown among them. It was a low area in the environs of

Rosemary-lane, with the smell of the river and of the docks hanging in the air as palpably as the strings of washing across narrow passages. The familiar perfume of rotting wood, bilge water and the foetid compost of the gutter seeped behind the peeling plaster and mouldy brickwork of the slowly decomposing streets that he called home.

Presently, he approached a ramshackle marine store with a jumble of rain-tainted furniture before its grimy windows. With one final glance behind him, he entered.

The dim interior of the shop was empty of people. He looked around him at stacks of mildewed books, coats hanging on hooks, brass hearth-ware, stopped clocks and smoky glass. A smell of oakum, furniture wax and sulphur pervaded all. The place was a metropolitan Sargasso, where the flotsam and jetsam of the larger ocean finds dead water and settles. Currents and winds move all about, but it remains undisturbed, uncharted, undiscovered – a seeming lake in a limitless sea.

A lucifer match flared in a dark corner of the shop filled with leaning shelves of books.

'General? Cast a glim, won't yer – it's precious dark in 'ere.' The bully squinted in that direction of the flame.

The flame moved to an oil lamp on a table and an arm appeared briefly in its guttering light. Then the arm withdrew into the shadows and a chair creaked. He was there somewhere among the books, looking out through their spines but hidden by cracked leather and winking gilt inscriptions. When he spoke, it was with an even and intelligent tone:

'Is it done?'

'Yes, General, I 'ave it. Alas . . . there was difficulties.'

'Speak. Do not make me ask.'

'Well, I found the paddin' ken jus' as yer directed. I went

jus' afore dawn as yer said. The door was no o'stacle for me and I made me way upstairs quiet as a cat with them special shoes yer give me. It were tarry dark. I was like a groper in that place. A piece of luck – they was all asleep. All but someone sittin' writin' at a desk by candle. It were two young girls sittin' close by each other and one on 'em was the one yer described. I crept quiet as you like to nab the letter. But the d— floor began singin' like a canary. One of 'em turns and I sees that it weren't two girls – it was one. *With two 'eads!* You didn't tell me nothing about no queer lully, General!'

'I told you what you needed to know. Continue.'

'Well, I fair screamed when I saw. I got out me blade, for they was a monster. I went to grab the letter but they covered it. One of 'em looked like she would scream so I cut her. Then I grabbed the letter and I ran. The second started up yellin' even as the claret was pourin' from the other and I was runnin'.'

'Where is the letter?'

'I must tell yer, General, that there was more in this than what I bargained for. I had to kill one on 'em and now there is a rope 'bove my 'ead. I 'eard the bobby settin' off his coffee grinder and now I 'ears there's a prime fuss. I'll need to leave the city for a good while.'

'You are asking for more money.'

'It's only fair. I've risked me neck for yer.'

'That business is your own idiocy. Where is the letter?'

'Shall we say twenty pounds?'

The man among the bookshelves leaned slightly forwards into the light so that his countenance was illuminated briefly by the lamp. His eyes were vitreous orbs of swirling grey smoke. He stared into the muddy eyes of Bully Bradford as if reading the smudgy text of his mind. Then he leaned back into writhing shadow. He sighed.

'Mr Hawkins!'

An unseen door opened and heavy footsteps entered the room. The man was easily six feet tall and hugely built about the shoulders. His nose was a mess of fractured and re-healed cartilage and one ear seemed a deformed fungal growth.

'Are you familiar with Henry Hawkins?' asked the voice from among the books. 'You might know him as "Butcher" Hawkins if you are one for "the fancy". Have you seen him fight, Mr Bradford?'

The bully attempted to puff his chest and stand taller. 'Aye, I've seen 'im fight. Pretty 'andy with his mawlies, too.'

'Henry is a good fighter because he fights with his head as well as his fists.'

'Aye, I've seen 'im use his 'ead in more than one fight.'

Here the bare-knuckle fighter spoke. It was a voice bubbling from the bottom of a two-storey gin barrel: 'There's no more of that now we've got the New Rules . . . though I make the occasional exception, heh-heh!'

'Mr Bradford is asking for more money, Henry. What do you think about that?'

'I have the letter here, General,' answered the bully. 'I 'ave not read it meself—'

'Because you cannot read. Place it on the table beside you there.'

'And if I 'ave somethin' else to offer?'

'Show me.'

'Well, it depends on what it might be worth, don't it?'

'Mr Bradford, my patience with you is exhausted. Show me what you have directly, or Mr Hawkins here will gladly instruct you in the finer points of bare-knuckle fighting, preferably that variety untamed by the New Rules.'

'I'm not a man to be threatened, General. Nor am I afraid of Mr 'Awkins.'

'Brave, but thoroughly dishonest. Give it to me.'

'It's a locket – the one what she were wearin'. It's bloody, as I grabbed it while she were sprayin' the claret.'

'I will you give you five pounds for it and you will accept my offer.'

'There may be another as would give more.'

'Mr Hawkins, retrieve that locket from Mr Bradford.'

The bully rapidly extracted the locket from his trouser pocket. 'I accept yer offer, General.'

'As I expected you might. Give it to Mr Hawkins. He will pay you for all. Good. Now – I suggest that you go to ground. That scar on your face is like a bell to identify your movements. If anyone saw you in Lambeth—'

'Not a soul, General.'

'*If* anyone saw you, the constables hereabouts will recognize the description in a moment. You will be in Newgate before you can draw breath, and we do not wish that on any man. Go to the country, or to Scotland. Wherever you go, stay there for at least six months.'

'I will, General. Yer talk good sense.'

'Go. You have been here too long as it is.'

The door clattered behind Mr Bradford and Mr Hawkins spoke:

'Should I follow him, General?'

'No – there is no need. To be sure, he will not take my advice. He could no more venture from these verminous streets that he could from his own skeleton. In one hour he will be in the gin palace or the bawdy house.'

'You should have asked me to get the letter.'

'No, you are too valuable for me to risk you on such a venture. Mr Bradford is expendable, especially now that the imbecile has committed a murder. The police will not shed a tear when *his* body is dredged out of the Thames or found stiff in an alley.'

'I should kill him?'

'The time for that will come. For now, I would like you to return to the house in Lambeth. Watch it and report to me who enters and leaves – discover their names if possible. I want to know who is investigating the case and what they know. Give me that locket before you go. Good.'

Alone now in the dust and detritus of the shop, the 'General' moved closer to the light and turned the necklace in his hands. It was the same one he had seen about the neck of the girl: a simple and unadorned oval of gold, worth very little of its own accord but invaluable to those who could read its contents correctly. He opened it and saw two differently coloured locks of hair – nothing other. That made him smile. Had Mr Bradford also opened the locket and did he know what was inside? That would soon not matter.

He turned his attention to the bloodstained letter. It was written in an ornate hand, most likely with a steel pen. There was no address on the reverse and the paper seemed odourless apart from the faint metallic tang of blood. The whole text was legible:

Dear Parent

We believe we may begin so after receiving your letter. You say we have met and spoken while we are in

*London, but we have met so many visiters at the house
and at our shows that the numbers are bewildering.
Nevertheless, we feel that we know in our heart who
you are because we saw an uncommon sympathy in
your eyes among the many that have gazed upon us.
And we share a striking similarity (or rather a family
trait if our assumptions are correct)!*

*We have kept the locket you allude to from our
earliest memory and know that the Lord Himself has
prevented it being taken from us in our childhood.
Surely He always intended for us to be united again
after our trials. We have hoped for nothing less in our
prayers.*

*You write that the time will soon approach when
you will make your true identity known to all and
reclaim us from the unpleasant Mr Coggins (who
has much to answer to when the Day of Judgement
arrives). We anticipate that day with joy and . . .*

The letter ended thus. That cretin Bradford had taken the
wrong letter: the reply rather than the original. Still, it was
valuable in its way. He flicked a match with his thumbnail
and watched the flame dance. No jewel was more attractive to him. He watched the flame work its way along the
wood until pinched extinct by his calloused fingers. Then he
opened the locket once more, taking out one of the curls
of hair and holding it closer to the light, turning it about
between thumb and forefinger to examine its colour and texture.

What he had intended as a theft – a minor and irrelevant
occurrence that would interest nobody – had become a
murder thanks to Mr Bradford and his ready razor. Now
everyone would be looking at what was previously under his

gaze alone. And it would be virtually impossible to gain access to the house to search for the original letter. Worse still, the investigation might – however inconceivable it might seem – lead back to him. Mr Bradford would be the first to be silenced. But not here, and not at this exact moment. Better to arrange for him to meet his end elsewhere, and in a manner more fitting his habits.

The shop door opened and a man in a broad-brimmed hat poked his head inside.

'The body of the girl is now at Bart's. The surgeons are arguing over her bones. I have not been able to learn anything more.'

'Very good. There may be a letter about her person. If you can obtain it, there will be five pounds for you. That is all.'

'Gen'l.' The man touched the brim of his hat and was gone.

When a bonneted woman walked into the shop shortly afterwards to enquire about a mantel clock in the window, she found the place completely empty. Only a sharp, sulphurous pall remained.

SIX

The prisoner lay sleeping on his mattress at Giltspur-street. He turned frequently and murmured indistinct words. Were we to enter his head and observe his feverish dreams, what would we see?

It is murky in the oneiric theatre of his mind. One has to stoop and fumble to find one's way in the darkness. There is a foetid stench of damp wood, tar and verminous bilge water. As our eyes become accustomed, we see double ranks of bunks astride a narrow aisle. There are dozens of faces and a reek of sour humanity. All is in motion and the very ground rises and falls precipitously like the sleeper's chest. It is a nauseating and claustrophobic place full of fear and foreboding. A boy can be heard crying . . .

He awoke with a start. He was again alone in the cell, lying prostrate and perspiring on the mattress. It was the day after the Lambeth murder, though he knew nothing of it. Just below his window, the street was going about its business, carrying the sounds and smells up to him: horse hooves and ironbound wheels; snatches of speech as people passed on the pavement; a dray pulling up and a consignment of rattling beer bottles being delivered to the gaol. The smell of the horses twitched at his nostrils and, as he cast his eyes towards the sky, he could see the tower of St Sepulchre raking the clouds. The mournful windows of its east wall looked blankly back at him. At the whimsy of the breeze, the bestiary of Smithfield market would, on Mondays, bring the mingled cries of innumerable sheep, cattle and swine to the cell on a hot wind of manure.

He cast a glance at the iron slat in the door. It was closed and there was no sound in the corridor outside. He reached for one of his cork-soled shoes and pulled firmly against the sole until it began to part from the leather. Between the two was secreted the means to communicate with the outside world.

He stood and clasped the cold iron bars of the window in his hands. They were sturdy and unmoving. The street was directly below him and he observed that the people passed by without casting a glance upwards. He might have been invisible, observing them so. It was common enough knowledge that the solitary cells of Giltspur-street gaol faced the street, but few people were bold enough to stop and converse with a criminal in daylight. Better to pretend that no eyes lurked there behind the bars, and to instead affect an animated conversation as one passed.

Someone, however, *was* looking. A street-sweeping boy on the corner with Skinner-street, too lackadaisical to attend to his labour, twirled his broom and looked into the windows of the solitary cells. His shoes were rags of leather about his feet and his man's jacket an oversized cloak around his bony shoulders. As he observed, a prisoner's arm extended through the bars and beckoned. The sharp-eyed lad could not help but notice a sovereign glinting between the fingers.

*

Nor was he the only sharp-eyed observer on the street. Inspector Newsome had stationed men about the gaol with exactly this sort of occurrence in mind. Detective Constable Bryant and the civilian-clothed PC saw the street-sweeper lean his brush nonchalantly against the wall of the gaol and set off west along Skinner-street.

Inspector Newsome had promised them traffic duty on London-bridge if the boy was lost, and, though such a Draconian punishment was not likely, failure would certainly have grave consequences.

As a denizen of these streets, the boy moved quickly and assuredly towards the thunderous noise of upper Farringdon-street where the confluence of traffic from Field-lane, Holborn-hill and Skinner-street swirled in a deafening maelstrom of hooves, iron-bound wheels and the cries of drivers. Only one born on the streets would attempt to cross the thorough-fare on foot, risking mutilation and death under the goods wagons and omnibuses.

Indeed, even as the two policemen attempted to follow the boy, a lurching omnibus caught the corner of a goods wagon and a wheel was wrenched loose with the fracturing crack of a falling tree. The wagon keeled over, one of its horses stumbled and a wave of oranges poured into the road. In a moment, the fruit was pulped beneath the traffic and a heady citrus tang filled the air. Pedestrians gasped and dashed recklessly between horses' legs to grasp the precious fruit. Pandemonium set uniformed police screaming at drivers, who in turn screamed at each other.

Through all of this, the boy slipped determinedly through, pausing only to stuff an orange in each voluminous trouser pocket. Then he was across the cacophonous gulf and up Holborn-hill, paying no heed to the inns, the saucy words of street girls and a staggering guardsman bringing his scarlet tunic into further disrepute. Whatever the boy was doing, wherever he was going, he had a great sense of purpose.

Along Holborn he strode, that conduit between east and west which might equally stand as a border between nations, dividing the tree-dappled shade of western squares and the grim masonry labyrinths of the east. On and on he walked, undistracted by the traffic or the shops. On and on, down on to Broad-street on the periphery of St Giles, where every dark alley holds an opportunity for sin or death, then up High-street and into the very *aorta* of the city's circulation: Oxford-street.

This pulsing artery of top hats and bonnets, carriages, cabs and omnibuses is London vivisected. See here the beggar with his pitiful card reading 'Lord help my poor soul', the liveried footman waiting patiently at the shop door, the seller of spaniels beneath the streetlight, the policeman dissuading fights between drivers, and the advertising men with boards on their backs telling interested passers-by that Ross & Sons, Perruquiers of Bishopsgate-street, have in stock the latest toupees and perukes.

But the purposeful boy walks on, distracted not by the smell of leather goods, or of meat pies, or of hot sugared confections from the doors he passes. Neither by the crack of the horseman's whip, or the cries of 'All right!' from the omnibus driver, of the dung flicked against his calves by those other boys of his trade – for he has a sovereign tight within his fist and stands to earn another when he reaches his goal, and yet another when returning to Giltspur. It is his fortune and he will yam meat pies until he grows a pig's curly tail.

Behind him, the two policemen hurry to keep pace and

lift their hats to wipe away sweat with their sleeves. In the rush of humanity, as the boy passes frequently from sight, they are forced to push past and through knots of people to follow him. And as they pass the chaos of Oxford-circus, the youngster, who is no doubt illiterate, is oblivious to the tapestry of signs and advertising hoardings that assault the eye and call for attention.

Almost lost amidst the noise, the lone voice of a running patterer shouts news of the latest scandal – one so new that he has not yet procured the printed sheets to sell: 'Hideous murder in Lambeth! Two-headed monster slain by killer! House of horrors in our midst!'

Finally, the boy turns right up Duke-street and on to Edward-street, a more sedate thoroughfare in the environs of Portman-square: a street of milliners, of Lazenby and Sons' famous fish-sauce warehouse, and, for those of the inclination, Miss Prince's Academy of Dancing. But he does not stop here – rather, he continues into Manchester-square: a small oasis of calm away from the cacophony of the city. It is the kind of place one might find the residence of an eminent physician, writer or composer.

And it was here that the boy approached a black door on the south side and knocked. It was answered by a Negro man. He listened as the boy explained something at length, nodded and took a coin from his pocket for the boy, who then set off back towards the east.

'And then I sent the PC in pursuit of the boy while I attended to the house. Nobody has entered or left the property as I waited for your arrival. I have made enquiries hereabouts as to who occupies the house and have received conflicting reports. One neighbour maintains that a writer lives there;

another says he is a businessman. All say that he is a quiet and unassuming man. All remarked on the peculiarity of his Negro manservant – and I'm sure you will recall that it was a black man who attacked PC Wiseman of Stepney. Both have lived here for about four years.'

Inspector Newsome, who had just arrived at Manchester-square by police carriage, nodded to himself and answered:

'Very good, Mr Bryant. The boy returned directly to Giltspur-street, where he received another coin. I admit I have no idea from where the prisoner produced these coins – he was thoroughly searched in his cell. I have ordered him searched again. Well, I wonder if this is our prisoner's address. Have you elicited any further information from any of the neighbours?'

'A strange thing, sir – none can agree on a name. One knows him as Henry Matthews, another as William Smart. Yet another has heard him called Harold Smith.'

'I see. I am not particularly surprised. Now – I intend us to enter the house and search it for anything that might throw light on our mysterious prisoner. Evidence of stolen goods would also be beneficial to our cause, though I do not expect to find it. If we are fortunate, the secret to the enigma will lie herein.'

Together, they crossed the road and Mr Newsome used the brass knocker to rap three times on the door. The Negro man who had answered previously opened it now. He was of a singular appearance:

There was no stock about his neck and the two police-men saw a quite horrific scar there, the skin evidently having been stretched and torn as if he had been hanged and sur-vived it. His left eye was also damaged, presenting an opaque film to the world. His build was that of a bare-knuckle boxer, an assumption reinforced by the flattened nose and scar tissue about the temples, but his manner was attentive. Mr Newsome saw him looking at their clothes and demeanour as closely as they were reading him. Evidently, he knew who they were before they spoke, though it did not seem to alarm him.

'I am Inspector Newsome of the Detective Force and this is Detective Constable Bryant. We are investigating a crime and must enter this place to seek evidence. You are obliged to permit us entrance, or risk being arrested yourself.'

The Negro said nothing. His hand moved to the scar tissue at his neck and he scratched absently at the skin there. He did not move from his position filling the doorway.

'Is your master at home?' enquired Mr Bryant.

The Negro shook his head.

'When do you expect him to return?' asked Mr Newsome.

Again, there was no answer, only a blank stare that might have been malevolence or indifference.

'Speak, man! We are officers of the law!' expostulated Mr Newsome.

And here the Negro smiled as if mocking the agitation of his interlocutor. He opened the mouth of large ivory teeth and pointed within. The two detectives, utterly perplexed, could not help but look where they were bidden, and observed the glistening stump where a tongue had once been. The man was a mute. Inspector Newsome could not contain himself.

'Aha! Now I respect our prisoner even more. We follow the clue and it leads to a man who cannot speak even if compelled to! No doubt this dusky fellow is illiterate as well, Bryant. His secrets are hidden and locked inside that fuzzy head as securely as in a safe.

'Is there anyone at home but yourself, sir?' he said to the Negro. 'Nod or shake you head accordingly.'

The dark head shook.

'I believe that your master is currently in a cell at Gilt-spur-street and that he has just sent a message to you . . . But I see from your expression that you already know this. Now – we aim to enter.'

And enter they did, to discover an abode of admirable *décor* and taste. The furniture was of good quality, the carpets clean and unworn, and the curtains seemed to be regularly dusted. Ornaments in the parlour suggested foreign travel, or at least an interest in it. Mr Bryant picked up an ornately carved club from the mantel and noted an amulet of jade hanging around a lamp, while Mr Newsome was taken with a slender sword that must have originated from the Far East. Though examples of weaponry, these trinkets were clearly not for use in the cracksman's profession. Was this indeed the home of the prisoner, or of an absent benefactor?

The Negro watched the two intruders with barely suppressed amusement as they walked deferentially about the room randomly handling objects that meant nothing to them. It was clear to him that they had no idea whom or what they were looking for. Inspector Newsome caught the glance of their observer and scowled, addressing his fellow policeman.

'What we are looking for, Mr Bryant, is not something hidden. What we are looking for is what lies in plain sight. A man's home says much about the man and his habits, his past and his acquaintances. What does this house tell us about our mystery prisoner? Look, and tell me what you see.'

Together, they combed through the house: from the

basement kitchen to the bedrooms, in drawers, upon shelves and in cupboards. The absence of female *accoutrements* and the lack of female hair in the bathrooms, on the seats or in the beds suggested that the gentlemen – and a gentleman he appeared to be – was a bachelor and did not entertain ladies at home. Swatches of old newspaper used to light the fire told them that the resident was a regular reader of *the Times*. Indeed, everything about the place bespoke a tenant of means and intelligence.

The book-lined study would not have disgraced a scholar. Its shelves held books on chymistry, biology and anatomy, as well as classical history, literature and poetry. Mr Newsome stroked his fingers along the leather spines of Demosthenes, Lucretius, Herodotus, Aristotle and Cicero. Framed maps of the South Seas and Antipodes adorned the walls and a handsome oak desk sat at the window, from which vantage point the writer might look down to the street. No letters, either sent or received, could be found apart from those necessary communications with tradesmen about the city, and among these the recipient was listed variously as Henry Matthews or William Smart. A letter from a costume maker of Haymarket was addressed to Harold Thackeray.

A number of wide drawers of the kind found in museums or libraries lined one wall of the study. They attracted Mr Bryant, who set about pulling each one to discern its contents. From one, he extracted a large map of London. A number of red points had been marked on both the Middlesex and Surrey sides, each appended with a date on a personally annotated legend attached to the map. Beginning in 1829, the dates ended in that very month of 1844 with a red point at the western end of Fleet-street.

'Sir, I think you should see this,' he said.

Inspector Newsome approached and gazed upon the map. He pointed to the most recent point. 'What happened at this location, Mr Bryant? And what does it have in common with these other points?'

'A fire, sir? I recall a fire in a milliner's on that date in Fleet-street.'

'Yes . . . yes, let me see.' The inspector traced a finger over the map and found a red point at each location he sought. 'Fires, Mr Bryant. Each red point represents a fire. Here we have the infamous warehouse blaze of Deptford, and here the brewery fire of Battersea. There is the Fenning's Wharf fire of 1838, the Horselydown and Rotherhithe fire of two years ago that destroyed three warehouses and fifteen dwellings. Are we dealing with an incendiary here, do you think?'

'He does not seem the type, sir. Though one can never be sure.'

'That is true. He has made his money somehow, and he does not strike me as a working man.'

Throughout all of this, the Negro butler, whose name was Benjamin, watched impassively. Like his friend imprisoned at Giltspur-street, he had learned from hard experience when to act and when not to act. The wise man holds his tongue (when he has one) and restrains his fist when silence is the better strategy. Nevertheless, his brooding presence was an unnerving influence on the policemen, who were no nearer to their goal.

The policemen even searched his quarters at the top of the house. His room was small but pleasantly appointed, with a level of comfort far beyond that of a typical servant's quarters. Indeed, it seemed as well furnished as the lower rooms and there were a number of personal possessions. An etching of a river steamboat hung on one wall and there were books on the shelves. Inspector Newsome read the title of one: *A Voyage to the Indies* by Captain Percival Hubert.

'So, you are not the dumb animal you appear,' remarked the inspector, almost to himself. 'There is something we are not seeing here, Mr Bryant. All of this silence – the silence of the prisoner and his man – disturbs me. They are hiding something. It may be criminal; it may not be, but I will not have something hidden from me, by G—! I maintain that there is something in this house that will provide a key to our man. If I have to look between every leaf of every book, I will find it.'

'Sir – I was thinking . . .'

'Well out with it! It's no use inside your head, is it?'

'Sir. If the prisoner had a policeman's uniform, might he have other such clothing to hide his identity?'

'Indeed.'

'So I was think— We have looked in his wardrobes but not yet examined his actual clothes.'

'You are correct, Mr Bryant. Let us descend.'

Mr Bryant opened the double doors of the large wooden wardrobe and beheld a fine selection of clothes that bespoke a man of the city who could afford good tailoring but who disliked ostentation. Upon further searching, the policeman withdrew a suit of base corduroy fabric that seemed at odds with its neighbours.

'What have we here?' remarked the inspector. 'That suit is more fitting for a costermonger than a gentleman. Keep looking.'

Searching further, Mr Bryant turned up the canvas attire of a sailor, a threadbare *ensemble* suitable for a beggar, and another policeman's tailcoat. At the foot of the wardrobe, behind a row of polished shoes, was a pointed staff like that used by the rag-picker, a basket that a pure-finder might use, and a walking stick which concealed a slender sword.

'Well, we have uncovered a veritable masquerade warehouse here, haven't we, my dusky fellow?' said the inspector to Benjamin. 'Does your master like to dress up when he goes out?'

Benjamin stared back with that unnerving milky eye and made no sound or gesture.

'I wonder what else we'll discover if we apply ourselves with more care to the library?' said Mr Newsome, to himself as much as to the other men. Whether he was acting upon his years of experience, or whether it was a mere guess, he was correct to think that more secrets would lie there. For where better to 'hide' an item than among other seemingly identical items?

And search they did, removing book after book from the shelves and checking it for inserts or false covers. History, poetry, art, biology, philosophy – all passed through the hands of the policemen, their thumbs fanning pages for secrets. Such knowledge was wasted on them; it was little more than ink on paper. But what they lacked in erudition, they compensated for with determination.

'This is odd,' said Mr Newsome, holding a brown leatherbound volume. 'The spine proclaims it to be *Anatomy of the Cranium* by a Doctor Herbert Malham but the contents are handwritten.' He looked to Benjamin and saw the Negro's jaw set in mute frustration.

Upon closer inspection, the book's entire contents proved to have been compiled by one man, and the pages loaded with sketches and maps, all of which were carefully dated. Lists of names and addresses filled pages, and there were more notes about fires. Articles from *the Times* that related to fires or other crimes had been cut out and catalogued. Inside the front cover was a list of men's names.

'What is it, sir?' asked Mr Bryant.

'I have no idea. The more I learn, the less I understand. The Negro showed apprehension at us finding this book, and it has a false description on its spine (a very dull one) – no doubt to deter the casual observer. We must try to discern what secret it holds. As for our prisoner, I admit I am at a loss. His address and his belongings are perplexing. Who is he? *What* is he? From where does he derive his income?'

'I cannot say, sir, but I think we have enough information to start applying wedges to prise open the safe of his silence.'

'In that, Mr Bryant, you are assuredly correct. We must talk to our prisoner further.'

'And the Negro?'

'You may arrest him under suspicion of the theft of a police uniform and he can ride in the carriage with us. Let us go.'

And with that, the three gentlemen left the house. Benjamin gave no fight, but submitted to the irons with seeming calmness. The policemen cannot have known, however, what anguish the cold metal brought to him, and what anger coursed through his body. Only his benefactor could save him now.

SEVEN

Sergeant Williamson paced the murder scene in Lambeth. The pitiful performers had been moved to another address the previous day, but the house retained the atmosphere of one still inhabited. Their breath and scent remained – as did the blood.

Does a place retain a memory of a murder? When the blood is scrubbed away, when the curtains are replaced and the furniture washed, can another occupy the same room with undisturbed sleep? When we walk the midnight streets, do we feel the chill fingers of those who have perished there in fires and fights? Are their spirits a hidden population among us?

No such thoughts entered the head of Mr Williamson, who was still simmering with indignation. The meeting with his superiors had not been amicable. He had entered that room at Giltspur-street with his eyes tired from lack of sleep, and had been in no mood for excessive deference.

'Inspector Newsome, Superintendent Wilberforce – I have been called from investigating the scene of a murder in Lambeth. The very room lies unattended as I stand here. May I enquire as to why I have been summoned?'

'Have some courtesy in the presence of the Superintendent,' warned Mr Newsome.

'Forgive me, sir, but you know my methods. In cases such as these, the critical thing is to strike quickly and gather clues before they are lost. There is too much laxity in the handling of crime to allow any further opportunities to the criminal.'

'All will be explained, Sergeant,' said Mr Wilberforce, restocking the bowl of his pipe.

And indeed all was explained: their scheme for expediting investigations, the discussions with Commissioner Mayne, and their possible plans for the unnamed prisoner in the solitary cell. As they might have expected, they did not find a willing participant in Sergeant Williamson.

'With respect, Superintendent Wilberforce, it goes against everything I stand for as a police officer and as a detective. The idea of working *with* a criminal rather than against him is preposterous.'

'And if it allowed you to catch a greater criminal or solve a greater crime in order to protect a greater number of people?' answered Mr Wilberforce. 'Is it so different from the information we occasionally receive from captured criminals in order to apprehend their cohorts?'

'A convicted criminal's place is in gaol or, if it is absolutely necessary, on the gallows, not on the streets in companionship with a detective.'

'I respect your opinion, Sergeant Williamson. You are one of our finest men. But if Commissioner Mayne decides that this scheme will be put into action, your consent will not be necessary. The reputation of the Metropolitan Police may one day depend upon the services of such a criminal. Should that be the case, he may be put in the charge of a trusted investigator such as you, Sergeant.'

'I am flattered by your words, sir, but I will—'

'You will follow your orders to the letter, as you always have. Now, please tell us the full details of your Lambeth murder case before you return. Omit nothing.'

A group of people loitered persistently outside the Lambeth house, no doubt waiting for it to give up further secrets. PC Cullen was still on duty and in dire need of being relieved. But for his presence, they would have been inside enjoying the horror.

Nevertheless, one piece of evidence had emerged from the onlookers: shortly after the police had arrived, a stranger had been among them asking what all the fuss was about. When he heard of the murder, he fled. The locals had described him variously as 'a toff', a 'west-end boy' or a 'foreigner'. To these people, however, anyone from across the river might well fit the latter appellation.

Sergeant Williamson cast his eyes over the mournful scene: the chair where Eliza-Beth had sat; the spatter of blood up the wall and on the floor; the beds of the performers with their still rumpled sheets. Daylight added little illumination to the place, but he had discovered some minor clues.

There were partial bloody footprints, presumably made by the killer as he stepped around the chair to grab the letter or the locket, neither of which could be found in the house. From the sole print, it appeared a curious species of shoe: completely flat (without a heel) and a little broader than typical. They had carried their taint of blood down the stairs, but become too faint to see beyond the front door. Upon close inspection, the door appeared to have been forced open, most likely with an iron jemmy. No razor had been found in or around the house.

Resorting to his usual method, he tried to reason through the little information that he had to hand, writing it in his notebook:

> *Victim: A two-headed girl, part of a 'freak show' – no known family.*

> *Location: A poor boarding house in Lambeth – a transient address.*

> *Clues: Shoeprints, a missing locket, missing letters, a broken lock, sundry visiters (and visiting cards).*

> *Suspect: The scarred man seen by the dog-child and heard by Miss Eugenia; the 'west-end boy' seen loitering outside.*

> *Weapon: Most likely a razor.*

> *Motive: To steal the locket? To steal the letters? Revenge?*

Such conclusions were unhelpful, even contradictory. The broken lock suggested a common burglar, while the shoes could have been the gutta-percha or cork soles utilized by highly skilled cracksmen. The killer's attire, however, indicated that he was more probably the former than the latter – so why did he wear silent shoes if he was planning to break the lock?

Since every man owned a razor, the choice of weapon was of no great consequence: it was quick to use and easy to conceal. Moreover, the house was in a poor district and was unlikely to contain anything of great value – unless the killer had foreknowledge of some other prize. The locket itself was worth little, except to poor Eliza-Beth, herself an unfortunate accident of nature with no other possessions of her own. Only the letters provided a possible link to some outside agency, but – until found – they appeared to be nothing more than an attempt by a parent to recommence his or her role after a prolonged period. In short, the avenues of investigation were more akin to *culs de sac* and the vicious murder seemed entirely unjustified.

Detective Williamson looked again at the visiting cards that Mr Coggins had given to him. The 'strange cove' doctor was Dr Cole of 26, Harley-street: a surgeon specializing in spinal deformities (to whom a constable had been dispatched to make an appointment for an interview). The writer was Mr Henry Askern MA (Oxon.) with an address in Portman-square. The detective would call on him presently.

Would either of those gentlemen be able to throw illumination on details of the girl's past life that might motivate someone to kill her? The possibility was a distant one.

There was a knock at the street door and PC Cullen called up the stairs: 'Reverend Josiah Archer here to see you as requested, sir!'

'Send him up, Constable.'

The clergyman stamped up the stairs and into the room. He was a fearsome-looking man in his flowing black robes and cloak. His head was a glabrous egg, framed above the ears with wiry grey hair, and his eyes had the roving intensity of the insane. In truth, he had once been a respected member of the Anglican Church until his doctrine had become warped with extremism and his sermons condemnatory of his very own flock. Under scrutiny, his robes, which most likely constituted his entire clothing, were soiled with mud, grease and food. His church was now the streets and his congregation the entire population of London. Mr Williamson inadvertently wrinkled his nose at the smell of his visiter.

'Thank you, Reverend, for agreeing to visit me here,' began the detective. 'I understand that this is your second visit to the house. May I ask what motivated your earlier visit?'

The clergyman spoke loudly, as if addressing a busy street corner: 'Are you familiar with scripture, Sergeant?'

'As well as the next man, I imagine. As to your visit-ing—'

'*And I stood upon the land of the sea, and saw a beast rise up out of the sea having seven heads and ten horns, and upon his horns ten crowns, and upon his heads the name of blasphemy!*'

'Well, quite.'

'The Book of Revelation, chapter thirteen, verse one. I'm sure you perceive the parallels.'

'Frankly, no. Why did you visit this house on Wednesday last?'

'The Book predicts the Apocalypse, Sergeant. Its warning signs are among us even now: many-headed freaks of nature, flames of fire in our midst. *Babylon is fallen, is fallen that great city because she made all nations drink of the wine of the wrath of her fornication.* Chapter fourteen, verse eight. London is the modern Babylon – a Sodom and a Gomorrah in one. The reek of its sin reaches Heaven Itself.'

'So you came here to see Eliza-Beth, the two-headed girl, for proof of the prophecy? Is that correct?'

'The beasts that dwelled here were an abomination in the eyes of the Lord! See how they multiply and mock Him. I am called to witness these things, to record them and preach them. The Redeemer is to return at any moment – the signs make it clear. Are you saved, Sergeant?'

'Reverend Archer – a murder has been committed. The girl that you saw is dead, her throat cut in that very chair.'

Mr Archer looked towards the chair and then at the gouts of dried gore on the wall and floor around it. He paled and supported himself on a nearby table.

'Reverend – have you been in this room before?'

'No. My viewing of the monsters was held in the down-stairs kitchen, under the supervision of Dr Zwigoff. He introduced them to me individually and described each infir-mity with great relish. The man will burn as assuredly as they.'

'Did you speak with Eliza-Beth?'

'I spoke to none of them. My purpose is to witness, to record and to preach.'

'Have you written a letter to any of the people you saw?'

'A letter? To them? Why? I would sooner write a letter to the Devil!'

'Then, did you see Eliza-Beth in possession of a letter during your visit?'

'Are you insane? I was looking at a natural aberration with two heads! She was flanked by a giant, a half-man and a human dog. Do you think I would stop to notice a letter tucked into someone's clothing?'

'I suppose not, Reverend Archer. Not everyone has the observation of a detective.'

'Quite right, Sergeant. Quite right. Now, is there any-thing further I can tell you? I am uncomfortable in this infernal place. It breathes the very vapours of Hell. I have witnessed; I have recorded; now I must preach.'

'Did you see anyone loitering about the building when you visited? Or perhaps you encountered another interested party here?'

'I believe a man was leaving as I arrived. I almost walked into him as he left the house. He did not apologize and I shouted after him that he should learn some courtesy.'

'What did he look like?'

'Our meeting was brief. He wore something over his lower face – a scarf perhaps. Have you finished now, Detective? I am unwilling to spend time here when there are souls to be saved elsewhere.'

'One more question, if I may. Have you any children?'

'What an absurdity! I am a man of God! I have taken a voluntary vow of chastity in order that I may remain untainted by the sin of fornication. My mind is pure. *Let not sin therefore reign in your mortal body, that ye should obey it in the lusts thereof.* Book of Romans, chapter six, verse twelve. Something more?'

'Nothing more. I will seek you if I need further information. Thank you.'

And the clergyman departed, offering a parting suggestion that Mr Williamson might reacquaint himself with the New Testament that his soul could be prepared. The man was clearly deranged. He had been preaching about London for years and had never hurt anyone. It seemed highly unlikely that he had committed the murder. Of course, that did not mean that he knew nothing about it.

The detective looked around once more at the scene. One of the beds had two pillows, one laid next to the other – presumably Eliza-Beth's bed. He walked over to it, trying to recall which head had belonged to which girl. A single strand of red hair lay on the left-hand pillow. As he reached down to take it between thumb and forefinger, he felt paper crackle beneath. The letter?

The stitching at the side of the pillow had been unpicked in order to hide the secret within. He opened the narrow aperture and delved into the horsehair to extract what he had been searching for.

The letter had no addresses, reinforcing the assertion that it had been delivered personally to the house. By her parent, or by a representative thereof? The hand was in standard copperplate and could have been written by a male or female hand. He sniffed the paper but could not identify any perfume, not even pipe smoke. Sitting on the bed, he read:

Dear Eliza-Beth

You do not know me, though you carry a part of me about your neck. It was I who left that locket with you when I shamefully abandoned you at the church door, hoping that, like Moses, you would be borne to safety.

I have followed your progress from afar, reading of your travels in the newspapers and hearing of your fame around the continent. Indeed, I have attended your shows at Vauxhall Gardens and seen the way you are exhibited like an animal. I have even spoken to you at your own abode and discovered your graceful, loving nature. Through all these years, my heart has been pierced with guilt.

In my heart, I have accepted that the time has come to accept you, regardless of my position and reputation. Very soon, I will come to claim you, even if I have to pay the rapacious Mr Coggins for the privilege.

Be patient, sweet child. You may communicate with me by passing a letter to the person who has delivered

this. He will return early on Monday morning. I
apologize for not revealing my true identity –
I cannot yet have it known should the letter
fall into a stranger's hand.
*   I send you my love.*

There was no signature. There were, however, some new questions to be answered. First among them was why the Reverend Archer, who confessed to his own poor observation, had alluded to '*a letter tucked into someone's clothing*' – just as it had been described by Miss Eugenia and Mr Coggins. Second was the identity of the messenger who was to visit that very morning. Was he the stranger identified by the locals? Or was the 'toff' an associate of the murderer come to see what was happening?

EIGHT

We will step momentarily away from the case itself to cast an eye over the sensation that the Lambeth Murder very shortly began to cause in the city. The facts of the case, like smoke from the chimney of that very boarding house, seemed to rise into the sky over the sea of rooftops. There, they intermingled with the carbonaceous effluvia of a million other chimneys: domestically burned wood and coal, the sulphurous billows of the copper manufactory, the acid clouds of the alkali works, the ferrous breath of the foundry, and the hot, malty outpourings of the distillery. They cooled, solidified, and then began to settle across the city in a fine particulate of scandal, rumour, gossip – and news. No corner of the metropolis could escape the story.

Of course, the newspapers covered every detail. But among the common man, it was the clever patterer who spread the news like a wind-borne fire through the streets. There he was at the street corner, shouting his wares with carefully emphasized words:

'HIDEOUS and UNNATURAL MURDER in Lambeth! TWO-HEADED-MONSTER slain by razor in den of abominable DEFORMITY . . .'

Called by his words, the people approached to buy his broadsheets, which were spiced with similar linguistic *bon-bons* to tantalize those who read them. Others who could not read listened in hushed congregations as the words were read to them, evoking the yearned-for terror of monsters and murderers in their midst. Thousands of people had already handed over their penny to see that sheet beginning, 'An authentic account of the recent events in Lambeth and the MURDER of Eliza-Beth, a two-headed girl . . .' Viewings of 'Dr Zwigoff's peculiarities had multiplied tenfold at the nightly Vauxhall extravaganza, and Mr Coggins was a deeply contented man.

I offer the following pieces in illustration of the official fascination and outrage caused (adding, with all modesty, that the first piece is my own work).

From page 7 of *the Times* that Wednesday:

In the early hours before dawn on Monday, a most diabolical murder was committed at a boarding house off Princes-street in Lambeth. The victim is a bicephalous girl known only as Eliza-Beth, a performer in the troupe of 'Dr Zwigoff's Anatomical Wonders', currently appearing at Vauxhall Gardens. The supposed perpetrator of the murder has been described by a witness as a working man wearing a cloth cap, a waistcoat and a jacket. He has a scar vertically traversing his left eye.

The following particulars appertaining to the murder may be relied upon as correct: The murderer entered the property by breaking the street-door lock, passed by the kitchen and silently ascended the stairs. On entering the sleeping quarters, he apprehended the deceased sitting at a writing desk. Evidently surprised, he exclaimed, 'Oh,

G—! A monster!' and assaulted her. The sleepers were awoken to discover the poor girl in the throes of death and a cry of 'murder' was raised. Police constable Cullen, 242 L, was the first to attend the scene and called for assistance. Sergeant George Williamson and Police Surgeon McLeod were soon on the spot and discerned that Eliza-Beth was dead, her throat having been cut by a razor. A description of the supposed murderer was elicited from one of the inhabitants and was immediately distributed to other watch houses around the city, but no progress has yet been made in his apprehension.

The reader will observe that no mention has been made of the letters or the locket. I was compelled to omit these details by a senior police officer so that the insane who habitually confess to such crimes may be eliminated on questioning.

Letter to *the Times* (the following day):

Dear Sirs

The late case of murder in Lambeth has captured the attention like so many infamous crimes before it, and the public scrutiny must naturally turn to the police force. Though they may be satisfactorily established as preventors of crime, their role as a detective force must still be in question. This is made evident by the following facts:-

Though a description of the killer has been released to watch houses around the city, and though his identifying characteristics are striking, no trace of the man has yet been found. The truth is that the local beat constable knows only the immediate territory and faces of his district. Should the murderer lurk elsewhere, he will languish in happy anonymity, unsought by men who are certain he does not reside there. The intelligent and skilled men of the Detective Force may have the wherewithal to rove the city without adherence to district boundaries, but they are few in number and cannot possibly have the requisite encyclopaedic knowledge of every face under their authority.

Unless the miscreant is apprehended while carelessly committing a lesser crime, it must be hoped that, as in previous cases, he will suffer a surfeit of guilt and voluntarily confess at his local watch house. If not, I fear the next we hear of him may be in connection with another murder.

A.D., Stoke Newington

Commissioner Mayne sat at the same table he'd headed those few months previously. Those very editions of *the Times* were spread before him, the letter of A.D. of Stoke Newington circled twice, somewhat brutally, and also partially underlined in black ink. Superintendent Wilberforce and Inspector Newsome sat either side of him.

'Superintendent. Inspector. I trust you have seen this . . . this slur. I have marked the most offensive passages. Let me quote: "Though they may be satisfactorily established as preventors of crime, their role as a detective force must still be in question." Or maybe you would prefer this: "They are few in number and cannot possibly have the requisite encyclopaedic knowledge of every face under their authority." Or should I mention the writer's hope that, "as in previous cases", the murderer will deliver himself to the police? What are we doing to catch this killer, gentlemen?'

Mr Newsome cleared his throat. 'Sir – a description of the killer has been distributed about the city—'

'He has a huge scar traversing his face, man! How can he not be known to the local constables? How can we not have found this man as easily as one finds a coffee vendor on the morning streets?'

'It is not so simple, sir. If he has gone to ground in one of the rookeries, no policeman will see him. No colleague will inform on him because the criminal brethren are united only in their hatred of the police. If we sent our men into St Giles or Rotherhithe or Whitechapel, we might spend weeks searching every grimy nook as the killer watches us from the very same darkness.'

'What of your detectives? Cannot they infiltrate these areas?'

'Only, perhaps, if they adopt the attire and habits of the local inhabitants, sir. But even then—'

'Yes, yes – I know about that. We have discussed it.'

Mr Wilberforce interceded: 'If I may make an observation, Sir Richard?'

'Go on.'

'The public attention upon this case is immense, as well it might be. All of London is looking to us to capture this criminal. The quicker it is done, the better. We have the means to do so rapidly and effectively.'

'Are you referring to the situation we discussed before?'

'Sir – the police force is being humiliated. The criminals are laughing at us. If I said I could have your killer in Newgate gaol within the week; if I said that the Detective Force could be covered with glory at the unprecedented rapidity of his pursuit and arrest, and if I said I could do this at no risk to any of our men – would you countenance my methods? You need not know how it is done, only that it is done.'

Sir Richard looked again at the newspaper. He stood and walked over to the window, casting his eyes down at the city of which he had made himself the guardian. A rag-picker was making his way along the street below, picking through the gutter with his pointed stick. The commissioner sighed heavily. He spoke without turning:

'Proceed.'

'The prisoner sleeps but fitfully. He sweats and shivers, and he speaks in his sleep.'

'What does he say?'

'"Fire!" He calls out that there is a fire and moves his limbs sluggishly as if he, too, were on fire.'

'Anything more?'

'Only much agitation, sir. He is calmer and more composed, in fact, when awake.'

'And the sovereigns? From where did he produce them?'

'It was most ingenious, sir. He had them secreted between his sole and shoe. True, he had to destroy the shoes to access them, but it was a masterful hiding place. I have seen nothing like it.'

Inspector Newsome concluded his interview with the warden at Giltspur-street Compter and returned to the room where Mr Wilberforce was contentedly smoking his pipe. He stood, and together they walked to the cell of their nameless prisoner, having discussed their strategy at great length following their short meeting with Sir Richard. There was no sound emanating from inside the cell as they exchanged glances and entered.

The prisoner was sitting cross-legged like an oriental idol, an expression of sublime calm upon his face. He looked up at the officers but gave no sign of recognition – indeed, no sign of any emotion. He was the very essence of impassiveness. Mr Newsome began:

'Henry Matthews, or should I say William Smart . . . or maybe you would prefer Harold Thackeray? Yes, we know you are using these names. We know many things about you.'

The prisoner merely adopted an amused expression.

'You might well smile,' continued Mr Newsome, 'but you are not in possession of all the facts, as we are. Did you know, for example, that the constable whose uniform you were wearing has passed away? Yes – he was accosted by a Negro matching the description of he who lives at the address you dispatched the boy to. Constable Wiseman did not recover from the blow to his head, and you appear to be the direct beneficiary of his assault.'

The prisoner's smile disappeared to be replaced with a stony blankness.

'This is enough to hang you, sir,' said Mr Wilberforce. 'Especially since you refuse to speak in your defence. But that is not all. We also have reason to believe that you are implicated in a series of incendiary attacks that have been fastidiously documented at your place of residence. You appear to know more about these crimes than any policeman in the city. Can you add illumination to any of these accusations? No?'

The prisoner shifted his position on the mat and looked to the window.

'Your man is not coming for you,' said Mr Newsome. 'We have the Negro under arrest on suspicion of the murder of PC Wiseman. You are quite alone now. We have your diamond and your house; you have no more sovereigns to bribe street boys; you stand accused of murder, of possessing a cracksman's tools, and of involvement in incendiarism. You will assuredly be transported. More likely, you will be hanged.'

At this, the prisoner evinced the first perceptible reaction of his waking time at Giltspur. He glared at his interrogators with an expression of fearsome malevolence.

Mr Wilberforce, as the two officers had agreed previously, adopted a more conciliatory tone: 'Prisoner – whatever your name might be – you could defend yourself. Tell us that you are not implicated in these crimes. Speak to us. You seem like an intelligent man – indeed, a gentleman, if yours was the house we visited.'

No response was given.

'No? Then there is nothing further we can do,' sighed Mr Wilberforce. 'The evidence will be presented in court and you will very probably find yourself in the hands of Mr Calcraft, or rather at the end of his rope. Your Negro manservant will also hang as your accomplice. I see that you have nothing to say, so we will leave you.'

The two policemen exchanged a look and made to exit the cell. Then, as the heavy oaken door swung open, they heard a cough behind them and turned to see their prisoner fixing them with an icy stare.

'He is not my manservant,' said the prisoner. 'He is a free man: an American named Benjamin. I will not have him hanged on my account.'

His voice was even, bearing the authority of a judge and the restraint of a confessor. There was a peculiar accent that neither policeman could place. He showed no fear at his situation.

'Aha! He speaks!' remarked Inspector Newsome. 'Are you ready to tell us all you know?'

'Officers – I am not the dullard you may think me to be. Your presence here is extraordinary and thus I adduce you have ulterior motives in detaining me and proffering these ludicrous charges, which you know have little foundation and could be refuted by even the most mediocre barrister.'

Mr Newsome attempted to show no surprise at the articulacy of his prisoner: 'Perhaps you speak the truth, but you underestimate the authority behind us. Any prosecution of ours would be successful.'

'You know that the diamond is my own – it could not be otherwise. I was seen by the arresting constable bending to pick up a set of tools – could not they have been dropped in the street by another? You implicate me in the theft of PC Wiseman's tailcoat and his murder, but are there not many Negroes in London and many shops where second-hand clothes can be bought? Your case is hollow.'

'Would you test your neck and that of your . . . your friend against that assumption? No? I see you are not so confident with that condition.'

'What do you want? I perceive that you have some reason for taking an interest in my case.'

'What we want in the first instance,' began Mr Wilberforce, 'is to know who you are and from where you come. In the second instance, we may have a proposal which may mitigate your case.'

'I see. A bargain. Well, if we are to bargain, I will use whatever value I have to seek advantages for myself. That is the essence of bargaining, is it not?'

'Continue.'

'Benjamin will not be prosecuted. He will be judged

innocent of all charges against him and released immediately. After you have finished with me, I, too, will be judged entirely guiltless all of the spurious charges you have prepared against me and I will be given my freedom. My property will be returned to me. Since I have no reason to trust you, these promises will be presented to me and to Benjamin in letters signed by Sir Richard Mayne himself. You will also outline your plans for me before I reveal a word about myself. On these points, I am unmovable.'

'You bargain like an Arab, sir,' said Mr Wilberforce, who knew something of Arabs and their tricks. 'And you value your worth highly.'

'Why does a superintendent and an inspector of the Detective Force examine a common prisoner? Yes – you might well evince surprise that I know who you are. Why search him and send men to his house in order to search it, as I perceive that you have? Why threaten him with the gallows and use the death of his friend as a tool of persuasion? Why? Because, for some reason that I cannot yet discern, I am clearly of inestimable worth to you.'

'Your demands are ambitious,' remarked Mr Newsome.

'And *you* seek to coerce a free and innocent man into some scheme that the police cannot manage by itself, using dubious methods into the bargain. I value myself at a suitable rate. Can you deliver my requirements? I would like to see Benjamin appear at these very bars and tell me in his own tongueless way that he is free. Next, I would like to see that letter from Sir Richard. Then we can speak again.'

'Why, you are an impertinent—' started Mr Newsome, but the superintendent held his arm and interrupted:

'We will approach Sir Richard. In the meantime, grant us the luxury of at least knowing your name.'

The prisoner seemed to ponder his decision for a few moments, holding his fingers to his temples and closing his eyes. He remained like this for some moments as the two officers exchanged perplexed looks. Then he opened his eyes and looked from one policeman to the other. He cleared his throat.

'My name is Noah Dyson.'

NINE

Haymarket after dark presents a glittering display, though its illuminations vary in brilliance. At its northern end, the muddy streets provide pleasures of a baser kind, its gin shops spilling raucous revellers out into the street to be enticed by prostitutes into alleys for a fumbled encounter – or a cudgel to the scull. Harsh words are exchanged under the influence of spirits, and blows are inevitably exchanged in a blasphemous Babel of expletives. At this end of the street, near Regents-circus, pickpockets lurk away from the identifying light of lamps, and coffee shops hide upper rooms that are rented by the quarter hour.

Compare, however, the southern end near Pall Mall, where swells in silk top hats and doeskin trousers strut arm-in-arm with ladies newly made acquaintance with. With its champagne and oyster bars, this locale exchanges grubby upper-floor rooms for well-appointed hotels, and common street girls for practised courtesans in fine silks and bonnets. Midnight sees the gaslit parade reach its apogee after the theatres have disgorged audiences into a street thronged with barrow vendors and peripatetic brass bands, rattling carriages and cabs, street-sweepers, lurkers and police. The unattended lawyers, students, tourists, lords and City men among them head immediately for the notorious dancing halls such as the Argyll Rooms and the Alhambra, hoping to meet locally residing 'ladies' at the polkas and waltzes.

And midway along this festive thoroughfare, between the glamour and the gloom, between profligacy and wantonness, lay Mary Chatterton's Night Rooms: a place for supper, a place for dancing – a place for illicit encounters engineered by the great lady herself.

It was a cool night, that Thursday – cool enough, per-haps, to warrant a scarf worn over the lower face and a broad-brimmed hat pulled low over the eyes. Cool enough, certainly, to be wearing a shapeless old overcoat large enough to distort one's true shape, especially when hunched and hobbling artificially like a knock-kneed beggar. Cool enough to strike a match to light a pipe, pausing just a little too long to watch the dancing flame burn out.

In a back room smelling strongly of *eau de parfum* and the sickly pall of dying flowers, Mary Chatterton herself held court. The muffled sounds of the orchestra and the thumps of a hundred dancing pairs of feet echoed through the walls to where she sat, enthroned on a gilt and scarlet velvet arm-chair. Two effeminate young men attended her: one offering cut strawberries to her mouth with a silver spoon, the other holding a glass of French champagne from which to sip.

Once a great beauty, she had lured many a man to the tempestuous seas of her rooms, her fiery red tresses and that pale bosom being the rocks upon which many a bark had foundered. It was said that she had been courted by men of rank and power. Now she was fat. Her soft fingers were gaudy with jewels and her second chin glistened stickily with strawberry juice. True, there might have been traces of hair about her upper lip, and that slender waist may have ballooned, but she was still a true voluptuary: a living embodiment of the shameless and always dubious pleasures of her Night Rooms.

'More champagne!' she shouted, as the last sluiced down her throat. 'More champagne, my boys! More strawberries!'

Her attendants scuttled to fetch more treats for their mistress, leaving her momentarily alone in the room. It was a shrine to her conquests: over-spilling boxes of *billets-doux*, jewellery lying carelessly on the mantel, and calling cards from countless men – most of them ignored. It was said that she held more secrets than anyone in London and that, as long as she lived, there would be men all over the city who would continue to seek her favour. She was an illustrious lover, but not a woman to have as an enemy. Who can forget the case of the young doctor who attempted to blackmail her over an alleged indiscretion? His dead body, pulled black and bloated from the river, was a warning to any who would slight her.

As she reached for the last of the strawberries, the handle began to rattle on the door leading to a rear courtyard: a heavy oaken door which was bolted and seldom used (and known to the *cognoscenti* as the 'lovers' door'). Indeed, a full-length mirror hung upon its back, half-disguising its existence. That mirror wobbled now as Mary shouted back at her own reflection.

'Use the front entrance, dear! This one is bolted. We don't use it.'

The door stopped rattling. Then a tremendous kick ripped the bolt and lock from the jamb. A man carrying a black canvas bag entered, pushing the splintered door closed behind him.

'Good evening, Mary.'

'You can't come kicking my f— door in!' replied Ms Chatterton in characteristically salty terms. 'Who are you, blackguard, to come bashing into my private parlour? I should box your ears!'

The man, who had a scarf pulled over his face and a hat worn low, stepped briskly towards her and slapped her hard across the face with the back of his gloved hand.

'Why, you —! I'll not be hit in my own f— Rooms!' she expostulated, struggling to haul her bulk to a standing position.

He hit her again, this time rocking her back into the chair. A trickle of blood emerged from her already fruit-reddened lips. Her eyes burned with humiliation and loathing: 'You —! Were I a man, I would rip out your eyes and fry them!'

And again he hit her, so that the tears in her eyes were those of pain rather than mere outrage. After this, he unbuttoned his coat and pulled a chair over to sit before her. She snivelled and mopped her bleeding lip with a silk handkerchief. He extracted a razor from an inner pocket.

'Now Mary, there is no need for theatricals. I want to talk to you. I trust that you will not call out further, or I will be obliged to cut your throat with this weapon and ruin that delightful dress with your blood.'

'Show your face, you cur, so that I might spit on it.'

'I have been watching you, Mary. They say you know many secrets about many powerful people. They say that if you were inclined, you could blackmail half of London with the pillow-whispered truths of your career.'

'I am sworn to secrecy. On my honour.'

'Your "honour"? That is amusing. They say that the greatest secrets are the ones you keep about yourself, Mary.'

'So, you are a blackmailer. You have no information about me, d— you. My boys will soon return to find you here – then you shall see my wrath!'

'No, they will hear a man's voice in here as they have so many times before and they will retire until morning, when they imagine your "visiter" will leave by this discreet door here. We will be quite undisturbed. Am I correct?'

'Blackguard! What are you, then? Come to blackmail me? Take some jewellery and leave, you petty criminal. You shall be found later and beaten beyond recognition.'

'I see I have not yet garnered your full attention. Perhaps you need something to focus on. Have you seen this before?'

At this, the man – who, by now, I am sure the reader has correctly identified as the 'General' who met Mr Bradford in the marine store – extracted Eliza-Beth's locket from his coat and held it before Mary's eyes. It twirled in the gaslight.

She became rigid in her throne and paled even further. She looked behind her to the other door, hoping vainly, per-haps, that a rescuer would enter.

'Ah, *now* I have your full attention!' he continued. 'Where have you seen this trinket before, Ms Chatterton?'

'I . . . I have never seen it. It looks too cheap to be of my possession.'

'Your expression says otherwise. Have you been to Lam-beth recently, or to see the shows at Vauxhall Gardens?'

'I have not.' Her lower lip began to quiver.

'Must I strike you again? I know that you have been to both.'

'Vauxhall is a pleasant place. Why wouldn't I go there for the music and the dancing?'

'Or to see "Dr Zwigoff's Anatomical Wonders", perhaps? No answer? Mary Chatterton lost for words? You have been there on three occasions, one of them being a private viewing of the wonders. And you have also visited the freaks at home—'

'They are not freaks!'

'No matter what the appellation, you have been to that boarding house in Lambeth. Tell me, have you been following the newspapers in the last couple of days?'

'I don't bother myself with the latest events in China, or the price of coal.'

'Yes, you are a queen in this tiny kingdom of yours. Nothing beyond its gaiety and popping corks exists. Gossip and rumour is your only news. Still, there can be few who have not already heard the news. Must I be the one to inform you of young Eliza-Beth?'

'What? What of her?'

'I perceive your concern. She is dead – most likely being boiled for her skeleton as we speak, her throat opened by a ruffian's razor—'

'*Liar!*' Fat tears swelled from those once beguiling eyes and her lips crumpled. 'Liar! She is alive! She must be alive.'

'No, she is dead. Murdered.'

'O! . . . I . . . I cannot bear it!'

He opened the locket and extracted the lock of red hair. He stood and held it next to Mary's head so that the strands became quite indistinguishable from her hair.

'A perfect match. I was curious, Mary, why you might have such an interest in the girl. When I met her for myself, the resemblance was striking. The locket merely confirmed my assumptions – it and the letter.'

'You have my letter?'

'*Your* letter? No, but I have hers. She made reference to a striking similarity that she shared with her anonymous parent. She believed she knew your identity.'

'My Eliza-Beth! . . . Show me the letter. Please.'

'Alas, it is in a poor condition. I have it in a secure place.'

'And now you will use it against me, is that right? Are you her murderer?'

'Tell me the story.'

'Why should I? Did you kill her?'

'The girl is dead. Only you and I and perhaps the father need know the truth. I have enough to blackmail you, if that was my purpose. Was it the shame that made you forsake her?'

'I was young and beautiful. I might have had London at my feet, but my lover – Love! What a dream! – filled my head with tales of houses and children. I was ready to settle: the mother hen. Can you imagine? He was a good man; perhaps he would have cared for me. But I did not want one man. One man could not buy enough jewellery or champagne for one as empty as I. One man could not supply the attention that I needed. A queen needs more than a king – she needs a country.

'He was away when I gave birth to the monster, that punishment from Heaven for my sin. I could not accept the child . . . nor could I bear to live with it. I told him it was stillborn . . . I left him also. All I had was my beauty and my dreams . . . and now . . . look what I have become. I am unworthy of the man and the child.'

'So you abandoned her. I would have done the same.'

'It is easy for you to say that! You are a man. You feel no guilt or emotion or connection with a child. She came from inside me!'

'And you abandoned her.'

'B—!'

'Indeed I am. Why did you try to contact your abandoned child now, after all these years?'

'You would not understand.'

'Guilt? Redemption? Or was it business? I have heard that the girl was quite—'

'Have you no soul? Have you no pity?'

'Maybe once, but I found such things superfluous, and then dangerous. What I am interested in at present, however, is the identity of the father. I have my suspicions, and you will confirm or deny them. Information is my currency, Ms Chatterton. I would have difficulty blackmailing one such as you, who has greater currency than I in the guilty secrets of important people, and whose character is as blackened as can be. The father may be a different matter. I suspect he has much to lose from these revelations.'

'Never!'

'Have you contacted him as you have contacted Eliza-Beth? Do you now aim to pursue that family life you once eschewed?'

'Ha! What man would acknowledge such a creature as Eliza-Beth as his own? What man would accept me, knowing what all of London knows about *my* reputation? I have not spoken to him for years. He may be dead for all I know, or living on the other side of the world.'

'Why do you protect him? You have no love for him now.'

'The love I had for him was the only love I ever truly gave

a man. I will take it to the grave, if only to spite you. You callous, heartless—'

'I anticipated such an answer. And if it is the grave you seek, you will find it soon enough – but not before you tell me what I require.'

'You will not get the better of me, you —!'

'We will see.' He stood and opened his black canvas bag, extracting a coil of rope from within. Then he took a silk handkerchief from his jacket pocket. 'I am going to put this in your mouth, Mary, and secure it in place. I can't have you screaming all night. You will speak when you are ready to speak. Do not be alarmed – it is clean.'

Naturally, she struggled as he tied her. But her cries were soon stifled and she was broken in body and in spirit. That was when he reached for the poker and began to stoke the coals so that an eruption of sparks reflected in his eager eyes.

TEN

Mr Williamson had just taken a carriage to Haymarket and was turning over the facts of the case in his head as he rattled across the night-time city. Who had delivered the letter to Eliza-Beth? And did that have anything to do with her murder? Since there was little apparent motivation for the crime, those few visiters were his only routes of investigation. Mr Coggins had listed the clergyman, the writer, Mary Chatterton and the doctor as callers during the current run at Vauxhall. Reverend Archer had already been filed in the detective's mind as a dubious case; Dr Cole was in Edinburgh and would not return for some days; Mary Chatterton, however, was the greatest anomaly in his mind.

This notorious woman of pleasure was famous for hardly ever leaving her Rooms, not least because of her unwieldy size and inability to be too distant from a bottle of champagne. She was a rare and gaudy flower that flourished only in the unique climate of her kingdom. And, in retrospect, the letter *had* had a vaguely feminine stroke, its letters just a little more rounded and its downward strokes more truncated than one might find in a man's writing.

Haymarket had passed the zenith of its revels as he

stepped from the cab. The streets were less populous and the gaiety had transformed into surfeit. He pursed his lips in distaste as a young girl hanging from the neck of her beau vomited forth the large quantities of brandy and water she had consumed that evening. Someone else was singing drunkenly unseen, no doubt having emerged from the penny gaff with its bawdy songs fresh in his gin-addled mind. Mr Williamson made for the passage that led to Mary's Night Rooms.

'There is an admission to be paid.' A thickset man barred the detective's way with a beefy arm.

'I am Sergeant Williamson of the Detective Force. I am not a customer.'

'It don't matter nothing to me. All who enters pays.'

'I know you. You are "Fancy" Harry. If I am not mistaken, you have spent some time in gaol for your violent temper. Are you committing a violent act upon me now?'

'I am not.'

'I fear that heavy arm of yours has done me some damage. I will be forced to arrest you—'

'I didn't touch you!'

'I'm sure there is a constable hereabouts who will aid me in your arrest . . .'

'All right! Enter! You police are—'

'Contain that thought in the limited drawers of your mind, Harry.'

Music made its way along the murky passage to meet him, and rose in volume as he opened the door to the ground-floor dancing hall. A few couples were still whirling across the wooden floor with intoxicated imprecision as the band worked their instruments in the final throes of exhaustion. Cigar smoke, perspiration and the scent of spilled drinks filled the humid air of the place. Murmured conversation precipitated from the tabled balconies above, punctuated with a pattering of lascivious laughter. Their pleasure was reaching its autumn, turning from sweetness to rot.

Mr Williamson approached the large horseshoe-shaped bar, which flashed with gas plumes reflected in multitudinous bottles and mirrors.

'You strike me as a brandy and water man,' chirped the hatless girl attending it. 'I always knows a brandy cove, I does.'

'You are mistaken. I am looking for Miss Mary Chatterton.'

'You and a hundred other gents! Miss Chatterton is seen only by appointment.'

'I am not . . . I am not seeking services of that kind. This is about an investigation I am conducting.'

'Well, you still can't see her. She's entertaining a gentleman as we speak.'

'How long will she be?'

'What a question!' The bar girl gave a saucy wink. 'The lucky gent will be leaving here at dawn if *I'm* any judge.'

'I cannot wait. Call her now or I will be arresting you and having you sent to Newgate before you can serve another drink.'

'Why? I haven't done anything wr—'

At that moment, one of the boys who had earlier been attending Mary burst into the room pale with horror and raised the cry that spelled free admittance to Mr Williamson:

'*Murder! O! Mary is murdered!*'

The boy then fainted where he stood and was fussed over

by the barmaid. At the cry of 'murder', the band stopped and the dancers stopped. The conversation upon the balcony diminished and a prickly silence settled. There was a single, strangled cry that could have been a laugh or a sob – then an urgent murmuring overtook the gathered revellers.

Mr Williamson strode over the fallen boy towards the door from which he had emerged. A stench of burned hair, flesh and clothing told him that the discovery would be an unpleasant one.

He was correct. The *boudoir* of Mary Chatterton presented a sorry scene. He immediately noted the shattered lock of the 'lovers' door' and also took in the chair placed opposite Mary's. Evidently a discussion had taken place. The lady herself was tied firmly to her chair, her head slumped on to her breast. Drops of her blood spattered the walls and furniture. There was not enough blood to have produced a clear footprint, but some of the drops had been smudged by a flat sole, which appeared very like the one he had seen at the Lambeth house. A balled and bloodstained handkerchief lay on the floor beside the chair and the poker remained in the fire, glowing red at its tip. Was that the gag that had stifled her shouts?

Mary herself was barely distinguishable, even to those who knew her. Her head had had its crown of red hair burned away like a stubble-scorched field, leaving that bloated face oddly naked. The effect thereupon was worsened by the bruises, swelling and crusted rivulets of blood that had evidently resulted from a systematic beating. Her arms showed the charred spots where the poker had been held against her. He checked her fingernails to see if she had managed to retaliate and found some blood there which may have been her own or her assailant's. None of these injuries had killed her, however. It was the gaping wound across her throat.

Brought back to awareness by an unadulterated brandy, the boy who had found her ventured gingerly into the room once more. His lip trembled with emotion.

'Is she really dead, sir? Is Mary dead?'

'Yes, quite dead. Her throat has been cut. She was badly treated before that small mercy, I fear. Tell me how you found her.'

'I heard the lovers' door go and thought she was again alone, the gentleman having left—'

'Who was with her? Did you see him?'

'I didn't, sir. There is a rule that if we hear a man's voice, we are to retire until morning.'

'And you never break that rule?'

'I . . . I admit I saw the fellow for the briefest moment through the door here. He was sitting before her and they were talking. I didn't see his face 'cause he had a wide-brimmed hat on and a scarf about his face. His clothes were all black. I dared not linger, so I retired to the dancing hall. If only I had—'

'And when did you find her?'

'As I said, I heard the door go. I waited about twenty minutes and came to see if she wanted champagne. I smelled the awful smoke and saw her sitting there . . . O! Her beautiful hair all gone!'

'What time was this?'

'Just now, before I came into the bar.'

Mr Williamson opened the lovers' door and stepped out into the alleyway. There was no sign of anyone – merely the stink of the stopped gutters. He stepped back inside and extracted his notebook.

'Can you tell me if anything has been taken from this room?'

'I would have to look.'

'Well, look then. Now.'

The boy crossed to the mantel and looked carefully where Mary's discarded jewellery still glinted dully. He seemed to examine each piece rapidly. Then he crossed to her body and examined her bejewelled fingers with a lachrymose tenderness. Next, he opened a wooden box on an ornate *escritoire* loaded with feminine unguents and found that it was still stocked with money. His eyes flicked among the bottles and Mr Williamson saw the reaction.

'The letter – the letter is gone.'

'Which letter?'

'She had been writing a letter. I was to deliver it personally this very night.'

'To whom was it addressed?'

'I don't know. I only saw her writing it and then saw it lying there. It was there when we left the room, I'm sure.'

'Tell me, boy, have you ever been to that house in Lambeth where the recent murder took place?'

'Never! O! I never have!'

'I perceive from your vehemence that that is not the truth. Your mistress has been slain and you are no longer bound by any oath you may have sworn.'

'I have never been there! I know nothing of the murder.'

'Which murder? The one sitting here before us? Or the one at the house where you delivered your letter? Yes – I know about it. I also believe that you were also sent to collect a letter. You were seen. Cease your crying, boy – you are

not suspected of any crime, but you might be able to illuminate one, and you might help to catch Mary's murderer if he
is the same who murdered young Eliza-Beth. Tell me the
truth.'

The boy fidgeted as he stood. His eyes watered afresh and
he chewed his bottom lip. He rested his hand on the chair
opposite Mary. Then he slumped upon it, staring at his feet.
'I . . . I did go there with Mary two nights before the murder,
but I waited outside. She had an audience with the curiosities. The next day I was sent there with a letter for Eliza-
Beth.'

'Is this the letter?' Sergeant Williamson extracted it from
a pocket and handed it to the boy.

'I didn't read it, but it is her writing and looks like the
paper she uses. But how did you—?'

'No matter. So it *was* Monday that you were to collect a
letter – the same day of the murder?'

'Yes, last Monday morning. I approached the house just
before dawn but saw a number of people there. I was under
instructions to collect the letter in secrecy and didn't want
anyone to see. They told me that a murder had been committed and I returned here empty-handed. Mary was angry
with me and said I could not be trusted. She said she would
send someone more faithful. I *was* faithful . . . but I couldn't
tell her about the murder when I learned the victim because . . .
I feared her reaction. She had such a terrible temper and I
only wanted her happiness. I *did*!'

'Quite, quite. Stop your snuffling, boy. Did you see anything suspicious as you loitered about the house? The
murderer exited the house mere minutes before you arrived.'

'O! I am sorry for my tears . . . no, I saw no murderer.
Only the people standing outside the house. I do not know

them. To my eyes, everyone in that area looks like a murderer.'

Mr Williamson made a note in his book and consulted his watch. The discovery had been made barely half an hour previously. The murderer had left perhaps half an hour before that and was walking the streets or riding in a coach somewhere in the vicinity at that very moment, unseen and undetectable.

'Can I go, sir? I feel quite faint again.'

'Tell no one else to enter this room. I must speak to anyone else who may have entered since the killer left.'

'There is no one, sir.'

'All right. Leave me.'

Alone again, the detective looked about the room and inhaled its feminine scents. Strange how a woman's room always had a scent and a sense of its own, as if her spirit remained even when she was absent. He walked to a large mirror and saw his sombre, pockmarked face reflected in a surface more used to beauty and gaiety. A brush with strands of red hair lay nearby, and he noticed a carelessly discarded letter that began '*My dearest Mary, I burn for you . . .*' He did not read further. Instead, he once again extracted his notebook and attempted to assess the scant evidence:

Victim: Mary Chatterton, bon vivant and woman of dubitable virtue.

Location: A back room in her Night Rooms.

Clues: Burned hair, matches, broken door, footprints, man with hidden face.

Suspect: The murderer of Eliza-Beth (disguised)? An ex- or spurned lover?

Weapon: Fire, a blunt instrument and a knife/razor.

Motive: To glean information? Revenge? Jealousy?
  Theft of a letter?

The nature of the murder was certainly curious. Nothing appeared to have been stolen, though the room was full of jewellery. Had the killer known about the 'lovers' door' and that Mary's attendants would leave him to complete his work in privacy? The fact that the door had been smashed indicated that Mary did not know, or at least was not expecting, her visiter. That, and his insistence on wearing a hat and scarf to cover his face while inside. And why had he maltreated her so before delivering the final blow – unless he was attempting to elicit information by force? That would explain the positioning of the chairs. The use of fire, in any case, was highly unconventional and unnecessarily cruel when the man in question already had his fists and a razor.

It was possible, of course, that the murder was completely unconnected with the Lambeth Murder. Mary was – or at least had been – a notorious *grande horizontale*. She held the secrets of many who would welcome her perpetual silence, though she was not reputed to be a blackmailer.

Nevertheless, the parallels with Lambeth were too clear to ignore: the broken lock, the razor, the seated victim and the lack of discernible motive. Mary was one of the last people to converse with Eliza-Beth, and the letters were a crucial link. Another question was why Mary's hair had been burned off. Was it pure malice? Then there was the murderer himself: careful to cover his face lest he be identified. Because he was known to Mary or the bar staff? Or because there was an obvious distinguishing mark on his face – a scar, for example?

All was supposition. With his experience, and his detective's mind, Mr Williamson knew that the truth of the case may prove to be something else entirely.

All he could say with certainty was that the murder of Eliza-Beth was at the centre of some larger pattern.

ELEVEN

It is some time since we heard of Bully Bradford, the murderer of Eliza-Beth. Had he followed his sponsor's advice, he would have been biding his time on the continent or in Scotland. But, true to character, he had not left the insalubrious streets of his youth. In fact, he could be found most nights in the close, smoky atmosphere of the penny gaff, his conspicuously scarred face reddened with gin and merriment. Let us enter that place unseen and watch him in his native environment.

An audience of a hundred or so people are gathered shoulder-to-shoulder on a wooden floor baptized with a sticky layer of beer and gin. The band plays a frenetic dance and four ladies stamp enthusiastically on the small *dais*, lifting and twirling their skirts so that the men in the audience can quite blatantly see their legs. Cat calls of 'Prime pins!' and 'Go on, girls!' ring out from men and boys alike, whose faces shine with the heat and intoxication of the place.

As for Mr Bradford, he shows no trace of remorse or sadness for the crime committed just four days previously. He jigs from foot to foot with a carious grin and loops an over-familiar hand around the waist of a woman beside him. The police could walk in at any moment and apprehend him, except that the police constable is not permitted to enter such a place. Even if he was, this unlicensed gaff, a recently abandoned shop, is located in the Minories, a sump of criminality drawn from all the nearby docks and river industries. A uniformed officer entering this place after dark was either an exceedingly brave, or a foolhardy, man.

And yet there *was* one man watching the bully. Towards the back of the heaving crowd, near the street entrance, the sometime bare-knuckle fighter Mr Henry Hawkins loitered. *His* countenance showed none of the grinning idiocy of the drunk, for he was at work on the orders of his employer. A hooked iron bar was secreted down one trouser leg, though one of his prodigious fists would have been sufficient to dispatch any victim, should that be his purpose.

As the girls left the 'stage' with their bonnets askew and hair in disarray, a portly man with a too-small top hat stepped up, causing an instant roar of approval with his ejaculation of 'B— h—, me eyes have steamed over!' He was a 'comedian' whose patter seemed to consist of little more than uttering expletives, each of which stimulated the crowd to greater laughter. Bully Bradford himself was weeping tears of mirth that ran down the channel of his scar and into his gin.

Henry Hawkins, however, was not laughing. He was observant and patient. Indeed, so intent was he on observing Mr Bradford that he had not noticed another man watching both himself and the bully. This man was also laughing along with the crowd and had the same glowing face, although a careful look at his eyes would have shown that he was neither intoxicated nor amused. Nor did the rough corduroy jacket and knee breeches represent his usual attire. He had followed the bully into the gaff an hour or so previously and then, very quickly, noted the presence of Mr Hawkins at the door.

With a final flourish, the band put down their instruments and reached for their glasses of ale as the proprietor shamelessly attempted to expedite the exit of one audience in favour of the next: 'Come along now! Out you go! There are others waiting!' And indeed there was a large gathering waiting at the street door to enter the hot fug for the third encore of the evening.

The bully emerged with the flow of people and, after some noisily cordial leave-taking among his friends, immediately turned south in the direction of Rosemary-lane. The street was alive at that time with the noise of public houses and girls in over-tight bodices asking gentlemen if they'd like to retire for a warming brandy. Vendors shouted their wares from the kerb: '*Coffee! Get yer coffee! . . . Kidney pies, good and 'ot! . . . 'Am sandwiches as thick as yer 'ead – get 'em fresh!*'

Thus with a meat pie in his hand and a clay pipe at the side of his mouth, the bully ambled along unsteadily past the glaring light of shops and coffee houses. Here, he was among his kind: the bawdy dredgers, ballast heavers, coal-whippers, watermen and sailors who were quick to drink and quicker to fight. Pipe smoke replaced the common air and hid the stench of the gutters.

The bully's footsteps were filled just a few feet behind by Mr Hawkins, still utterly oblivious that he himself was being followed. *His* pursuer appeared to be staggering under the influence of the gin he had not drunk, and to the casual passer-by he was one of the many working men of the neighbourhood enjoying an evening out in such a conventional manner that he might well have been invisible.

But as the bully turned the corner on to Rosemary-lane, Mr Hawkins's pursuer changed his gait and posture, standing more erect and affecting alertness. Now he appeared a late-night shopper at the marine stores and second-hand clothing emporia. Gazing into windows and handling the hanging garments, he remained as inconspicuous as he had before.

Henry Hawkins, however, was known to many of the residents from his time in the fights and, even in this area, he radiated a threat of violence that repulsed people for yards around him. All, that is, except for one bleary-eyed 'fancy' lover who called out:

'Butcher 'Awkins, is that you? Look! It's 'Awkins of the fancy!'

Mr Hawkins looked malevolently at the man who had called attention to his presence. But it was too late to maintain anonymity and Bully Bradford had turned round on hearing the name. His eyes met those of Hawkins and filled with justifiable dread. He turned quickly, hoping perhaps to give the impression that he had not seen his nemesis – though his increasing velocity demonstrated otherwise. Hawkins, too, quickened his pace.

The bully cut rapidly down Cartwright-street, puffing heavily at his pipe and perspiring freely. A prostitute would later report seeing him rush past her in a most agitated state, pursued first by a 'big bruiser' and then shortly after by 'a man of no particular distinction'. The bully turned into a *cul de sac* and waited there, panting, in the vain hope that his pursuer had lost him. It was a stinking and forgotten alley of the city, rank with the corpse of a rotting dog and alive with rats scuttling away from his approach.

'Good evening to you, Mr Bradford,' said a smiling Mr Hawkins.

'Why yer following me? What d'yer want?'

'I have a message from the General.'

'*Do* yer? I've 'ad enough on 'im. What's 'e want?'

The ex-fighter reached forward and grabbed Mr Bradford by the stock, jerking him within range of his fearsome breath. The clay pipe fell from the bully's mouth and crunched under Hawkins's boot.

'General says your existence is no longer required.'

'*Did* 'e? Well . . . well . . .'

'Short of insolence now, aren't you, maggot?'

With his spare hand, Hawkins extracted the iron bar and raised it above his head to smash the bully's scull like a boiled egg. Its descent was halted only by the voice of the third man – he who had been following Mr Hawkins.

'Henry Hawkins! Put down that bar.'

Hawkins turned, Mr Bradford's throat still in his fist. 'Who the — are you? A detective? Be on your way, or you'll also be found in the river tomorrow.'

'I told you to set him free. I am taking him.'

'We'll see about this,' said Hawkins. He shoved the bully towards the end of the alley, where he stumbled and fell to the muddy ground. Then the fighter turned fully to face his challenger, a man of a much slighter build than he. 'You may have heard of me, if you follow the fancy.'

'I have heard of you. And I tell you once again to deliver Mr Bradford to me. You need not fight about it.'

Mr Hawkins adopted the pose of the fighter, fists held high, and approached his opponent.

'I have no interest in harming you, Hawkins.'

Hopping from foot to foot now as if he were in the ring, Mr Hawkins snorted at the idea that any man could hurt him, but noted with some surprise that the stranger evinced no alertness of danger. Nor did the man raise his fists to fight. Somewhat insulted by the lack of fear he was inspiring, he lunged with a formidable right . . .

But the man was not where his fist had aimed. Instead, the fighter felt a stinging blow to the side of his head that made his eyes flash and his ears ring. He had not seen where it had come from and did not know whether it had been a hand, a foot or a weapon. He flicked around and saw the man standing behind him, hands empty.

Again, the fighter lunged with a prodigious punch. His combatant did not move his feet. Rather, he deflected the approaching arm away from him at the elbow and aimed a staggering blow to Mr Hawkins's throat with the edge of his hand. The latter clutched his neck in agony and stumbled, gurgling and frankly stunned. As he knelt struggling for air, the heel of the other man's hand connected solidly with his forehead and he fell quite unconscious to the muddy ground, where a well-placed kick at his upper abdomen seemed to empty all of the air from his body.

'Come with me, Mr Bradford, if you wish to live longer,' said the stranger.

''Ow d'yer know me . . .? *Yer bested Butcher 'Awkins!*' replied Mr Bradford, clearly dumbfounded.

'And I will do the same for you unless you accompany me immediately.'

The bully approached his saviour in wonder, uncertain

whether to be afraid or amazed. At this point, a pair of handcuffs were locked deftly about his wrists.

'Oi! What's this? Are yer a buzzer?'

'I am not. But you are under arrest and I have some questions for you. Do not try to resist or I will be obliged to injure you considerably.'

The two men walked back towards the busier streets, not noticing another – a fourth man – who had observed the whole proceedings from the shadows, and who was following them now back towards Rosemary-lane.

Mr Bradford looked nervously around him for a chance to run, or perhaps for a friend to free him.

'You are captured now. Your fate is known,' warned his 'saviour'.

'Yer not a detective. Let me free and we'll both profit. I 'ave money.'

'What happens to you is of no concern to me. The police will discern if you are guilty of the Lambeth murder.'

The gin-addled brain of Mr Bradford struggled to comprehend his situation. 'I . . . 'ow do they—? No one saw . . . It weren't me! I was made to do it!'

'By whom?'

'I . . . I cannot tell. 'E'd kill me sure as a dog kills a rat. Or set light to me, more likely.'

'Stop. What did you say?'

'Why, that 'e'd kill me sure as—'

'You said he would set light to you. Why did you say that?'

'Nothin'. Just, 'e plays with lucifer matches—'

'What is his name?'

'What's it worth to yer? If I'm in a position to—'

'It is worth your miserable life to tell me directly. Nobody need know that I have found you tonight. I could snap your neck like a twig and toss you in the river without a sorrowful feeling. It will be no worse than your appointment with Mr Calcraft.'

'Yer won't know 'im. They call 'im General, though I've 'eard others call him Mister Ball or some such . . .'

'Where? Where have you seen him?'

'Well, to tell the God's 'onest, I don't often see 'is face—'

'*Where?*'

'Last was at the marine store jus' off Rosemary. Use to be "Wilson's".'

'I know it.'

'Will yer set me at liberty now?'

'No, you will certainly hang. I am taking you to the nearest watch house. In the meantime, you will tell me everything you know of this man and you might survive the journey.'

They continued along the night streets, Mr Bradford occasionally being pulled by the handcuffs like a recalcitrant ass.

The reader will have no doubt surmised that in this latter scene Henry Hawkins's conqueror and Mr Bradford's apprehender can have been none other than Noah Dyson. It will be necessary, therefore, to fill the lacunae.

Noah had indeed been presented with his letter from Sir Richard (an occurrence occasioning unprecedented rancour at Scotland Yard), and seen Benjamin freed to his satisfaction. Then he had been informed of the conditions of his release by Inspector Newsome:

'Mr Dyson, we are to engage you as a species of detective in the pursuit of a murderer. You have perhaps heard about the case in Lambeth from the turnkeys? It is he. The details of your arrest, and our investigations into your life, have led us to believe that you are a man of some resource—'

'Albeit a criminal in your eyes.'

'No matter. You have the skills we seek. Our witness statement describes a man with a perpendicular scar crossing his left eye: a working man wearing a cap and knee breeches.'

'That describes innumerable men in London – if he is still in London.'

'The scar narrows our search. You presumably have intelligence of the criminal classes. Do you know of such a man?'

'No. But I may know where to ask.'

'You are to find this man and bring him to the nearest watch house. There he will be handed over to Detective Sergeant Williamson, who is handling the case.'

'And thereafter I will be free.'

'You will remember that the conditions of your release are dependent on you providing us with information about yourself.'

'You know my name. I was born in this city in the parish of St Giles and spent time as a sailor in the South Seas, hence my tattoo and the lash marks you have seen. I recently resettled in London.'

'That is hardly a biography, Mr Dyson. How do you come to live in Manchester-square? From where do you draw your income? Why do your neighbours know you by different names? Why have you documented fires in the city and who is the man you seek? Why were you so reluctant to speak when you were captured? The questions multiply!'

'I see no necessity for you to know these things. My usefulness to you is not affected by the answers and you know it.'

'Call it curiosity, then. We are not about to release a man who may be a greater criminal than we already think you to be. Are you an incendiary?'

'I am not. I take an amateur's interest in crime and cata-logue it as another man might pin butterflies to a board. I may compile a monograph on the subject.'

'I see. And who is the man you appear to be seeking? You need not look so confused. We discovered the book in your study: that handwritten book in which you have docu-mented your researches. We have been looking through it and discerned that you are looking for a man: an incendiary, a man who seems to have no address but the entire city itself. Who is this man?'

'My researches have demonstrated that a single man may be responsible for many of the fires in London. If I am able to find him, I will be happy to turn him over to the police. In the meantime, it is an idle hobby of mine.'

'A hobby? It seems more like a mania.'

'It is a hobby. Might not one man's hobby seem an obses-sion to another?'

'And what of your income? How is it that you – a retired sailor, if we are to believe you – have such wealth?'

'You saw the diamond about my neck. It is the last of many precious stones I acquired during my travels – enough to make me self-sufficient when diligently invested. That is enough. I agreed to pursue your man to the best of my abil-ity, not to sell you my soul. As long as I am in your custody, he is free. When he is in custody, I will be free.'

'You will see in Sir Richard's letter that you are to be engaged until the case has been concluded to the satisfaction of the police. The scarred man is our only suspect at present, but if he proves—'

'Wait. Am I to understand that I could be under obligation to the police as long as this case remains unsolved?'

'We are hoping that your role will lead to its rapid resolution. If you wish to be free, you will do all in your power to bring the perpetrator or perpetrators – whomever they may be – to justice as quickly as you can.'

'I see I have little choice. You will have considered, of course, the possibility that I will simply flee my obligation and disappear?'

'Naturally. But the cost to you would be too great. You would have to flee this city. You would lose your home and possibly your wealth. You would be a fugitive. Alternatively, you could do what is required of you and consider it little more than a minor irritant. Your letter from Sir Richard is your guarantee.'

'And my alternative is to be tried for crimes for which there is no strong evidence. Perhaps I should wait for justice to take its course.'

'I believe I can promise you that you will be found guilty,' said Inspector Newsome. 'This choice of action is your only one.'

'It seems I am compelled to agree.'

And so – to expedite the story – the man calling himself Noah Dyson was released from Giltspur-street. He returned home in the company of Mr Bryant (Inspector Newsome's man) and Benjamin; he changed his clothes, and within half an hour was in the eastern districts in pursuit of the scarred man and his own eventual freedom. Though he did not know Mr Bradford from his description, he did indeed know whom to ask.

Let us not imagine, however, that he was at all trusted by the police officers merely because they held a noose above his neck. Mr Bryant stayed with Benjamin until Noah returned, and other more covert measures had been put in place to ensure complicity in the agreement.

TWELVE

I need hardly describe the public phrensy that attended the capture and trial of Mr Bradford towards the end of that week. Sir Richard Mayne had caught his murderer, and the Metropolitan Police enthusiastically released a version of the story so that the newspapers could glut themselves on the already infamous case. Sketches of the bully – looking variously brutal and bemused depending on the artist – appeared in *the Times*, the *Illustrated London News* and the *Observer*, not to mention the broadsheets being sold by patterers on every street corner of the metropolis. As might be expected, many of these scandal-mongering sheets emphasized sensation at the expense of verity. The following – by my own hand, and written for the common taste – is a finer example than many of the less literate specimens abroad at that time:

CUT-THROAT MURDERER CAPTURED!
Will hang at Newgate

The Lambeth murderer of the two-headed girl Eliza-Beth has finally been captured by the fearless men of the Metropolitan Police! Mr Harold Bradford, a sometime boatman and coal-whipper of the Parish of St Paul, has been charged with the murder and will hang at Newgate on the morning of Monday October 14th.

Upon interrogation at the hands of Inspector Newsome of Scotland Yard, the prisoner revealed the horrible details of his crime. With his razor in his hand, he stalked the pre-dawn streets of his victim as the Highlander stalks the blameless deer. Insensate with an indiscriminate lust to kill, he tried different doors along the night-time streets, passing slumbering residences like the Angel of Death. What mark on their doors saved them from his blade is not known, or why the ill-fated door of 'anatomical performers' was the one he stopped at.

Like a shadow, he passed through the dark and silent hallways and stairways of that house . . . until he came upon his victim: an innocent girl born with two entirely different heads joining her body via two separate necks. Did she have a moment to utter a final prayer as the steel sliced into her flesh? Did a childish cry of outrage escape her lips? Did her four eyes, as the life passed from them, meet the two of her killer? Only Harold Bradford can answer these questions, and he may take the answers to his tomb.

With his hands be-gored and his murderous intent slaked, he crept from the building and back to the twisting streets where men of his kind lurk and boast of their crimes. There, the murderer – walking among those who were reading with horror of his exploits – remained at liberty, until the intrepid men of Scotland Yard sought him out and brought him to justice. He will meet Mr Calcraft soon enough.

We know the facts of the case to be somewhat different. After Noah had delivered the bully to a watch house, Inspector Newsome had been notified and had arranged to interrogate the prisoner. Mr Williamson had also been summoned, the questioning had taken place and the guilt of Mr Bradford had been satisfactorily decided upon. In rapid succession, his fate had been sealed by a judge and Newgate gaol was to be his temporary home until the day of his execution.

The public had naturally attended every step of the process, for the 'Lambeth Murder' had eclipsed even that of Daniel Good in the popular imagination. The streets were animated with the cry of the patterers and the brisk trade in their broadsheets. The murderer himself had become evil incarnate, walking invisibly among the innocents of London, likely to strike again at any moment. It was the very motivelessness of his crime that evoked the common fear. Not for theft did he kill, nor jealousy, nor any explicable reason that might give hope to those who barred their doors at night. What manner of monster was it who would slaughter for no reason and how many more like him peopled the midnight streets?

They could not know, of course, that the murderer was the simple, red-faced Bully Bradford, that lumpen instrument of a darker force, who was a murderer only by ineptitude. In the nightmares and fear-thrilled narratives of the milliner's girls, the magdalenes and below-stairs gossips, he was Death himself. Murder itself had stalked the back alleys during that period of his brief liberty, and the murderer was the demon in every shadow.

In such times, it is the writer who emerges triumphant.

The literate clamour for information of the crime: its details, its effects, its investigation. The illiterate look to the patterer for their lurid narrations and fanciful elaborations: the poetry of Mr Bradford, his true confession, his final letter to his poor mother in which he thoughtfully delineates every horrific image of his crime. And it was men such as I supplying the lines, feeding the hunger for information and the thirst for sensation.

For Sir Richard Mayne, the Metropolitan Police was covered with glory – but there were others for whom the case was far from closed. Indeed, another crime was already smouldering, set alight by a spark from the first: the murder of Mary Chatterton.

Two such horrific murders had seldom occurred in rapid succession, and the metropolis was soon to be a-fire with the news of more murder, the fear of murder, the anticipation of murder. Yes, Bully Bradford had been captured, but his impending execution and the grisly details of his crime had created an insatiable appetite for the macabre and violent. Mary Chatterton's death had come like a welcome meal to feed that hunger.

Unlike poor Eliza-Beth, whose appearance was so rare as to be something worth paying for, Mary was known to many – and feared by more. She was a 'character' whose name – at least wherever London's smoke drifted – was as well known as Nelson. There were street girls who might not know Her Majesty the Queen herself if they met her outside the King's Arms, but who revered 'Mother' Mary Chatterton as a greater monarch. Those of them who could read would have seen the following in *the Times*.

MURDER AT HAYMARKET

Shortly after three o'clock on Wednesday morning, Mary Chatterton, proprietor and resident of a night rooms in Haymarket, was found murdered. The discoverer of the crime, just moments after its commission, was Sergeant Williamson of Scotland Yard.

The likely killer has been described as being of average height, wearing a wide-brimmed hat pulled low over his face, and a scarf covering his mouth and nose. His clothes were of a black colour. No sign could be found of him following a brief search of the area.

The murderer entered the parlour of Miss Chatterton by a rear door, and was glimpsed by one of her attendants. Over the next hour or so, Miss Chatterton was shamefully and brutally mistreated before her throat was cut. There is no evidence of theft and no motive has yet been discerned.

Sergeant Williamson said, 'The recent arrest of Mr Bradford is a warning to all murderers that the Metropolitan Police will not rest until the criminal is brought to justice. The investigation is proceeding at this moment.'

It was not only the gin shops and penny gaffs that were animated by the news. There were men in private clubs and men in robes of one sort or another who paled when they read of the murder. Certainly, Mary was dead, but the nature of her murder and the liberty of the murderer was something to bring pallor to the cheeks of those men with secrets – men, more to the point, who had the ear of Sir Richard Mayne. The police commissioner was informed personally by a number of them that the capture of this villain was of the utmost priority.

As for Mr Bradford, he was safely ensconced in the 'Stone Jug' to think about his crime. Though gaol was an occupational risk for men of his sort, he could not help struggling with the enormity of his situation. In a very short time, he would be standing at the gallows with many thousands of eyes staring at him and Mr Calcraft fitting the noose to his neck. Perhaps people would throw fruit and harsh words, as he himself had done at many a hanging. This, even more than the fear of death, was what filled him with fear and turned his legs weak: to stand before all those people and bear their derision. It was not dignified! He would be humiliated! He would be nothing! People he knew would be there and see him trussed like a chicken ready for death. For a man who had lived his life unknown in the alleys and darkened drinking dens of the east, there was horror in becoming the sole focus of an entire city. It would be akin to nakedness.

The fact of his actual hanging was, at this stage, too enormous for him to adequately conceive, mortality being too abstract a concept for the lumpen bully that he was. Illiterate, godless, unmarried and childless, he had never contemplated the nature of his existence, nor its end. For men of his ilk, time never stretched further than the next fair. It would come to him soon enough – sooner than he would like, and yet very much too late.

And we should also not overlook the fact that the murderer of Mary Chatterton held that very same edition of *the Times* in his sulphurous grasp, smiling as he read of Sergeant Williamson's earnest promises of early capture. The very thought of the city's constables searching fervidly for a man whose face was entirely covered but for his eyes was enough to make any criminal smile – even if he burned with anger at the new attention cast in his direction by the capture of Mr Bradford.

The bully would tell the police whatever they wanted. True, he did not know enough about his sponsor to bring the police to his door, but now the name of 'General' would be abroad, and soon enough they would know his real name. That was a nakedness he feared more than any other – one that he could not hide.

He had indeed learned the identity of Eliza-Beth's father. Mary Chatterton had told him in her final, gasping, bubbling moments of agony – as he knew she would. Not only that, but while searching her writing desk for any correspondence with Eliza-Beth, he had discovered a most invaluable piece of information tucked away between tawdry love letters: a finished but unsealed and undated letter from Mary to the father of their child, informing him of his paternity. The address was written on the envelope. So the old strumpet *had* thought about the man during her long years of harlotry. It was, perhaps, the one pure love she had kept in her corrupted heart: a pressed flower that affected the blush of life whilst long dead.

So the General had posted Mary's letter to its addressee, intending that he receive it as if from her. And he had also sent one of his own a day later, a deft and subtle note saying only what was necessary and building upon the inevitable reaction to the letter from Mary. It was enough to instil fear in the recipient:

Dear Sir

I am the murderer of Mary Chatterton. It is only courteous that I introduce myself. Before you think

*about acting and revealing my letter to a third party,
perhaps you would first like to reflect on its purpose.*

*I wonder if the death of Mary had any personal
meaning to you? You were, after all, an 'acquaintance'
of hers some years ago – approximately the same
number of years that the two-headed girl Eliza-Beth
had attained before she, too, was murdered. Indeed,
I spoke at some length with both ladies and they both,
in their own way, had something to say of you. The
latter kept a memento of you, which I think perhaps
you know of.*

*I believe that you perceive my meaning. Shortly,
I will contact you in person to see how our shared
information can be of benefit to us both. Do not try
to locate me in the meantime, for it will end badly
for you.*

Sincerely,

Your Observer.

Who was the father of Eliza-Beth and how did he react
to these letters? Assuredly, he did not react well. The letter
from Mary opened a wound that had long ago healed
over. She had been a different woman then: a pretty girl over-
impressed with the big city and the attention she could gar-
ner. The news of a daughter, a girl – *that* girl – at once sick-
ened and saddened him. If it was true. If it was not some
grubby hoax. He knew by now that the mother was dead.
She had meant nothing to him for decades, and now – in a
rush – she and a child were thrust back at him as corpses.

He felt that everyone was looking at him, that everyone
knew. He heard their whispers: *There is the man who had a
child with Mary Chatterton, the Haymarket whore. There is*

132

the man whose child was a monster, slain among other monsters. The gutter newspapers would make him famous and drag him into the mire of gossip and calumny if they knew his identity. Innocent as he was, they would besmear him with the infamy.

Thus, the second letter set his blood running cold. Who was this man observing him and what did he know? It could all be an elaborate joke, but it did not feel so. It felt as if his life was under a glass and that the eye above him was the sky itself.

THIRTEEN

'Nothing, Ben! *Nothing!* I could smell his presence there – that sulphurous, infernal whiff – but the shop was quite abandoned. He will never set foot there again.'

Noah stared fixedly from his study window to the street below as Benjamin poured tea from a silver pot.

'I have never been this close,' he continued. 'It's as if he is taunting me, as if he knows I am searching for him and gives me glimpses just to play with me. It would be like him.'

The Negro caught Noah's attention with a guttural cough and proceeded to make a series of brief but complicated gestures with his hands, describing shapes in the air with his paler palms and punctuating the words with fine finger movement. He raised his shoulders interrogatively in conclusion.

'Yes, yes – you are right. He has no idea I am even in the country. At least, he has no reason to know. It is only my fancy and my anger that make it seem otherwise. You know I am not like you, Ben. I cannot forget. I will not forget.'

Again, Benjamin made his curious language of signs.

'No. The police business is over as far as the detectives are concerned. They have their murderer and we have our letters. The case is closed. The only good thing to come from it is that it brought me closer to finding him. Indeed, I was think—'

Noah was interrupted by a decisive knocking at the street door. He peered down from the window and saw the stovepipe hats of two policemen.

'G— confound them! It is the police, Ben. No Sabbath for them. Be good enough to let them in. Evidently, they want more value from me.'

The two officers entered the room with their hats in their hands and waited patiently for Noah to bid them sit. He did not do so, leaving them instead to stand as he scrutinized them from his stance at the window. He recognized Mr Newsome, of course, but the other man was a stranger to him.

Assuredly, the man was a policeman – his posture was unmistakable. He looked like a man who might have grown up among the barrows and barges, the gin shops and chandlers of the city as Noah himself had. But he had risen above them. Whoever he was, he was making a detailed examination of the room as if gauging what kind of man might inhabit it. His voice was quiet, but carried authority:

'I perceive you seek to make us uncomfortable by not asking us to sit. I expected nothing less. My name is Sergeant George Williamson. I will not shake your hand because I do not shake the hands of criminals.'

Noah nodded to himself and smiled slightly. 'Sit, gentlemen. I await with interest the reason for your presence here, especially since I have a letter from your commissioner naming me as an innocent man.'

'The case is not over and you know it,' said Mr Newsome, sitting on a large leather sofa. 'We may have Mr

Bradford in custody, and the public may think the crime solved, but you know there is more to it.'

'I know nothing of the sort.'

'Did you question him when you arrested him?' enquired Mr Newsome.

'I had little time. Another man was about to kill him, as I'm sure he has told you. I rescued him and took him to the nearest watch house. I returned here afterwards, exhausted after my ordeal at your hands.'

'You did not discuss the circumstances around his committing the murder?' enquired Mr Williamson. 'You did not venture to a marine store off Rosemary-lane once you had delivered our prisoner?'

Noah looked again at this detective who had delivered what were evidently rhetorical questions. Sitting there beside Mr Newsome, he did not seemed cowed by the decorous surroundings, by the books and furniture of a gentleman. In his eyes, Noah was a cracksman: a criminal, albeit an uncommon one. If Mr Bradford had been questioned carefully (and the murderer was not a man of strong will), the police would know what had passed between him and Noah. What Mr Bradford couldn't know for sure was whether his 'rescuer' had actually gone to the marine store they had discussed. Either the detective was guessing, or . . .

'I did not go to the store, though I did discuss it with the man.'

'Hmm.' Mr Williamson appeared to smile. 'So you will know what we know: that although we have the murderer in our custody, the man behind the crime remains at liberty.'

'Indeed, but he has committed no crime himself. Your case is closed, as is my involvement with it.'

'He has benefited from the murder, or at least from Mr Bradford's primary intention in visiting that address.'

'And what was that?'

'That is no business of yours.'

'Is it not? Why, then, do I have two detectives sitting in my study telling me that the murderer is to be hanged but that I am still involved in some way?'

Inspector Newsome observed with evident satisfaction the verbal sparring of these two men whom he had planned to put together. They reminded him of two dogs that will cease fighting only when – bleeding and exhausted – they perceive they have met their match. But turn those two dogs on a third fierce creature and they will together bring it down decisively. He addressed their host:

'Mr Dyson, you perceive correctly that we have not finished our business with you. Let us lay pretence aside for a moment and address the issue: the man you seem to have been seeking for some years past is very likely the man we also seek. You know much about this man that we do not, and we know things you do not. I would like you to work with my colleague Sergeant Williamson to bring this man to justice. It is in all our interests to have this man at the gallows.

'Now, if you will excuse me, I have business to attend to. I leave you together to discuss how you are going to collaborate. This man must be caught with all haste. I trust Benjamin will see me to the door?'

After a brief glance of enquiry at Noah, Benjamin escorted Mr Newsome out of the room. The two remaining men heard the street door close and appraised each other in silence. An awkwardness settled, as when young gentlepeople of opposite genders are left alone together for a moment. It being Noah's own house, he had the advantage of home territory.

'Would you like a cup of tea, Detective? Benjamin has just poured one for himself, but you are welcome to it.'

'No, thank you. And I am surprised that you take tea with your servants.'

'He is not my servant, and I am not his master.'

'Hmm. He is certainly a curious specimen. I perceive that he has been hanged, a fate that may one day befall you. Only, you will not survive the ministrations of Mr Calcraft.'

'You do not like me, Mr Williamson. May I call you George?'

'You may not.'

'I see. You do not like me, but you know nothing about me.'

'I know that you are a cracksman—'

'You know nothing of the sort. You know only that I was arrested in possession of a cracksman's tools. No stolen property has been discovered in my possession. Nor can there be any provable link between that uniform of mine and the one stolen from the unfortunate constable.'

'PC Wiseman.'

'Indeed. Such items can be bought at any shop along Rosemary-lane, or made by a tailor. In short, you must know as a detective that, however dubious the circumstances of my arrest, there is no proof of my guilt.'

'You mean that we have not yet discovered it.'

Noah smiled and sipped his tea, noting that his guest had elected not to drink his cup. 'Do you play chess, Detective?'

'I prefer draughts . . . Mr Dyson, may we omit this delicate conversation and proceed to the heart of the matter. I am obliged to cooperate with you and I do not relish the opportunity. There is a criminal behind this crime and we believe you know who he is.'

'Why do you believe so?'

'You have been searching for a man who is likely an incendiary. The man described to us by Mr Bradford goes by the name of 'Lucifer' Ball, or Boyle, named for his odd attraction to the eponymous matches. We also have other evidence that the man who initiated this chain of crimes is—'

'What other evidence?'

'That is none of your concern.'

'You said we were working together on this case. If so, we are both compelled to collaborate against our will, so you need not maintain your injured air, or that of superiority. I already know – as you must – that the bully was sent to Lambeth to obtain a letter, and that the subsequent murder was the result of fear rather than malice. There are more things in Heaven and Earth than are dreamed of in Mr Bradford's philosophy.'

Mr Williamson pursed his lips in distaste. He did not perceive the origin of the literary reference – merely that it was one. His fingers worked unthinkingly at the brim of his hat. 'So you know as much as we do.'

'I may know more, Detective. I know what was inside the locket.'

'Hair. Mr Bradford revealed that to us.'

'Of two colours: red and brown.'

'Quite. But you know nothing of the letters.'

'Lett-*ers*, plural? I know only of one letter: the one that Mr Bradford took from Eliza-Beth, but which he could not read. We can assume that Boyle has read it.'

'Indeed he has, much to my regret. I discovered the second letter myself, inside the pillow on Eliza-Beth's bed.'

'What were its contents?'

'Let us proceed with less haste. Before I reveal to you the secrets of the Detective Force, I would like to know – indeed, I demand it – why you seek this man and what his capture means to you.'

'He once did me an evil turn, which I promised I would avenge. That is all. Now – to the matter of this second letter.'

'What was the nature of this evil turn?'

'What were the circumstances of your disfigured face? I presume it was the smallpox.'

Mr Williamson's face reddened and showed all the signs of rising anger.

'Forgive me, Detective, but I seek only to illustrate that some things are best left unspoken. Our subject is the case at hand – nothing more. I pursue this man for personal reasons; you seek to enforce the law. Now – the contents of that letter.'

The detective clenched his jaw. 'It appears to be from Eliza-Beth's absent mother. No name was appended, and no return address given. It was delivered by hand, by the same person who was to collect the reply. I have it here.'

He handed the letter to Noah, who smelled it and then rapidly read the contents. He thought for a moment.

'So the red lock of hair in the locket belonged to the writer of this letter, the mother. I have seen Dr Zwigoff's show at Vauxhall and seen the girl for myself. Her hair was flame red . . . Wait – you spoke of other evidence.'

'A number of people visited the house during the period of the Vauxhall shows. I have been contacting them to see if they can shed any light on the case. One of them has recently been murdered – an occurrence which cannot be attributed to coincidence.'

'Because Mary Chatterton was red-haired. Yes, I have read of it. I presume she is the victim you are referring to. She was one of the visiters to the house . . . and the writer of the letter. Tell me, how was she killed?'

'Quite horribly. The full details are known only to a few. She was beaten, burned about the body and the head, and then her throat cut. Our surgeon, Dr McLeod, tells me that none of the burns were fatal in themselves, and that the burning of her hair and scalp most likely took place *post mortem* . . . it means "after death".'

'I know what it means. How do you know that the bully did not commit the crime?'

'Mr Bradford denies all knowledge of it, except what he has heard in the street. I am inclined to believe him.'

'Yes, I feel sure it is the man you seek. His name is Lucius Boyle. The bully may be a killer, but he does not have the stomach for torture. And only Boyle would use fire in such a way. It fascinates him. But why—'

'Why would he kill her? I have my own ideas but I would like to hear yours.'

'She was a singular woman. She could have angered him so much that . . . But, no, he would not lose his temper. He would not have murdered her if he wanted to blackmail her over the maternity of Eliza-Beth . . .'

Noah lapsed into contemplation, playing out different scenarios in his mind. For a few moments, the only sound in the room was the distant clatter of hooves and wheels. Despite the closed window, the pungent smell of Lazenby's fish-sauce warehouse found its way into the room, adulterated occasionally with the infernal ferrous tang of the Panklibanon foundry over at Baker-street.

'Which other people visited the house, Sergeant?'

'A clergyman named Josiah Archer.'

'Ha! The man is quite insane. I am surprised he is not yet preaching at Bedlam.'

'Quite. He visited to satisfy himself that the performers were correctly fulfilling the predictions of the Apocalypse. Then there was a doctor, whom I have not yet been able contact. He is teaching in Edinburgh. And a writer by the name of—'

'Henry Askern?'

'Do you know of him?'

'He is often to be found about the rookeries and the low public houses. I understand he is researching a new book on the underworld of London. I have seen him on my peregrinations about the city. Which of these have you spoken to?'

'Mr Archer only. I am to meet Mr Askern this afternoon.'

'And which of these do you suspect is the father?'

'What . . .? Ah, very good, Mr Dyson! I see that you have followed the same pathways of my own thoughts. There is no reason to believe that any of them fathered Eliza-Beth. I am sure that each has his legitimate reason for visiting the place. Our only indication that the father is close by is Mr Boyle's seeming interest in the poor girls' parentage. *He* evidently believes that the man can be found, whomever and wherever he is. Our goal is the same as our quarry – but only he knows where to look.'

'If Mary told him. If indeed Mary *knew*. She was quite a phenomenon in her youth.'

'If she knew, no mortal would have withstood the treatment he dealt her. I believe he knows the father's identity and will act on the information.'

'What is your plan, Sergeant?'

'What do *you* suggest? You have been searching for this man for many years, with no apparent success. Why have you been unable to find him?'

'He is a child of the city and knows it like few others. I believe he wears disguises. There may be men who live side by side with him and do not know his true identity . . . why do you smile?'

'You have described yourself.'

'Mmm . . . What knowledge have you gained from *your* witnesses?'

'One of Mary's boys said that he was covering his face with a scarf and hat. Mr Bradford said that he has only ever seen the man in shadow or with a face-covering of some kind. It would seem that he is unwilling to be seen even by the people he converses with. Such a mania for anonymity seems odd, does it not? Unless he has some highly recognizable facial feature that he wishes to hide. You have seen him – is this the case?'

'The truth is that covering one's face is likely to attract *more* attention—'

'You have evaded my question, Mr Dyson. We are sharing information and you are attempting to retain some of yours, no doubt to give yourself an advantage in the pursuit. If I apprehend the man, he will hang. Is that not revenge enough for you? Our aim is the same. Do not treat me as a fool.'

Noah smiled stiffly, acknowledging his opponent's insight whilst simultaneously resenting it. It was true that the entire apparatus of the police was indeed his best chance thus far of locating his enemy . . . although Boyle would never be – as he had not yet been – caught by a mere policeman.

'I capitulate, Sergeant Williamson. Boyle's lower face is disfigured by a birth defect. His skin is violently red, hence his scarf. I do not know why he wears a low hat – it could be that he has acquired further distinguishing marks in the intervening years. His eyes are grey, the light grey of wood smoke.'

'Thank you. This information may prove invaluable in our pursuit.'

'I do not see how. He has remained entirely unknown to the police for years, and I – who know the man by sight – have been unable to find him. How do you intend to locate this man who has evaded the notice of the authorities for a lifetime?'

'I see a few possibilities. Firstly, he will make a mistake and be apprehended quite by chance as you were—'

'*I* was not committing a crime, Sergeant. Nor am I a murderer.'

'The second possibility is that we will divine his actions with sufficient foresight to be waiting for him when he acts again, although you have failed singularly in this for some years.'

'They are both slim possibilities.'

'Indeed, but I see a third. Is it not plausible that Mr Boyle will overextend himself in theatricality? There have been murderers who became intoxicated with public attention as if by gin, and trapped by that perceived glamour.'

'Not Boyle. He is too clever for that. Anonymity is his protection. How do you imagine he has escaped the notice of the police since his criminal childhood?'

'You know of his childhood?'

'I know *him*.'

'And I would wager that he would know you if he saw you. Or if your presence was made known to him. Would he, I wonder – knowing that he was being pursued by one who knows him, one who may know his secrets – make an uncharacteristic error?'

'What are you suggesting, Mr Williamson?'

'Mr Bradford will be hanged on Monday, as you know. I will be there, and Mr Boyle may also make an appearance. You know that a hanging brings out the entire criminal fraternity for entertainment, and he may want to satisfy himself that this fragile link to his identity is finally deceased. How would it affect Mr Boyle to see you standing beside me near the gallows? Would he recognize you?'

'Frankly, I cannot say. We have not looked each other in the eye for . . . for many years. I might have passed him in the street a dozen times . . . but . . .'

'But if you saw him, you would know him.'

'If I could see his face uncovered – or even his eyes – I am certain, yes.'

'And I think he would know you. Moreover, a hanging is an exceptionally suitable occasion for our purposes.'

'How so?'

'Think on it. Just before the prisoner is hanged, the entire audience removes their hats – supposedly out of respect, but in actuality to provide an unobstructed view. All faces are turned on a single point: the rope and the neck within it. For us, situated on or near the gallows, a sea of twenty or thirty thousand faces presents itself. Would we not notice – in such a crowd – a man with a scarf about his face and a hat pulled over his eyes? Or a man with a highly visible red mark? He cannot possibly hide his features in such a crowd. Were he to try, he would become eminently visible.'

'Which is why it would be pure foolishness on his part to attend. And discerning one face in a multitude is no easy task. I see no reason why he should be there.'

'Nor I. But I have a strange intuition that he might. There is much attention on the recent murders and he is in danger of being exposed as never before. Also, we have no other options. After the hanging – if he attends and if any identification is made – we must discern the rules of the game as he sees fit to play them. He may vanish forever, or he may embark on a new course of action. I hope for the latter.'

'What do you expect him to do?'

'I think Mr Boyle, like many of the "greater" criminals, has an exaggerated sense of self-regard. It is necessary for him to feel himself superior to lesser men, and to the police in general. It is a kind of game to him, an entertainment if you like.'

'You speak as if you know him.'

'I know his kind. The circumstances of Mary's murder have certain curious similarities to the Lambeth case although the killer was different: the door which was broken when a man of his ability could have gained access more easily; shoes that bore a similar imprint to those worn by Mr Bradford; and the cut throat, most probably with a razor.'

'Do you think he was leaving clues to misdirect your investigation? To make you think—'

'I do not know. The manner of Mary's death could not have been the work of Mr Bradford . . . unless . . . well, I am confused as to what Boyle's intentions were.'

'Perhaps that was his intention – we will discover eventually. As for our endeavours, what are we to do before the hanging?'

'I am to see Mr Askern, the writer, later today. I suggest that you search out Reverend Archer and learn what you can from him.'

'But you have questioned him previously. Do you suspect him?'

'I think he knows more than he told me.'

'On what authority am I to question him? I am not a detective; he is not obliged to speak to me.'

'I will say only that you were able to glean all of the information that Mr Bradford held in that under-worked brain of his. Catching this murderer is more important to me than the outraged ravings of a street evangelist.'

'So you will see the law bent, though not broken – if I understand you?'

'When a man has no respect for the law, he has no respect for his common man.'

'Mmm. What does the Reverend Archer know?'

'If he is entirely innocent, only what has been in the papers: that Eliza-Beth was killed by Mr Bradford. I asked him about a letter, of which he denied all knowledge – while inadvertently revealing he had seen it peeping from her dress. Concerning the locket, he may have seen it but he says he knows nothing of its theft. At least, he should not.'

'Can you trust this Dr Zwigoff when he says that these are the only people who visited Eliza-Beth?'

'One cannot trust the man – his real name is Coggins – any more than one could trust a Haymarket bar girl to keep a secret. It may prove necessary to call on him again, this time with a more persuasive approach. I must also ascertain when the good Doctor Cole is to return from Edinburgh. We will meet again at the scaffold and compare our findings.'

'Take care, Sergeant Williamson.'

'I always do, Mr Dyson.'

FOURTEEN

Henry Askern, aged forty-two, was the writer who had visited that ill-fated house in Lambeth in the week before the murder. One would think that his education at Westminster School and Oxford University would have provided a comfortable, affluent lifestyle for this undoubted gentleman, but he had a fatal flaw: his romantic sensibility. Not for him the secure position at his father's legal practice; no, he sought adventure (and ruin) in India and the islands of the South Seas. Returning to London was a rude awakening to disownment and the perils of having chosen a fanciful path.

What vocation for an intelligent man of limited means? Why, the greatest of them all: to write! His plays were judged harshly by the critics and his novel was a carcase that no galvanism could revive. So he turned to journalism and found his *métier* in social study. You may have seen his *Pieceworkers of the East End* or his *Street Children of the Metropolis*, both of which were minor successes drawn from his fearless travels about the city's filthier environs.

Sergeant Williamson was escorted into Mr Askern's study by a slightly frayed servant and saw the writer himself rising from a writing desk to extend a dry hand. The detective noted the man's clean linen and ink-stained fingers, the prematurely greying hair at his temples and the perceptiveness behind those tired eyes. He looked a little underweight and sickly. A faint chymical smell pervaded the room and made the detective wrinkle his nose.

'Thank you for agreeing to see me, Mr Askern.'

'It is my pleasure, sir. My Sundays are days of rest. I must apologize for the smell – chymistry is a hobby of mine and I have been conducting experiments this morning. Well, I have heard and read many things about the men of the Detective Force. I believe that your job is very similar to mine in a number of respects.'

'Really?'

'Please – be seated.' Mr Askern sat again at the desk as his guest settled into a wing-backed leather chair. The writer laced his fingers in his lap. 'Yes, we both seek information. You seek it in pursuit of a crime, I in the pursuit of knowledge – for my books. We are both obliged to search the city for our subjects, and elicit answers from those who may be unable or unwilling to share them. It is a skill.'

'Quite.'

'I am certain that you have observed the number of researchers about the darker streets. I myself regularly meet members of sundry charities and other writers being escorted to lodging houses or brothels as if visiting darkest Africa rather than the pre-eminent city of the entire earth. We are all detectives of a sort, are we not?'

'I understand that you recently visited a house in Lambeth—'

'Ah yes. Dr Zwigoff's collection . . . or rather Mr Coggins's. A terrible case.'

'What do you know of it?'

'Only what I have read in the newspapers: that the girl Eliza-Beth was murdered for no discernible motive and that the perpetrator has just recently been apprehended.'

'Why did you visit the house?'

'I am preparing a new book on the London underworld. Though Mr Coggins is not strictly a criminal, his business has that *frisson* of the macabre that readers publicly abhor and privately consume with fervour. I'm afraid I am little better than Mr Coggins in this respect, but the clamour surrounding the case is proof enough of its interest. I spoke briefly with some of his "exhibits" about their personal histories.'

'And what did you learn of Eliza-Beth?'

'A moment. I have my notes here somewhere . . . ah, here we are.'

'May I see them?'

'I would be happy for you to, but it is written in "shorthand": a kind of code which allows the writer to rapidly transcribe. Do you know it?'

'No. Mr Coggins thought it might be Greek.'

'Oh? Do you read Greek, Sergeant?'

'I do not. Please tell me what you learned from the unfortunate girl.'

'You are right to call her unfortunate, for hers was a doleful story even in life. She was left at a church door and never knew her parents. She was raised by a succession of physicians who considered her nothing more than a study in abnormal development. Mr Coggins insinuated to me that he bought the girl. Or rather, that is what I inferred from his winks and knowing nods. The others at that house were the only family that she ever knew.'

'Do you have a family, Mr Askern?'

'No. I am a bachelor. The truth, Sergeant, is that I have little to offer a bride. My father saw to that. This new book might make my fortune, but . . . well, we will see.'

'I wonder, Mr Askern, if you have any ideas on what might have motivated Eliza-Beth's killer? You know more than many others about the criminal classes of the city. Do you have a theory?'

'Of course I have thought about it, from the viewpoint of a writer as well as a researcher. But I am curious at your question: you have the killer in custody and must know his motive.'

'Indeed we do. But I am interested in your answer.'

'Well, in that case I will satisfy your curiosity to satisfy my own. There are men – and, yes, women, too – who would kill you for your watch—'

'Eliza-Beth had nothing.'

'True . . . well, no, she did have a gold locket about her neck when I spoke with her, though I do suspect it was worth too little to be killed for. Then, there are also men who are quite insane, men who kill because they hear voices telling them to do so, or because they are angry, or because it is a Thursday. There is no rational explanation and perhaps not even any evil in their actions, for they are insensible to their crimes. Then again, there are men who become monsters when drunk, which accounts for most of the lower classes much of the time.'

'So you are telling me that Eliza-Beth could have been killed virtually by accident, a victim almost of chance.'

'You must know from your experience that such things are possible. I am sure they account for the majority of victims dredged out of the Thames . . . and I see from your nods that I am right. But let us explore other possibilities. Could it be that Eliza-Beth knew Mr Bradford in some context? Maybe they were romantically linked . . .'

'I think that your creativity is getting the upper hand, Mr Askern.'

'Yes, yes . . . I suppose so. Let me think. What if Mr Bradford had intelligence of Eliza-Beth's lost parents? Being the man he undoubtedly is, he would have asked for money to not reveal the information. Perhaps they fought. She refused his price and threatened to expose him as a blackmailer. In the passion of the moment, he slashed her throat . . . Oh, I don't know, Sergeant! Please, tell me the truth – I see from your expression that I am speaking absurdly.'

'Your ideas are certainly interesting. But you are quite correct in your original suggestion. The murder was quite random. Mr Bradford was no doubt intoxicated and broke into the house to steal. He was startled and reacted with a razor instead of his mind. Now he will hang.'

'A tragic waste. The girl was quite articulate, you know. At least one of them was, I forget which.'

'Was Eliza-Beth your daughter, Mr Askern?'

'I . . . I beg your pardon!' Mr Askern stood as if the interview were terminated. 'I will *not* accept such impudence, even if you *are* a detective! Did I not tell you that I have no family? Are you accusing me of being—?'

The writer began to cough. It was no normal cough – it was the glutinous rattle of the consumptive. He leaned against the seat back and reached for his handkerchief as his body was wracked with convulsions. His eyes watered and his face became scarlet as he covered his mouth and strained for control. Presently, he managed to calm himself and looked ominously into the handkerchief, folding it with a dark look.

'Forgive me. I have not been entirely well since I returned from the east. It was just . . . I was—'

'I understand. My questions are not my own, but part of an investigation. Please, sit down. I am certain that you have experienced anger from interviewees in your own researches, so you will understand.'

'Well . . . well . . . a gentleman is not accustomed to such questions, Sergeant Williamson.'

'Indeed. Please be seated. Let us proceed. Have you ever, in your travels about the underworld, heard the name "Lucius Boyle" or "Lucifer Boyle"?'

The writer sat, grudgingly accepting the truth of Mr Williamson's words: questions *could* often cause offence – most especially those questions that the inquisitor sought answers to. 'Mmm, "Boyle" you say? The name is not familiar. What is he?'

'We cannot be sure. It may be a clue. We have heard the name. We know that he is a criminal, perhaps a master criminal with others working for him. I thought that he would be known to others of the fraternity.'

'It is rare for criminals – serious, professional criminals, that is – to work together, or for others. They are too distrusting. It is true that children will work for a kidsman, but they soon escape from his authority and become independent. It is also highly likely that any "master criminal" would soon be challenged or killed by a rival. I'm afraid that the figure of the master criminal is all too often a literary conceit.'

'What kind of man would be a "master criminal", if you were to portray such a man in a book?'

'Well, if we are to consider him as a character in a fiction, he would have to be uncommonly intelligent. A university education would be of very little use to him (though I sup-

pose it would help him to enter the confidence of gentlemen).
No, his intellect would be one bred by the city itself: a sly
cunning, a labyrinthine mind as dark and unmappable as the
streets that raised it. He would be involved in diverse criminal enterprises – theft, robbery, blackmail, prostitution –
but not personally. He would have too much to risk.'

'So he would have men working for him. What of loyalty?'

'Well, quite. What could buy the loyalty of men whose
very existence is based upon lies and deception? Any such
criminal mastermind would have to inspire unwavering loyalty, and history teaches us that there is only one thing that
engenders such loyalty.'

'Money?'

'Fear. Our man must be brutal in his authority, punishing
the merest breach of trust with death, or something worse.
But, as I say, such a man is an unnatural monster. He would
have to be almost insane, and bloodthirsty to an extreme
degree, in order to maintain his power for any period.'

Mr Williamson seemed to ponder these answers for a
moment, working the brim of the hat in his lap. An idea
occurred to him:

'Mr Askern, has any of your research focused on the
attire of our city's inhabitants?'

'Your line of questioning is quite odd, Sergeant. I am not
entirely sure what you require of me. Nevertheless, yes, a
man's clothing is a particular interest of mine. Indeed, it is
one that I intend to write about very shortly. What is it that
you would like to know?'

Where would one find the turbulent clergyman? His peripatetic ways took him all over the city to rant at passers-by

about Revelations already made flesh, and those to come. Noah was forced to agree that one merit of the Metropolitan Police was the efficacy of its beat system. No matter how ineffectual the police divisions as a collaborative whole, the individual constables knew their territories better than any other – at least, almost as well as the criminals they pursued.

A letter from Inspector Newsome to all of the watch houses in the city had resulted in a map compiled from the knowledge of numerous beat constables. It pinpointed the Reverend Archer's most common pulpits and when he might be found at each. Thereafter, it was merely a matter of going from one to the next in the hope of meeting the man.

Thus, as Sergeant Williamson was quizzing Mr Askern, Noah was crossing Hyde Park Corner and passing through the Ionic columns of the triumphal arch into Hyde Park itself. Though autumn was passing into winter and it was not a Sunday, traffic in the park was plentiful. Carriages rattled through the arches and passed along parallel to Park-lane or Knightsbridge and nursemaids led excitable children across the grass. Casting a respectful glance at the colossal statue of Achilles, Noah set off towards the Serpentine.

Even before reaching that stretch of water, its rank odour drifted to meet him. A memory shuddered momentarily through his body, stimulated by that compost of sewage and dead flesh – a memory as palpable as the scars on his back. Just as the whitened skin would sometimes stretch tightly, or itch with remembered pain, so a familiar smell would return shards of recollection to him. He fought the momentary impulse to vomit and continued.

Children were launching their miniature barks and cutters on to the putrid waters as their nursemaids exchanged gossip on the benches. Less respectable children waded thigh deep among the mud and occasional animal corpse which had bobbed gaseously obscene to the surface. Though some called it a lung of the city, it was in that case a tubercular organ. The smoke of a million chimneys had laid their soot over all, and it drifted still, high above the trees.

A familiar voice began to make itself heard to Noah. Then, as he approached, he saw the flailing black figure of Reverend Archer standing on a bench, and began to discern words:

'. . . *Come here and I will show unto thee the judgement of the great whore that sitteth upon many waters, with whom the kings of the earth have committed fornication . . .*'

Drawing closer, Noah saw that a wide circle of people had formed around the preacher – not to listen, but to be distant from him. It was a space of fear rather than fascination surrounding him, and children's ears were covered as the man in black robes spat forth his warnings of immanent oblivion. Upon closer inspection, he cast a sorry figure, his bony frame lost within the swirling folds and his bald head glistening red with exertion.

'. . . *And the woman was arrayed in purple and scarlet colour, and decked with gold and precious stones and pearls, having a golden cup in her hand full of abominations and filthiness of her fornication . . . !*'

Noah stood before the clergyman and watched. It was clearly the only interest the speaker had attracted all day and he paused to look back at this audience of one. He stepped down from his improvised pulpit and assailed Noah with sour breath.

'The End is upon us, sir. Have you welcomed Christ into your heart?'

'Christ has done nothing for me. May I speak with you privately, Reverend Archer?'

'*Nothing for you?*' thundered Mr Archer. 'Nothing for you? He *died* for you, sir! Died for you. What manner of human are you that rejects his Lord and Master?'

'I am master of myself. Jesus might have saved himself the trouble of dying for me. I have "died" many times, but have returned to life. Now, if you—'

'*Blasphemer!*' The clergyman's face contorted into scarlet apoplexy. 'The Apocalypse is upon us, sir, and you are set to burn in everlasting fire in company with the sin-soaked fornicators of this city of Babylon.'

'I am interested in your choice of text. The book of Revelation, chapter seventeen, if I recall.'

'Aha! So you *do* know your scripture.'

'Have you read of the murder of Mary Chatterton at Haymarket?'

'It is a sign. *And the ten horns which thou sawest upon the beast, these shall hate the whore, and shall make her desolate and naked, and shall eat her flesh and burn her with fire.*'

'Did you ever meet Mary, Mr Archer? Did you know her?'

'She was a whore. *Upon her forehead was a name written, MYSTERY, BABYLON THE GREAT, THE MOTHER OF HARLOTS AND ABOMINATIONS OF THE EARTH.*'

Noah sighed, his patience now strained to its limits. He looked about him and saw what he expected to see: a dozen or so people assiduously not looking in his direction. It was human nature that when something caused embarrassment, it became curiously invisible. Without a word of threat, Noah's fist flashed rapidly into the cavity beneath the clergyman's bony chest and the man collapsed to the ground in a flutter of dark drapery. As he lay there pale and panting, Noah knelt by his side.

'Listen carefully, Mr Archer. I have neither the time nor the inclination for your scripture, much as I admire its lyrical qualities. You will answer my questions, or I will be forced to cast your body into this pestilential Styx here, without the benefit of Charon's steerage. I prefer the Greek to the Hebrew, you see. Now, let us begin again – in your own words, if you please.'

Passers-by turned away from the scene and nursemaids called children away from the vicinity. Only one man, sitting at a bench with an unread newspaper, watched the tableau with interest.

'A street girl – as I'm sure you fully comprehend – is one of the most astute judges of attire in the city, for it is necessary that she be able to discern a client and his wealth at a glance. She will charge what she thinks she can get away with, and approach only he who is likely to patronize girls of her sort. She knows that the judge or aristocrat keeps his own seclusive in high style at Regent's-park and would not lower himself to associate with a common prostitute. I hope I am not patronizing you, Sergeant Williamson.'

'Please, go on, Mr Askern.'

'Well, as I say, the street girl knows at a glance and to within a fraction of an inch how fashionable a man's hat is and whether it is made of silk, rabbit skin or beaver. She knows if his gloves are kid or pigskin. She can see if his boots have been made to order by a bootmaker, or handed down via a Rosemary-lane shop. She knows from a man's very coat buttons how much he will pay. Of course, we all notice such things if we are sapient, but the street girl *reads* them as we might read *the Times*. Indeed, let us conduct a game just for our amusement.'

'What manner of game?'

'Imagine that you are not a man of London. Imagine that you had just arrived here from the country. You would not know how to read a man's attire as we city dwellers do. So, if you saw . . . let me see . . . a dirty boy with his hair shorn—'

'I would imagine him a recently released convict, although if his hair is very short, I would be inclined to think he has escaped.'

'Of course, of course. But a newcomer would not know this. Let us say that he saw a man with mother-of-pearl buttons on his blue jacket, a coarse checked shirt and a long moustache oiled to its tips—'

'A sailor, naturally. Most likely a Spaniard or Lascar – you were going to mention his dark complexion, no doubt.'

'I see that you understand. A man's clothes represent a kind of language, but you must know that language. For example, a cap-wearing man with his broad trouser bottoms turned up—'

'—would be a boatman or dredgerman.'

'I see I do not have to illustrate further. Such examples are simple enough. I might add, unnecessarily I suppose, that location is also an important consideration.'

'In what sense?'

'Well, a Chinese sailor – no matter how odd his appearance – is liable to attract little or no attention along the Minories, but he would be a curiosity on Oxford-street. Likewise, a man in a silk top hat might as well wear a bell if walking through St Andrews-street, whereas a beggar would attract no attention at all in the same place. Rather obvious examples, I'm afraid, but I am trying to answer a question I do not clearly understand.'

'In fact, you have made an important point. You say that it is a language. Might it not be possible that a man might learn to speak this language? Not only to recognize, but to adopt the identity of others?'

'Again, I do not quite follow you, detective.'

'Let me ask you this: what would you think if the sailor you described, or the beggar, was stopped by a constable and was discovered to be not a sailor or a beggar but a barrister.'

'How absurd! Why would a barrister dress as a sailor? Costume is reserved for the stage.'

'You have already demonstrated that a man is known by his clothing. If a man wanted to hide his identity, could he not use these same assumptions against those who sought him? Thus, a sailor who was wanted for murder – if he was cunning – could adopt the appearance of, say, a beggar or a costermonger. Who would know him? He could remain in the city and yet be invisible. When one asks the local constable if he has seen an unknown sailor on his beat, he is not likely to answer "Yes, he is disguised as a beggar." He will look for a sailor and not find him.'

'What you say is true, but I have not seen any evidence of the phenomenon.'

'You may have heard about a recent case of a lady who arrived at fashionable shopping areas in a smart carriage with her own footman. This elegant and well-dressed woman would purchase items at a series of shops and tender counterfeit money. Naturally she was not suspected because "ladies" do not do such things. However, a quick-witted constable followed her and discovered that she was working for a gang of thieves from one of the lowest areas of the city. All were imprisoned.'

'Well, yes, I can see how that deception might have been effected. However, I still fail to see the direction of your argument.'

'Let us take the fictional master criminal we were speaking of. How would he dress?'

'Aha! Now I see! Yes . . . I admit he would have to change his appearance to render himself invisible. But those who had contact with him would know his face, would they not? Nothing remains secret for long in the gin shops and penny gaffs . . . and yet I have never heard mention of a character such as the one you describe.'

'I have no answers, Mr Askern – only questions. I had hoped your particular knowledge of the city would provide me with some.'

'I am sorry I cannot be of more help. If I have learned anything in my researches, it is that there are areas of London that might as well be those blank spaces on old marine maps: "Here be Monsters". We know the names of the streets; we may map and catalogue them, but the wretched lives that exist there are beyond our comprehension. There is crime and bestiality that is barely human, walking barefoot in the filth as if Christ had never trod the earth and science had never opened our eyes. There are people who barely know how to speak, let alone pray. Indeed, there *are* monsters among us.'

Mr Williamson only nodded. Mr Askern's latter statement was perhaps truer than he knew. Sometimes the detective wished that the Thames could rise and wash away the detritus at its banks, or that fire would once again cleanse the city. It was a tree whose roots and branches were tainted with canker. He shook his head slightly and stood.

'Thank you for your time, sir. It has been enlightening. Please contact me at Scotland Yard if you should receive any intelligence concerning what we have discussed.'

'I will, Sergeant. I am amongst the population almost every evening. Perhaps I could ask a few pertinent questions.'

'By all means do so. I do have one final question. Did you meet any other visitors on the night you visited the house in Lambeth?'

'Let me think . . . Well, I did not meet one, but I did see a gentleman arrive by carriage. He had Eliza-Beth with him and escorted her into the house.'

'Indeed? You have not mentioned this previously.'

'I suppose you have reminded me.'

'Hmm. What did he look like?'

'I did not pay him much attention. I cannot recall seeing his face.'

'Because it was covered?'

'It was dark, but . . . yes, perhaps his lower face *was* obscured by a cape or a stock.'

FIFTEEN

It is almost one week to the hour since we met Mr Coggins, alias Dr Zwigoff. In the interim, he has become a much wealthier man. The furore over Eliza-Beth's death was the publicity he had always dreamed of but been too parsimonious to buy. The shows at Vauxhall Gardens had been extended to cater for the greater numbers of customers, and his pockets had been further swelled by the increase in private viewings. In short, business was good. It was a pity, therefore, that this day would be his last on earth.

Now he was on his way – along with many thousands of others – to see Bully Bradford hang. It was four o'clock in the morning on that momentous Monday morning and Henry Coggins gurgled like a wineskin as he walked, so full of gin was his portly stomach. A light mist hung low over the city, settling glassily on roofs and chimneys – chimneys which had momentarily paused in their almost unceasing sooty exhalation. At this hour of the morning, after the gin shops had closed and before the respectable retailers opened their doors, one might imagine oneself in a different, more innocent place. An earthy compost of wet earth drifted from a nearby park, and a lamb, escaped from Smithfield, trotted lost through pastures long subsumed by cobbles and brick, bleating its own futile lament.

Countless others were also moving towards Newgate. Along Fleet-street, Cheapside and Aldersgate; across Black-friars, Southwark and London bridges they came. The crim-inals and workers walked, while the well-to-do travelled by carriage and cab. How would it look, were one to float above the scene in a balloon? Like ants converging in multi-tudinous paths on a tasty morsel dropped in the forest? No morsel this, however. This was the gallows – already in situ before the implacable *façade* of Newgate gaol.

And as Mr Coggins entered that broad thoroughfare, a hundred or so others were already loitering there, some of whom had been in attendance since the previous evening. The barricaded area around the black-painted scaffold itself was dark with people – the worse kind of people, naturally. Gap-toothed boys in fustian and their 'gals' with cotton shawls tight about their shoulders to keep out the pre-dawn chill, all stamping their feet and breathing on hands while exchanging banter about previous 'shows'. Between puffs of pipe tobacco, the rapscallions boasted knowledgeably in front of the girls:

'I was ther for the Frenchy manservant – Cor-Voosi was 'is name. Blubbed like a girl, he did. I wod take it like a man.'

'He did not! He prayed to God even as he dropt. I saw it from the very spot.'

'Aye, and his legs moved after he was dead, doing the Newgate hornpipe!'

At this piece of intelligence, and at the jerky simulation accompanying it, the girls squealed. This prompted more gruesome lore from the boys, which drifted into the properties of the rope used, and how much Mr Calcraft might charge afterwards for a few inches of that dread cord.

More arrived: a steady flow of humanity from all over the city and from as far afield as Bristol and Norwich, where news of the horrific murder had been the only topic of conversation for weeks. Mr Coggins took his place, feeling no cold in his intoxicated state.

Inside the prison itself, the Mr Bradford lay disconsolate and insomniac upon his bed. His clothes had been taken from him the night before and thoroughly searched lest he should take his own life in the night and cheat the hangman. They had found nothing – no message to a loved one, no fragment of scripture for comfort, no sharpened splinter of wood with which to open a vein. He would exit this world in those same empty clothes.

He shivered. Having attended a few executions, he knew that the streets would already be filling with people come to see him. Not knowing his face, they nevertheless knew his name and infamy. By eight o'clock, the streets before the gaol would be full of people, all of their faces turned upon one point. They would be waiting to see his face and execrate him as a killer, to watch his life jerked quickly from his body.

He would not blub, he was sure of that. He had already decided that he would focus upon his shoes until the blessed grace of the hood gave him privacy. Until that moment, innumerable thousands of eyes would bore into him, unmanning him. He would not blub, he was sure of that.

Voices echoed coldly through the stone corridors towards his cell. It was the prison clergyman, a solicitous old gent come to give the prisoner his final sacrament. For Mr Bradford, who had never ventured inside a church unless for nefarious purposes, the ceremony was one of almost mute incomprehension, the bully murmuring unfamiliar 'amens' just slightly after the other men. He knew there was a heaven, and perceived dimly that this softly worded ritual was his means of entry. It was of little consolation, for the devil himself lurked just out of eyesight beyond the cell: Mr William Calcraft, the hangman.

On the exit of the clergyman, the hangman entered. Expecting a demon, Mr Bradford was surprised to see that the countenance of his executioner was in fact kinder than that of the priest. Its very calmness and lack of expression was, indeed, a palliative influence. This man who had extinguished the lives of more than a hundred was as famous to the criminals of England as the Queen or Lord Nelson, and Mr Bradford showed him more deference than he had ever shown any other man. 'Tell me how to die well,' he said, his voice an arid croak.

'It is quite simple. I will show you where to stand; then I will apply the hood. You will have no problems breathing – many ask me that. I will place the rope around your neck and attach it to the chain on the beam.'

'Will it be quick?'

'Quick enough. You will have a moment to consider your crime.'

'Thank you.' It came out as a whisper.

The absurdity of thanking his killer was lost on the bully, and went unremarked upon by the hangman, who had heard it numerous times. There was a bond between criminal and executioner that went beyond common understanding, and which only the latter truly understood. Mr Calcraft's eyes were not evil. Nor were they kind. He could have been a coach-builder or a tailor going about his business as a matter of routine. Now the clergyman had finished with the soul of this man, Mr Calcraft took charge of his body.

Producing a rope from a bag, he took the bully's hands and tied the wrists firmly in front of his body. At this, Mr Bradford felt the prickling burn of tears and coughed to hide them. Shuffling footsteps echoed in the corridor: the prison governor, the sheriff, under-sheriffs and clergyman.

And there was another, much more disturbing, sound. It was something akin to wind buffeting the building – a low rumble, something at once natural and yet highly unnatural. It was half-past seven.

Outside, the street was thick with people and the gallows stood as a solitary dark mast in a sea of humanity. Perhaps thirty thousand persons extended from the barriers around the scaffold to a distance from which nothing of worth could possibly be seen. Rather, news from the front telegraphed through human wires to the audience's extremities – so when a series of hammerings emanated from within the dread structure, they rippled through the people as the wind ripples heads of wheat. Smoke drifted up from innumerable pipes and cigars.

Hundreds of constables were distributed within the crowd, which laughed and chatted as if at Greenwich fair. Ruffians, clerks, manservants and street girls commingled, the women protected solicitously from the crush by their menfolk. Here and there, a patterer sold penny 'cocks' describing the crimes or purporting to be confessions of the illiterate bully. Those who had not managed to obtain such copy made do with handbills printed in excess for previous executions. All were purchased. The thirst for information was unquenchable.

Indeed, the atmosphere was very like that before the theatre curtain opened on a much-praised show. Chatter, laughter and general conversation hummed like a distant river in a gorge. Up on the 'balcony', people who had paid to gain access to the upper floors of private houses peered from windows, and men settled upon rooftops for an aerial view. Inside the prison itself, sundry gentlemen who had been granted special (and expensive) rights watched from the stone *façade*.

The audience was excited to such a pitch that they were ready to see any spectacle. Were the very Apocalypse to be announced in place of the *matinee* hanging, they would have applauded its arrival. In its absence, their eyes sought out whatever show presented itself.

Thus, when a cab driver lashed out in frustration with his whip at the impenetrable multitudes surrounding him, a tremendous jeer went up and the crowd shivered *en masse* at the opportunity of a performance. Coarse words were uttered by the driver, and were responded to with good-natured catcalls as if the city itself had become a penny gaff. A constable pushed his way through to calm the situation and the collective attention scattered to whatever else might be available.

'This man's life is nothing to the people but another distraction,' said Sergeant Williamson, almost to himself.

'As were the deaths of Eliza-Beth and Mary Chatterton,' agreed Noah.

The two men stood in the barricaded space between the door of the gaol and the scaffold. The sergeant wore a police uniform and Mr Dyson a dark suit that might pass as a uniform from a distance. Before them, a selection of London's worst people was gathered at the wooden barrier, jostling for position and heaving like a single, vast organism. Here at the front, the crush was such that a man's feet might be lifted involuntarily from the ground by the pressure. One of these people, a costermonger lad with a corduroy hat pushed cockily back on his head, called out to the police:

'Oi, bluebottles! Mind yer don't get yer own 'eads caught in Calcraft's noose!'

His friends giggled and jeered their approval.

'I would respond,' said Noah to Mr Williamson, 'but I'd wager most of them will be dead or on the scaffold themselves in a few years.'

'Hmm.'

'Have you attended many executions, Sergeant?'

'I have been obliged to, but I would not voluntarily do so. They are bestial.'

'I, too, have seen my share. More than my share.'

'It is almost time.' Mr Williamson looked at his pocket watch. 'When the prisoner ascends, we will ascend with him and cast our eyes about the crowd. Nobody will give us a second glance when Mr Bradford steps on to the trap, but our observation may prove productive.'

'So you still imagine that he will attend?'

'We will see.'

At that moment, the bell of the gaol began to toll eight.

A galvanic ripple went through the crowd: terror, awe and fascination equally mixed. As one, they removed their hats or bonnets and gazed fixedly upon the small door of the gaol. Where before there had been a rumbling murmur of voices, silence now settled. Tens of thousands of gazes settled on that exit. The door opened and the prisoner emerged, followed by his attendants.

Mr Coggins stood up on his toes to see the man who had killed his Eliza-Beth. In the *mêlée*, his peruke had been knocked askew and his face shone with the exertion of trying to maintain his place. Yes, that was the murderer! The facial scar was quite visible.

'Murderer!' screamed Mr Coggins. 'Evil cur, you will burn in Hell, you d— —! You will swing for it now. Oh yes!'

Others around him looked askance at this bewigged vision of loathing and addressed him with the respect he deserved:

'Show some restraint, sir. A man is to die here today.'

'Quiet there! He might give some last words.'

To which the *impresario* answered with his usual delicacy: 'I will not be quiet! That man killed my girl! He deprived me of my livelihood! I will shout if I—'

His words were halted by a vice-like grip on his upper arm that seemed to close around the very bone. Turning, he saw a tall man with familiar eyes whose lower face was partially covered with a scarf, perhaps because of the early morning chill. On closer inspection, however, Mr Coggins recognized the man who had come to visit the house in Lambeth.

'Why, Dr Cole! Fancy meeting you here. I heard you were in Edinburgh. Come down for the hanging, have you? I see you are wearing your scarf against the bad air. There is much of it about, eh?'

'Hush, Mr Coggins. We are drawing attention from the show,' replied the man.

*

So many people! Bully Bradford blinked, flinched and stepped back at the vision of mass humanity before him. He felt himself weakening under the relentless stares. He stumbled into the clergyman, who held his elbow in support. Fear stiffened his limbs and he felt his face freezing into an absurd rictus of embarrassment. His legs would not move.

Someone took his other elbow and they walked him somnambulistically to the steps leaned against the scaffold. Like an automaton, he climbed. His hands clasped and unclasped within their bonds. Up on the platform, a veritable ocean of faces gazed upon him. He was vaguely aware of others there with him – Mr Calcraft, the clergyman, two policemen – but it was the restless masses that mesmerized him. Under the weight of their relentless eyes, he felt himself stripped naked and reduced to nothing – no longer a man, but a spectacle. His name, his history, his friendships and his voice were nothing to them. He tried to speak, to say that he had not meant to kill the girl, but his throat was constricted and dry. Only a rasp emerged. And now Mr Calcraft was holding the hood.

Mr Williamson had been quite correct. Though the two of them stood upon the platform, they might have as well been invisible. All eyes were upon the bully and Mr Calcraft, the only two performers. Even Mr Bradford was oblivious to their presence, being understandably distracted.

Noah reflected on the impossibility of their task. Ten faces might allow a degree of individual recognition; twenty would be more difficult – but here were thirty thousand or more. They merged into one indistinguishable blur. As soon as he looked at one, it seemed to be absorbed by the others. Only a bald head or a flash of white hair provided any point of focus. Boyle could have been standing within yards of them and remained unseen. It seemed hopeless.

Noah turned to look at the prisoner, who was now wearing the hood. It fitted quite tightly over his face so that the nose and chin pressed the material outwards. He was positioned beneath the beam and Mr Calcraft was attaching the rope to the chain already in place there. Short, percussive breaths emanated through the black hood and the prisoner's hands held each other, perhaps in prayer.

'Pay attention to the crowd, Mr Dyson,' warned the sergeant.

And the people stared back, unblinking lest they miss the moment. An impossible quiet had stilled them – an eerie, unearthly silence from such a huge audience. Indeed, Mr Bradford's breathing seemed the loudest sound within that amphitheatre of expectation. He stood, unmoving, knees slightly bent in anticipation.

The mechanism was pulled free and the trap dropped. A soundless wave of attention fluttered through the tens of thousands, punctuated only by a single, distant shriek. Mr Coggins's eyes telescoped upon the hooded figure as it fell, hands still clasped in prayer or terror. The body jerked to a halt, neck twisted, and hung – a dead weight. Time stopped. The legs gave a reflexive twitch and were still. Mr Calcraft's infamous 'short drop' had been long enough to do its job.

The voice of Mr Coggins, raucous and gin-laden, fractured the moment:

'Good — riddance!'

Both Noah and Sergeant Williamson looked instinctively in the direction of the lone voice. The latter squinted over the rows of heads and pinpointed the ludicrous blond peruke of Mr Coggins as the source of the cry. Other people, too, were looking towards the source of the disrespectful yell. The spectacle they had come to see was over and yet their hunger to see a show was as yet unsated. Some turned away from the scaffold and looked towards Mr Coggins.

And Noah felt the jolt of recognition. Beside the risible figure of 'Dr Zwigoff' was a man wearing a scarf about his lower face. As if drawn by magnetism, the be-scarfed man caught the glare of his nemesis, noticing this anonymous 'policeman's' face for the first time. Their stares met. Boyle's smoke-grey eyes widened at the same instant that Noah's arm raised and pointed across the crowd:

'Seize that man!'

Sergeant Williamson looked confusedly at Noah and then again at the focus of his gaze, perceiving for the first time the man with the scarf. His recognition of Mr Coggins had blinded him to the peripheral faces. In a burst of uncharacteristic excitement, he shouted to a constable standing on duty just a few yards from Coggins and Boyle:

'You there! Yes, you, constable! Seize the man in the scarf beside the bewigged blond man. Take him – now!'

A phrensy of sensation animated the crowd and all eyes sought the new show. Murmurs and shouts transmitted the news to distant fringes where people could not see. A space began to form around Coggins and Boyle as the constable shouldered his way through towards them.

Mr Coggins blinked in bewilderment at the sudden turn of events and dimly perceived that the focus of the attention was not he but 'Dr Cole', whom the police were attempting to arrest. His prime instinct – the prospect of financial gain

– pierced the dull alcohol fug of his mind and he turned to grasp Boyle's arm:

'If you are a criminal, I apprehend you in the name of the law.'

At this, Boyle struck Mr Coggins in the stomach with a formidable blow, but the drunken *impresario* was too stubborn to fall. They struggled with a flurry of arms and the scarf was pulled free, revealing Boyle's empurpled jaw. A collective exclamation went up from the surrounding observers. Consternation showed in the whites of the incendiary's eyes.

From the platform, Noah watched in frustration. Even if he had wanted to, he could not have penetrated the density of people to reach the fighting pair before the constable. The object of his sleepless, ceaseless searches stood before him now, inaccessible even within sight.

The constable had almost reached them when Boyle reached left-handed into the folds of his coat and – unperceived by his assailant – produced a dark-handled pistol with a short barrel. He pressed it into the soft skin under Mr Coggins's jaw.

The muffled explosion was heard only by those closest, but everyone within sight saw the peruke leap vertically from the blond man's head and the geyser of thick red matter that erupted forth immediately thereafter. The pistol was withdrawn as the *impresario* collapsed, and the circle around the two men widened suddenly at the sight of the weapon, people pushing maniacally backwards to flee danger. A woman wailed and a strangled cry of '*Murder!*' went up. The news spread like fire through the vast congregation, a murmur erupting outwards to those who could not see.

Lucius Boyle brandished the weapon at the constable arriving out of breath at the edge of that horrifyingly silent circumference. Its single shot was spent, but a gun is a gun to the non-military man and its lethality infinite. Was not Mr Coggins proof of that, lying there with a spreading pool of coagulate about his splintered scull?

'Seize him! The weapon is empty!' shouted Noah from the platform, but his words were dissipated like smoke amid the growing clamour. Sergeant Williamson shouted orders to the constables around the platform who could see little of what was happening.

The constable looked at the pistol and at the demoniacal countenance of the man who held it. He looked at the prone body of Mr Coggins and felt the circle receding behind him so that he faced the gunman alone within it.

'I will kill you with as little compunction as I would kill a fly,' said the red-jawed man with cold imperiousness. And he began to back away from the policeman, who stood frozen to the spot. The crowd parted around Boyle, transfixed by the gun and by the man. As he moved, they parted silently before him and closed around him again so that he walked as in a bubble. Any one of them could have struck him, but his status as a murderer seemed almost supernatural to them. Murders happened in the dark, unseen – not in plain sight amid a crowd of thousands on a Monday morning at Newgate. The enormity of it was too much to conceive. The space around him was as uncrossable as a castle moat, a force that emanated from him. This man was not a mortal. This occurrence could not be real. His fearsome appearance struck terror into the witnesses as if he were the very Devil himself, turning and turning again within his circle to touch all with his baleful glare.

And as Noah watched futilely from his balcony seat, Boyle moved spectrally unmolested through the buzzing crowds towards the alleys north of Paternoster-row, the distance between them stretching and stretching until the receding figure passed suddenly out of sight and down into those narrow passages. Constables from different parts of the crowd pushed in multiple paths towards that spot, but too late. Too late. Before they arrived there, Lucius Boyle had become – out of sight – just another body on the city streets, his gun, jaw and identity once again concealed.

The throng seemed to exhale, and a swelling cacophony began to reverberate between the buildings. Noah stamped ferociously on the boards of the scaffold and let forth a bestial, spittle-flecked profanity that attracted the startled looks of many.

The body of Mr Bradford hung motionless for a further hour before being cut down and taken within the gaol.

SIXTEEN

Detective Sergeant Williamson

I apprehend that your pursuit has begun in earnest. I congratulate your intuition in standing sentinel at the scaffold on the slim chance that I would materialize before you. Simultaneously, I curse my own foolish curiosity in playing the hand you expected. That will not occur again.

I also applaud your coercing (for I believe it cannot be otherwise) of my erstwhile companion Mr Noah Dyson into your scheme. Few others could recognize me, and no other could thirst for my capture with such keenness, except perhaps your hapless superior. In truth, I thought him long dead. The sight of him there, across that field of bared heads, was a shock even to me. Now we know the stakes of our game.

Naturally, I will have to go to ground and disappear. That is most inconvenient. You came close to me. That was laxity on my part. Soon, all other connections will be broken and your

hounds will lose the scent. Much as I respect you,
you will be humiliated – and I will be free.
    Regards
    Lucius Boyle

Commissioner Sir Richard Mayne pounded the letter against the broad tabletop with the flat of his hand. Also arrayed there were a selection of newspaper reports on the astonishing events of the previous day's hanging.

Sitting around that same table were Inspector Newsome and Superintendent Wilberforce, who had first approached Sir Richard with their scheme; those three men were now joined by Mr Williamson and Noah. The commissioner's anger seemed to hang in the cigar smoke above the table. Nobody but Sir Richard dared speak.

'This man Boyle murdered another in plain sight of thirty thousand citizens *as hundreds of policemen looked on!* At this solemn exhibition of the price of crime, a criminal is bold enough to *scorn* the Metropolitan Police by murdering a man even as the prisoner Bradford is dropping through the trap! It is an *insult*, gentlemen. And now this letter . . .'

His exasperation strangled the words once more. The other men looked down at the table, willing another to speak first.

'What are we to do, gentlemen? What do we know? I want to hear everything and I want to hear how we are going to catch this man with the rapidity with which Mr Bradford was brought to justice. Do you know that the Queen has been asking questions about this? It has gone that far.'

'With all respect, Sir Richard,' began Superintendent Wilberforce, 'there was no way we could have foreseen or prevented the occurrence with Mr Boyle. Any man could have taken a pistol to the execution. There are often numerous crimes at a hanging: pockets picked, petty violence, theft from shops, burglaries—'

'But murder! Do not tell me that *that* is common. There were hundreds of policeman within feet of the man.'

'The crowd was unprecedented, sir,' added Mr Newsome. 'More even than with Courvoisier.'

'You should have foreseen that, especially since you tell me that Sergeant Williamson had an intuition that this Boyle would attend. Did you not make plans for this?'

'If I may speak, Sir Richard . . .'

'You are the man who had me sign my name to a letter of exculpation, yes? The cracksman who captured Mr Bradford – Noah Dyson? I will say now that I experience great unease entertaining you at this table, sir. This is a police matter – you would be advised to keep your silence.'

'Nevertheless,' continued Noah, unconcerned, 'the situation was not remotely typical or predictable. The facial appearance of Boyle, the unique character of the occasion and the choice of murder weapon all combined to create a climate where he was able to escape. Nobody here is at fault.'

Sir Richard seethed with a barely contained fury at the head of the table. Had this common thief just disregarded his order to remain silent? Not only disregarded it, but with an air of disdain at the gravity of the situation and a complete lack of respect for the commissioner of police. He looked from Mr Wilberforce to Mr Newsome, then he stood, and without a word, left the room.

The others stood, too late, as he exited the room with a formidable slam of the door. A humiliated Mr Newsome jabbed a finger at Mr Williamson and Noah:

'Find Boyle. Do whatever you must do. We cannot have any more murders by this man. The newspapers are intoxicated with it, and now this . . . this letter of his. The very Queen herself is asking questions! I hold both of you responsible. And let us agree that the name of Lucius Boyle will go no further than this table, do I make myself clear? We don't want the papers to get hold of it or we'll be inundated with letters from a thousand Lucius Boyles!'

And then he and Mr Wilberforce hastily left the room to placate Sir Richard.

Noah and Mr Williamson sat once more, facing each other across the table. The air of the room was charged with lingering anger and accusation. Cigar smoke hung in a grey-blue pall above them.

'It was foolish of you to speak like that to the commissioner,' said Mr Williamson.

'It was foolish of the police to utilize me in the first instance. I am not bound by any oath.'

'You are melancholic because Boyle slipped through our fingers yesterday. I understand that. His escape and the murder of Mr Coggins is as much an injury to me, I can promise you.'

'I think not.'

The detective reached across to the letter and placed it between them. It was written in black ink, most likely with a steel pen, on standard writing paper. It had been handed to a beat constable on Westminster-bridge by a street boy who had vanished into the traffic just as quickly as he had appeared. The letter was addressed to 'Sergeant George Williamson of the Detective Force, 4 Whitehall Place'.

'The physical letter can tell us little. The handwriting is copperplate with good spelling and grammar, but we already know he is intelligent. I have looked over its entirety with a magnifying glass and found nothing that can help us. That leaves us only with the content . . . Noah? Are you listening?'

'We will never see him again. You are wasting your time in any further investigation.'

'You are being melodramatic – and you are wrong. You will see Boyle again, because he will not rest until you are dead. He knows that you are working with the police – that is why he has revealed his name to us. He knows that we know him; he knows that you, more than most men, can identify him; he knows that you are alive when he once thought you – or wished you – dead . . . I see from your expression that the latter is the more correct.'

'Why would he kill me?'

'I am beginning to think that he has determined to kill everyone connected with this case – however tangentially – just as he seems to kill everyone who has seen him or who can implicate him. First was Mary Chatterton, then Mr Coggins—'

'Wait. I assumed Mr Coggins was merely an unlucky victim. His coarse shouting attracted unwanted attention. Then he made the mistake of grappling with Lucius.'

'I thought so too, initially. But is it not too great a coincidence that Boyle should have been standing next to Mr Coggins in a crowd of thousands?'

'Why a coincidence? Boyle may have attended the show at Vauxhall Gardens and seen Eliza-Beth, but we have no evidence that the two men ever met or knew each other.'

'Perhaps we do not have evidence, but I think we may make a certain assumption. When I first spoke to Mr Coggins, he described a Dr Cole.'

'But you told me this Dr Cole is a legitimate doctor, a

well-respected specialist of Harley-street. This has been veri-fied.'

'No. What we have established is that a man claiming to be a doctor visited the Lambeth house, that a doctor of that name exists at Harley-street and that he is currently in Edin-burgh.'

'There is something you have not told me.'

'The doctor who visited Mr Coggins was wearing a scarf about his face to "prevent against bad air". And Dr Cole left for Edinburgh two days *before* the murder of Eliza-Beth took place. To the knowledge of his household, he has not returned.'

'Boyle.'

'It is hardly conclusive, but the evidence suggests it. We may assume that Mr Boyle followed Mr Coggins to New-gate.'

'Why did you keep this from me?'

'I learned the date of Dr Cole's departure to Scotland only this morning. He was the sole connection to the case that remained truly unknown. Evidently our Mr Boyle showed more foresight than you – *his* calling card named a real person with a real address. A person, moreover, who could not be immediately contacted.'

'You should keep me informed of the enquiries you make.'

'Mr Dyson, I told you that I have only just confirmed this information. Nevertheless, I am still not sure I can trust you. I believe you want to capture Mr Boyle for your own revenge. I, on the other hand, want to bring him to justice.'

'What I plan for him is justice enough.'

The two stared unblinking at each other across the table. A low murmur of congregated people was carried up to the window. They had gathered at the police headquarters for news, for gossip, for a glimpse of the policemen conducting the case. The bare facts in the newspapers were not enough to feed their hunger.

'Mr Dyson, we must apprehend this man by any means necessary, and as rapidly as we can. After that, we need never meet again. I am sure we will not. Now – let us consider the letter. What are your opinions?'

'He is amused rather than perturbed by the situation. My continued existence, however, is a genuine surprise to him.'

'That much is clear. What of his promise to "go to ground"? What could he mean by that?'

'I am not sure. He has been in hiding for most of his life. I cannot comprehend what more he could do to be invisible, apart from disassociating himself from those few that know him. In that case, how is he to function? The newspapers are full of descriptions of his face, both covered and uncovered.'

'Hmm. And what of this "all other connections will be broken"? Is it not a promise, the "connections" being the other people connected to this case?'

'What connections? Mary is dead. Mr Coggins is dead. Who else is there for him to kill? The rest of the performers?'

'You. Me. The father of Eliza-Beth, the search for whom may have been the reason why all of this started. He is an incendiary – he is accustomed to razing things to the ground and destroying them utterly so that not a trace remains.'

'Sergeant, do you really believe that he would try to kill you and me?'

'Would you have believed that he would kill Mr Coggins amid thirty thousand people?'

'Frankly, no. It was highly visible and out of character.

So, if we are to keep a watch on possible victims, who are we to watch? Ourselves?'

'That is something we must ascertain. I will return again to Mr Coggins's troupe and see if Mr Hardy – the half-man – recalls the visit of "Dr Cole". We know that both Mr Askern and the clergyman saw Boyle at the Lambeth house, so we may consider them also to be in danger. Indeed, we may consider all of the performers to be in danger . . . I hope we are not facing more slaughter.'

'What exactly did you learn from the writer?'

'He believes he saw the "doctor" returning Eliza-Beth to the house. What do you make of that?'

'He cannot have been easily mistaken. It is possible Mr Coggins had other lucrative uses for the girl . . . What of Mr Askern's paternity?'

'He appears to be what he claims and gave me no reason to believe that he is the father of Eliza-Beth.'

'I do not mean to be coarse, but how would he know? When a man is young, he may know many women – just as many men knew Mary Chatterton.'

'I will trust your experience on that subject, Mr Dyson. Mr Askern is a gentleman. What of the Reverend Archer? Did you locate him?'

'Yes, and he was as full of wind as usual. I questioned him about the letter and he admitted he had seen it. Only that. Perhaps he was ashamed to have been looking at that area of her anatomy and therefore lied to you about it. He also provided me with a new piece of information – one that has added weight now that you have told me about the doctor and Eliza-Beth. Mr Coggins offered him the services of Eliza-Beth.'

'Services? What services? Do you mean . . . ?'

'Yes. He was prostituting the girl. She was pretty in her own way, and there are men in London so debauched that they perpetually crave something new—'

'You do not need to elaborate.'

'You are blushing, Sergeant. I would expect a man of your experience to have seen everything on the streets.'

'Hmm. Hmm. This new intelligence complicates matters greatly. It means Eliza-Beth may have had contact with a larger number of men than we know. Perhaps Boyle was indeed one of them. Yet she is dead, and so is Mr Coggins. What of Mr Archer? Did he partake of her . . . services?'

'I believe he has never had carnal experience of any woman, save the Virgin perhaps—'

'I'll thank you not to blaspheme in my presence, Mr Dyson. So, we must certainly visit the performers once again before they scatter. I do not know what is to become of them now that their "protector" is dead. They may be in imminent danger.'

At that moment, there was a knock at the door and a clerk entered with a letter. He handed it to Sergeant Williamson and left without a word. The detective looked at his name and the Whitehall address written on the front.

'Boyle?' asked Noah.

Mr Williamson opened the letter with care and quickly read through its contents. His jaw set with determination and he handed the letter to Noah, who passed his eyes fervidly across the copperplate writing.

'I will make the arrangements,' said Mr Williamson. 'In the meantime, we must go to the house where Mr Coggins's performers are currently residing. I have insisted that they stay in the city until this case is solved. All of us will meet there.'

'What of the clergyman? He may also be in danger.'

'Yes. We must attempt to find him again and inform him. Now, let us go.'

'The crowds outside have increased since we arrived. Are we to drag them with us to the house?'

'No. I will leave first and speak briefly to the newspaper-men. Wait for an hour and make your own way there, preferably unseen. You know the address.'

And with that, Mr Williamson exited the room.

Noah rose and walked to the window. He could see a group of people – journalists, gossip-mongers, avid readers of broadsheets and newspapers – too impatient to wait for the printed news. Indeed, I was one of them – there to gather news. Had I looked up, I would have seen him looking down at me and we might have exchanged gazes. Instead, Sergeant Williamson appeared at the door and we clamoured around him, oblivious to the man above us.

Somewhere out there across the roofs and the chimneys, Noah's quarry was hiding. He saw those smoky eyes again, staring at him over the bared heads of the execution crowd. The moment was frozen as a painting in his mind: a para-lysing shock of recognition, undimmed by the years they had spent apart.

Naturally, he remembered Boyle as the boy. The man was broader and more muscular, taller and more weathered. But there was a familiarity of movement and demeanour which meant that Noah would have recognized that gait had he seen Boyle from the rear walking down a street. It was the boy's face that he had carried with him all those years as a *totem* of revenge, and the adult enemy was an unexpected image. In truth, he wondered if he had ever really expected to find his betrayer. Boyle had been, for so long, merely an idea: an origin towards which Noah was perpetually returning in order to begin again.

Now they had met again. Boyle had become everything his character as a boy had promised: amoral, fiery, deranged, homicidal . . . almost a myth. Noah extracted the dagger from inside his coat and tested the edge against his thumb. It scraped razor-sharp against the tiny swirls of skin.

The reader must have been wondering about the past of Noah Dyson. The police would never know. Only I know. It would be impertinent to ask how, but I have my methods and my sources. I pull at them gently and they emerge from darkness like the endless roots of a plant tapering off beneath our feet. Shall we look together at the rhizotomous past of the man, that we might understand him better?

His father had been a sailor plying the Northern and Southern Oceans, sometimes beneath the red and white pennant of the convict ships to New South Wales, sometimes on a reeking American whaler, sometimes carrying pungent spices from India. The baby Noah, dandled on the paternal knee, had delighted in tracing the tattooed lines across his father's arms and chest, following an imagined map of those travels through valleys of scars and lines etched by rope and salt – travels that he would one day make himself. Regrettably, that father was seldom in London, and seldom sober when he was. One day, he never returned, no doubt lost to a saline tomb or a navy brig's overzealous disciplinarian.

His mother was the poor daughter of an unsuccessful

printer, with the one mitigating result that the young man was never short of reading matter. Indeed, among his kind, he was considered something of a prodigy for his reading ability and knowledge of foreign parts. To his peers, Achilles or Troy might well have been characters from the Bible, had they ever seen a bible. Before he had friends, he had a cast of hundreds in his head and a world spanning eons in which to play. Then, in his eleventh year, the maternal care that had so tenuously kept him from running with the shoeless boys of his district was taken by the cholera. Her family could not afford to keep him.

Extinction beckoned, but he – as so many of our orphaned boys – chose freedom and crime. He became a street Arab, sleeping in doorways and living from nimble-fingered pilferings. Wherever a back was turned to enter a carriage, wherever a wallet was carelessly opened, wherever there was a soft heart to be gulled with an artificial snivel, young Noah was there – surviving.

And he became a leader among the boys on account of his patter. With the gentlemen, he could flatter with classical titbits and Latin puns. With the ladies he could wring tears even from the bitterest and most desiccated widow with his earnestly delivered passages of scripture. Had the charitable organizations known of him, he may have been directed into schooling by some benefactor. Instead, he met Lucius Boyle.

Lucius was indeed an odd name for a child of the streets. The man himself had no idea that his parents had been well-born residents of Park-lane, whose horror at his birth defect was sufficient to banish the baby boy from their lives forever. He was sent – as many children of that class are – to a nurse-maid and was simply never returned. A steady (if small) supply of money found its way to his surrogate mother, most of which went directly to the manufacturers and purveyors of brandy. It ceased once his parents' guilt had been sufficiently assuaged.

He grew: undernourished, effectively orphaned and cruelly marked by fate. Some cursed him as the Devil's spawn; others treated him as one would a street dog. Indeed, his only salvation was that the fine stock of his birth had blessed him with a quick wit. As soon as he could escape the spirit-addled woman who had negligently 'raised' him, he fled to the streets, where he learned the universal law of nature: that the most vicious, most cunning creature usually survives.

Every 'head boy' meets a rival on the streets. Fiefdoms cross and reputations are bandied by followers. 'Dyson earned a sovvy by speaking Roman to a toff!' boasts one tribal member. '*Did* he?' ripostes a rival. 'Well, Boyle stole a ten-guinea watch from a gent up Haymarket – didn't even feel it!' Fights ensue over whose leader is superior. Domination is hard won, the loser being cast into shameful obscurity.

Boyle and Dyson met finally near Southwark-bridge. They gauged each other against their exaggerated reputations, neither one as tall nor as fierce as the gossip implied – both still children. Noah was a wiry youth, fast rather than strong. Other boys might hit harder, but he was seldom in the space where the fist had been aimed. Lucius was more of a physical presence, his lower face disfigured quite terrifyingly by an enflamed purple birthmark that seemed to trace his jawline almost exactly, bubbling angrily at his cheeks and neck like port or venous blood. To his followers, it was a supernatural thing, at once intimidating and fascinating. It gave him a look of perpetual wrath.

'Achilles and Odysseus fought on the same side,' said Noah.

'I don't know no Romans, but a good fighting dog knows when to attack and when to bide his time,' said Boyle. 'We are doubled together and halved apart – that is simple 'rithmatic.'

Both smiled. They spat in their grubby palms and shook. An empire was born. They called themselves 'the Generals', the Napoleons of London. What Boyle lacked in learning at that time, he compensated for in a cunning born of a lifetime on the streets. What Noah lacked in callousness, he made up for with intelligence. Together, they became legends among the urchins, mudlarks, chimney boys, street-sweepers and boot-blackers. Not for them the adult kidsman who orchestrates a horde of child thieves – they were their own masters. They knew the best places and the best 'lays'. It was Smithfield at dusk for a gristly chop, Billingsgate at midday for a turning fish, closing time at the Whitechapel bakers for a stale crust. With Noah's patter and Boyle's slyness, their boys were the lords of juvenile crime.

Alas, boys grow. They become men and they become proud. It is often their baser instincts that grow unchecked. Boyle's native cruelty fermented in his growing vessel, while Noah began to argue for the more honest living he knew his intelligence could easily procure. Boyle sought criminal means; Noah looked to commerce. Any historian knows that force and deception always overcome rationality and truth.

The *coup d'état* came as they were conducting a 'campaign' on the Surrey side. Boyle had received intelligence of how a certain brewery could be accessed after dark, and their boys had a taste for beer. Prepared with bags, they entered a store and began to remove the bottles, acting silently because Boyle had thought to fill each bag with straw to muffle the glassy clinks.

In the musty dimness of those vaults, the two head boys held oil lamps to guide their troops. Only one man knows whether it was accident or intention that caused Boyle's lamp to crash into a nest of tinder-dry straw, striking the fatal spark that would bring the brewery crashing down in a raging inferno later that night. Only two men know for certain that it was perfidy that closed the sole means of safe egress while Noah was still trapped inside at the mercy of the already intractable flames.

To the alarm raised by Noah's loyal followers outside, Boyle offered only a chilling sentence: 'There was only one Napoleon, boys . . .'

Despite his best and frantic efforts, young Noah was unable to escape from that place until the door was battered in by a constable attending the attempts to extinguish the flames. On finding the boy there, the policeman immediately concluded that he had discovered the thief and incendiary in the act. A particularly violent arrest was effected and, omitting the predictable legal proceedings, Noah found himself gaoled at the tender age of thirteen.

His articulacy could not save him now. Boys of a similar age were routinely being transported for as slight a crime as taking a loaf of bread. He expected no clemency from the magistrate, and received none: the sentence was transportation to New South Wales, to be carried out as soon as the next transport ships left London. In the meantime, he would be incarcerated at the hulks in Woolwich.

I need hardly inform the reader of the conditions he must have experienced there. Even today, there are regular deaths from cholera, influenza and countless other brutalities. The pestilential atmosphere of those rotting hulks, the scuttle of rats, the stink of men, the bilge miasma and the ever-present threat of violence make them unbearable for an adult; for a child, they must have seemed Hell.

Young Noah was expected to fulfil his work duty at the arsenal until the transports set sail: back-breaking work that would prepare him for the slavery of his destination. And, each day, people would come to watch the prisoners work as if they were animals reduced to inhuman labour. How he felt the burning shame of their eyes upon his humiliation! Throughout his many weeks there, the only thing that sustained him – excepting the wormy beef and sprouting potatoes – was the futile hope that his boys would come and rescue him. That, and the burning desire for revenge against his enemy Lucius Boyle. Every outrage at the hands of his fellow prisoners, every bruise and knock stoked his hatred of the boy who had betrayed him. Unable to escape and unlikely to be rescued, he survived each day with thoughts of revenge.

The many months at sea did nothing to diminish his passion. As people died around him, he drew strength from the hope that he would soon return to London. A passage to the Antipodes is punishment enough for many crimes, and through roaring tempests, thirst and the briny swill of vomit in overheated lower decks, another man might have forgotten. But Noah's bestial treatment at the hands of fellow prisoners reminded him daily of the injustice of his punishment. True, he had stolen from the brewery, but the fire (and the betrayal) was Boyle's crime. Boyle should have been the one locked in that verminous hull. Boyle should have been the one with iron chafing at his bones and the suffocating nausea blocking his senses. It was the motivation that kept Noah alive.

SEVENTEEN

Mr Hardy lowered the newspaper from which he had been reading aloud to the gathered 'performers' and folded it neatly into his lap. Though his feet did not reach the ground in the adult-sized chair, and though the opened newspaper had stretched his arms to their limit, he maintained an air of dignity and authority that was much needed under the circumstances.

A muffled sobbing came from Miss Eugenia and the dog-child nuzzled her considerable thigh, oblivious for the time being to the situation. It was only the emotion she sensed with her anthropocanine intuition. The fire crackled in the grate and lamps cast their flickering illumination upon the group, even though it was daylight beyond that curtained room.

'We are lost. What is to become of us?' sniffed the giant lady. 'Mr Coggins may have been a vile, despicable man – but he provided us with a life. We are at the mercy of the mob. They will be here at any moment to *crash down the door*!'

The dog-child whimpered in response to the tone of her mistress.

'Nonsense, Eugenia,' replied Mr Hardy calmly. 'We must reflect rationally on our situation. We hold in our very bodies the means to live profitably. Once this case is solved and the perpetrator caught, we may venture out once more. All we need is someone to organize the shows and protect us from the common gaze.'

'*You* can do it, Mr Hardy.' The *basso profundo* voice was that of the giant man, folded as usual upon too small a chair. 'You are the most "normal" of us all.'

'I thank you for that, Edgar, but I am afraid the majority of citizens would disagree. No, we must find another sponsor.'

'We must leave this city! We must leave now or else we will all be killed,' wailed Eugenia.

'Now, now – there is no need for such histrionics. Why would we all die?'

'*He . . . he* will come for us. The doctor man.'

'Why, what on earth are you talking about, Eugenia?'

'Do you not recall how Missy responded to his presence?' The giant lady felt for the hirsute face of the dog-child and stroked her nose. 'She growled and bared her teeth something terrible . . . and when he glared at her, she whimpered and ran to hide. Have you seen her behave so on other occasions?'

'I hardly think you can—'

'She knew he was evil, I tell you. She has a heightened sense for these things, like a real dog. *And* she sees spirits.'

'That is really enough nonsense for one evening, Eugenia. I am sure—'

A knock stopped him. All heads turned towards the door. Then another three knocks came in rapid succession, followed by a further single knock: the signal they had agreed with those who helped them. Mr Hardy jumped down from his chair and made a series of rapid little steps to open the door.

'Sergeant Williamson! Welcome. I was expecting a visit from you. Come in, come in. Take my seat there by the fire and you will be able to speak to everyone.'

The group shuffled uncomfortably at the intrusion, even though they had met Mr Williamson before. The sunken-faced man reached instinctively for his hat and pulled it low over his brow, while Missy, the dog-child, ventured tentatively to smell the detective's trouser leg – an action that occasioned him some mild embarrassment.

'*Ahem* . . . I apologize for disturbing you all, but I have a number of questions I would like to ask.'

'It was the doctor!' shrieked Eugenia.

'Hush! This is serious business!' admonished Mr Hardy, taking a seat. But the sudden look of attention upon the detective's face stopped him from going further.

'What of the doctor? Tell me everything you know,' urged Mr Williamson.

'He made Missy growl.'

'Why did you not speak to me before about this doctor?'

'Why, because you didn't ask me, Constable.'

'Hmm. Why do you say that he was evil?'

'It was in his eyes. They were not human. I have seen many eyes look upon me, Constable. More eyes than you have felt – but this man looked *through* me as if my life was worth less to him than a pinch of salt.'

'Was his face covered the entire time?'

'Yes. To protect against the bad air, he said. I think he meant my wind—'

'Eugenia!' warned Mr Hardy, 'let us avoid vulgarity.'

'Did he speak to each of you in turn?' enquired Mr Williamson to the group in general.

'Yes,' answered Mr Hardy, 'we all spoke with him, but I believe he expressed greater interest in Eliza-Beth and spoke to us, I believe, only out of courtesy. We may be "monsters" but we perceive human nature as well as any other – perhaps better.'

'Of what did he speak to you?'

'Oh, the usual things: whether our parents shared the same features, whether we knew our parents, if we felt pain and where – it was almost as if he was following a script. Certainly there was nothing especially sinister or suspicious about him, excepting his medicinal scarf.'

'Was that the extent of his communication with you? Did he speak further with Eliza-Beth?'

'I do not believe so.'

A suppressed moan came from Eugenia, who appeared to be in a state of some inner turmoil. Missy wheedled and pawed empathetically at her mistress's leg.

'Miss Eugenia, have you something to tell us?' asked Mr Williamson. 'I must inform you that I have discovered things about Eliza-Beth that you may not know – shocking things. Anything you can tell me may help to trap the murderer, who is assuredly not a doctor. Indeed, the man you spoke to – if you have not already surmised – is the same man who murdered your Mr Coggins at the hanging of Mr Bradford.'

A flutter of muttered comment passed through the room as the performers reflected on the fact that they had entertained a murderer in their midst. Eugenia let forth a blubbery sob and dabbed at her eyes.

'And not only Mr Coggins. Your "doctor" is also wanted for the murder of Mary Chatterton. Indeed, all of you find

yourselves by coincidence or pattern at the centre of a series
of murders that has no precedent in the annals of this city –
a series that, I fear, is not completed. Though you may not
realize it, you may hold the key to catching this man.'

The performers sat in silence, contemplating what they
had heard.

'Sergeant Williamson, I am sure we are all eager to help
you,' responded Mr Hardy, 'but I cannot think that we can
tell you more than we have already revealed. It is we who are
the objects of observation, such that we often become blind
to those who view us.'

'I would like to speak with Miss Eugenia alone, if I may.
Mr Hardy, would you be so kind as to escort your fellows to
the kitchen for a cup of tea. And the dog . . . I mean, little
Missy, also.'

'Certainly, Sergeant. I understand. I will listen for your
call should you need me.' The tiny man glared briefly in
warning at the giant lady, then jumped down from his chair.

And the performers shuffled away to the kitchen, muttering to each other about the situation they found themselves
in.

'Miss Eugenia. Forgive me for my frankness: Eliza-Beth
was a whore – and you know very well that was the case.'

'*She was not!* She was the purest, most gentle girl you
could care to meet, but that . . . that gutter-filth Mr Coggins
sold her to the young gentlemen who were curious. Yes, she
told me – only me. I was her confidante. Oh, the shame! The
shame of that poor, poor child! She was *not* a whore.'

'Calm yourself. Here, take my handkerchief.' The detective handed Eugenia his kerchief and took out his notebook
as she was attending noisily to her face.

'She was not like those girls you see on the street, sir. She was pure of heart but defiled of life.'

'I have no doubt. Tell me – was this Dr Cole one of her "visiters"? Do not keep anything from me or you tarnish her memory. I am sure she acquitted herself with honesty and morality.'

'She did! And he was . . . but how did you know?'

'I surmised. Tell me of it.'

'He was an odd one. He took her after our show at Vauxhall and returned her to the house later that night – that was how they arranged it. He did not want to use her as the other men did, though. He wanted only to talk to her. He took off his scarf and showed her his face – terribly red, it was (that's when I knew he was the murderer). He tried to tell her that they were alike in their difficulties, can you imagine!'

'Of what did they speak?'

'He asked her more about her family, but of course she knew nothing. He asked about some important gentlemen, but she had not heard of them. He said that he knew many people in society and that he could help to discover her true parents if only she could give him some clue. She told him about the letter she had received, but did not show him.'

'Are you sure about that?'

'Certain, for he became quite violent in manner when she refused to show him the letter or reveal how she had come into possession of it.'

'What "important gentlemen" did he speak of?'

'I cannot recall. The names were unfamiliar to Eliza-Beth and unknown to me. I have forgotten them completely.'

'Could it have been "Archer" or "Askern"?'

'I cannot recall . . . I . . .'

'Could it have been a "sir" or a "lord"?'

'You are confusing me now! I do not know these names!'

'What else did they speak of?'

'I believe Eliza-Beth may have told him that her parents were important people. It was always a dream of hers – long before she received any letter. Is it not the dream of us all?'

'Hmm. Did the other performers here know of Eliza-Beth's shame?'

'They might have guessed. They knew she was escorted by gentlemen after the show . . . they knew Mr Coggins. It does not take a schoolmaster to understand. But she spoke of it only to me – of that I am certain. She would not speak to a gentleman of it.'

A knock was heard at the street door: three rapid raps. The kitchen door opened and Mr Hardy appeared there below the handle.

'Sergeant Williamson? That is not the code.'

'Do not be concerned, Mr Hardy. I am expecting someone. Perhaps Edgar could answer the door. That way, any idle visiter is likely to be dissuaded. And I think we can have everyone back together now.'

The giant lumbered from the kitchen, half bent to pass through the doorway, and moved to the street door. When he opened it, Mr Williamson saw Noah standing there. The sight of the huge man before him did not seem to startle or unnerve him. Indeed, he smiled. 'Good day – I have arranged to meet Sergeant Williamson here.'

'Come in!' called the detective. 'We are in the sitting room.'

Noah walked into the room and cast his eyes across the curiosities gathered there. He had seen them at Vauxhall Gardens, of course, transmogrified by make-up and theatrical illumination into greater monsters than they were. In this be-curtained room, however, they seemed fragile specimens, cowering away from the world. Missy began to sniff loudly from her accustomed place beside Eugenia, and let forth a guttural snarl at the newcomer, baring her teeth in an alarming way. Unafraid, Noah walked slowly towards the child and held out a hand, whereupon she sniffed the fingers and began to lap at them. The performers could not help but be amused.

'Did anyone follow you?' asked Mr Williamson of Noah.

'It would be a formidable pursuer who could have traced my steps here,' answered Noah, now stroking Missy's head. 'I came along the Strand, cut up Drury-lane, took a cab through Long-acre – then I walked here, seemingly wearing a different coat than before I entered the cab. It is double-sided, you see?'

At this, the performers remarked amongst themselves upon the odd design of the coat, which was indeed green on the outside and dark blue on the inside – both materials featuring the buttons and *accoutrements* of an exterior.

'Well, that is enough of fashion. Shall we proceed?' said Mr Williamson.

'Is he arrived yet?' asked Noah, taking a vacant seat beside Eugenia.

'No.' The sergeant consulted his pocket watch. 'But he will be here shortly. I sent him a message to arrive here with clothes enough to be away from home for some time. I think we agree that he cannot return home until this business is finished?'

'Assuredly. Have you informed these good people of your intentions?'

'I will do it presently.'

By now, the performers appeared quite confused and

were exchanging glances of dubiety. Their spokesman, Mr Hardy, felt compelled to speak:

'Excuse me, gentlemen, but what is going on here? Who is this man, Mr Williamson, and why does he speak of your "intentions" for us?'

'I apologize, Mr Hardy. This is Mr Dyson, a . . . an associate of the Detective Force. He has been working with me on the pursuit of the man who killed Eliza-Beth. We arranged to meet here on another matter, but I am also obliged to inform you that I intend you all to move.'

A general clamour arose.

'Mr Williamson!' ejaculated Mr Hardy, 'I do not know if you realize the upheaval we experienced at the last move. Why, just moving Eugenia is no easy task. And there are those among our number who experience great distress when exposed to the possibility of being surrounded by a braying mob. Our isolation is our solace . . . we are shepherdless without Mr Coggins—'

'I understand completely. But if you stay here, you are all in danger of imminent death. The same man who has killed so many now appears to be seeking out any who can identify him. Since you have seen him, albeit half-concealed, you know about him and he cannot leave to chance that you may see him again.'

'O! We are to die!' wailed Eugenia. 'Are our unhappy lives to have no respite!' And Missy again began to whine.

'Fear not,' said Noah with a firm voice that stilled the tremulous mood. 'There are places in the city where not a soul will see you, and where you will be safe. If your nemesis's power lies in his anonymity and stealth, you must use the same methods against him. You will be safe.'

'Mr Dyson is quite correct,' added the detective. 'You will

be moved this evening and there will be no more Vauxhall shows until this matter is resolved. That is the end of the discussion.'

'But who is this man you speak of who will come here?' enquired Mr Hardy.

It is a question the reader must also have been asking, and which some will no doubt have answered with the identity of Mr Henry Askern, the writer. His letter to the police had proved to be the elusive clue they had been seeking. Mr Williamson extracted it and handed it to Mr Hardy (I make no apology for the style of the letter – these writers of 'literature' are prone to prolixity):

Dear Sergeant Williamson,

On the very same night that we spoke together, I was about my researches in the environs of Oxford-street and spoke to a common pickpocket about his life. He was quite inebriated on account of having visited a 'gin palace' and so his tongue was loosened perhaps more than it usually would be – a state of affairs I encouraged by plying him with brandy and water.

On the subject of crime, he spoke of a man he knew only as 'the General' – a man who pays sundry men of the pickpocket's ilk to run occasional errands and to do diverse jobs about the city. Though he claimed personally to have been such an employee, my interviewee had never seen 'the General' in person. He averred, however, that the man was the single greatest criminal mind of London and had been for many years. It is said that he knows more, and sees more, of what goes on in (and beneath) society than the police or the politicians or the newspaper writers.

It may, of course, have been hyperbole, but I was told that this 'master criminal' is seldom seen by anyone and trusts only a handful of men he has known from childhood. He is apparently feared even by those criminals who know him and execute his will. Indeed, even in the depths of his drunkenness, my interviewee evinced great apprehensiveness about speaking of 'the General' on the grounds that 'the walls has ears'.

I wonder if this General fellow is the mythical 'master criminal' you were alluding to during our meeting. It would be exciting to think so, and I would value the opportunity to hear your thoughts on the subject.

If you would like to discuss the matter further, please pass your reply to me via the same man who has delivered this. He will wait, and can be trusted.

Respectfully yours,
Henry Askern Esq.

'So this "General" is the same man who is to murder us, I presume?' enquired Mr Hardy.

'I do not know. That is why I have arranged for the gentleman to come here where all of those most closely acquainted with the case reside.'

'At least, those still living,' added Noah, with macabre precision.

'Quite. Mr Dyson here has . . . has special knowledge of the case and, together, we will attempt to take the greatest advantage of this new avenue. It may lead us to another *cul de sac* – we will see. Until the gentleman in question arrives, I have some more questions for the people here.'

'We are happy to help,' said Mr Hardy, jumping up to his accustomed perch on the chair.

'Then tell me – did the doctor visit more than once?'

'Let me think . . .'

'Yes! Yes!' Eugenia flapped her arms like an immense chicken. 'That evil man *was* here another time. When he returned Eliza-Beth from their "carriage ride". He did not enter, but I remember the writer gentleman was leaving about the same time – maybe a little before. They may even have seen each other.'

'Why, what are you talking about, Eugenia?' said Mr Hardy.

'*You* don't know! None of you know! Only I know. You all chose not to see what anyone could see. You are as guilty as those who spoiled that young girl!'

The large lady dissolved into bubbling sobs and an atmosphere of uneasy embarrassment settled in the room. Mr Hardy – ever the tiny gentleman – made a brave attempt to salvage some decorum, albeit without entirely convincing himself or those gathered there.

'Well, Detective . . . I . . . I'm sure I have no idea what she is talking about.'

'Prostitution, Mr Hardy,' replied the detective. 'And the series of degradations poor Eliza-Beth underwent during her short and unhappy life. She may not have told you of them, but I feel everyone here knew of them.'

'Well, I . . . well . . .'

'Quite.'

Silence reigned again, but for the lachrymose snuffling of Eugenia. Then Missy began to sniff, and footsteps were heard crunching outside the window. A rasping cough rattled, and then there was a rapping at the door.

'I will answer it this time,' said Mr Williamson to the giant Edgar, who was making to unfold himself once more.

EIGHTEEN

The reader, like the police, must be wondering about the escape and the whereabouts of Mr Lucius Boyle. In truth, there were many accustomed to reporting to him who now could not locate him in the places he usually resided. Those divers criminals of the city had of course heard about the sensation at the hanging of Mr Bradford and surmised that their 'General' had decided to vanish.

Stepping back a moment, we might discover what had occurred in the immediate aftermath of Mr Boyle's extraordinary exit from the scene at Newgate. How had he made his escape and where had he ventured thereafter?

Due to the immensity of the crowd, there were many who had not seen Boyle, or the murder of Mr Coggins. They were aware only of some remarkable occurrence that quivered through the multitude as through a single organism. Thus, when the people packing the entrance to those alleys beheld an odd, red-jawed man approaching them through the crowd, they can only have been stricken by the strange and unnerving nature of his appearance. They did not know him as a murderer, even if they marvelled at the ease with which he had moved through the people in a space of his own. If he moved calmly, and if people all around him seemed to stare fixedly at him, there was nevertheless a wildness in his eyes that forbade any interaction. By the time he entered the dark and narrow lanes where printers and bookbinders toil at their labour, his face was again covered and he was part of the general exodus returning to work or to the gin shop – just another faceless city dweller about his business. From those alleys, he would have slipped easily on to Warwick-lane or Paternoster-row and thence into the nearest cab.

But he was angry. That imbecile Coggins had almost cast him into the hands of the mob – a far more serious prospect than capture by the police. After shadowing the *impresario* the previous evening, his plan had been to lure him to a gin shop after the hanging and thereafter dispose of him quietly. It was not advisable to let one so garrulous and acquisitive stay alive when the entire city was talking about the recent series of murders.

The commingled rage and excitement of the events boiled inside him. Killing Mr Coggins had alleviated that to a small extent, but a savage rage was burning. If he had been able to see clearly through his ire, he would have admitted that seeing Noah there on the platform had shocked him more that he cared to admit.

Though he had seldom spared a thought for his trans-ported childhood companion over the years, he had always regarded Noah as his only equal: a boy very like himself, who had emerged from the gutter stronger and better than he had entered it. That was why he had had to betray his fellow 'General' – Noah was his only obstruction to unri-valled supremacy, the only threat he would be afraid to encounter. The other boys may have feared Lucius, but they admired Noah.

He thought back to those days. After his victory against Noah, his notoriety had spread . . . and his violence had blossomed. When one of his boys tried to steal from him, Boyle's retribution exceeded all previous limits. It was his first murder. How loyal were his boys now? Would they keep his crime secret? *Could* they, when gossip was the currency of the street boy? Ever cautious, he did the one thing he could to save himself: he disappeared.

Such a thing is not as difficult as it may seem. Lucius Boyle's face may have been a common feature in the environs of Smithfield, say, but a migration to Whitechapel or Stepney would have been little different to a move to the continent as far as the constables and his boys were concerned. Criminal fiefdoms and police divisions were as islands in an archipelago. Moreover, the continuous influx of people from the country, the ever-changing residents of lodging houses, and the daily ingress and egress of tradesman made a new face nothing odd. He could be at home anywhere – and nowhere.

Of course, his was no ordinary face. Its distinctiveness was a curse. He would have to become a phantasm of the shadows, venturing out mostly at night and braving daylight only with concealed features. Thus light and dark became his special concern, and fire his obsession.

Who knows what prompted his incendiarism? No doubt there are doctors of the troubled mind who could ascribe it to some impulse or other. Was it a symptom of his suppressed rage? Or was he simply insane? Whatever the cause, he found a twisted solace in the breathing of the inferno, the crackle of timbers and the inevitable collapse, with its billowing exhalations of sparks and embers cast skyward. There was beauty and drama in such a show, and he was the conductor of this symphony of fire.

And let us not imagine that he had learned nothing from his brief partnership with Noah. He had understood that brawn is all very well, but it was doubled with brains. He stole books, or had them stolen by his minions, and tried to learn. There were ladies and gentlemen at that time, as now, who sought grace through the charitable education of wretched street children. Perhaps he was one of them. Perhaps his virulent face marked him out as an especially pitiful specimen. He learned to read and write, collecting words like weapons. Had he not seen how Noah had beguiled the boys with his fancy words? They were like incantations to the unlearned. Had he taken interest in history, he would have known that the combination of rhetoric and violence are an irresistible force.

And now Noah had returned. Not only had he returned, but he appeared to be allied with the police. The coincidence was too strong to ignore: the police had somehow discovered Noah and employed him in the pursuit of his erstwhile friend. It made no difference whether Noah was a willing accomplice or not – the capture of the man who had betrayed him was the desired conclusion, presumably driven by an entire adult life tainted with the canker of unfulfilled revenge.

Such were the thoughts that crackled in his overheated mind as he returned to one of his many hiding places, there to write the letter to Sergeant Williamson that we have already seen. For a full day he remained alone, not even contacting his trusted servant Henry Hawkins. All of London was now looking out for his vermilion jaw, or for any man wearing a conspicuous scarf.

Ever the tactician, he considered what he must do. There were people who had seen him at the Lambeth house and who could link him to the case. There were people who were pursuing him and who would not cease until he was captured. There were people who might seek to benefit from their marginal knowledge of him. These people had to be dealt with, and would be. More alone now than he had ever been – excepting perhaps during those early days on the streets – he was a cornered animal facing survival or death.

Despite the even tone of the letter he had sent to Scotland Yard, he was much agitated and felt the visceral urge to destroy. It resonated in his very sinews like a maddening bass note struck upon some dark instrument, throbbing and humming interminably. Throughout his childhood and adulthood, when these unfathomable dark humours came upon him, there was only one balm to soothe his rage, only one release for the tension: fire. In those hours spent alone, concealed, he stared into the grate and watched the coals spark and flicker, poking at them savagely with an iron bar.

On the Tuesday, Mr Hawkins arrived with food, drink and coal for the fire. He found his master in a smouldering mood.

'I have been looking all over for you, General, lugging this coal about the city. Nobody has any intelligence of you.'

'Do you wonder why?'

'Well, no. I have seen the papers. I have one here . . .'

'You were not at the execution?'

'I thought I might be identified.'

'That was astute of you. Tell me with certainty that you were not followed. People know of your connection to me.'

'I was careful. I took cabs and went back on myself as you told me to. But . . . I am becoming nervous. People know my face—'

'*Your* face? That is good, Mr Hawkins. No matter – I will be leaving this place shortly.'

'Where will you go? Out of the city?'

'That is no concern of yours. It is better that you do not know. In the meantime, there are things that you must do for me. I have made a list of instructions for you, which you are to follow to the letter. Destroy it once you have finished.'

'Of course. General . . .'

'What? There is something you are hesitating to tell me. Out with it.'

'I heard talk of a man asking after you. He didn't know your name, but he seemed to know of your reputation.'

'Tell me everything you know.'

'The gentleman was a writer. He said he was writing a book about the "underworld". He was asking about a criminal "master". It was along the gin shops of Oxford-street.'

'Did anyone speak?'

'I heard that Razor Bill was talking to the gent. As usual, he was half-cut, and the gent was plying him with brandy and water like it was tea.'

'What was said?'

'I don't know, General. I wasn't there. Razor Bill has never seen you as far as I know. What could he say?'

'Enough.'

'What would you have me do?'

'Find Bill – he will be in his usual place with a glass in his hand – and enquire what was said. Find out also where I can find this writer – I believe I have come across him before. If Bill proves difficult, you know what to do.'

'Yes, General.'

'If he has said anything that compromises me to the slightest degree, make sure that he will never speak another word. And if you discover the writer himself, let him know in no uncertain terms that his researches are to end immediately. In no uncertain terms, do you understand?'

'Yes, General.' Mr Hawkins rubbed his ossified fists absently. 'Where can I contact you?'

'I will contact you.'

Mr Hawkins left, and Lucius Boyle opened out the newspaper to see a rather dramatic sketch of himself brandishing a gun amid the execution crowds. The artist had exaggerated his height and given him a vaguely skeletal appearance so as to maximize the sense of threat and terror. But there was his own face for all the city to see. Its hideous mark was a badge of terror that was now the discussion of London.

We should not imagine, however, that he was cowed and beaten. The cornered rat is the most dangerous. It leaps for the throat.

And as darkness fell on that Tuesday night, there were others venturing out across the city streets. The pickpockets migrating from their daytime workplace of Oxford-street and Regents-street to Haymarket's pleasure-seeking crowd; the base bullies loitering in the shadows of Whitechapel and Rotherhithe; the street girls of various degrees walking out in the parks and the evening shopping streets. And, of course, the beat constable whose uniform and rattle might protect him from, or lead him to, a brutal death.

Among all of these gaudy characters, one also found the wretched: the rag-and-bone finders with their forked sticks and perpetually bent backs, and the destitute beggars shuffling endlessly about the city, never reaching any destination but the hoar embrace of an open grave.

Here is one of the latter now, bare head bowed and with

his soles peeling away from fourth-hand boots. His ribs are occasionally visible through the rents in his greasy black top-coat and he carries a long staff to support himself. He could be Death Himself, wrapped in the rotten lineaments of the grave. As he walks stolidly through the crowds of shoppers about Regents-circus, he is no more notable than a horse or a dog. There are many of his ilk, filthy hands out for money and a guttural plea uttered so frequently that it has become an incantation. Should a man want to pass unseen through the beating heart of London, he could do no better than to be one of these 'scavagers' – or to adopt the appearance of one.

For this derelict man was not as he seemed. The averted eyes of others magnified the effectiveness of his own gaze, since every face he saw was one turned away either in rejection or embarrassment. The astute observer would have noticed, however, that, unlike the true beggar, he passed before the gaudily lit and steaming windows of coffee houses and the gas-flare illumination of shops without pausing to gaze longingly at their wares.

Nor was he alone in his deception. Another followed his movements from twenty paces to the rear, observing with ease the movement of his target. This pursuer understood just as well that what is invisible to the majority is highly conspicuous to the few.

Noah had ventured out from his own home at Manchester-square with the sole intention of locating Razor Bill, whose description Mr Askern had provided with sufficient clarity for Noah to recognize him. On discovering the pickpocket, he would conduct a more efficacious cross-examination. There was also the very likely possibility that news of Mr Askern's first interview had already reached Boyle and that

Noah would come across an associate of his conducting precisely the same task, albeit with greater fatality intended.

The gin shops of Oxford-street are of a different calibre to those in the East End. Here, vulgar meretriciousness is the *décor* of choice: gilt and crystal, gas *chandeliers* and polished mahogany bars give an impression of great luxury much appreciated by those who like to affect a certain sophistication as they slide into oblivion. The place where Mr Askern had seen Razor Bill, the Rose and Crown wine-vaults at the corner of Gilbert-street, was just emerging from its renovation and was a glittering example of its kind.

Noah – for it was he who was the 'beggar' – pressed his nose against the large plate-glass window and looked inside. The gin 'palace' was indeed impressive, with its Ionic columns, stucco fittings, rich burgundy carpets and large horseshoe bar. Colossal vats of spirits rose up two storeys to support a gallery of carousing spirit drinkers, while the ground floor was populated with dozens of adults and children sipping with much self-conscious enjoyment at their brandies, their gins, rums and other divers liquors.

There among them was Razor Bill, just as Mr Askern had described him: a rather rodent-faced man of slight build and with one of the tricorn hats favoured by carriage drivers. Were it not for the hat, Bill might not have spent so much time in gaol. As it was, the constables never had any trouble locating him when his description was passed on by a victim. The man's face was flushed with heat and intoxication – and about his shoulders was the beefy arm of Henry Hawkins, who looked sober and lethal of intent.

Noah glared at the boxer. Now he knew that the hand of Boyle was at work, just as it had been with Mr Bradford, and that the incendiary was still in London manipulating events. His first urge was to enter the gin shop and deal with Mr Hawkins immediately, but his cool head triumphed.

Entering in the garb of a beggar would draw all eyes upon him, whereas outside he maintained his advantage – just another worthless, nameless, faceless member of the bustling crowd. Mr Hawkins would not attempt anything rash on the premises. So the 'beggar' turned his back on the bacchanalia within to face the night-time street, his grubby hand out and a sub-audible mumbled plea for alms falling from his lips.

Waiting there, he watched the carriages rattle past and people visiting shops brilliant with light. He wondered, as he had many times, at the idea of the city going about its business in this way during his many years of absence. Shops had changed hands, fortunes had been made and lost, new buildings had appeared – and the show had been played out countless hundreds of times, oblivious to the torturous journey and travails of one of its sons. A man on these streets was nothing but a mote of dust to be ground under the wheels of time, and the span of a single life was but another year's layer of verdigris or lichen on the city's immortal fabric.

As Noah stood there lost in inward vision and absently muttering his counterfeit penury, a heavy coin dropped into his gloved hand and drew him back from his thoughts. It was a sovereign – a highly unlikely donation to a street beggar. He had not even noticed which direction his 'benefactor' had been walking. He looked quickly to each side, hoping to see a smiling face, but saw only retreating backs and averted eyes.

The coin seemed newly minted and flashed brilliantly against the dirty leather. And he felt the first twinges that something was amiss. Until that moment, he had been an inanimate feature of the busy street – then someone had seen him and made that fact known to him. It was too unlikely that the charity was genuine. Such virtuous gentlemen or ladies liked their 'unfortunates' to speak for their alms, spinning shocking tales of destitution and illness. No – he had been, or was being observed. He could feel it. And the observer was playing with him.

At that moment, the door to the gin palace opened with a billow of pipe smoke and sweet spirit fumes, and Mr Hawkins emerged with his arm around an unsteady Razor Bill. Heedless of Noah, they weaved off towards Regents-circus, knocking against top-hatted gentlemen and bonneted ladies as they went.

Noah looked around once more to see if anyone was watching. Shoppers and early pleasure seekers flowed un-seeing around him. He set off in pursuit of Razor Bill, easily following the havoc they caused as they wobbled drunkenly through the ceaseless flow. Surely at any moment, they would cut left or right where a lull in the traffic and an opportune shadow would allow Bill's neck to be snapped like a twig in Hawkins's grasp.

But something else arrested Noah's pursuit and turned him around – something that seemed somehow inevitable, as if everything thus far that evening had been a prelude to it. With a horripilating chill, he knew suddenly where the coin had come from. A screech went up in the vicinity of the gin shop he had just left.

'*Fire!*'

He paused in momentary indecision, knowing that he was certain to lose both Razor Bill and Hawkins if he turned back. The incendiary was as palpably present as if he had been resting his hand on the nape of Noah's neck. He dropped his staff and began to run back towards the Rose and Crown, all pretence of indigence now vanished.

People were flooding from the smoke-filled rooms when he arrived. There were screams and coarse words as they poured through the too narrow doorway into the street, gin glasses still in their hands and sprits splashed to the ground in the *mêlée*. Passers-by paused to watch, increasing the congestion so that people spilled on the road and even the traffic was forced to pause. Those on the opposite side of the road also stopped to observe, and shoppers emerged for a better view. More voices joined the cry.

'Fire! Fire! Call the engines!'

The first flames began to flash at the widows of a room adjoining the gin palace, where the fire had evidently started. Smoke was now curling out into the street.

Noah looked at the faces surrounding the stricken building, hoping to see the be-scarfed face of Lucius Boyle. Scores of people were now gathering, swelling out into the road, where cab drivers shouted profane threats and horses snorted into their reins. Frenziedly, Noah pushed among the crowds to see every face. Then he turned to gaze up into the lit windows in case Boyle had sought a higher vantage point. But there seemed no sign of him.

A colossal crash emerged from inside the gin palace and a dividing wall toppled down with an explosion of flame and sparks. The plate-glass window juddered, rippling light across its surface, and the gathering throngs scrambled still further back so that a large semicircle now formed around the windows. Distant shouts heralded the approach of the engines.

'The barrels! The spirits will catch alight!' yelled a voice.

This sent a shiver through the massed observers, for it was true that the immense barrels were full of volatile spirits and might rupture if damaged by the fire . . . which was even now flaring at the small pools of gin or brandy spilled on the floor, and at the carpets and curtains, which burned with thick billows of smoke.

To Lucius Boyle, it was a beautiful vision. The large window of the Rose and Crown was as a brilliant picture frame in which the conflagration danced and sang in vivid orange flames. He almost had to restrain himself from applauding. The smoke was a fine *bouquet* to him, carrying with it charred hints of juniper and grape, velvet and mahogany – the aromas of sweet destruction.

And there – as an extra character in the piece – was Noah himself, dressed ludicrously as a beggar and searching phrenziedly about him for the incendiary who had outrageously dropped a sovereign into his hands just moments earlier.

A piercing scream came from one of the floors above the bar and a window swung open to reveal an unbonneted young lady wreathed in smoke.

'I am trapped!' she shrieked. 'A ladder! Fetch a ladder!'

By now the engines were arriving. First the St Marylebone engine, then the King-street brigade, then that of Well-street and Baker-street – seven engines in all – disgorging their hoses and preparing to enter. The barrels within were now alight and burning like individual torches.

'We should break the window!' shouted one of the fire officers, but at that moment the structure seemed to shift on its foundations with a masonry roar and the large pane began to wobble in its frame. A flare of heat erupted inside, and the thick sheet of glass shuddered once more before toppling silently out of its frame to hit the street as a vitreous hail. A blistering wave of heat and smoke emerged and scattered the crowds in fear. Lucius Boyle felt the scorching breath upon his upper face and squinted against it; his smile was concealed.

Again, Noah gazed over the faces illuminated by the flickering inferno, each one a dancing orange mask of fear and fascination. None of them was covered or concealed in any way. Their top hats and bonnets were all quite normal. Indeed, only some of the engine operators had their mouths covered with dampened cloth to prevent them from inhaling the smoke. All of them were busy working the engines . . . all except one who seemed to be standing inert, mesmerized by the light of the conflagration – a man with smoke-grey eyes widening in recognition. This time there would be no escape.

But as Noah made his first step, there was a terrific gasp from the observers and a vast barrel toppled slowly to the ground inside the gin palace, spilling its super-heated spirit to the ground, where it became a molten flood pouring hundreds of gallons of liquid fire out into the street.

A fire engineer stooping to position a hose was caught in the inundation and thrashed ecstatically as the flames consumed him. Burning gin rushed into the gutters and leaped at the legs of fleeing shoppers. The entire street was illuminated by flowing fire and the burning spirit filled the air. Boyle was already ahead of the running people as Noah felt his beggar's boots wetted with flaming liquid and the flashing pain of burning. He jumped clear of the flames and shrugged off his coat, wrapping it hastily about his lower legs and cursing while trying to keep Boyle in view. Tears filled his eyes from the acrid smoke, though they might as well have been tears of frustration. The space between himself and the receding Boyle was now an uncrossable lake of shimmering flame, its heat warping all shapes into indistinct chimerae.

Lucius Boyle walked away from the scene still dressed as a fire engineer. His veins flowed with the exhilaration of the conflagration and he could not suppress a smile beneath his 'smoke scarf'. As long as there was a scent of smoke in the air, he might go unchallenged. The Oxford-street fire had cast a pall across most of that part of London, protecting him within its compass.

He made his way towards a nearby square until he came to a short flight of stairs leading up to a black door. There, he used the brass knocker to rap three times.

A gentleman rather than a manservant appeared at the door. He beheld the 'fire engineer' reeking of smoke and assumed from the scent of the evening air that the fire was close. 'Is the property in danger?' he asked.

'That depends.' Boyle unwrapped his smoke-scarf and allowed the gentleman to behold his uncovered face.

'*You!*'

'Indeed.'

Boyle pushed the gentleman into the house and kicked the door closed behind him. Though clearly perturbed, the gentleman led the intruder towards a parlour, looking over his shoulder all the way lest a weapon be suddenly produced.

The room was decorated in the good taste of the moderately wealthy. Shelves of books revealed their owner to be a man of limited but expert interests, and some of the books lay open alongside written notes on a large wooden table. A fire burned in the grate, crackling into the silence between the two men.

'So you are the writer of that nicely written letter – my "observer",' said the house owner.

'I am.'

'You take a formidable risk appearing in person like this. Are you not afraid? Someone may have seen you on the doorstep and bring constables here *en masse*.'

'Not at all. It is you who have reason to be afraid, sir. Afraid of me and of what I know. Shall we be seated?'

'What do you want?'

'What does anyone want? Freedom, wealth . . .'

'I am not a wealthy man.'

'Maybe not, but you have position – at least, more position than one such as I. You are able to do things that I cannot, and you know things that I do not. I wonder what the newspapers would make of it? It is one thing to consort with a woman of Mary Chatterton's sort, but quite another to produce progeny of Eliza-Beth's kind: illegitimate and abandoned in addition to her other woes. I fear you would not be so welcome at your club if such details were known.'

'You d— scoundrel! I could kill you right this moment and be a hero in addition to being rid of you.'

'You are welcome to try. Only you have no conception whether I am the only man to know what I know, or what mechanisms are in place for making it known should I be harmed.'

'Hmm. You are a practised blackmailer. So – for my amusement, then – what do you expect from me if not money?'

'I am a highly visible man at the moment. I need a place to hide where nobody will think to look. You will provide it . . . wait! I have not finished. You will also do everything in your power to see that those who pursue me will not find me. These are the preliminaries.'

'Preposterous! The outrageousness of it . . . do you understand the implications of my hiding *you*? And what can I possibly do to hinder the police investigation? Your demands are unrealistic.'

'Nevertheless, they shall be met.'

'And if I refuse? What will you do – kill me also? What evidence have you got against me? At least demonstrate the proof you base so much expectation upon.'

'Well – first, I have the testimony of Mary Chatterton herself, delivered under circumstances not conducive to dishonesty. She spoke of a great love tainted by ambition, of abandonment and of bitterness . . . and I see from your face that you still carry the guilt.'

'Mary Chatterton is dead. Imbecile that you are, you have killed the one person who might corroborate what you say.'

'Take care with your words, sir. You need not die tonight, but you are still of value to me wounded. I also have the locket from about the girl's neck, which contains a lock of your hair. It is the same colour still.'

'Like many men (or women, I might add) in London and in the entire British Isles. Is this all you have?'

'I have the letter penned by Eliza-Beth herself. It is covered in the blood of her own execution and names both you and Mary as parents. I believe that Mary communicated these facts to the child in anticipation of welcoming her back. Then, of course, there is the letter you have in your possession from Mary herself, informing you of your fatherhood.'

'What letter . . . you are speaking nonsense . . .'

'Your pallor would suggest otherwise. In fact, it was I who sent the letter. I found it on her writing desk. I thought it would make a fitting complement to my own. So, let us not waste any more time discussing your situation.'

'I must see the letter from Eliza-Beth. How else should I believe in its existence.'

'Why, when it is printed in *the Times*?'

'You — blackguard! I should kill you now.'

'That is certainly one solution. Have you much personal experience of murder? I sit here quite unarmed. No? Well – let us consider where I will be staying henceforth. Certainly not here.'

'I am ruined.'

'Not yet. As long as you are my protector, you are safe.'

'And I am also d—d.'

'We are all d—d. Now – I will be venturing out again in a moment. Before then, there are some other things I will have you do. First among them is a change of clothes.'

NINETEEN

Let us retrace our steps for a moment and venture back before the Oxford-street fire to the house of Mr Hardy and his unusual colleagues, where we left Noah and Detective Williamson welcoming the writer Mr Askern. It was there that Detective Williamson had agreed with Noah that the latter would venture out in search of Razor Bill and learn from him what he could.

It was also decided there that Mr Askern, as with the performers, must go to ground that very day for his own safety – no matter how unlikely they thought the threat from Lucius Boyle. The writer had only seen the murderer in passing, but that might be enough justification for attack. Without even returning home, the writer was to be taken away by carriage to a place where he might be unseen until Boyle was captured or killed. Mr Williamson would accompany him there after dark and be one of only four – being himself, the carriage driver, Inspector Newsome and the owner of the place – who knew the whereabouts of the writer. Not even Noah would know.

Where was the house? Confidentiality forbids me from revealing its precise location, but I may say that it was a property known to a select few of the higher-echelon police and used by them for various purposes. Shall we follow the detective and Mr Askern as they approach the property and make themselves familiar with its arrangements?

The carriage stopped outside the house and Mr Williamson stepped down into the street, casting his eyes about for any signs of observation. A cab was coming from the opposite direction and he waited until it passed out of sight before opening the carriage door and beckoning Mr Askern to exit.

They walked briskly to the street door of the house, which opened in anticipation and closed behind them in a moment. The carriage left immediately.

The two gentlemen were welcomed by the housekeeper, a man of about fifty years with a military bearing and greying hair. When he moved, however, he manifested a curious off-centre gait and a slight limp. Mr Williamson knew that the man had been one of the first recruits to the Metropolitan Police, and one of the many to be almost killed while doing his duties, set upon by a gang of ruffians and left for dead in Deptford.

'Mr Askern, may I introduce you to Mr Charles Allan. He will be your host until this business is over. He does not know why you are here, and nor should you tell him. He is accustomed to accommodating men for various times and purposes and will provide you with meals, newspapers and anything you might reasonably require.'

'I thank you, Mr Allan, for your kindness,' answered the writer. 'I wonder if it would be possible to receive some writing materials and books.'

'Certainly, sir,' answered Mr Allan. 'But you will not be

permitted to send letters from this address, by post or by personal messenger. They could be intercepted.'

'Why, whatever you think best.'

'Mr Allan has long experience in these matters,' said Mr Williamson. 'You may trust him completely, as do I. Will you show us to the room, Mr Allan?'

'I have chosen the safest room in the house, if you will follow me downstairs. It is a cellar room beside the kitchen, which only I use. There is one door, a thick wooden one reinforced with iron bands. It would take half a dozen men some time to demolish it – in the unlikely event that half a dozen men were able to enter this kitchen. The door locks from the inside only, with double locks.'

They came to the door, which did indeed seem impressively stout. It was ajar and Mr Allan pushed it – whereupon a bell rang loudly behind it.

'That is to alert me that the door has been opened,' said Mr Allan, demonstrating the mechanism. 'I can hear it all over the house. There is also a wedge here to place under the door lest someone attempt to force the two locks. It is quite unnecessary, but might provide you with a sense of added security.'

The room itself was simply but adequately furnished: a single bed with blankets, a desk and a chair, a wardrobe, and coal already in the fireplace. There was a small window – too small to admit a person – which was barred with thick iron rods fastened securely to the interior masonry.

'It is a little spartan, I'm afraid, but I trust you will not be here long,' said Mr Williamson. 'I will see that you are well supplied with books. Perhaps it will be an opportunity for you to begin something new.'

'Yes, yes – perhaps.'

'Do not be disheartened, Mr Askern. These measures are for your safety – perhaps for your survival.'

'Who else resides here?'

'That is not for you to know. Even I do not know. Only Mr Allan knows the identity of the other residents, if such currently exist. He delivers their food, and supplies all their needs. This is the safest way.'

'Who knows about this house?'

'A very few – a handful of senior detectives and the police superintendents. Constables know nothing of it. Naturally, those who have stayed here know of it, but they owe a debt of gratitude to the police and maintain their silence – or at least we trust them to. In truth, the place is seldom used.'

As the two men spoke, Mr Allan busied himself at the grate and soon had a hearty fire burning. A little smoke had entered the room and Mr Askern began to cough. Fortunately, he was able to stifle the fullness of his convulsion with a handkerchief pressed tight to his mouth. His relief was palpable.

'Forgive me, sir,' said Mr Allan. 'It is a narrow chimney, but once the fire is burning there will be no smoke. You will need a good fire as it gets cold here during the night. You have sufficient blankets, however, so you will not be chilled once the fire has burned out.'

'I thank you, Mr Allan. You are most kind.'

'It is nothing. You may bathe in exactly one hour on the floor above – for no longer than forty minutes. I will ask you to be punctual as other tenants have their own specified times so they will not meet inadvertently. I will serve dinner after you have bathed and then you may retire.'

'Good,' said Mr Williamson. 'Everything is in order, then. I will leave. I have important matters to attend to. You will not see me again, Mr Askern, until it is safe for you to leave. It will be just a few days, I am sure.'

Thus did the detective leave Mr Askern in the capable care of Mr Allan and return home. Finally, it seemed, he was gaining the upper hand in the case: Mr Askern was safe, the performers were safe (at another location on the periphery of the city) and the criminal Boyle was a hunted animal, his face sketched upon thousands of newspaper pages distributed across London. Noah was searching out the garrulous Razor Bill. Only the Reverend Archer remained at liberty and at risk. Whatever his role in the case, whatever his innocence or guilt, his life may be in danger and he would have to be traced – traced and persuaded to go into hiding.

Mr Williamson was tired as he returned home for the first time in what seemed like days. The fire in his grate had been cold for a long time and he shovelled some coal into its white ash. His home was simple but clean. A frame above the mantel in the parlour contained a piece of embroidery that faded year after year despite being under glass. A clock ticked methodically.

He made a pot of tea and ate a meat pie he had purchased from a street vendor, then sat in one of two chairs facing the flames. The other chair had not been sat in for some years. He thought of Noah and Lucius Boyle, of Inspector Newsome and Commissioner Mayne and their expectations of him. It was a difficult case – perhaps the most difficult he had ever dealt with.

First, the murder of Eliza-Beth by Mr Bradford, himself a tool for a greater criminal in the form of Boyle. *That* man was an enigma, his emotions and motivations lost entirely in the fumes of rumour and supposition surrounding him. Until the murder of Mr Coggins, the nature of Boyle's crimes was ambiguous. Rather he *was* Crime: lurking unseen in every unknown face and rank alley.

By the time the fire had burned to nothing, the detective was asleep.

When he was awoken in the early hours of the next day by a wild knocking at his door, his first thought was one of foreboding. He stumbled to the door.

'What is it that cannot wait until morning, Constable?'

'Sorry, Sergeant. I was sent on the orders of Inspector Newsome. He said it was most urgent that you accompany me as you are investigating the case.'

'Well, what is it?'

'There has been another murder.'

'Who?'

'I don't know. All I was told is that I should fetch you and escort you to St Giles's Church. The carriage is waiting.'

St Giles's Church. Its spire was an inverted arrow marking a part of the city that could boast squalor unchanged since medieval times. It was one of the few buildings in the parish that was not decaying, decrepit and overloaded with stinking humanity – an island of holiness in a tumultuous sea of sin.

The slate-grey sky was just beginning to lighten into a smoky dawn as Mr Williamson arrived, its clatter a startling awakening call to that crapulously slumbering *locale*.

A handful of people had gathered around the lofty masonry gate leading to the graveyard and the church steps. Two constables were holding them back from satisfying their curiosity, and they seemed relieved to see the detective.

'Good morning, Constables. What have we got here?'

They directed their lamps at a shadowy presence just inside the gate. The body lay face down, half on the church steps and half on the ground as if in supplication at the foot of the building. A trail of blood had flowed down from its cut throat to pool around the legs, soaking into the dirty black robes where they touched. The Reverend Archer, in death, appeared a frail old man – all vigour and righteousness gone and his emaciated frame lost in the folds of his only clothes.

'Murdered on holy ground, sir,' said one of the constables. 'Who would do such a thing, even in this area?'

'One who has no fear of Divine or mortal observation.'

Was Boyle there at that moment? wondered the detective. Was he watching from a window, or loitering in the guise of a beggar? He looked around, not expecting to see any sign of the man. Of late, it felt as if the incendiary – the murderer – was everywhere, seeing everything. It should have been *he* who was hidden away in fear of police scrutiny.

'Have you touched the body, Constables?'

'Not we, sir. But there was a man bending over him as John here was passing on his beat. The gent ran off as I set my rattle going.'

'Has Dr McLeod been sent for?'

'As soon as we found the body, sir.'

Have you looked around the church for a weapon?'

'Yes, sir. But it was dark and we couldn't see everything with our lamps. The church itself is locked up tight as you like.'

'Good. We will be able to move the body shortly and you shall be relieved.'

'Who is it, Detective, that is killing all these people? Is it him who killed the cove at the execution – Red Jaw?'

'Is that what they are calling him now? "Red Jaw"?'

'Aye, on account of his jaw.'

'Thank you for that, Constable. In truth, we do not who committed this crime. It could have been anyone, especially in this parish.'

'But the gent's throat was cut. That was the method with Mary Chatterton. And the murderer of her had his face covered to hide his face. Why would he hide his face but to hide his red jaw?'

'Perhaps you have a future as a detective, Constable. Mr Coggins, however, did not have his throat cut. How do you explain that?'

'A pistol is better than a razor, is it not?'

'That rather depends on the intentions of the killer. Be mindful of these loiterers at the gate. We do not want the body disturbed further.'

Mr Williamson turned back to look once more at the pitiful aspect of the clergyman. The man had done nothing more than glimpse Boyle and had been killed for it. Only for that reason? Or as a message to the investigating detective: to show him that no one was safe and that the pursuers were the pursued? If this was the case, his own life (and that of Noah) were equally under threat.

He was unafraid. Rather, he was grievously fatigued. The following day's newspaper headlines would be damning; the police would be further humiliated and more pressure would be exerted from above. In this game, the rules were constricting – and those who broke them could be the victors. Men like Mr Dyson and Lucius Boyle were rule-breakers. Men like Mr Williamson trailed them almost blindly, the marked path being the safest and the most moral.

These thoughts were disturbed by the rattle of an approaching carriage conveying the police surgeon.

'Morning, Mr Williamson.'

'Good morning to you, Doctor. It is a murder, I'm afraid.'

'So I see . . . and quite a recent one from the looks of the blood. Here, help me to turn him over. Ah, yes – a slashed throat. Very likely a razor. There is some damage to the face, perhaps from falling – or from fists. It is difficult to be sure in this light.'

'Wait. What is that in his left hand?'

'Why, yes. It is a piece of paper.'

The doctor carefully extracted the paper, unfolded it and read the contents. He seemed to pale a little, though the sickly dawn light made all look cadaverous.

'I think it is intended for you, Detective.'

Mr Williamson took the scrap of paper and saw the black copperplate writing, most likely done with a steel pen. Its message was brief:

I am watching. You will do my bidding.

'Is it he?' asked the doctor. 'The impertinence of the man is breathtaking.'

The detective held the note in his hand and resisted the urge to crumple it tightly in his palm. He looked at the two constables, who were frequently looking over their shoulders to remember as much detail of the scene as possible. Tonight, they were part of a criminal legend and this would be part of their anecdotes for years to come.

'Constable! Yes, you who saw a man bending over the corpse. Come here.'

'Sir?'

'What did he look like, the man you saw?'

'His face wasn't covered if that's what you mean. Though I was too far away to see if his jaw was red. It could have been, though I can't swear to it.'

'That was not my question.'

'Well, he was tall, sir. Burly and big about the shoulders. That's all I can say. He might have been Red—'

'Thank you, Constable. You may go back to your duties.'

'Do you know the man he speaks of?' the doctor asked Mr Williamson.

'It could be anyone. Will you oversee the formalities with the body? I will look about the vicinity in case there is anything to be found.'

Mr Williamson began to walk around the church, among the cold grey tombstones and with the dew dampening his boots. The first chimneys of the day were now billowing smoke and he smelled the coal on the morning air – a smell that had become to him like that of coffee or freshly baked bread to other inhabitants of the city. Before that hour, London seemed to retain some ancient innocence; after it, all innocence was burned.

The ground at his feet was littered with the expected detritus: an empty bottle (no doubt tossed there that very evening), a recently deceased dog (starvation the evident cause), a piece of sodden newspaper carried by the wind some days previously. He was about to return to the gate when he saw another small piece of paper.

It was the size of a letter, and folded as if it had been kept in a pocket. The dew had made it damp, but the writing was legible: copperplate writing in black ink, probably with a steel pen. With feverish fingers he held it under a gas lamp and read its contents:

Mr Hawkins

You are to follow these instructions to the letter and report back to me personally that they have been carried out as I say.

First: You will locate the Reverend Josiah Archer – you know his face. I have intelligence that he frequents the low drinking dens of St Giles on this night to preach his doom-saying. Discover if he knows anything of me, or if he has spoken to anyone about the time he saw me at the Lambeth house. Then dispose of him as you see fit. I have enclosed a slip of paper within the folds of this note. Insert that slip into the palm of the deceased.

Second: Seek out Detective George Williamson. The best place to find him will be the very same place you leave the body of the clergyman (so choose your time and location carefully). See to it that he understands the importance of not pursuing me too closely. Make clear to him that it would be easy enough for him to procure a disfigured body from the river or a fire and claim it as mine. Be certain that he understands his life depends on these things.

Should you learn the whereabouts of Noah Dyson, act on that knowledge before returning to me.

That is all.

Mr Williamson looked rapidly around him, suddenly aware that he was out of sight of the other policemen. He felt for the truncheon that he had started carrying and held it tightly in his hand as he walked around the gate where the doctor was overseeing the removal of the body.

'He is here, Doctor McLeod. The murderer is here at this very moment.'

'It is possible, I suppose. Though it hardly seems likely—'

'No – he *is* here. Look, I have found this note. He must have dropped it. Be on your guard. Constables! Be alert – the burly man you saw before is close by.'

The two constables withdrew their truncheons in readiness, and the handful of observers looked fearfully about them. Although the surrounding streets were still empty, the sense of threat was suddenly palpable to the few gathered there.

'Have you considered, Mr Williamson, that this note was left purposely to unnerve you and hamper your investigation?' asked the doctor, who was holding the piece of paper. 'The murderer could be miles away and is hoping to keep you here chasing his phantom. Only a fool would let such a piece of evidence drop from his pocket.'

'Are not most criminals fools? I think he is here.'

'So let us ride away together in the carriage. You will be quite safe.'

'If the man is here, I will take him and question him.'

'Unless he attacks you first, as he is bidden to. If he is this Hawkins, he has little compunction about following his instructions to the letter.'

'No. I will not leave this place. You should go, Doctor, and take the body where you can examine it in more detail. Take the letter also, and see that Inspector Newsome receives it. The two constables should be relieved and I will linger here alone. A greater number of people may deter Mr Hawkins from his duties.'

'You go gladly to your death, Mr Williamson. Allow one of the constables to remain at the corner there. He will be unseen in the shadows and may come to your aid.'

'I will not die. I will speak with the man, and perhaps arrest him. An appointment with Mr Calcraft might be just what he needs to focus his loyalties.'

'Mr Williamson . . . George, this is not a man to debate with. This is not an area to stand alone. Please, return with us. We have evidence and we can search out this Hawkins fellow.'

'Why seek him when we know where he will be?'

'Then let one of the constables stay out of sight . . .'

'If that will persuade you to leave me, I agree. Now – go quickly, for the murderer may be close.'

And so, with much foreboding – but in acknowledgement of the detective's stubbornness – the doctor left Mr Williamson there, standing at the gate of St Giles. A constable waited in a dark alcove at the corner, his fingers twitching with nervousness and excitement at his part in the drama.

The sound of wheels and hooves receded and silence settled over the area. Lights were appearing in some windows, but it was still not quite daylight. Mr Williamson clenched the truncheon in his hand and waited.

Presently, a coster lad pushed a trolley of produce along the road, its wooden wheels clattering so that the detective could not hear any possible footfalls. He looked around him until the lad was out of earshot and he was once more alone. At least, he assumed so.

'Good morning, Detective.'

The calm voice came from behind him. He turned and saw the crushed nose and looming figure of Henry Hawkins, who had evidently approached through the graveyard.

'Mr Hawkins, I presume.'

'Have you seen me fight?'

'No, but I found the slip of paper in the clergyman's hand, and your note from Lucius Boyle, your master.'

At this, the fighter paled and felt in his trouser pocket, discovering the detective's words to be true. A meaty palm was held out.

'I'll thank you to return that note to me, Detective. Now.'

'Alas, I do not have it. It was taken from here by the police surgeon and will be in the hands of Inspector New-some in no time. That is unfortunate for you, as your name is on it – along with instructions to kill the Reverend Archer. I perceive from the blood on your sleeve that you have carried out that instruction.'

'You are very calm, sir, for a man in your position.'

'I have the power of the law on my side, Mr Hawkins.'

'Stop using my name like that, by G—!'

'Are you familiar with the Royal Proclamation of October 1843? It was circulated in *the Times*.'

'You are alone here. Only you have seen me.'

'Not quite alone, Mr Hawkins.'

'Are you thinking of the constable over there in the doorway? The one lying unconscious with his scull bashed in?'

Mr Williamson darted a glance at the doorway and perceived two legs jutting from it. The passing coster lad must have covered the sound. Mr Hawkins gave a predatory grin.

'Hmm. Hmm. In that proclamation, Mr Hawkins, Her Majesty promises that, "any person or persons who shall discover and apprehend, or cause to be discovered and apprehended, the authors, abettors, and perpetrators of any such incendiary fire . . . so that they, or any of them, shall be duly convicted thereof, shall be entitled to the sum of five hundred pounds for each and every person who shall be so convicted, and shall receive our most gracious pardon for the said crime." In short, Mr Hawkins, there is five hundred pounds for you if you help bring Mr Boyle to justice for even one of his fires – and a pardon for you if you were involved.'

Henry Hawkins smiled. Then he began to laugh his glutinous bass-note laugh. His eyes showed little mirth. It was at that moment that Mr Williamson realized the depth of his miscalculation and truly felt the inadequacy of his own diminutive stature next to the brawn and sinew of his interlocutor. And he felt the first tremors of fear.

TWENTY

Inspector Newsome sat at his desk in Whitehall, his head in his hands. The note that Mr Williamson had found in the graveyard of St Giles's was on the desk before him, as was the slip of paper from the dead clergyman's hand – both supplied by a concerned Dr McLeod.

News of Mr Williamson (and that of the wounded constable) had arrived shortly after eight o'clock that Wednesday morning. The other constable had returned to the church when he had gone off duty and found a group of people surrounding the prone figure of the detective, bloodied and immobile in the very same place where the Reverend Archer had lain.

Shortly before this, intelligence of another body had arrived: that of a man known as Razor Bill, a petty criminal who had had his throat cut in Hanover-square. Mr Newsome recognized the name from Mr Williamson's most recent report: the drunken interviewee who had made mention of a certain 'General'. That 'General' was almost certainly the murderer, blackmailer and incendiary Lucius Boyle, who had largely carried out his promise to 'break the connections' between himself and the pursuing police.

The others, though safe in their respective hiding places, were quite useless in aiding the investigation further. Only their status as murder victims in waiting made their concealment necessary. The police could hardly sustain *more* damaging newspaper coverage.

'What are we to do now? He has disabled our detective, murdered our witnesses and made a mockery of the police. This is no longer a matter of a two-headed girl and Mary Chatterton. It is a matter of our abject humiliation. Do you realize that the future of the Detective Force could be at risk – not to mention our good names?'

The question was addressed to Sir Henry Wilberforce, who was sitting in a leather armchair by the fire and smoking a pipe. His grey hair looked a little whiter in the light from the window.

'The situation is bleak,' he replied. 'The whole of London – indeed, the entire nation – is now talking about this "Red Jaw".'

'D— the man! Had I been waiting there at St Giles, I can assure you that I would not be the one left on the ground. No doubt Williamson tried to explain the finer points of law to this Hawkins even as the blows rained down!'

'Mr Williamson is a good man. What is his condition?'

'I spoke with him earlier this morning. He was badly beaten about the head and chest, though no bones seem to be broken. He refused to stay at the hospital and has returned home under the protection of two constables. Dr McLeod has advised him to remain in bed for at least a week. I certainly do not think he is ready for duty, but he says he will lead the investigation from his bed. What investigation, I say? There is no investigation.'

'There is the man Hawkins: a bare-knuckle fighter by all

accounts. He is a big man and his face is known. We will find him, Mr Newsome. With that letter already in our possession, we will compel Mr Hawkins to provide us with certain means of sending this Boyle to the gallows. In order to expedite that piece of investigation, however, I have a more pressing question. Where is Noah Dyson?'

'The last we heard, he was in pursuit of this Razor Bill – the very same man found dead this morning. Since then, we have no indication as to his whereabouts.'

'What of your man Mr Bryant who has been following Mr Dyson these past days?'

'That is the curious thing, sir. After the fire in Oxford-street, Mr Bryant continued to follow his man as usual when Mr Dyson suddenly darted around a corner and simply vanished into the crowd. It is as if he had known all along that he was being followed and simply chose the moment to elude his pursuer. He has not returned home.'

'Do you suspect him in the murder of this Bill fellow?'

'I see no benefit for Mr Dyson in that murder, but I do wonder why he chose now – of all times – to vanish.'

'Perhaps he is also dead. This Boyle is proving highly effective in fulfilling his promises to cut all connections.'

'I do not believe that Mr Dyson is dead. Whatever my feelings about the man, he is like a street dog. He lives by his wits and has already survived what might kill others.'

'No matter. We know where he lives. If he is alive, he must return there for clothes – and he has a manservant, does he not? A Negro?'

'Indeed. Mr Bryant is observing the property as we speak.'

'Do you think that Mr Williamson gave anything away during his beating? I am sure this Boyle would appreciate knowing Mr Dyson's address, for instance, or what we know so far about Boyle himself.'

'I asked him that and he said he believed he had not said anything damaging to the case – although he did lose consciousness. I do not believe he would speak. You know him.'

'Let us hope he is correct in his assumption.'

A knock at the door interrupted the officers' conversation and a clerk, on being beckoned by Inspector Newsome, entered with a sheaf of papers.

'Do you remember our initial interrogation of Mr Dyson?' said Mr Newsome to his colleague. 'You will recall that he gave us scant personal details. Since then, I have had my men investigating these and other questions I had. Let us see what we have.' Mr Newsome indicated that the clerk should present his information.

'Ahem . . . well, sirs, his claim that he was born in the parish of St Giles is not true. At least, there is no record of the birth of a Noah Dyson. We checked for twenty years either side of his probable age and found only a Noel Dyson, who died aged three months.'

'I see,' said Inspector Newsome, giving Sir Henry Wilberforce a knowing glance. 'And what of his sailor's service in the South Seas?'

'We could find no evidence of his having been in the Royal Navy, sir.'

'Indeed? I cannot say that I am surprised. No doubt he sailed under another flag. What of his other claims?'

'The house in Manchester-square was paid for in cash, sir, in the name of Henry Matthews. Of that gentleman, we can find no evidence.'

'So – we have nothing. *Nothing*. The man vanishes like a ghost. It was foolish of us to—'

'Sir? We did discover one piece of information . . .' offered the clerk.

'Then speak of it, man!'

'In 1829, a boy called Noah Dyson was transported to New South Wales for incendiarism and theft. He was initially sentenced to hang, but received a royal pardon on account of his tender years. We are trying to discover if any ticket of leave or pardon was issued to permit him to return to England. It may take some time.'

'Ha! I'm certain you will not find evidence of a legitimate departure from those shores. Good work, Jones. You may go back to your researches. What do you think of that, Sir Henry? Our man is an escaped convict from the Antipodes. That would explain his multiplicity of scars.'

'That remains to be seen. What is of greater interest – if he is our man – is the nature of the crimes: incendiarism and theft.'

'Indeed.'

'What do you intend to do? Noah is apparently a greater criminal than we thought. And this man Boyle must be apprehended with all haste. Neither can remain at liberty.'

'Mr Dyson will not remain away from his home indefinitely. My Mr Bryant and his colleagues are watching the place for any signs of contact as we speak. And we will endeavour to locate this Hawkins, who himself is no doubt also searching for Noah. A bulletin will be sent out to all stations and watch houses for both, though I am sure that wherever Boyle or his instrument Hawkins are to be found, we will also find Noah.'

'What about this writer fellow, Askern? Do you think that Boyle will make an attempt on his life? We cannot afford another murder.'

'Mr Askern is quite safe. Only we know where he is.'

'Are you sure that Sergeant Williamson did not speak to Hawkins?'

'He says not and I believe him. He has no reason to lie. No, Sir Henry – even Boyle cannot find a man we have purposely hidden.'

'One week ago, I might have believed you. Check on it personally.'

Benjamin sat in the study at Portland-place and stroked the scarred skin at his throat absent-mindedly. A mantel clock ticked stolidly through the silence. Whenever Noah did not return home, the Negro man could not rest until a letter or other communication arrived with information or instructions.

Some would say – if they knew the full details – that Benjamin stood to benefit greatly from the death or disappearance of his benefactor, for he was named sole beneficiary in Noah's will. The house and all of Noah's considerable assets would go directly to him. But would one wish the death of one's brother for financial gain? Wealth and property meant little to a man cast friendless, speechless and alone upon the metropolis. A dark face was a badge of foreignness, however well-to-do it might be. In truth, he would have laid down his life for Noah, as Noah had risked his own to save Benjamin. Theirs was an unbreakable bond.

He thought back to their early acquaintance on a ship – the *Bluebird* out of Nantucket – plying the Southern Oceans. Noah already had his stripes from the cat, and Benjamin was tongueless and scarred about the neck. Both outcasts and fugitives, they were drawn together and were bunkmates.

Crews could be volatile. Both men knew how to defend

their names or their honour. Benjamin could knock any man into oblivion with his powerful fists, but his wits were not as sharp as his friend. Noah was as patient and strategic as a spider, but was not made for the seas. He was a city boy thrown to the winds and he would not rest until he was back within the shadow of a building.

Of course, Benjamin knew something of hate and retribution. His neck was proof enough of that. How long had he hung until they'd cut him down thinking he was a corpse? And didn't he still carry in his inner eye the face of the instigator of that lynching? The man had pleaded for his life like a child as Benjamin had tightened a rope around *his* neck until the last strangulated cry was twisted out. It had been an empty victory – a shameful loss of control that had cast him beyond the coasts of America for a life of outlawry.

A timid knock at the street door started him from his thoughts and he rushed down the stairs to open it, hoping for good news but fearing another visit from the police.

On the doorstep stood a ragged urchin, who recoiled to see a black man with a ghostly eye opening the door to him. The boy's feet were bare and caked in filth, and his clothes showed pale skin and bruises through their rents. He was evidently a long way from his accustomed streets. A letter was clutched in his hand.

'Is you Ben?' he said.

Benjamin nodded.

''E said as you should show me yer licker first.'

Benjamin opened his mouth and bent down so that the boy could peer into the darkness.

'O! Did it 'urt bad?'

Benjamin nodded once and held out his hand for the letter.

"Ee said there was a sovvy in it for me.'

Benjamin took out a sovereign from his waistcoat pocket and held it up to the light. The boy's eyes focused on it as if it was the largest diamond in the world, and acquisitiveness twisted a smirk across his vulpine features.

'What if this letter is worth more than a sovvy to you and the gent?'

He had hardly finished expressing that base consideration when a meaty black palm like one of those enormous spiders sometimes encountered by men working at the ports settled gently on his shoulder and exerted just enough pressure to promise crippling pain.

'I'll take the sovvy.'

And he handed over the letter. Benjamin opened it quickly and looked at the *postscriptum* to assure himself that it was indeed from Noah. Then he handed the sovereign to the boy, who snatched it and danced away with a cheeky 'Thanking you, chimney chops!'

Benjamin closed the door and the boy walked jauntily and newly wealthy back along the street, moving eastwards. He had hardly gone more than a hundred yards around the corner when a man in a top hat and dark-blue clothes ran up behind him and grasped his grimy ear.

'Halt there, boy! What do you have in your hand?'

'Ow! Yer 'urtin' me lug! It's a sovvy – and I earned it fair an' square, so get off me, bluebottle!'

'So, you recognize me as a policeman.'

'I smelt yer!'

Mr Bryant slapped the boy none too gently with an open palm while keeping hold of the ear. 'Who gave you that letter to deliver, boy?'

'What letter? Ow! Stob 'ittin' me like that! It was a gent

down on the Mall. Gave me a sovvy an' says there's another in it if I took a letter to this address.'

'So why didn't you just take the first sovereign and throw the letter in a dustheap, you rapscallion?'

'Two sovvies is better than one, ain't it?'

'What did he look like, this "gent"?'

'I don't know – like any gent. Only 'e had manners . . . ow! Stobbit! 'E was nothin' paticlar, I tell yer!'

'Did you read the letter? Be honest now!'

'I can't do readin'. I only knows some words like "gin" an' "meat pie" an' the like. Will you let go of me b— lug now?'

'Not yet. What did he tell you? His exact words, mind.'

''E said "Take this letter to this address an' there's another sovvy in it for yer." 'E said a blacky man will open the door and you must look in 'is gob cos 'e's got no licker. If it is 'im, 'e said, give 'im the letter an' 'e'll give yer another sovvy. An' that's all.'

'Are you sure? I could have you in gaol in a moment if you are lying to me.'

'Ow! Me — lug! Wait. There was somethin' other – I think 'e meant it for you. He said someone might stop me an' ask me about the letter, an' if they did I must tell 'em paticlar this message: "The pusood is now the pusoor." Made me repeat it 'bout ten times to remember, 'e did.'

'"The pursued is now the pursuer?"'

'S'what I said, isn't it? Ow! Stobbit, I tells yer!' And the urchin twisted free to escape the grasp of Mr Bryant, who in any case was in a state of some surprise. He looked about him and made his way quickly back to a point where he could view Mr Dyson's house.

Benjamin was locking the door. The Negro tilted his top

hat at an angle and began to walk with an athletic gait down Duke-street and along Edward-street towards the east.

Mr Bryant followed, signalling to his colleague standing on the corner that he should watch the house.

Mr Allan, it will be remembered, is the worthy who was overseeing the anonymous address where Mr Askern was safely ensconced. That very same morning, he was frying eggs and bacon in the kitchen for the benefit of his various guests, some of whom might very much surprise the reader, and even the police themselves.

In its time, that unassuming address in an unremarkable area of London had accommodated thieves, informers, fallen women, potential victims like Mr Askern, and at least one murderer. Though it might seem incredible, even the commissioners themselves did not know of its existence – or rather, they had not been told and affected not to know. What went on there was legally expedient but judicially suspect. A man's residency was no guarantee either of innocence or immunity from the gallows. It was a place – and a state – of temporary invisibility from which one might emerge free, or damned.

Mr Allan started at the top of the building, knocking at a selected door and leaving breakfast and a newspaper before it before moving on to the next, always being careful that no resident might see another. With each opening door, a bell rang out. A few in the past had been curious, but most were there in fear of their lives and were grateful for the anonymity. When he reached the basement room of Mr Askern, he repeated the practised ritual again, knocking on the door with a 'Breakfast, sir!' and laying the plates and cups on the stone flags at his feet.

However, when he set about collecting the breakfast things an hour or so later, he was surprised, but not alarmed, to see Mr Askern's food untouched. People reacted differently to their stay, and a temporary loss of hunger was the least of their symptoms. So, honest Mr Allan simply took away the crockery and went about his daily business: taking delivery of coal and beer, receiving his shopping in packages throughout the morning and fulfilling his role as amanuensis in the divers police correspondence he was obliged to read and write.

When the writer did not emerge from his room or eat his lunch, Mr Allan was still not alarmed. Such things had happened before. Nor did he feel any compulsion to notify Mr Williamson (of whose unfortunate encounter he was completely ignorant). Indeed, it was only when the dinner remained untouched that Mr Allan thought to knock on the door – a gesture of personal concern rather than of fear for the man inside.

'Sir? I do not mind whether you eat, but I must ask you for a sign that you are healthy and not in need of aid. Sir?'

Silence.

'Sir? You need not speak. Simply rap upon the table or make a sound if you are all right.'

Silence.

'I am afraid I must forcibly enter if you do not give me a sign. Sir? Sir?'

Silence.

Mr Allan banged on the door to be sure that the inhabitant was not in a deep slumber. Still there was no answer. The situation was still not unprecedented: a man had once taken his own life in the house and the door had been broken down. This Mr Askern did not seem the kind to kill himself, but any man discovers parts of himself that perhaps he had never before explored when forced to spend time alone in the silence of an unfamiliar room. Mr Allan sighed and went to fetch his hammer and chisels. He hoped there would not be blood on the new mattress.

The Negro named Benjamin made his way on foot and uninterrupted towards Leicester-square. Among the shops there, he looked in the window of a tobacconist and stood to read a large street display of advertisements and playbills before entering a shop on Castle-street. This establishment was Mr Nathan's Masquerade Warehouse, where the Negro purchased two costumes – a Greek and a Moor – and two masques, all of which he arranged to have delivered later. I discerned this on returning to this shop after I was relieved.

Mr Newsome put down Mr Bryant's report and nodded to himself. Mr Bryant was a dedicated and thorough man. The inspector was reading the report in the back of a carriage on his way to the safe house to which Mr Williamson had escorted Mr Askern, there to ask the writer what he knew of the bare-knuckle fighter Henry Hawkins. The swaying motion and start-stop traffic was making him nauseous.

. . . Then he made his way towards Whitehall – passing within mere yards of headquarters – to cross the river at Westminster-bridge, whereupon he continued south along the water's edge until he came to the very same alley where the girl Eliza-Beth was murdered. Here, he paused a while as if in contemplation of the property and presently extracted a sheet of paper from his coat. He folded it, slipped it under the door and turned to retrace his steps back towards Westminster-bridge. (I attempted to extract the letter from under the door but it was locked tight and I was afraid of losing the Negro, so I continued to follow him.) He walked all the way back to the house in Manchester-square, where PC Jackson told me that no-one had entered or left the property since. This is the extent of my latest report.

Mr Newsome folded the report and returned it to his coat pocket. It was clear to him, if not to Mr Bryant, that Benjamin had taken his curious route in full knowledge that he was being followed and that there was some message to be gleaned from that strange peregrination. The letter would of course have to be recovered from the (now empty) Lambeth property with all haste. If Noah Dyson did not show himself very shortly, *his* house would have to be searched again and the Negro interrogated more persuasively than on the last occasion.

These thoughts were still in his mind when the carriage stopped outside the secret house where Mr Askern was staying. He stepped down on to the street and bade the driver wait. The door opened before he could knock, and the expression on Mr Allan's face told him that the news was dire. The housekeeper beckoned him in and closed the door behind them.

'Mr Newsome, sir! Thank G— you have come. I was about to send a boy for you. It is most strange . . . most dreadful and most strange.'

'What is it, man? Is it Mr Askern?'

'I cannot explain it, sir. There is no indication . . . there is no clue . . . I am at a loss . . .'

'You are dithering! Speak plainly!'

'Inspector Newsome – Mr Askern is dead. And my most recent resident has fled.'

TWENTY-ONE

Sergeant Williamson sat in bed with that day's copy of *the Times* spread before him. His face was a gruesome sight. One eye was swollen and empurpled, while the other was barely a slit amid a circle of bruising. His bottom lip bore a congealed cut where it had been split by Henry Hawkins's fist, and his jawline was blotched red (which struck him as ironic under the circumstances). He had lost a couple of teeth and it also hurt when he breathed, thanks to the energetic kicks of his assailant.

All of London was now talking about Lucius Boyle and the series of murders attributed to him, though they were still referring to him as 'the General' or the increasingly common and popular 'Red Jaw'. There had been only one reference to a 'Lucifer', in *the Observer*, but the name had not yet caught on. Mr Williamson squinted through puffy eyes at the letter in *the Times*:

Dear Sirs

The current situation is both unacceptable and unbearable. That a callous murderer walks free among the streets of the city when upwards of thirty thousand have seen and know his face is a matter that can only reflect upon the Metropolitan Police in the blackest manner. How many more murders must he commit before he is brought to justice? First, it was the unfortunate Mary Chatterton, then the theatrical agent Mr Henry Coggins (alias Dr Zwigoff) at the execution of Eliza-Beth's murderer. My wife is afraid to venture out alone and doors across the metropolis are bolted even during daylight.

What are the Police doing to catch this man? Does he not have associates? Does he not buy food and coal? Does he not have neighbours? How much longer must we live in fear of our lives?

He smiled grimly, imagining the apoplexy of Commissioner Mayne on reading the letter. The smile made him wince. When the newspapers discovered the murder of the Reverend Archer, the scandal would reach historic proportions and the pressure upon the Detective Force would become even more impossible.

The frustration of inaction itched under his bandages. Boyle was free. With each murder, he was rendering himself ever more invisible until the last tenuous connection to him was severed. No one was safe, not even his closest associates – something Henry Hawkins would be wise to consider. Then the man would vanish again, most likely to another town or another country.

And what of Mr Dyson? The vacuum of information was quite infuriating. Until that night's grievous beating, Mr Williamson himself had been the one who held all the knowledge. Indeed, his gravest concern now was what he may have revealed during the encounter with Henry Hawkins.

He recalled falling to the floor and a heavy boot striking his stomach and ribs. He recalled the boxer's face just inches from his own, that deep voice drifting to him through waves of pain. Noah's name was mentioned, as was Mr Askern's. Then more blows and he had fallen into an oblivion of agony. Had he spoken as he lapsed? Had he given a word or a phrase – spoken in his very anxiety not to speak – that had helped the criminal? He had told Inspector Newsome that he had said nothing. Only subsequent events would show if that was true.

Police Constable John Cullen knocked at the door and entered the room with a cup of tea, which he laid on the table next to the bed. 'Here you go, sir. A nice fresh one for you.'

'Thank you, PC Cullen.'

'I would like to meet him that did this to you, sir. I'd show him the mettle of the Metropolitan Police, I can tell you.'

'I am sure of it, but that is not how we enforce the law. What news is there? Have you heard anything from the other men in your division? I know how you constables talk.'

'A very busy night, sir. A huge fire in Oxford-street – a gin palace went up like an arsenal. A lady burned to death in an upper floor and a fire engineer was badly burned.'

'Where on Oxford-street?'

'A place called the Rose and Crown wine vaults – a new place by all accounts. And there was a murder: a fellow of no great consequence found at Hanover-square. Most probably a drunken brawl.'

'In Hanover-square? Do you have a name?'

'I am not certain. I heard the name "Bill" but it's not someone known to me.'

'Hmm. Hmm.'

'Bad news, sir?'

'That seems to be the only kind these days, Constable. Tell me, when is Inspector Newsome expected? I need to speak to him urgently about the case.'

'He said he would come today, sir, but did not say what time.'

'Thank you, Constable. You may leave me now. Please show Inspector Newsome in the moment he arrives, even if I am sleeping.'

'Yes, sir.'

Alone now, Mr Williamson reclined with difficulty and dabbed a handkerchief to his lip, which had split again. He attempted to apply his concentration once more to what little he knew. He had been worrying at the facts since the doctor had left.

The most pressing question was why Boyle wanted him to live when Hawkins could so easily have extinguished his life. The letter had made reference to the detective making an artifice of Boyle's death, which would certainly have been a neat ending to the affair for the incendiary. Death was the greatest anonymity. But did the criminal really imagine that the police would believe or accept it? Such a scheme would require the collaboration of more than just Sergeant Williamson. Others would have to participate, and such a thing was quite unthinkable of Mr Newsome or Mr Wilberforce or Commissioner Mayne. Unless . . .

A feverish thought brought colour to his face and he struggled to stand, though nausea washed over him in dizzying waves. He took off his night shirt and put on his clothes, every movement causing burning pain.

'Constable Cullen!' he called.

The constable appeared at the door. 'Is everything all right, sir . . . Are you sure you should be up? The doctor said—'

'There are things I must do. You will accompany me.'

'Yes, sir . . . but Inspector Newsome will be calling. Shouldn't we—?'

'Do not worry about that. There are more pressing matters. Here, take my arm – I am unsteady.'

Amid all of this confusion, the reader must share the curiosity of the police as to Noah's whereabouts. We last saw him illuminated by the inferno at Oxford-street, as consumed with frustration and anger as the gin palace was itself consumed.

He understood then that he must do something to change the balance. Until that stage, Boyle had been leading proceedings. The police were simply reacting to his crimes and slamming closed numerous stable gates as horses raced over the brows of numerous hills. The man seemed to know more about their investigation than they did.

So, as the smoke billowed and the fire engine crews laboured to spray water over hissing beams, Noah looked around him and saw the policeman who had been (rather clumsily) following him since the whole business had begun. And he set off walking, all pretence of being a beggar now abandoned. At the first corner, he rapidly took off the charred topcoat and reversed it, turning it from black to bottle green. He pulled out a soft cap, and, placing it low over his forehead, he immediately changed his gait and posture, and reversed direction so that he soon passed the man following him.

Did his pursuer stop in confusion, scanning the crowds? Did he register, too late, the scent of juniper-infused smoke on the man who had passed him in the green coat and discern what had happened? No matter – Noah had been absorbed once more into the city. Nobody knew where he was.

But nor did he know the whereabouts of Boyle or his man Hawkins. That would have to be remedied. Since he could not yet return home, he took a cab to a lodging house in the vicinity of Long-acre. There, he wrote the letter which – as we now know – the street urchin was to deliver to Benjamin the next day:

Benjamin

I saw him tonight at Oxford-street, and, again, I lost him. The police investigation is proving quite futile and the time has come to change strategy.

I have escaped that heavy-footed gentleman who has been loitering outside our house for so long. No doubt he will return there in order to await my return. I will not return. Instead, he will follow you. This is my intention.

You will lead him a merry dance across the city. Go to the costumier that we have used before and purchase two costumes – a Greek and Moor – and two masques. Have them delivered. Then make your way to that ill-fated house in Lambeth and slip a note under the door (I enclose the text separately). After that, return home and go about your normal business.

Naturally, you will be followed by the policeman. If my suppositions are correct, you will also be followed by one of Boyle's men. Fear not – I will be with you all the way. Until now, it is they who have been observing us. Now I will follow them and trace them to their source. Burn this message before you leave. If challenged, defend yourself.

Noah

PS You will know that I am the true author of this letter when I mention the iron band you wear about your ankle.

After negotiating the letter's delivery, Noah followed the boy to observe the effects. Sure enough, the police dullard saw Benjamin receive the note and made a ham-handed interrogation of the boy, who no doubt recounted the message Noah had provided him with for that very eventuality. Then Benjamin put his instructions into action.

Naturally, the policeman followed. And within a few yards, another man emerged from the glove shop on the corner of Spanish-place and took up the pursuit. It was Henry Hawkins, that increasingly ubiquitous tool of Lucius Boyle. Perturbed as he was, Noah was unsurprised. Indeed, it was exactly the outcome he had hoped for.

To Leicester-square and Whitehall, across Westminster-bridge and to Lambeth, the trio followed Benjamin, who played his role to the letter. When they arrived at that notorious and unfortunate address where Eliza-Beth had been murdered, Mr Hawkins evidently faced a dilemma: whether to continue his pursuit or risk losing sight of his targets to acquire the note that had been posted under the door. Having lost at St Giles the letter Mr Boyle had forbidden him to lose, he must have reasoned that claiming this piece of evidence would bring him leniency. So he wasted no time in knocking down the door with a prodigious kick and grabbing the sheet of paper before hurrying after Benjamin and the policeman.

Throughout the curious journey, Noah maintained a safe distance. He was still wearing his 'beggar' attire and utilized it in busier streets, adopting a shuffling gait or limp that would cause people to immediately look away lest he asked for money. As long as he was constantly 'moving on' to another division, the street constables would not stop him. On less frequented streets, he would revert to his usual athletic gait and modify his appearance to some degree: going bareheaded or wearing his cap, choosing black or green for the exterior hue of his coat. By these small gestures, and with slight changes in posture (walking tall or going round-shouldered), he could minimize his visibility, for – as we have already seen – a man's appearance in the common crowd is as much a matter of rhythm and pace as colour and size.

When the pursuit led back to where it had started, Noah took a suitably inconspicuous vantage point and saw the policeman make a report to his colleague, who presumably went off to the Detective Force with his bulletin. Noah waited. He watched Mr Hawkins return to the glove shop he had emerged from. And Noah continued to wait.

Was Mr Hawkins still in the shop? Was Boyle himself in the shop receiving Hawkins's account? People walked in and out of the shop, none of them lingering for a sustained period. Was one of them a messenger carrying news from Hawkins to Boyle? A curtain twitched on the first floor. Was there access to an upper floor from within the shop, from which Hawkins was watching him? Or perhaps the fighter had already left? The whole charade would come to naught if Noah ventured into the shop now. It was imperative that the details of Hawkins's pursuit of Benjamin – and the contents of that note – find its way back to Lucius Boyle. But . . .

He could wait no longer. Even if his police pursuer was to catch sight of him again, he needed to follow Hawkins. He strode around the square and pushed open the shop door, whose small bell tinkled his entrance. A counter of massed gloves in different colours and hides faced him, their scent filling the air. There was no one in the shop but a pretty girl in an apron behind the counter.

'Can I help you, sir?'

'Yes. I wonder if you can repair a pair of gloves for me.'

'Of course, sir. You live just opposite there, don't you? You are dressed rather odd today – not your usual elegance.'

'Yes. Tell me, who was that man who entered a few moments ago? It looked very like the bare-knuckle fighter Henry Hawkins. He did not exit from the same door.'

'The gentleman with the scars? I don't know his name but he was here earlier today causing no end of trouble.'

'Oh? What kind of trouble?'

'Well, he came in asking about repairing gloves, just as you have, but then he didn't seem to want to leave. He just looked out into the street as if waiting for someone. Mr Jedson asked him to leave if he did not want to produce his gloves or purchase more – it isn't such a big shop, as you see – but the man said he would beat us senseless if we spoke to him again and would kill us if we went for a constable. He showed us an iron bar. It was very unpleasant, I can tell you.'

'Where is he now?'

'He asked if there was another exit. I told him only through the stitching room, but that was not for the public.

Then he used language I will not repeat and I was obliged to show him the exit.'

'Is it this door here?'

'Yes, sir, but it is not for the public . . . Sir!'

Noah pushed through the door and entered an area of many tables where five or six men toiled over innumerable scraps of cow leather, suede and pigskin. They looked up from their work, but Noah was moving towards another door that stood ajar. He exited and found himself in a tiny, malodorous courtyard. Crossing this, he emerged on to Thayer-street. Hawkins was nowhere to be seen.

Noah cursed and hailed a cab. He was satisfied, as the cab clattered off, to see his police shadow emerging from the same courtyard – too late to follow and with no other cab immediately available. The expression on the man's face was one of extreme anger as Noah smiled broadly.

Inspector Newsome was caught between impatience and dread of hearing more. The kindly Mr Allan seemed to regard the death of one of his residents as no more inconvenience than misplacing a cup. Commissioner Mayne would see it very differently, as would the infernal newspapers.

'Did he take his own life?' asked the inspector.

'I do not think so, sir.'

'Well, how did he die if not by his own hand? The room was quite secure, was it not?'

'Yes, sir. Perhaps you'd better see for yourself.'

The two men walked down to the basement room, whose door had been hacked from its jamb by Mr Allan. Splinters lay about the floor and the tools were where they had been dropped. The men entered the room.

The writer lay pale and quite dead on his bed. In his borrowed nightshirt, he could have been sleeping but for the lack of breathing and heartbeat. There was no sign of injury to his person, no disturbance of furniture and no sign of forced access. The bars over the window were intact and the glass was unbroken. Mr Newsome tested the ironwork with a forceful pull and found it quite secure.

'Did the bell ring at all during the night, Mr Allan?'

'Ah, you are thinking that Mr Askern allowed access to another in the night. No – the bell did not ring. And anyone venturing downstairs would have passed my door and woken me first. I know the sounds of this house like no one else, Mr Newsome.'

'Was this wedge in place when you forced the door?'

'Indeed. I looked under the door before I began to dismantle it and saw the wedge there.'

'Did you find anything strange on entering? Think carefully – the slightest oddity may be of note.'

'Nothing at all, sir.'

'Think! Anything you would not expect upon opening the door. Anything at all.'

'Nothing, sir. I know this house like . . . wait . . . there *was* a faint smell. It smelled sweet, like burned sugar, but not exactly. More acrid. I have never smelled anything like it before and I cannot smell it any longer. I have heard that a dead body can often smell sweet.'

'I think not.' Mr Newsome looked into the grate and prodded the cold ashes with a poker. There did not seem to be anything sugary that had been burned there. The window could not be opened, so the scent could not have entered there.

'Did Mr Askern smoke a pipe or cigars, Mr Allan?'

'No, sir.'

'I suppose it is possible that Mr Askern died of natural causes, but he was a young man and seemed healthy.'

'He had a terrible cough, sir. I believe he was consumptive, although I didn't hear him coughing in the night. Indeed, I heard no sound at all from his room after dark, and I was up 'til after midnight. There was a light under his door, so perhaps he was writing.'

Mr Newsome walked over to the simple table and looked at the sheets of paper there. The writer had evidently been making plans for places he intended to visit once he was released, for the papers showed little other than lists of streets and characters he would like to interview. Only the candle presented a curious sight: it had burned right down to its brass holder rather than being blown out. He looked again at the corpse.

'He does not look like he has coughed himself into an early grave, Mr Allan. I have seldom seen a more composed cadaver. Have you sent for Doctor McLeod? Maybe he can resolve this.'

'I have.'

'Good. Now – what of this other man you say fled last night?'

'Yes, sir. I heard the street door close before dawn and went to investigate. I could see no one, so I went up to the rooms and found all doors closed except the attic. The man had only been here for a few hours. He had cut the bell free from the door jamb so as to make no noise on leaving.'

'What man was he?'

'Why, you should know, sir, for it is the man you sent.'

'What gibberish are you talking now? I did not send any

man except Mr Askern, and Sergeant Williamson escorted him here.'

'But there was your letter, sir.'

'What letter? Tell me everything, for I am sure I do not understand a word you are saying.'

'A constable knocked at the door late last night with a man in irons. He said that he had orders to render the man unto my care. Naturally, I denied all knowledge of my special services here – I knew that no common policeman would know of it. But then he produced a letter from you.'

'Do you have this letter?'

'Yes. I will fetch it.'

Mr Allan limped off to retrieve the letter and the inspector looked about him at the death scene. His confusion was giving way to a rushing fear.

'Here it is, sir. It has your signature on it.'

Mr Newsome snatched it from Mr Allan's hands.

Sir

Please take this gentleman into your care in my name. It will only be until tomorrow, and then I will come for him. Please extend him every courtesy, but do not attempt to speak to him. He has a partially severed tongue and cannot speak.

Until tomorrow.

Detective Inspector Newsome

'That signature is not mine. And did you not wonder that the letter was addressed to "Sir" and not "Mr Allan" as I would have addressed it?'

'No, sir . . . as I said, it was late. After midnight. Perhaps I was a little tired.'

'What did he look like, this man who was brought here?'

'Well, he was of average build—'

'His face, Mr Allan – what of his face?'

'He had grey eyes – quite startling. But I did not see the rest. He wore a bandage about his lower face that quite hid his features. No doubt for his injured tongue. He smelled quite badly of smoke, as if he'd been near a fire, and he carried a canvas bag such as sailors carry . . . Mr Newsome, sir? Are you all right? You have become very pale.'

'Do you read the newspapers, Mr Allan?'

'Why, yes, of course I read them. One has to be well informed.'

'Could you tell me, then, what the biggest news story of the moment is?'

'I am sure you know better than—'

'Just tell me.'

'Well, it is the pursuit of this fellow they call "the General": murderer of Mary Chatterton and the theatrical agent Coggins, and more besides if the rumours are to be believed.'

'Indeed. Indeed. You are quite right on that latter point. In fact, the latest murder has very likely taken place just feet from where we are standing. And just this very night.'

'Sir? I . . .'

'The man who was brought here last night had his lower face covered, did he not? Let us add to that piece of information the fact that he was fraudulently brought here in my name. Let us further note that in the same house was one whom this man with the "injured tongue" would like to see dead.'

'Red Jaw was in this house? L— preserve me!'

'It seems highly probable. Two things still perplex me, however. First: there are no signs at all that Mr Askern was murdered, and indeed no possibility of it. And, second, how did this "Red Jaw" come to know of this house and its residents?'

A knock at the street door echoed down to where they stood.

'Dr McLeod, no doubt,' said Mr Newsome. 'Please show him to this room and let us discover what – or who – killed poor Mr Askern.'

TWENTY-TWO

Noah paid the driver and got down from the cab. He'd had to pay extra to tempt the cab south of the river at that time of day, and more to hurry the man along.

The carriage had set him down before Sergeant Williamson's home, which had a policeman posted at the front door. Noah approached the door and saw the policeman stand to attention, ready to accost this man who looked so like a street beggar yet walked like a gentleman. Fortunately, the sergeant himself opened the door at that moment, supported on the sturdy arm of PC Cullen.

'My G—, Williamson! What happened to you?'

'Mr Dyson – I was about to venture out to call on you.'

'You would not have found me at home.'

'Come inside. We have very important things to discuss.'

The two men established themselves in Mr Williamson's parlour, the latter propped upright in his chair and evidently in a state of great discomfort. PC Cullen prepared tea.

'Was it Hawkins?' asked Noah.

'Yes. He murdered the Reverend Archer and then waited for me at the scene. He told me in no uncertain terms that I was to procure a disfigured body and claim it as Boyle's, thereby ending the case.'

'And you did not acquiesce, I presume.'

'Hmm. You are quite the detective, Mr Dyson. I have heard that you were unsuccessful in your attempts to locate Razor Bill alive. Unless it was you who killed him and left his body in Hanover-square?'

'Hawkins again.'

'I must take your word for it. Why are you dressed like that?'

'Because your men have been following me since I was first released from Giltspur-street and I must escape them to do my job properly.'

'I told Mr Newsome that you would discover that piece of duplicity in no time. I would have been disappointed if you had not. Just now, you said that I would not find you at home – why is that?'

'Recent events have shown that Boyle is always ahead of the game. With that buffoon of Inspector Newsome's following me about, I might as well have had a beam of gaslight upon me. And Mr Hawkins knows where I live – could you explain that to me, Mr Williamson?'

'We will come to that in a moment. What have you been doing?'

'I shrugged off my shadow last night after the fire. Boyle caused it – he was there. I almost had him again. Until now, he seems to have been following our every move, so I made the choice to disappear. When he cannot follow, he must lead.'

'What did you discover?'

'I discovered nothing – but I have left a trail of clues that,

I hope, he will act upon and which will lead him directly into our hands.'

'Tell me.'

'Wait. Do I know that I can trust you? The Detective Force has not trusted me from the outset. I was surprised to find that Hawkins – and therefore Boyle – knows where I live. Hawkins may have followed the policeman, but how would Hawkins know to follow *him*?

'Mr Dyson . . . Noah . . . I will be frank. I have grave concerns about my own superior.'

'Inspector Newsome? I have my own. Tell me.'

'From the beginning, I have wondered why he has gone to such lengths to employ one such as you, stretching and sullying everything that the police stand for in order to solve a murder. What would make the man so maniacal in his pursuit of a criminal, unless he had something personal at stake?'

'What are you thinking?'

'I believe – and I have no evidence for this except for my detective's nose – that Inspector Newsome may be the father of Eliza-Beth and the lover of Mary Chatterton. I believe that he had had some indication of this prior to Eliza-Beth's death. Perhaps Mary was trying to blackmail him. Perhaps it was Mr Boyle doing the blackmailing. Whatever the impetus, the inspector persuaded those at Whitehall to agree to his scheme to save his own name. He can be a persuasive man. And now the pursuit of Mr Boyle has become a veritable mania for him.'

'Have you considered that it was Mr Newsome himself who orchestrated the murder of Eliza-Beth? To remove the evidence of his dalliance, so to speak.'

'I could not think that of him. There are, however,

numerous questions. Do you recall the letter that was sent to me at Whitehall? Mr Boyle wrote: "Few others could recognize me, and no other could thirst for my capture with such keenness, *except perhaps your hapless superior*." What did Boyle mean by that latter part? Was it a personal message to the inspector? And why did Boyle sign his name? Perhaps we knew it was he, but a man so careful did not have to make it clear – unless he wanted Mr Newsome to know particularly that he was the author.'

'You make a reasonable case. However, you forget that there is no possibility that Mr Newsome can have known about my past with Boyle, or that I had been looking for him.'

'That is true. It would be the oddest piece of luck on his part. Or it could be that in his own attempts to find Mr Boyle and curtail the blackmail, he found you also searching – your own records show that for a long time you could be found wherever Mr Boyle's fires took place.'

'I suppose it is possible. Whatever the background, it seems that Boyle and Mr Newsome are engaged in a game and that we are pieces in it. The inspector wants to catch his enemy, but in order to placate him, he offers the man opportunities to elude us. I think he would prefer me to find and kill Boyle rather than you to find and arrest him. It is a double-faced game he is playing: attempting to maintain the *façade* of a detective and yet following his own agenda. Thus, Hawkins attacks you but doesn't kill you; Hawkins knows my home yet does not kill me – unless he had only just received the information and was not able to act on it. What are we to do? Can you go to the commissioner?'

'I have considered going to Commissioner Mayne or to Superintendent Wilberforce with my suspicions, but with what evidence? I have nothing but surmises. I have no idea who is involved in this. I am afraid that the decisive agent in the case will be you.'

'I have made the first step. I have interrupted their game with a move neither Boyle or Mr Newsome expected, and which neither will understand. They can only react. Then we have them. Neither knows where I am. That will remain the case if your constables here do not speak.'

'What have you done?'

'I will not tell you now lest I put you in a position where you have to choose your loyalties. I will say only that I have presented them with the means for proceeding, move by move, into a trap that I have laid for them. Even if they suspect it, they have little other option.'

'I hope you are right, Noah.'

'I am not a gambling man. Now – I have taken a risk in coming here. I must leave.'

'Wait. Why *did* you come to me?'

'Mr Williamson, you are good man, an honest man. I have not known many in my life. Whatever your other faults – being a policeman among them – you are the only one who can help me. Perhaps I am the only one who can help you.'

'Hmm. Hmm. If you are planning to remain invisible, you must leave. I am expecting Mr Newsome here. Go – find Boyle. But bring him to me alive. It is his testimony that will entrap Inspector Newsome also. Both are guilty. Can you promise me that?'

'I would like to, but I fear the game has become a fatal one.'

'Noah – why must you kill him? Whatever evil he did to you was a lifetime ago. You are a different man now. Killing him will change nothing, will repair nothing.'

'What do you know of loss and pain, Mr Williamson?'

'I . . . I know more than you think. But I bear it like a Christian.'

'I am no Christian. You do not know what I have suffered for Lucius Boyle.'

'I know that killing him will not cleanse your mind of it.'

'I have lived half a life thinking of nothing else.'

'You are wrong to think so. You are his prisoner by thinking so.'

'I have had my fill of being a prisoner while he has been free . . .'

'Then why don't you allow me to capture him alive? Then you can live the rest of your life knowing that you saw him tried, imprisoned and hanged.'

'I must leave. Mr Newsome may look for me here. How will we communicate?'

'Find PC Cullen, the burly man who brought us tea. He is a beat officer in this division and I can trust him. He will pass on messages. Now go.'

The sound of a carriage stopping outside the house caused both men to exchange glances. PC Cullen's voice called out:

'Inspector Newsome is arrived, sir.'

'Can I leave the house without him seeing me?' asked Noah.

'Yes. To the rear. Down the corridor there.'

Noah pulled a folded piece of paper out of his pocket and held it out to the detective: 'Quickly – take this. You will discern my plan.'

Then he was gone. Mr Williamson thrust the paper, unread, into his jacket pocket and shifted uncomfortably in his seat as the door was opened by PC Cullen.

'Good afternoon, Sergeant Williamson!' said Mr Newsome entering. 'Up and about, I see. Is that advisable? We
need you fit as soon as possible. I trust you have heard about
the other events of last night: the fire, the death of Razor
Bill . . .?'

'What do you mean?'

'From the constables, of course. I know how they talk.
One has no need of a newspaper if one knows a constable. I
expect PC Cullen knows more about the criminal headlines
of London that does the editor of *the Times*.'

'Yes, yes – I expect so. I have heard the news. Was it
Lucius Boyle?'

'That we cannot say. It may be that this man Noah Dyson
has a hand in it.'

'Oh? Why do you say so?'

'Well, you sent him to Oxford-street in search of this Bill
and a few hours later there is a conflagration and a dead body
at Hanover-square. I will let you draw your own conclusions,
bearing in mind Mr Dyson's documented interest in incendiary matters. I might also add that we have discerned some
surprising facts about the man, first among them that he
seems to be a convict escaped from New South Wales. What
we knew of him appears now to be a web of untruths . . . you
look surprised. I thought that your opinion of him was lower
even than mine.'

'It is the pain that makes me grimace.'

'I sympathize. I have sent a bulletin to all stations and
watch houses with a description of Hawkins *and* of Noah.
He did not return home last night and so we know what
clothes he is wearing. If either man shows his face, we will
have him.'

'I do not believe Hawkins will reveal anything, even if

captured. I offered him five hundred pounds for information leading to the capture of Boyle and he just laughed. There is nothing we can do to him that Boyle cannot do twofold.'

'You are quite the pessimist after your beating, Mr Williamson. Alas, I have worse news. Mr Askern is dead.'

'What? *How?*'

'Yes. Last night. His body was discovered this morning. A man was brought to the house at around midnight with a letter purporting to be from me. Mr Allan foolishly admitted the man, whose lower jaw was covered on account of an "injured tongue". He had grey eyes and was carrying a sailor's canvas bag.'

'Boyle. How did he know about the house?'

'How indeed? But do we know it was Boyle? No red jaw was seen – only a *covered* jaw. Who is to say that it was not merely someone with his jaw covered? Who is to say it was not Noah Dyson? His movements during the night are completely unaccounted for and even now we do not know where he is.'

'What of your man Bryant?'

'Noah escaped him. We were able to follow his manservant, the Negro, on a jaunt around London to costumiers and the like – but the man himself remains at large.'

'I did not tell Noah where I was taking Mr Askern – only that it was to a completely secure place. What else do we know of this man who stayed there?'

'Only that he fled at dawn.'

'Hmm. How did Mr Askern die? It was quite impossible for anyone to gain access to that room; I checked everything personally. What did you find? What did Doctor McLeod say?'

'He examined the body and proclaimed a natural death.

There was no bodily injury, no blood – no sign at all of violence. I could see all of that for myself. The room was locked from the inside and there was no sign of forced entry either by door or window. The man simply passed away in his sleep with no indications of agitation, struggle or discomfort.'

'That seems a remarkable coincidence, especially if there was an anonymous intruder in the house.'

'My thinking exactly, Mr Williamson.'

'Which room was the other man accommodated in?'

'In the attic – the furthest possible room from Mr Askern's. Even if he had wanted to descend to attack the writer, he would have alerted Mr Allan in doing so.'

'I cannot believe that the death was natural. Not in light of all that has happened.'

'Nor I, but there is no evidence to suggest otherwise.'

'At least, no evidence that has yet surfaced.'

'What do you mean?'

'I do not know. I am tired . . . tired of all of this. What else is left? Is there is any chance of us finding Boyle now? Perhaps Noah himself is dead and we will find him rotting on the mudbanks in a day or two. Mr Boyle and Henry Hawkins will vanish.'

'Come, Sergeant. That is not the spirit I expect from you.'

'I am trying to be realistic. Mr Boyle may have finished his series of killings – except perhaps for mine. Would it be so reprehensible if I were to follow his instructions and dredge up a suitable corpse to satisfy the newspapers and Commissioner Mayne? A phial of clothier's dye applied to the jaw . . .'

'Enough of that talk! He must be caught. The reputation – no, the continued *existence* – of the Detective Force depends on it. How can we survive if we allow this man to escape? How can we respect ourselves, Mr Williamson? He is in London somewhere. We are many and he is one. I would like you – even in your frail condition – to pay a visit to Mr Allan's house and conduct your own investigation. Tomorrow morning at the very latest. It may be our only remaining link to Mr Boyle.'

'Your fervour is admirable, sir. How do you maintain it?'

'Justice, Mr Williamson: my thirst for justice.'

'Only that?'

'Of course. What else would it be?'

The two men stared at each other for a moment.

'There is also the fact of my own pride and reputation,' added Mr Newsome. 'I am sure you can imagine how Commissioner Mayne has reacted to recent events. It is I who bears the onslaught of his doubts and remonstrations, his daily trawl through the newspapers for derogatory stories about the police, his insinuations of my own personal responsibility for recruiting a thief to catch a murderer. If the whole business is not brought to a satisfactory conclusion very shortly . . . well . . . the consequences will be more to my detriment than to yours. Thank G— I will be able to keep Mr Askern's death away from the newspapers for the time being.'

Muffled shouts were heard at the front door and a voice asked for Mr Newsome. Heavy footsteps clattered towards the room where the two detectives sat, and there was a knock at the door.

'Enter,' said Mr Williamson.

The door opened to reveal Noah standing between two constables, his wrists bound in handcuffs. The faces of the three showed that a struggle of some magnitude had taken place. All were perspiring and the two policemen were bleeding freely from the lips and nose.

'Well, good afternoon to you, Mr Dyson,' said Mr Newsome.

'It took four of us to apprehend him,' said the constable to Noah's right. 'Jones is still unconscious.'

'Well done, Constable. You have apprehended an escaped convict.'

Noah stared at Mr Newsome with animal ferocity. Sergeant Williamson looked with incredulity between Noah and his superior.

'You are making a mistake, Inspector Newsome,' said Noah. 'I am your only means of apprehending Lucius Boyle.'

'Indeed you are, Mr Dyson. But I am fatigued trying to run around after you. I think it would be easier if you were kept in one place where both I and Mr Boyle can be sure that you reside. If he wants you, he will know where to come – and a gaol is exactly where I want him. I am placing you under arrest and returning you to the very same cell at Giltspur-street where we first met.'

'On what charges?'

'As I say, I have evidence that you are an escaped convict from New South Wales. Then there is the matter of Razor Bill and the fire in Oxford-street. Should these crimes prove insufficient, I believe I will think of something else.'

'—!'

'Ah, the convict vocabulary emerges! Constables – take him away.'

And as Noah was once again thrown into gaol, it is apt that we cast our eyes back once again to the story of his previous life, of his early transportation and the events that were to set the direction of his future.

After finally leaving Woolwich, the months at sea were an

education, albeit not the kind he would have experienced in books. In calm seas, the convicts would be allowed on deck to fully extend their legs and expose sickly skin to a sun of unprecedented ferocity. It was here, amid the scent of tar and hemp, that Noah first beheld the violent blue immensity of the sea. It was here that he saw sharks longer than a man, and distant behemoths breaching. For a city boy, it was what he had imagined Heaven to be: a limitless vault of sea and sky and light.

Sydney would be more wretched, though he was one of the lucky ones. While older men went directly into government service to break their backs building roads, he was assigned to a settler out at Parramatta. The benevolent gentleman in question was one Henry Matthews, himself an ex-convict from the first transportations, and a modest landowner who was kinder to his convicts than most.

Young Noah was put to work on the land, where the sun blistered his skin and the labour raised calluses on his hands. And not only his hands; he had accepted – there at the rim of the world – that he was truly abandoned as London continued without him, so far away as to be in a dream. It was only in his dreams that he walked its streets, pursuing Lucius Boyle into blind alleys where the enemy would disappear.

It was a book that saved him – at least for a period. Mr Matthews was quite illiterate and used the books in his possession for lighting fires. When Noah unfolded a page and began to read to himself, his master was astounded and bade Noah read aloud from the scrap. Thereafter, when his daily work was done, he would read to delight Mr Matthews. And, foreseeing a time when the reading matter would end, Noah began to elaborate upon the lines before him, lengthening and embellishing the stories so that one of 'his' pages lasted two normal pages. It pleased his master and it earned him a few extra pennies.

It continued like this for a year or so, the young boy turning into a young man. Mr Matthews, who was perhaps sixty, became less able to work and requested another convict. The man who arrived – John Carter – was a brutal sort: a thief and bully from London who immediately resented Noah. Nor was it coincidence that this man had arrived at this settlement.

Through machinations unknown, Lucius Boyle had managed to send out a message to Noah. Perhaps he had contacted a number of criminals bound for the Antipodes, or perhaps it was just John Carter. Perhaps money had exchanged hands as convicts were allocated. But within a few days, as the two convicts worked to saw down trees, the message was passed on:

'The General says you are never to return. London belongs to him now. Return and you will die.'

As one might imagine, Noah boiled with anger. Even here, beyond the seas, his enemy and betrayer mocked him. Thereafter his fortunes would decline rapidly, but there is no room here for the murder of Henry Matthews, the flight of Noah and his escape upon a Dutch East India vessel bound for China. That story, and the multitude that followed across the world's trade routes, is for another book.

TWENTY-THREE

Sergeant Williamson sat on the bed of the attic room at Mr Allan's house that next morning and looked again at the paper Noah had handed to him. It was nothing but a common advertising flyer of the type handed out in the street or pasted to the sides of buildings:

GRAND MASQUERADE AND CARNIVAL
AT VAUXHALL GARDENS

The promoters of this most popular choice of galas have, in response to an urgent and repeated demand, determined on a splendid masquerade and carnival to take place on Friday night next, October 18, the last night that the gardens will be opened, when the immense resources of the illustrious venue will be brought into requisition to render the carnival one of the most magnificent to have occurred in this city, combining all the splendour of a Neapolitan carnival with humour of an English masquerade. The Rotunda Theatre and Hogarth Picture Gallery will be converted into a grand pavilion for dancing. Ticket 5s.

In itself it meant nothing, but with the information Inspector Newsome had given him about the pursuit of Benjamin, it suggested obvious conclusions. Now, however, he felt his loyalties torn.

His initial desire – before Noah's surprise visit and the business with Mr Newsome – to solve the curious case of Mr Askern's death had been replaced with a sense of futility at the whole endeavour. Lucius Boyle had no doubt gained access to the house through some intervention of Inspector Newsome, no matter what the latter said about the letter being forged. Still, there may a clue that could entrap at least one of the possible perpetrators.

No personal belongings had been left behind by the murderer. The bed had not been slept in and there were no obvious physical clues. Much as he hated to admit it, the only hope of finding the man was Noah, now locked away at Giltspur-street gaol. Would Mr Newsome allow Henry Hawkins or Boyle himself into the cell late one night and end the case with a final corpse? And was there any truth in what Mr Newsome had said about Noah being an escaped convict? Despite his better judgement, Mr Williamson had begun to believe that Noah might be an innocent man after all.

'You look at a loss, sir,' offered PC Cullen, who was still under orders to guard Mr Williamson's life as if it were his own.

'I have much on my mind, Constable Cullen.'

'Aye, this Red Jaw or "General" is the scourge of London.'

'What do you know of him?'

'What I have read, and what people say. They say he has the power of not being seen, taught to him by a Chinese magician. He can influence men's thoughts with only the power of his mind. Nobody is safe from him; even if they were locked away in the depths of Newgate, he would find out his victim and vanish. I'm not saying I believe such things myself – it's just what is being said.'

'Hmm. *I* do not have magic on my side.'

'Is this latest murder the work of Red Jaw?'

'Very possibly, though I would thank you not to advertise the fact.'

'Of course, sir.'

'Hmm. Tell me, Constable – if you wanted to kill a man in the basement, how would you do so from this room without actually going downstairs and entering the room by the door or window? What do you think our myth-makers would make of that?'

'Why, if we are to accept what is said – which, as I say, I don't fully believe – Red Jaw might do it with his mind alone. Or he would assume a different shape and float like a vapour without making a peep of noise.'

'Well, that is quite ridic—'

Mr Williamson paused and made his way awkwardly to the dormer window, where he looked around the interior of the frame and then out over the city's fields of chimney pots. He opened the sash window and leaned out to peer upwards and backwards at the house's own vertiginous chimneys.

'Constable Cullen, I think you may have hit upon something there.'

'Really, sir?'

'The route between the basement and the attic may be the longest on foot – but the shortest by another, more direct, route.'

'I don't quite follow you, sir . . .'

'Come here. Do you see what I see, Constable? The soot about the chimney base there has been disturbed and there is a little freshly broken mortar here in the gutter. There are lines in the grime of the tiles where knees or feet have passed.'

'He went down the chimney, sir?'

'No – a boy could not slip down there. Even a cat would have trouble.'

'What are you saying, sir?'

'I believe a rope was thrown up to the apex of the roof, most likely with a corked hook on it, and a man clambered up the tiles to reach the pots. That would explain the contents of the canvas bag he carried. Constable, I would like you to follow in his footsteps.'

'Me, sir?'

'Yes. Mr Allan will procure us some rope and a grappling iron. I want you to climb up there and report to me anything you can find – anything at all out of the ordinary.'

And so the rope was obtained and Constable Cullen was able, with some difficulty, to eventually cast a line and ascend with trembling knees over the gritty tiles to the pre-eminent position.

Few have seen London from such a privileged viewpoint. Up there in the smoky aether, one is alone with the birds. Sounds swirl around one, echoing up from the deep gorges of the streets: a hawker shouting his wares, the rumble of a goods wagon (quite a different noise to the phaeton or hackney carriage), and the ceaseless murmur of a million souls at work. One might be atop the main spar of a brig, looking out across the empty ocean, for not a single human presence could be seen in that murky and smut-smeared sea of baked clay and slate.

It proved quite simple for Constable Cullen to locate among the six the one chimney pot belonging to the basement room that Mr Askern had slept in. The clay pot itself had been wrenched free and tied to an adjoining one with a length of weak hempen twine, no doubt so it would not roll away and alert residents. In time, the rope would rot and the broken chimney would roll down to shatter on the street below. He peered into the jagged hole, which vanished into sooty darkness after less than a yard. It was clear, however, that something had scratched away the accretions of carbonaceous matter either going down the chimney or coming up it.

PC Cullen, who regarded the detectives with awe and imagined his own career navigating in that direction, did not, however, possess their acuity. He theorized upon what could have caused the scratches. Some manner of animal, perhaps, that had been trained to deliver a lethal attack? A phial of noxious material dropped down to befuddle the unfortunate writer? There seemed nothing to report to Sergeant Williamson but the scratches.

Making to return to the window, he put his hand into a wad of matter on the tiles by the chimney base and cursed. The quantity, if not the texture, suggested a duck was responsible. He wiped it on his trouser leg with a grimace and began to lower himself back to safety. Once back in the room, retrieving the hook proved to be as simple as whipping the rope to dislodge its purchase on the apex. A little mortar ratted down after it and landed in the gutter.

'Scratches, you say?' said Mr Williamson. 'What kind of scratches? Long and unbroken? Multiple like a man's fingernails? Like an animal's claw?'

'No, sir. They were not regular at all. It looked like something had fallen and simply touched the sides on its way down – or up, I suppose. It was not possible to tell.'

'Something big? Were the scratches distributed all around the inside of the shaft?'

'No, sir. I would say that the object fitted quite easily within the diameter but brushed against it slightly on descending.'

'I think we can rule out any animal. I cannot think of any that would be able to find its way down and then back up in addition to killing Mr Askern without a sign.'

'I thought the same thing myself, sir.'

'Hmm. It cannot have been something dropped, for it would be in the fireplace to be found. Inspector Newsome looked there and found only ashes. In which case, the only logical conclusion is that something was lowered and then pulled back up. Did you say that the broken chimney was tied to its neighbour with a thin piece of rope?'

'Yes, sir. Too thin for the man to have gained access to the chimneys in the first place. Perhaps it was an off-cut from the other rope?'

'You have read my mind, PC Cullen.'

'Thank you, sir.'

'Let us go down to that room and look again at the fire-place.'

The body had of course been taken away and Mr Allan had evidently made some attempt to tidy the room. The door, splintered and now quite useless, stood beside the doorway. The constable shivered at the thought of a dead body having lain there just hours ago – killed most probably by Red Jaw himself.

'Yes. Do you see here, Constable Cullen? If you look around the edge of the grate you can see the darker soot of the inner chimney quite black against the grey of the other combusted materials. I would say that whatever caused those scratches occurred after this fire had burned itself out.'

'I see it. But—'

'Quite – what was the cause? There is nothing here now to indicate that any object living or dead was lowered down. Whatever it might have been, it no longer exists.'

'Perhaps some kind of noxious gas, sir?'

'What is that, Constable?'

'Well, sir. I was thinking that—'

'No – what is that stain on your trouser leg. It was not there when we arrived at the house. Was there something on the roof?'

'A bird, sir . . . I wiped my hand—'

'Show me your hand . . . the palm. Let me smell . . . Hmm. Do you know that smell, Constable?'

PC Cullen sniffed gingerly at his soiled palm.

'No? I am surprised you have not come across it before. That is opium, Constable. Opium mixed with something else that sailors are prone to smoke along with it: *hashish* – a highly soporific combination.'

'Sir?'

'Where did you find it?'

'Beside the chimney base, sir. On the tiles.'

'It seems unlikely that a passing bird dropped it there. I think we have our solution to this little mystery.'

'I don't follow . . .'

'Of course, we cannot be sure, but I would say that the events unfolded thus: the resident of the attic room – most likely your Red Jaw – waited until sometime just before dawn, when the fires had burned out, and clambered up to the roof. There, he wrenched off the chimney pot for easier access and lowered some kind of device down to this room. Perhaps it was a censer of the kind used in Catholic or Orthodox churches. Whatever it was, it was loaded with opium and possibly other narcotics, which, when lowered into this small room gave off a quantity of intoxicating smoke. Most likely he covered the chimney to seal the room completely.'

'But wouldn't the gentleman have woken up?'

'Perhaps under normal circumstances, but we have evidence enough to suggest otherwise (not least his death). The candle on the desk had burned out, which tells us Mr Askern was possibly too tired to extinguish it. Let us also remember that the effect of these narcotics is extreme relaxation. Some men have simply never woken after overindulging in such a combination. There is no sudden shock of waking to smell smoke. Indeed, if he had woken at all, it would have been to a warm stupor of sleepiness. Two or three hours breathing such smoke would have been quite enough. And, finally, let us recall that Mr Askern had a weak chest – a factor that the murderer most likely knew when he chose this ingenious plan.'

'Sir? You sound as if you admire the murderer.'

'The plan is quite perfect: to kill a man by smoke alone, leaving a corpse that not only shows no injury but in fact gives every impression of peace. Evidently the smoke had dissipated by the time Mr Allan broke down the door – and what if it had not? The deed had still been done and the criminal fled. A man who concocts such a plan is to be feared, even by the Detective Force.'

'Will you catch him, sir?'

'I do not know. Naturally we can make investigations

among the opium dens, and among the churches or ecclesiastical suppliers to see if a censer has been recently stolen or bought. The sources of such a thing are rare enough. But I fear it will do us little good.'

'Sir . . . have you lost heart? The men say that if anyone can catch this man, it is you.'

'No, that is no longer the case. I am beginning to think Mr Newsome – wherever his loyalties lie – was correct in at least one of his initial assumptions: a criminal like your Red Jaw will seldom be caught by a policeman such as me. He does not observe the rules – or rather, he knows the rules and how to break them in a way they would never be broken.'

'I am not sure I follow you, sir. What was that about Inspector Newsome?'

'The surgeon in the field hospital must often decide to let one man die so that he can direct his attentions to one who may live. Can one break a law in order to uphold a greater one – if the outcome is the greater good?'

'Sir?'

'There is another, PC Cullen, who can catch Red Jaw. He is the man who came to the house earlier and was dragged there again by the other constables. He is very likely a criminal . . . In fact, I have no idea at all who he truly is or what he may be . . . Constable – if I asked you to perform a duty that goes against your training and your duty as a policeman . . . if I asked you to break the law in the name of catching a murderer, would you follow my orders?'

'To catch Red Jaw, sir, and play my part in this case, I would walk into Hell itself and shackle the Devil if you ordered me to.'

'That will not be necessary. Although the task I have in

mind may be of comparable difficulty. The man I speak of is in Giltspur-street gaol. And he must be free by tomorrow evening.'

The reader will recall that the last we saw of Lucius Boyle was his appearance to the subject of his intended blackmail, a man who had been reached by a bloody path – a path which in turn had begot yet more blood.

It had indeed been Lucius Boyle who had spent a brief, sleepless night at Mr Allan's house, easily admitted with the letter written by his poor victim. And the murder had proceeded to exactly the pattern surmised by Mr Williamson. Much as he would have enjoyed staying at the house even longer – right under the nose of the Detective Force – he was not a man to take risks.

Now, twenty-four hours or so after the conflagration and the numerous events of the previous night, he was sitting beside a flaming iron stove on a coal barge just east of the Pool, near Bell Wharf. The vessel creaked rheumatically at its mooring, bearing no lights save the flickering illumination of the iron stove on Mr Boyle's uncovered face. It was there, among the aqueous forest of midnight masts and serried hulls, that he awaited a visit from Henry Hawkins.

As he waited there in the gloom, what thoughts occurred in that smouldering mind? Was he afraid of capture? Did he consider the possibility that Mr Hawkins had been captured and would arrive with the police? Was there a mob gathering on the sludgy banks at that very moment, having seen a man with a covered jaw board the barge? A man's mind is a curious thing; it can be as shallow and murky as a puddle, or as clear and unfathomable as the open ocean. We may

assume that Mr Boyle's was of the latter variety, its levia-
thans sounding where no light penetrates.

'General! Are you here, General?'

Henry Hawkins's nailed boots thudded on to the deck
and down the steps to the coal blackness.

'Why not shout to the whole of London, Mr Hawkins, to
let everyone know that I am here?'

'Sorry. I—'

'Where have you been all this time? I told you to report
back to me with news.'

'I've been very busy, sir. Here is a newspaper.'

'I have heard about the clergyman. Did he have anything
to say?'

'The police have questioned him twice. The first one was
Williamson, who asked Mr Archer whether he had a family.
He didn't ask about you. The second was this man Noah
Dyson, who assaulted the clergyman in Hyde Park and asked
him about you. Fortunately, the old gent had nothing to say
except he saw another man at the Lambeth house. He'll be
seeing nothing more now.'

'I see. What of the detective?'

'He offered me five hundred pounds for your location
and said I would not go to prison.'

'And?'

'I said no, of course.'

'Of course. Did he talk?'

'I beat him properly, but he will live. At the last, he was
whispering something that sounded like "square". He said
it over and over. Well, it could have been any square in
London. So I gave him some more boot and he started to
drift off—'

'Spare me the preamble, Mr Hawkins.'

'I asked him about Noah Dyson and he said something about Noah and "Manchester". Then he was gone. I could not revive him. Was he trying to tell me that Noah had gone to Manchester? But then I had it: Manchester-square! So I went directly there the next morning. Of course, I didn't know what I was looking for. I didn't see anything of that Dyson cove, but I did see a man who looked like the police. He was hanging around the square obviously waiting or looking for something. So I decided to watch him from the glove shop on the corner of Spanish-place. Do you know the one?'

'Are you a penny-a-liner to weave out the account? *To the matter of the story.*'

'Well, after some time, a black man comes out of a house in the square and this police gent starts to follow him. So I followed, too, and I followed the two of them all over London. The dusky fellow went into a costume shop at Leicester-square and came out shortly after. And would you believe where he went next? To that very house in Lambeth where the girl was killed! And the black man puts a piece of paper under the door before setting off right back to the house at Manchester-square.'

'Did you discover what was written on that paper?'

'I have it here in my pocket. Why do you look at me so? I thought you'd be pleased.'

'The fact that you brought it here means the recipient will not receive it, and, therefore, that its contents may now be nullified.'

'I had to kick the door down to get it.'

'The subtlety increases. Give it to me. Good. I trust you returned to the costume shop to discover if anything was purchased?'

'Yes. Two costumes – a Greek and a Moor – and two masques to be delivered to the address in Manchester-square. The gent in the shop said I was the second to ask about the black man's order.'

'Indeed? You will return to that address and watch that policeman and that house. It seems here is something that Detective Williamson tried to protect with what he thought was his dying breath. It may be Noah Dyson. It would be ideal if you could waylay the delivery of those costumes if they have not already been delivered. You could become the deliverer yourself if you are clever about it. You know what to do if you find Noah. That will conclude our business. If you do not find him, try to discover why the police are watching that house. Can I trust you to do these things, Henry?'

'Yes, General. You can trust me. Are we to leave London after? People are looking at me. People know my face from the fights.'

'Perhaps. Now, where is that piece of paper I gave you concerning last night's duties? I trust you have burned it?'

'Yes.'

Lucius Boyle looked at Mr Hawkins with precisely that look which had sustained his reign of intimidation for so long: a blank, unblinking expression in which those smoky eyes became embers. No matter that the recipient of that stare was a bigger man, or a force of ten men – being its focus was often a prelude to fatality.

'Are you lying to me, Henry?'

'I . . . I lost it. No doubt it has already been carried to a dust heap or to the riv—'

'Your name is on that piece of paper, as are the crimes

you committed in my name. And you are quite correct in what you said: people *do* know your face.'

'I know that.'

'If that piece of paper is found, and if you are captured, you will certainly hang.'

'They will ask me about your whereabouts.'

Silence.

The tainted skin of Lucius's jaw seemed alive in the light from the stove, seething incarnadine as if bubbling up from his neck.

'What are you saying, Mr Hawkins?'

'Nothing. I would never tell. You know it. We have been together for so long. I would rather die than betray you. You know it.'

'Yes. I know it, Henry.'

'You believe me, don't you? I didn't mean anything—'

'I am sure of your sincerity. Now, go to Manchester-square. And try to be discreet when you leave this place.'

'What will you do?'

'I will follow my own route towards Noah Dyson. You know where and when to find me again if you discover any-thing.'

Mr Hawkins left. Lucius Boyle opened the folded piece of paper retrieved from the Lambeth house and read its con-tents. It was difficult to discern from his expression whether the contents pleased or displeased him, for there was no change in his countenance. Rather, he opened the door on the stove and touched the paper to the eager flames, holding on until the dancing yellow-blue edge touched his fingertips and the spent fragments fluttered to the ground.

He was not so dull-witted as to be unsuspicious of the

letter and its means of delivery. The entire episode was distinctly dubious. True, the intended recipient may not have received the letter, but the information therein was nevertheless useful for his own purposes – and the Negro had no way of knowing whether the letter had reached its destination.

The newspaper carried the now familiar sketch of the man the police were seeking for the murders of Mr Coggins and Mary Chatterton (the murders of Razor Bill and Josiah Archer would not appear until the next day). Were Lucius to venture into any of the riverside bars at that moment, he would have been ripped limb from limb. Already, men had been attacked merely for covering their faces for whatever innocent reason. A coal delivery man had been beaten half to death in the early hours as he protected his face from the coal dust. All of London was looking for Lucius Boyle – and seeing him everywhere.

Something dramatic would have to be done to change the state of play – and on the very next day. There, cradled in the glassy blackness of the Thames and surrounded by the brittle perfume of the coal, he made a decision. Someone would have to be forgotten, someone would have to be faced – and someone would have to die.

TWENTY-FOUR

'How else are you to apprehend Boyle without my help?' said Noah, back in his Giltspur-street cell. 'He does not play by your rules. You have seen what he did to your finest detective.'

'I see that a poor night's rest has done little to soothe your mood,' replied Inspector Newsome. 'So tell me – what successes have you achieved since you left this cell? Perhaps you recognize no rules, but you have twice been within touching distance of the man and let him go free. Am I to put my trust in you? The only thing I can be sure of is that he wants you. If he comes for you, I will have him.'

'And if he does not? What then, Inspector? Will I rot in this cell? Do you not remember that I have a letter from your own commissioner absolving me of any guilt?'

'That letter absolves you of house-breaking and the aggravated theft of a police uniform. Fleeing Her Majesty's penal colony is not mentioned. It is an entirely different charge – one that I think you will not be able to escape. You may well find yourself on your way back to Botany Bay.'

'What if Boyle *does* discover me here? Is he to kill me? It would not be difficult to gain access to me through the window here.'

'I am hoping that he will think so. I will be stationing a man outside to look out for Mr Boyle or his associates.'

'Your plan is weak, Mr Newsome. Of the two things Boyle could wish for me, you grant him at least one: my imprisonment. What is to stop him simply forgetting me? I am no threat to him in irons. Or are you to contrive an execution for me and capture him there with as much success as the last such episode?'

'I am willing to hear your suggestions, Noah.'

'You will have no doubt heard from your man – the one who was following me like a forlorn goat with a bell about its neck – that I "disappeared" yesterday. You will also know that Benjamin led your man about the city on a curiously circuitous route. Have you yet worked out the truth behind those facts, Detective Inspector?'

'I know about the costumes. I know about the note at the Lambeth address.'

'Oh, you do? Do you know where it is now?'

'It will be in my hands shortly.'

'No – it is already in Lucius Boyle's hand. Henry Hawkins delivered it there, as I intended. He was following your man and I was following them both. It was my intention that Boyle be given a trail to follow. Only I know that trail and where it leads.'

'And if I let you free, you will take me to Boyle, yes? You must think me very gullible. I have believed too much of what you have told me and found myself in a worse position than ever as a result. You will remain here and the situation will, I hope, not become any worse.'

'I tell you: Lucius Boyle is going to be in a particular

place at a particular time. So will Henry Hawkins. Only I know these things.'

'Do you take me for a fool? The costumes you ordered indicate a masque ball. There is to be one tonight at Vauxhall Gardens. You have admitted that Boyle is expecting a Greek and a Moor – you and Benjamin – to be there. And I will be there to apprehend him. It is a perfect opportunity for him to venture out of hiding. On that piece of inventiveness, I congratulate you.'

'And, of course, there will be *only* two men so dressed. Have you ever been to such a ball, Inspector? The Greek, the Turk and the Scotsman are the most popular costumes every time. There will be dozens so attired. And how are you to find him in a crowd of disguised people? Will you unmask everyone there? You must know that there will be many men there who wish to remain anonymous as they consort with women not their wives. The letter slipped under the door at Lambeth is the key to where Boyle will be, when, and why. Only I and Boyle know of its contents. What of that?'

'I could make you tell me.'

'Inspector – you have seen my scars. I have not lived a life like yours. I have seen and experienced things that you cannot imagine. I have been strapped to the triangle and flogged until my shoes filled with blood and strips of my back flicked wetly at my face. I made no sound. Few could break my spirit.'

'And it seems Lucius Boyle is one of them. You are as much a prisoner of his as you are mine, Noah. Can you not see that? He has already won the battle between you by dominating your every thought. Even if you were to kill him, he will always be with you.'

'I will find him.'

'No, you will remain here until I decide otherwise. I will leave you to think about that, Noah. If you feel at any time that you would like to reveal more information to me, call the turnkey and he will notify me. I will be attending the *bal masqué* to see whether Mr Boyle has been tricked by you. We might discuss that tomorrow.'

The door banged shut and the key rattled in its lock.

Noah fought a surge of anger and frustration. It would not help him to break the irons binding his ankles, nor to bend the bars at the window. To be incarcerated there by a man like Inspector Newsome was an insult indeed. To have his actions curtailed by the police had become an intolerable imposition, especially now as bait to the predator.

He had had more experience of incarceration than most men. The leaden weight of time; the eroding silence of solitude; the humiliation of beatings; the cold; the damp; the massy closeness of stone all around – he had promised himself never again to endure such things. When this was over – if he was still alive at that time – he would take measures to see that his freedom was unassailable.

Before then, there was the more pressing matter of Lucius Boyle. If Sergeant Williamson's suspicions about Mr Newsome were correct, there was every reason to believe that Henry Hawkins or some other weapon would be arriving shortly. What game was the inspector playing now? Was he working in concert with his blackmailer, or against him? Shuffling to the window with his chains scraping, Noah was able to see the top hat of Mr Bryant standing sentinel there lest the prisoner try to attract the attention of a passer-by. He coughed and the policeman turned around.

'It should be easier to keep me in your sight now,' said Noah.

'I should say so. Are your irons comfortable?'

'Sufficiently. A pity you didn't manage to acquire the letter from the Lambeth House. You helped me greatly with that piece of ineptitude.'

'How did you—?'

'Never mind that. Worry more about what is to happen at half-past seven this evening.'

Mr Bryant made to answer, but then paused and turned back to the street. Noah waited to see whether the man would check his pocket watch, and was rewarded some minutes later when, unable to resist, the policeman looked surreptitiously inside his coat as if buttoning it.

Nothing was due to happen at half-past seven – at least not as far as Mr Bryant was concerned. That was the time the ball would begin, but it might prove useful to have his overseer thinking about some unspecified threat for the rest of the day while Noah thought of some way to get a message to either Benjamin or Mr Williamson (if the latter was inclined to trust him any longer).

He was lying on his rough horsehair mattress and considering his options when Mr Bryant evidently encountered someone on the street outside the window:

'Good afternoon, Mr Bryant.'

'Do I know you, sir? You have the bearing of a policeman.'

'I *am* a brother officer – from L division. Is it true that they have Red Jaw locked up here?'

'What is your name?'

'I have heard a rumour that Red Jaw is caught by Inspector Newsome and has been locked in this very cell. Is it true? I will not tell a soul if it is true.'

'Move along, Constable. I am working. I cannot tell you anything.'

'May I have a quick look?'

'Move along I tell you, or there will be trouble.'

'Your words are truer than you know.'

The sound of a carriage stopping just outside caused Noah to venture once more to the bars. There, he beheld a police carriage with the door open but nobody inside. As Mr Bryant readied himself for some imagined rescue attempt, a truncheon caught him not too softly at the tip of the jaw and he dropped unconscious to the ground, whereupon Constable Cullen – for it was he – lifted him with ease and carried him to the open carriage. The door was slammed shut and the carriage set off, leaving Mr Cullen to place Mr Bryant's too-small top hat on his own head for all the world as if he had just relieved the other officer rather than assaulted him. He spoke *sotto voce* without turning fully around to the bars:

'Sergeant Williamson sends his regards. Do not speak to me in case the turnkey is listening. In a moment, your manservant Benjamin will come with a package and instructions for you. There will be a pencil and paper if you want to write to the sergeant. In the meantime, do not fear. Everything has been planned. Mr Williamson says I am to tell you that you will be attending the *bal masqué* this evening, just as you planned.'

Noah returned to the mattress, his mind awhirl. Could it be true that Sergeant Williamson – upright, rule-abiding and criminal-loathing Mr Williamson – was about to abet an escape from one of Her Majesty's gaols? And that he had inveigled PC Cullen into the scheme? His fingertips itched with anticipation and he wondered at how the escape would be accomplished.

The street-facing wall of the gaol was of Portland stone and the bars were quite solid, so no possibility of escape presented itself there. Likewise, the door was of oaken planks, banded with iron and locked from the outside. An eyehole covered with an iron slide could be used at any time to observe the prisoner inside, and there was a similar space at the bottom, wide enough to slide a plate of food through.

It would also be quite senseless to be given any kind of weapon, for although it might be possible to shoot or stab the turnkey through the eyehole, he would still be locked inside the room. Perhaps Benjamin would bring enough money to tempt the warders into the cell for a moment, but Noah knew from experience that even warders are not that foolish. They would just confiscate the money and leave him worse off than before. Whatever the detective had in mind, it would have to be something very good.

A cough from outside brought him again to the window. PC Cullen was still standing there, and Benjamin was crossing the road towards him with a package under his arm. On seeing Noah at the bars, he smiled but did not wave or make any obvious gestures. Instead, he continued to walk and handed a paper-wrapped package to PC Cullen without breaking his stride. In moments, he had gone. Although there were people in the street, the transaction had occurred just as a carriage had passed before the window and it seemed that no one had seen. The constable tucked the package under his arm and looked around to make sure.

Then, when he was certain that there were no observers, he made a quick backwards glance and tossed the package through the bars on to the floor of the cell. Noah retrieved it rapidly and returned to the mattress, checking that none of this had been seen through the eyehole.

He opened the package carefully, trying not to rustle the paper (and cursing this oversight on the part of Mr Williamson). Inside it, neatly folded, was a pair of his own dark-blue trousers from home, a shirt and a police tunic complete with the insignia of Lambeth division. A tiny knife with a blade of no more than one inch was secreted inside one trouser pocket, and a blank sheet of paper with a pencil occupied the other. A roughly circular muslin bag completed the package. There was no saw to cut his chain. Perplexity and anger overtook him. What kind of ridiculous charade was this? Dress as a policeman and persuade the guard that they had locked up the wrong man? Squeeze through the bars and take PC Cullen's place?

He snatched a letter from the folds of the clothing and read Sergeant Williamson's regular hand. As he did so, a key wrapped in its folds fell to the stone floor. A smile appeared on his face and, as he read the letter, he had to fight the urge to laugh. The plan was sheer genius! It had potential for failure, true, but in conception it was a work of a great mind. If Mr Williamson's life had had a similar beginning and followed a similar route to Noah's, he might have been a criminal to rival Lucius Boyle. Only one thing was missing . . .

And it came through the bars at that very moment: about three yards of rope and a further three yards of thin twine, all within a canvas bag. He coiled it all swiftly and put it under the mattress along with the clothes. Now would come the most difficult part of the plan: waiting.

Henry Hawkins was also waiting. Earlier that morning, he had ventured into Mr Nathan's Masquerade Warehouse, pretending to be one of Noah's household, and asked if the costumes had yet been delivered. On hearing that they had not, he offered to take them himself but could not provide satisfactory evidence that he was of that household.

So now he was waiting within sight of the house in Manchester-square for the delivery to arrive. The policeman watching the house had gone, but this made Mr Hawkins more comfortable about waiting in front of various shops. By and by, a young man with a large parcel descended from a hackney carriage and made to approach the door. In a moment, Mr Hawkins was at the young man's side.

'Let me help you with that heavy package, lad. Are you going to the address here? It is the house of my master. These will be the costumes he is expecting.'

'Please let go, sir. I am to deliver these myself.'

'Worried about your pennies, are you? Here, take this half-sovereign and be gone. I will take the package.'

'Please, sir! Let me alone.'

'I have told you, he is my master. *Do you understand me?*'

With these final words, Mr Hawkins jabbed the blade of a considerable dagger against the ribs of the poor man with the package.

'O! You will murder me!'

'No, you idiot. I will take this package and you will take the money and run back to your employer. If you go for a constable, I will come to your place of work and kill you. Now – hand me those costumes like a good boy.'

And so it was that Henry Hawkins stood on the doorstep knocking at the large brass knocker as if he were the delivery lad from Mr Nathan's.

The door opened to reveal the same Negro man he had

followed the day before, only he seemed much taller and sturdier close to. The black man's eyes bore into his own as if he knew him. And a long-forgotten sensation from the prize-ring flashed into his mind, one that he had not experienced since he had first stepped on to the blood-spattered floor amid the yelling crowd: the knowledge that he had met his match.

'I have this delivery from Mr Nath—'

He did not speak further because he had just seen Sergeant Williamson appear below and behind the formidable shoulder of the Negro. The detective's face was a mass of cuts and multi-hued bruising from the beating Mr Hawkins had administered two nights previously. But in the time it took for him to register this, a large black hand had grasped him by the jacket and jerked him into the house, whereupon a black fist exploded in his face with a force that rocked him back on his heels and knocked him clear unconscious – an impact coinciding exactly with the door slamming behind him.

When he awoke on the parlour floor, it was to discover his hands and feet bound, and the two men looking down at him.

'Well, Mr Hawkins. Our roles are now reversed,' said Mr Williamson.

'I will not say a word to you, Detective.'

'You need not speak at all. Neither are you in a position to bargain. We have enough evidence against you to see you hang: your attack upon me, your murder of Reverend Archer, abetting Lucius Boyle in his various crimes . . . Yes, you will certainly hang.'

At this realization, Mr Hawkins began to struggle against

his bindings. But Benjamin stepped forward and kicked him hard under the ribs so that the air rushed out of his body.

'It is a waste of energy to struggle so,' said the detective. 'If you persist, I will have to ask Benjamin here to render you inert once more.'

'What . . . what about that five hundred pounds you promised me?' asked Mr Hawkins.

'Ah, *now* you want to bargain! It is too late for that.'

'I will tell you where he is. It is a coal barge—'

'How quickly the loyalties change. All I need to know from you is whether you have arranged to meet him again and what information he is expecting to receive.'

'Ha! You will hang me anyway.'

'I am not a murderer like you. I do not agree with execution. If what you tell us proves to be true, I could have your sentence commuted to fourteen years' transportation.'

'You wouldn't. You are lying.'

'It is entirely your choice, although it seems to me that there is very little choice in the matter: certain death, or the possibility of transportation. I must ask you for an instant decision.'

'He will kill me.'

'And so will the judge's sentence. Choose your murderer.'

'You are a heartless —.'

'No, I am a detective in pursuit of a criminal who should not be allowed to survive in this city any longer. Now, what is your choice? Should I ask Benjamin to help you with your considerations?'

Mr Hawkins looked at Benjamin, who stood over him with expressionless malice. Whatever the Negro had experienced in his life, wherever he had acquired those scars, the death of another violent white man clearly held no distress for him. He had long ago passed any threshold of pity for those who would threaten him or those he protected.

'Mr Hawkins? I cannot wait all afternoon.'

'All right, d— you! I am to meet him and tell him what I found at this house.'

'Where and when?'

'There is a marine store—'

'Off Rosemary-lane? I know about it. He has been there before. What time?'

'At dusk. He will not be seen during the daylight. Don't expect me to take you there . . .'

'You will do exactly as I bid you. Tell me, who is the gentleman that Mr Boyle has been blackmailing? We know that he is a policeman of some significance . . .'

'I know nothing about that. He tells me nothing but what I am to do.'

'Yes. You are his tool. Just a dumb animal to do his bidding.'

'I am no dumb animal. My name is known across the city as a fighter.'

'And now as a murderer. Soon they will whisper your name in the silent seconds before the trap falls and the rope tautens.'

Mr Hawkins looked at the swirling scars about Benjamin's neck and knew, finally, that his fate lay upon the gallows.

Noah sat on his mattress in that same idol posture that Inspector Newsome and Superintendent Wilberforce had seen before. It had grown dark outside and the illumination from the gas lamps cast bars of shadow over his body. He was calm and ready. At six o'clock the turnkey would look through the eyehole and slip that evening's meal under the door. Noah had thirty minutes to prepare.

As quietly as he could, he used the key to unlock his ankle irons. Then he changed into the clothes brought to him by PC Cullen and used the small knife to make a slit down the entire side of the mattress. The corridor outside the cell was quiet as he began to tie the hems of the discarded trousers closed with the twine, followed by the cuffs of the shirt he had taken off.

Casting a wary eye at the eyehole, he began to scoop the musty horsehair from the mattress and stuff wads of it into the legs of the trousers and the arms of the shirt until the empty clothes began to take on a corporeal form. When the 'legs' and 'torso' were sufficiently filled and shaped, he attached the two at the 'waist' with more twine. The circular muslin bag was the head: an unsatisfactory substitute, but hopefully effective when stuffed and used in concert with the rest of the plan.

When the parts had been combined, he looked critically at the effigy of himself with disappointment. It didn't look like it would fool a child. Nevertheless, he fashioned a noose from the rope and put it around the 'neck' of the horsehair Noah. He tied the whole to the bars at the top of the arched window so that, from the eyehole, the turnkey would see the clear silhouette of a hanging man when he peered through. As a final touch, Noah attached the remaining twine to the ankles of the effigy. If he jerked on the twine from his position beside the door, its legs would twitch as if in the final throes of asphyxiation.

But would it work? From where he sat, it looked a pretty poor spectacle. However, it would make a sudden impression through the aperture in the door. Who would question the sight of a prisoner hanging in the window with his legs twitching? Who would pause to ask where the rope had come from? And if Inspector Newsome had made it explicit to all concerned that the prisoner in that solitary cell was important, wouldn't they be more inclined to pay more attention? The effectiveness of the plan would depend on these assumptions.

What was the time? Noah crouched beside the door with the twine in his hands. Perhaps Mr Newsome had instructed the warders not to feed him. Perhaps they would come later, after the masque ball had already started. Perhaps Mr Bryant had escaped and was at that moment reporting to an apoplectic Mr Newsome. Perhaps a passer-by would see the figure in the window and raise the alarm prematurely. Noah flexed his fingers.

Voices. Noah heard the rattle of keys in locks and the ceramic scrape of plates going under doors down the corridor. He tautened the twine. The adjoining door rattled. He heard boots scratching outside and the iron eyehole cover slid back. He began to twitch the twine and the figure in the window jerked spasmodically as if expending the final dregs of life.

Silence.

It hadn't worked.

Noah kept jerking the twine. How many seconds had passed? One? Two? A carriage was arriving outside. Mr Williamson – or Mr Newsome?

Then a tremendous shout:

'*He's gone and hanged himself!* Merrill! Come quick! He's still alive! Smith – go and fetch the inspector!'

The key clattered into the lock and the door swung open. The turnkey rushed to grasp the horsehair figure, realizing, perhaps, only when he was halfway to it that it was not a real man. By that time, he had heard a rattle of chains behind him and the door slamming, its lock clicking with the key he had carelessly left outside. He cried out:

'*Escape! Escape!*'

Noah raced down the corridor, the chains swinging in his hand like a life preserver. Mr Merrill, the burly turn-key, paused in surprise at the seeming 'policeman' rushing towards him. It was all the time Noah needed to strike the man in the throat with the chains so that he collapsed to the ground. A further guard, having seen this and heard the cries, went to grab the truncheon at his hip. Noah simply continued running and used his momentum to strike the man's face with his head. There was a crunch of cartilage and the second man fell, clutching a bloodied nose.

Noah dropped the chains, turned right and pulled open the street door. PC Cullen was waiting there and ran with him to the waiting carriage's open door. They boarded, slammed the door and the horses were off with a crack of the whip and sparking hooves.

Sergeant Williamson sat in the carriage and regarded the two new arrivals with a smile. 'Shall we go to the ball, gentlemen? I have our costumes and masques here.'

TWENTY-FIVE

As the carriage headed south, rocking the three men from side to side, they reflected on the manner of the escape.

'I congratulate you on your criminal mind, Mr Williamson,' said Noah. 'And I thank you for aiding my escape.'

'I thought that having you out of gaol would serve justice better than Mr Newsome using you as bait to catch Mr Boyle.'

'Quite right. Where is Benjamin?'

'He is waiting at your home on the chance that Mr Boyle goes there. I presume he is quite able to deal with the murderer?'

'Quite able. And it is likely people will be wasting energy looking for Ben at Vauxhall. Have you learned anything more about the inspector's role in this?'

'Perhaps, but first I think there is some information that you have for me. I have signalled my good faith and risked my position on the understanding that you have the means to apprehend Lucius Boyle.'

'I believe I have. He knows that I will be at the *bal masqué* tonight – or at least he will have surmised this. If he knew of my arrest, he will soon also hear of my escape.'

'How do you know that Mr Boyle knows you will be at Vauxhall?'

'The letter I had Benjamin deliver. It was addressed to Mr Hardy, the diminutive gentleman who seems to have replaced the late Mr Coggins as leader of that curious *troupe*. In it, I made clear that I was going to visit him at Vauxhall Gardens tonight in order to discuss Lucius Boyle further.'

'But Mr Boyle must already know that Mr Hardy is no longer resident at the house – and that the tiny gentleman has not received the note.'

'Quite, but he does not know that I know that. As far as he is concerned, I will be there tonight. It is the last night of the season at Vauxhall and the human curiosities will make one final appearance. It is perhaps Boyle's final chance to find me – and them, if he wishes them harm. And what could be a greater opportunity for him than an occasion where disguises are *de rigueur*.'

'Still, you have no guarantee he will be there. He may perceive that it is a trap.'

'No, no guarantee. And, yes, he will be aware that it may be a trap. But he was not deterred from attending the execution of Mr Bradford, was he? He is bold. Fear of discovery has made him so.'

'Hmm. I still fail to see how this is a plan. He may be there, but so will thousands of others. How will we know him from his costume?'

'We know that he is interested in Mr Hardy and friends, and in finding me. Thus, he is most likely to be found near that show. Also, I believe I will be able to discern his gait and presence, if not his costume. I do, however, have one concern: the possibility that he will send his lackey Hawkins in his stead.'

'I do not think so. Mr Henry Hawkins is imprisoned at this very moment.'

'Yes? Tell me what happened.'

'It seems your plan worked. When the delivery of costumes arrived, the fool tried to pass himself off as the costumier's boy. Benjamin dealt him a rousing blow and we questioned him. He told us about the same marine store you once searched for him at—'

'But he wasn't there.'

'No. I went there before coming to Giltspur-street but found the premises quite empty. I have left a man there. Either Mr Hawkins was lying, or Mr Boyle has decided there is now no one he can trust. Mr Hawkins will hang.'

'So it seems even more likely that Boyle will be there tonight. He has nothing to lose and perhaps something to gain. If he cannot kill me there, I am sure he will flee London. He can no longer stay in the city.'

'There is also, of course, the question of Inspector Newsome. Now you have escaped, he will also be heading to Vauxhall. I am afraid that if you cannot capture Mr Boyle, you, too, will have to leave the city – or face being transported. Again . . .'

'Yes, it is true, Mr Williamson. Do you regret allying yourself with me now that you know for certain that I am – or was – a criminal?'

'I always thought you were a criminal. But the foregoing weeks have made clear to me that criminality is not the unequivocal beast I thought it.'

'I was sentenced to fourteen years' transportation. I was betrayed by Lucius Boyle. We were partners – almost brothers. I was just a boy. But I was a boy from the streets of London, a boy with a library within his head. The period between that time and this has been one that you could not imagine, Mr Williamson, and one that you would not believe even if I had time to tell you. I have seen Heaven and Hell, and I carry them with me always.'

'And what of the cracksman's tools you were arrested with? Are you really a thief?'

'The tools were mine, it is true. But I do not steal valuables. My search has always been for information, for Lucius Boyle. If I break a safe, it is for the documents inside it – not the gold.'

The two men looked at each other across a gulf of experience, Lucius Boyle the bridge across that chasm of time and understanding.

As witness to the conversation, PC Cullen held his own thoughts. He strained to remember every historic word, every nugget of information, that he might recount them to hushed bar audiences for decades to come. And he would.

'So much for my fate, Mr Williamson,' said Noah, 'what of yours? If Inspector Newsome is indeed what we think he is, how are you to continue in your role?'

'Simple – I must prove his guilt and bring him to justice, ideally before he can capture you. Perhaps tonight will bring us both men working in collusion.'

'So. Our plan of action must be thus: we will change into our costumes when we arrive at Vauxhall. We will separate and look out for both Boyle and Inspector Newsome. There are only four of us among thousands, but we can be reasonably sure that our targets will be mobile. They will not be at supper or dancing; they will be walking around as we are. When a man is searching for something, his gait and demeanour cannot be hidden by a costume. Whoever finds their man will stay with him like a shadow and not permit him to leave the gardens without being waylaid. If our targets pose a threat to our scheme, we will incapacitate them. I will go directly to Mr Hardy and await Boyle.'

'It seems an impossible task, Noah.'

'I think not. The inspector is unlikely to be in costume. He has not had time to prepare, and he will be there as a policeman. Boyle is looking for me and knows where I will be. The greatest risk is his seeing us before we see him. That could be fatal. Only PC Cullen here is unknown to him. That may be to our advantage.'

At this, the constable's face flushed and he unconsciously swelled his chest. 'I will do all in my power, sirs.'

'I'm sure you will,' said Mr Williamson. 'I have all faith in you.'

Silence settled again as the three considered what lay before them. PC Cullen felt for his truncheon at his hip. The inspector looked twice at his pocket watch in the space of three minutes, while Noah closed his eyes and breathed deep regular breaths, his palms resting in his lap.

'There is another possibility,' said Noah, opening his eyes after some minutes. 'Boyle may attend the ball to kill Mr Newsome. If he has heard of my arrest (a likely assumption), he may reason that the inspector will be there. In cutting that link, he could rid himself of the whole sorry business. His blackmail plot has proved more complicated than he expected and it is time to stand away from the game. There will be other opportunities for him.'

'That would be neither a satisfactory solution nor a just one,' said Mr Williamson. 'Though I admit it would be fortuitous to have Mr Boyle thus engaged as we search for him.

As for Mr Boyle, what manner of costume do you think will be his choice?'

'Presumably the same kind I chose: something that is common enough to be unremarkable; something neither too accomplished nor too lacking in effort. In other words, something very like the common reveller.'

'That is suitably vague.'

'Indeed, Detective. It is exactly that.'

The carriage came to a halt and the driver rapped on its roof. They had arrived at Vauxhall Gardens.

And what a spectacle presented itself in the streets. Innumerable carriages were disgorging ladies and gentlemen intent on merrymaking, while still others arrived on foot. The air was animated with laughter and conversation, and massed revellers presented a gaudy display in their costumes. There were the usual Greeks, Highlanders, Turks and clowns, as well as *postillons*, huntsmen, Leperellos and countless other curious incarnations identifiable neither by clime nor age. Some wore masques over their faces, while others wore 'masques' of intoxication and frivolity. Like streams flowing inexorably to the ocean, they poured through the gates of the Gardens, paying their five shillings and being welcomed by jovial masters of the ceremonies resplendent in court costume.

It was, in short, a faithful imitation of a Neapolitan ball of the sort never seen but known from anecdote. True, the weather was cooler, and the aristocracy had deigned not to attend (Vauxhall having long been considered *passé*). Many of the bonneted young ladies were there 'professionally', and many of the married gentlemen's masques were as much to conceal identity as to embrace the spirit of the evening.

Though the entrance fee had deterred the lowest beggars and bullies, there were nevertheless countless tricksters, prigs, fakers and cutpurses commingled among those costumed carousers.

Who is that gentleman in the garb something like an Old Testament prophet? Is he a barrister making merry, or a counterfeiter come to spend his base metals? Who, that elegant lady with her swishing black silks and alabaster masque reminiscent of the Venetian? Is she the wife of the famous architect, or his kept woman brought hither in her own carriage from her Park-lane apartment (paid for with his annuity)? Who is yonder Greek in his flowing white robes and laurel wreath? Who is that manic Scotsman in his red peruke and tartan kilt? And who is that gentleman dressed in the very cerements of the grave, dusty and torn as if recently disinterred from the sarcophagus or mausoleum? His costume is particularly effective in the pale light of the full moon. No doubt he is some dark-humoured medical student.

Music drifts from multiple locations – from the Rotunda where dancing feet thunder hollowly on a floor etched by a professional *artiste* with chalk arabesques; from the orchestra performing in the gazebo at the Grove, and from fiddlers and drummers in Moorish costumes wandering the arboreal pathways of the Gardens.

And yet amid the hordes of duplicitous bacchanals, those imprudent imbibers of champagne, punch and sherry cobbler, there are some whose demeanour is sober and whose costume is purely professional – the police. Particularly those half-dozen surrounding a gesticulating and red-faced Inspector Newsome.

'Men – you are to stop any and every tall and burly

Negro you may find. He is likely to be dressed as a Moor or a Greek. Look at his eyes if his face is covered and you will see a filmy left eye. At his neck is a gallows scar. Do *not* apprehend him, but follow him. You are looking for his colleague, a man with grey eyes who is also dressed as a Greek or a Turk. If you find *him*, arrest him. He is violent and will fight, so take care. PC Nelson – you are to wait here at the entrance and scour those entering and leaving. Now, all of you, go!'

The policemen set off in different directions to parade the colonnades and supper rooms, the dance-floors and the audiences in search of that burly Negro. As for the inspector himself, he had somewhere else to look and someone else to find. He proceeded towards the firework ground.

PC Cullen, now wearing his regular uniform, had observed and overheard Inspector Newsome's whole exchange with the other constables. He looked around him and, seeing that his dark-blue attire might as well be a shadow or a painted effigy in such ostentatious company, he followed the inspector.

Mr Newsome did not stop to observe the Calcutta juggler or to marvel at the native dances of the chamois-clad Ojibbeway Indians encamped there among the trees. He stalked onwards, his brow perspiring despite the coolness of the evening, scanning the faces and bodies around him for a Greek or a Moor. When he saw one – and there were many – he would approach them and brusquely ask them to remove their masque before moving relentlessly on without pausing to explain his purpose to the perplexed revellers in his wake.

PC Cullen was close behind, easily observing Mr Newsome's ragged progress through the crowds. At the same time, he looked out for his colleagues, none of whom, it seems unnecessary to say, were dressed as either Greeks or Moors. And as he walked, the constable was joined by a portly 'judge' in flowing black robes and ornate grey peri-wig, his nose and cheeks reddened to suggest an over-indulgence in port.

'Have you seen any of them, Constable?' muttered the judicial Mr Williamson.

'Yes, sir. Ten yards ahead is the inspector.'

'Ah, yes, I see him.'

'He has told his men to look for a Greek and a Moor. He described Benjamin and Mr Dyson.'

'Good work. Keep following him. Prevent him in his duty if you can. If you see any of his constables, tell them you have seen Benjamin at the entrance. Keep them looking awry.'

'Yes, sir—'

But the 'judge' had taken a different path and was heading for the Grove, where an audience was gathered around the gazebo for a vocal performance supported by a small orchestra. The gathered people had hushed momentarily in anticipation of the first notes, and all eyes were bent upon the singer, an attractive lady with curled blonde hair spilling from her bonnet.

Mr Williamson did not look at the lady, however. He cast his eyes across the people for one that was out of rhythm, one that was not behaving in a like manner, one that (like himself) had an alternative purpose. He was looking for a man in a costume much like everyone around him, most probably with a full-face masque – an almost futile task in that environment.

There were couples; there were groups; there was the occasional unaccompanied person – but all were occupied with the pleasures around them. With a drink or a ham sandwich in hand, they observed the musicians or the various shows. They moved leisurely directionless and observed what went on around them without excessive concern or agitation. In short, they were having fun.

All except for one man, a man moving purposefully away from the crowd and heading towards the firework ground – a man whose gait and build seemed familiar, and who seemed quite uninterested in all that was happening around him.

Mr Williamson pushed his way through the people and tried to keep sight of the other man. Though the tree-lined walkways were brilliantly lit, the shadows between them were dark enough, and those recesses not yet occupied by illicit lovemaking could harbour the man at any moment.

As for the object of Mr Williamson's pursuit, his costume was that of the Greek or Roman orator: sweeping folds of white drapery and the obligatory laurel at his temples. Over his face was a tragedian's masque fashioned from brass and frozen into a perpetual grimace of agony. It was polished to such a degree that any interlocutor would simply gaze back at his own distorted reflection. Only the eyes were visible.

As Mr Williamson followed, the man walked without pause in his chosen direction. He did not look at the other carnival-goers, even those dressed as Moors and Greeks. Whatever he was looking for, he seemed to know where he would find it.

Together and apart, they crunched along the gravelled pathways towards the open area at the eastern end of the Gardens, where the firework ground could be found, and where two enormous balloons swayed in their fully inflated state, tethered complainingly to the earth by numerous ropes and pegs. One of them was the balloon of the famous Mr Lyme, its red and gold stripes held like a sub-marine behemoth within a vast net. A crowd of people gathered admiringly around its wicker car.

This was also the area where Mr Hardy and his *troupe* could be found, located a safe distance from the good taste and *decorum* of the dancing halls and supper tables, at an outer perimeter reserved for oddities and wonders: the very edge of Eden, where illumination strained to reach.

The theatrical *façade* of their show – otherwise an enclosed structure of shoddy gimcrackery – was as gaudy as one might expect. Wooden boards depicted lurid representations of the performers themselves: Edgar the giant pictured perhaps a foot higher than his already miraculous (or cursed) height and with a midget loaf of bread in his palm; Eugenia in full beard and inflated like a ball in her specially constructed throne; Mr Hardy dwarfed by a conventionally proportioned dog, who on closer inspection proved to be Missy herself with a bone between her teeth. The man with the destroyed face was not pictured at all (perhaps because no exaggeration could do justice to his woe). There was, however, a conspicuous space in the gallery of dysmorphia, an undecorated area no doubt once occupied by poor Eliza-Beth's cruel effigy.

The Graeco-Roman paused for a moment outside the frontage, as did Mr Williamson. A hawker stood before the entrance regaling hesitant onlookers with titbits of what they might see if they parted with their money:

'Come inside! Come inside! See the prodigious man-giant Edgar who was three feet tall *at birth*, ladies and gentlemen – not a word of a lie. He could hold your head in his palm like you hold a wine cork. Come inside! Cast your eyes upon

Eugenia the bearded behemoth – as heavy as an elephant and as hirsute as an ape. But not, ladies and gentlemen, as hairy as her child . . . or should I say *dog*, for the creature is both simultaneously. The wonders of nature reside within. No tricks here – you may touch and converse with them if you don't believe. Just a shilling!'

Mr Williamson's mouth turned down at the artless patter and at the vulgarity of the thing. A number of people were hesitating whether to venture inside, weighing their repulsion and dubiety against their fascination for the hideous. One of them was dressed as an ancient warrior, perhaps Achilles. His polished breastplate and greaves glinted dully in the gaslight and a gladiator's iron mask covered his face. A dagger was sheathed at his hip. Presently, a number of people walked forward to the entrance with their coins ready, and the Graeco-Roman, too, took his opportunity to enter with them. The 'judge' followed.

Inside, there was a small, dimly lit area for a dozen or so observers, and a raised stage illuminated on both sides by long plumes of flickering gas. An unclean green velvet curtain hung at the rear of the stage. The audience murmured among themselves and waited.

Then the curtain parted in the middle and Mr Hardy emerged to gasps and mutterings from the people. He was immaculately turned out in a tailored suit and carried a tiny cane.

'Ladies and gentleman, my name is Goliath. I welcome you to my world of anatomical curiosities,' he began in his odd falsetto voice. 'Here you will find wonders . . .'

But a number of his audience were not paying attention to the speech. Sergeant Williamson kept his eyes on the laurel wreath of his target. The ancient soldier looked at the judge and discerned from that venerable personage's gaze that he, too, should be looking in the same direction. Noting this, he began to move slowly back towards the entrance to prevent anyone else from leaving or entering. But before he arrived there, another pushed inside, a man not in costume but in his conventional attire: Inspector Newsome.

'. . . Let me introduce Edgar the man giant,' continued Mr Hardy. And the lumbering gentleman emerged from the curtain with his head brushing the roof. As the exclamations of wonder burst forth, Mr Hardy cast a sly glance at both the judge and Achilles and saw the direction of their gazes.

When the audience reaction had subsided, Mr Hardy continued: 'Let me stand beside Edgar to show his full height. But, no . . . the comparison is unfair. Who among you will come to stand beside Edgar to properly show his enormity? How about you there – the gentleman dressed as Socrates or perhaps Herodotus. You are of a conventional height. Come up on to the stage, won't you?'

All eyes turned to the Graeco-Roman. All eyes including those of Inspector Newsome, who focused intently on the man.

'Don't be shy, sir. You may keep on your masque. Just stand here beside Edgar for us to compare.'

The Greek shook his head but did not speak. A few of the audience began to clap and encourage him to go on stage that they might not themselves become the focus of attention. Still he shook his head, adamant that he would not go.

'Have you something to hide, sir?' chided Mr Hardy in a mild mocking tone. 'What could *you* have to be ashamed of in comparison to us, anomalies of nature that we are. I perceive that you are normal in every way . . . unless your masque hides a terrible secret.'

At this, the audience laughed and called out variously to the silent gentlemen:

'Go on – stand next to the giant!'

'Don't be shy, sir.'

'Take off your masque and show us your deformity!'

'A big nose, I'll bet!'

'Or a red jaw.'

The latter comment was from Achilles, standing behind them all at the entrance. The Greek jerked round to stare in his direction – and an unnerving, silent stillness settled over that murky space. The theatrical atmosphere was replaced with one of confinement. Breathing was the only sound. The people looked between the soldier and the Greek, then back to the Greek.

'Take off your masque, sir,' said a 'Scotsman', all trace of good-natured goading now gone. 'You are making the ladies nervous.'

'I am Detective Inspector Newsome of the Detective Force,' said the inspector. All eyes turned upon him. 'I demand that you remove that mask.'

Edgar stepped down from the stage and approached the Greek through the people, who moved fearfully away. But the Greek did not flinch or show fear. Instead, he reached inside his folds and produced a pistol. And still the giant advanced on him.

'Put that gun down! You have no conceivable escape!' shouted Inspector Newsome.

Edgar continued as inexorably as a fully laden Thames barge and reached out a colossal hand towards the Greek's masque. The pistol cracked: a staggering detonation in that small space.

A general clamour of screams and shouts went up and

people rushed to the exit, the Greek among them. But Edgar was no more inconvenienced by the bullet than by a fly upon his belly. He clamped his hand upon his target's shoulder and halted the gentleman's flight as an obstructing tree might.

Inspector Newsome closed in upon the pair, as did Mr Williamson and Achilles. In a moment, they were the only remaining persons, forming an awkward tableau of conflict: the giant Edgar holding the Greek's upper arm as in a vice; the miniature Mr Hardy watching intently from the stage; the Homeric warrior, now holding a dagger; the judge holding up placating hands; and Inspector Newsome, oblivious to the identity of any but the Greek.

'Noah Dyson! Remove your masque. You are under arrest,' said the inspector to the pinioned Greek.

TWENTY-SIX

'I am here,' replied Noah, removing the gladiatorial mask and showing himself as Achilles.

The inspector looked at him in bewilderment.

'Did you really think I was going to dress as a typical Greek when both you and Boyle expected me to? I am not the fool you take me for, Inspector.'

Edgar used his free hand to snatch the Greek's masque away, revealing – as the reader has long ago surmised – the virulent countenance of Lucius Boyle. His face was so scarlet with rage that the jaw was almost consumed within it.

'So – two criminals caught in one evening,' said Mr Newsome with evident satisfaction.

'Three.'

The speaker was Mr Williamson. He removed his judge's wig and wiped the *rouge* from his nose and cheeks with a sleeve. 'I aided Noah in his escape. Therefore I am also a criminal in your eyes. Will you arrest me also?'

The inspector stared incredulously at his fellow detective.

'Four.'

This voice came from behind. All except Lucius Boyle

JAMES McCREET

turned to see PC Cullen at the entrance. He was holding his truncheon.

'What in d— is going on here?' said Mr Newsome.

'I also aided Detective Williamson in the escape of Mr Dyson, sir. Therefore, I, too, am guilty. As are you, Inspector.'

'Are you quite mad, Constable? Do you realize what you are saying, and to whom?'

'The constable speaks for us all,' said Mr Williamson. 'We have reason to believe that you have been in contact with Mr Boyle here for some time, that he has been blackmailing you, that his access to Mr Allan's house was gained with your help and that you recruited Noah to end the blackmail by any means within your power.'

'You are all bereft of your senses! What you say is sheer nonsense.'

'We can ask Mr Boyle himself about that.'

Lucius Boyle had remained quiet throughout this exchange. He had ceased his struggles and stood observing the scene playing out before him. Of his pursuers, only one seemed to be of any significance to him. He looked at Noah constantly.

For his part, Noah glared at his enemy with an unbroken stare. The dagger was still grasped in his hand. In an instant he could spring forward and bury the steel in Boyle's heart. But would he, in that instant, receive payment for his years of imprisonment, his humiliations, his violations, his lashes, his losses? Was death retribution enough?

'Noah! Put away that dagger. That is not the way,' said Mr Williamson, who had just discerned the hatred sparking between the two.

'You are *all* under arrest,' said Mr Newsome. 'I have six constables with me. They will be here momentarily.'

'No, sir,' said PC Cullen. 'They are waiting for you at the entrance to the Gardens. I took the liberty of passing the news among them that you had captured your men and would meet them there.'

The inspector reined in his apoplexy and breathed deeply. The tableau remained frozen. 'Mr Williamson, I can assure you that your accusations are baseless. However, I am certainly not about to ask a multiple murderer to provide my alibi. If you wish to charge me with anything, you will present your evidence in a court and I will answer it – as I will present mine against you. Now is not the time.'

'Sir, I cannot allow you to arrest Noah. Much of what he has done has been in your service and with the sole aim of capturing Mr Boyle. We would not be standing here now without his efforts.'

'This whole business has been a mistake on my part. I am glad it will end with the capture of the criminal.'

Noah was still holding the dagger in a white-knuckled palm. Lucius Boyle was still watching Noah intently. He knew something that nobody else had yet discerned in their heated claims and counter-claims.

Unnoticed by all except Mr Boyle, Edgar had been bleeding constantly since the shot had been fired. The bullet had entered his abdomen and caused severe damage there. A lesser man would have collapsed instantly. Now his grip on his prisoner was gradually loosening and Lucius could feel it. Inevitably, the giant would not be able to withstand the loss of blood, which had been seeping relentlessly from the wound, for much longer.

'Arrest Mr Boyle – he is the murderer that the newspapers and Commissioner Mayne have been baying for,' urged Mr Williamson. 'He is your blackmailer and the one who has almost succeeded in sullying your name and reputation.'

'How many times must I repeat it? *He is not my blackmailer!* That is pure fantasy on your part. You have misread your evidence!'

Noah alone, who had been disregarding the policemen's debate lest his enemy flee once more, noticed Edgar wobble. The giant's eyes rolled back. His mouth opened dumbly. He fell forward like a sawn pine, hitting the wooden planks a with resounding crash.

And Lucius Boyle was off. He sprinted for the entrance, not pausing for the obstruction of PC Cullen, whom he brutally dispatched with the empty pistol swung underarm like an iron bar to connect with the policeman's jaw. Immediately, a commotion was heard to strike up beyond the doorway.

'*Stop him!*' roared Noah.

All three charged outside, where the fugitive audience had been waiting *en masse* for the outcome of the drama within. Some pointed in the direction that Boyle had taken. His pursuers raced there.

'He cannot escape!' panted Inspector Newsome. 'All exits are covered!'

But he had not reckoned on every manner of escape. Lucius Boyle would not knowingly have entered a trap unless every means of flight had been fully considered. Shouts and screams from the nearby balloon ground showed the direction of his progress.

One balloon was rising as the three men arrived. The tethers had been severed and a prone body lay surrounded by concerned revellers on the flattened grass where the car had sat.

'It's Boyle,' said Noah, arriving at the scene first and looking up at the receding car. 'We'll take the other balloon.'

'You will not, sir!'

The man barring his way was none other than the illustrious Mr Charles Lyme, he who had flown from this very spot to Germany and who had risen to heights unthought-of by lesser aeronauts. Naturally, he did not want to lose a second balloon.

'This flight has already been reserved. You may not board.'

Inspector Newsome spoke: 'Listen, man! That other who has fled with your balloon is the man they call "Red Jaw" or "the General": the murderer of Mary Chatterton, Mr Coggins and the Reverend Josiah Archer. Tonight he has killed another. Will you let him drift away? I command you to aid the Detective Force in this matter.'

Noah, the dagger still clasped in his hand, was watching Boyle drift higher and further beyond his grasp. For him, it was no longer a matter of asking permission.

Perceiving this, Mr Williamson added his weight to the argument: 'Mr Lyme – I am a keen admirer of yours, but I will be forced to arrest you if you do not aid us. I suspect that you are working in collusion with the killer in this matter.'

'Well, I declare—' began the aeronaut indignantly, but Noah had already boarded the car and was hacking at the ropes with a hatchet presumably provided for the purpose.

'Take us, Mr Lyme, or watch us leave without you,' added Mr Williamson, himself heading for the car.

'Stop! You cannot navigate alone! You need an experienced pilot,' yelled the aeronaut.

'And you are he,' added Mr Newsome, roughly taking him by the arm and pulling him towards the car.

Perhaps Mr Lyme saw that the only way to protect his balloon was to accede to the demands of the policemen. Certainly, it would be safer with him aboard. He climbed in the car, where Noah was still hacking frenziedly at their restraints.

'Not that one!' cried Mr Lyme, halting Noah's arm. 'That is the guide rope. Throw those three bags of ballast overboard – he is only one and we are four. He has the advantage of buoyancy, but he lacks the skill.'

With the last rope loosed, the balloon rose soundlessly. Or rather, from the point of view of the passengers, the earth seemed to fall away beneath them without jolt or judder. The faces around them retroceded, becoming smaller and more distant until they appeared mere characters upon the illuminated night-time canvas of Vauxhall Gardens itself, whose gaslit walkways and concert areas gleamed like chains of pearls amidst the inky foliage.

Mr Lyme bade the four men sit around the car's rim, which was only four feet tall. A hoop hung down from the horizontal ring above them where the balloon's net was fastened, and upon this hoop were located the various brass and teak aeronautical instruments necessary for flight: a barometer, a compass, a telescope and others unnameable which were in an experimental state. Now becalmed and in his natural element, Mr Lyme consulted his needles, dials and mercury readings as another might look upon the commodities listing in *the Times*.

'The wind is taking us north across the river,' he said. 'We are currently rising past two hundred feet. The full moon will reach its apogee at around one o'clock and it is a fine clear night for flying.'

Noah peered through the telescope and focused upon Lucius Boyle, who appeared to be consulting the instruments in his balloon with considerably less proficiency. He turned and looked at his pursuers often, confident in the knowledge, at least, that there was nothing they could do to go faster. They were all at the mercy of the wind.

Mr Williamson clutched the edge of the car as if he were in a boat. He peered down to the dark ribbon of the Thames that had appeared on his left and saw the stone flower of Millbank penitentiary glowing spectrally in the moonlight. As they rose, the city seemed more and more like a map spread below him, Westminster-bridge a mere strand across the water and St James' park a great black lung sliced silver by lunar reflection. His city. Seeing it thus was like floating in a febrile state above his own prostrate form, recognizing and yet not recognizing. Up here, amid the smoke of count- less hearths and manufactories, he had entered the very *pneuma* of London.

'He is rising faster than we,' said Noah, pointing to the other balloon, which was a good hundred feet higher against the starry sky.

'Of course. He has less weight,' said Mr Lyme. 'But he cannot go faster. And he must come down.'

'Can we do nothing?' asked Inspector Newsome.

'We are at the mercy of the breeze, sir. I recommend that you enjoy the view and allow me to worry about the flight.'

'Enjoy the view, man? Do you understand the urgency of our pursuit?'

'Science will not be rushed.'

'He is manipulating the valve,' interrupted Noah. 'Here, look through the telescope.'

Mr Lyme took the instrument and beheld Lucius Boyle within its glassy eye. He was indeed touching the valve as if trying to understand the mechanism. As Mr Lyme watched, Lucius seemed to perceive the gaze upon him and glared back with a look that magnified its hate through the lenses into the blinking eyeball at the end. The aeronaut shivered.

'Yes, he is perhaps trying to release gas and descend. If he does so over the city, there will be casualties for certain. And if the balloon is ruptured, the coal gas will escape and . . . well, it could be very nasty.'

He applied himself once more to the telescope: 'Wait. He has stopped with the valve and is checking his instruments. Perhaps he has understood that he has the advantage of levity.'

'Just do as he does,' advised Inspector Newsome. 'If he descends, descend. Do not let him escape us. The pursuit is in your hands.'

Mr Williamson seemed mesmerized by the passing city. They were crossing the river now, just south of Waterloo-bridge. Moored boats were as twigs at the edge of a stream-let and he fancied that he could smell the water itself: a muddy exhalation of wet wood, waste and damp stone. Even at this height, the sounds of the city could be heard quite clearly from the spider-web of gaslit thoroughfares.

For a moment, the four men paused there in the eternal aether and listened to snatches of sound brought to them on breaths of air: cart wheels on stone; the chorus of a drunkenly bellowed song; a scream that could have been of pleasure or of death; and beneath it all, seemingly, the ghostly murmur of manifold invisible lives rising on the smoke.

'What is that?' asked Inspector Newsome, pointing to their left at a patch of relative darkness like a bloodstain upon the urban fabric.

'St Giles,' mumbled a lugubrious Mr Williamson.

'Are you still brooding on your ludicrous suspicions about me, Mr Williamson?'

'Until I have evidence to the contrary.'

'You have no evidence *now* – only supposition. Do you really think I would have allowed you to undergo a beating such as you experienced there in that inky parish? I abhor this man Boyle as much as you. Unlike you, I vowed to do anything to catch him, even if it meant utilizing another criminal.'

'So you are not the father of Eliza-Beth? You have no personal investment in this case at all, other than seeing justice done?'

'I have no children. You know that. The only personal aspect of this case is my desire to see the man at the end of a rope.'

'Which man?' said Noah.

'Boyle, of course. I will be frank – you mean nothing to me, Mr Dyson. One criminal is the same as another to me. You are all worthy of the gaol and the gallows. But that man . . . that man has plagued me like no other.'

'And me? I, too, am a criminal in your eyes,' said Mr Williamson.

'Yes. Yes, you are. You broke the law when you allied yourself with Noah.'

'Will I be prosecuted when we land?'

'What would *you* do, Mr Williamson? You are the rigid backbone of the Detective Force. You are the one who lives by the rules and regulations. You are the one who would reason with a fist-fighter using only Royal proclamations in your defence. What would you do in my position? Tell me and I will be guided by your superior morality.'

Mr Williamson looked out again over the limitless charcoal smudge of the city. It might be a sea of ashes from this altitude, all consumed. The British Museum was a masonry oasis of civilization down there, amid the holocaust. He closed his insubstantial judge's robes about him for warmth.

'Well, Mr Williamson? Have you been taken in by the rhetorical patter of Mr Dyson here, our gentleman thief? But a thief all the same. Where is the young policeman I knew who would send a boy to Botany Bay for taking a loaf of bread? Where is *he* now?'

All eyes were upon Mr Williamson. But he did not speak. Mr Lyme, who was oblivious to the convoluted tale that had brought these men to his balloon, cleared his throat and took the telescope once more.

'The man is again attempting to loosen the valve!' he said.

'Let me see.' Noah looked through the telescope at the balloon ahead and above them. 'Yes. Do you think he will try to descend? There is a patch of open land there near the Regent's Canal.'

'It is not possible to descend so quickly or accurately. He would be foolish to try.'

'Not foolish – desperate,' said Inspector Newsome.

'If he is descending,' said Noah, 'we must do likewise.'

'One cannot simply let the gas escape. It would be too slow. We must first rise to a higher altitude to use the air-pressure differential.'

'If *he* is doing it, so must we,' said Noah.

'You are insane – all of you! This is not a carriage to stop anywhere you choose. We could be cast against a roof and fall to our deaths. We must first rise – and so must he.'

'Sergeant Williamson, do you have your handcuffs there?'

'Indeed, Noah.'

'Listen to me, gentlemen!' pleaded Mr Lyme, 'one cannot cheat science. We must rise before we fall. Look – your man is still rising. Would you have us descend?'

'All right. All right,' said Inspector Newsome, 'do what you must, but do not lose sight of that man.'

The balloon continued to rise as they passed over Islington. By now, the city might equally have been the sky: an immeasurable darkness pinpointed with light, an unknown galaxy that might or might not contain life. Breath billowed from the mouths of the four men in the chill upper atmosphere and Mr Lyme produced woollen cloaks to drape around their shoulders. They sat thus in impotent silence, thinking their separate thoughts and waiting for gravity and pressure to aid their pursuit. Inspector Newsome extracted a pipe and made to light it.

'Do not light that match in this balloon!' yelled Mr Lyme. 'Don't you know that we have thousands of cubic feet of coal gas above us? I will not have you be Icarus to my Daedalus!'

Noah smiled slightly at the classical reference. But it was a cold smile. He could not take his eyes off the other balloon and its lone occupant. The two of them might have been satellites – but which revolved around the other? Whose gravity was strongest?

'Will you kill him, Noah?' asked Mr Williamson.

Noah made no answer.

'You had the chance at Vauxhall. You had your knife –

you could have sprung at him and sliced his throat as he sliced Mary's. And yet you did not. Why? Surely you were not dissuaded by the presence of the police.'

Again, Noah made no answer. Instead, he stared out across the chill air to the other balloon.

'Have you decided, perhaps, that killing him will not solve anything?'

'I have decided nothing,' answered Noah.

And Lucius Boyle? He was more Antaeus than Daedalus; he derived his power from contact with the ground, where shadows and solidity hid his presence. Up here he was exposed and in full view. He was no aeronaut. Though the barometer told him his altitude, the thermometer the temperature and the compass his direction, he was still powerless. He continued to rise and the policemen continued to follow him according to the immutable laws of science.

Having read of such flights in the newspapers, he knew as much as the rest of the public about guide ropes, gas and ballast. Nevertheless, the chill of altitude and the dizzying effect of ascent were almost as unnerving as being in full view of the moon's objective eye.

His ascent was slowing. Had Mr Lyme been there to explain, Lucius would have known that this was due to a partial equalization of pressure within and without the balloon, combined with increased atmospheric moisture adding to its weight. At the same time, his linear progress also ceased. The effect was that the other balloon – travelling in another stratum of air – began to move directly underneath.

Lucius Boyle looked down upon the netted globe and understood what he must do. He picked up one of the smaller ballast bags – sand or gravel inside a coarse canvas bag – and retrieved an ever-present box of lucifers from beneath his robes. He struck a match and held it to a corner of the canvas until flames began to lick at the material, then he leaned over the edge of the car and dropped it.

The burning bag plummeted towards the other balloon and connected with the outer curve, bouncing off the surface with a shower of sparks.

'My G—! What was that?' shouted Inspector Newsome.

'I believe it was a flaming bag of ballast,' said Mr Lyme. 'He is attempting to set us alight.'

'Can he do that? How secure is the surface of this machine?'

'It is nothing but silk coated with liquid gum. It will burn quite readily if one of those bags settles on the surface. There may be one there now. We must descend.'

'We must not.'

'Mr Newsome, would you rather flutter burning to the ground hundreds of feet below us?'

'Descend if you must,' said Noah. 'He will still be visible to us on this cloudless night. We can follow on the ground if necessary. Descend, Mr Lyme.'

'Mr Dyson – you have no authority—'

The inspector's sentence was cut short by Noah's dagger glinting in the moonlight.

'Inspector – tell me: what have I to lose? You say I am guilty and will go back to gaol when we land. What is to stop me cutting your throat and tossing your body over the edge? Who knows you are in this balloon? Who knows that *I* am?'

'Sergeant Williamson knows. Sergeant – speak to this man. Tell him. Mr Williamson? Detective? That is an order!'

Mr Williamson looked impassively between the two men. A second flaming bag of ballast sailed past the car, trailing a tail of sparks.

'Take us down immediately, Mr Lyme,' said Mr Williamson. 'Or I will have Noah here deal with you as he would deal with Inspector Newsome.'

'Think carefully what you say,' warned Mr Newsome.

Mr Williamson made no answer. The aeronaut quickly attended to the valve and the acrid stench of coal gas began to fill the car. At first, there was no discernible change in height, but the balloon of Lucius Boyle soon emerged above them, moving across the moon in a dark eclipse. It diminished in size as they descended.

'Throw out the guide rope,' said Mr Lyme, now all business.

Noah tossed the coil and watched it unravel into the void. They had left the city behind and the earth below was now a blanket of darkness punctuated infrequently by light. As they moved lower, the hedges and trees of rural Middlesex became distinguishable in the moonlight.

'Can we not fasten the valve once more and follow from a lower altitude?' asked Inspector Newsome, half covering his face to avoid breathing the gas.

'That depends on whether there is an ember currently burning atop the balloon, sir,' said Mr Lyme. 'If there is, we may all die shortly. Would you like to test that hypothesis?'

The question was rhetorical, as the treetops were growing closer and the guide rope was now trailing among them.

'Be ready with the grappling iron,' Mr Lyme warned Noah.

Now that the features of the ground were clear and able to give scale to their height, Mr Williamson once again became tense. A collision with a treetop could tip them out into space. They seemed to be moving much faster than they had in the upper aether.

'Brace yourselves, gentlemen! Throw out the iron there!'

The hook sailed over the edge and all four gripped the edges of the car. Below them, the land anchor struck soft earth and ploughed a furrow, jumping and skipping along the surface. It leaped at a stone wall and pulled the first two layers down after it. Then it snagged through a patch of thorns and caught upon an exposed root. The car jerked violently and was pulled to the ground by the tautened rope, where it connected roughly, rocked over on one edge and finally settled upright.

'Everybody out!' shouted Mr Lyme.

The four clambered frantically over the edge and made some distance between themselves and potential explosion. But the balloon just wobbled limply in the moonlit field it had landed in, apparently undamaged by its unorthodox flight.

The silence – to the two policemen who were used to the unsleeping city – was uncanny. They looked about them warily, as if set down upon the shores of an undiscovered continent. No streets here to guide their paths; no spires by which locate oneself; no passing omnibus; no advertising posters adorning walls. Even the scent was something other-worldly: a curious aroma of damp earth and leaves untainted by smoke. Was this how London had once smelled?

'There is no burning bag! We could have stayed in the air!' raged Inspector Newsome.

'The benefit of retrospection, sir,' said Mr Lyme.

'Look. He is descending beyond that hill,' said Noah.

And, indeed, the other balloon was a dark shape against

the sky. Noah set off across the field, his Homeric hero's boots rapidly becoming soaked by the clinging grass. The others followed less sure-footedly uphill and over unfamiliar terrain until all were panting and sweating freely. As the fittest of them all, Noah raced ahead until his lungs ached and his legs throbbed with the heat of effort. Lucius Boyle's balloon had descended out of sight on the other side of the hill.

Then, as Noah approached the crest, a false dawn blossomed before him. A ball of fire and smoke rose into the night sky and cast his martial silhouette against its redness so that he appeared almost a statue to those following.

Reaching the peak, he looked down to see the ruptured and burning remains of the balloon. Flaming tatters were falling around the car, itself half-consumed in the conflagration.

'The gas! He must have ignited the gas with all that fire play. Any breach of the skin could have set it off,' said Mr Lyme, the first to catch up to Noah.

But Noah was not there to hear. He continued on to where the car lay upright and crackling. From a distance, he could make out a form slumped over its edge: a body evidently consumed in its attempts to escape.

The smoke billowed into his eyes, obscuring his view. Not until he was within embracing distance did he see the body with clarity. Its clothing had been partially burned away, but what scraps remained bespoke once-white Greek robes. Its skin was a blackened papyrus and the face a charred rictus of death so that no trace of a red jaw remained. A sickly stench of scorched flesh emanated from it.

The flame-scarred eyeballs of the corpse mocked him

even in death and he felt an urge to strike the face. The dagger was clutched furiously in his hand.

'So, he has met his end,' said Inspector Newsome from behind. We can all be happy, Noah. Justice has been done.'

Noah did not reply. Nor did he turn away from the face of the incendiary. He threw the dagger into the ground so that the blade buried itself in the soft soil.

TWENTY-SEVEN

NOTORIOUS MURDERER KILLED
IN BALLOON DESCENT

The man sought by police for the murders of Mr Henry Coggins and Miss Mary Chatterton, and wanted in connection with the murders of the girl Eliza-Beth, of Reverend Josiah Archer and of a certain 'Razor' William Barley, has been killed in a balloon accident, his body burned almost beyond recognition owing to ignition of coal gas.

The gentleman, previously known as 'Red Jaw' or 'the General', and now identified as Mr Lucius Boyle, had been lured to Friday's *Bal Masqué* by officers of the Metropolitan Police. There, it was surmised, he would try to silence by murder those few remaining who might know his identity, viz. the performers of Mr Coggins's theatrical *troupe*.

Inspector Newsome of A Division lay in wait with a group of constables for the murderer to appear and confronted the man with his crimes, whereupon Mr Boyle extracted a pistol (the same used to kill Mr Coggins) and shot Edgar Grimes, the man-giant of the show, killing him. In the *mêlée*, Mr Boyle made his escape and purloined one of Mr Charles Lyme's two balloons, rendering an aeronaut unconscious and grievously injuring him the process.

Inspector Newsome gave chase in the second balloon, taking Mr Lyme himself as pilot and navigator for the flight. There followed a heated pursuit across the skies of London, followed by many inhabitants on that clear, moonlit night. During the pursuit, Mr Boyle attempted to destroy his pursuers' balloon by dropping flaming ballast bags upon it, but Mr Lyme evaded these and managed to land safely.

Owing to the extreme volatility of the gas, and the inexperience of the pilot, Mr Boyle's balloon was subsequently brought down by a fire that destroyed both it and the pilot. His burned body was discovered and identified by Inspector Newsome.

Information given by an associate of Mr Boyle's, a bare-knuckle fighter named Henry Hawkins (now in police custody and charged with murder), has revealed the former's complicity in the murder of Eliza-Beth and the Reverend Josiah Archer, in addition to numerous documented cases of incendiarism.

CLEAR CASE OF SUICIDE – Dr Alexander McLeod, esteemed surgeon to the Metropolitan Police, was discovered dead by a coal deliveryman early on Saturday morning. He had died by his own hand, taking an overdose of opium. No letter was left to be discovered.

The deliveryman arrived to discover the street door open, and, knowing this to be strange and knowing the doctor to be a careful man, called inside to ask if there was any problem. Alarmed by the smell of smoke, he entered the corridor and followed the scent to the parlour, whereupon he found the body of the doctor sitting in a high-backed chair. The smoke had been caused by documents being burned in a metal urn. A doctor was called and pronounced Mr McLeod deceased. The police do not suspect foul play.

'Good news and bad news,' said Commissioner Mayne solemnly, putting down the newspapers with their circled articles. 'I am glad that this lamentable tale has finally come to an end. You are to be congratulated, Inspector Newsome, though the result has been tardy.'

'Thank you, sir.'

'Dr McLeod was unmarried, is that correct?'

'Indeed. He was a bachelor and lived alone without domestic help.'

'Do we know why he might have killed himself? What is this about the burned documents?'

'Frankly, we have little idea. The documents were burned to ash and quite illegible. Evidently he did not want anyone to read them, and he has succeeded in that.'

'Do you think there is any connection to this case? I would like to be certain that all loose threads are neatly severed. I do not want to be reading about further atrocities in a few days' time. Are you absolutely sure that this was not another subtle murder like that of Mr Askern, or that those documents do not have darker implications?'

'I am as sure as I can be. The doctor certainly had the means to kill himself in a painless way. He lived an impeccable and utterly blameless life. Perhaps, as is sometimes the case, he simply became fatigued with the death he encountered almost daily. It affects men in different ways.'

'Well, he was a good man. He will be missed. Now – what is this about Sergeant Williamson?'

'Yes, he was also at Vauxhall Gardens that night. His own investigations had led him to believe that he would find Lucius Boyle there and we met at Mr Hardy's show—'

'Mr Hardy?'

'The miniature gentleman . . . he has taken over from Mr Coggins as—'

'I remember. Proceed.'

'Well, we boarded the balloon together, he and I, and joined forces in the pursuit. On landing, he was quite badly injured. These injuries, in addition to those he sustained at the hands of Mr Henry Hawkins, mean that he is not currently fit for duty. We have agreed that he will take some time away from the Detective Force in convalescence.'

'Is that advisable? He is one of our finest men; we need men like him on the streets of the city pursuing crime, not malingering in bed.'

'The injuries were quite serious, sir, and, I fear, not restricted to the body. This case has shaken him like no other. It may have reduced his faith in his own abilities, Commissioner. When a policeman is afraid to venture into a dark alley, whether actual or metaphorical, he has lost his worth.'

'I will thank you not to wax poetical with me, Inspector. I'm sure we will be seeing more of Sergeant Williamson, whatever you say. There will certainly be no more of this regrettable activity with known criminals.'

'Certainly not, sir.'

'It has been a most curious case, has it not? I feel that there are still parts of it that I do not understand. Much of it seems purely motiveless.'

'Indeed. From what Mr Hawkins deigned to tell us, it appears that the original murder of Eliza-Beth was in order to procure evidence for a case of blackmail, either of the mother or father. Mary Chatterton was evidently the mother and yielded nothing but her life. The murders of Mr Coggins, the clergyman and Mr Askern were evidently aimed at eradicating witnesses of Boyle's visits to Lambeth – a rather drastic set of measures.'

'And still we have no idea who the victim of this supposed blackmail was? Is he somewhere in the metropolis, joyful at Boyle's death and yet stricken with the slaughter committed to protect his name?'

'We have no idea, sir. I am afraid it is a thread we cannot and, perhaps, should not pursue.'

'I fear you are correct. However, there is one "thread" I am keen to sever. I presume that Mr Dyson is on his way back to New South Wales.'

'Ah. That is an issue I wanted to discuss with you . . .'

Mr Williamson was sitting alone at home. He put down the newspaper with a mirthless smile. Both articles were thoroughly incorrect in their own way, but they told the story they intended to, making appropriate heroes and villains of the characters in the whole murderous tale. As for Mr Williamson himself, which was he?

Needless to say, he had not been injured in the balloon landing. That piece of artifice had been Inspector Newsome's idea – or rather his insistence. Mr Newsome had come to the house on the Sunday after the balloon chase and found Mr Williamson in a confrontational humour.

'Have you come to arrest me for aiding Noah's escape, Inspector Newsome?'

'I am reassured that you would think so. That is the George Williamson I know: the one who would arrest his closest friend if he proved to be a criminal.'

'You are not my closest friend, and I am not that George Williamson.'

'Indeed. Indeed you are not. And that is why I have come. Not to arrest you, but to discuss your future in the Detective Force.'

'Am I to be suspended? Or expelled completely?'

'I think we can find another solution, one that is less drastic. I will tell Commissioner Mayne that you were injured in the balloon chase. You still have visible injuries from your beating so this will be quite plausible. I will recommend a period of convalescence which will, in time, grow into your retirement from the Metropolitan Police.'

'I have given my life to the police. How am I . . .?'

'Mr Williamson, the alternative is a trial and gaol, possibly transportation. The other convicts would not take kindly to an ex-detective in their midst.'

'Why are you doing this to me?'

'You did it to yourself the moment you stepped on to the side of the criminal.'

'And you have never stepped across that dividing line, Albert? Not when you recruited Noah to do your work for you? Not when you allowed Noah to be locked in Giltspur-street as bait to draw a murderer who would have slain him?'

'What I did, I did in the interests of justice.'

'As did I, but you obviously cannot see that. Lucius Boyle was caught and the matter is over. We approached the same conclusion from different paths.'

'My path did not involve two gaolers and three constables

brutally injured at the hands of Mr Dyson. It involved the breaking of no law – only the stretching of it.'

'Since I clearly have no option in what you suggest, at least do me the honour of being truthful about your motivations in removing me from the police. What intrigue are you involved in now?'

'George, do you still suspect me of complicity with that man?'

'No, I do not. I admit I was following the wrong path. Even if I did believe you were the victim of his blackmail, there is little now that I could do to prove it. I wonder if it is selfishness that you would like all the acclaim to fall upon your shoulders for this success?'

'It is not. It is the simple fact that I believe you have lost your sense of right and wrong. I am sure that even you understand we cannot have a serving detective who has aided a criminal to break out of prison. We would become the joke of the entire nation. It is better that you disappear gradually from view.'

'Hmm. Hmm.'

'It is really the best solution.'

'Hmm. Have you behaved similarly with PC Cullen? Is he to be hanged?'

'You need not be so melodramatic. The man is a capable policeman; he was following your orders and cannot be blamed for his actions. He is a simple man and quite in awe of the detectives. I have been no harsher with him than having him transferred to traffic duty on London-bridge.'

'Where he may be trampled, crushed or maimed at any moment.'

'If you say so. I can see you are tired, but I do have one further question before I leave. Have you had any contact with Noah Dyson since Friday night when we all came back to the city?'

'I have not seen him or heard from him since that night – nor do I have any wish to. It was only through your machinations that we were introduced and there is no need for any further contact. Perhaps you will find him at home.'

'Well, that is the thing. We went to his house the very next morning but there was no answer. We forced entry and discovered – it appears – that the man and his manservant have fled. The furniture remains, but the books and clothing have gone. I suspect that this occurred at the hands of the Negro even while we were at Vauxhall. The two of them seem to have vanished . . . do you find something amusing, Mr Williamson?'

'Nothing.'

'If you have any information about his whereabouts, you are bound to deliver it. If he sends you a letter or one of his cryptic communications via a street boy or fancy-dress impostor, I trust you will contact me immediately. I must find him. He belongs on the other side of the world where he cannot damage the reputation of the Detective Force.'

'Of course I will give you any information I have.'

'Well . . . good. I trust you have heard about Dr McLeod?'

'Yes. A tragic loss.'

'Why would he kill himself? Do you suspect anything suspicious? He was connected to this case, however tangentially.'

'I have no idea. I did not know him well. I suspect that few did. I was sorry to hear the news.'

'Quite. Well, I will be leaving. I hope that we will remain

in contact; if not professionally, then at least for the occasional cup of tea.'

'I think not.'

'That is a pity. Goodbye.'

Now alone, Mr Williamson unfolded the letter he had received by post that very morning: the last letter written by Dr McLeod:

Dear George

I have no doubt that by now you have heard of my death and, adept detective that you are, have discerned the reason for it. I am the man you sought: the father of Eliza-Beth, the subject of Lucius Boyle's blackmail and the unwilling accomplice in the murder of Mr Askern.

These facts alone are enough to condemn me to eternal damnation, but they are nothing compared to my guilt over your treatment at the hands of Henry Hawkins. My part in a murder – hideous though it is – pales against the assault on my friend and colleague. Had I been a stronger man – had I not been motivated by the selfish desire to protect my name from infamy and taint – I would have come to you immediately. My death is my belated gesture of honesty. Now he can do nothing more against me.

I do not know if you know the story of my past – of my youth. Mary Chatterton was – to my immature and romantic mind – a vision of beauty and perfection. I thought it was love. It was not. I knew nothing of the child until she wrote to me prior to her own murder. The blackmail started shortly thereafter.

You will have guessed that he came to me on the night of the Oxford-street fire and compelled me to aid

*him in the murder of Mr Askern. Inspector Newsome
had told me of Mr Allan's secure address many times
and I knew the protocol of entry. No doubt you have
seen the note I wrote in Boyle's name. It was also I
who formulated the method of the killing – though I
had hoped the combination of narcotics would merely
stupefy Mr Askern. I was wrong.*

*Boyle was in my house when the constables came
to notify me of the Reverend Archer's murder. He knew
then what your fate would be. I tried to warn you that
night, but you had to see justice done. If only my
resolve had been so strong.*

*I should have known that no man escapes his
destiny. No man escapes his punishment. Mine came
before the Judgment, and I will face it again at that
time. I only hope that the motivations of my self-
killing may be understood in its righteous context.*

*Forgive me, George. Do with this letter as you see
fit. My name is nothing to me now but an entry on a
document and iron-chiselled marks on stone.*

Alexander McLeod.

Mr Williamson held the letter in his hand with a feeling of
commingled pity, sorrow and anger. He reserved the anger
for himself for not having discerned the facts sooner. Had he
done so, he might have prevented multiple deaths, including
that of the doctor.

Were there clues? In retrospect, he had to admit that
there were, if only he had been able to piece them together.
There was the body of Josiah Archer. Was the slip of paper
in his dead hand – 'I am watching. You will do my bidding'
– addressed to Mr Williamson as he had thought – or to the
man who would very likely see it first, the man who actually

did find it first: the doctor? Mr McLeod had paled at the sight of the handwriting. And he had just left the man who had written it.

No doubt Inspector Newsome had told Dr McLeod of Mr Allan's secret house and the means of entry to it. The letter accompanying Lucius Boyle to that address had claimed he had a 'partially severed tongue' – a decidedly medical-sounding explanation. Why not simply an 'injured mouth'? Why any reason at all? Only Mr Newsome's name was required to gain entry, but Dr McLeod had not known that when he wrote the letter. And the choice of murder weapon – a mixture of opium and hashish delivered to a man with respiratory problems – had a clinical genius to it that even Lucius Boyle might not have considered. Had the doctor also been forced to supply the change of clothes that Boyle had found before visiting the house?

It was a ragged collection of clues that carried weight only after the death and confession of the doctor. And yet, hadn't it seemed there was an equal quantity of clues against Inspector Newsome?

Mr Williamson rubbed his eyes and looked into the hearth. The fire was dying and required more coal. His thoughts turned to Noah and he smiled again at the seem-ingly miraculous disappearance of the man. Where was he now? On a ship bound for the Indies or America? Or was he standing on the street outside dressed as a rag-picker, a cabman or a swell about town, watching over his erstwhile colleague? The man might well be everywhere – or nowhere: London's very *genius loci*.

The detective reluctantly left the warmth of his chair and bent to the bucket of coal before the fire died completely.

*

With what emotions had Noah gazed upon the blistered countenance of his enemy? Had it been with relief? With anger? With pity? The face staring back at him had hardly been human. Rather, it was a liquescent parody of anatomy: bone and cartilage showing through black paper skin, eyes clouded with film, all trace of identity wiped clean by the purifying flame. It could be none other than Lucius Boyle. Nobody else had been in the balloon.

There must have been no satisfaction in it. To have Boyle killed in a mere accident was a hollow victory. The cadaver seemed unreal – a mere effigy of the man Noah had known and carried with him as a talisman of vengeance for years. All vitality and threat had been purged from the body by the cleansing flame. Only ash was left.

The men had travelled back to the city in a carriage provided by the assistants of Mr Lyme – the usual method of retrieving aeronauts. Few words had been exchanged on that trip, for the pursuit of Boyle had consumed each man in its way and worked its own web of animosities between them. No further mention of guilt or arrest was made; no more accusations were thrown. They would come later, as we have seen.

On reaching the City-road, Noah had simply opened the carriage door as they turned a corner and stepped out into the night. Inspector Newsome had shouted after him, but he was gone. Gone back to the streets and the invisibility he had cultivated before his inadvertent capture. Gone so completely that even I did not know where he had gone – at least, for some time.

Was there a second house that he had kept for years in anticipation of the necessity to flee? No doubt the loss of his property in Manchester-square was a painful one, though he had taken everything of personal value. The police could – and would – search it for clues to his whereabouts. They would search in vain. And then, suddenly, they would cease their attempts on the orders of Inspector Newsome, who would ascribe his unwillingness to continue to the futility of the search and the lack of manpower. The true reason, however, was quite different.

Returning home late one night a few days after his meeting with Mr Williamson, the inspector ate a light meal and drank a gin and hot water, as was his habit. He performed his toilet, changed into his night shirt, extinguished the gas and got into bed.

As soon as his head touched the pillow, he felt the object beneath. Sitting up with a jerk, he stepped out of bed and fumbled to light the gas lamp. Then he took a pair of brass tongs from the hearth and lifted the corner of the pillow as if a deadly serpent lurked there beneath.

The object was a dagger. Noah Dyson's dagger: the one that the inspector had confiscated all those weeks ago and later been obliged to return. The same one that Noah had held at Vauxhall Gardens and in the balloon.

Mr Newsome looked phrenziedly around him, expecting to see the man emerging from the shadows intent on bloody retribution. But there was only silence. He moved to the window and pulled the curtains aside to look into the street, but saw nothing. He looked inside the wardrobe and under the bed and even in the bathroom before realizing he was overreacting. Noah was not in the house.

Back in the bedroom he lifted the pillow completely and saw that there was also a note. He unfolded it with trembling fingers:

Inspector Newsome

You cannot change addresses as I can. Nor can you hide. Your pursuit of me will end immediately and I will suffer no further attention from the Metropolitan Police for as long as you live.

I wish you a long and healthy life.

Sincerely yours.
Noah Dyson

And thus the story concludes with Mr Hawkins's hanging before the gates of Newgate. The patterers made more money on that day than ever before, hawking their tales and verses of Bully Bradford, Lucius Boyle and the third in that infamous trinity of murderers. And even today, the characters in that bloody parable stir memories of the two-headed girl, the woman of pleasure, the notorious murder of Mr Coggins, the death of a giant, the slaying of a priest. By and by, even the details of Mr Askern's death emerged to further embellish the tortuous tale, which in some circles took on supernatural interpretations.

Was Lucius Boyle *really* dead? they mused. He could not be killed, they said. He was still among them: wherever a face was covered, wherever unease rippled through a crowd, wherever flames crackled and smoke rose – he was there.

Nonsense, of course. I have presented it all here as it truly happened. I may have taken the occasional liberty and embroidered the tale a little more than others who have sought to document it. But what is a writer without a little fancy in his pen? What is the city – or the man – that can be seen only at its surface? My ink flows within it, above it, below it. I, the writer, am its beginning, its middle and its end.

Acknowledgements

Thanks to the following, without whose help . . .

My parents, for waiting
Monika Wolny, for reading
Jennifer White – card holder
Jill Carey, for reading
Barry Nicholls, for nurturing
Will Atkins, for the chance
Martin Bryant – unsung hero
EAP – Lord help your poor soul

An Atlas of Investigation and Management
HIV/AIDS

An Atlas of Investigation and Management

HIV/AIDS

Alison J Rodger
MBChB, MRCP, FFPH, MSc, DipHIV, MD
Senior Lecturer and Honorary Consultant in HIV and Infectious Diseases
Royal Free NHS Trust, London, UK

Tabitha W Mahungu
BMedSci, BM BS, DTM&H, MRCP
Speciality Trainee in Infectious Diseases and Medical Microbiology
Royal Free NHS Trust, London, UK

Margaret A Johnson
MBBS, MD, FRCP
Consultant Physician in Thoracic Medicine, Professor of HIV Medicine
Royal Free NHS Trust, London, UK

CLINICAL PUBLISHING

OXFORD

Clinical Publishing
an imprint of Atlas Medical Publishing Ltd
Oxford Centre for Innovation
Mill Street, Oxford OX2 0JX, UK

Tel: +44 1865 811116
Fax: +44 1865 251550
Email: info@clinicalpublishing.co.uk
Web: www.clinicalpublishing.co.uk

Distributed in USA and Canada by:
Clinical Publishing
30 Amberwood Parkway
Ashland, OH 44805, USA

Tel: 800-247-6553 (toll free within US and Canada)
Fax: 419-281-6883
Email: order@bookmasters.com

Distributed in UK and Rest of World by:
Marston Book Services Ltd
PO Box 269
Abingdon
Oxon OX14 4YN, UK

Tel: +44 1235 465500
Fax: +44 1235 465555
Email: trade.orders@marston.co.uk

A catalogue record of this book is available from the British Library

ISBN print   978 1 904392 90 3
ISBN e-book 978 1 84692 629 7

The publisher makes no representation, express or implied, that the dosages in this book are correct. Readers must therefore always check the product information and clinical procedures with the most up-to-date published product information and data sheets provided by the manufacturers and the most recent codes of conduct and safety regulations. The authors and the publisher do not accept any liability for any errors in the text or for the misuse or misapplication of material in this work.

Clinical Publishing and Atlas Medical Publishing Ltd bear no responsibility for the persistence or accuracy of URLs for external or third-party internet websites referred to in this publication, and do not guarantee that any content on such websites is, or will remain, accurate or appropriate.

Back cover, top image: reproduced with permission from Cornelia Büchen-Osmond, Columbia University

Colour reproduction by Henry Ling, Dorchester Press, Dorset, UK
Printed by Marston Book Services Ltd, Abingdon, Oxon, UK

Contents

vi   Contents

Preface

The advent of effective antiretroviral therapy 15 years ago has led to a dramatic improvement in the life expectancy of patients with HIV infection. Consequently, our wards now have many fewer admissions of patients with opportunistic infections and AIDS-related malignancies. As we now see very few of these complications on a regular basis together with new clinical problems that our patients face, there is a real need for an atlas of this kind. Increasingly, we are looking after patients with the complications of living long-term with HIV infection and the complications of antiretroviral therapy, and these are covered in this atlas.

Many admissions are now due to late diagnosis and so there is a very pressing need for our clinical colleagues in both primary and secondary care to advocate testing of their patients whenever HIV could be considered as part of a differential diagnosis.

This atlas will be a valuable resource across the spectrum of medicine and, as with any publication with many contributors, this is a posy of other man's flowers and I wish to thank all the contributors for their huge effort in producing this book.

Margaret A Johnson

Acknowledgements

We would like to extend our heartfelt thanks to the HIV-infected individuals without whom publication of this atlas would have been impossible. We are grateful to Andrew Gardner, Head of Medical Illustration at the University College of London Medical School and his colleagues for their expert help with the preparation and processing of the images. We thank all our colleagues in the Department of HIV Medicine at the Royal Free NHS Trust for supporting this project and giving their time to contribute to this publication.

We are also grateful to the following individuals for providing images from their personal collections for inclusion in this publication:

Ian Cropley, Consultant in Infectious Diseases, Royal Free NHS Trust, London; Amar Dhillon, Consultant Histopathologist, Royal Free NHS Trust, London; Malcolm Galloway, Consultant Neurohistopathologist, Royal Free NHS Trust, London; Lucy Melly, Consultant Histopathologist, Royal Free NHS Trust, London; Colm O'Mahony, Consultant in HIV, Countess of Chester Foundation Trust Hospital, Chester; John Williams, Senior Principal Clinical Scientist, London School of Tropical Medicine and Hygiene, London; Pauline Wilson, Consultant Ophthalmologist, Royal Free NHS Trust, London; James Kalmakoff, Associate Professor, Department of Microbiology and Immunology, University of Otago, New Zealand; Victor Hoffbrand, Professor, Department of Haematology, Royal Free NHS Trust, London; Rob Shorten, Clinical Scientist, Royal Free NHS Trust, London.

Contributors

Sanjay Bhagani
Department of Infectious Diseases
Royal Free NHS Trust
London, UK

Claire Booth
Department of Virology
Royal Free NHS Trust
London, UK

Cristina Cellerai
Department of Immunology
Royal Free NHS Trust
London, UK

Christopher Collis
Department of Oncology
Royal Free NHS Trust
London, UK

Ian Cropley
Department of Infectious Diseases
Royal Free NHS Trust
London, UK

Kate Cwynarksi
Department of Haematology
Royal Free NHS Trust
London, UK

Anna Maria Geretti
Department of Virology
Royal Free NHS Trust
London, UK

Justin Green
Department of Infectious Diseases
Royal Free NHS Trust
London, UK

Marc Heller
Department of Haematology
Royal Free NHS Trust
London, UK

Margaret A Johnson
Department of HIV Medicine
Royal Free NHS Trust
London, UK

Sabine Kinloch-de Loes
Department of HIV Medicine
Royal Free NHS Trust
London, UK

Miranda Kronfli
Department of Oncology
Royal Free NHS Trust
London, UK

Marc Lipman
Department of Respiratory Medicine
Royal Free NHS Trust
London, UK

Tabitha W Mahungu
Department of HIV Medicine
Royal Free NHS Trust
London, UK

Neal Marshall
Department of HIV Medicine
Royal Free NHS Trust
London, UK

Devaki Nair
Department of Clinical Biochemistry
Royal Free NHS Trust
London, UK

Alison J Rodger
Departments of Infectious Diseases and HIV Medicine
Royal Free NHS Trust
London, UK

Rimi Shah
Department of HIV Medicine
Royal Free NHS Trust
London, UK

Abbreviations

ABC abacavir
ADAMTS-13 ADAM metallopeptidase with thrombospondin type 1 motif
ADC AIDS dementia complex
ADCC antibody-dependent cellular cytotoxicity
ADI AIDS-defining illness
AFB acid-fast bacilli
AFP alpha-fetoprotein
AIDS acquired immunodeficiency syndrome
AITP autoimmune thrombocytopenia
ALT alanine aminotransferase
AMI acute myocardial infarction
ARL AIDS-related lymphoma
ART antiretroviral treatment
AST aspartate aminotransferase
ARV antiretroviral
ATV atazanavir
AUC area under curve
AUROC area under the receiver operating characteristic curve
AXR abdominal X-ray
AZT azidothymidine (zidovudine)
BAL bronchoalveolar lavage
BBB blood–brain barrier
BCG bacillus Calmette-Guérin
BHIVA British HIV Association
BMI body mass index
CAP community acquired pneumonia
CCR5 chemokine receptor type 5
CDC Centers for Disease Control and Prevention
CHOP cyclophosphamide, doxorubicin, vincristine, prednisolone
CM cryptococcal meningitis
CML chronic myeloid leukaemia
CMV cytomegalovirus
CNS central nervous system
CPAP continuous positive airway pressure
CRAG cryptococcal antigen
CRF circulating recombinant form
CRP C-reactive protein
CSF cerebrospinal fluid
CT computed tomography
CTL cytotoxic T lymphocyte

CVD cardiovascular disease
D4T stavudine
DAT direct antiglobulin (Coombs) test
DBP diastolic blood pressure
DC dendritic cell
DDI didanosine
DLBCL diffuse large B-cell lymphoma
DM diabetes mellitus
DNA deoxyribonucleic acid
DRV darunavir
EACS European AIDS Clinical Society
EBV Epstein–Barr virus
ECS elective caesarean section
EFV efavirenz
eGFR estimated glomerular filtration rate
ELISA enzyme-linked immunosorbent assay
EMU early morning urine
FBC full blood count
FDA Food and Drug Administration
FDG fluorodeoxyglucose
FNA fine-needle aspirate
FPV fosamprenavir
FTC emtricitabine
G6PD glucose-6-phosphate
GIST gastrointestinal stromal carcinoma
GUM genitourinary medicine
H&E haematoxylin and eosin (stain)
HAART highly active antiretroviral therapy
HbA1c glycosylated haemoglobin
HBeAg hepatitis B e antigen
HBsAb hepatitis B surface antibody
HBsAg hepatitis B surface antigen
HBV hepatitis B virus
HCC hepatocellular carcinoma
HCV hepatitis C virus
HDL-c high-density lipoprotein cholesterol
HHV human herpesvirus
HIV human immunodeficiency virus
HIVAN HIV-associated nephropathy
HPA Health Protection Agency
HPLC high-performance liquid chromatography

HSCT haematopoietic stem cell transplantation
HSR hypersensitivity reaction
HSV herpes simplex virus
HT hypertension
HTN hypertension
HUS haemolytic uraemic syndrome
ICP intracranial pressure
IFAT immunofluorescent antibody test
IFN interferon
IGRA interferon gamma release assay
IGT impaired glucose tolerance
IHD ischaemic heart disease
IL interleukin
IRIS immune reconstitution inflammatory syndrome
ITU intensive care unit
IVDU intravenous drug user
KS Kaposi's sarcoma
KSHV Kaposi's sarcoma-associated herpesvirus
LDH lactic dehydrogenase
LDL-c low-density lipoprotein cholesterol
LFT liver function test
LGV lymphogranuloma venereum
LP lumbar puncture
LPV lopinavir
LTBI latent TB infection
LTR long terminal repeat
MAC *Mycobacterium avium intracellulare* complex
MAI *Mycobacterium avium intracellulare*
MC&S microscopy, culture, and sensitivity
MCD multicentric Castleman's disease
MCV mean cell volume
MDR multidrug-resistant
MDT multidisciplinary team meeting
MRI magnetic resonance imaging
MSM men who have sex with men
MTB *Mycobacterium tuberculosis*
MTCT mother-to-child transmission
NAb neutralizing antibody
NASBA nucleic acid sequence based amplification

NHL non-Hodgkin's lymphoma
NK natural killer (cell)
NNRTI non-nucleoside reverse transcriptase inhibitor
NPA nasopharyngeal aspirate
NPV negative predictive value
NRTI nucleoside reverse transcriptase inhibitor
NtRTI nucleotide reverse transcriptase inhibitor
NVP nevirapine
OD opportunistic disease
OGD oesophagogastroduodenoscopy
OHL oral hairy leukoplakia
OI opportunistic infection
PACTG Pediatric AIDS Clinical Trials Group
PAP Papanicolaou (stain)
PCP *Pneumocystis jiroveci* pneumonia
PCR polymerase chain reaction
pegIFN pegylated interferon
PEP post-exposure prophylaxis
PEPSE PEP after sexual exposure
PET positron emission tomography
PGL persistent generalized lymphadenopathy
PI protease inhibitor
PK pharmacokinetic

PML progressive multifocal leukoencephalopathy
POEMS polyneuropathy, organomegaly, endocrinopathy, monoclonal gammopathy, and skin changes
PORN progressive outer retinal necrosis
PPD purified protein derivative
PPV positive predictive value
PrEP pre-exposure prophylaxis
PUO pyrexia of unknown origin
RAL raltegravir
RCC red cell count/renal cell carcinoma
RNA ribonucleic acid
RT reverse transcriptase
RVR rapid virological response
SBP systolic blood pressure
SIV simian immunodeficiency virus
SJS Stevens–Johnson syndrome
SOL space-occupying lesion
SPECT single photon emission computed tomography
SQV saquinavir
STI sexually transmitted infection
SVD spontaneous vaginal delivery
SVR sustained virological response

TB tuberculosis
TBM tuberculous meningitis
TC total cholesterol
TDF tenofovir
TDM therapeutic drug monitoring
TEN toxic epidermal necrolysis
TG triglyceride
Th helper T lymphocyte
TLR Toll-like receptor
TNF tumour necrosis factor
Treg T regulatory cell
TST tuberculin skin test
TTP thrombotic thrombocytopenic purpura
ULN upper limit of normal
URF unique recombinant form
VDRL Venereal Disease Research Laboratory
VEGF vascular endothelial growth factor
VL viral load
vWF von Willebrand factor
VZV varicella zoster virus
WHO World Health Organization
XDR extensively drug-resistant
ZDV zidovudine
ZN Ziehl–Neelsen (stain)

Chapter 1

Introduction

TW Mahungu

History of the HIV epidemic

The first cases of acquired immunodeficiency syndrome (AIDS) were reported in 1981 by the Centers for Disease Control and Prevention (CDC) after the emergence of biopsy-confirmed *pneumocystis* pneumonia in five young, previously healthy male homosexuals[1]. Incidentally all five patients had a history of cytomegalovirus infection and candidiasis. These initial reports were subsequently followed by a cluster of cases of *pneumocystis* pneumonia with Kaposi's sarcoma also in male homosexuals. In Uganda, physicians were confronted by an equally baffling fatal, wasting, diarrhoeal illness which they referred to as 'slim disease'[2]. The aetiology of this devastating illness remained unknown until 1983 when the retrovirus was isolated by Luc Montagnier's[3] and Robert Gallo's[4] group, linking human immunodeficiency virus (HIV) to AIDS.

The HIV epidemic is just under three decades old. During this period, there have been several leaps and bounds (**1.1**). The greatest has been the advent of highly active antiretroviral therapy (HAART) in the mid-1990s resulting in the transformation of HIV infection from a terminal illness into a manageable chronic disease. Unfortunately, despite the fact that many resource-poor countries have made considerable progress in improving access to HIV prevention and treatment, universal access is yet to be achieved. According to the Joint United Nations Programme on HIV/AIDS (UNAIDS) there were approximately 33 million people living with HIV infection at the end of 2009 (**1.2**). Sub-Saharan Africa continues to account for over two-thirds of the epidemic (**1.3**). Despite these alarming figures, the prevalence of HIV infection in adults appears to have levelled off over the last 7 years. We remain hopeful that by 2015 universal access will become a reality to all affected populations in line with the Millennium Development Goals.

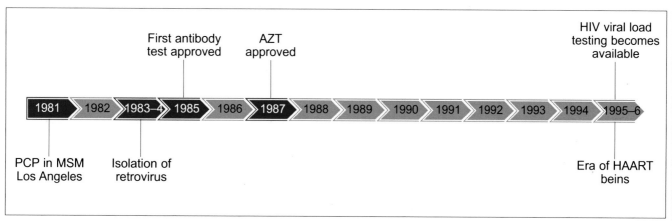

1.1 Key events leading up to the era of HAART. AZT: azidothymidine; HIV: human immunodeficiency virus; MSM: men who have sex with men; PCP: *Pneumocystis jirovecii* pneumonia.

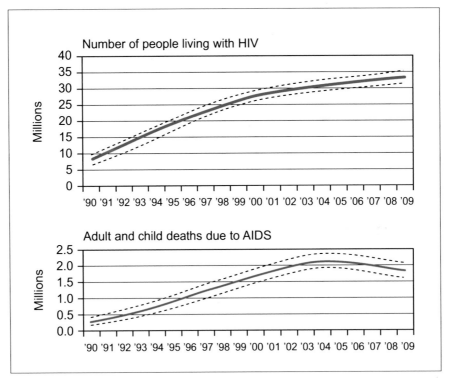

1.2 Number of people living with HIV and percentage adult HIV prevalence. Solid lines, estimates; dotted lines ranges. (Adapted from UNAIDS data 2010.)

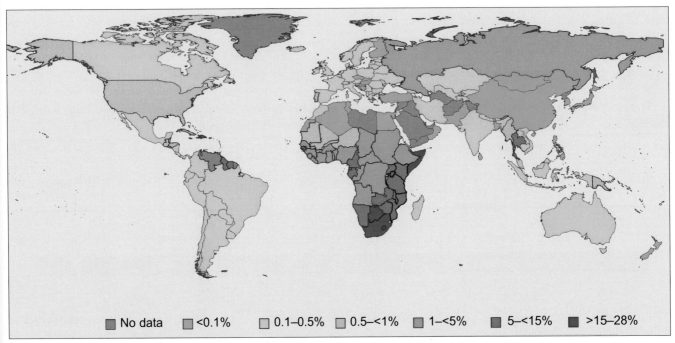

1.3 Adult (age 15–49 years) prevalence of HIV by geographical regions. (Adapted from UNAIDS data 2010.)

Transmission of HIV infection

HIV infection can be transmitted via
Sexual intercourse
Unprotected sexual intercourse is the most common route of HIV transmission, accounting for up to 85% of all infections[5]. There is no doubt that an individual is at their most infectious during primary HIV infection when the virus undergoes extensive, uncontrolled replication with HIV viral loads frequently exceeding a million copies per millilitre. The risk of transmission is amplified in receptive anal intercourse and by the presence of concurrent sexually transmitted infections. Studies in serodiscordant heterosexual couples have shown that in established HIV infection, the risk of transmission is highly dependent on the plasma HIV viral load[6].

Contaminated blood and blood products
After the development of the first HIV antibody test in 1985, most industrialized countries adopted universal screening of all blood donations for HIV infection. Unfortunately, due to financial constraints the risk of acquiring HIV infection from contaminated blood and blood products remains a reality in many resource-poor countries. Outside sub-Saharan Africa sharing unsterilized needles and syringes remains an important route of transmission in intravenous drug users.

Mother to child transmission
The prevention of mother to child transmission (MTCT) remains one of the most successful HIV prevention strategies. In an antiretroviral-naïve pregnant mother, there is a 30% risk of transmitting HIV infection *in utero* or at delivery. Most of the transmission occurs in the third trimester and at delivery but there remains a residual risk of infection through breastfeeding. Where the appropriate measures are taken to prevent MTCT, the risk of vertical transmission falls to less than 1%[7]. As the rate of transmission is governed by the availability of effective antiretroviral therapy, the rates of MTCT in other parts of the world reflect local practice.

The factors determining HIV infectivity and the risk of HIV transmission by route of exposure are summarized in *Tables 1.1* and *1.2*.

Table 1.1 Factors determining HIV infectivity

Host	*Agent*
Genetics • Host genetic factors determine susceptibility, e.g. CCR5-Δ32 deletion confers high level of protection	*HIV virus* • HIV-2 less easily transmitted than HIV-1 • *In-vitro* studies have shown that some subtypes are more infectious
Environment *Barriers* • Direct inoculation into blood stream more efficient than via mucous membranes • Transmission determined by the integrity of the mucous membrane, e.g. STIs increase transmission, circumcision reduces transmission *High-risk practices* • Risk increases with number of high-risk sexual partners, contaminated needles	*HIV viral load* • HIV viral load is one of the strongest predictors of transmission

Table 1.2 Risk of HIV transmission by route of exposure

Exposure	Estimated risk of transmission per exposure (%)
Blood transfusion	90–100
Mother to child	30
Anal intercourse	
Receptive	0.1–3.0
Insertive	0.06
Vaginal intercourse	
Receptive	0.1–0.2
Insertive	0.03–0.09
Receptive oral sex (fellatio)	0–0.04
Needle stick injury	0.3
Sharing injecting equipment	0.67

(Adapted from Fisher M, *et al. Int J STD & AIDS* 2006;**17**:81–92)

Natural history of HIV infection

There are three distinct phases in the natural history of untreated HIV infection (see **1.4**).

Primary HIV infection is often missed or misdiagnosed as patients may be asymptomatic or the clinical presentation resembles a nonspecific viral illness. This period lasts from the time of HIV transmission to the moment an individual mounts a detectable antibody response. During this phase, there is extensive viral replication resulting in a marked drop in CD4 cells. The CD4 count normally bounces back up but to levels lower than the pre-infection count.

Following acute HIV infection, a *viral set point,* which is governed by the unique immune response of the host to the virus, is reached. Patients now enter the next phase of **chronic HIV infection**. During this phase there is a steady decline of CD4 cells. Towards the end of this phase patients may begin to experience constitutional symptoms and develop illness referred to as *indicator diseases*. The rate of CD4 cell decline is variable with a small minority never progressing to AIDS, i.e. *'long term nonprogressors'*. Within this group lies a subset of individuals who control HIV replication to undetectable levels, i.e. *'elite controllers'*.

Once an individual's CD4 count drops below 200 cells/mm^3, they have **advanced HIV infection** and are at risk of developing a number of opportunistic diseases. Although rare, there are well documented reports of opportunistic infections occurring in patients with CD4 cell counts above 200 cells/mm^3.

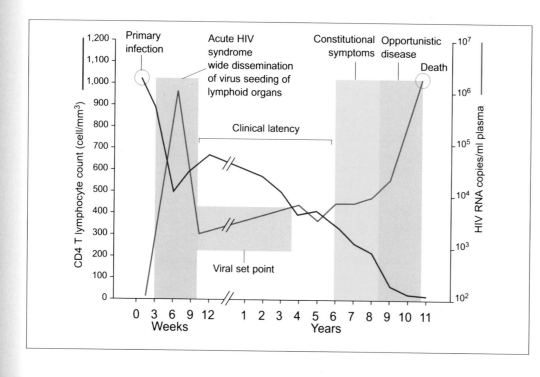

1.4 Natural history of untreated HIV infection. RNA: ribonucleic acid.

Classification of HIV infection

The Centers for Disease Control and Prevention (CDC) and the World Health Organization (WHO) have developed staging systems that classify patients on the basis of certain clinical conditions and infections. The WHO system is reliant on clinical symptoms as laboratory evaluations are not always available in resource-poor settings. The CDC system on the other hand consists of a composite of associated clinical conditions and infections and the CD4 count. These are summarized in *Tables 1.3–1.5*.

Table 1.3 WHO clinical staging of HIV infection

Primary
- Asymptomatic
- Acute retroviral syndrome

Clinical stage I
- Asymptomatic
- Persistent generalized lymphadenopathy (PGL)

Clinical stage II
- Weight loss (<10% of body weight)
- Mucocutaneous disease, e.g. seborrhoeic dermatitis, recurrent oral ulceration
- Herpes zoster (within last 5 years)
- Recurrent upper respiratory tract infections

Clinical stage III
- Weight loss (>10% of body weight)
- Chronic diarrhoea (>1 month)
- Unexplained fever (>1 month)
- Oral candida
- Oral hairy leukoplakia
- Pulmonary tuberculosis (within past year)
- Severe bacterial infection

Clinical Stage IV
- HIV wasting syndrome
- *Pneumocystis jirovecii* pneumonia
- Cerebral toxoplasmosis
- Diarrhoea secondary to cryptosporidiosis (exceeding 1 month)
- Extrapulmonary cryptococcosis
- CMV disease (of any organ other than liver, spleen, and lymph nodes)
- Herpes simplex
- Progressive multifocal leukoencephalopathy
- Disseminated endemic mycosis
- Oesphageal, tracheo-bronchial candidiasis
- Disseminated atypical mycobacteria
- Nontyphoid salmonella septicaemia
- Extrapulmonary tuberculosis
- Lymphoma
- Kaposi's sarcoma
- HIV encephalopathy

(Adapted from WHO data: http://www.who.int/hiv/pub/guidelines/HIVstaging150307.pdf)

Table 1.4 CDC classification system of HIV infection

CD4 (cells/mm^3)	A Asymptomatic PGL Acute HIV	B Symptomatic conditions (excluding A or C)	C AIDS-defining conditions
≥500	A1	B1	C1
200–499	A2	B2	C2
<200	A3	B3	C3

(Adapted from CDC data: http://www.cdc.gov/mmwr/preview/mmwrhtml/00018871.htm)

Table 1.5 CDC symptomatic and AIDS-defining conditions

Symptomatic conditions

- Bacillary angiomatosis
- Oropharyngeal candidiasis
- Vulvovaginal candidiasis, persistent or resistant
- Pelvic inflammatory disease
- Cervical dysplasia/cervical carcinoma in situ
- Oral hairy leukoplakia
- Idiopathic thrombocytopenic purpura
- Constitutional symptoms, such as fever or diarrhoea lasting >1 month
- Peripheral neuropathy
- Herpes zoster (≥2 episodes or ≥1 dermatome)

AIDS-defining conditions

- Recurrent bacterial pneumonia
- Candidiasis of the bronchi, trachea, or lungs
- Oesophageal candidiasis
- Cervical carcinoma, invasive, confirmed by biopsy
- Coccidioidomycosis (disseminated or extrapulmonary)
- Extrapulmonary cryptococcosis
- Chronic intestinal cryptosporidiosis
- CMV disease (other than liver, spleen, or nodes)
- HIV encephalopathy
- Herpes simplex: chronic ulcers or bronchitis, pneumonitis, or oesophagitis
- Histoplasmosis (disseminated or extrapulmonary)
- Chronic intestinal isosporiasis
- Kaposi's sarcoma
- Lymphoma
- Atypical mycobacteria (disseminated or extrapulmonary)
- *Mycobacterium* tuberculosis, pulmonary or extrapulmonary
- *Pneumocystis jirovecii* pneumonia (PCP)
- Progressive multifocal leukoencephalopathy (PML)
- *Salmonella* septicaemia, recurrent (nontyphoid)
- Cerebral toxoplasmosis
- HIV wasting syndrome due to HIV (involuntary weight loss >10% of baseline body weight) associated with either chronic diarrhoea (≥2 loose stools per day ≥1 month) or chronic weakness and documented fever ≥1 month

(Adapted from CDC data: http://www.cdc.gov/mmwr/preview/mmwrhtml/00018871.htm)

Primary HIV infection

Primary HIV infection is classically described as an 'acute mononucleosis-like illness' occurring between 2 and 6 weeks after HIV infection[8]. It normally lasts for between 1 and 2 weeks but can last considerably longer in a minority of cases. Unfortunately, the seroconversion illness is often missed. The diagnosis of HIV infection is often late with a significant number of patients presenting with an opportunistic infection several years after seroconversion.

Presentation

Acute HIV-I infection is symptomatic in 40–90% of all cases. The most common symptoms include:
- A triad of fever, maculopapular rash (upper trunk), and lymphadenopathy.
- Oropharyngeal ulceration.
- Other manifestations are summarized in *Table 1.6*.

Important differential diagnoses include: Epstein–Barr virus (EBV) infectious mononucleosis, toxoplasmosis,

Table 1.6 Signs and symptoms of acute HIV infection

Generalized/constitutional

- Fever
- Lymphadenopathy
- Arthralgia
- Myalgia
- Loss of appetite
- Weight loss
- Malaise

Gastrointestinal

- Abdominal pain
- Nausea and vomiting
- Diarrhoea
- Transaminitis

AIDS-defining illnesses

- Rare

Neurological

- Headache
- Aseptic meningitis
- Transverse myelitis
- Encephalitis
- Peripheral neuropathy
- Guillain–Barré-like syndrome

Dermatological/mucosal

- Rash
- Oral ulceration
- Pharyngitis

(Adapted from BHIVA, *UK National Guidelines for HIV Testing 2008,* BHIVA 2008)

rubella, measles, secondary syphilis, influenza, primary herpes simplex virus (HSV)/cytomegalovirus (CMV), and viral hepatitis.

Diagnosis

The diagnosis is dependent on the demonstration of HIV-1 replication in the absence of HIV-1 antibodies. Following clinical suspicion, individuals should have both an HIV-1 antibody test and HIV-1 ribonucleic acid (RNA) quantification. A new diagnosis must be confirmed with a follow up HIV-1 antibody test during the next 12 weeks. There is often a marked increase in CD8-positive T-cells during primary HIV infection, indicating increased immune activation.

Treatment

Treatment is often supportive. However, there is considerable interest in the use of antiretroviral therapy to shorten the duration of the acute syndrome, thereby reducing the number of infected cells and preserving HIV-1 specific immune responses[9]. The results of the first randomized trial (SPARTAC) powered to investigate the benefits of early antiretroviral treatment (ART) are eagerly awaited. In the meantime, any patients being considered for ART during this period should be treated within a clinical trial. Recognition of acute HIV infection allows the early diagnosis of HIV infection before patients present with opportunistic disease. It also provides an opportunity to decrease onward transmission, as patients tend to be at their most infectious at this time point.

HIV testing

Throughout the world, HIV infection continues to be diagnosed late. In industrialized nations most of these late diagnoses are in ethnic minorities and marginalized groups where heterosexual transmission remains the primary route of HIV infection. In the United Kingdom (UK) the Health Protection Agency (HPA) reported that of the estimated 86,500 people living with HIV in the UK at the end of 2009, 26% were unaware of their infection. Unlinked, anonymous prevalence surveillance reveals that men who have sex with men (MSM) and sub-Saharan-born heterosexuals account for the highest proportions of undiagnosed HIV infection (**1.5**). Furthermore, 30% of the individuals newly diagnosed with HIV were diagnosed late, i.e. with a CD4 count below 200 cells/mm^3. The proportion of late diagnoses was highest in heterosexual women and men (**1.6**).

Unfortunately, individuals presenting with advanced disease are more likely to present with opportunistic infections and have suboptimal clinical outcomes. A significant proportion of these 'late presenters' have had contact with medical services prior to their diagnosis where the opportunity to offer an HIV test has often been missed. There is therefore a need to increase the uptake of HIV testing in non-HIV clinical settings.

Since the United States of America (USA) Food and Drug Administration (FDA) approved the first HIV antibody test in 1985, HIV testing has evolved from a tool that was designed to screen blood supplies to a voluntary test that is offered in healthcare settings. At the beginning of the AIDS epidemic, the fear of stigma and discrimination

as well as the very poor prognosis of an AIDS diagnosis resulted in a test that was only performed if an individual had received pre-test counselling and provided informed consent. It may be argued that in the long term, in an era where HIV is now considered to be a chronic disease, these measures may have contributed to the slow uptake of HIV testing outside HIV specialist settings. The benefits of early HIV testing include:

- Identification of HIV-infected individuals as early into their infection as possible.
- Reduction of the onward transmission of HIV infection to others.

In most healthcare systems, HIV testing occurs in a number of settings. In one setting, individuals may self-present to genitourinary medicine (GUM) or same-day testing centres. In another setting, individuals seeking medical care in specific settings are informed that an HIV test is routinely performed on everyone unless they explicitly decline (**opt out**). This is common practice in UK GUM

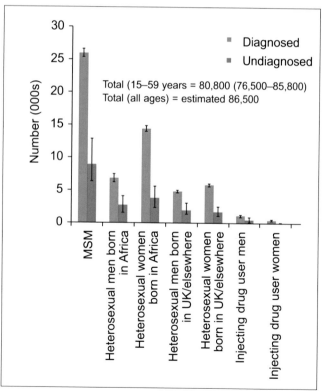

1.5 Estimated number of adults living with HIV (both diagnosed and undiagnosed). (Adapted from HPA data, 2010.)

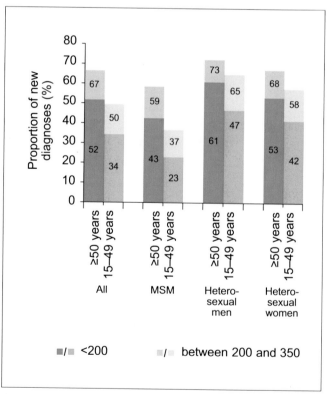

1.6 Estimated late diagnosis of HIV infection by prevention group, 2007. (Adapted from HPA data, 2010.)

and antenatal services, where the uptake of HIV testing is up to 77% and 95% respectively. More frequently, individuals presenting with suggestive symptoms or high-risk behaviour are offered a diagnostic HIV test (**opt in**).

Since 2006, the CDC recommends universal testing of ALL individuals presenting to a medical facility. In the UK and Europe, there is a move towards more targeted testing where local HIV prevalence data as well as the presence of indicator diseases determine whether HIV testing is routinely performed[10]. The British HIV Association

(BHIVA) guidelines are summarized in *Table 1.7*. This information must be disseminated to healthcare workers outside HIV specialist centres, as this is where patients are likely to present.

In all settings it is important that the offer of an HIV test remains voluntary and the results confidential. As with any other medical test it is important that individuals understand the implications and results of the test. It is therefore important that patients are counselled **before** and **after** the test. See *Tables 1.8*, *1.9* for BHIVA recommendations.

Table 1.7 British HIV Association (BHIVA) guidelines for HIV testing

Universal testing
- Genitourinary medicine clinics
- Antenatal care
- Termination of pregnancy services
- Drug dependency programmes
- Patients with TB, hepatitis B/C, lymphoma

Routinely perform (Department of Health Guidance)
- Blood donors
- Dialysis patients
- Organ transplant donors and recipients

Routinely offer
- All sexual partners of individuals known to be HIV positive
- All patients diagnosed with a sexually transmitted disease
- All patients with *indicator diseases*
- All injecting drug users
- All female and male sexual contacts of men who have sex with men
- All men and women from countries with an HIV prevalence of >1%
- All men and women reporting sexual contact (locally or abroad) with individuals from countries with an HIV prevalence of >1%

If local HIV prevalence >2/1,000, *consider testing*
- All patients registered in general practice
- All general medical admissions

(Adapted from BHIVA, *UK National Guidelines for HIV Testing 2008*, BHIVA 2008)

Table 1.8 Components of the pre-test discussion

- Explain indication for test
- Obtain a thorough and chronological history of sexual and other high-risk practices
- Ascertain whether individual is within 'window period'
- Explain practicalities of test, i.e. how it will be performed, how and when results will be given
- Explain implications of positive test
- Give an opportunity to ask questions
- Obtain informed consent

(Adapted from BHIVA, *UK National Guidelines for HIV Testing 2008*, BHIVA 2008)

Table 1.9 Components of the post-test discussion

Provide results (should be confidential)

If positive:
- Reinforce implications of positive test
- General education regarding the natural history of HIV infection and the current treatment options
- Establish whether there is a need for psychological support
- Discuss the need for testing partners or children if appropriate
- Discuss risk-reduction behaviour
- Obtain blood test for confirmation of diagnosis
- Book patient into new patient clinic within a week

If negative:
- Establish whether there is a need for retesting if individual 'within window period'
- Establish whether post-exposure prophylaxis is indicated
- Discuss risk-reduction behaviour

(Adapted from BHIVA, *UK National Guidelines for HIV Testing 2008*, BHIVA 2008)

Table 1.10 Clinical indicator diseases for adult and paediatric HIV infection

AIDS-defining conditions	Other conditions where HIV testing should be considered	AIDS-defining conditions	Other conditions where HIV testing should be considered
ADULT HIV INFECTION *Respiratory* • Tuberculosis • Pneumocystis	• Bacterial pneumonia • Aspergillosis	**ADULT HIV INFECTION (cont.)** *Other*	• Mononucleosis-like syndrome (primary HIV infection) • Pyrexia of unknown origin • Any lymphadenopathy of unknown cause • Any sexually transmitted infection
Neurology • Cerebral toxoplasmosis • Primary cerebral lymphoma • Cryptococcal meningitis • Progressive multifocal leukoencephalopathy	• Aseptic meningitis/encephalitis • Cerebral abscess • Space-occupying lesion of unknown cause • Guillain–Barré syndrome • Transverse myelitis • Peripheral neuropathy • Dementia • Leukoencephalopathy	**PAEDIATRIC HIV INFECTION** *ENT*	• Chronic parotitis • Recurrent and/or troublesome ear infections
Dermatology • Kaposi's sarcoma	• Severe or recalcitrant seborrhoeic dermatitis • Severe or recalcitrant psoriasis • Multidermatomal or recurrent herpes zoster	*Oral*	• Recurrent oral candidiasis • Poor dental hygiene
Gastroenterology • Persistent cryptosporidiosis	• Oral hairy leukoplakia • Oral candidiasis • Chronic diarrhoea of unknown cause • Weight loss of unknown cause • Hepatitis B infection • Hepatitis C infection • Shigella, salmonella, or campylobacter	*Respiratory* • Pneumocystis • CMV pneumocystis • Tuberculosis	• Recurrent bacterial pneumonia • Lymphoid interstitial pneumonitis • Bronchiectasis
		Neurology • HIV encephalopathy meningitis/encephalitis	• Developmental delay • Childhood stroke
Oncology • Non-Hodgkin's lymphoma	• Anal cancer or anal intra-epithelial dysplasia • Lung cancer • Seminoma • Head and neck cancer • Hodgkin's lymphoma • Castleman's disease	*Dermatology* • Kaposi's sarcoma	• Severe or recalcitrant dermatitis • Multidermatomal or recurrent herpes zoster • Recurrent funagal infections • Extensive warts or molluscum contagiosum
Gynaecology • Cervical cancer	• Cervical intraepithelial neoplasia (Grade 2 or above) • Vaginal intraepithelial neoplasia	*Gastroenterology* • Wasting syndrome • Persistent cryptosporidiosis	• Unexplained persistent hepatosplenomegaly • Hepatitis B infection • Hepatitis C infection
Haematology	• Any unexplained blood dyscrasia including: – lymphopenia – neutropenia – thrombocytopenia	*Oncology* • Lymphoma • Kaposi's sarcoma	
		Haematology	• Any unexplained blood dyscrasia including: – lymphopenia – neutropenia – thrombocytopenia
Ophthalmology • Cytomegalovirus retinitis	• Any unexplained retinopathy • Infective retinal diseases, including herpes viruses and toxoplasma	*Ophthalmology* • Cytomegalovirus retinitis	• Any unexplained retinopathy
ENT	• Lymphadenopathy of unknown cause • Lymphoepithelial parotid cysts • Chronic parotitis	*Other* • Recurrent bacterial infections, e.g. meningitis, sepsis, osteomyelitis, pneumonia • Pyrexia of unknown origin	

(Adapted from BHIVA, *UK National Guidelines for HIV Testing 2008,* BHIVA 2008)

Indicator diseases (1.7–1.11)

In the HIV context, indicator diseases are defined as diseases associated with a co-morbid HIV incidence of significance. *All AIDS-defining illnesses are included in this list.* BHIVA in conjunction with the British Association of Sexual Health and HIV, and the British Infection Society have compiled a list that contains a number of clinical conditions that if present should alert the clinician to consider HIV infection in the differential diagnosis (*Table 1.10*).

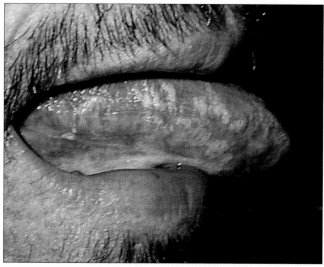

1.7 *Oral hairy leukoplakia.* This is one of the most common oral diseases in HIV. It is caused by EBV and is characterized by asymptomatic white plaques on the lateral borders of the tongue as well as on the buccal mucosa and the gingiva.

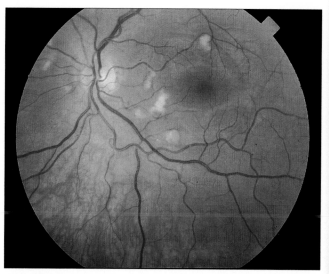

1.8 *AIDS retinopathy.* Characteristic indented ('hourglass') cotton wool spots with an otherwise normal fundus caused by immune complex microthrombi in the retinal vasculature.

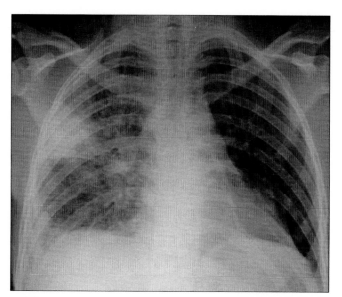

1.9 *Bacterial pneumonia.* Community acquired pneumonia is 10 times more common in HIV-infected patients in comparison to the general population.

1.10 *Acute retroviral syndrome.* Maculo-papular rash predominantly affecting the upper trunk. Often associated with fever and lymphadenopathy.

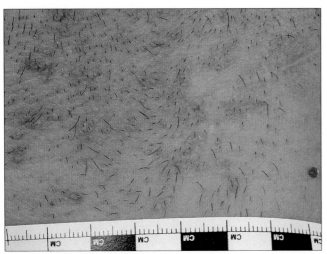

1.11 *Molluscum contagiosum*. Characteristic waxy, dome-shaped, umbilicated, flesh coloured papules caused by the DNA pox virus. They are commonly located on face, neck, axillae, and ano-genital region. Although not listed as an indicator disease in the BHIVA guidelines, in advanced HIV infection lesions tend to be multiple, larger, and persistent.

References

1 Pneumocystis pneumonia – Los Angeles. *MMWR Morb Mortal Wkly Rep* 1981 Jun 5;30(21):250–2.
2 Serwadda D, Mugerwa RD, Sewankambo NK, Lwegaba A, Carswell JW, Kirya GB, et al. Slim disease: a new disease in Uganda and its association with HTLV-III infection. *Lancet* 1985 Oct 19;2(8460):849–52.
3 Chermann JC, Barre-Sinoussi F, Dauguet C, Brun-Vezinet F, Rouzioux C, Rozenbaum W, et al. Isolation of a new retrovirus in a patient at risk for acquired immunodeficiency syndrome. *Antibiot Chemother* 1983;32:48–53.
4 Gelmann EP, Popovic M, Blayney D, Masur H, Sidhu G, Stahl RE, et al. Proviral DNA of a retrovirus, human T-cell leukemia virus, in two patients with AIDS. *Science* 1983 May 20;220(4599):862–5.
5 Royce RA, Sena A, Cates W, Jr., Cohen MS. Sexual transmission of HIV. *N Engl J Med* 1997 Apr 10;336(15):1072–8.
6 Gray RH, Wawer MJ, Brookmeyer R, Sewankambo NK, Serwadda D, Wabwire-Mangen F, et al. Probability of HIV-1 transmission per coital act in monogamous, heterosexual, HIV-1-discordant couples in Rakai, Uganda. *Lancet* 2001 Apr 14;357(9263):1149–53.
7 Mother-to-child transmission of HIV infection in the era of highly active antiretroviral therapy. *Clin Infect Dis* 2005 Feb 1;40(3):458–65.
8 Jolles S, Kinloch de LS, Johnson MA, Janossy G. Primary HIV-1 infection: a new medical emergency? *BMJ* 1996 May 18;312(7041):1243–4.
9 Fidler S, Fox J, Porter K, Weber J. Primary HIV infection: to treat or not to treat? *Curr Opin Infect Dis* 2008 Feb;21(1):4–10.
10 Gazzard B, Clumeck N, d'Arminio MA, Lundgren JD. Indicator disease-guided testing for HIV – the next step for Europe? *HIV Med* 2008 Jul;9(Suppl 2):34–40.

Further reading

HIV in the United Kingdom: 2010 report. Health Protection Agency. Available at: http://www.hpa.org.uk/

Joint United Nations Programme on HIV/AIDS (UNAIDS). 2010 report on the global AIDS epidemic. Available at: http://www.unaids.org/

WHO case definitions of HIV for surveillance and revised clinical staging and immunological classification of HIV-related disease. World Health Organization 2007. Available at: http://www.who.int/hiv/pub/guidelines/HIVstaging150307.pdf

Centers for Disease Control and Prevention (CDC). 1993 Revised classification system for HIV infection and expanded surveillance case definition for AIDS among adolescents and adults. *MMWR Recomm Rep* 1992 Dec 18;41(RR-17):1–19. Available at: http://www.cdc.gov/mmwr/preview/mmwrhtml/00018871.htm).

Centers for Disease Control and Prevention (CDC). Revised Recommendations for HIV testing of adults, adolescents, and pregnant women in health-care settings. *MMWR Morb Mortal Wkly Rep* 2006;55(RR14):1–17. Available at: http://www.cdc.gov/mmwr/preview/mmwrhtml/rr5514a1.htm

British HIV Association, British Association of Sexual Health and HIV, British Infection Society. UK National Guidelines for HIV Testing 2008. Available at: www.bhiva.org

Chapter 2

Pathogenesis of HIV infection

HIV virology

AM Geretti and C Booth

Virus classification

Like all members of the *Retroviridae* family, HIV-1 and HIV-2 share a common step in their replication cycle, i.e. transcription of single-stranded genomic RNA into double-stranded complementary DNA by the viral reverse transcriptase (RT) enzyme.

HIV-1 and HIV-2 represent cross-species, zoonotic infections[1–3]. All known strains of HIV-1 are closely related to SIV$_{cpz}$ (simian immunodeficiency virus of chimpanzees), while the origin of HIV-2 has been traced to SIV$_{sm}$ found in sooty mangabeys (**2.1**).

The molecular epidemiology of HIV-1 infection is complex and in continuous evolution[4]. Phylogenetic analyses identify *nine* genetically equidistant subtypes within group M of HIV-1, which diverge by 20–30% in the *env* gene and 15–22% in the *gag* gene. Multiple inter-subtype circulating and unique recombinant forms (CRFs and URFs) have also been identified (**2.2**). In Western Europe several HIV-1 strains co-circulate, whereas subtype B accounts for most infections in North America (**2.3**).

HIV-1 subtypes show important differences in their genetic sequences and responses to gene expression regulatory factors, which influence cellular tropism, kinetics of viral replication, rate of disease progression, susceptibility to antiretroviral drugs, and drug resistance pathways. The classification of HIV-1 and HIV-2 is summarized in *Table 2.1*.

Table 2.1 Classification of HIV-1 and HIV-2

	HIV-1		*HIV-2*
Family	*Retroviridae*		*Retroviridae*
Genus	*Lentivirus*		*Lentivirus*
Prevalence	Global		West Africa
Group	M (major)	>90% of infections worldwide	–
	O (outlier)	West Africa	
	N (non-M/O)	West Africa	
Subtypes	A–D, F–H, J, K (all within Group M)		A–H
	Circulating recombinant forms (CRFs)		
	Unique recombinant forms (URFs)		
Related to:	SIV$_{cpz}$		SIV$_{sm}$
	Found in chimpanzees native to West Africa		Found in sooty mangabey
	(*Pan troglodytes troglodytes*)		(*Cercocebus atys*)

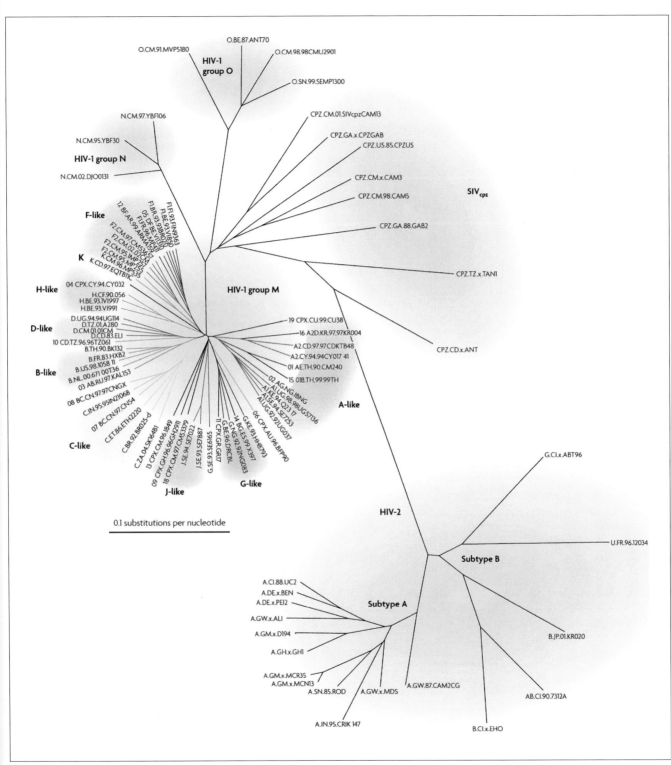

2.1 Phylogenetic tree; genetic relationship between HIV-1, HIV-2, and SIV$_{cpz}$. (Reprinted by permission from Macmillan Publishers Ltd: *Nature Reviews Microbiology* **5**(2):141–151, copyright 2007.)

2.2 Global prevalence of HIV-1 group M subtypes and CRFs. (Adapted from Osmanov S, *et al.*, 2002[5].)

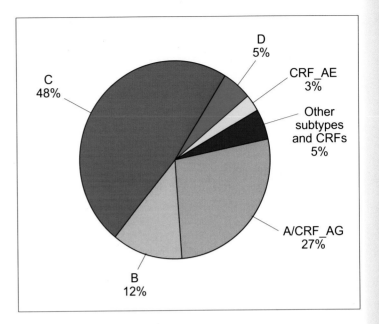

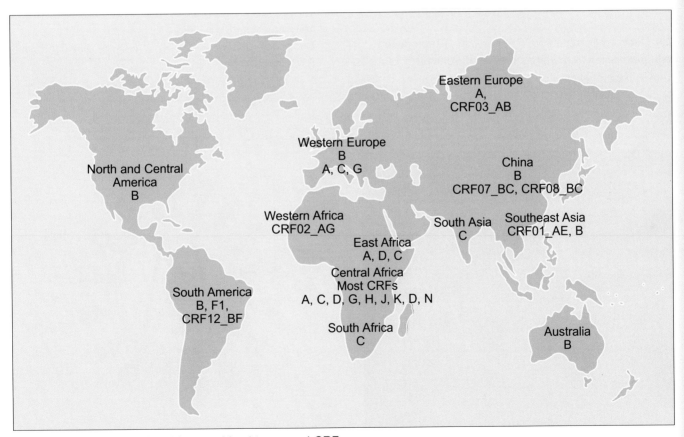

2.3 Global distribution of HIV-1 group M subtypes and CRFs.

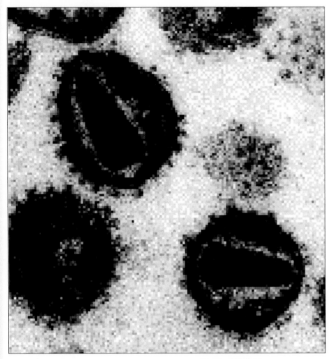

2.4 Electron micrograph of HIV particles. (Reproduced with permission from James Kalmakoff, University of Otago, New Zealand.)

Virus structure

The HIV particle has a diameter of 120 nm (**2.4**). It consists of:
- The *core,* which contains two single strands of positive-sense RNA surrounded by a conical capsid, composed of the viral p24 protein. The *matrix,* which is composed of the viral protein p17, surrounding the capsid.
- The *envelope,* which surrounds the core and is composed of two lipid layers derived from the host cell membrane and containing the viral glycoproteins (gp) 120 and 41 (**2.5**).

Viral genome

The RNA genome is 9.8 kb in size and contains (**2.6**):
- Three structural genes: *gag, pol,* and *env.*
- Six accessory and regulatory genes: *tat, rev, nef, vif, vpr,* and *vpu* (*vpx* in HIV-2).
- Long terminal repeat (LTR) sequences that flank each RNA strand.

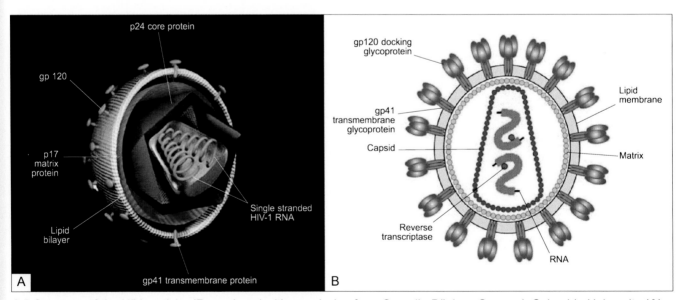

2.5 Structure of the HIV particle. (Reproduced with permission from Cornelia Büchen-Osmond, Columbia University (**A**), and the National Institutes of Health, Bethesda (**B**), NY, USA.)

The *gag* gene encodes a precursor protein, p55, which is cleaved into the smaller core proteins MA (matrix, p17), CA (capsid, p24), NC (nucleocapsid, p9), and p6.

The *pol* gene encodes the viral enzymes protease, RT, ribonuclease (RNAseH), and integrase, which are expressed within the context of a gag-pol precursor polyprotein (p160). The *env* gene encodes gp120 and gp41.

The LTR regions control virus production in response to viral or cellular proteins.

The structure and function of major HIV enzymes are summarized in *Table 2.2*.

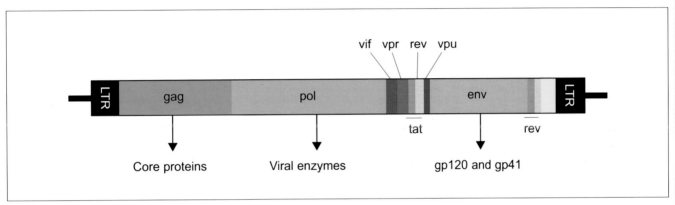

2.6 Organization of the HIV-1 genome.

Table 2.2 HIV enzymes

	Structure	Function
Protease	Homodimer Each half composed of 99 amino acids	Cleavage of gag (p55) and gag-pol (p160) precursor proteins into core proteins and viral enzymes
Reverse transcriptase	Heterodimer with two subunits: • p66: polymerase domain (440 amino acids) + C-terminal RNAse H domain (120 amino acids) • p51: corresponds to polymerase domain of p66	Reverse transcription (RNA-dependent DNA polymerase), ribonuclease (RNaseH), DNA-dependent DNA polymerase
Integrase	288 amino acids 3 domains: N-terminal, catalytic core, and C-terminal	Integration of proviral DNA into host genome, through exonuclease, endonuclease, and strand transfer/ligase functions

HIV replication

The life-cycle of HIV comprises six main steps (**2.7**).

1 Virus *entry* begins with binding of the viral gp120 to both the CD4 receptor and one of two main co-receptors (CCR5 or CXCR4) on the target cell. This is followed by a conformational change that allows gp41 to mediate *fusion* of the viral envelope with the host cell membrane.

2 Once viral nucleic material is released into host cytoplasm *reverse transcription* of the viral RNA occurs in the cytoplasm producing double-stranded DNA.

3 and 4 The double-stranded DNA migrates to the nucleus where it is *integrated* in to the host genome and *transcribed*.

5 *Assembly* of the newly produced viral proteins and genomic RNA occurs in the cytoplasm, and the new virus particle is released by *budding* from the cell surface.

6 *Cleavage* of the viral polyproteins is required for the functional maturation of the virus particle.

HIV tropism

Tropism is defined by the virus's preferential use and the cellular distribution of co-receptors. Although several co-receptors can mediate HIV entry, most strains bind to either CCR5 or CXCR4[6,7]. Three main phenotypes are recognized:

1 CCR5-using (R5) strains: R5 viruses play a key role in infection (*Table 2.3*, **2.8**).

2 CXCR4-using (X4) strains: X4 viruses tend to become dominant in advanced infection, but it is still debated whether their emergence is the cause or consequence of disease progression[8–11].

3 Dual tropic (R5/X4) strains: which can use both co-receptors.

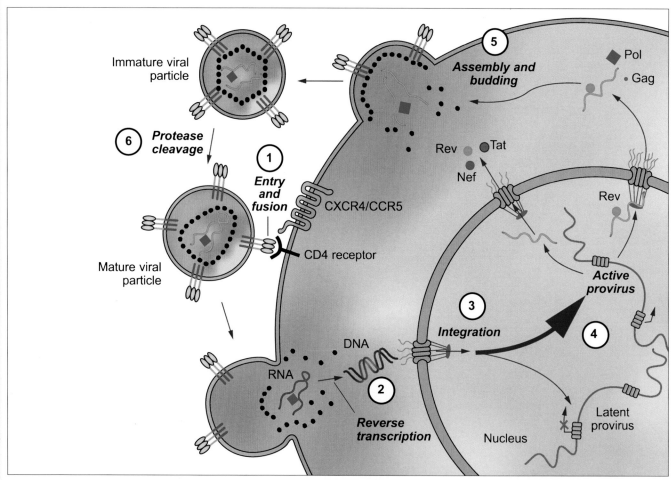

2.7 The life cycle of HIV. (Adapted from a figure supplied by the Gladstone Institute, University of California San Francisco, USA.) Drug action points (see Chapter 3): **1**: Entry inhibitors (Appendix 3.7); **2**: NRTIs (Appendix 3.2), NtRTI (Appendix 3.3), NNRTIs (Appendix 3.5), **3**: integrase inhibitors (Appendix 3.6); **5**: protease inhibitors (Appendix 3.1).

Table 2.3 HIV tropism

	R5	*X4*
Co-receptor	CCR5	CXCR4
Natural ligands	MIP-1α, MIP-1β, RANTES	SDF-1

Cellular targets	Macrophages
	Subset of memory CD4 T-cells
	Naïve CD4 T-cells must be activated to a memory phenotype to become a target
		Many cell types including:
		  naïve CD4 T-cells
		  memory CD4 T-cells
		  macrophages

Acute infection	Dominant	Rare
Chronic infection	Dominant	Rare
Advanced disease	Reduced dependence on high CD4/CCR5 levels for entry, decreased susceptibility to inhibition by RANTES, enhanced pathogenicity	Emerge in 40–60% of infected patients, coinciding with expanded cell tropism, increased viral replication, immunological deterioration, and disease progression
Host genetics	Homozygotes for a 32 bp deletion in CCR5 (CCR5-Δ32) are resistant to infection, heterozygotes have delayed disease progression	

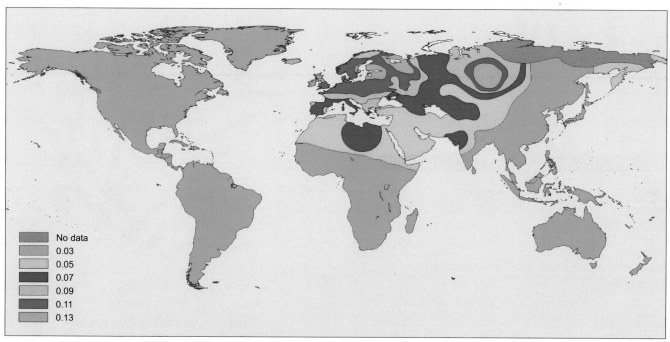

No data
0.03
0.05
0.07
0.09
0.11
0.13

2.8 Distribution of the HIV-resistant CCR5-Δ32 allele. Only the frequencies in native populations have been evidenced in America, Asia, Africa, and Oceania. (Adapted from Faure E, *et al.*, 2008[13].)

HIV tropism can be determined *in vitro* using recombinant viruses containing the *env* gene sequence from the patient's plasma viral RNA to infect cells expressing the CD4 receptor with either CCR5 or CXCR4[12]. Results are reported as R5, X4, or dual tropic/mixed (D/M), and do not distinguish between dual tropic virus and mixed populations of R5 and X4 strains. HIV tropism can also be predicted from the sequence of the V3 loop in gp120 (**2.9, 2.10**). This is the major determinant of co-receptor use, reflecting the structural homology between the crown of the V3 loop and the beta2-beta3 loop in the natural chemokine ligands[14].

HIV replication dynamics, genetic variability, and fitness

HIV infection is characterized by:
- High levels of virus replication.
- Ongoing genetic diversification.
- Rapid virus clearance by the immune system[18,19].

The RT enzyme, which is responsible for the production of double stranded DNA from the viral RNA template during virus replication:

- Has low fidelity, with an estimated error rate of 10^{-4} nucleotides.
- Lacks proof-reading activity therefore nucleotide *mis-incorporations* become fixed in the newly produced genome as point mutations. All mutations can occur daily, and while some mutants are not functional, others persist in plasma and within integrated proviral DNA. *Duplications* and *insertions* also occur.
- A further mechanism of genetic diversification is recombination between virus strains infecting the same cell to produce *hybrid progeny virus*, mediated by RT jumping between RNA templates during replication[20].

Because of the continuous genetic diversification, each infected person hosts a variety of related but diverging virus strains referred to as the viral 'quasispecies'. Within the circulating quasispecies, some virus strains predominate whereas others are present as low-frequency species. At any given time, dominant strains are those with the best ability to infect and replicate, properties defining the viral 'fitness'. Due to its diversity, the quasispecies can adapt rapidly to changing 'environmental' circumstances such as immuno-logical or drug pressure, or availability of cell targets. The dynamics of HIV infection are described in *Table 2.4*.

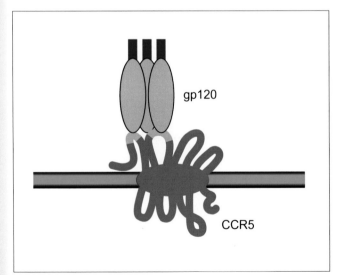

2.9 Interaction between gp120 and the CCR5 co-receptor.

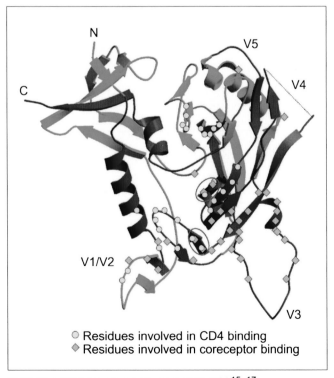

○ Residues involved in CD4 binding
◆ Residues involved in coreceptor binding

2.10 The HIV envelope glycoprotein 120[15–17].

Table 2.4 Dynamics of HIV infection

Virus production:	10^9–10^{10} virus particles per day
Half-life of free virus in plasma:	A few hours
Half-life of virus-producing cells:	Less than 1 day
Frequency of latently infected cells:	1 in 10^6 resting CD4 T-cells
Loss of infected cells:	10^8–10^9 per day
Reverse transcriptase error rate:	~1 mis-incorporation per genome round
Recombinant events:	7–30 events per genome round
Quasispecies:	Swarm of related but divergent strains
Viral fitness:	Ability to replicate and infect
Mutant virus:	Virus carrying a mutation of interest
Wild-type virus:	Virus not carrying a mutation of interest
Recombinant virus:	Hybrid progeny of two different parental strains

HIV replicates preferentially in activated CD4 T-cells. Although most infected cells have a short lifespan, a fraction of cells survive long enough to revert to a resting memory state, thereby allowing HIV persistence as a stable, integrated, and transcriptionally silent provirus, which is unaffected by antiretroviral therapy[21,22]. In viraemic individuals, the reservoir is continuously replenished, creating an archive for all viral quasispecies. Latently infected cells can resume full virus production once activated, which represents the main barrier to eradicating the infection[23–25].

Virological assays used to diagnose and monitor HIV infection

The virological assays listed in *Table 2.5* below are used in clinical practice for diagnosis, staging, and monitoring of the infection[26].

Plasma viral load
Virological monitoring is required during therapy to ensure early detection of treatment failure and optimal long-term outcomes. Plasma HIV RNA load ('viral load') provides an immediate measure of treatment success, acting as a surrogate marker for immunological and clinical responses[29]. Commercial assays show excellent correlation and reliably detect and quantify all major HIV-1 group M subtypes and CRFs[30]. The Abbott assays also detect group O viruses, but no commercial assay is available for the quantification of group N HIV-1 or for HIV-2.

Molecular viral load assays in routine use in high-income countries require expensive instruments and reagents, sophisticated laboratory facilities to minimize the risk of contamination, regular and stable electricity supply, and highly skilled laboratory technicians proficient in molecular biology techniques (*Table 2.6*). These factors limit their implementation in resource-limited settings. The Cavidi ExaVir™ Load assay employs a modified ELISA format to measure the viral RT enzymatic activity, which in turn correlates with plasma RNA levels. The assay is suitable for use in settings with limited infrastructure as it requires simple equipment and is relatively inexpensive and easy to perform.

Table 2.5 Assays commonly used to diagnose and monitor HIV-1 infection

Assay	Application	Comment
Antibody	Diagnosis	Detected 21–25 days after infection
		Detects HIV-1 groups M and O
Combined antibody/p24 antigen	Diagnosis	p24 detected ~6 days earlier than antibody
p24 antigen	Diagnosis	
Antibody avidity	Disease staging	Low avidity identifies infection within the previous 4–6 months[27,28]
Plasma HIV-1 RNA load 'viral load'	Diagnosis	Acute infection Detected 9–11 days after infection Detects HIV-1 groups M ± O
	Monitoring	Predicts rapidity of CD4 decline Measures treatment success Correlates with infectivity
Proviral DNA	Diagnosis	No commercial assays Vertical HIV transmission or indeterminate antibody status
Resistance testing	Monitoring	Detection of drug resistance
Tropism testing	Monitoring	Prior to using CCR5 antagonists

Table 2.6 HIV-1 viral load assays

Assay type	Assay model	Quantification range (copies/ml)
Branched chain DNA	Bayer VERSANT HIV-1 RNA assay v. 3.0	50–500,000
Reverse-transcription PCR	Roche Amplicor Monitor assay v. 1.5	400–750,000 or 50–75,000
Ligase chain reaction	Abbott LCX assay	50–1,000,000
Nucleic acid sequence based amplification (NASBA)	BioMérieux Nuclisens HIV-1 QT assay	50–3,000,000
NASBA + real-time molecular beacon detection	BioMérieux NucliSens EasyQ assay	50–3,000,000
Real-time reverse-transcription PCR	Roche COBAS® TaqMan® HIV-1 v.2 assay Abbott RealTime HIV-1 assay	20–10,000,000 40–10,000,000
RT enzymatic activity measured in ELISA format	Cavidi ExaVir Load v.3 assay	~200–600,000

Table 2.7 Point-of-care HIV antibody tests

Advantages	*Disadvantages*
Rapid, provide results in <30 min	Expensive
Detect antibodies against: Group M and Group O HIV-1 and HIV-2	Show reduced sensitivity in early infection compared with laboratory assays
Require simple equipment	Prone to operator errors
Easy to perform and interpret	Subjective interpretation of results
Avoid venopuncture	May give false-positive results
Include a positive control	Reactive results require immediate laboratory confirmation
Perform well compared with laboratory methods	Quality assurance requires complex arrangements

Rapid HIV antibody assays for point-of-care testing

Rapid HIV tests for point-of-care or near-patient testing use either capillary blood collected by finger-prick or the crevicular transudate from capillaries collected beneath the tooth-gum margin ('oral fluid'). They are most useful:

- In settings where rapid availability of results can immediately guide management (e.g. in pregnant women who present during labour, or prior to the use of post-exposure prophylaxis).
- In clinical settings where a significant proportion of persons tested by laboratory methods fail to return for their results.
- Or in out-reaching initiatives to provide testing outside of traditional clinical settings[31].

Second-generation assays combine the detection of antibodies and p24 antigen, thereby increasing sensitivity in early infection.

The advantages and disadvantages of point-of-care HIV antibody tests are shown in *Table 2.7*.

References

1 Hahn BH, *et al*. AIDS as a zoonosis: scientific and public health implications. *Science* 2000;**287**(5453):607–14.

2 Lemey P, *et al*. Tracing the origin and history of the HIV-2 epidemic. *Proc Natl Acad Sci USA* 2003;**100**(11):6588–92.

3 Keele BF, *et al*. Chimpanzee reservoirs of pandemic and nonpandemic HIV-1. *Science* 2006;**313**(5786):523–6.

4 Geretti AM. HIV-1 subtypes: epidemiology and significance for HIV management. *Curr Opin Infect Dis* 2006;**19**(1):1–7.

5 Osmanov S, *et al*. Estimated global distribution and regional spread of HIV-1 genetic subtypes in the year 2000. *J Acquir Immune Defic Syndr* 2002;**29**(2):184–90.

6 Feng Y, *et al*. HIV-1 entry cofactor: functional cDNA cloning of a seven-transmembrane, G protein-coupled receptor. *Science* 1996;**272**(5263):872–7.

7 Berger EA, Murphy PM, Farber JM. Chemokine receptors as HIV-1 coreceptors: roles in viral entry, tropism, and disease. *Ann Rev Immunol* 1999;**17**:657–700.

8 Connor RI, *et al*. Change in coreceptor use correlates with disease progression in HIV-1-infected individuals. *J Exp Med* 1997;**185**(4):621–8.

9 Kinter A, *et al*. Chemokines, cytokines and HIV: a complex network of interactions that influence HIV pathogenesis. *Immunol Rev* 2000;**177**:88–98.

10 O'Brien SJ, Moore JP. The effect of genetic variation in chemokines and their receptors on HIV transmission and progression to AIDS. *Immunol Rev* 2000;**177**:99–111.

11 Kwa D, *et al*. Increased in vitro cytopathicity of CC chemokine receptor 5-restricted human immuno-deficiency virus type 1 primary isolates correlates with a progressive clinical course of infection. *J Infect Dis* 2003;**187**(9):1397–403.

12 Coakley E, Petropoulos CJ, Whitcomb JM. Assessing chemokine co-receptor usage in HIV. *Curr Opin Infect Dis* 2005;**18**(1):9–15.

13 Faure E, Royer-Carenzi M. Is the European spatial distribution of the HIV-1-resistant CCR5-Delta32 allele formed by a breakdown of the pathocenosis due to the historical Roman expansion? *Infect Genet Evol* 2008;**8**(6):864–74.

14 Soulie C, *et al*. Comparison of two genotypic algorithms to determine HIV-1 tropism. *HIV Med* 2008;**9**(1):1–5.

15 Kraulis PJ. MOLSCRIPT: a program to produce both detailed and schematic plots of protein structures. *J Appl Cryst* 1991;**24**:946–50.

16 Merritt EA, Bacon DJ. Raster3D: photorealistic molecular graphics. *Methods Enzymol* 1997;**277**:505–24.

17 Neurath AR, *et al*. *Punica granatum* (Pomegranate) juice provides an HIV-1 entry inhibitor and candidate topical microbicide. *BMC Infect Dis* 2004;**4**:41.

18 Wei X, *et al*. Viral dynamics in human immuno-deficiency virus type 1 infection. *Nature* 1995;**373**(6510):117–22.

19 Markowitz M, *et al*. A novel antiviral intervention results in more accurate assessment of human immuno-deficiency virus type 1 replication dynamics and T-cell decay *in vivo*. *J Virol* 2003;**77**(8):5037–8.

20 Ramirez BC, *et al*. Implications of recombination for HIV diversity. *Virus Res* 2008;**134**(1-2):64–73.

21 Chun TW, *et al*. Quantification of latent tissue reservoirs and total body viral load in HIV-1 infection. *Nature* 1997;**387**(6629):183–8.

22 Wong JK, *et al*. Recovery of replication-competent HIV despite prolonged suppression of plasma viremia. *Science* 1997;**278**(5341):1291–5.

23 Siliciano JD, *et al*. Long-term follow-up studies confirm the stability of the latent reservoir for HIV-1 in resting CD4+ T cells. *Nat Med* 2003;**9**(6):727–8.

24 Strain MC, *et al*. Heterogeneous clearance rates of long-lived lymphocytes infected with HIV: intrinsic stability predicts lifelong persistence. *Proc Natl Acad Sci USA* 2003;**100**(8):4819–24.

25 Han Y, *et al*. Experimental approaches to the study of HIV-1 latency. *Nat Rev Microbiol* 2007;**5**(2):95–106.

26 Branson BM. State of the art for diagnosis of HIV infection. *Clin Infect Dis* 2007;**45**(Suppl 4):S221–S225.

27 Suligoi B, *et al*. Precision and accuracy of a procedure for detecting recent human immunodeficiency virus infections by calculating the antibody avidity index by an automated immunoassay-based method. *J Clin Microbiol* 2002;**40**(11):4015–20.

28 Chawla A, *et al*. Human immunodeficiency virus (HIV) antibody avidity testing to identify recent infection in newly diagnosed HIV type 1 (HIV-1)-seropositive persons infected with diverse HIV-1 subtypes. *J Clin Microbiol* 2007;**45**(2):415–20.

29 Mellors JW, *et al*. Prognosis in HIV-1 infection predicted by the quantity of virus in plasma. *Science* 1996;**272**(5265):1167–70.

30 Schutten M, *et al*. Multicenter evaluation of the new Abbott RealTime assays for quantitative detection of human immunodeficiency virus type 1 and hepatitis C virus RNA. *J Clin Microbiol* 2007;**45**(6):1712–17.

31 Roberts KJ, Grusky O, Swanson AN. Outcomes of blood and oral fluid rapid HIV testing: a literature review, 2000–2006. *AIDS Patient Care STDS* 2007;**21**(9):621–37.

HIV and the immune system

S Kinloch-de Loes and C Cellerai

HIV transmission and immunopathogenesis

Infection with HIV-1 is characterized by chronic viral replication and progressive immunodeficiency with the loss of CD4 T-cells. In the absence of combination antiretroviral treatment (ART), continued loss of CD4 T-cells results in the development of opportunistic infections and malignancies, ultimately leading to death[1].

Dendritic cells are the earliest targets of HIV-1. They are found within the mucosal epithelium and act as antigen-presenting cells. Within the first 48 hours of successful transmission via skin or mucosal surfaces, HIV-1 can be detected in regional lymph nodes and by 72 hours, HIV-1 can be detected in the plasma (**2.11**)[1].

Immunopathology occurs within the first few weeks of infection following viral entry and sets the scene for the chronic phase. Although historically T-cells (in particular CD4 T-cells) have been viewed as the main target of the virus, all major lymphocyte populations and components of the immune system, including B cells, are affected by HIV-1.

Apart from a small minority of patients known as *HIV-1 controllers* or *long-term nonprogressors*, prolonged long-term control of viral replication with the maintenance of CD4 T-cell counts and the absence of clinical progression is not achieved in the absence of ART or after the discontinuation of treatment. In recent years, progress has been made in understanding the immune correlates and genetic factors involved in the protection against AIDS. Great insights in particular have been gained from studies in the population of HIV-1 long-term nonprogressors (**2.12**)[2–4].

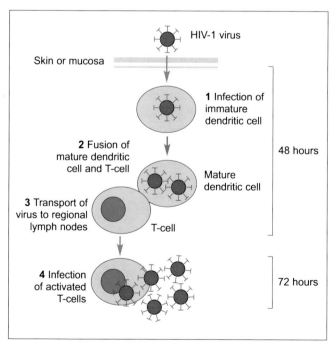

2.11 HIV transmission and early immunological events.

2.12 Natural history of HIV infection in: (**A**) untreated progressors; (**B**) untreated nonprogressors; (**C**) treated progressors.

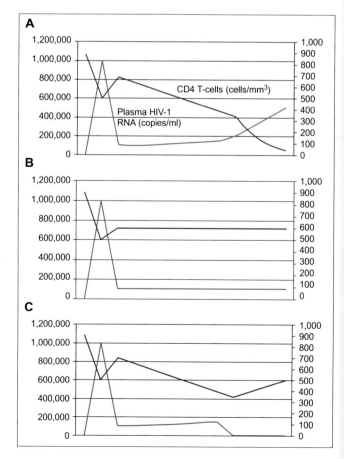

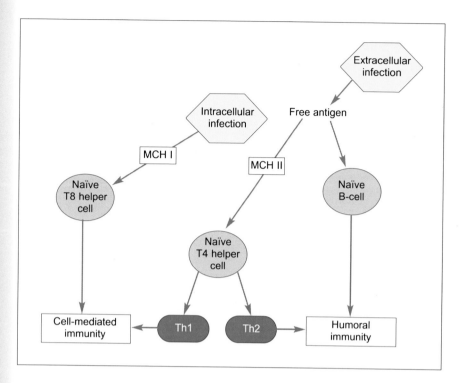

2.13 Overview of adaptive immune responses.

With effective ART on board, the control of viral replication is achieved and some HIV-related immune abnormalities are reversed as immune reconstitution occurs. The extent of immune recovery, however, largely depends on the stage of the infection when treatment is initiated and on its duration[5].

Immune responses

In general terms, the human host is protected from infectious pathogens by two types of defence mechanism:
- Innate immune responses.
- Adaptive immune responses.

The *innate immune response* provides an immediate, nonspecific response to infection while the *adaptive immune response* is a delayed antigen-specific one. Although equally important, most studies seeking to understand the immunopathogenesis of HIV-1 infection have focused on the adaptive immune response.

Adaptive immune responses
These consist of both cell-mediated (cytotoxic T-cells) and antibody-mediated (humoral) responses (**2.13**).

Cell-mediated immune responses
CD8 cytotoxic T lymphocytes (CTL) and CD4 helper T lymphocytes (Th) play a very important role in cell-mediated responses. CTLs arise from naïve T-cells and are able to eliminate infected cells. Th cells, on the other hand, enhance CTL-mediated activity by helping CD8 lymphocytes to differentiate into active CTLs[2,6,7].

Although HIV-1 specific T-cells are unable to fully suppress viral replication, they are understood to have an important role in virological control. Initial studies looking at interferon-gamma (IFN-γ) production by T-cells and their effector function found no correlation between the magnitude of IFN-γ-producing HIV-1-specific T-cell responses and virological control or clinical progression.

More recently, the emphasis has shifted on to the functional qualities rather than the frequency of virus-specific T-cells. The term 'monofunctional' is used to define the type of HIV-1-specific T-cells with sole effector function (IFN-γ or TNF-α production and cytotoxic activity) in contrast to 'polyfunctional' cells that in addition to typical effector function, also produce interleukin-2 (IL-2) upon stimulation and retain proliferative capacity. These 'polyfunctional' cells are often associated with disease control and therefore represent a correlate of protective antiviral immunity[6,7].

The importance of genetic factors in generating protective virus-specific T-cells and their association with some HLA-B alleles (B*5701/02/03, B*2705, B*5801, B*5101, and B*1302) has recently been highlighted (*Table 2.8*)[8]. HLA-A and -C may play a role in host control as well, although the evidence is not as strong as HLA-B.

Table 2.8 HLA-B alleles associated with slow or rapid progression of HIV infection

Slow	Fast
HLA-B*2705	HLA-B*3502/03
HLA-B*5701/02/03	HLA-B*5301
HLA-B*1302	HLA-B*5802
HLA-B*5801	HLA-B*18
HLA-B*5101	

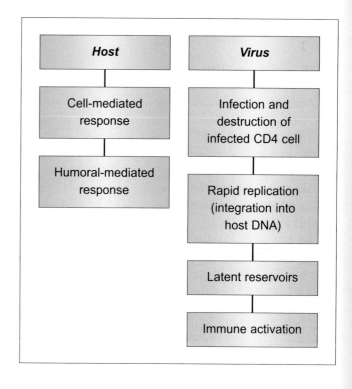

2.14 HIV replication and immunity.

Both HIV-1-specific CD4 and CD8 T-cells have a reduced ability to proliferate upon antigen encounter in HIV-progressors, which has been ascribed to their impaired ability to secrete IL-2. Defective cytotoxic activity of HIV-1-specific CD8 T-cells is also observed in chronic HIV infection and may result from mechanisms such as skewed maturation, senescence, and exhaustion.

Humoral immune responses

The role of B-cells and neutralizing antibodies in the control of HIV remains unclear. B-cell exhaustion has recently been described in association with a reduced ability to produce high-quality antibodies in the context of HIV infection. Some but not all of these abnormalities recover with ART, potentially explaining the improvement in humoral immunity with virological control[9–11].

The role of neutralizing antibodies (NAb) in the control of HIV replication remains controversial. Some studies have shown higher titres of heterologous NAb in HIV-controllers compared with HIV-progressors, but these may have only a limited effect *in vivo* on viral replication.

The role of antibody-related mechanisms, such as antibody-dependent cellular cytotoxicity (ADCC), where antibodies stimulate natural killer (NK) cells to destroy infected cells still deserves further investigation[12].

Although the host mounts an HIV-specific cell-mediated and antibody-mediated response, viral replication is not halted in the absence of treatment. The eventual outcome of infection is governed by a balance between the immune response generated and attempts by the virus to escape detection and destruction (**2.14**)[13].

Innate immune response

NK cells and dendritic cells (DC) are important components of the innate immune response. NK cells rapidly expand in number during acute infection, preceding the development of adaptive HIV-1-specific CD8 T-cells. However, NK cell defective cytotoxicity and cytokine secretion occur during the course of chronic infection and appear to be correlated with viraemia. It remains unclear whether effective suppression of viral replication by ART can fully restore NK cell function[14,15].

Recent data have demonstrated slower disease progression in patients who express KIR3DS1, a killer immunoglobulin-like receptor in conjunction with HLA-Bw4-80I (a putative ligand with an isoleucine at position 80), suggesting a role for NK cells in chronic viral control. Several studies have described an impairment in the interaction between NK cells and DCs that is proportional to the level of viraemia and has been suggested to interfere with the development of an effective immune response.

CD4 T-cell depletion

During the acute phase of the infection, CD4 T-cells decrease in the peripheral blood as a result of high levels of viral replication. However, the most dramatic loss of these cells occurs at the gut level (**2.15**)[1], and although numbers in peripheral blood tend to temporarily recover in the ensuing weeks, the decline in effector memory CD4 T-cells remains a hallmark of chronic infection. While CD4 T-cells decrease during chronic infection, the number of CD8 T-cells in peripheral blood remains increased and results in an inverted CD4/CD8 ratio.

The extent of CD4 T-cell loss during the course of the infection is more profound than the estimated number of HIV-1-infected cells (estimated at 1 in 100 to 1 in 1000 cells). In addition to the direct cytopathic effect of the virus, other mechanisms such as immune activation as well as virally-derived and autoimmune factors have been put forward to explain the dramatic loss of these cells. Among these, *immune activation* is now considered to be the major player in HIV-induced immune dysregulation and progressive loss of CD4 T-cells leading to AIDS[16,17].

Chronic immune activation

Generalized and persistent immune activation is one of the hallmarks of chronic HIV infection (**2.16**). Its main manifestations include:

- Increased T-cell turn-over.
- Increased expression of markers of activation on T lymphocytes.
- High levels of activation-induced apoptosis in uninfected T-cells.
- Polyclonal B-cell activation.

The above occur in a context of increased proinflammatory cytokines and chemokines. B-cells, NK cells, and macrophages also show an increased rate of proliferation.

One of the strongest arguments in favour of the direct role of chronic immune activation in AIDS pathogenesis comes from animal models where it is a prerequisite for the progression to AIDS in the presence of high viral loads. In these models, the predictive value of immune activation in terms of disease progression is higher than that of HIV-1 viral load.

Events taking place at the gut mucosal level (the site of major CD4 T-cell destruction and intestinal barrier damage) during primary HIV infection set the scene for

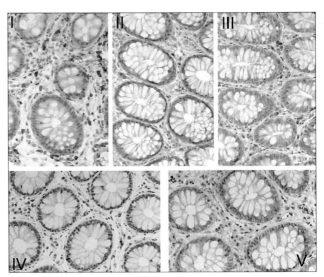

2.15 CD4 depletion in the gut. (From Plos Med 2006. 3(12), with permission.)

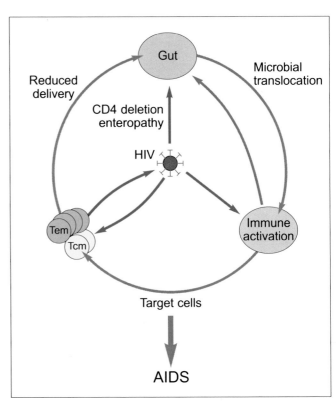

2.16 Chronic immune activation. Tem: effector memory T-cells; Tcm: central memory T-cells. (Adapted from Douek D. *Immune Effects at HIV-infected Mucosal Surfaces.* Abstract 20. 18th CROI; 2009; Montreal, Canada.)

later immune dysregulation. Infection and depletion of the critical central memory CD4 T-cell pool result in reduced tissue delivery of effector memory CD4 T-cells and further loss of immune control at mucosal level. These events are understood to lead to chronic microbial translocation with the involvement of the Toll-like receptor (TLR) pathway and to contribute to chronic immune activation. There have been contradictory reports regarding the role of T regulatory cells (Tregs) in this phenomenon[18-22].

HIV-1 prophylactic vaccine

Unfortunately efforts at developing an HIV-I prophylactic vaccine have not been successful. Over the last few years the emphasis has shifted from the development of vaccines able to generate NAbs towards a cell-mediated type of vaccine that would generate HIV-specific T-cells.

In a recent phase-IIb trial (STEP trial) a vaccine containing Merck's adenovirus serotype 5 vector (MRK Ad5) was tested in 3,000 high-risk individuals. Unhappily, the results were disappointing – the vaccine did not work and individuals with pre-existing immunity to Ad5 appeared to have an increased risk of HIV transmission. However, the positive results from the RV144 trial performed in Thailand with a canary pox-based vaccine (ALVAC-HIV [V1521]) and AIDSVAX B/E showed a 31% decrease in the rate of infections in vaccinated subjects versus those who received placebo will help to provide correlates of protection to help vaccine development[23].

Renewed efforts are focusing on different types of vector and viral antigen combination in the vaccine. A prime-boost strategy has been used in recent trials in an effort to increase the levels of immune response towards the virus. Progress in the understanding of neutralization sites could promote this line of vaccine development and produce new vaccine candidates[24].

Conclusion

Although great progress has been made recently in the understanding of the mechanisms underlying HIV-1 immunopathogenesis, there remain large gaps in our understanding of the main immune correlates of protection against the development of AIDS. Efforts continue to concentrate on the development of an HIV-1 vaccine using both innate and adaptive immunity.

References

1 Brenchley JM, Price DA, Douek DC. HIV disease: fallout from a mucosal catastrophe? *Nat Immunol* 2006 Mar;**7**(3):235–9.

2 Pantaleo G, Koup RA. Correlates of immune protection in HIV-1 infection: what we know, what we don't know, what we should know. *Nat Med* 2004 Aug;**10**(8):806–10.

3 Fellay J, Shianna KV, Ge D, Colombo S, Ledergerber B, Weale M, et al. A whole-genome association study of major determinants for host control of HIV-1. *Science* 2007 Aug 17;**317**(5840):944–7.

4 Betts MR, Nason MC, West SM, De Rosa SC, Migueles SA, Abraham J, et al. HIV nonprogressors preferentially maintain highly functional HIV-specific CD8+ T cells. *Blood* 2006 Jun 15;**107**(12):4781–9.

5 Robbins GK, Spritzler JG, Chan ES, Asmuth DM, Gandhi RT, Rodriguez BA, et al. Incomplete reconstitution of T cell subsets on combination antiretroviral therapy in the AIDS Clinical Trials Group protocol 384. *Clin Infect Dis* 2009 Feb 1;**48**(3):350–61.

6 Rehr M, Cahenzli J, Haas A, Price DA, Gostick E, Huber M, et al. Emergence of polyfunctional CD8+ T cells after prolonged suppression of human immunodeficiency virus replication by antiretroviral therapy. *J Virol* 2008 Apr;**82**(7):3391–404.

7 Addo MM, Yu XG, Rathod A, Cohen D, Eldridge RL, Strick D, et al. Comprehensive epitope analysis of human immunodeficiency virus type 1 (HIV-1)-specific T-cell responses directed against the entire expressed HIV-1 genome demonstrates broadly directed responses, but no correlation to viral load. *J Virol* 2003 Feb;**77**(3):2081–92.

8 Kiepiela P, Leslie AJ, Honeyborne I, Ramduth D, Thobakgale C, Chetty S, et al. Dominant influence of HLA-B in mediating the potential co-evolution of HIV and HLA. *Nature* 2004 Dec 9;**432**(7018):769–75.

9 Moir S, Fauci AS. Pathogenic mechanisms of B-lymphocyte dysfunction in HIV disease. *J Allergy Clin Immunol* 2008 Jul;**122**(1):12–19.

10 Moir S, Ho J, Malaspina A, Wang W, Dipoto AC, O'Shea MA, et al. Evidence for HIV-associated B cell exhaustion in a dysfunctional memory B cell compartment in HIV-infected viremic individuals. *J Exp Med* 2008 Aug 4;**205**(8):1797–805.

11 Moir S, Malaspina A, Ho J, Wang W, Dipoto AC, O'Shea MA, et al. Normalization of B cell counts and subpopulations after antiretroviral therapy in chronic HIV disease. *J Infect Dis* 2008 Feb 15;**197**(4):572–9.

12 Deeks SG, Schweighardt B, Wrin T, Galovich J, Hoh R, Sinclair E, *et al*. Neutralizing antibody responses against autologous and heterologous viruses in acute versus chronic human immunodeficiency virus (HIV) infection: evidence for a constraint on the ability of HIV to completely evade neutralizing antibody responses. *J Virol* 2006 Jun;**80**(12):6155–64.

13 Huber M, Trkola A. Humoral immunity to HIV-1: neutralization and beyond. *J Intern Med* 2007 Jul;**262**(1):5–25.

14 Kottilil S, Chun TW, Moir S, Liu S, McLaughlin M, Hallahan CW, *et al*. Innate immunity in human immunodeficiency virus infection: effect of viremia on natural killer cell function. *J Infect Dis* 2003 Apr 1;**187**(7):1038–45.

15 Mavilio D, Lombardo G, Kinter A, Fogli M, La SA, Ortolano S, *et al*. Characterization of the defective interaction between a subset of natural killer cells and dendritic cells in HIV-1 infection. *J Exp Med* 2006 Oct 2;**203**(10):2339–50.

16 Hazenberg MD, Otto SA, van Benthem BH, Roos MT, Coutinho RA, Lange JM, *et al*. Persistent immune activation in HIV-1 infection is associated with progression to AIDS. *AIDS* 2003 Sep 5;**17**(13):1881–8.

17 Sousa AE, Carneiro J, Meier-Schellersheim M, Grossman Z, Victorino RM. CD4 T cell depletion is linked directly to immune activation in the pathogenesis of HIV-1 and HIV-2 but only indirectly to the viral load. *J Immunol* 2002 Sep 15;**169**(6):3400–6.

18 Rowland-Jones S, Dong T. Dying T cells trigger autoimmunity in HIV. *Nat Med* 2007 Dec;**13**(12):1413–15.

19 Grossman Z, Meier-Schellersheim M, Sousa AE, Victorino RM, Paul WE. CD4+ T-cell depletion in HIV infection: are we closer to understanding the cause? *Nat Med* 2002 Apr;**8**(4):319–23.

20 Sodora DL, Silvestri G. Immune activation and AIDS pathogenesis. *AIDS* 2008 Feb 19;**22**(4):439–46.

21 Chang JJ, Altfeld M. TLR-mediated immune activation in HIV. *Blood* 2009 Jan 8;**113**(2):269–70.

22 Holmes D, Jiang Q, Zhang L, Su L. Foxp3 and Treg cells in HIV-1 infection and immuno-pathogenesis. *Immunol Res* 2008;**41**(3):248–66.

23 Koff W, Berkley SF. The renaissance in HIVE vaccine development – future directions. *N Engl J Med* 2010.

24 Barouch DH. Challenges in the development of an HIV-1 vaccine. *Nature* 2008 Oct 2;**455**(7213):613–19.

Treatment of HIV infection

AJ Rodger, N Marshall, AM Geretti and C Booth

Initial assessment of the new HIV patient

The aim of initial consultation is to assess the patient's understanding of HIV natural history, address issues such as stigma and disclosure, the need for professional counselling, routes of transmission, potential contact tracing and testing of partners and children, promotion of safe sex practices through the use of condoms, and to assess stage of HIV disease and patient health (*Table 3.1*).

Table 3.1 Initial assessment of the new HIV patient (adapted from EACS and DHHS)[1,2]

History	Physical examination (3.1–3.11)	Laboratory evaluation
• HIV testing history • Routes of exposure – in UK or overseas • Evaluation of social and psychological support • Smoking, alcohol, and recreational drug histories • Family history – CVD, HT, diabetes • Social history • Details of partners and children and their HIV testing history • Sexual health history • Vaccination history (see *Table 3.2* for recommended vaccinations) • Complete medical history including cardiovascular risk assessment • Current medications • Current symptomatology	• General: height, weight, BMI, waist to hip ratio, blood pressure • Skin: KS (see Chapter 7) (**3.7–3.9**), *Molluscum contagiosum* (**3.1–3.3**), seborrhoeic dermatitis (**3.4**), shingles scar, fungal infection (**3.5**) • Lymph nodes – site, size, consistency (**3.6**) • Mouth – OHL, *Candida*, gum disease, palatal KS (**3.10**) • Cardiovascular, respiratory, abdominal, and neurogical examinations as standard • Women: cervical pap smear • Urine dipstick for protein and sugar • Sexual health screen	• Confirmation of HIV antibody-positive • Avidity and detuned assays if available • Plasma HIV RNA • Resistance testing (genotype) with determination of HIV subtype • CD4 absolute count + percentage (optional: CD8 and %) • Full blood count, AST, ALT, alkaline phosphatase, calcium, phosphate, glucose, creatinine, calculated creatinine clearance • Antibody tests for Toxoplasma, CMV, VZV, hepatitis A, B, and C, and syphilis • Fasting blood glucose and lipids including fasting total LDL and HDL cholesterol, and triglycerides • G6PD status If relevant: • HLA-B*5701 determination • HIV tropism

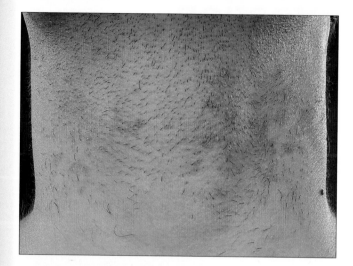

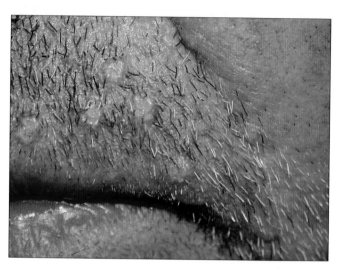

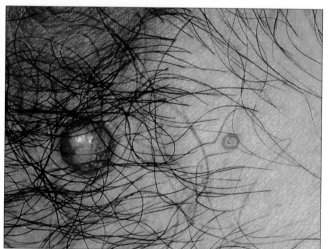

3.1–3.3 *Molluscum contagiosum.* Characteristic waxy, dome-shaped, umbilicated flesh-coloured papules caused by the DNA pox virus. They are commonly located on the face, neck, axillae, and ano-genital regions.

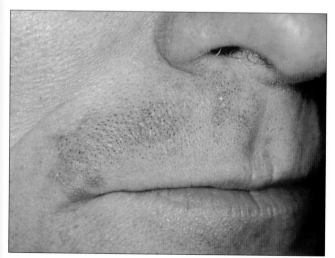

3.4 HIV-related seborrhoeic dermatitis.

Vaccinations that are recommended for all HIV-infected adults found to be susceptible on serological screening are hepatitis B (HBV), measles, mumps and rubella (if CD4 count >200/mm^3) and varicella (CD4 count >400/mm^3). Further details on vaccination in HIV-positive adults is given in *Table 3.2*, adapted from the BHIVA guidance on vaccination (2008)[3].

When to start treatment

Primary HIV infection

Guidelines do not currently recommend treatment in acute infection unless symptoms are neurological in nature or severe, as there is some indication that this may lead to more rapidly progressive disease[4]. Duration of treatment is unclear, as is its effect on outcome or prognosis. The Short Pulse Anti Retroviral Therapy at HIV Seroconversion (SPARTAC) trial, which is a randomized prospective study

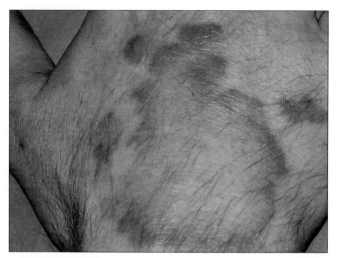

3.5 Cutaneous fungal infection in advanced HIV.

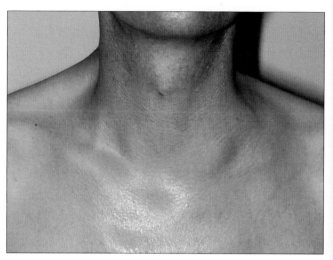

3.6 Cervical lymphadenopathy.

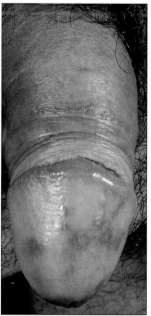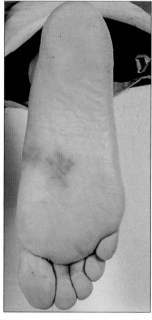

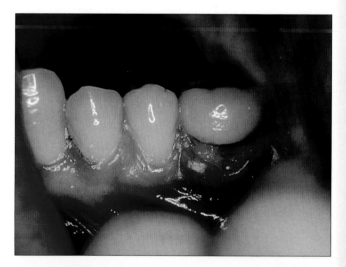

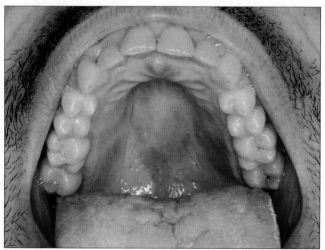

3.7–3.10 Kaposi's sarcoma. KS on penis (3.7), sole of the foot (3.8), gum (3.9), and hard palate (3.10).

Table 3.2 Vaccination in the HIV-positive patient[3]

Inactivated vaccines that may be used safely in HIV-positive adults if indicated	***Recommended in all HIV-positive adults*** Hepatitis B Pneumococcus (PPV23) Influenza – parenteral ***Can be used in selected risk groups*** Cholera (WC/rBS) Hepatitis A *Haemophilius influenzae* Meningcoccus (MenC and ACWY) Rabies Tetanus – diptheria – parenteral poliomyelitis (Td/IPV) Typhoid (ViCPS)
Live vaccines that may be indicated in HIV-positive adults, but should not be used if CD4 is <200 cells/mm³	Measles, mumps, rubella Varicella Yellow fever
Live vaccines contraindicated in HIV-positive adults regardless of CD4 count	Cholera (CVD103-HgR) Influenza (intranasal) Oral poliomyelitis (OPV) Typhoid (Ty21a) Tuberculosis (BCG) Smallpox (Vaccinia)

comparing three different strategies of antiretroviral treatment (ART) in patients recently infected with HIV, is testing the hypothesis that short-course treatment in acute infection confers a long-term survival benefit. SPARTAC is due to report at the end of 2011.

Asymptomatic infection

Data suggest that the average time from infection to development of AIDS is approximately 10 years. The likelihood of an individual developing an AIDS-defining event can be predicted from viral load (VL) and CD4 count (*Table 3.3*)[5].

Current treatment guidelines

Current guidelines on the treatment of HIV are updated regularly, both with respect to when to treat and what to treat with. The USA (DHHS), UK (BHIVA), EU (EACS), and International AIDS Society (IAS) Guidelines should be consulted for regular updates[1,2,4].

EACS: http://www.europeanaidsclinicalsociety.org/
DHHS: http://www.aidsinfo.nih.gov/
BHIVA: http://www.bhiva.org/
IAS: http://jama.ama-assn.org/

For details on when to treat according to UK BHIVA, DHHS, and IAS Guidelines see *Table 3.4*.

For symptomatic patients or those with opportunistic disease, ART should be commenced regardless of CD4 count. Once HIV patients have commenced ART generally it should be taken life long unless taken to prevent mother-to-child transmission (MTCT) or during seroconversion. The SMART trial (Strategies for Management of Antiretroviral Therapy) demonstrated that there was increased morbidity and mortality in patients who interrupted therapy compared to continuous ART, regardless of CD4 count. In the main analysis, those randomized to the intermittent arm had a 2.6 times (95% confidence interval [CI]: 1.9–3.7) increased hazard of

Table 3.3 Predicted 6-month risk of AIDS according to age and current CD4 cell count and viral load, based on a Poisson regression model[5]

Table 4. Predicted 6-month risk of AIDS according to age and current CD4 cell count and viral load, based on a Poisson regression model.

Viral load (copies/ml)	Predicted risk (%) at current CD4 cell count ($\times 10^6$ cells/l)[a]									
	50	100	150	200	250	300	350	400	450	500
Age 25 years										
3000	6.8	3.7	2.3	1.6	1.1	0.8	0.6	0.5	0.4	0.3
10 000	9.6	5.3	3.4	2.3	1.6	1.2	0.9	0.7	0.5	0.4
30 000	13.3	7.4	4.7	3.2	2.2	1.6	1.2	0.9	0.7	0.6
100 000	18.6	10.6	6.7	4.6	3.2	2.4	1.8	1.4	1.1	0.8
300 000	25.1	14.5	9.3	6.3	4.5	3.3	2.5	1.9	1.5	1.2
Age 35 years										
3000	8.5	4.7	3.0	2.0	1.4	1.0	0.8	0.6	0.5	0.4
10 000	12.1	6.7	4.3	2.9	2.0	1.5	1.1	0.9	0.7	0.5
30 000	16.6	9.3	5.9	4.0	2.8	2.1	1.6	1.2	0.9	0.7
100 000	23.1	13.2	8.5	5.8	4.1	3.0	2.3	1.7	1.3	1.1
300 000	30.8	18.0	11.7	8.0	5.7	4.2	3.1	2.4	1.9	1.5
Age 45 years										
3000	10.7	5.9	3.7	2.5	1.8	1.3	1.0	0.7	0.6	0.5
10 000	15.1	8.5	5.4	3.6	2.6	1.9	1.4	1.1	0.8	0.7
30 000	20.6	11.7	7.5	5.1	3.6	2.6	2.0	1.5	1.2	0.9
100 000	28.4	16.5	10.6	7.3	5.2	3.8	2.9	2.2	1.7	1.3
300 000	37.4	22.4	14.6	10.1	7.2	5.3	4.0	3.1	2.4	1.9
Age 55 years										
3000	13.4	7.5	4.7	3.2	2.3	1.7	1.2	0.9	0.7	0.6
10 000	18.8	10.7	6.8	4.6	3.3	2.4	1.8	1.4	1.1	0.8
30 000	25.4	14.6	9.4	6.4	4.6	3.3	2.5	1.9	1.5	1.2
100 000	34.6	20.5	13.3	9.2	6.5	4.8	3.6	2.8	2.2	1.7
300 000	44.8	27.5	18.2	12.6	9.1	6.7	5.0	3.9	3.0	2.4

[a]Shading distinguishes risk: < 2%, no shading; 2–9.9%, light gray; 10–19.9%, mid-gray; ≥ 20%, darkest gray.

(Reproduced with permission from Phillips A, et al., 2004[5])

opportunistic disease (OD) or death compared to those in the continuous arm[6].

There is now a trend to start treatment at higher CD4 counts due to evidence that morbidity and mortality from both HIV and non-HIV-related events are reduced if treatment is started in the region of 350 cells/mm[3].

Although there is overall agreement that HIV should be treated at CD4 counts of <350 cells/mm[3], the differences in the BHIVA Guidelines and other guidelines lie in when to start treatment at CD4 counts of >350 cells/mm[3]. Cohort studies have suggested likely health benefits of earlier treatment with ART including both HIV and non-HIV-related adverse outcomes[7,8].

The DHHS, EACS, and IAS Guidelines suggest treating everyone with a CD4 count between 350 and 500/mm[3] (Table 3.1). At CD4 counts >500 cells/mm[3], 50% of the DHHS panel suggest that commencing ART should be optional while the BHIVA Guidelines suggest that the evidence is not yet sufficient to recommend ART at this level and that patients should be entered into the START trial (Strategic Timing of Antiretroviral Therapy), which is recruiting worldwide and which will evaluate, using a randomized controlled design, the potential health benefits of starting ART at a CD4 count above 500 cells/mm[3].

Immune reconstitution inflammatory syndrome (IRIS)

Timing of the start of ART for symptomatic patients with opportunistic infection (OI) can be problematic due to interactions between ARVs and some of the drugs used to treat OI (e.g. tuberculosis [TB] treatments) and the increased risk of an immune reconstitution reaction or inflammatory syndrome (IRIS).

IRIS is a paradoxically increased severity of a clinical condition due to improved immune response (3.11–3.13) and it occurs in an estimated 10–40% of HIV patients (based mainly on retrospective studies), and is more common in those starting ART with a low CD4 count.

Table 3.4 When to start treatment for HIV – BHIVA (2008 with addendum in 2009), DHHS, and IAS Guidelines (2009)[2,4]

HIV disease stage	CD4 count (cells/mm³)	BHIVA Guidelines	DHHS Guidelines	IAS Guidelines
Early (primary) infection	Any CD4 level	Treatment in clinical trial; or neurological involvement; AIDS-defining illness; or CD4 <200 cells/mm³	Treat	Treat
Established (chronic) infection without symptoms	CD4 >500	Consider enrolment into 'when to start' trial	50% panel defer 50% of panel ART optional	ART should be considered, unless patient is an elite controller (HIV-1 RNA <50 copies/ml) or has stable CD4 cell count and low-level viraemia in the absence of ART
	CD4 351–500	Treat in specific situations with higher risk of clinical events: • AIDS-diagnosis • Hepatitis B infection, where treatment for hepatitis B is indicated • Hepatitis C infection • Low CD4 percentage (e.g. <14%) • Established CVD or a very high risk of cardiovascular events (Framingham risk of CVD >20% over 10 years)	Treat	Treat
	CD4 201–350	Treat	Treat	Treat
	CD4 <200	Treat	Treat	Treat
Established (chronic) infection with symptoms	Any CD4 count	Treat	Treat	Treat
Pregnancy	Any CD4 count	Treat	Treat	Treat
HIV-associated nephropathy (HIVAN)	Any CD4 count	Treat	Treat	Treat

With mycobacterial disease the development or worsening of lymphadenopathy is the most commonly reported manifestation and can be accompanied by fever.

The ACTG A5164 study team performed a randomized strategy trial to look at risk factors for IRIS and mortality in patients with acute OIs who received either early (within 14 days of OI treatment) or deferred (at 4–32 weeks, i.e. after OI treatment completed) ART. They reported decreased rates of AIDS progression and death in patients initiating early ARVs after diagnosis of opportunistic infection, although the majority of cases (63%) were *Pneumocystis jirovecii* pneumonia (PCP) and the study was not powered to look at outcomes with other OIs such as cryptococcal meningitis (CM), as only 12% of enrolled patients had CM. They concluded that early ART resulted in better outcomes with no increase in adverse events[9].

However, a prospective study randomized HIV-positive patients with CM to initiate ART within 72 hours of diagnosis or to delay initiation until 10 weeks after fluconazole monotherapy. They found that mortality rate due to CM was high overall at 62%, but that mortality rate in the early treatment group was 82% compared with 37% in the delayed treatment group, with most mortality occurring early after initiation of ART[10].

Current practice in countries such as the UK is usually to wait for 1–4 weeks with acute opportunistic infections that are inflammatory and whose treatments are potentially toxic and metabolically interactive, such as TB, PCP, cytomegalovirus (CMV) retinitis, CM (usually wait >3 weeks) and toxoplasmosis. For patients with advanced HIV who are clinically very unwell or who have multiple OIs, ART is likely to be started early and any interaction or IRIS managed as it arises.

For infections such as herpes simplex virus (HSV) or *Candida* there is no reason to delay ART, and for other opportunistic disease such as lymphoma or progressive multifocal leukoencephalopathy (PML), treatment should be started immediately as highly active antiretroviral therapy (HAART) will influence outcome positively.

HIV treatment and guidelines

There are now six licensed licensed classes of ARVs which inhibit the virus at different stages of its life cycle(see **2.7**). Initial treatment regime success impacts on outcomes, including development of HIV resistance mutations. The aim when commencing treatment is to maximize adherence, limit toxicities and drug interactions, and take account of individual patient factors and other co-morbidities.

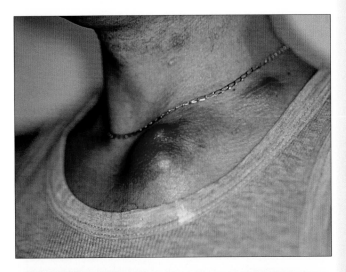

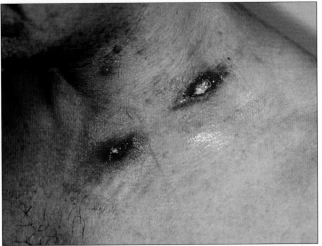

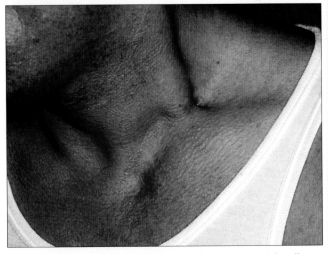

3.11–3.13 Enlargement, rupture and subsequent healing by scarring of lymph nodes in a patient with advanced HIV and MAI started on ART and antimycobacterial treatment.

Table 3.5 Drug selection (naïve). BHIVA Treatment Guidelines (2008)[3]

Drug 1	Drug 2	Drug 3
Preferred: • Tenofovir[1]; or • Abacavir[2] (but see comments[4])	Lamivudine[2,3] or Emtricitabine[1]	Preferred: • Efavirenz[1]
Alternative: • Zidovudine[3]; or • Didanosine		Alternative: • Lopinavir/r • Atazanavir/r • Fosamprenavir/r • Saquinavir/r • Darunavir/r[7] Specific groups: • Nevirapine[5] • Atazanavir (unboosted)[6]

Notes

[1] Tenofovir and emtricitabine available as the co-formulated Truvada, and in combination with efavirenz as Atripla (for patients with VL<50 copies/ml with no resistance to constituent drugs)

[2] Abacavir and lamivudine available as the co-formulated Kivexa

[3] Zidovudine and lamivudine available as the co-formulated Combivir, however dose of zidovuidne is higher

[4] Abacavir – consider alternatives in patients with high cardiovascular risk (D:A:D & SMART data) and those with VL >100,000 copies/ml (ACTG 5202). Should not be used if test positive for HLA-B*5701

[5] Nevirapine should be avoided in women with CD4 >250 cells/mm^3 and males with CD4 >400 cells/mm^3 with detectable viral load due to significantly increased risk of hepatitis and severe rash

[6] Where there are established cardiovascular disease risk factors and a PI is required. Unboosted atazanavir should not be used in combination with tenofovir due to drug interactions. Unboosted atazanavir is not licensed within the EU

[7] Darunavir/r was licensed in naïve patients in 2009

Triple combinations of drugs are now the standard of care, usually composed of a dual nucleoside reverse transcriptase inhibitor (NRTI) backbone with a third drug, *either* a non-nucleoside reverse transcriptase inhibitor (NNRTI) or ritonavir-boosted protease inhibitor (PI). The aim of treatment is to suppress the virus to undetectable levels with minimal toxicity for the patient.

The standard regimen – recommended in the UK – is shown in *Table 3.5* and consist of two NRTIs with a preference for the NNRTI efavirenz as the third drug[4]. PIs should be reserved for specific groups of patients such as those with NRTI or NNRTI resistance, women who wish to become pregnant, and some individuals with psychiatric problems.

The recommended regimen for naïve HIV patients in the American DHHS Treatment Guidelines is given in *Table 3.6*.

Different classes of drugs have differing side-effect profiles, interactions, and toxicities (for information on individual ARV drugs see Appendices at the end of this chapter). Some combinations of ARVs are contraindicated, e.g. zidovudine (AZT) and stavudine (D4T) share a common metabolic pathway and are antagonistic; lamivudine (3TC) and emtricitabine (FTC) have a common mechanism of action; tenofovir (TDF) and didanosine (DDI) increase toxicities; and TDF and unboosted atazanavir (ATV) lead to reduced plasma levels of ATV. Combination of D4T and DDI carries increased risk of peripheral neuropathy, pancreatitis, and lactic acidosis.

Monitoring treatment response

HIV viral load

The aim of ARV therapy is to reduce the HIV viral load (VL) to undetectable levels. Decrease in VL after starting ART has a biphasic response, with an initial rapid response

Table 3.6 Drug selection (naïve). DHHS treatment guidelines (2009)[2]

Preferred	Alternative
Regimens with optimal and durable efficacy, favourable tolerability and toxicity profile, and ease of use	Regimens that are effective and tolerable but have potential disadvantages compared with preferred regimens
NNRTI-based • EFV/TDF/FTC	**NNRTI-based (in alphabetical order)** • EFV + (ABC or AZT)/3TC • NVP + AZT/3TC
PI-based (in alphabetical order) • ATV/r + TDF/FTC • DRV/r (once daily) + TDF/FTC	**PI-based (in alphabetical order)** • ATV/r + (ABC or AZT)/3TC • FPV/r (once or twice daily) + either [(ABC or ZDV)/3TC] or TDF/FTC • LPV/r (once or twice daily) + either [(ABC or ZDV)/3TC] or TDF/FTC • SQV/r + TDF/FTC
INSTI-based • RAL + TDF/FTC	
Preferred for pregnant women • LPV/r (twice daily) + AZT/3TC	

INSTI: integrase strand transfer inhibitor; NNRTI: non-nucleoside reverse transcriptase inhibitor; PI: protease inhibitor; ABC: abacavir; ATV: atazanavir; 3TC: lamivudine; DRV: darunavir; EFV:efavirenz; FPV: fosamprenavir; FTC: emtricitabine; LPV: lopinavir; NVP: nevirapine; RAL: raltegravir; r: low-dose ritonavir; SQV: saquinavir; TDF: tenofovir, AZT: zidovudine.

Notes:
EFV should not be used during the first trimester of pregnancy or in women trying to conceive or not using effective and consistent contraception.
ATV/r should not be used in patients who require >20 mg omeprazole equivalent per day.
NVP should not be used in patients with moderate to severe hepatic impairment (Child-Pugh B or C). NVP should not be used in women with CD4 >250 cells/mm^3 or men with CD4 >400 cells/mm^3 with detectable HIV load. However, those with low CD4 cell counts when ART was initiated, but who had high CD4 count and undetectable VL at the time of switching, tolerated the switch to nevirapine as well as ART-naïve subjects with low CD4 counts whose initial therapy included nevirapine[112]
ABC: should not be used in patients who test positive for HLA-B*5701. Use with caution in patients with high risk of cardiovascular disease or with pre-treatment HIV-RNA >100,000 copies/ml

occurring in the first few weeks of treatment followed by a slower phase to undetectable levels within 3–6 months[12]. VL should fall by approximately 2 logs after 1 month. Most patients should be undetectable by 6 months, however, some patients with very high baseline HIV VL may fail to reach undetectability by 6 months and should be monitored closely[4]. VL should be monitored every 4 weeks until it is undetectable, when every 3–6 months is adequate.

Sustained VL rebound is defined as VL >400 copies/ml at least 1 month apart. Regime intensification or change may be necessary. The patient's adherence should be assessed and drug resistance testing conducted. See page 46 for discussion of ARV resistance. Any patient failing therapy should be discussed in a multidisciplinary team (MDT) meeting involving pharmacists and virologists, as well as the treating physician.

CD4 response

This also occurs in two phases; rapid rises in CD4 in the first few months of HIV virological suppression occur due to circulation of existing CD4 reserves. Further rises are slower and depend on new CD4 cell production. The lower the CD4 nadir the less complete the restoration of CD4 count, with recent data suggesting that patients who start with lower CD4 counts may take up to 6 years to reach reconstitution and some patients never achieve normal CD4 levels, particularly if they start with very low nadir CD4 counts[13]. Age is also associated with a less complete immune response to treatment. Once the CD4 count has normalized it is unlikely to change much if the patient's VL

remains undetectable, and many clinicians are now measuring it less frequently.

Besides the CD4 count and VL several other investigations are required to monitor the HIV-positive patient (*Table 3.7*). This should be adapted depending on the immune status and condition of the patient. At each visit patients should be assessed for adherence and possible side-effects from therapy.

Therapeutic drug monitoring

Plasma levels of ARVs may vary considerably depending on compliance, metabolism, and absorption. Adequate levels of ARVs are essential for virological suppression and too high levels of ARVs can be associated with increased side-effects. Measurement of drug concentrations has become an important tool for monitoring therapy and the indications for therapeutic drug monitoring (TDM) include:

Table 3.7 Monitoring the HIV patient on treatment[1,2]

Treatment initiation
- Assess and support patient's readiness to start ART
- Physical examination, including height, weight, BMI, blood pressure
- Baseline plasma HIV RNA, repeated at 2 weeks, 4 weeks, 3 months into therapy and then 3 monthly
- Resistance testing (genotype) with determination of HIV subtype if not yet obtained
- CD4 absolute count + percentage (optional: CD8 and %)
- Full blood count, AST, ALT, alkaline phosphatase, calcium, phosphate, glucose, creatinine, calculated creatinine clearance
- Antibody tests for Toxoplasma, CMV, hepatitis A, B, and C, and syphilis
- Fasting blood glucose and lipids including fasting total LDL and HDL cholesterol, and triglycerides
- HLA B*5701 determination (if using abacavir)
- Tropism (if considering CCR5 antagonist)
- Fasting glucose and lipids
- Urine dipstick for protein and sugar
- Other laboratory parameters may be useful according to selected first-line regimen, e.g. protein creatinine ratio, amylase, lipase
- Cardiovascular risk assessment

3–6 monthly visits when established on therapy
- Plasma HIV RNA
- CD4 count and % (optional: CD8 count and %) – may be done less frequently if patient VL consistently <50 copies/ml
- Complete blood count, creatinine, calculated creatinine clearance, AST, ALT, bilirubin
- Other laboratory parameters according to selected regimen
- Fasting glucose and lipids
- If HBsAg positive or cirrhotic (regardless of cause): alpha-fetoprotein + ultrasound examination 6 monthly
- If HBsAg positive, HBV DNA to assess response to treatment

Every patient annually
- Physical examination
- Evaluation of social and psychological support
- Smoking cessation and diet evaluation
- Repeat serologic testing (syphilis, CMV, toxoplasmosis, hepatitis B, hepatitis C) if previously negative
- AST/ALT
- Women: cervical pap smear
- Fasting lipids and blood sugar

- Suspected/predicted drug–drug interactions.
- Concerns about suboptimal response (slow virological response).
- Unlicensed dosing regimens such as once daily nevirapine/etravirine or unboosted fosamprenavir/ atazanavir (take > 7 days post-initiation).
- Possible toxicity (e.g. CNS toxicity with efavirenz).
- Liver impairment.
- Pregnancy (PIs).
- Suspected noncompliance (only indicates if most recent dose has been taken).

In clinical practice TDM is limited to the PI and NNRTI classes. Although TDM is available for certain NRTIs (tenofovir), entry and integrase inhibitors, the clinical utility is not well defined in practice. Sample timing is critical to interpretation. In general a pre-dose trough allows the most accurate interpretation; however, some commercial service providers are able to offer predicted trough levels or percentile-based interpretations based on population kinetics. This allows more flexibility with sample timing (taken at least 4 hours after the prior dose). Peak levels may be useful with suspected toxicity; however, there are limited data to guide interpretation.

Toxicities and side-effects

Side-effects are common although most resolve in the first month of therapy. Patients should be asked about side-effects at each visit and given agents to minimize these, i.e. antiemetic and antidiarrhoeal agents. Inadequate management of side-effects can impact on a patient's risk of nonadherence. Some toxicities will require discontinuation of the relevant ARV drug or a regime change. The commonest ARV side-effects and toxicities are given in *Table 3.8*.

Table 3.8 Commonest side-effects and toxicities of ARV therapy

Toxicity	*Associated ARVs*
Haematological toxicity	Drug-induced bone marrow suppression is most commonly seen with AZT (anaemia, neutropenia): 5–10% of patients on AZT develop anaemia. MCV is elevated[14]; leucopenia may also rarely be associated with ART
Psychiatric	Efavirenz can cause dizziness and sleep disturbance. More severe psychiatric problems include depression, depersonalization, paranoid thoughts, and suicidal ideation. In most cases side-effects are mild and occur in the first 4 weeks of treatment and then resolve. Discontinuation due to side-effects is required in <5%[15]. Side-effects can be associated with higher plasma levels of EFV. EFV is metabolized by CYP2B6. An allelic variant of this is more common in those of African origin and is associated with significantly higher plasma levels of EFV. Depression, insomnia, and psychosis may rarely occur on 3TC or ABC therapy
Renal toxicity	Renal tubular dysfunction is associated with TDF. Proximal tubular damage manifests as proximal tubular acidosis, hypophosphataemia, hypokalaemia, glycosuria, and proteinuria[16]. Risk factors for TDF toxicity are pre-existing renal impairment, low body weight, and co-administration of other nephrotoxic drugs
Mitochondrial dysfunction	Primarily seen with the NRTI drugs, including lactic acidosis, hepatic toxicity, pancreatitis, peripheral neuropathy, lipoatrophy, myopathy[17]
Peripheral neuropathy	This is mainly caused by DDI and D4T. Symptoms occur after several months of therapy and usually present with a distal symmetrical sensory motor neuropathy. Other causes of peripheral neuropathy such as B12 deficiency, diabetes, alcohol, thyroid disease, other drugs, or HIV itself should be excluded[18]

Continued overleaf

Table 3.8 Commonest side-effects and toxicities of ARV therapy (*continued*)

Toxicity	Associated ARVs
Metabolic abnormalities (see Chapter 4)	More common with PIs. Include hyperlipidaemia, fat accumulation, insulin resistance, diabetes, and osteopaenia
Allergic reactions	Skin rashes and hypersensitivity reactions are more common with the NNRTI drugs, but are also seen with NRTI drugs, such as ABC (less likely if HLA B*5701-ve) and some PIs (in particular atazanavir). Nevirapine causes a rash in up to 30% of patients and in up to 25% of patients with efavirenz[19]. The NNRTI-related rash presents as a maculopapular, pruritic, confluent rash mainly over trunk and arms (**3.14, 3.15**). HLA-DRB1*01 status is associated with cutaneous hypersensitivity induced by nevirapine and efavirenz[20]. Fever may precede the rash and other signs may include mucosal ulceration and fatigue. The rash usually begins in the second to third week of treatment and women are more commonly affected. Severe reactions such as Stevens–Johnson syndrome (SJS) are rare (**3.16**). Approximately 50% of reactions resolve despite continuation of therapy. Treatment should be discontinued immediately if there is mucous membrane involvement, exfoliation, hepatic dysfunction (transaminases >5 times ULN) or fever >39°C. Steroids confer no benefits and may increase risk of infection in SJS A newer NNRTI, etravirine, has also been rarely associated in post-marketing reports with cases of SJS, toxic epidermal necrolysis (TEN) and erythema multiforme, as well as a rash. Any NNRTI therapy should be immediately discontinued when signs and symptoms of severe skin or hypersensitivity reactions develop
Allergic reactions	Abacavir can cause a life-threatening hypersensitivity reaction (HSR). In most cases the HSR occurs at an average of 8 days and usually within 6 weeks. There is a strong association between HLA*B5701 and HSR. HLA-B*5701 testing is recommended pre-treatment with abacavir after the results of the PREDICT study. This study found that the prevalence of HLA-B*5701 was 5.6% (109 of 1956 patients) and that screening eliminated immunologically confirmed HSR with a negative predictive value of 100% and a positive predictive value of 47.9%[24]. The rash with abacavir is often mild (30% have no rash) and more frequent symptoms are fever, malaise which progressively worsens, and gastrointestinal symptoms. Elevations of LFTs may occur. There is no eosinophilia. HSR may be fatal if not diagnosed. Once a diagnosis of HSR is established re-challenge with ABC may be fatal and is contraindicated[4]
Hepatotoxicty	Reported with all classes of drugs. With NNRTIs it is reported with 8% in EFV and 15% NVP, the risk being greater among persons with chronic viral hepatitis and those prescribed concurrent PIs[22]. Hepatotoxity with NVP is associated with HLA-DRB*0101 status and CD4 counts[23]. In PIs hepatotoxicity occurs in up to 30%, especially associated with ritonavir. Screen for HBV and HCV pre-treatment is advised. Grade 1–3 elevations in ALT/AST may resolve, but monitor closely. With Grade 4 ↑ALT stop drug. DRV administered with ritonavir during clinical trials and post-marketing data collection caused drug-induced hepatitis in 0.5% of patients. Liver injury including fatality was more associated with patients on multiple medications or who had hepatitis co-infection or IRIS[24]

Continued

Table 3.8 Commonest side-effects and toxicities of ARV therapy (*continued*)

Toxicity	Associated ARVs
Osteopaenia/ osteoporosis	HIV-infected individuals have a lower bone density than uninfected individuals. Bone density is measured by measurement of X-ray absorption (e.g. DEXA scan) (**3.18**). Results are given as the number of standard deviations (the T score) from the mean value in young and healthy adults. Values between -1 and -2.5 standard deviations (SD) are referred to as osteopaenia and values above -2.5 as osteoporosis. In addition to HIV other factors are associated with bone thinning and these include excess alcohol, steroid treatment, hypogonadism, smoking, immobilization, hepatitis C co-infection, and also ART, especially PIs[25,26]. The SMART study[27] found that compared with people taking intermittent ART, those on steady ART had significantly greater drops in bone mineral density as measured by DEXA, indicating an apparent negative effect of treatment, without a link to specific drugs or classes
	The following tests should be done in all HIV patients to look for disorders of bone metabolism: bone function tests (serum calcium, phosphate, and alkaline phosphatase), serum 25-hydroxyvitamin D and parathyroid hormone, serum testosterone (men), bone mineral density (DEXA scan)
	Osteopaenia should be treated with adequate calcium intake (around 1 g/day), dietary or as supplement and vitamin D repletion if required (up to 2,000 IU/day)
	Advice on weight-bearing exercise and stopping alcohol and smoking should be given. Patients with osteoporosis can be treated with bisphosphonates (usually alendronate) with calcium and vitamin D as adjunctive therapy[28]

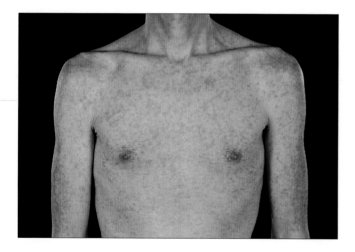

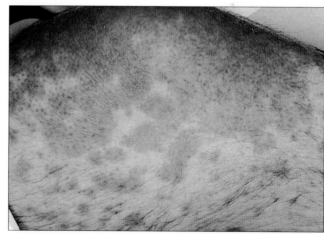

3.14, 3.15 Efavirenz hypersensitivity rash.

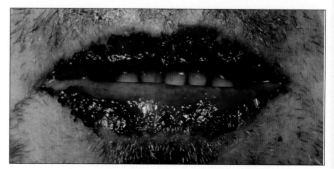

3.16 Nevirapine hypersensitivity: Stevens–Johnson syndrome.

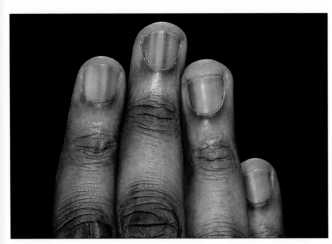

3.17 Longitudinal melanonychia has been attributed to the use of zidovudine but has also been described in patients not receiving ART. Possible mechanisms include increased levels of melanocyte stimulating hormone[29].

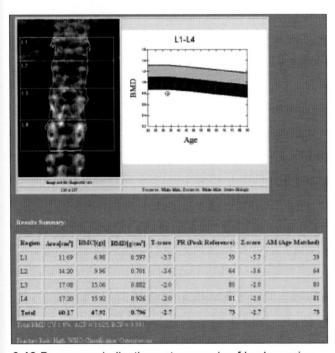

Results Summary:

Region	Area[cm²]	BMC[g]	BMD[g/cm²]	T-score	PR (Peak Reference)	Z-score	AM (Age Matched)
L1	11.69	6.98	0.597	-3.7	59	-3.7	59
L2	14.20	9.96	0.701	-3.6	64	-3.6	64
L3	17.08	15.06	0.882	-2.0	80	-2.0	80
L4	17.20	15.92	0.926	-2.0	81	-2.0	81
Total	60.17	47.92	0.796	-2.7	73	-2.7	73

3.18 Bone scan indicating osteoporosis of lumbar spine.

Drug interactions

Assessing for potential drug interactions with ART is required every time new drugs are prescribed. This is best done through the use of specialist websites such as the University of Liverpool, HIV drug interaction site (www.hiv-druginteractions.org/).

The future

There are a vast number of new therapeutic compounds in development which may enter clinical practice within the next few years both from existing classes and new drug classes, although as in all fields of medicine the majority of drugs in early stages of development do not reach clinical use. The Treatment Action Group (TAG) in conjunction with i-base (www.treatmentactiongroup.org) provides a comprehensive overview of the current state of ARV development. The major compounds likely to impact on clinical care are outlined below.

NNRTIs

Rilpivirine (Tibotec) is a new NNRTI currently in phase III studies in HIV-1 treatment-naïve patients. Initial phase II studies indicate similar overall efficacy to efavirenz with fewer CNS side-effects; however, the development of mutations which are cross resistant with etravirine are a possible concern. A once-daily fixed dose combination with tenofovir/emtricitabine is likely.

Lesivirine (Pfizer/ViiV Ltd) is a new NNRTI in phase IIB trials in both antiretroviral-naïve (vs. efavirenz on backbone of Truvada) and experienced studies (vs. etravirine on backbone of darunavir/r + NRTI).

Integrase inhibitors

Elvitegravir (Gilead Sciences Ltd) is a new once-daily integrase inhibitor tested for efficacy in naïve and experienced patients. Unlike raltegravir, elvitegravir requires pharmacokinetic boosting either with ritonavir or one of the new pharmacokinetic (PK) boosters (most likely cobicistat). Small studies comparing cobicistat-boosted elvitegravir formulated in a 'quad' pill (tenofovir/emtricitabine/elvitegravir/cobicistat) compared with Atripla are promising and phase III studies are currently under way.

GSK1349572 (ViiV/Shionogi) is another new once-daily integrase inhibitor which may have activity against raltegravir-resistant virus. Phase III experienced and naïve studies are currently enrolling patients.

New pharmacokinetic boosters

There are a number of new PK boosters in development as an alternative to ritonavir. Gilead's cobicistat (GS9350) is furthest in clinical development, with a small phase II study suggesting similar outcomes as a PK booster as that of ritonavir; however, the side-effect profile is also similar. Although cobicistat may not provide a side-effect advantage over ritonavir, it may be a cheaper alternative to co-formulate with other PIs. Gilead also plan to combine cobicistat with their integrase inhibitor elvitegravir, which requires PK boosting.

SPI-452 (Sequoia), PF-3716539 (ViiV) and TMC558445 (Tibotec) are potent CYP3A4 inhibitors in phase I studies in conjunction with PIs.

Other drugs and new classes

Bevirimat (Myriad Genetics) and vivecon (Myriad Genetics) are maturation inhibitors that block viral assembly leading to production of noninfectious viruses. Bevirimat's development has been hindered by formulation issues and efficacy concerns in patients with certain gag polymorphisms. Vivecon is entering phase IIA clinical trials in drug-naïve HIV-1-positive patients.

LEDGINS are a new class of integrase inhibitor which are unlikely to show cross resistance as they do not bind to the same active site. TBR-652 is a new CCR5 antagonist which also blocks CCR2, a cellular receptor involved in inflammation. The clinical safety and utility of CCR2 blockade are as yet unknown.

Ibalizumab (TNX-355, TaiMed) is a new type of monoclonal antibody that acts as an entry inhibitor by binding to CD4 receptors preventing attachment of HIV-1. It is currently in phase II development, where it is given as a fortnightly injection.

Patent expiry (3.19)

The NRTIs zidovudine, lamivudine, and abacavir as single agents are now off patent, as is the PI saquinavir. The patent for the NNRTI nevirapine is due to expire in 2011, with efavirenz following in 2014. The impact of patent expiry in the western world is as yet unknown, with many of the drugs in declining use due to the availability of newer, preferable agents or the availability of fixed-dose combination still within patent.

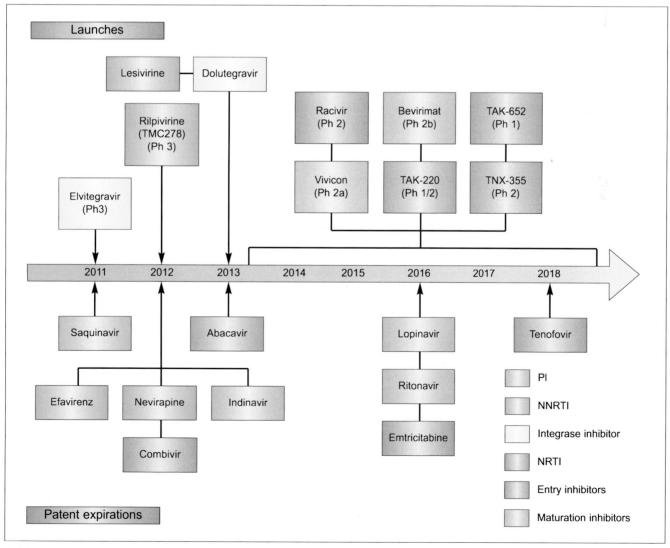

3.19 HIV landscape: launches and patent expiries.

Antiretroviral drug resistance

Treatment changes may be required for side-effects and toxicities or virological failure due to antiretroviral drug resistance.

Principles of resistance

- Drug-resistant mutants are generated spontaneously during virus replication and pre-exist the introduction of ART (*Table 3.9*).
- It has been estimated that the prevalence of pre-existing single drug-resistant mutants is relatively high within the quasispecies, whereas double and especially triple mutants are considerably less frequent.
- Ongoing virus replication during therapy leads to the selection and evolution of resistant mutants with accumulation of mutations on the same viral genome and growing levels of resistance and cross-resistance (**3.20**).

Drug-resistant mutants display changes in viral proteins such as protease, RT, or integrase, which play a key role in virus replication and infectivity. Drug resistance therefore carries a fitness cost, which is related to the number and type of resistance mutations.

There are potential clinical benefits associated with maintaining selective pressure on mutations that carry a significant fitness cost for the virus[30]. Impaired pathogenicity can translate in partial viral load reduction and improved CD4 counts despite ongoing virus replication. The effects are especially apparent with mutations associated with resistance to the nucleos(t)ide RT inhibitors, most notably the lamivudine resistance mutation M184V, and variably with protease resistance mutations[31-34].

For highly drug-experienced patients with limited or no remaining drug options, continuing therapy is preferred to a complete treatment interruption in order to delay disease progression while waiting for new drug options. The benefits may be short-lived however, if compensatory mutations emerge within the *pol* gene or other genetic regions that restore viral fitness and pathogenicity (**3.21**).

Resistance mutations may also exert an antagonistic effect on the emergence of certain other resistance mutations or partially restore susceptibility to certain drugs while causing resistance to others. For example, co-treatment with lamivudine tends to delay the emergence of resistance to zidovudine by maintaining selective pressure

---

Table 3.9 Principles of antiretroviral drug resistance

Resistant mutants before therapy is introduced
- Are generated spontaneously during virus replication
- Pre-exist the introduction of antiretroviral therapy
- Usually display reduced fitness in the absence of drug pressure
- Are present as low-frequency variants within the quasispecies

Resistant mutants during therapy
- Are selected, not created, by drug pressure if virus suppression is incomplete
- Acquire a selective advantage over wild-type virus
- With ongoing virus replication become dominant within the quasispecies
- Continue to evolve under drug pressure with increasing levels of resistance
- Over time acquire mutations that compensate for reduced fitness

Resistant mutants after therapy is discontinued
- Lose the replication advantage
- Are outgrown by wild-type virus
- Persist as low-frequency species in plasma and in latently infected cells
- Can re-emerge rapidly if drug pressure is re-introduced

on M184V. Once zidovudine resistant mutants emerge, the presence of M184V confers high-level resistance to lamivudine but reduces the levels of zidovudine resistance. The M184V mutation also increases susceptibility to stavudine and tenofovir.

Resistance testing

There are two main approaches for detecting drug resistance in routine practice: genotypic and phenotypic testing (*Table 3.10*). Both methods are typically applied to the viral RNA recovered from the patient's plasma.

In genotypic testing, automated population sequencing of the viral genomic region of interest (e.g. RT or protease) allows the identification of resistance mutations within the dominant quasispecies (**3.22**). Resistance mutations are classified as primary or major, and accessory, secondary or minor according to their impact on drug susceptibility (*Table 3.11*). The interpretation of genotypic test results is performed through algorithms that assign scores to individual mutations or apply specific rules to certain mutation patterns.

In phenotypic testing, viral genetic regions of interest are transfected into a laboratory vector to generate a

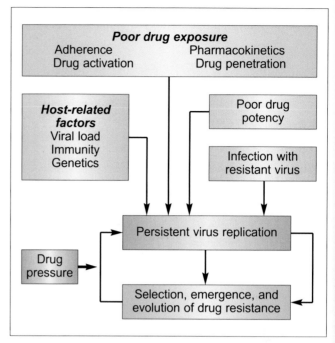

3.20 Antiretroviral treatment failure and drug resistance.

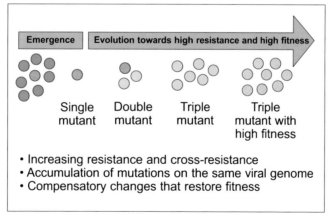

3.21 Emergence and evolution of drug resistance.

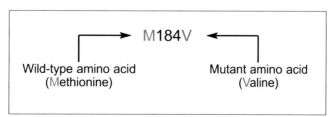

3.22 Nomenclature for drug-resistance mutations. The example shows the lamivudine-resistance mutation M184V.

Table 3.10 Resistance testing in clinical practice

	Genotypic test	*Phenotypic test*
Principle	Sequencing of genetic region of interest to identify resistance mutations	Growth of recombinant virus containing the genetic region of interest
Availability	Wide	Limited
Turn-around time	1–2 weeks	3–4 weeks
Cost	++	++++
Commercial assays	Yes	Yes
In-house assays	Common	Uncommon
External quality assurance	Available	Not available
Sensitivity	Detects variants representing >20–30% of quasispecies	May require a high proportion of resistant strains to measure significant shifts in susceptibility
Output	Consensus sequence of dominant quasispecies	Average susceptibility of dominant quasispecies
Results	Mutations, deletion, insertions compared with reference sequence	Fold-changes in drug concentration required to suppress patient's virus compared with reference virus
Interpretation	Known effect of mutations on viral phenotype and clinical responses	Known effect of fold-changes on clinical responses

recombinant virus that can be grown *in vitro* in the presence of escalating concentrations of antiretroviral agents. The virtual phenotype is a genotype interpretation method that matches the patient's derived viral sequence to genotype–phenotype pairs within a large dataset to predict the phenotype.

With appropriate interpretation of results, both resistance testing methods can provide useful information in different clinical scenarios (*Table 3.12*). One limitation is that the assays cannot detect resistance present at low frequency (<20–30%) within the quasispecies. Therefore, testing should be performed while the patient is still receiving therapy to ensure optimal performance, as resistant mutants decay below the assay detection threshold after therapy is discontinued. The clinical significance of low-frequency mutants is currently under investigation and several ultrasensitive resistance testing methods have been developed in research settings (e.g. sensitive real-time PCR, ultra-deep sequencing), although they remain currently too laborious or expensive for routine practice.

Transmitted drug resistance

Transmitted drug-resistant mutants show different kinetics from mutants selected during therapy. The absence of wild-type virus and the high fitness of the mutant virus as a prerequisite for efficient transmission mean that resistant mutants decay very slowly and may remain detectable for years after infection in the absence of drug pressure[35].

Reported prevalence of transmitted drug resistance varies widely, due in part to differences in study design and inclusion criteria, geographical location, sample population, and interpretation systems. Data reported in 2008 and 2009 show rates ranging from 1.8% among pregnant women in South Africa[36] to 16.7% among untreated patients in Spain[37] (*Table 3.13*). The highest prevalence is observed in geographical areas with well established use of ART, including western Europe, North America and regions of Latin America such as Brazil. In these regions, historical use of mono- and dual therapy in the pre-HAART era, use of suboptimal treatment regimens in the early HAART era, and ongoing difficulties with adherence

Table 3.11 Major drug-resistance mutations

Nucleos(t)ide RT inhibitors

ZDV, d4T, ddI, ABC, TDF	M41L, D67N, K70R, L210W, T215Y/F, K219Q/E
ABC, ddI, TDF, 3TC, FTC	K65R, K70E/G
ddI	T69D
ABC, ddI	L74V/I
d4T, ddI	V75T/M
ABC	Y115F
3TC, FTC, ABC	M184V/I
MDR	T69ins, Q151M complex

Non-nucleoside RT inhibitors

NVP	A98G, K101E, V106A, Y188H/C, K238N/T
NVP, EFV	L100I, K103N/S, V106M, G190A, M230L
NVP, ETR	Y181C/I/V
ETR	E138K, V179F, F227C
MDR	K101P, Y188L, G190S/E

Protease inhibitors

NFV	D30N, I54A/L/M, N88S/D
FPV	I32V, I47V/A
LPV	I47A, I50V
ATV	G48V, I50L, N88S
NFV, SQV	G48V, L90M
DRV, FPV	I50V, I54L/M, I76V
IDV, LPV, NFV	I54V, V82A/F/T/S
TPV	V82F/T/S/L
MDR	I84V

ZDV: zidovudine; d4T: stavudine; ddI: didanosine; ABC: abacavir; TDF: Tenofovir; 3TC: lamivudine; FTC: emtricitabine; NVP: nevirapine; EFV: efavirenz; ETR: etravirine; NFV: nelfinavir; FPV: fosamprenavir; LPV: lopinavir; ATV: atazanavir; SQV: saquinavir; DRV: darunavir; IDV: indinavir; TPV: tipranavir; MDR: multidrug resistance

Table 3.12 Clinical applications of resistance testing

Clinical scenario	Genotypic	Phenotypic	Comments
Primary infection New diagnosis	✓ ✓		Genotypic testing has higher sensitivity for the detection of transmitted drug resistance
Treatment failure	✓	✓	Genotypic testing is generally more cost-effective. Phenotypic testing is useful in the presence of complex resistance patterns
Pregnancy	✓		Before starting therapy or in the presence of detectable viraemia during therapy

and tolerability have led to a pool of patients carrying drug-resistant virus which is available to seed new infections. Patients newly infected with drug-resistant virus represent a further important source of onward transmission of drug resistance. In other regions rates of transmitted drug resistance currently remain low. However, emerging data suggest that this pattern is changing in countries currently scaling up access to ART[38].

Table 3.13 Prevalence (%) of antiretroviral drug resistance among drug-naïve HIV-1 infected persons worldwide*

Population	N	Year of survey	Country	%	Reference
Untreated pregnant women	113	2002, 2004	South Africa	1.8	36
New diagnoses	1903	2003–2007	Japan	4.2–7.7	39
	474	2002–2007	Greece	5.0	40
	611	2000–2007	Switzerland	6.2	41
	189	2007	Ireland	6.8	42
	433	2004–2007	London	7.2	43
	2555	2002–2005	Europe, Israel	8.5	44
	530	2006–2007	France	9.6	45
	102	2006–2007	Spain	10.8	46
	261	2004–2007	Spain	11.1	47
Recent infection	1174	1996–2007	Germany	12.6	48
	504	1997–2007	Spain	13.8	49
	224	2003–2007	USA	16.0	50
Untreated patients	1690	1996–2007	Italy	13.7	71
	358	2007	Spain	16.7	37

*Studies including >100 patients

References

1 European AIDS Clinical Society (EACS) Guidelines for the Clinical Management and Treatment of HIV Infected Adults In Europe (2009). Version 5-2. Available at: http://www.europeanaidsclinicalsociety.org/guidelinespdf/EACS-EuroGuidelines_FullVersion.pdf

2 Panel on Antiretroviral Guidelines for Adults and Adolescents. Guidelines for the use of antiretroviral agents in HIV-1-infected adults and adolescents. Department of Health and Human Services. December 1, 2009; 1–161. Available at: http://www.aidsinfo.nih.gov/ContentFiles/AdultandAdolescentGL.pdf

3 British HIV Association Guidelines for Immunization of HIV-Infected Adults 2008. *HIV Med* 2008;9(10): 795–848.

4 British HIV Association guidelines for the treatment of HIV-1-infected adults with antiretroviral therapy 2008. *HIV Med* 2008;9:563–608. Available at: http://www.bhiva.org/files/file1031815.pdf

5 Phillips A, Pezzotti P; CASCADE Collaboration. Short-term risk of AIDS according to current CD4 cell count and viral load in antiretroviral drug-naive individuals and those treated in the monotherapy era. *AIDS* 2004 Jan 2;18(1):51–8.

6 The Strategies for Management of Antiretroviral Therapy (SMART) study Group. CD4+ count guided interruptions of antiretroviral therapy. *N Engl J Med* 2006;355:2283–96.

7 When To Start Consortium. Timing of initiation of antiretroviral therapy in AIDS-free HIV-1-infected patients: a collaborative analysis of 18 HIV cohort studies. *Lancet* 2009 Apr 18;373(9672):1352–63.

8 Wilkin TJ, Gulick RM. When to start antiretroviral therapy? *Clin Infect Dis* 2008 Dec 15;47(12):1580–6.

9 Zolopa A, Andersen J, Powderly W, et al. Early antiretroviral therapy reduces AIDS progression/death in individuals with acute opportunistic infections: a multicenter randomized strategy trial. *PLoS One* 2009;4(5):e5575.

10 Makadzange AT, Ndhlovu CE, Takarinda K, et al. Early versus delayed initiation of antiretroviral therapy for concurrent HIV infection and cryptococcal meningitis in sub-saharan Africa. *Clin Infect Dis* 2010;50(11):1532–8.

11 Wit FW, Kesselring AM, Gras L, Richter C, van der Ende ME, Brinkman K, et al. Discontinuation of nevirapine because of hypersensitivity reactions in patients with prior treatment experience, compared with treatment-naive patients: the ATHENA cohort study. Clin Infect Dis 2008 Mar 15;46(6):933–40.

12 Rizzardi GP, De Boer RJ, Hoover S, Tambussi G, Chapuis A, Halkic N, et al. Predicting the duration of antiviral treatment needed to suppress plasma HIV-1 RNA. J Clin Invest 2000 Mar;105(6):777–82.

13 Moore RD, Keruly JC. CD4+ cell count 6 years after commencement of highly active antiretroviral therapy in persons with sustained virologic suppression. Clin Infect Dis 2007 Feb 1;44(3):441–6.

14 Moyle G. Anaemia in persons with HIV infection: prognostic marker and contributor to morbidity. AIDS Rev 2002;4(1):13–20.

15 Hawkins T, Geist C, Young B, et al. Comparison of neuropsychiatric side effects in an observational cohort of efavirenz- and protease inhibitor-treated patients. HIV Clin Trials 2005 Jul-Aug;6(4):187–96.

16 Izzedine H, Launay-Vacher V, Deray G. Antiviral drug-induced nephrotoxicity. Am J Kidney Dis 2005 May;45(5):804–17.

17 Moyle G. Mechanisms of HIV and nucleoside reverse transcriptase inhibitor injury to mitochondria. Antivir Ther 2005;10(Suppl 2):M47–52.

18 Gonzalez-Duarte A, Cikurel K, Simpson DM. Managing HIV peripheral neuropathy. Curr HIV/AIDS Rep 2007 Aug;4(3):114–18.

19 Manosuthi W, Thongyen S, Chumpathat N, et al. Incidence and risk factors of rash associated with efavirenz in HIV-infected patients with preceding nevirapine-associated rash. HIV Med 2006;7(6):378–82.

20 Vitezica ZG, Milpied B, Lonjou C, et al. HLA-DRB1*01 associated with cutaneous hypersensitivity induced by nevirapine and efavirenz. AIDS 2008 Feb 19;22(4):540–1.

21 Mallal S, Phillips E, Carosi G, et al. HLA-B*5701 screening for hypersensitivity to abacavir. N Engl J Med 2008 Feb 7;358(6):568–79.

22 Sulkowski MS, Thomas DL, Mehta SH, et al. Hepatotoxicity associated with nevirapine or efavirenz-containing antiretroviral therapy: role of hepatitis C and B infections. Hepatology 2002 Jan;35(1):182–9.

23 Rivero A, Mira JA, Pineda JA, et al. Liver toxicity induced by non-nucleoside reverse transcriptase inhibitors. J Antimicrob Chemother 2007;59(3):342–6.

24 DRV REF: FDA Medwatch: Prezista (darunavir), March 12, 2008. Available at: RelatedDrugLabelingChanges/ucm116300.htm.

25 Glesby MJ. Bone disorders in human immunodeficiency virus infection. Clin Infect Dis 2003;37(Suppl 2):S91–5.

26 Duvivier C, Kolta S, Assoumou L, et al. Greater decrease in bone mineral density with protease inhibitor regimens compared with non-nucleoside reverse transcriptase inhibitor regimens in HIV-1 infected naive patients. AIDS 2009 Apr 27;23(7):817–24.

27 Grund B, Carr A. Continuous antiretroviral therapy (ART) decreases bone mineral density: results from the SMART study. 48th ICAAC, 25–28 October 2008. Washington. Abstract H-2312a.

28 Clay PG, Voss LE, Williams C, et al. Valid treatment options for osteoporosis and osteopenia in HIV-infected persons. Ann Pharmacother 2008;42(5):670–9.

29 Cribier B, et al. Nail changes in patient infected with HIV: a prospective study. Arch Dermatol 1998;134:1216–20.

30 Geretti AM. The clinical significance of viral fitness. J HIV Ther 2005;10:6–10.

31 Eron JJ, Benoit SL, Jemsek J, et al. Treatment with lamivudine, zidovudine, or both in HIV-positive patients with 200 to 500 CD4+ cells per cubic millimeter. N Engl J Med 1995;333:1662–9.

32 Deeks SG, Hoh R, Neilands TB, et al. Interruption of treatment with individual therapeutic drug classes in adults with multidrug-resistant HIV-1 infection. J Infect Dis 2005;192:1537–44.

33 Castagna A, Danise A, Menzo S, et al. Lamivudine monotherapy in HIV-1-infected patients harbouring a lamivudine-resistant virus: a randomized pilot study (E-184V study). AIDS 2006;20:795–803.

34 Geretti AM. Clinical implications of HIV drug resistance to nucleoside and nucleotide reverse transcriptase inhibitors. AIDS Rev 2006;8:210–20.

35 Bezemer D, de Ronde A, Prins M, et al. Evolution of transmitted HIV-1 with drug-resistance mutations in the absence of therapy: effects on CD4+ T-cell count and HIV-1 RNA load. Antivir Ther 2006;11:173–8.

36 Pillay V, Ledwaba J, Hunt G, et al. Antiretroviral drug resistance surveillance among drug-naive HIV-1-infected individuals in Gauteng Province, South Africa in 2002 and 2004. Antivir Ther 2008;13(S2):101–7.

37 Viciana I, Mora L, Palacios R, et al. Prevalence of HIV-1 drug resistance mutations and non-B subtypes in treatment naïve patients in Andalucia (Spain) during year 2007. Abstracts from the 6th European HIV Drug Resistance Workshop, Budapest, Hungary, 2008. Abstract 17.

38 Aghokeng AF, Vergne L, Atem-Tambe A, et al. Evaluation of transmitted HIV drug resistance using the

WHO HIV drug resistance threshold survey model in four Central African countries. Abstracts from the XVII International HIV Drug Resistance Workshop, Sitges, Spain, 2008. *Antivir Ther* 2008;**13**(S3):A149.

39 Yoshida S, Gatanaga H, Itoh T, *et al*. Prevalence of drug resistance associated mutations in newly diagnosed HIV/AIDS patients in Japan from 2003 to 2007. Abstracts from the XVII International HIV Drug Resistance Workshop, Sitges, Spain, 2008. *Antivir Ther* 2008;**13**(S3):A162.

40 Paraskevis D, Magiorkinis E, Hatzitheodorou E, *et al*. Prevalence of transmitted drug resistance mutations in newly diagnosed HIV-1 infected patient in Greece during the period 2002-2007. Abstracts from the 6th European HIV Drug Resistance Workshop, Budapest, Hungary, 2008. Abstract 22.

41 Yerly S, Junier T, Boffi E, *et al*. drug resistance in newly diagnosed individuals: transmission rate, clusters and persistence. Abstracts from the XVII International HIV Drug Resistance Workshop, Sitges, Spain, 2008. *Antivir Ther* 2008;**13**(S3):A167.

42 De Gascun CF, Regan C, Coughlan S, *et al*. Transmitted HIV-1 antiretroviral drug resistance surveillance in Ireland 2007. Abstracts from the 6th European HIV Drug Resistance Workshop, Budapest, Hungary, 2008. Abstract 24.

43 Booth CL, Garcia-Diaz AM, Smith C, *et al*. Trends in transmitted antiretroviral resistance in London. Abstracts from the 6th European HIV Drug Resistance Workshop, Budapest, Hungary, 2008. Abstract 7.

44 Vercauteren J, Wensing AMJ, Van de Vijver, *et al*. Trends in transmitted drug-resistance HIV-1 in Europe (Sept 2002–Dec 2005). Abstracts from the 6th European HIV Drug Resistance Workshop, Budapest, Hungary, 2008. Abstract 5.

45 Descamps D, Montes B, Chaix ML, *et al*. Prevalence of resistance mutations in antiretroviral-naïve chronically HIV-infected patients in 2006/2007: a French nationwide study. Abstracts from the XVII International HIV Drug Resistance Workshop, Sitges, Spain, 2008. *Antivir Ther* 2008;**13**(S3):A154.

46 Aguilera A, Rodriguez-Calvino J, Cortizo S, *et al*. Trends of resistance transmission and HIV-1 non-B subtypes in newly diagnosed patient in Galicia (Spain) over time (2006–2007). Abstracts from the 6th European HIV Drug Resistance Workshop, Budapest, Hungary, 2008. Abstract 20.

47 Cuevas MT, Perez-Alvarez L, Munoz-Nieto M, *et al*. HIV-1 genetic forms, transmission clusters and drug resistance mutations in newly diagnosed patients from the Basque Country, Spain. Abstracts from the 6th European HIV Drug Resistance Workshop, Budapest, Hungary, 2008. Abstract 19.

48 Kuecherer C, Schuenadel L, Somogyi S, *et al*. Transmission and persistence of HIV-1 with thymidine analogue resistance mutations in HIV-1 infected patients with documented date of infection. Abstracts from the 6th European HIV Drug Resistance Workshop, Budapest, Hungary, 2008. Abstract 1.

49 De Mendoza C, Rodriguez C, Aguilera A, *et al*. Virological characterization of HIV strains in recent seroconverters in Spain. Abstracts from the XVII International HIV Drug Resistance Workshop, Sitges, Spain, 2008. *Antivir Ther* 2008;**13**(S3):A152.

50 Jain V, Pilcher C, Deeks S, *et al*. Increasing prevalence of NNRTI-associated drug-resistance mutations in patients with acute, early HIV in San Fransisco. Abstracts from the 16th Conference on Retroviruses and Opportunistic Infections, Montreal, Canada, 2009.

51 Bracciale L, Colafigli M, Romano L, *et al*. Prevalence of primary HIV-1 drug resistance in HIV-1 infected patients in Italy: evolution over 12 years and predictors. Abstracts from the 6th European HIV Drug Resistance Workshop, Budapest, Hungary, 2008. Abstract 11.

Further reading

British HIV Association guidelines for the treatment of HIV-1-infected adults with antiretroviral therapy 2008. *HIV Medicine* 2008;**9**:563–608. Available at: http://www.bhiva.org/files/file1031815.pdf

European AIDS Clinical Society (EACS) Guidelines for the Clinical Management and Treatment of HIV Infected Adults In Europe (2009). Version 5-2. Available at: http://www.europeanaidsclinicalsociety.org/guidelinespdf/EACS-EuroGuidelines_FullVersion.pdf

Panel on Antiretroviral Guidelines for Adults and Adolescents. Guidelines for the use of antiretroviral agents in HIV-1-infected adults and adolescents. Department of Health and Human Services. December 1, 2009; 1–161. Available at: http://www.aidsinfo.nih.gov/ContentFiles/AdultandAdolescentGL.pdf

Hoffmann C, Rockstroh JK, Kamps BS (eds). *HIV Medicine*, 15th edn. Flying Publisher, 2007. Available at: http://www.HIVMedicine.com

Appendices to Chapter 3: antiretroviral drug dosing guidelines

Appendix 3.1 Protease inhibitors

Drug name	Key prescribing information	Food restrictions	Side-effects
Atazanavir (Reyataz) 150 mg caps 300 mg caps 200 mg caps	• NNRTIs: Increase ATV/r to 400 mg/100 mg od with EFV & NVP • PPIs: Do not co-prescribe where possible as reduced ATV levels • H2 antagonists: Rx ranitidine 150–300 mg od 3–12 hours post dose • Avoid indigestion remedies at same time	With/after food	Hyperbilirubinaemia: clinical jaundice in 4% of patients Nephrolithiasis
Darunavir (Prezista) 600 mg tablets 400 mg tablets 150 mg tablets 75 mg tablets	• Once daily licensed in ART-naïve patients plus patients without darunavir-associated mutations • Caution with sulphonamide allergy	With/after food	Skin rash Liver toxicity in 0.5% especially in advanced HIV-1 disease taking multiple concomitant medications, co-morbidities including hepatitis B or C co-infection
Fosamprenavir (Telzir) 700 mg tablets 50 mg/ml liquid	• Viral failure with presence of (fos) amprenavir mutations may lead to suboptimal response to darunavir as salvage PI • Significantly increase fosamprenavir levels when combined with etravirine: avoid • Caution with sulphonamide allergy	None	Nausea/vomiting, GI disturbances, skin rash
Indinavir (Crixivan) 200 mg caps 400 mg caps		With/after food	Renal stones, renal dysfunction, nausea/vomiting Fluid intake at least 1.5 litres (6 glasses each day)
Nelfinavir 250 mg tablets	• Does not require ritonavir boosting • May not be as effective as other boosted PIs	Must be taken with meals every 2 hours	Diarrhoea

Continued overleaf

Appendix 3.1 Protease inhibitors (*continued*)

Drug name	Key prescribing information	Food restrictions	Side-effects
Ritonavir (Norvir) 100 mg tablets 80 mg/ml liquid	• Used as a PK booster at doses of 100–200mg in combination with other PIs	With/after food	Nausea/vomiting Liver toxicity
Saquinavir (Invirase) 500 mg tablets 200 mg capsules	• Only licensed twice daily • Use with caution in drugs which prolong QT or PR intervals	Take within 2 hours after a meal	Nausea/vomiting PR + QT prolongation
Tipranavir (Aptivus) 250 mg caps 100 mg/ml solution	• Not recommended in treatment-naïve patients • Requires ritonavir 200 mg BD • Contraindicated with etravirine • Caution in liver disease • Possible increased risk of intracranial haemorrhage • Requires refrigeration	With/after food	Liver toxicity, ↑lipids
Lopinavir/ritonavir (Kaletra Tablets) 200 mg/50 mg tablet 100/25 mg tablet 80 mg/ml liquid	• Once daily lopinavir/r licensed in naïve patients • Use with caution with NNRTIs (consider dose increase) • Liquid contains propylene glycol and 42%v/v alcohol, and requires refrigeration	None with tablets, with/after food for liquid	Diarrhoea, headache, nausea/abdominal pain Lipid elevation

Appendix 3.2 Nucleoside reverse transcriptase inhibitors (NRTIs)

Approved drug name	Key prescribing information	Food restrictions	Side-effects
Zidovudine (AZT) 250 mg caps 100 mg caps 10 mg/ml liquid 10 mg/ml inj	• 300 mg bd when used as a part of Combivir or Trizivir (more anaemia than with lower dose) • Commonly used during pregnancy/labour to prevent MTCT. See BHIVA pregnancy guidelines *Drug interactions:* overlapping myelosuppression with septrin/ganciclovir	None	Nausea/vomiting/headache, anaemia and neutropenia, mitochondrial toxicity

Continued

Appendix 3.2 Nucleoside reverse transcriptase inhibitors (NRTIs) (*continued*)

Approved drug name	Key prescribing information	Food restrictions	Side-effects
Didanosine (DDI) 400 mg caps 250 mg caps 200 mg caps 25 mg tabs	• Weight-dependent dosing • If given with tenofovir (not an advised combination): >60 kg: 250 mg OD <60 kg: 200 mg OD *Specific drug interactions:* • Tenofovir: DDI levels are increased; use with caution, not recommended • Renal dose adjustment needed in eGRF<50 ml/min	2 hours before/ after food (no food restrictions when given with tenofovir)	Abdominal pain/nausea, peripheral neuropathy, mitochondrial toxicity, pancreatitis *Monitoring:* always check amylase in patient with abdominal pain/GI disturbance taking DDI, consider sending pancreas-specific amylase to a major hospital testing laboratory
Stavudine (D4T) 40 mg/30 mg/ 20 mg caps 1 mg/ml liquid	• Weight-dependent dosing • Do not co-prescribe with isoniazid or AZT • Not advised with DDI due to increased risk of peripheral neuropathy, lactic acidosis, and pancreatitis	None	Peripheral neuropathy, abnormal LFTs, associated with lipodystrophy, mitochondrial toxicity
Abacavir (ABC) 300 mg tablets 20 mg/ml liquid	• Caution in patients with high cardiovascular risk • Caution with VL >100,000 cps/ml • *Caution with ribavirin:* Reduced intracellular levels of ribavirin may lead to inferior response to HCV treatment if not dosed according to weight	None	Hypersensitivity reaction (5–7% - HLA-B*5701) NB: hypersensitivity typically presents with **rash**, or one or more symptoms from at least two of the following groups: • Fever • SOB, sore throat or cough • Nausea or vomiting or diarrhoea or abdominal pain • Severe tiredness or achiness or generally feeling ill Symptoms typically start within first 6 weeks *Before starting abacavir:* order HLA-B*5701 test for predicted HSR before prescribing (7 day lag time); do not prescribe if HLA-B*5701-positive *If suspected do not re-challenge, record in patient's notes. Record HLA-B*5701 positive results*

Continued overleaf

Appendix 3.2 Nucleoside reverse transcriptase inhibitors (NRTIs) (*continued*)

Approved drug name	Key prescribing information	Food restrictions	Side-effects
Emtricitabine (Emtriva) (FTC) 200 mg caps 10 mg/ml liquid	• Predominantly used with tenofovir in fixed dose combination Truvada • Renal dose adjustments needed at eGFR<50 ml/min • 200 mg caps = 240 mg (24 ml) liquid	None	Peripheral neuropathy/headache
Lamivudine (3TC) 150 mg tablets 100 mg tablets 10 mg/1ml Epivir 5 mg/1ml Zeffrix	• Combined in FDC in Kivexa, Combivir, and Trizivir • Renal dose adjustment needed if eGRF<50 ml/min	None	Skin depigmentation, possible mitochondrial toxicity

Appendix 3.3 Nucleotide reverse transcriptase inhibitors (NtRTIs)

Approved name	Key prescribing information	Food restrictions	Side-effects
Tenofovir disoproxil 245 mg tablets (Rx as tenofovir 300 mg od)	*Drug interactions:* • Nephrotoxic agents: potential overlapping toxicity, especially with cidofovir and possibly foscarnet • Atazanavir: not advised with unboosted atazanavir *Baseline renal assessment:* • SrCr & eGRF • Spot urinary electrolytes and protein/creatinine ratio If decline in renal function repeat above with urine dipstick (protein + glucose) Dose reduction if eGRF <50 ml/min	Licence suggests after food but not essential	Renal dysfunction, including Fanconi's; osteomalacia

Appendix 3.4 Combined preparations

Brand name	Contents	Dose	Strength	Comments
Truvada	Tenofovir/emtracitabine	1 tablet od	245 mg/200 mg	*Food restrictions*: take after food, but not essential Can be dispersed in water See comments for tenofovir and emtricitabine
Kivexa	Lamivudine/abacavir	1 tablet od	300 mg/600 mg	*Food restrictions*: none See comments for abacavir and lamivudine Possible inferior response compared to Truvada at VL >100,000 copies/ml
Combivir	Zidovudine/lamivudine	1 tablet bd	300 mg/150 mg	*Food restrictions*: none, but nausea reduced with food Higher dose of zidovudine than when prescribed alone, with increased risk of anaemia Inferior to Truvada in combination with efavirenz
Trizivir	Zidovudine/lamivudine/abacavir	1 tablet bd	300 mg/150 mg/300 mg	*Food restrictions*: none, but nausea reduced with food Higher dose of zidovudine than when prescribed alone, with increased risk of anaemia See comments for zidovudine, abacavir, lamivudine above
Atripla	Tenofovir/emtracitabine/efavirenz	1 tablet nocte	300 mg/200 mg/600 mg	*Food restrictions*: take on an empty stomach

Appendix 3.5 Non-nucleoside reverse transcriptase inhibitors (NNRTIs)

Approved name	Key prescribing information	Food restrictions	Side-effects
Nevirapine (Viramune) 200 mg tablets 50 mg/5 ml susp	*Interactions:* CYP inducer: decrease levels of PIs (+ other drugs) which may need dose adjustment *Initiation:* Initial therapy 200 mg od for 14 days then bd *CD4 exclusions:* not advised in patients with detectable VL when CD4 is >250 cells/mm^3 (women) or >400 cells/mm^3 (men) *Stopping NNRTI:* long half-life, care when changing from any NNRTI, consider using PI cover for 2–4 weeks	None	Skin rash/ SJS/TEN, hepatitis Monitor hepatic function and signs of rash (18 weeks)
Efavirenz (Sustiva) (EFV) 600 mg tablets 200 mg caps 100 mg caps 50 mg caps 30 mg/ml susp	Combined with Truvada as Atripla 600 mg tablet = 720 mg (24 ml) liquid *Interactions:* Predominant CYP inducer: decrease levels of PIs (+ other drugs) which may need dose adjustment 800 mg OD when used in combination with rifampicin and wt >50 kg (see TB guidelines) *Caution:* history of depression *Pregnancy:* contraindicated in first trimester (neural tube defects reported); avoid in women with high pregnancy potential *Counselling:* take at night. Initial dizziness after taking and drowsiness next morning for 4–7 days. Vivid dreams and sleep disturbances for 2–4 weeks *Stopping/swapping from NNRTI:* long half-life, care when changing from any NNRTI, consider using PI cover for 2–4 weeks	Empty stomach	CNS – vivid dreams, altered mental state (first 2–4 weeks), rash (usually after 10–14 days) Monitor hepatic function
Etravirine (Intelence) 100 mg tablets	*Drug interactions:* Contraindicated with fosamprenavir/r, tipranavir/r and unboosted atazanavir *Stopping/swapping from NNRTI:* long half-life, care when changing from any NNRTI, consider using PI cover for 2–4 weeks Tablets can be dispersed in water	With/after food	Rash including SJS

Appendix 3.6 Integrase inhibitors

Approved name	Key prescribing information	Food restrictions	Side-effects
Raltegravir (Isentress) 400 mg tablet	• Once daily dosing not currently advised • When using with rifampicin, consider doubling raltegravir dose	None	Minimal

Appendix 3.7 Entry inhibitors

Approved name	Key prescribing information	Food restrictions	Side-effects
Enfuvirtide (Fuzeon) 90 mg injection	• For highly treatment-experienced patients • Very limited data for once-daily dosing	None	Injection site reactions common, rotate injection sites
Maraviroc (Celsentri) 150 mg tablet 300 mg tablet	• CCR5 viral tropism determination required prior to initiation (genotypic and phenotypic tests available) • Caution in ART-naïve patients • Dose dependent drug interactions, consult product literature for detailed dosing information	None	Miminal

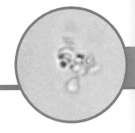
Clinical management issues in HIV patients

Common clinical scenarios

AJ Rodger, TW Mahungu, M Heller, K Cwynarski, S Bhagani, J Green and N Marshall

Pyrexia of unknown origin

Patients with HIV frequently present with pyrexia of unknown origin (PUO). Infectious causes are more likely in the HIV-positive population than the HIV-negative population and the likely organism is CD4 dependent. Approximately 80% of PUOs in HIV-positive patients are infectious in nature (compared to 30% in the HIV-negative population), and the remainder are largely due to lymphomas or drug reactions[1] (*Table 4.1*).

Most PUOs occur in patients with advanced HIV and are less likely in patients with good CD4 counts who are stable on antiretroviral treatment (ART). Some HIV patients may have more than one cause for the fever. There are also geographical differences in likelihood of infectious causes, and tuberculosis (TB) is more common in Europe than in the USA[1]. The commonest cause of PUO in HIV-positive patients identified in a case series from the USA from 1992 to 1997 was disseminated MAI infection (31%), followed by *Pneumocystis jirovecii* pneumonia (PCP) (13%), cytomegalovirus (CMV) (11%), disseminated histoplasmosis (7%), and lymphoma (7%)[2]. A case series from London found that infections caused 79% of episodes of PUO in inpatients with HIV and the commonest causes were mycobacterial infection (53%) and bacterial infection (15%)[3]. A Spanish case series found that TB was most common (48%), followed by visceral leishmaniasis (16%) and infection by *Mycobacterium avium* complex (7%). They also found that the most useful diagnostic tests were liver biopsy (68.9%) and bone marrow aspirate/biopsy (39.7%)[4].

Table 4.1 Differential causes of PUO in HIV-positive individuals

Infective
- Mycobacterial: MTB (tuberculosis) at any CD4 count (**4.1, 4.2**); MAC and other non-TB mycobacteria (i.e. *M. kansasii, M. sulzgi*) at very low counts (CD4 <100)
- Viral: CMV (CD4 <100), VZV, HSV, adenovirus, hepatitis
- Fungal (usually CD4 <200) cryptococcosis, histoplasmosis (**4.3**) and penicillinosis, PCP
- Bacterial: abscesses (including liver), syphilis, endocarditis, urinary tract infection, osteomyelitis, brucellosis, salmonella, bacilliary angiomatosis
- Protozoan parasites: visceral leishmaniasis (**4.4**), malaria, cryptosporidium

Tumours
- Hodgkin's lymphoma, NHL, KS, solid tumours (RCC)

Others
- Adverse drug reactions, Castleman's disease, connective tissue diseases, thyrotoxicosis, factitious fever, sarcoidosis, immune reconstitution disease

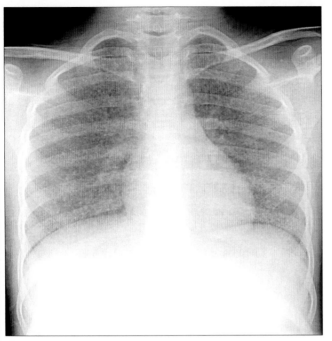

4.1 Miliary TB in a patient with advanced HIV.

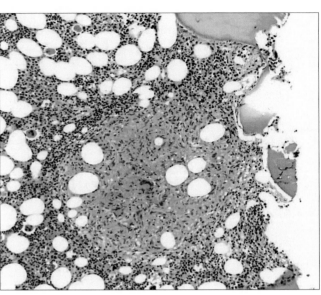

4.2 Bone marrow examination in an HIV-positive patient with MTB demonstrating a granuloma.

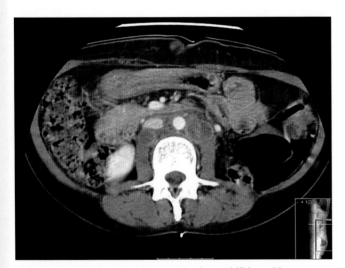

4.3 Abdominal lymphadenopathy in an HIV-positive patient with histoplasmosis.

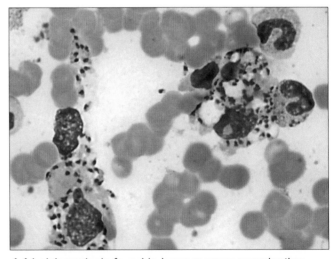

4.4 Leishmaniasis found in bone marrow examination.

Investigation and differential diagnosis of PUO in HIV

A full history is required from the patient including travel, vaccinations, sexual history, medications, and use of recreational drugs, and a complete examination is important. Geographical location and travel history are important for many infectious diseases, e.g. leishmaniasis and the Mediterranean region, histoplasmosis and east-central USA, central and South America, east Africa, and parts of Asia, and penicilliosis in South East Asia.

Investigations for PUO

Initial investigations include:
- Full blood count (FBC), C-reactive protein (CRP), biochemistry, liver function.
- Pulse oximetry (rest/exercise).
- Blood cultures for MCS, two sets from different sites and patient off antibiotics if possible.
- Mycobacterial blood cultures, mycobacterial stool cultures, EMU.
- Sputum for microscopy, culture, and sensitivity (MC&S) and acid-fast bacilli (AFB).
- Stool and urine cultures.
- CMV DNA (if CD4 <200), viral throat swab if ulcerative lesions.
- CRAG.
- Chest X-ray.
- Consider computed tomography (CT) and lumbar puncture (LP) if clinically indicated.
- Serologies as dictated by history, presentation, and travel history.

If there is no obvious cause of the PUO, further investigations to consider include:
- CT scan of chest, abdomen, and pelvis.
- Bronchoscopy.
- Consider lymph node biopsy, liver or bone marrow biopsy.
- Autoantibody screen.
- Echocardiography.

Management

Antibiotics should be avoided until adequate cultures are obtained. This can be done quickly if necessary in the form of blood, urine, and throat cultures in the patient who appears septic after which broad-spectrum antibiotics can be given. If the patient is not acutely septic further relevant samples (in particular tissue samples for histology and microbacterial investigation, as in *Table 4.1*) should be obtained. It should be remembered that some antibiotics in common use have some antimycobacterial activity, i.e. quinalones. Management depends on the underlying cause, and supportive therapy with fluids and antipyretics should be used. Once tissue samples are obtained empiric treatment may be warranted based on clinical and radiological features and this may include empiric antimycobacterial treatment while awaiting the results of mycobacterial cultures.

Dyspnoea

With the breathless HIV patient especially at lower CD4 counts or low CD4 percentages (<12%) always consider PCP (see page 105). With PCP there are often minimal signs on examination although the chest X-ray is abnormal in 90% of cases and the patient will usually give a history of several days to weeks of exertional dyspnoea with dry cough and often weight loss (**4.5**). Elevated serum LDH levels can be associated with PCP.

The presence of high fever, purulent sputum, pleuritic chest pain, and localizing signs will point to bacterial pneumonia (**4.6**). Lung involvement with viruses, fungi, and mycobacteria also occur in HIV-positive patients. The presence of a pleural effusion is more often associated with mycobacterial disease or malignancies (**4.7**).

Investigations for dyspnoea or other respiratory symptoms

Initial investigations include:
- Oximetry: rest and exercise (if desaturates to <92% on air then good evidence for alveolitis, which occurs not only with PCP and but also with viral, protozoal, fungal, mycobacterial, and bacterial involvement of the lungs). Do not exercise if O_2 desaturates to <92% at rest on air.
- Chest X-ray looking for interstitial/alveolar shadowing or consolidation or pleural effusions.

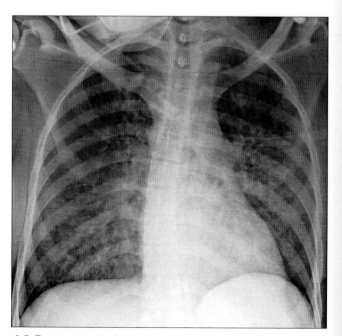

4.5 *Pneumocystis jirovecii* pneumonia.

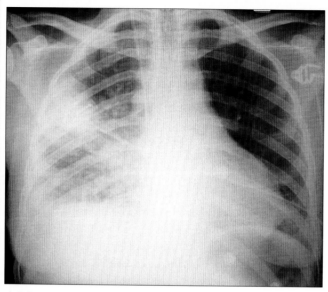

4.6 Pneumococcal pneumonia.

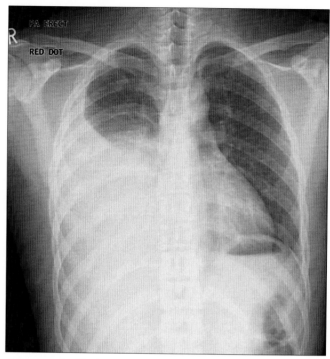

4.7 Pleural effusion in a patient with MTB.

- Blood cultures.
- Urine antigen tests (pneumococcal, *Legionella*).
- Serology for atypical infections (with follow-up titre at 4 weeks).
- Sputum smear and cultures (MC&S, *Mycobacteria*).
- Nasopharyngeal aspirate (NPA) for virus detection (influenza, para-influenza, rhinovirus, metapneumovirus, respiratory syncytial virus).
- Isolation if suspect TB, i.e. any of previous history of TB or abnormal chest X-ray or fever.

If there is no obvious cause of dyspnoea, further investigations to consider include:
- Pleural tap if appropriate.
- Pleural biopsy can also be considered for mycobacterial disease.
- CT chest.
- Bronchoscopy:
- Check clotting, platelets, and FBC. Nil by mouth 3 hours before, 2 hours post-procedure.
- Send samples to microbiology for MC&S, AFB, fungi (and TB polymerase chain reaction [PCR] if clinically suspected and available), cytology, virology for respiratory viruses (CMV, HSV, and histology if transbronchial biopsy is performed).

Management

If this is felt to be PCP, allergies should be checked, then the patient started on high-dose co-trimoxazole 120 mg/kg in 3–4 divided doses for 21 days; bronchoscopy can be deferred for up to 5 days if necessary. If O_2 saturation is <92%, IV hydrocortisone 100 mg qds should be started, or oral prednisolone 40 mg bd. Oxygenation should be maintained at >92% with increased inspired O_2. (The patient may need a CPAP circuit if tiring, or ITU assessment.) If pneumonia is diagnosed it should be treated with broad-spectrum antibiotics and atypical cover with total duration of 7–10 days:
- Nonsevere community acquired pneumonia (CAP) (CURB-65 score <1): amoxicillin +/- clarithromycin; if penicillin allergic use clarithromycin alone.
- Severe CAP (CURB-65 score >1): co-amoxiclav + clarithromycin; if penicillin allergic clarithromycin PO 500 mg bd + ciprofloxacin PO 500 mg bd.

The CURB score comprises the following features:
- **C**onfusion: new mental confusion defined as an Abbreviated Mental Test score <8.
- **U**rea: raised >7 mmol/l.
- **R**espiratory rate: raised >30 breaths/min.
- **B**lood pressure: low blood pressure (systolic <90 mmHg and/or diastolic <60 mmHg).

References

1 Hot A, Schmulewitz L, Viard JP, Lortholary O. Fever of unknown origin in HIV/AIDS patients. *Infect Dis Clin North Am* 2007 Dec;**21**(4):1013–32.
2 Armstrong WS, Katz JT, Kazanjian PH. Human immunodeficiency virus-associated fever of unknown origin: a study of 70 patients in the United States and review. *Clin Infect Dis* 1999;**28**(2):341–5.
3 Miller RF, Hingorami AD, Foley NM. Pyrexia of undetermined origin in patients with human immunodeficiency virus infection and AIDS. *Int J STD AIDS* 1996;**7**(3):170–5.
4 Lozano F, Torre-Cisneros J, Bascuñana A, *et al.* Prospective evaluation of fever of unknown origin in patients infected with the human immunodeficiency virus. *Eur J Clin Microbiol Infect Dis* 1996;**15**(9):705–11.

Diarrhoea

Diarrhoea is extremely common in HIV-positive patients and may occur for a variety of reasons both infective (including HIV-related colitis) and also as a side-effect of treatment (*Table 4.2*). In the acute setting, the aetiology is often very similar to that of the immunocompetent host.

In HIV-positive patients with CD4 counts <200 it is usually caused by opportunistic infections. Diarrhoea that is from the small bowel is usually large in volume, accompanied by weight loss and is offensive in smell. Large-bowel causes tend to be smaller in volume and may be associated with left lower quadrant pain or tenesmus and can contain blood. Diarrhoea is usually defined as chronic when the patient has had diarrhoea for more than 4 weeks.

Investigation and management

The patient will need isolation in a side room and may need aggressive rehydration whilst awaiting results. A stool chart should be initiated to monitor severity.

Diarrhoea should be investigated in stages:
- Initial investigations include stool specimens to:
- Microbiology: Microscopy, culture and sensitivity, ova, cysts, and parasites, *Cryptosporidium*, *Isospora*, *Microsporidia*, AFB, *Clostridium difficile* toxin; consider *Chlamydia* swab for LGV.
- Virology: Viral culture +/- electron microscopy (CMV, HSV, adenovirus).

If no organisms are identified after the first 3 days, stage 1 should be repeated and further investigations (stage 2) initiated as indicated clinically:
- Blood and urine cultures for MC&S and virology (see PUO).
- AXR: megacolon, ischaemia.
- Sigmoidoscopy and rectal biopsy with samples to histopathology (in formalin), virology (in viral transport medium) for viral culture, and a fresh specimen to bacteriology.
- Endoscopy with biopsy of macroscopic lesions with samples to histopathology (in formalin), virology (in viral transport medium) for viral culture for CMV and adenovirus PCR, and a fresh specimen to bacteriology and to immunology if lymphoma is being considered.
  +/-   if appropriate, brushings to cytology.
  +/-   jejunal sample (aspirate/brushings) to cytology and to microbiology for *Cryptosporidium* and *Giardia*.
- Colonoscopy with sampling of macroscopic lesions as for endoscopy.

Common gastrointestinal pathogens in HIV

Tables 4.3–4.7 and Figures **4.8–4.12** present information on parasitic protozoa associated with chronic diarrhoea in HIV-infected individuals.

Further reading

Lewthwaite P, Gill GV, Hart CA, *et al.* Gastrointestinal parasites in the immunocompromised. *Curr Opin Infect Dis* 2005 Oct;**18**(5):427–35.
Stark D, *et al.* Clinical significance of enteric protozoa in the immunosuppressed human population. *Clin Microbiol Rev* 2009;**22**(4):634–50.

Table 4.2 Important causes of diarrhoeal illnesses in HIV-positive patients

Acute
Bacterial
- Salmonella
- Shigella
- Campylobacter
- Clostridium difficile
- Clostridium jejuni
- Escherichia coli

Viral
- Adenovirus
- Norovirus

Medication
- Protease inhibitors

Chronic
Bacterial
- Mycobacterium avium intracellulare

Viral
- CMV
- HIV enteropathy

Protozoa
- Cryptosporidium
- Microsporidium
- Isospora
- Giardia
- Entamoeba histolytica

Medication
- Protease inhibitors

Table 4.3 Giardiasis

Infectious agent
- Giardia lamblia (a flagellate protozoan)

Transmission
- Faecal–oral
- Oral–anal

Clinical manifestation
- Usually infects the upper small intestine; Giardia does not cause invasive disease
- Patients typically present with: steatorrhoea, abdominal cramps, flatulence, nausea, and anorexia
- *HIV-positive patients are not thought to be more susceptible to infection or the development of more severe disease*

Diagnosis
- Identification of cysts or trophozoites in stool samples
- Identification of trophozoites in duodenal aspirates or intestinal mucosa
- Giardia antigen detection tests

Treatment
- Gold standard (>90% efficacy):
- Metronidazole   2 g daily orally for 3–5 days
- Tinidazole   2 g orally stat
- Alternatives (less efficacious):
- Paromomycin
- Furazolidone (not be used in patients with G6PD-deficiency)
- Albendazole
- Quinacrine

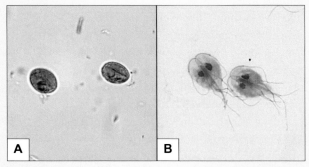

4.8 *Giardia lamblia* cyst (**A**) and trophozoites (**B**).

Table 4.4 Amoebiasis

Infectious agent
- *Entamoeba histolytca*

Transmission
- Faecal–oral
- Oral–anal

Clinical manifestation
- Acute dysentery with mucoid diarrhoea; or
- Amoebic colitis; or
- Liver abscess

HIV-positive patients are not thought to be more susceptible to infection or the development of invasive infection

Diagnosis
- Demonstration of cysts* or trophozoites in 'hot' stool samples
- Identification of motile trophozoites containing red blood cells is indicative of invasive disease
- Liver abscess aspirate characteristically resembles 'anchovy paste'
- Serology – IFAT and CAP. A positive CAP is indicative of invasive disease

*Morphologically indistinguishable from nonpathogenic Entamoeba dispar, but can be differentiated using ELISA or PCR

Treatment
- Amoebic dysentery and invasive disease:
- Metronidazole followed by a luminal agent:
- Diloxanide
- Paromomycin
- Iodoquinol

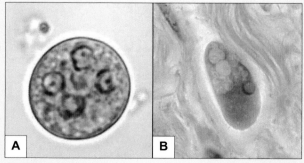

4.9 *Entamoeba histolytica/dispar* cyst (**A**) with quadruplicate nuclei and trophozoite (**B**) in a gut biopsy.

Table 4.5 Cryptosporidiosis

Infectious agent
- *Cryptosporidium parvum* and *C. hominis* are the most common species
- Intracellular coccidian protozoa with worldwide distribution closely related to *Plasmodium* species

Transmission
- Faecal–oral

Clinical manifestation
- Most common cause of chronic diarrhoea in HIV-infected patients with CD4 counts below 200 cells/mm^3
- ***AIDS defining if chronic***
- Large volume diarrhoea accompanied by significant electrolyte loss; occasionally associated with abdominal cramps and nausea
- Rare but other presentations include acalculous cholecystitis and pancreatitis

Diagnosis
- Identification of oocysts in stool smears
- Antigen detection assays and PCR

Treatment
- The illness tends to be self-limiting in immunocompetent patients
- In HIV-positive patients HAART is the definitive treatment
- Symptom control:
- Antiperistaltics, octreotide
- Antiparasitics. The agents below have been used with poor results:
- Paromomycin   – Azithromycin
- Nitazoxanide

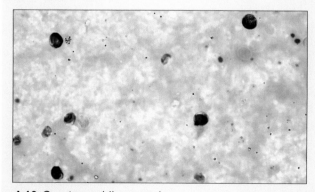

4.10 *Cryptosporidium* species.

Table 4.6 Isosporiasis

Infectious agent
- *Isospora belli* (coccidian parasite)
- Distribution mainly in tropical regions

Transmission
- Faecal–oral

Clinical manifestation
- Large-volume diarrhoea accompanied by abdominal cramps and nausea
- Hepatobiliary disease and reactive arthritis have been reported (rare)
- **AIDS-defining if chronic**

Diagnosis
- Identification of oocysts in stool smears, duodenal aspirates
- PCR

Treatment
- The illness tends to be self-limiting in immunocompetent patients:
- Antiparasitics:
    Septrin
    Sulfadiazine
    Pyrimethamine (if sulphur allergic)

Table 4.7 Microsporidiosis

Infectious agent
- *Enterocytozoon bieneusi* most important species
- Obligate intracellular parasite

Transmission
- Unclear

Clinical manifestation
- Chronic diarrhoea accompanied by abdominal cramps and nausea
- *E. bieneusi* is the 2nd most common cause of chronic diarrhoea in HIV-infected patients
- Biliary disease frequent
- Dissemination is rare
- **Not AIDS-definining** (but often occurs in patients with CD4 counts <50 cells/mm^3)

Diagnosis
- Identification of oocysts in stool smears, duodenal aspirates by:
- Electron microscopy
- Modified trichrome stain
- IFAT
- PCR

Treatment
- HAART is the definitive treatment
- Antiparasitics:
- Albendazole is modestly effective
- Fumagillin and nitazoxanide have also been used with variable results

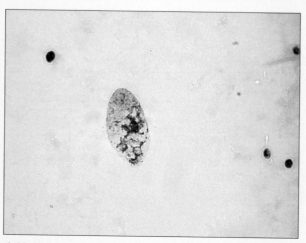

4.11 *Isospora belli* oocyst (ZN stain).

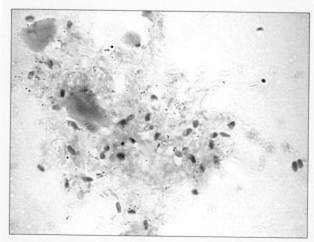

4.12 *Microsporidia* cyst (trichrome stain) ×1,600.

Haematological abnormalities

M Heller and K Cwynarski

Cytopenias

Anaemia

The incidence of anaemia is related to the stage of HIV disease. Anaemia is positively associated with clinical AIDS and a CD4 count of < 200 cells/μl, and indirectly is related to median survival. Recovery from anaemia is significantly associated with decreased risk of death.

The incidence of anaemia may also depend on the subtype of HIV prevalent in the studied population: HIV-1 subtype B, found predominantly in Europe and North America, appears to have considerably less capacity to infect haematological progenitor cells and to impair erythroid progenitor survival, than HIV-1 subtype C, found in sub-Saharan Africa.

Once a diagnosis of anaemia has been established, investigations are guided by history, clinical features, and laboratory markers. Treatment depends on the cause of anaemia (*Tables 4.8*).

Table 4.8 Investigation of anemia caused by decreased/inefficient production

CAUSES OF ANAEMIA	INITIAL INVESTIGATION
Direct effect of HIV on haematopoietic stem cells and bone marrow stroma and accessory cells	
Initial infection	Blood film – normocytic normochomic anaemia Often lymphopenia, occasionally thrombocytopenia
Anaemia of chronic disease (most frequent cause of anaemia in HIV infection)	Blood film, reticulocyte count, inflammatory markers, erythropoietin, iron status
Infection Parvovirus infection (transient reticulocytopenia – pure red cell aplasia	Parvovirus serology (IgM), parvovirus, DNA PCR
Cytomegalovirus (CMV)	CMV serology, CMV DNA, PCR
Mycobacterium (**4.13A, B**)	Chest radiograph, ELISpot assay, bone marrow aspirate and culture
Malaria (**4.14A–C**)	Thick and thin blood film, rapid antigen agglutination text
Leishmaniasis (**4.15A, B**)	Serology, bone marrow aspirate and culture
Haemophagocytosis (presenting as pancytopenia) (secondary to infection or malignancy)	Bone marrow aspiration and trephine biopsy culture for mycobacteria, HSV and EBV DNA PCR

Continued

Table 4.8 Investigation of anaemia caused by decreased/inefficient production (*continued*)

CAUSES OF ANAEMIA	INITIAL INVESTIGATION
Nutritional deficiency Haematinic deficiency (**4.16–4.18**)	Iron status (ferritin, serum iron, transferrin saturation, total iron binding capacity) Vitamin B12, folic acid levels
Trace elements: selenium, copper	Serum Cu^{2+} and Se^{2+} levels
Drugs Antiretroviral drugs: Azidothymidine	(Replace with equivalent alternative) (Direct bone marrow suppression)
Antimicrobial agents: Ganciclovir	(Direct bone marrow suppression)
Primaquine, sulfonamides, nitrofurantoin (and others)	(Oxidative haemolytic anaemia) Blood film, G6PD assay, Heinz body stain Withdrawl of drug
Frequently: penicillins, cephalosporins, quinine, quinidine	(Drug induced immune haemolytic anaemia – often mimicking immune red cell alloantibodies) DAT, LDH, bilirubin, haptoglobin, urinary haemosiderin Specific tests for drug induced haemolysis Withdrawl of drug
Haemoglobinopathies Thalassaemia (**4.19**) (α- and/or β-chain gene deletions)	Haemoglobinelectrophoresis, HPLC
Amino acid substitutions (sickle syndromes: HBS (**4.16**), C, D, etc)	Sickle solubility test Haemoglobinelectrophoresis, HPLC
Immune haemolytic anaemia Autoimmune haemolytic anaemia	DAT, LDH, bilirubin, haptoglobin, urinary haemosiderin
Bone marrow infiltration Haematological malignancy (such as HIV-associated lymphoma)	Bone marrow aspirate, trephine, flow cytometric and cytogenetic analysis
TTP/HUS	Blood film, clotting, ADAMTS13 assay

DAT: direct antiglobulin (Coombs) test
TTP/HUS: thrombocytopenic purpura/haemolytic uraemic syndrome
ADAMTS13: A disintegrin and metallopeptidase with thrombospondin type 1 motif
Haemolytic screen: blood film, retinculocyte count, indirect (unconjugated) bilirubin, lactic dehydrogenase (LDH), DAT, haptoglobin level, urinary haemosiderin (in intravascular haemolysis)

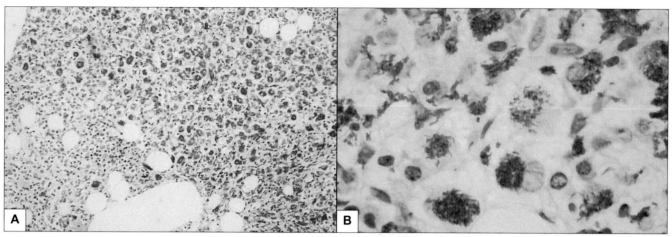

4.13A: *Mycobacterium avium intracellulare* (BMT ZN ×100); **B:** *Mycobacterium avium intracellulare* (BMT ZN ×600).

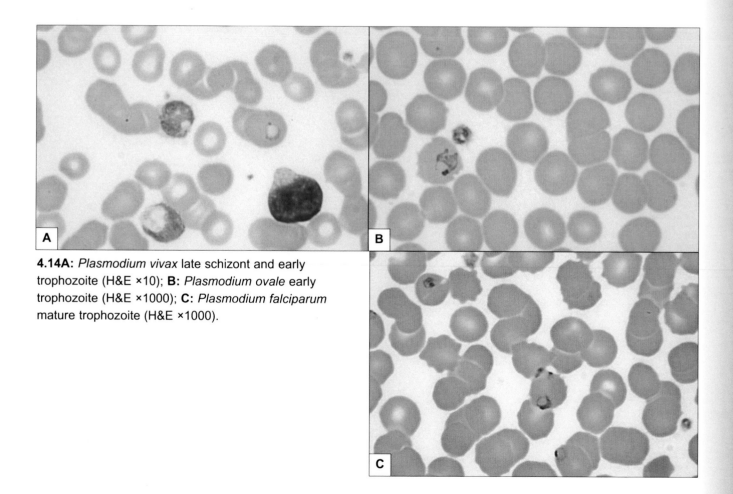

4.14A: *Plasmodium vivax* late schizont and early trophozoite (H&E ×10); **B:** *Plasmodium ovale* early trophozoite (H&E ×1000); **C:** *Plasmodium falciparum* mature trophozoite (H&E ×1000).

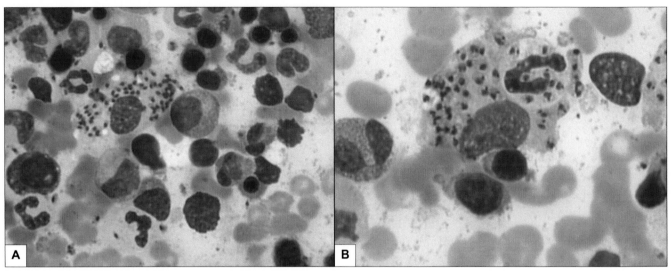

4.15A: Leishmaniasis (BMA H&E ×600); **B:** Leishmaniasis (BMA H&E ×1,000).

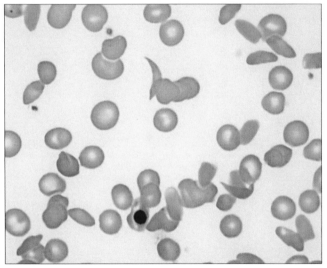

4.16 Haemoglobin SS disease (BF H&E ×600).

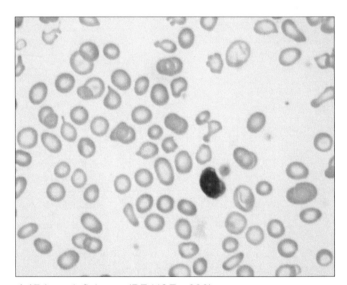

4.17 Iron deficiency (BF H&E ×600).

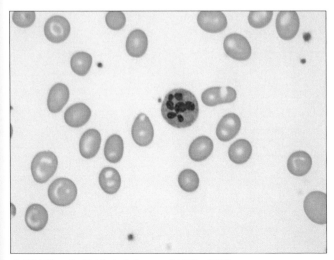

4.18 Vitamin B12 deficiency (H&E ×600).

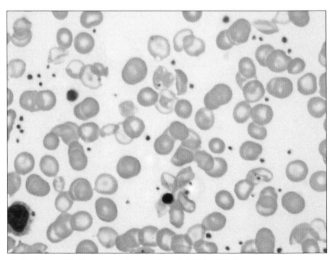

4.19 Beta thalassaemia major (H&E ×600).

Thrombocytopenia

Approximately 10% of HIV-infected individuals present with thrombocytopenia. Epidemiological studies suggest that the incidence of thrombocytopenia is partially dependent on disease burden. Of all patients with AIDS, approximately 21% develop thrombocytopenia, compared to only 9% without clinical AIDS.

HIV-associated thrombocytopenia developing early after infection is mediated primarily by peripheral destruction and resembles autoimmune thrombocytopenia (AITP). In contrast thrombocytopenia in patients with immunologically advanced HIV is predominantly due to impaired megakaryopoiesis.

Bleeding is rarely severe. Classical treatment modalities for AITP work better in patients with less advanced HIV, whereas treatment with azidothymidine (AZT) or highly active antiretroviral therapy (HAART) works in patients at all disease stages. Treatment modalities for AITP, initiated with the involvement of a haematologist, include IV Ig, anti-D therapy (in RhD+ patients), corticosteroids, splenectomy, and immunosuppressive therapies.

Clotting disorders

Thrombosis

Thrombosis has been reported in up to 2% of all HIV-infected patients. Acquired protein C deficiency has been demonstrated in up to 75% of HIV-infected patients. Elevated factor V, VIII, and X levels, and acquired protein C, S, and antithrombin III deficiency have been demonstrated in HIV-associated nephropathy, causing a prothrombotic state. The significance of the presence of antiphospholipid and anticardiolipin antibodies in HIV patients remains unclear, but can be demonstrated in up to 50% of HIV-infected patients.

Thrombotic thrombocytopenic purpura/ haemolytic uraemic syndrome

Thrombotic thrombocytopenic purpura (TTP) and haemolytic uraemic syndrome (HUS) are characterized by microthrombi formation in small vessels, red cell fragmentation, haemolytic anaemia, and thrombocytopenia. Vascular endothelial damage, due to viral infection and bacterial toxin, and circulating large von Willebrans multimers, are thought to be of pathogenetic relevance. A deficiency of ADAM metalloprotease with thrombospondin type 1 motif (ADAMTS-13), which normally cleaves von Willebrand factor (vWF), appears to be implicated, often due to the presence of an autoantibody.

Fever, neurological symptoms, and liver dysfunction occur in TTP and renal failure in HUS. Clotting parameters remain normal. Treatment consists of plasma exchange using cryo-depleted fresh frozen plasma, and initiation of HAART. Platelet transfusion should be avoided and can worsen microthrombi formation.

Further reading

Marti-Carvajal AJ, Sola I. Treatment for anaemia in people with AIDS. *Cochrane Database Syst Rev* 2007;CD004776.

Morelli P, Bestetti G, Longhi E, *et al*. Persistent parvovirus B19-induced anaemia in an HIV-infected patient under HAART. Case report and review of literature. *Eur J Clin Microbiol Infect Dis* 2007;**26**:833–7.

Redd AD, Avalos A, Essex M. Infection of hematopoietic progenitor cells by HIV-1 subtype C, and its association with anemia in southern Africa. *Blood* 2007;**110**:3143–9.

Sullivan PS, Hanson DL, Chu SY, *et al*. Epidemiology of anemia in human immunodeficiency virus (HIV)-infected persons: results from the multistate adult and adolescent spectrum of HIV disease surveillance project. *Blood* 1998;**91**:301–8.

Liver disease and viral hepatitis co-infections

AJ Rodger and S Bhagani

Viral hepatitis co-infection

With the introduction of HAART there have been dramatic reductions in HIV-related morbidity and mortality[1]. However, hepatocellular failure and hepatocellular carcinoma (HCC), complicating hepatitis C (HCV)/hepatitis B (HBV)-related cirrhosis, have become increasingly significant causes of morbidity and mortality in HIV-infected individuals[2].

HIV/HBV co-infection

Because of their shared routes of transmission, it is estimated that across Europe 9% of HIV-positive patients are co-infected with HBV[3] and 5–15% worldwide. HBV co-infection is more common in those from high HBV prevalence areas, intravenous drug users (IVDUs) and men who have sex with men (MSM). HBV is preventable by vaccination, but response rates to the vaccine are CD4 count dependent, with approximately 80% response at >500 CD4 count and less than 15% at <200[4]. HBsAb levels >100 IU/l are considered protective post vaccination.

There is increasing evidence that HIV leads to increased HBV viral replication, more rapid progression to advanced stages of hepatic fibrosis[5] and an increased rate of liver-related mortality[6]. Moreover, as a result of HIV-associated immune suppression, much of this fibrosis may not be related to immunopathology, and hence there may be a poor correlation with hepatic enzyme elevations. Hepatitis delta virus can exist as a co-infection with HBV and is mainly seen in IVDUs. The prevalence of delta co-infection in the UK is low (~5%), but can be associated with more rapid progression of disease with lower HBV DNA levels[7]. All HIV/HBV co-infected patients should be tested for delta virus.

The aim of treatment in chronic HBV is to suppress viral replication. Guidelines on the use of HBV therapy in co-infected patients have been published (BHIVA 2009 Guidelines) and include long-term therapy with a combination of nucleoside analogue and a nucleotide analogue to maintain sustained viral suppression. Current BHIVA algorithms on management of chronic HBV are given in Figure **4.20**. The updated EACS guidelines are very similar and can be obtained on-line: http://www.europeanaidsclinicalsociety.org/

The key determinants for treatment are levels of HBV DNA, CD4 count, and presence of liver fibrosis.

HBV is directly carcinogenic and can promote the development of HCC in the absence of cirrhosis. All HBV and HIV co-infected patients must be entered into an HCC screening programme that should consist of 6-monthly AFP measurements and screening ultrasound scans, which have been shown to increase survival in non-HBV mono-infected infected patients[8].

HIV/HCV co-infection

It is estimated that across Europe 34% of HIV patients are co-infected with HCV[3]. Rates are traditionally highest in individuals with haemophilia and in IVDUs. Recently a rise in acute HCV in HIV-positive MSM has been reported in Western European countries, North America, and Australia. A European-wide sexual network has been identified and HCV infection in MSM has been associated with higher-risk sexual behaviour, concurrent sexually transmitted infections, and drug use[9,10].

HCV is usually detectable in the blood by PCR within 1–3 weeks after infection, and antibodies to the virus are generally detectable within 3–15 weeks. HIV-positive individuals, especially those with a low CD4 count, can have delayed HCV seroconversion. In one case series the median time from HCV ribonucleic acid (RNA) detection to anti-HCV positive was 91 days (range 0–1206) and 5% remained anti-HCV negative after 12 months[11].

In HCV/HIV co-infected patients there is evidence that accelerated hepatic fibrosis is associated with lower CD4 counts, older age, male sex, and alcohol use[12]. Data suggest that combination ART may protect against accelerated fibrosis progression in these patients[13].

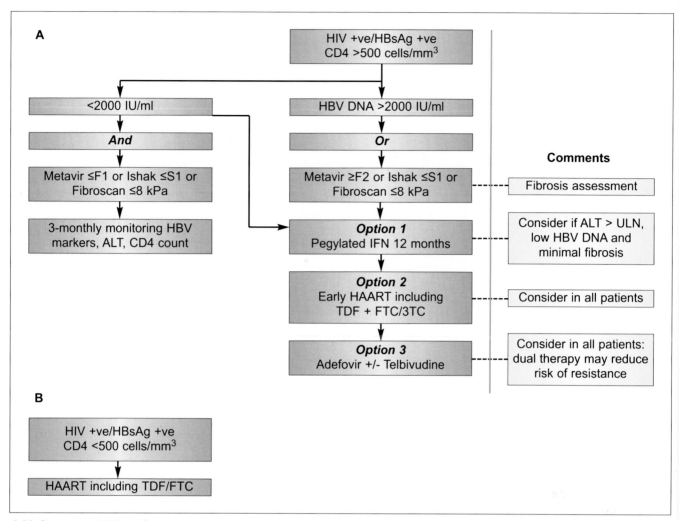

4.20 General guidelines for the management of co-infection with HIV-1 and chronic hepatitis B 2009. **A:** If CD4 count >500 cells/mm^3; **B:** if CD4 count <500 cells/mm^3. (Adapted from BHIVA data: http://www.bhiva.org/files/file1031815.pdf.)

Treatment for HCV

Randomized controlled trials have confirmed the activity of pegylated interferons (pegIFNs) and ribavirin in achieving sustained viral clearance in patients with HCV and HIV co-infection[14,15]. However, the responses in patients with genotype 1 infection and high HCV viral loads were generally poor (<30% sustained virological response [SVR]) (**4.21**).

Current guidelines for treatment of chronic HCV in HIV-positive patients are available on the web: (http://www.europeanaidsclinicalsociety.org/). The recommended durations of pegIFN and ribavirin are given in Figure **4.22**. If required, HIV should be treated first with antiretrovirals (ARVs) before HCV treatment if required, as

there may be a drop in CD4 counts of up to 150 cells/mm^3 during interferon treatment. Interactions between ARVs and pegIFN and ribavirin may occur. Didanosine (DDI) and stavudine (D4T) may interact with the ribavirin to cause significant toxicity and should be avoided. Ribavirin and IFN may cause additive myelosuppression if used with AZT, which should be avoided. Efavirenz may increase CNS disturbance in association with IFN, and abacavir may impair the anti-HCV effect of ribavirin (**4.23**). In addition ribavirin may cause haemolytic anaemia and require dose adjustment.

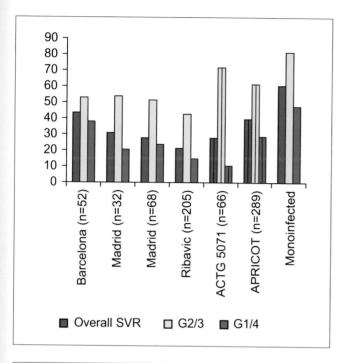

4.21 Response to pegIFN and ribavirin in chronic HCV/HIV co-infection. Studies outlining SVR in HIV/HCV co-infected patients according to genotype. Red: overall SVR; yellow: genotype 2/3; blue: genotype 1/4. Vertical stripes: PegIFN alpha 2b; others: PegIFN alpha 2a. Overall responses 30–40% compared to mono-infected patients. Much lower SVRs in G1/4 co-infected patients. (Adapted from Fried TA, *et al., NEJM* 2004;**347**:975–82; Torriani FJ, *et al., NEJM* 2004;**351**:438–50; Chung R, *et al., NEJM* 2004;**351**:451–9; Carrat F, *et al., JAMA* 2004;**292**:2839–42; Laguno M, *et al., AIDS* 2004;**18**:F27–F36; Nunez M, *et al., JAIDS* 2007;**45**:439–44.)

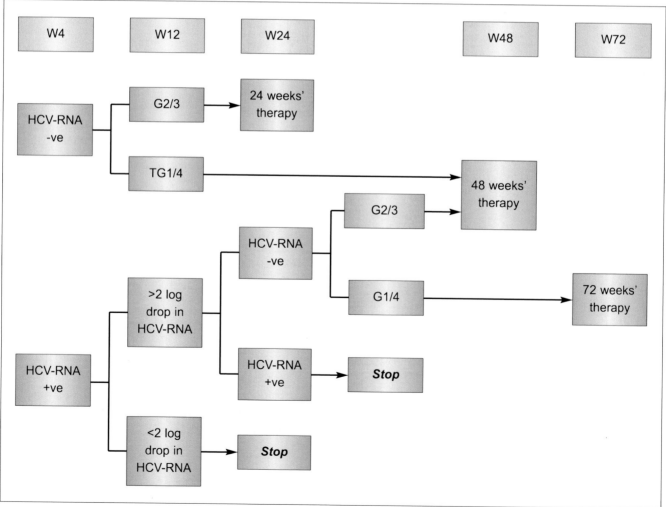

4.22 Proposed optimal duration of HCV therapy in HIV/HCV co-infected patients. (Adapted from EACS data: http://www.europeanaidsclinicalsociety.org/guidelinespdf/3_Treatment_chronic_hepatitis_co_infection.pdf.)

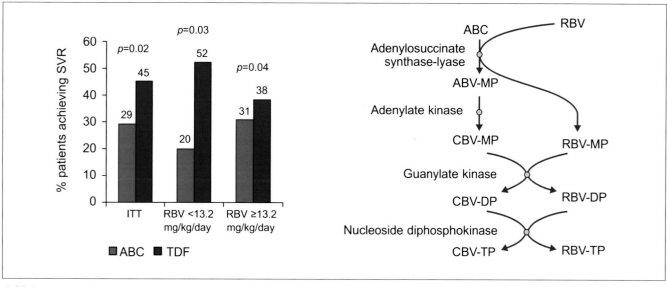

4.23 Interaction between ribavirin and abacavir. (Adapted from Mira JA, *J Antimicrob Chemother* 2008;**62**(6):1365-73.)

Acute HCV

Higher rates of SVR (62%) have been recorded in HIV co-infected patients with acute HCV infection undergoing early anti-HCV treatment[16]. In this group treatment should also be with pegIFN and weight-based ribavirin. Duration of treatment should be based on RVR (negative HCV RNA at week 4) regardless of HCV genotype. In patients with RVR, treatment duration should be 24 weeks and in patients without RVR, treatment duration of 48 weeks should be considered[17].

Genetic variation in IL-28B and response to HCV treatment

A link between clearance of acute HCV infection and achieving SVR with pegIFN/ribavirin treatment and two single-nucleotide polymorphisms in the gene region on chromosome 19 that encodes IL-28 has been described. The IL-28B rs12979860 SNP has two variations, or alleles, known as C and T. The C allele, which is favourable for SVR, is found at a much higher frequency in white populations than in black populations; those with homozygous pattern (CC) are most likely to clear HCV spontaneously and have the best treatment outcomes, while those with TT are associated with poorer response. These data suggest that host genetics and IL-28 genotypic testing might in future help guide treatment decisions and may be useful for the prediction of IFN-α response in the treatment of HCV, although this is not yet fully elucidated[18].

Cryptogenic cirrhosis and noncirrhotic portal hypertension

There have been a number of case-series reported recently of HIV-positive patients presenting with complications associated with cryptogenic cirrhosis or noncirrhotic portal hypertension[19–21]. The incidence varies from 1–8%. In those where liver biopsies were performed the histology was variable and included micro- and macrovesicular steatosis, cirrhosis, periportal fibrosis, and features of nodular regeneration hyperplasia (**4.24, 4.25**). A proportion of these patients presented with portal venous thrombosis[19–22] and many were associated with thrombophilic states[21,22]. Although the aetiology and pathophysiology of this condition may be multifactorial, an over-riding association in all these patients was the current or previous use of didanosine (**4.26**).

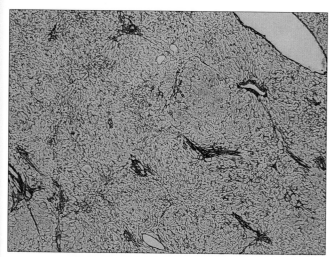

4.24 Histology of nodular regeneration hyperplasia and portal vein thrombosis.

4.25 Explant liver demonstrating nodular regeneration hyperplasia.

Noninvasive investigation of liver fibrosis

There is concern that up to one-third of HIV/HCV co-infected patients in one analysis progressed from minimal to advanced fibrosis within 3 years[23], which is the recommended interval between biopsies in HIV/HCV co-infected patients not going on to HCV treatment (EACS and BHIVA). There is a need to identify 'difficult-to-treat' patients with minimal fibrosis and monitor them closely while new treatments and treatment strategies are being developed for optimal responses.

The established gold standard for the evaluation of liver disease has traditionally been a percutaneous liver biopsy. Liver biopsy is used predominantly for the diagnosis, prognosis, and staging of liver disease. Biopsy is also useful for determining prognosis, usually by confirming the presence or absence of cirrhosis. More recently, biopsy has been used for staging fibrosis in viral hepatitis and for decision analysis as to the need for treatment. Many treatment algorithms recommend treatment for patients with septal fibrosis or greater (METAVIR stage ≥2). Figure **4.27** explains the staging of fibrosis.

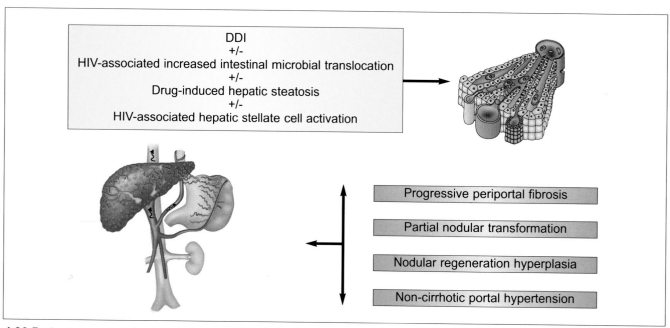

4.26 Pathophysiology of noncirrhotic portal hypertension.

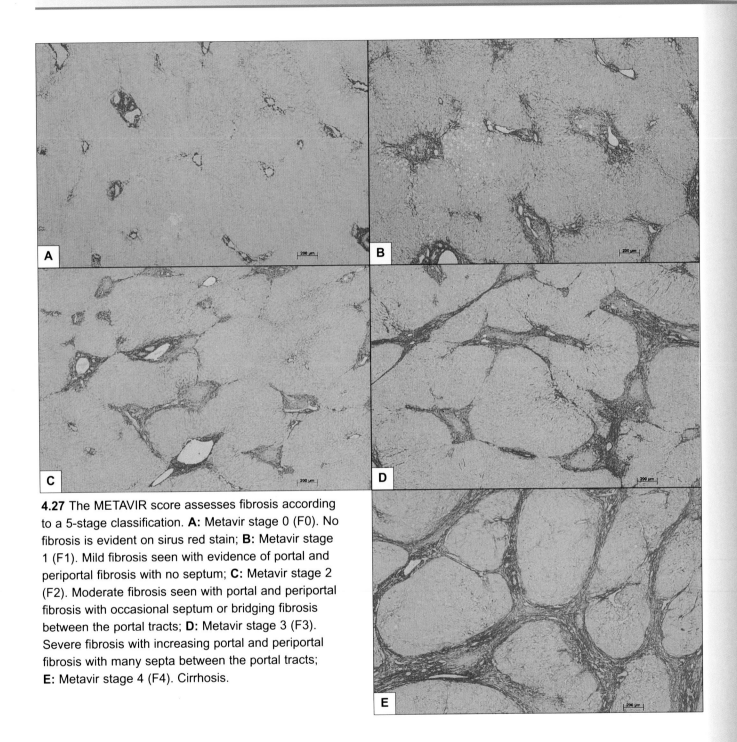

4.27 The METAVIR score assesses fibrosis according to a 5-stage classification. **A:** Metavir stage 0 (F0). No fibrosis is evident on sirus red stain; **B:** Metavir stage 1 (F1). Mild fibrosis seen with evidence of portal and periportal fibrosis with no septum; **C:** Metavir stage 2 (F2). Moderate fibrosis seen with portal and periportal fibrosis with occasional septum or bridging fibrosis between the portal tracts; **D:** Metavir stage 3 (F3). Severe fibrosis with increasing portal and periportal fibrosis with many septa between the portal tracts; **E:** Metavir stage 4 (F4). Cirrhosis.

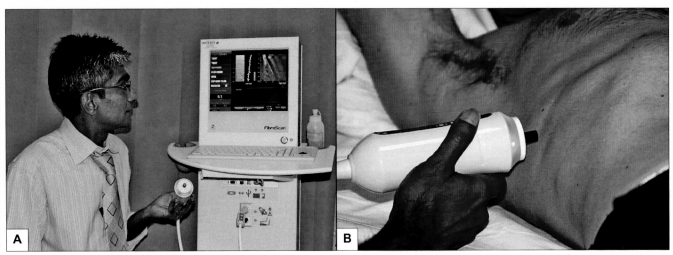

4.28A, B: A FibroScan™ in use.

An alternative noninvasive technique for staging liver disease is to measure liver stiffness or elasticity using a FibroScan™ [24] (Echosens, Paris, France). The principle is relatively simple and involves measuring the shear velocity of a 50 MHz wave propagated through a 2–5 cm segment of the liver, and converting this into a stiffness value in kilopascals (kPa). The procedure is simple to undertake, noninvasive and painless (**4.28**). An ultrasound transducer probe is mounted in the axis of a vibrator and vibrations of mild amplitude and low frequency are emitted by the transducer. The probe is held against the skin overlying the liver and induces an elastic shear wave which propagates through underlying tissue. Velocity of the shear wave through tissue is measured and directly relates to tissue stiffness, as the harder the tissue the faster the wave propagates.

Established thresholds are >7.9 kPa for ≥F2, ≥10.3 kPa for ≥F3, and ≥11.9 kPa for F4[25–28].

References

1 Palella FJ, Jr, Delaney KM, *et al.* Declining morbidity and mortality among patients with advanced human immunodeficiency virus infection. HIV Outpatient Study Investigators. *N Engl J Med* 1998;**338**(13):853–60.

2 Rosenthal E, Poiree M, Pradier C, GERMIVIC Joint Study Group. Mortality due to hepatitis C-related liver disease in HIV-infected patients in France (Mortavic 2001 study). *AIDS* 2003;**17**(12):1803–9.

3 Rockstroh J, *et al.* Hepatitis B and hepatitis C in the EuroSIDA Cohort: prevalence and effect on mortality, AIDS progression, and response to HAART. Abstract 799 (poster). Program and Abstracts of the 11th Conference on Retroviruses and Opportunistic Infections (11th CROI). February 8–11, 2004. San Francisco, CA.

4 Veiga AP, Casseb J, Duarte AJ. Humoral response to hepatitis B vaccination and its relationship with T CD45RA+ (naïve) and CD45RO+ (memory) subsets in HIV-1-infected subjects. *Vaccine* 2006 Nov;**24**:7124–8.

5 Di Martino V, Thevenot T, Colin JF, *et al.* Influence of HIV infection on the response to interferon therapy and the long-term outcome of chronic hepatitis B. *Gastroenterology* 2002 Dec;**123**(6):1812–22.

6 Thio CL, Seaberg EC, Skolasky R Jr, *et al.*; Multicenter AIDS Cohort Study. HIV-1, hepatitis B virus, and risk of liver-related mortality in the Multicenter Cohort Study (MACS). *Lancet* 2002 Dec;14;**360**(9349):1921–6.

7 Cross TJS, Rizzi P, Horner M, *et al.* The increasing prevalence of hepatitis delta virus (HDV) infection in South London. *J Med Virol* 2008;**80**:277–82.

8 Zhang BH, *et al.* RCT of screening for HCC. *J Cancer Res Clin Oncol* 2004;**130**:417–22.

9 Gambotti L, *et al. Euro Surveill* 2005;**10**:969–74.

10 Van der Laar T, Pybus O, Bruisten S, *et al.* Evidence of a large international network of HCV transmission in HIV positive men who have sex with men. *Gastroenterology* 2009;**136**(5):1609–17.

11 Thomson E, *et al. AIDS* 2009;**23**:89–93.

12 de Torres M, Poynard T. Risk factors for liver fibrosis progression in patients with chronic hepatitis C. *Ann Hepatol* 2003 Jan–Mar;**2**(1):5–11.

13 Qurishi N, Kreuzberg C, *et al*. Effect of antiretroviral therapy on liver related mortality in patients with HIV and hepatitis C virus coinfection. *Lancet* 2003;**362**(9397):1708–13.

14 Torriani FJ, Rodriguez-Torres M, *et al*. Peginterferon alfa-2a plus ribavirin for chronic hepatitis C virus infection in HIV-infected patients. *N Engl J Med* 2004;**351**(5):438–50.

15 Carrat F, Bani-Sadr F, *et al*. Pegylated interferon alfa-2b *vs*. standard interferon alfa-2b, plus ribavirin, for chronic hepatitis C in HIV-infected patients: a randomized controlled trial. *JAMA* 2004;**292** (23): 2839–48.

16 Vogel M, Dominguez S, Bhagani S, *et al*. Treatment of acute HCV infection in HIV-positive patients: experience from a multicentre European cohort. *Antivir Ther* 2010;**15**(2):267–79.

17 Rockstroh JK; The European AIDS Treatment Network (NEAT) Acute Hepatitis C Infection Consensus Panel. Acute hepatitis C in HIV-infected individuals – recommendations from the NEAT consensus conference. *AIDS* 2010 Dec 6. (Epub ahead of print.)

18 Ge D, Fellay J, Thompson AJ, Simon JS, *et al*. Genetic variation in IL28B predicts hepatitis C treatment-induced viral clearance. *Nature* 2009;**461**:399–401.

19 Maida I, Núñez M, Ríos MJ, *et al*. Severe liver disease associated with prolonged exposure to antiretroviral drugs. *J Acquir Immune Defic Syndr* 2006 Jun;**42**(2):177–82.

20 Mallet V, Blanchard P, Verkarre V, Vallet-Pichard A, Fontaine H, Lascoux-Combe C, Pol S. *AIDS* 2007 Jan 11;**21**(2):187–92.

21 Maida I, Garcia-Gasco P, Sotgiu G, *et al*. Antiretroviral-associated portal hypertension: a new clinical condition? Prevalence, predictors and outcome. *Antivir Ther* 2008;**13**(1):103–7.

22 Saifee S, Joelson D, Braude J, *et al*. Noncirrhotic portal hypertension in patients with human immunodeficiency virus-1 infection. *Clin Gastroenterol Hepatol* 2008;

23 Sulkowski MS, Mehta SH, Torbenson MS, *et al*. Rapid fibrosis progression among HIV/hepatitis C virus-co-infected adults. *AIDS* 2007;**21**(16):2209–16.

24 Sandrin L, Fourquet B, *et al*. Transient elastography: a new non-invasive method for assessing hepatic fibrosis. *Ultrasound Med Biol* 2004;**29**(12):1705–13.

25 Foucher J, Chanteloup E, Vergniol J, *et al*. Diagnosis of cirrhosis by transient elastography (FibroScan): a prospective study. *Gut* 2006;**55**(3):403–8.

26 Kelleher TB, Afdhal N. Assessment of liver fibrosis in co-infected patients. *J Hepatology* 2006;**44**:S126–31.

27 Ziol M, Handra-Luca A, Kettaneh A, *et al*. Noninvasive assessment of liver fibrosis by measurement of stiffness in patients with chronic hepatitis C. *Hepatology* 2005 Jan;**41**(1):48–54.

28 de Lédinghen V, *et al*. Diagnosis of hepatic fibrosis and cirrhosis by transient elastography in HIV/hepatitis C virus-coinfected patients. *J Acquir Immune Defic Syndr* 2006;**41**:175–9.

Further reading

European AIDS clinical Society guidelines for the management of co-infection with HIV-1 and chronic hepatitis B 2009. Available at: http://www.europeanaidsclinicalsociety.org/guidelinespdf/3_Treatment_chronic_hepatitis_co_infection.pdf

British HIV Association (BHIVA) guidelines for the management of co-infection with HIV-1 and chronic hepatitis B 2009. Available at: http://www.bhiva.org/files/file1031815.pdf

HIV and the central nervous system

J Green, AJ Rodger and N Marshall

Introduction

A number of central nervous system (CNS) pathologies are almost universally HIV-specific and it is estimated that approximately one-third of all patients with AIDS develop neurological complications at some stage of their illness[1]. Although mortality and morbidity can be significant from these conditions, early recognition should afford the opportunity for influencing an improved outcome.

The CNS immune system differs from the rest of the body in that the innate immune system is well represented by microglial cells, resident CNS macrophages, but it does not have a well established adaptive immune arm. Nevertheless, T-cells do traffic in and out of the CNS under normal conditions[2]. In addition, the blood–brain barrier (BBB), a complex physiological and physical barrier made up of astrocyte foot processes, basement membrane, and tight junctions, adds a further level of complexity to CNS immune responses[3].

Many inflammatory conditions are characterized by BBB breakdown, allowing migration of both innate (e.g. neutrophils and monocytes) and adaptive cells (e.g. T-cells) into CNS tissue and the subarachnoid space. The CNS inflammatory response is thus responsible both for microbial elimination and also tissue destruction that can lead to disability. These two processes are imbalanced in HIV; hence opportunistic infections and unusual clinical manifestations of disease occur[4]. CNS infection occurs during primary viraemia as HIV-infected leucocytes cross the BBB and subsequently infect microglia, macrophages, and possibly astrocytes. Neuronal injury and death occur through exposure to viral proteins and host neurotoxic molecules such as CXCL-12 and tumour necrosis factor-alpha (TNF-α)[5]. Typically as the peripheral CD4 cell count falls so the spectrum of CNS-infecting organisms widens (*Table 4.9*).

This section will focus on both diagnostic pathways unique to HIV patients, such as the approach to space occupying lesions (SOLs), as well as more didactic sections on common diseases and the treatment options available to clinicians. Key areas to be covered include HIV-specific effects (e.g. HIV dementia), opportunistic infections, malignancy, and newer manifestations of disease associated with immune reconstitution inflammatory syndrome (IRIS).

Table 4.9 CD4 count and typical presentation of CNS disease

CD4 cell count	Organism	Common manifestations
> 500 cells/mm^3	HIV	Aseptic meningitis
200–500 cells/mm^3	*Mycobacterium tuberculosis*	TBM, tuberculomas
	Streptococcus pneumoniae	Bacterial meningitis
<100 cells/mm^3	*Toxoplasma gondii*	Encephalitis, focal neurology
	Cryptococcus neoformans	Meningitis
	Mycobacterium tuberculosis	Disseminated disease with CNS involved
	Epstein–Barr virus	Primary CNS lymphoma
	Cytomegalovirus/VZV	Encephalitis
	HIV	Meningoencephalitis, ADC, myelopathy

Presentation of disease and general management

The clinical presentation of CNS disease in HIV can broadly be divided into those with meningitis or those with SOLs; however, encephalitis will also be considered. The current absolute value and recent trend in the patient's CD4 count is important but any intercurrent chemotherapeutic agents received will have a bearing on presentation and aetiology. Pathogen-specific responses are also important. For example, SOLs are rarely due to cryptococcal disease, unlike toxoplasmosis, which in turn rarely causes meningitis. Outcome from some diseases, such as CNS tuberculosis (TB), is poorer in HIV-positive individuals than in HIV-negative ones but clinical presentation is often the same[6]. In addition the timing of commencement of ARVs currently remains unclear as immune reconstitution can further confuse the clinical picture and is therefore an area of active research.

Meningitis is the commonest neurological emergency in HIV medicine. Although bacterial pathogens are seen much more frequently than in age-matched controls, opportunistic pathogens, e.g. fungi such as *Cryptococcus neoformans*, are numerically the most common aetiological agents along with *M. tuberculosis*. Fortunately clinical presentation of bacterial and CNS TB is similar to that in the immunocompetent host but cryptococcal meningitis has an indolent onset and often there is little evidence of a CSF inflammatory response (*Table 4.10*).

SOLs can present with fits, headache, nausea, and vomiting, and decreased level of consciousness, as well as focal signs such as limb weakness. No specific clinical features help differentiate diagnoses, but epidemiological considerations are important. In the developed world setting, toxoplasmosis and primary CNS lymphoma are the most common diagnoses, but TB is an important consideration, especially in patients who may have spent part of their life in TB endemic areas. Encephalitis presents as an altered conscious state, associated with fever and headache in the majority of patients, but the differential diagnosis is wide, making exhaustive testing of limited CSF samples difficult. Nevertheless, primary HIV (especially at seroconversion), HSV, VZV, CMV, and toxoplasmosis are the most common pathogens.

Meningitis

Cryptococcal meningitis

Cryptococcus neoformans is an encapsulated yeast that rarely causes infections in seemingly immunocompetent hosts. Meningitis caused by *C. neoformans* is the commonest meningitis in HIV-positive patients in developed nations and is thus one of the commonest presentations of AIDS. Its diagnosis usually leads to a subsequent positive HIV antibody test in those patients not already known to be HIV positive. With a more indolent rate of onset than bacterial meningitis this infection nevertheless carries a significant level of both mortality and morbidity (**4.29**). Patients present with headache of a longer duration than in bacterial disease, 10 days being common. Focal signs may be present as cerebral SOL (cryptococcomas) are described (**4.30**).

Although classically described as a disease of patients with CD4 count <50 cells/mm^3, median CD4 counts at presentation are rarely above 20 cells/mm^3. CSF opening pressure at first LP is usually about 25 cm water, but can

Table 4.10 Comparison of the main clinical features of cryptococcal, tuberculous and bacterial meningitis in HIV-positive patients

Aetiology	Prodrome (days)	CSF cell count (cells/mm^3)	Differential neutrophil (%)	Protein (g/l)	Glucose ratio	CSF culture + (%)
Cryptococcal	10	<20	<10	1	0.3	80
Tuberculous	10	<500	10–60	1.3	0.3	40–90
Bacterial	3	>1000	>90	4.5	0.1	65

exceed 40 cm. CSF white cell count is usually mononuclear and often below 10 cells/ml. All laboratories will perform an India-ink stain to look for cryptococci in CSF specimens and can measure cryptococcal antigen titres in CSF and peripheral blood. Non-CNS manifestations of cryptococcal diseases do occur; blood cultures are positive in 60% of cases and pulmonary involvement is not unusual[7]. Features associated with poorer outcome include a high CSF organism load as measured by quantitative culture or cryptococcal antigen (CRAG) titre in the CSF >1:1024, the lack of a CSF inflammatory response manifest by low CSF leucocyte counts, being India-ink positive, reduced conscious level on presentation, and increased intracranial pressure (ICP). Optic atrophy and subsequent blindness are well recognized complications of prolonged raised ICP (**4.31**).

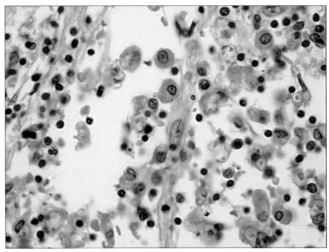

4.29 Cerebral cryptococcosis. H&E staining of the post-mortem sampling of the meninges of a 24-year-old African male who presented with a 13-day history of headache, fitting, and decreased level of consciousness.

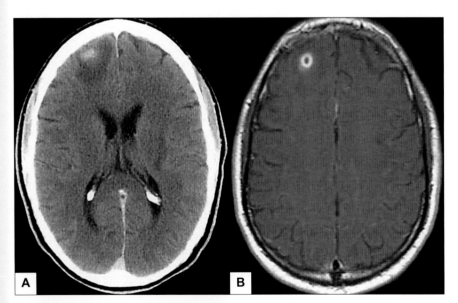

4.30 Contrast enhanced CT (**A**) and MRI head (**B**, T1 with gadolinium) of a 35-year-old Zimbabwean male, who presented with personality change and fitting. Scans demonstrate a well circumscribed right frontal lobe ring-enhancing lesion. This patient underwent stereotactic brain biopsy of the lesion, which revealed encapsulated yeast, later identified as *C. neoformans* on culture.

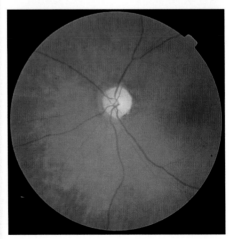

4.31 Optic atrophy after treatment for cryptococcal meningitis despite repeated LPs and lumbar drain insertion. Note the pale optic disc due to irreversible loss of nerve fibres caused by the mechanical stress of raised ICP. This patient was rendered permanently blind in both eyes.

Table 4.11 Treatment of cryptococcal meningitis

		Treatment	Comments
Acute treatment	1st line	At least 2 weeks of: • Liposomal amphotericin B 4–6 mg/kg IV daily • Flucytosine 25 mg/kg qds then maintenance treatment	*Lumbar puncture:* repeat LP with measurement of opening pressure critical to management of increased ICP. Maintain opening pressure <25 cmH₂0. May need daily LP or consider insertion of lumbar drain or shunt for CSF drainage if not contained by repeat LPs
	Alternative	Intolerance of flucytosine, or fully amphotericin sensitive (d/w microbiology), at least 2 weeks of: • Liposomal amphotericin B 4–6 mg/kg IV daily • (Consider adding fluconazole 800–400 mg od) then maintenance treatment	*Amphotericin test dose:* infuse 1 mg over 10 minutes. Stop the infusion and then observe the patient carefully for signs of anaphylaxis for 30 minutes. If no reaction occurs continue the infusion
	Alternative	If intolerant of amphotericin at least 2 weeks of: • Fluconazole 400–800 mg po/IVdaily • Flucytosine 100–150 mg/kg/day then maintenance treatment OR: • Itracaonazole 400 mg daily (but less effective)	*Flucytosine:* dose reduced to 100 mg/kg/day as additive effect with amphotericin. Trough levels 25–50 mg/l (200–400 mmol/l) and peak <80 mg/l (620 mmol/l)
Consolidation and maintenance	1st line	Fluconazole 400 mg daily for up to 8 weeks; then fluconazole 200 mg daily maintenance	Continue maintenance treatment till CD4 >100–200 cells/mm³ for at least 6 months (restart if CD4 <100 cells/mm³)
	Alternative	• Consolidation liposomal amphotericin (4 mg/kg/weekly), or itraconazole (200 mg bd) • Maintenance prophylaxis with itraconazole (200 mg od) or liposomal amphotericin B (4 mg/kg/weekly) • Little/no data on voriconazole & posaconazole	Itraconazole is less efficacious than fluconazole in clinical trials

Treatment of cryptococcal meningitis is usually with a combination of liposomal amphotericin and flucytosine (*Table 4.11*). Whilst standard formulation amphotericin B (0.7–1 mg/kg) is as efficacious as liposomal preparations its use can be limited by nephrotoxicity. However, pre-loading with intravenous saline can reduce this effect. Myelosuppression, gastrointestinal disturbance, and peripheral neuropathy are the main adverse events associated with flucytosine use. Treatment can be complicated by extremely high ICPs, with LP opening pressures of >40 cmH$_2$0 not infrequently recorded. These patients require either repeated LPs or lumbar drain insertion aiming to keep the pressure at <25 cmH$_2$O. Ventriculoperitoneal shunts have been used with success if pressure remains high for >2 weeks but the risk from blockage or infection is high. Consolidation therapy is usually with fluconazole, which is generally well tolerated, but abnormalities in liver function tests necessitating temporary cessation of therapy can occur. IRIS occurs in up to 20% of patients with cryptococcal meningitis. A prospective study randomized HIV-positive patients with cryptococcal meningitis to initiate ART within 72 hours of diagnosis or to delay initiation until 10 weeks after fluconazole monotherapy. They found that the mortality rate due to cryptococcal meningitis was high overall (62%), but that mortality rate in the early treatment group was 82% compared with 37% in the delayed treatment group, with most mortality occurring early after initiation of ART (p<0.01). Whether this was due to IRIS disease is not clear as many of the deaths occurred in the first few days after initiation of ART[8].

Tuberculous meningitis

TB of the CNS is one of the most important clinical presentations of TB. Untreated it is rapidly fatal and the degree of neurological impairment at presentation predicts outcome. Treatment is often complicated by ongoing inflammation and frequently hampered by a lack of microbiological information such as isolate drug susceptibility. It takes two main clinical forms: meningitis (TBM, **4.32**) and tuberculomas (**4.33**). Cerebral abscesses are rare, but described in the literature. TBM is frequently a manifestation of disseminated TB in HIV patients. Thus extra-pulmonary manifestations of disease such as concurrent pulmonary infection or lymphadenopathy should be sought during the initial work-up to aid diagnosis (**4.34**). The clinical presentation of TBM in HIV-positive patients is little different from HIV-negative disease. Patients present in the same fashion as pyogenic meningitis with headache, neck stiffness, and photophobia but symptoms tend to have been present longer (median 10 days) and the CSF leucocytosis is predominantly lymphocytic, although neutrophils may predominate very

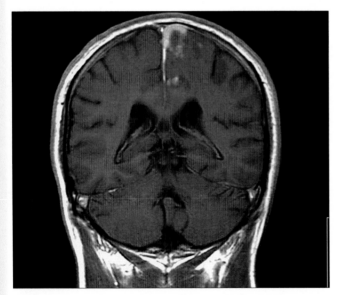

4.32 An extensive meningeal plaque of inflammation in TBM. A 42-year-old Ugandan male presented with symptoms of headache, fever, and neck stiffness of 12 days' duration, with past pointing. This T1-weighted transverse cranial MRI demonstrates significant parasagittal enhancement of the meninges. In addition the basal meninges enhance and multiple small posterior fossa tuberculomas are demonstrated. AFB culture was positive in CSF, confirming the diagnosis of CNS TB. CD4 count was 128 cells/mm^3 at presentation.

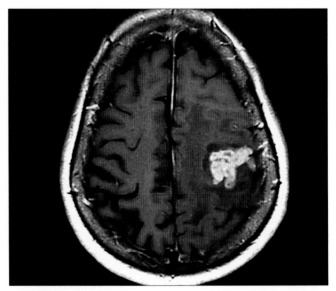

4.33 Large cerebral tuberculoma on MRI. This 34-year-old Ukranian woman presented with a 3-week history of partial-complex seizures involving her right hand and arm. Note the significant surrounding cerebral oedema and mild midline shift. Isoniazid-resistant *M. tuberculosis* was cultured from a brain biopsy specimen after 25 days of culture.

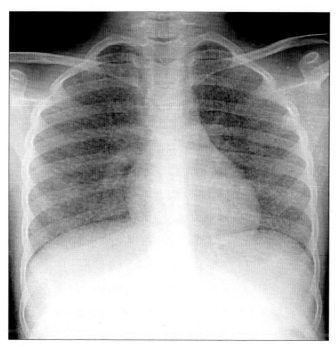

4.34 Miliary TB. PA chest radiograph from a 20-year-old Namibian migrant who underwent routine health screening at the port of entry. On questioning he gave a 3-week history of a dry cough, associated with fevers and night sweats. He had lost 5 kg in weight. AFB smear of bronchoalveolar lavage fluid was negative but he was empirically commenced on quadruple antituberculous chemotherapy with good resolution of his symptoms by day 7 of hospital admission. Culture of fully sensitive *M. tuberculosis* was subsequently confirmed in both sputum and CSF.

early in disease. Cranial nerve palsies are common with III, IV, and VI being more common than VII or VIII nerve palsies. Even in centres managing a lot of TBM cases, AFB are only found in the CSF of approximately 60% cases, the others being treated empirically based on high clinical suspicion. Cultures are positive in up to 90% if the laboratory has a large volume of sample that is processed appropriately. Although the use of adjuvant dexamethasone has a good evidence base in HIV-negative TBM, data are less convincing in HIV-positive cases. Treatment with antituberculous chemotherapy is usually for between 9 and 12 months. (See section on tuberculosis in chapter 6 for treatment regimes.)

Bacterial meningitis

Bacterial meningitis in HIV-positive patients is about 20 times more common than in the general population and mortality exceeds 50% in developing world settings where the greatest burden of disease (usually from *S. pneumoniae*) occurs. Clinical presentation is very similar between HIV-positive and -negative patients, with a 3-day prodrome most common. The classical triad of headache, fever, and neck stiffness is present in three-quarters of patients irrespective of HIV status. Nevertheless, differences in CSF findings are found, with lower white cell counts and higher glucose concentrations being frequent findings in those who are HIV positive. Recent randomized, placebo-controlled studies have suggested that adjuvant steroids are not of benefit in HIV-associated bacterial meningitis[9].

Space-occupying lesions

SOLs can present diagnostic challenges to the HIV physician, even with modern imaging and laboratory facilities. Patients who present with fitting, persistent headache, nausea and vomiting, falling level of consciousness, as well as focal signs such as limb weakness ought to undergo urgent cranial imaging. Unfortunately no specific clinical features help differentiate diagnoses but epidemiological information and laboratory test results can narrow the possibilities somewhat. Toxoplasmosis and primary CNS lymphoma are common diagnoses in the developed world, newly diagnosed HIV-positive patient, who has presented late in the course of their illness, with low CD4 counts. Often these patients will give a preceding history of shingles or pneumonia some months ago when the diagnosis of underlying immunosuppression could have been made. Importantly toxoplasmosis is very unusual in patients who are compliant with co-trimoxazole PCP prophylaxis. TB tends to occur in patients from high incidence TB endemic areas, although it often remains in the differential diagnosis as culture of (difficult to obtain) specimens is prolonged. Most laboratories will only give a negative result for TB culture at 6 weeks.

Toxoplasmosis

Falling immunity leads to reactivation of latent *Toxoplasma gondii* brachycysts, with primary disease acquired early in life. Although a diagnosis of severely immunosuppressed patients, with median CD4 counts of <100 cells/mm³, patients typically have strong serological evidence of past infection, being anti-*Toxoplasma* IgG positive. Multiple lesions can be apparent on cerebral imaging, usually with significant surrounding oedema (**4.35**). Rarely diffuse encephalitis in the absence of ring-enhancing lesions is seen, where the CT can be normal. CT scans have a lower level of sensitivity than MRI. Thus if the index of suspicion is high, or a single lesion is present on CT, this latter modality of cerebral imaging should be performed. Nevertheless, just occasionally you can be caught out by the patient with toxoplasmosis and a single CNS lesion (**4.36**).

CSF *T. gondii* PCR has a high specificity but variable sensitivity and is not always possible in those patients with mass effect on cerebral scans who cannot have an LP. Recent research findings suggest that use of peripheral blood PCR coupled with high titres of anti-*T. gondii* IgG

antibodies for the diagnosis of cerebral toxoplasmosis might be useful clinically[10]. In patients with the correct clinical features a trial of anti-*Toxoplasma* treatment is usually instituted with clinical improvement seen rapidly (2–3 days) in those with disease. A failure to respond to treatment is an indication for brain biopsy (**4.37**).

The treatment of toxoplasmosis and subsequent necessary maintenance therapy are summarized in *Tables 4.12* and *4.13*. The main initial adverse events are nausea

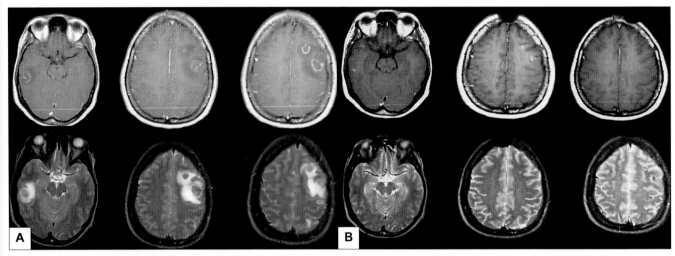

4.35A, B: This set of paired T1-weighted (top) and Grase (bottom) MRIs were performed in a 37-year-old HIV+ patient who had defaulted from follow-up for 2 years and presented with a decreased level of consciousness having been found fitting at home. CD4 count was 76 cells/mm³ on admission. Although there are multiple lesions in these transverse scans, compare the two left frontal lobe lesions in the pre- and post treatments. **A:** Pre-treatment: these scans highlights multiple ring-enhancing lesions with moderate peri-lesional cerebral oedema, especially in the left frontal lobe.
B: T1-weighted and Grase MR images performed in the post-treatment phase demonstrate that the two lesions in the left frontal lobe have regressed after 6 weeks' treatment with pyrimethamine/sulfadoxine, but illustrate that small calcified scars may persist.

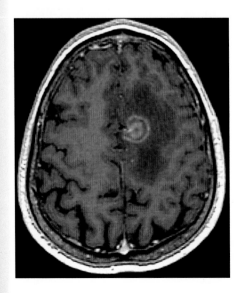

4.36 MRI of a 42-year-old Indian male, who presented with right arm partial-complex seizures. There is a large ring-enhancing lesion with significant surrounding oedema. He underwent stereotactic brain biopsy, having been told he was likely to have a cerebral tumour. After pus was aspirated from the lesion an HIV test was performed, which was positive. CD4 count was 34 cells/mm³. The histopathology confirmed a diagnosis of toxoplasmosis. Review of the MRI revealed no other lesions.

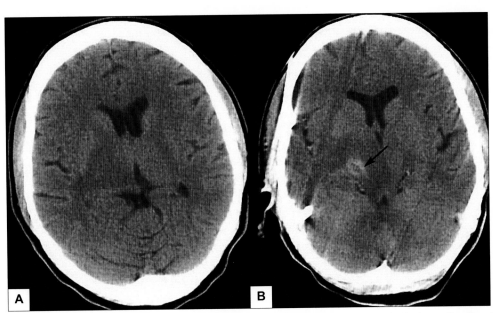

4.37A, B: This set of paired CTs demonstrate why a contrast-enhanced scan is essential in investigating CNS symptoms in HIV+ patients. **A:** An unenhanced CT head demonstrates a right-sided lesion deep in white matter with some midline shift. **B:** The contrast-enhanced scan highlights a ring-enhancing lesion (arrow) in the middle of moderate peri-lesional cerebral oedema that responded to anti-*Toxoplasma* therapy.

Table 4.12 Treatment of cerebral toxoplasmosis

	Treatment	*Comments*
1st line	6–8 weeks treatment with: • Sulfadiazine 1–1.5 g qds (IV currently not available) • Pyrimethamine 200 mg stat then 75 mg od (>60 kg) or 50 mg od (<60 kg) • Folinic acid 10–15 mg od	*Corticosteroids:* Adjunct steroids should be given for treatment of mass effect attributed to focal lesions or associated oedema Use dexamethasone 4 mg qds, and taper according to response NB: Steroids will lead to reduction in size of a CNS lymphoma (differential in cerebral toxoplasmosis)
Alternative (preferred)	At least 8 weeks' treatment with: • Clindamycin 600 mg IV/po qds • Pyrimethamine 200 mg stat then 75 mg od (>60 kg) or 50 mg od (<60 kg)*	
Alternative	Co-trimoxazole 60 mg/kg in divided doses	*Anticonvulsants:* Consider if history of seizures during the acute phase; but should not be used prophylactically
Alternative	Atovaquone 1500 mg po bd (with food); plus either: • Pyrimethamine (dose as above)* OR • Sulfadiazine 1–1.5 g qds	*With folinic acid 10–15 mg daily
Alternative	• Azithromycin 900–1200 mg po • Pyrimethamine (dose as above)*	

Table 4.13 Suggested maintenance treatments for _Toxoplasma_ encephalitis

		Choice of therapy
Secondary prevention	1st line	Sulfadiazine 1 g bd Pyrimethamine 25–50 mg od*
	Alternative (preferred)	Clindamycin 600 mg tds Pyrimethamine 25–50 mg od*
	Alternative	Atovaquone 750 mg bd (with food) alone, or with either: • Pyrimethamine 25 mg od* • Sulfadiazine 1 g bd
	Alternative	Co-trimoxazole 960 mg od (with ART)

Comments

Continue till CD4 >200 cells/mm^3 for at least 3 months (restart if CD4 <200 cells/mm^3)

NB: Nebulized pentamidine is not active against _T. gondii_ and should not be used as maintenance after toxoplasmosis treatment if CD4 <100 cells/mm^3 and IgG-positive _Toxoplasma_ serology

NB: Clindamycin + pyrimethamine is not effective for prophylaxis against PCP

*With folinic acid 10–15 mg daily

and vomiting but the most serious problem is an allergic rash due to the sulfadiazine, which can be so severe that Stevens–Johnson syndrome occurs.

Tuberculomas

TB can also present with CNS mass lesions. Tuberculomas present with typical symptoms and signs of any SOL, such as focal neurological deficits and seizures, often with few prodromal symptoms. Lesions can be solitary or multiple and both nodular and ring-enhancing patterns can be observed. Tuberculous abscesses are rare and tend to be larger than tuberculomas with a more accelerated clinical course. As TB resistance rates continue to rise a tissue diagnosis and samples for microbiological culture should be the gold standard. Search hard for TB in other sites such as the lungs (sputum, lavage) and lymph nodes (CT chest, abdomen, and pelvis) and take samples as an acceptable alternative to brain biopsy if neurosurgery is not possible. Nevertheless empiric anti-tuberculous therapy is often commenced. The role of steroids in the treatment of tuberculomas is far from clear and is thus usually decided on a case by case basis, but they are usually prescribed when a paradoxical reaction occurs. Paradoxical

reactions to antituberculosis therapy are especially poorly tolerated in lesions involving the CNS and occur in about 20% of cases between 1 and 3 months into treatment (**4.38**).

Primary CNS lymphoma

In addition to the clinical features of any SOL patients with PCNSL, a condition almost unique to HIV patients, may have the classical B symptoms such as fever, night sweats, and weight loss. Although features such as presence of a single lesion or lesions of size >4 cm are seen in about 80% cases, neither feature can reliably distinguish PCNSL from toxoplasmosis or CNS TB. Thus brain biopsy should be performed if a trial of anti-_Toxoplasma_ therapy fails to give clinical improvement in 1–2 weeks (**4.39**). The median CD4 count is usually <20 cells/mm^3. Molecular tests have not really improved diagnostic accuracy. Although EBV DNA is frequently present in the CSF of patients with PCNSL it is not a specific enough test to be relied upon in clinical practice for diagnosing PCNSL, despite using a >10,000 copies/ml cut-off. The mean prognosis is only 2–3 months from diagnosis despite treatments such as chemotherapy and cranial radiotherapy. However, there are

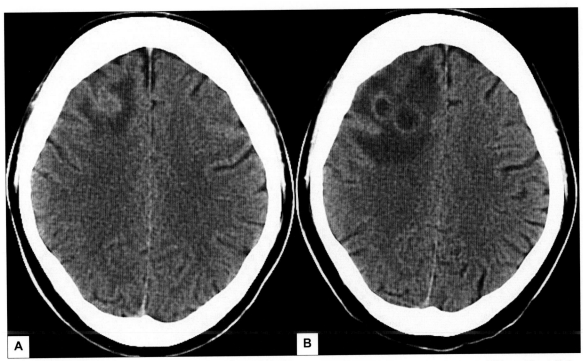

4.38 Paradoxical enlargement of tuberculomas. **A:** CT head of a 24-year-old Bangladeshi-born UK resident 5 months into antituberculous chemotherapy showing resolving oedema around a right frontal tuberculoma. **B:** Paradoxical enlargement of this lesion was seen with appearance of a second tuberculoma and further oedema in the same patient 3 months later when he presented with recurrent partial-complex seizures involving his left arm. This patient responded very well to the introduction of oral prednisolone 60 mg/day, tapering over the ensuing weeks.

some data suggesting institution of ARV therapy may improve outcome marginally.

Other diagnoses to consider for a SOL

It is not possible to produce an exhaustive list of the causes of SOL in HIV patients, but awareness that CNS symptoms and signs may be presenting features of a more generalized disease will enable diagnosis of disseminated bacterial infections, carcinomas, and inflammatory conditions. The list includes histoplasmosis, bacterial abscess (e.g. nontyphoidal salmonella as well as staphylococci and streptococci), nocardiasis, aspergillosis, and syphilis (**4.40**). In South American and Indian patients differentiating neurocysticercosis (infection with the larval form of the human tapeworm *Taenia solium*) from other pathogens can pose a diagnostic challenge if the typical radiological findings of either calcified cysts or a scolex within a cyst are absent. Conditions such as nocardiasis, coccidioidomycosis, histoplasmosis, and penicilliosis can all cause purely CNS disease and usually require confirmation by a tissue diagnosis.

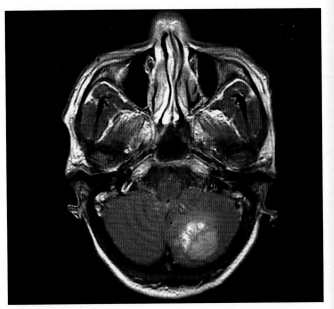

4.39 Single large left posterior fossa lesion in a 35-year-old Ugandan female who presented with a tonic–clonic seizure, aberrant gait, and past pointing on examination. CD4 count was 4 cells/mm³.

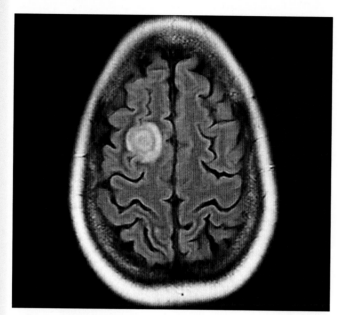

4.40 Cerebral aspergilloma on T1-weighted cerebral MRI. Septated and hyaline hyphae were observed in the direct microscopy of the pus from this cerebral abscess. Unfortunately the patient died despite aggressive therapy with amphotericin and voriconazole.

Encephalitis

Inflammation of brain parenchyma can result from primary HIV infection itself, as well as opportunistic pathogens, including CMV, HSV-1 and -2, VZV, and rarely toxoplasmosis. There are few specific features that distinguish these conditions besides PCR analysis of CSF and tissue. In addition up to 10% of patients with CMV encephalitis may also have HSV detected in CSF. Peripheral blood PCR for CMV is a useful recent additional diagnostic aid. HSV-2 is more common in HIV-positive patients, as is concurrent oro-genital ulceration with HSV encephalitis.

Cytomegalovirus

Although a relatively rare presentation of clinical CMV disease, CMV encephalitis can occur in advanced HIV and usually presents with peri-ventricular inflammation on cerebral imaging. It has a high morbidity and mortality if misdiagnosed. Prior to the development of HAART, 2% of HIV-infected patients with CD4+ counts less than 50/mm³ developed CMV neurologic disease. The incidence has decreased since HAART became available. CMV encephalitis can present with acute onset of confusion and lethargy which progress rapidly. It can also rarely cause focal neurological deficits such as cranial nerve palsies and

cauda equina syndrome. CNS disease is sometimes associated with CMV disease of other target organs such as the gut, eyes, and peripheral nerves. Adrenal insufficiency resulting in Addisonian crisis has been reported. Treatment is with intravenous ganciclovir or foscarnet if not tolerated, usually because bone marrow suppression occurs. (See page 126 for full details.)

VZV

Although usually causing shingles VZV is an important cause of meningoencephalitis and can be associated with cerebral vasculitis in HIV. It should be considered in the work-up of an HIV patient with strokes or cranial nerve palsy even in the absence of a classical rash. Treatment is with IV acyclovir 10 mg/kg tds for 1–2 weeks.

HIV encephalopathy

Since HIV seroconversion can present in a myriad of ways any patient with unexplained aseptic meningitis, cranial nerve palsy (e.g. Bell's palsy) or encephalitis should be offered an HIV test and potentially PCR analysis of CSF for HIV RNA if available. Cranial nerve palsies, encephalopathy, myeloradiculopathy, and Guillain–Barré syndrome can all present during the early course of HIV disease. Typically CD4 counts are well preserved in the 400+ cells/mm³ range, but these clinical features are indications for commencement of ART before counts fall towards the levels more commonly associated with ARV need, as neurological disease at seroconversion is associated with more rapid progression of HIV disease[11].

HIV associated neurocognitive impairment

Cognitive impairment has long been recognized as a consequence of chronic HIV infection[12]. Criteria for the definition of HIV associated neurocognitive disorders (HAND) were updated in 2007 by the American Academy of Neurology into three categories[13]: (1) asymptomatic neurocognitive impairment (ANI, mild-to-moderate neuropsychological [NP] impairment in at least two cognitive domains without day-to-day difficulties); (2) mild neurocognitive impairment (MNI, documented mild-to-moderate NP impairment in at least two cognitive domains with mild everyday difficulties); and (3) HIV associated dementia (HAD, moderate-to-severe NP impairment in two cognitive domains with moderate-to-severe everyday life difficulties). MRI may demonstrate patchy, diffuse and symmetrical lesions in the white matter. Brain atrophy is also a common finding in patients with AIDS, but the relationship of atrophy to HIV-associated dementia is unclear (**4.41**).

Although HAD is rarely seen in patients receiving effective cART, varying degrees of neurocognitive impairment are increasingly recognized in HIV patients both on and off cART. Such impairments can be associated with evidence of ongoing HIV replication in the CNS, degree of immunosuppression, age, and infection with other viruses, such as HCV[14].

Cross-sectional studies report very high prevalence of milder disease in the USA. In the CHARTER study, 53%

had HAND (21% with ANI, 30% with MND and 2% with HAD)[15]. Neurocognitive functioning generally improves following commencement of cART, but other studies suggest that cognitive impairment can progress despite cART[12]. Penetration of anti-retroviral drugs into the nervous system has also been a focus of research in recent years and there is evidence that drugs that penetrate better into the CNS result in greater improvements in neurocognitive function[12] although other studies are inconclusive[16–17]. The relative CNS penetrating abilities of ARVs are given below (*Table 4.14*). No adjunctive therapies have ever been shown to benefit these patients.

4.41A, B: Cerebral atrophy in a 55-year-old white male, who had been HIV positive for 21 years and presented with slowly progressive cognitive impairment.

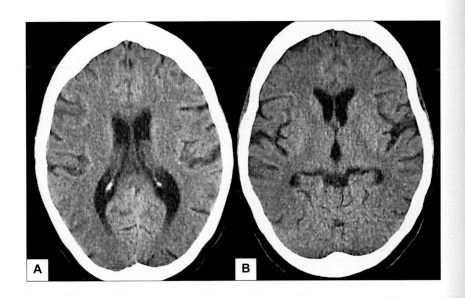

Table 4.14 CNS penetration of common ARV medication[18]

CNS penetration	Antiretroviral therapy
Low (1)	Tenofovir (TDF), nelfinavir (NFV), ritonavir (RTV), saquinavir/r (SAQ/r), tipranavir (TPV), enfuvirtide (T20)
Low–medium (2)	Didanosine (DDI), lamivudine (3TC), stavudine (D4T), etravirine, atazanavir/r (ATZ/r), fosamprenavir/r (FPV/r)
Medium–high (3)	Abacavir (ABC), emtricitabine (FTC), efavirenz (EFV), darvnavir/r (DRV), fosamprenavir/r (FPV/r), indinavir (IDV/r), lopinavir/r (LPV/r), maraviroc (MVC), raltegravir (RAL)
High (4)	Zidovudine (AZT), nevirapine (NVP), indinavir (IDV/r)

Progressive multifocal leukoencephalopathy

Progressive multifocal leukoencephalopathy (PML) is a multifocal white matter-based demyelinating disease driven by reactivation of JC virus replication, usually presenting in patients with CD4 counts below 200 cells/mm^3. Symptoms very much depend upon where the lesions are but motor, sensory, and cerebellar signs predominate (**4.42–4.44**). The only treatment available is ART and response to therapy is variable. Some patients continue to decline inexorably to death, whereas in others disease progression halts, although few get full recovery of function.

Immune reconstitution disease of the CNS

Immune reconstitution inflammatory syndrome (IRIS) is one of the major adverse effects of ARVs[19]. It is associated with significant morbidity and mortality and has been described in relation to all the major HIV-related CNS pathologies. The immunopathology is poorly understood and therefore current treatment regimens remain dependent upon anecdote and steroids. As in other organ systems immune reconstitution in HIV takes two forms and usually occurs between 4 and 12 weeks into ARV therapy.

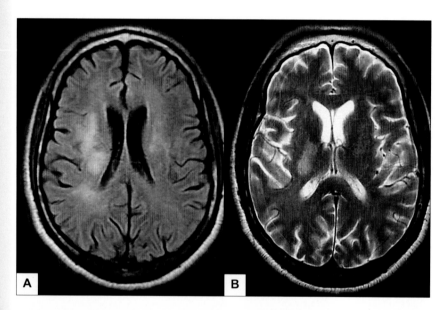

4.42 T1- (**A**) and T2- (**B**) weighted transverse MR images from a 48-year-old white male who presented with increasing confusion and was found to have widespread upper motor neuron signs on examination, with a spastic gait. Multiple white matter-based lesions are seen, more on the right than left, with little surrounding oedema. This patient had moderate reversal of symptoms after 3 months of ARVs.

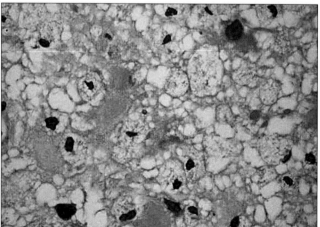

4.43 Histopathology of PML from a brain biopsy specimen. There is marked demyelination associated with a prominent infiltrate of foamy macrophages. Lymphocytes are sparse. Reactive astrocytic atypia is prominent.

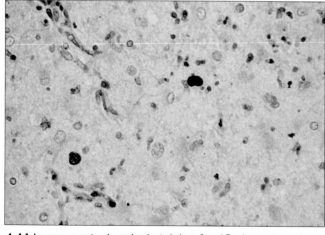

4.44 Immunocytochemical staining for JC virus strongly labels some glial nuclei.

4.45A, B: CNS IRIS after ARV initiation. T2-weighted transverse MRI scans of the same patient taken just 8 weeks apart. Left-hand scan was performed because the patient had developed widespread neurological symptoms, including slurred speech, cortical blindness (complex visual field defects), and left arm weakness about 7 weeks into ARV therapy. Scan demonstrates multiple, mainly white matter-based lesions in the occipital lobes, right paraventricular region and left frontal lobe. The right-hand scan was repeated because he had had worsening of all of these symptoms, confirmed by increased oedema and inflammation in the original lesions. Biopsy of one of these lesions showed a marked CD8 cell inflammatory infiltrate, with associated demyelination in keeping with PML.

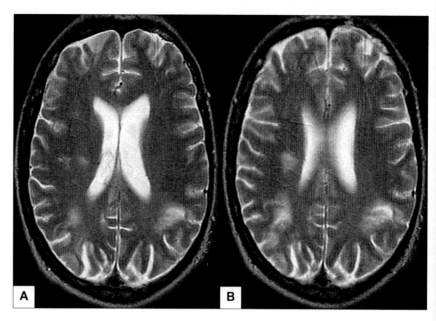

Unmasking of established infection

When patients, seemingly well when starting ARV therapy, mount an immune response to pathogens already present they get new symptoms and signs of inflammation and infection (**4.45**). Typically such symptoms include headache, fever, nausea, vomiting, and worsening level of consciousness. The exact timing of initiation of ARVs in CNS disease is not as clear as in systemic infections; ACTG 5164 reported decreased rates of mortality and death in patients initiating ARVs <14 days after diagnosis of opportunistic infection but the study was not powered to look at outcomes with CNS disease, as only 12% of enrolled patients had CNS infection, principally cryptococcal meningitis[20].

Dysregulated inflammatory response to retained antigen

Worsening of established, often partially treated disease can occur when ARVs are commenced early in the course of treatment for opportunistic infection. Up to 20% of cryptococcal meningitis patients will get IRIS, with worsening headache and raised ICP as typical clinical features. Predicting who will get IRIS is difficult but it appears to be dependent upon the speed of recovery of the CD4 count[21]. In CNS TB, either lesions expand or meningitis worsens (**4.46**). However, the outcome from TB IRIS appears to be more benign than from cryptococcal disease.

Spinal cord disease

Acute spinal cord disease can occasionally occur during HIV seroconversion but usually viruses such as CMV, VZV, HSV, and HTLV-1/-2 cause a radiculomyelitis (**4.47**). Other differential diagnoses include toxoplasmosis, neurosyphilis, and mechanical compression from an abscess (e.g. TB) or tumour (e.g. lymphoma, **4.48**).

HIV-associated myelopathy is also called vacuolar myelopathy due to the histological hallmark of vacuoles which are generally most prominent in the thoracic and cervical spinal cord. Occurring mainly with advanced immunosuppression it may be associated with ADC or HIV encephalopathy. Presentation is typically with subacute motor symptoms including spastic gait and brisk reflexes. The differential diagnosis is as above for acute spinal disease and investigations would include spinal imaging with MRI and CSF examination.

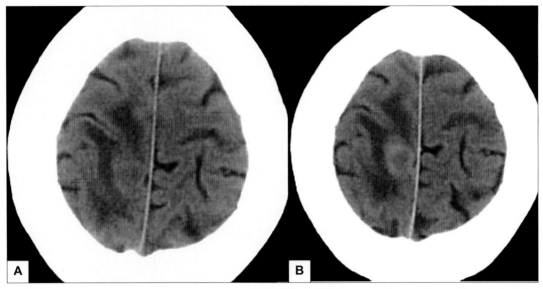

4.46A, B: Cerebral tuberculoma with a paradoxical reaction in HIV. A 35-year-old South African female presented with symptoms of headache, fever, fitting, and left-leg weakness. The left-hand enhanced CT scan demonstrates that there is a right-sided lesion in the motor cortex, with surrounding oedema and sulcal effacement. She was treated for 8 weeks with antituberculous chemotherapy and steroids and recovered well. ARV therapy was then commenced and then she re-presented 4 weeks later with worsening symptoms of right hemiplegia due to immune reconstitution disease. The right-hand repeat CT head with contrast shows that although the oedema is much the same the intensity of enhancement of the tuberculoma is increased, suggesting more intra-lesional inflammation.

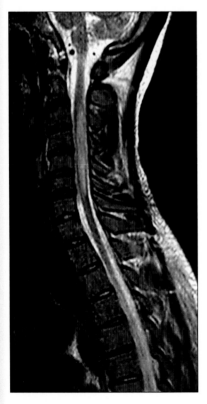

4.47 Diffuse hyperintensity signal representing central cord oedema and swelling in the cervical region of a 28-year-old female presenting with a transverse myelitis.

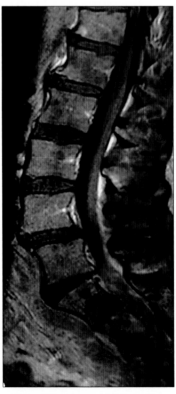

4.48 MRI of the lumbar-sacral spine of a white male who had been HIV positive for 25 years and had an undetectable viral load and CD4 count of 454 cells/mm^3. He gave a 6-month history of difficulty when walking that was initially diagnosed as sciatica. The scan demonstrates the lower lumbar spine and sacrum are encased by abnormal soft tissue that extends through the bone and into the spinal canal. At operation a tumour was seen encapsulating the conus. Histology of this lesion showed a diffuse large B-cell lymphoma.

Peripheral neuropathy

Peripheral nerve disease as a direct result of HIV infection can occur in up to one-third of patients and tends to present as symmetrical distal polyneuropathy. Commonest symptoms are of a painful burning sensation and numbness in the feet which progresses proximally over time. Examination generally reveals absent ankle reflexes and reduced fine touch and vibration sense. Other viral causes of peripheral neuropathy include herpes viruses, principally CMV, which can be associated with a mononeuritis multiplex picture. ARV drug toxicity, most commonly associated with DDI, AZT, and D4T, is an important cause of peripheral neuropathy. Other causes such as non-ARV drugs e.g. dapsone or isoniazid, as well as concomitant alcohol use or vitamin deficiencies (B12) should also be considered.

References

1 Mandell GL, Douglas RG, Bennett JE, Dolin R. *Mandell, Douglas, and Bennett's Principles and Practice of Infectious Diseases.* 2005. New York: Elsevier/Churchill Livingstone.

2 Hickey WF. Basic principles of immunological surveillance of the normal central nervous system. *Glia* 2001;**36**:118–24.

3 Abbott NJ, Ronnback L, Hansson E. Astrocyte–endothelial interactions at the blood–brain barrier. *Nat Rev Neurosci* 2006;**7**:41–53.

4 Langford TD, Letendre SL, Larrea GJ, Masliah E. Changing patterns in the neuropathogenesis of HIV during the HAART era. *Brain Pathol* 2003;**13**:195–210.

5 Zhang K, McQuibban GA, Silva C, *et al.* HIV-induced metalloproteinase processing of the chemokine stromal cell derived factor-1 causes neurodegeneration. *Nat Neurosci* 2003 **6**:1064–71.

6 Thwaites GE, Duc Bang N, Huy Dung N, *et al.* The Influence of HIV infection on clinical presentation, response to treatment, and outcome in adults with tuberculous meningitis. *J Infect Dis* 2005;**192**:2134–41.

7 van der Horst CM, Saag MS, Cloud GA, *et al.* Treatment of cryptococcal meningitis associated with the acquired immunodeficiency syndrome. National Institute of Allergy and Infectious Diseases Mycoses Study Group and AIDS Clinical Trials Group. *N Engl J Med* 1997;**337**:15–21.

8 Makadzange A, Ndhlovu C, Takarinda K, *et al. Early vs Delayed ART in the Treatment of Cryptococcal Meningitis in Africa. Abstract 36c Late Breaker.* Conference for Retrovirology and Opportunistic Infections. 2009; Montreal, Canada.

9 Scarborough M, Gordon SB, Whitty CJ, *et al.* Corticosteroids for bacterial meningitis in adults in sub-Saharan Africa. *N Engl J Med* 2007;**357**:2441–50.

10 Colombo FA, Vidal JE, Penalva de Oliveira AC, *et al.* Diagnosis of cerebral toxoplasmosis in AIDS patients in Brazil: importance of molecular and immunological methods using peripheral blood samples. *J Clin Microbiol* 2005;**43**:5044–7.

11 Gazzard BG. British HIV Association Guidelines for the treatment of HIV-1-infected adults with antiretroviral therapy 2008. *HIV Med* 2008;**9**:563–608.

12 Letendre SL, Ellis RJ, Everall I, *et al.* Neurologic complications of HIV disease and their treatment. *Top HIV Med* 2009;**17**(2):46–56.

13 Antinori A, Arendt G, Becker JT, *et al.* Updated research nosology for HIV-associated neurocognitive disorders. *Neurology* 2007;**69**(18):1789–99.

14 Skinner S, Adewale AJ, DeBlock L, *et al.* Neurocognitive screening tools in HIV/AIDS: comparative performance among patients exposed to antiretroviral therapy. *HIV Med* 2009;**10**(4):246–52.

15 R Heaton, D Franklin, D Clifford *et al.* HIV-associated Neurocognitive Impairment Remains Prevalent in the Era of Combination ART: The CHARTER Study. Abstract 154, 16th *CROI* 2009.

16 Bhaskaran K, Mussini C, Antinori A, *et al*; CASCADE Collaboration. Changes in the incidence and predictors of human immunodeficiency virus associated dementia in the era of highly active antiretroviral therapy. *Ann Neurol* 2008;**63**(2):213–21.

17 Marra CM, Zhao Y, Clifford DB, *et al.* Impact of combination antiretroviral therapy on cerebrospinal fluid HIV RNA and neurocognitive performance. *AIDS* 2009;**23**:1359–66.

18 Letendre S, *et al. CROI* 2010;poster *430.*

19 Torok ME, Kambugu A, Wright E. Immune reconstitution disease of the central nervous system. *Curr Opin HIV AIDS* 2008;**3**:438–45.

20 Zolopa A, Andersen J, Powderly W, *et al.* Early antiretroviral therapy reduces AIDS progression/death in individuals with acute opportunistic infections: a multi-center randomized strategy trial. *PLoS ONE* 2009;**4**: e5575.

21 Bicanic T, Meintjes G, Rebe K, *et al.* Immune reconstitution inflammatory syndrome in HIV-associated cryptococcal meningitis: a prospective study. *J Acquir Immune Defic Syndr* 2009;**51**:130–4.

Metabolic complications

D Nair and AJ Rodger

Epidemiology

The use of highly active antiretroviral therapy (HAART) has resulted in unquestionable reductions in HIV-related morbidity and mortality. However, as HIV-infected individuals live longer, it has become apparent that both HAART as well as HIV infection itself are associated with metabolic syndromes. Since the advent of HAART in 1995, there have been significant increases in metabolic disease in HIV-infected individuals (**4.49**)[1].

Cardiovascular risk factors in patients with HIV infection

The 'DAD (Data Collection on Adverse Events of Anti-HIV Drugs) Study' is a large, prospective observational study on a cohort of HIV-infected patients that showed that combination antiretroviral treatment (ART) was associated with a 26% increased incidence of AMI per year of exposure. The prevalence of cardiovascular risk factors in this cohort at baseline is shown in Figure **4.50**.

Further analysis of this cohort revealed that cumulative exposure to protease inhibitors (PIs) (and *not* non-nucleoside reverse transcriptase inhibitors [NNRTIs]) was independently associated with an increased risk of AMI. Although lipid abnormalities are the most frequent treatment-associated adverse risk factors, the long-term clinico-pathological consequences of PI exposure remain speculative.

A recent subanalysis of this cohort has shown that recent (but not cumulative) exposure to both abacavir and didanosine is also associated with an increased risk of myocardial infarction in the absence of dslipidaemia or insulin resistance. The mechanisms underlying this observed association also remain speculative. It is worth noting that the prevalence of smoking in this cohort is higher than that in the general population.

HIV infection and HAART influence the modifiable primary cardiovascular risk factors in a number of ways.

Lipids

A proatherogenic lipid profile is not unusual in antiretroviral-naïve HIV-positive patients. Studies on antiretroviral-naïve HIV-infected individuals have shown that high-density lipoprotein cholesterol (HDL-c) and low-density lipoprotein cholesterol (LDL-c) drop significantly after HIV seroconversion. Hypertriglyceridaemia subsequently develops with more advanced disease. The prevalence of dyslipidaemia in patients receiving ART varies between 15% and 30%, with some studies reporting prevalence of up to 60%. The most common treatment-related abnormality is a high triglyceride (TG) level, most often associated with exposure to PIs.

Lipodystrophy (4.51)

The term lipodystrophy describes a syndrome which consists of:

- Fat redistribution (peripheral limb and facial lipoatrophy and central obesity).
- Abnormal lipid metabolism.
- Insulin resistance.

Diabetes mellitus (DM)

Impaired glucose tolerance (IGT) has been reported to occur as early as 2 weeks into starting ART[3]. In addition, up to 40% of those with lipoatrophy have IGT or frank DM. Speculative mechanisms for insulin resistance include interference with glucose receptors Glut-4 in adipocytes and muscle and Glut-2 in the pancreatic islet cells[4].

Hypertension

There are conflicting data on the prevalence of hypertension in patients treated with antiretroviral drugs. There is some evidence suggesting higher prevalence of hypertension in patients with antiretroviral drug-induced insulin resistance.

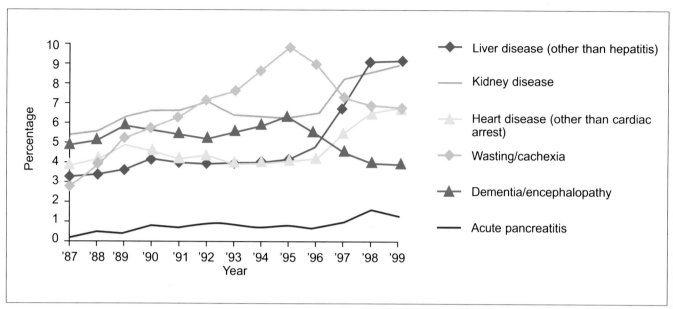

4.49 Non-HIV related complications in patients with HIV infection. (Adapted from Selik RM, *et al.*, 2002[1].)

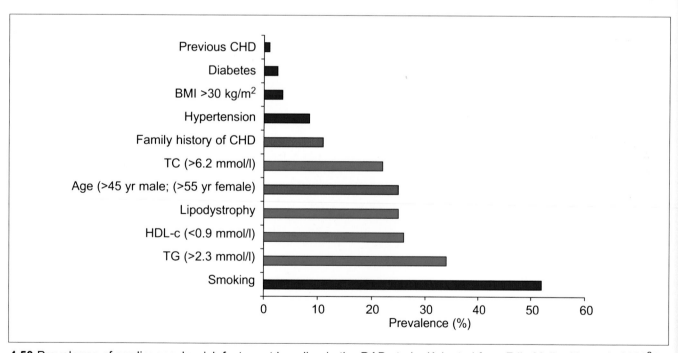

4.50 Prevalence of cardiovascular risk factors at baseline in the DAD study. (Adapted from Friis-Moller N, *et al.*, 2003[2].)

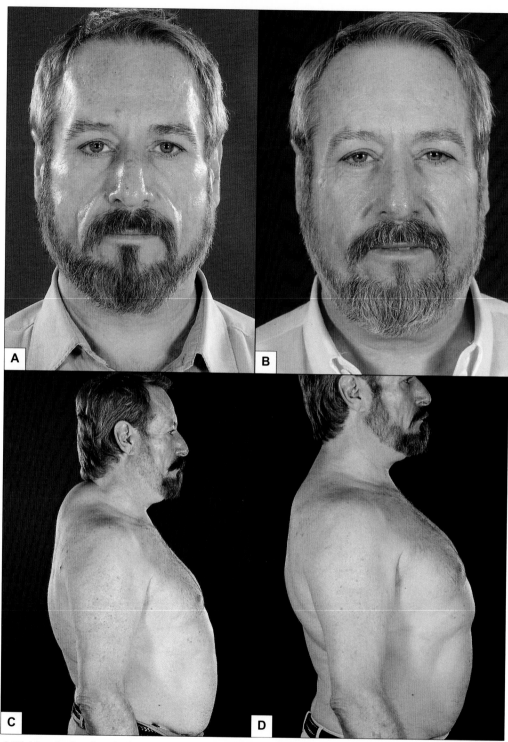

4.51 Lipodystrophy. **A**: Facial lipoatrophy (pre Nufill™); **B**: facial lipoatrophy (post Nufill™); **C**: buffalo hump and truncal obesity; **D**: post buffalo hump excision and abdominoplasty.

Screening for metabolic disease

A thorough assessment of cardiovascular risk factors is mandatory in this population. All subjects should have regular assessments of cardiovascular disease (CVD) risk. The European AIDS Clinical Society (EACS) Guidelines are presented in *Table 4.15*. In patients found to be dyslipidaemic, it is important to rule out secondary causes of abnormal lipid metabolism.

Table 4.15 EACS Guidelines for the screening of metabolic disease

	Assessment	*Frequency*
History	*Family history of:* • Premature IHD (in 1st degree relative) • Diabetes • Hypertension *Drug history:* • Concomitant therapy with: lipid-lowering therapy, antihypertensives, hypoglycaemics • Concomitant therapy with medication with risk of precipitating diabetes or dyslipidaemia *Lifestyle factors:* • Smoking, alcohol, exercise	• At HIV diagnosis • Before starting HAART • Annually
Lipids	• Fasting total cholesterol • Fasting TG • Fasting LDL-c and HDL-c	• At HIV diagnosis • Before starting HAART • Annually
Glucose	• Fasting glucose	• At HIV diagnosis • Before starting HAART • Annually
Body composition	• BMI • Waist circumference • Waist-to-hip ratio • Clinical lypodystrophy assessment	• At HIV diagnosis • Before starting HAART • Annually
Hypertension	• Blood pressure	• At HIV diagnosis • Before starting HAART • Annually
Cardiovascular disease	• Risk assessment • ECG	• Before starting HAART • Annually

Management of dyslipidaemia

The EACS Guidelines suggest that if lifestyle interventions (*Table 4.16*) and possible changes in ART to less lipogenic agents do not reduce LDL to below the target level (<4 mmol/l), then use of lipid-lowering medication should be considered. The EACS Guidelines for use of lipid-lowering medication are summarized in *Table 4.17*.

Table 4.16 Lifestyle interventions (adapted from EACS Guidelines)

Smoking

- Encourage patients to stop smoking with discussion of short- and long-term health benefits
- Consider referral to specialist Stop Smoking Centres and use of nicotine replacement therapies (patch, chewing gum, spray), varenicline, or bupropion (NB: bupropion may interact with PI and NNRTI)
- Explain that relapses are common before final discontinuation of smoking

Diet

- Limit intake of saturated fat and cholesterol
- Reduce total fat intake to <30% and dietary cholesterol to <300 mg/day
- Emphasize intake of vegetables, fruits, grain products with fibre
- Emphasize consumption of fish, poultry (without skin), and lean meat
- Consider referral to dietitian, keep a 1 week food and drink diary to assess calorific and fat intake
- Patients with BMI >30 kg/m² should be advised to lose weight. (NB: normal BMI range: 18.5–24.9; overweight: 25.0–29.9; obesity: >30.0 kg/m²)
- Starvation diets are not recommended in an HIV-positive person

Exercise

- Promote an active lifestyle with an emphasis on regular moderate intensity exercise rather than vigorous exercise
- Achieve cardiovascular fitness (e.g. 30 minutes brisk walking 5/7 days a week)

Table 4.17 EACS Guidelines for treatment of dyslipidaemia in HIV-infected patients

Type of dyslipidaemia	First choice	Combination therapy
Isolated hypercholesterolaemia (LDL-c >4 mmol/l)	Statin	+ Ezetimibe
Combined hyperlipidaemia (LDL-c >4 mmol/l) and TG 5–10 mmol/l	Statin	+ Fibrate (/nicotinic acid derivative)
Isolated hypertriglyceridaemia (TG 2.3–10 mmol/l)	Diet, alcohol abstinence	–
Severe hypertriglyceridaemia (>10 mmol/l)	Fibrate	+ Omega 3 acid ester (/nicotinic acid derivative)

Statins: drugs of choice

- Total cholesterol <6 mmol/l, pravastatin 20–40 mg/day; use as first-line treatment.
- Total cholesterol >6 mmol/l, atorvastatin 10–20 mg/day; use as first-line treatment. Avoid using any dose of simvastatin or atorvastatin higher than 20 mg dose.
- High-risk patients, rosuvastatin 5 mg or 10 mg may be used.
- If patient tolerates the above dose of statin but is still not to target, add ezetimibe.

Drug interactions and management of dyslipidaemia

As lipid-lowering and antiretroviral therapy are metabolized by common cytochrome P450 enzymes, there is an increased risk of adverse events or suboptimal drug levels when these compounds are co-administered. PIs inhibit the metabolism of simvastatin, and co-administration is contraindicated as it can lead to severe rhabdomyolysis. Low-dose atorvastatin or pravastatin appears to be safe. The Liverpool HIV Pharmacology website provides comprehensive, up-to-date information on potential drug–drug interactions and advice on dosing adjustments: http://www.hiv-druginteractions.org/.

Management of hypertension

Lifestyle interventions

Advice on behavioural interventions should be given including the importance of smoking cessation, reducing or stopping alcohol intake, and improving diet with reduced intake of saturated fat and salt and increased intake of fresh fruit. Patients should be encouraged to increase aerobic exercise and patients with BMI >30 kg/m^2 should be motivated to lose weight. Normal BMI range is 18.5–24.9, overweight is 25.0–29.9, and obesity is >30.0 kg/m^2.

Drug treatment

A suggested algorithm from NICE for drug treatment for hypertensive patients is given in Figure **4.52**[5].

The suggested target for adequate blood pressure control is <140/90 mmHg and in patients who are diabetic or have renal or cardiovascular disease, a level of <130/80 mmHg should be achieved.

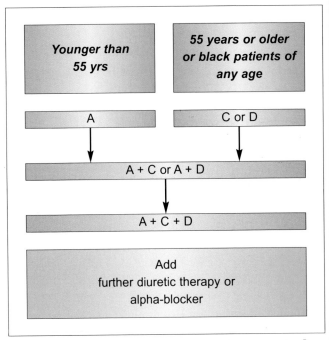

4.52 NICE algorithm for the treatment of hypertension[5]. A: ACE inhibitor (consider angiotensin-II receptor antagonist if ACE intolerant); C: calcium-channel blocker; D: thiazide-type diuretic. Note: black patients are those of African or Caribbean descent, and not mixed-race, Asian or Chinese patients.

Conclusion

Cardiac risk assessment is essential in patients with HIV infection on therapy regardless of the regimen. Use of ART is likely to change metabolic profiles (lipids and glucose) thus increasing the cardiac risk. However, the CVD risk *should not* influence timing of initiation of ART. If inflammation and atherosclerosis are related, then HIV is a risk factor and aggressive management is essential. Those with high risk for CVD should have aggressive intervention targeting risk factors.

References

1 Selik RM, Byers RH, Jr., Dworkin MS. Trends in diseases reported on U.S. death certificates that mentioned HIV infection, 1987–1999. *J Acquir Immune Defic Syndr* 2002 Apr 1;**29**(4):378–87.

2 Friis-Moller N, Sabin CA, Weber R, *et al.* Combination antiretroviral therapy and the risk of myocardial infarction. *N Engl J Med* 2003 Nov 20;**349**(21):1993–2003.

3 De WS, Sabin CA, Weber R, *et al.* Incidence and risk factors for new-onset diabetes in HIV-infected patients: the Data Collection on Adverse Events of Anti-HIV Drugs (D:A:D) study. *Diabetes Care* 2008 Jun;**31**(6):1224–9.

4 Murata H, Hruz PW, Mueckler M. The mechanism of insulin resistance caused by HIV protease inhibitor therapy. *J Biol Chem* 2000 Jul 7;**275**(27):20251–4.

5 National Institute for Health and Clinical Excellence. NICE Clinical Guideline 34, 2006. Hypertension: management of hypertension in adults in primary care (partial update of NICE Clinical Guideline 18). Available at http://www.nice.org.uk/nicemedia/pdf/CG034NICEguideline.doc

Further reading

Lundgren JD, *et al.* European AIDS Clinical Society (EACS) guidelines on the prevention and management of metabolic diseases in HIV. *HIV Med* 2008;**9**(2):72–81.

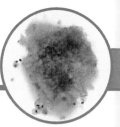
HIV and opportunistic infections

AJ Rodger, TW Mahungu, M Lipman and N Marshall

Introduction

In the post highly active antiretroviral therapy (HAART) era many opportunistic infections (OIs) such as cytomegalovirus (CMV) retinitis have become rare in countries such as the UK with access to antiretroviral drugs (ARVs). In these settings OIs are mainly seen in those unaware of their HIV infection status. In the UK 25% of patients presenting with acquired immunodeficiency syndrome (AIDS) were unaware of their HIV infection[1]. Diagnosis of OIs can be guided by the immune status of the individual (*Table 5.1*).

Pneumocystis jirovecii pneumonia (PCP)

Aetiology

PCP is still one of the commonest OIs and is caused by *Pneumocystis jirovecii*; it tends to occur at CD4 count of <200/mm³. It was originally thought to be protozoan, but is now classed as a yeast. PCP is almost completely preventable using prophylaxis (see *Table 5.3*) and tends to occur in those unaware of their diagnosis or those who do not comply with prophylaxis.

Clinical presentation

PCP usually presents over weeks or months with dry cough, night sweats, progressive dyspnoea, and weight loss. Clinical examination is often unremarkable although oral thrush may be present. Reduction in oxygen saturations on exercise is suspicious of PCP. Chest X-ray demonstrates ground-glass shadowing and perihilar interstitial infiltrates initially in the middle and lower zones (**5.1, 5.2**). Upper lobe involvement can be seen in patients who have been on pentamidine prophylaxis who may also demonstrate extrapulmonary involvement. Poor prognostic features are hypoxia, elevated lactic dehydrogenase (LDH) and presence of neutrophils on bronchoalveolar lavage (BAL) obtained at bronchoscopy.

Table 5.1 Common CD4 ranges at which certain OIs occur

CD4 range	Opportunistic disease
Any	Tuberculosis, Kaposi's sarcoma, HZV, lymphoma, bacterial pneumonia
<250 cells/mm³	PCP, oesophageal candidiasis, PML, HSV
<100 cells/mm³	Cerebral toxoplasmosis, HIV encephalopathy, cryptococcosis, miliary TB
<50 cells/mm³	CMV retinitis, atypical mycobacteria

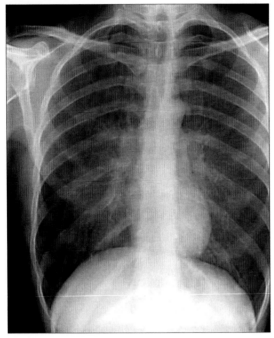 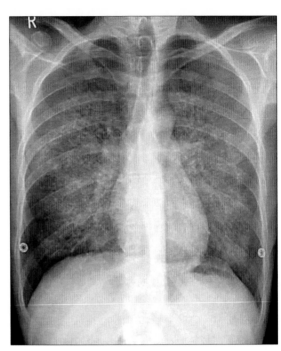

5.1, 5.2 PCP pneumocystis pneumonia with progression on serial chest X-rays.

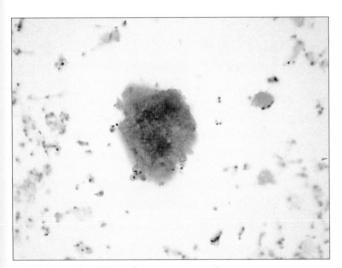 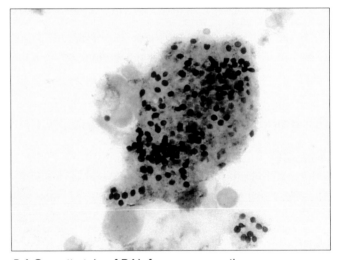

5.3 PAP stain of BAL for pneumocystis.

5.4 Grocott stain of BAL for pneumocystis.

Diagnosis

Diagnosis is by BAL. BAL can still lead to positive results even after up to 5 days of treatment so it is not essential to wait for the BAL prior to commencing treatment. Different stains (Papanicolaou [PAP], Grocott, Toluidine blue, Giemsa) are performed on smears of respiratory samples or tissues to demonstrate PCP cysts (**5.3**, **5.4**). Flourescent stains also have good sensitivity.

Treatment

Treatment should be instituted immediately on clinical suspicion of PCP. Mainstay of treatment is high-dose co-trimoxazole plus steroids in severe disease with pO_2 <9.3 kPa (*Table 5.2*). Patients may deteriorate even after treatment is started and may require respiratory support using continuous positive airway pressure (CPAP) or invasive ventilation. Pneumatocoeles and cysts may develop (**5.5**) leading to spontaneous pneumothorax, which should be considered in any patient who deteriorates acutely. Prophylaxis regimens for PCP are presented in *Table 5.3*.

Table 5.2 Treatment of *Pneumocyctis jirovecii* pneumonia

	Treatment	Comments
First line	*Co-trimoxazole* • 120 mg/kg in 3–4 divided doses for 21 days as follows: • 40 mg/kg IV tds till clinical improvement, then switch to PO (renal adjustment needed if GFR <30 ml/min) *Calculation of oral dose:* • (120 × wt)/960 = number septrin 960 mg tablets per day. Divide number of tablets to three divided doses	*Use of corticosteroids:* If arterial PaO_2 <9.3 kPa on room air or oxygen use: • Prednisolone 40 mg PO bd 3–5 days then taper over 7–10 days, OR • Hydrocortisone 100 mg IV tds, then switch to oral prednisolone *Side-effects:* • Septrin: GI disturbances – nausea, rash, myelosuppression, hepatotoxicity, haemolytic anaemia (G6PD deficiency), renal impairment, hypoglycaemia
Second line: mild to moderate	• Clindamycin 600 mg IV/PO qds + primaquine 30 mg PO od for 21 days (preferred), OR • Dapsone 100 mg PO od + trimethoprim 20 mg/kg/day, OR • Atovaquone 750 mg (5 ml) PO bd with food	• Clindamycin: GI disturbances (*C. difficile*), diarrhoea, hepatotoxicity • Primaquine: nausea, vomiting, bone marrow suppression, haemolytic anaemia (G6PD deficiency), methaemoglobinaemia
Second line: severe	• Pentamidine 4 mg/kg IV od for 21 days Note: If switching from septrin due to suspected treatment failure, continue septrin for 3 days overlap	• Atovaquone: rash, neutropenia, hepatotoxicity

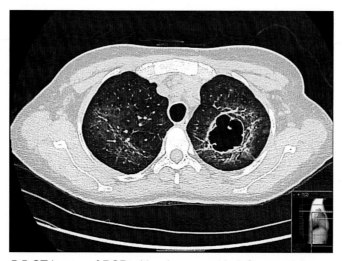

5.5 CT image of PCP with a large cyst in left upper lobe.

Table 5.3 Prophylaxis for *Pneumocyctis jirovecii* pneumonia

		Choice of therapy	*Comments*
Primary prevention	First line	• Co-trimoxazole 960 mg daily (alternatively 480 mg od, 960 mg three times a week) • Any patients with CDC IV symptoms or asymptomatic patients with CD4 counts persistently below 200 cell/mm^3	• Discontinue when CD4 >200 cells/mm^3 for at least 3 months + undetectable HIV load • Usual reasons for intolerance: bone marrow suppression, skin rash/fever, noncompliance, but consider desensitization if skin rash/fever
	Second line	• Nebulized pentamidine 300 mg monthly via modified Acorn nebulizer and compressor unless patient has a system at home and is proficient in its use OR • Dapsone 100 mg od orally	• Discontinue when CD4 >200 cells/mm^3 for at least 3 months + undetectable HIV load • For dapsone check G6PD status • If toxoplasmosis cover is required use dapsone 50–100 mg od plus pyrimethamine 50 mg once weekly (CD4 <100 cells/mm^3 and IgG positive for *Toxoplasma*)
Secondary prevention	First line	• Co-trimoxazole 960 mg daily (any patient with a prior episode of PCP)	• Discontinue when CD4 >200 cells/mm^3 for at least 6 months + undetectable HIV load • Usual reasons for intolerance: bone marrow suppression, skin rash/fever, noncompliance
	Second line	• Dapsone 100 mg od orally OR nebulized pentamidine 300 mg fortnightly as above	• Discontinue when CD4 >200 cells/mm^3 for at least 6 months • For dapsone check G6PD status • If toxoplasmosis cover required use dapsone 50–100 mg od + pyrimethamine 50 mg once weekly (CD4 <100 cells/mm^3 and IgG positive for *Toxoplasma*)

Candidiasis

Aetiology

Candida species are the most common cause of fungal infections in the immunocompromised patient. There are over 100 *Candida* species of which approximately 20 are pathogenic. The most common species is *C. albicans*. Other species include *C. glabrata*, *C. parapsilosis*, *C. tropicalis*, *C. krusei*, and *C. dubliniensis*.

Clinical presentation

Mucocutaneous

This is by far the most common presentation, occurring in up to 90% of individuals with untreated, advanced disease. Patients usually present with oropharyngeal thrush which is usually asymptomatic but may occasionally cause a burning sensation on the tongue as well as altered taste sensation. The white plaques are classically located on the buccal mucosa, throat, tongue, and gums (**5.6**). Individuals may also present with *atrophic candidiasis* where the only presenting feature is an erythematous mucosa, or *angular cheilitis*, which is characterized by erythema and fissuring of the corners of the mouth.

In more severe cases, infection with *Candida* results in oesophageal candidiasis. In most cases patients present with dysphagia, odynophagia, and retrosternal discomfort. Unlike oropharyngeal disease, oesophageal candidiasis is an AIDS-defining illness.

In women, vulvovaginal candidiasis is not uncommon. The incidence is comparable to that of HIV-negative women.

It must be remembered that in the immunocompetent host, diabetes mellitus, treatment with steroids and antibiotics, as well as alcohol excess may result in oropharyngeal or vulvovaginal thrush.

Disseminated

Invasive candidiasis is relatively uncommon (<1%) in HIV infection, even in advanced disease. Candidaemia is more likely to occur in patients with indwelling catheters, total parenteral nutrition, and additional immunosuppression from chemotherapy.

Diagnosis

The diagnosis of oropharyngeal candida is often made clinically due to its characteristic appearance. An upper gastrointestinal (GI) endoscopy can confirm oesophageal candidiasis as well as exclude other causes of oesophagitis (mainly CMV disease) in advanced HIV infection.

Treatment

There are a number of antifungal agents available for the treatment of candidiasis. Oropharyngeal and vulvovaginal

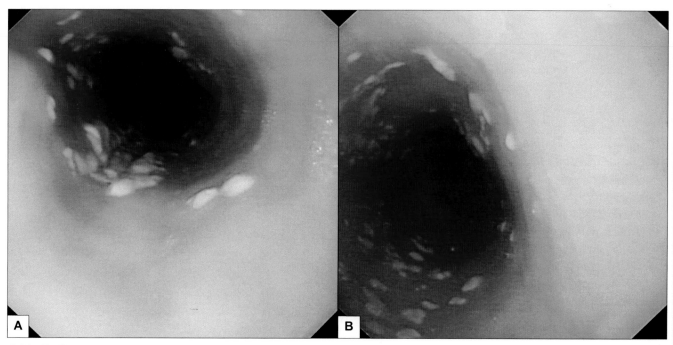

5.6A, B: Oesophageal candidiasis.

Table 5.4 Treatment of candidiasis

	Choice of therapy
First line	Oropharyngeal candidiasis: • Fluconazole 50–100mg PO od 7days, OR • Fluconazole 200 mg od 3 days Oesophageal candidiasis: • Fluconazole 150–200 mg od 14 days Vulvovaginal candidiasis: • Fluconazole 150 mg PO stat • Clotrimazole 1% topically for 3–7 days
Alternative	Oropharyngeal candidiasis: • Itraconazole liquid 200 mg od 7–14 days Oesophageal candidiasis: • Itraconazole 200 mg PO/IV od 14 days Uncomplicated vulvovaginal candidiasis: • Itraconazole liquid 200 mg PO od 3–7 days
Fluconazole-refractory disease	Oropharyngeal candidiasis: • Itraconazole liquid 200 mg bd 7–14 days Oesophageal candidiasis: • Liposomal amphotericin, e.g. Ambisome 3–5 mg/kg IV od, OR • Voriconazole 200 mg IV/PO bd (interactions possible)

Comments
• Chronic use of azoles may promote development of resistance
Interactions:
• Itraconazole: Levels are significantly reduced by NNRTIs/rifamycins and increased by ritonavir
• Fluconazole doubles levels of nevirapine
Topical antifungals:
• May be used in addition to systemic therapy, but may be of limited benefit if used alone

candidiasis can be adequately treated with topical preparations while oesophageal candidiasis requires systemic treatment. Patients on prolonged courses of the azoles should have their liver function monitored regularly (*Table 5.4*).

Prophylaxis

The benefits of antifungal prophylaxis are yet to be demonstrated. The reversal of colonization through the restoration of immune function with the use of HAART appears to be the most effective measure.

Mycobacterium tuberculosis

Worldwide, the HIV pandemic has been associated with an unprecedented re-emergence of tuberculosis (TB) (**5.7, 5.8**)[1]. According to the World Health Organization (WHO), of the 33 million individuals living with HIV worldwide, at least one-third are believed to be infected with MTB. Sub-Saharan Africa bears the brunt of this co-epidemic where it is the leading cause of death in HIV-infected patients[2]. There are however, worrying trends in eastern Europe and Asia.

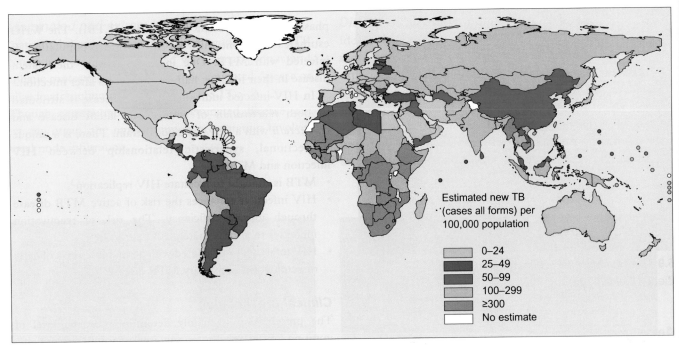

5.7 Estimated TB incidence rates by country 2009. (Adapted from WHO data.)

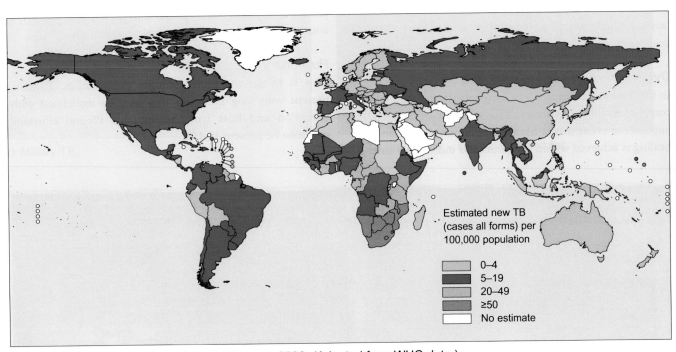

5.8 Estimated HIV prevalence in new TB cases 2009. (Adapted from WHO data.)

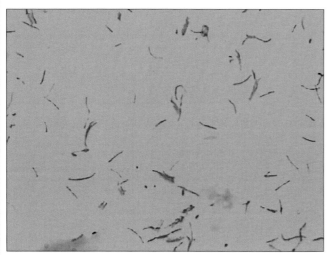

5.9 Acid-fast *Mycobacterium tuberculosis* in Ziehl–Neelsen stain.

Aetiology

Mycobacterium tuberculosis (MTB) belongs to the *Mycobacterium tuberculosis* complex group, which also includes *M. bovis and M. africanum*. MTB is an intracellular aerobic bacillus. *Mycobacteria* are classified as 'acid-fast' as they retain staining dyes in the presence of acid (**5.9**).

Dynamics of HIV/TB co-infection

In the immunocompetent host, aerosol infection with MTB complex results in *primary* TB, an often asymptomatic pneumonic event that is usually self-limiting. Spontaneous healing is achieved within 6 months and individuals enter a phase of clinically latent TB infection (LTBI). The WHO estimates that one-third of the world's population is infected with MTB. One in ten reactivate their latent disease in their lifetime: half within 2 years after infection.

In HIV-infected individuals, active disease is attributed to both *reactivation* of endogenous latent disease and *reinfection* with a new exogenous strain. There is a unique bidirectional, synergistic relationship between HIV infection and MTB:

- MTB is thought to facilitate HIV replication[3].
- HIV infection enhances the risk of active MTB disease through immunodeficiency. The risk of reactivation increases to approximately 10% per year.
- HIV infection is associated with an increased risk of early dissemination in primary MTB disease.

Clinical presentation

The presentation is mainly determined by the level of immunodeficiency[4]. Profoundly immune-deficient patients often have atypical presentations with systemic symptoms, extrapulmonary disease, and immune reconstitution inflammatory syndrome (IRIS) when exposed to anti-retroviral therapy, while those with well preserved CD4 counts tend to have a fairly typical presentation.

Pulmonary disease

This is by far the most common presentation. Patients present with lung infiltrates that may be associated with cavitation and hilar lymphadenopathy. Pleural effusions may also be present (**5.10**).

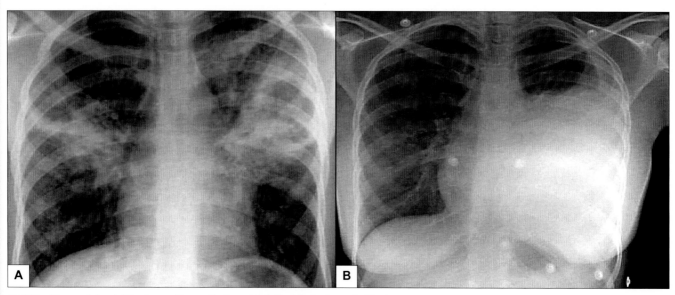

A   B

5.10A: Upper lobe infiltrates with cavitation; **B:** left-sided pleural effusion.

Disseminated and extrapulmonary disease

As patients become progressively immunodeficient, MTB infection is more likely to spread via haematogenous and lymphatic routes resulting in either disseminated disease or localized extrapulmonary disease (**5.11–5.13**).

Though extrapulmonary or disseminated disease can affect any organ, the most common presentation involves cervical node infiltration.

Diagnosis of active pulmonary disease

Ideally three sputum samples obtained on consecutive days should be examined (*Table 5.5*). In patients unable to expectorate, sputum induction with inhaled nebulized hypertonic saline or BAL is often useful. Studies have shown that sputum induction in experienced hands is as sensitive as BAL in terms of diagnostic yield[5]. However, bronchoscopy should be performed if other pulmonary diseases need to be excluded and a tissue biopsy is required.

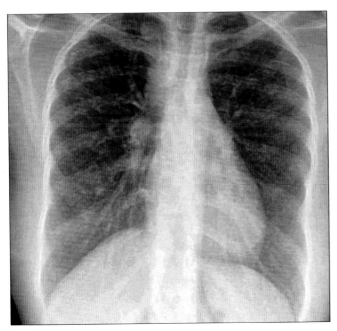

5.11 Miliary TB.

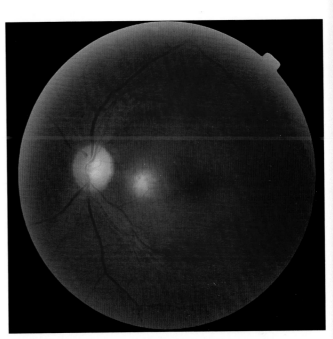

5.12 TB granuloma – choroidal tubercules.

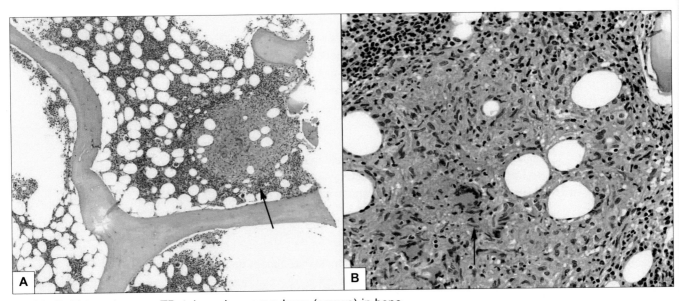

5.13A, B: Extrapulmonary TB: tuberculous granuloma (arrows) in bone.

Table 5.5 Diagnosis of active TB infection

Method	Comments
Sputum smear microscopy	*Advantages* • Rapid diagnostic test • Cheap • Does not require sophisticated laboratory equipment *Disadvantages* • Does NOT distinguish between mycobacteria species or live and dead bacilli • Requires 10,000 bacteria per ml • Sensitivity ranges between 31 and 80% in HIV infection[6] NB: Smear-negative pulmonary TB accounts for 24–61% of TB in patients with HIV infection[7]
Sputum culture	*Advantages* • More sensitive than sputum smear microscopy • Requires >10 bacteria per ml • Allows species identification • Allows drug-susceptibility testing • Inexpensive *Disadvantages* • Slow – can take 6 weeks or longer (liquid culture is much faster) • Laboratory cross-contamination
Chest X-ray	*Advantages* • Rapid • Cheap • Good for monitoring established disease *Disadvantages* • Atypical presentations in individuals with advanced HIV[8] • Interpretation of film highly dependent on quality of film • Interpretation of film prone to inter-individual variability • Hence sensitivity and specificity poor
TB nucleic acid probes (MTB PCR)	*Advantages* • Rapid • More sensitive and specific than acid-fast staining • Can differentiate between mycobacteria species • Can incorporate genotypic drug resistance assays for e.g. isoniazid and rifampicin *Disadvantages* • Expensive • Decreased sensitivity if sputum samples are smear negative • Not validated for nonsputum samples

Diagnosis of extrapulmonary TB

It is essential that tissue and body fluid samples from suspected extrapulmonary disease are obtained and subjected to microscopy, culture, and histology/cytology. Extrapulmonary samples are often smear negative so the diagnosis is often as a result of a combination of suggestive history, imaging, and subsequent culture results.

Diagnosis of latent infection

The diagnosis of LTBI is especially important in HIV infection due to the significant increased risk of transformation of latent infection to active disease. The oldest diagnostic test is the tuberculin skin test (TST), which dates back to 1890 (*Table 5.6*)[9]. The purified protein derivative which contains antigens to *Mycobacterium tuberculosis* (as well as other mycobacteria species) is administered intra-dermally and read 48–72 hours later after the development of a delayed hypersensitivity reaction. The use of the TST is not recommended in HIV-positive patients due to the high rate of false-negative results in patients with low CD4 counts[11].

More recently, there have been exciting developments in the use of interferon gamma release assays (IGRA) for the diagnosis of LTBI[10]. These tests measure the antigen-specific cell-mediated immune response through the amount of interferon gamma released. At present, there are two licensed diagnostic tests:
- T-spot TB Test (ELISpot-based method)
- Quantiferon-TB Gold in-tube (ELISA-based method)

Treatment
British HIV Association (BHIVA) Guidelines[12]
Patients with uncomplicated active disease normally require treatment for 6 months.

The first 2 months of treatment is referred to as the *initiation phase*. Patients are initiated on a quadruple regimen consisting of rifampicin, isoniazid, pyrazinamide, and ethambutol once the diagnosis is confirmed. It is recommended that rifamycin-based regimens are used. Once drug sensitivity has been established, if MTB isolate is fully susceptible to first-line agents, ethambutol may be dropped from the regimen.

Table 5.6 Diagnosis of latent TB infection

Method	Comments
Tuberculin skin testing (purified protein derivative, PPD)	**Advantages** • Inexpensive **Disadvantages** • Poor follow-up (some patients do not return) • Subject to wide range of inter-individual variability in terms of administration of PPD and interpretation of results • Cannot distinguish between active and latent infection or previous BCG immunization • Does not distinguish between mycobacteria species • High rate of false-negative results in HIV disease due to anergy[11]
Interferon γ release assays (IGRA)	**Advantages** • Rapid; provide results within 24 hours • More specific than TST • Limited cross-reactivity with nontuberculous mycobacteria **Disadvantages** • Expensive • Cannot distinguish between latent infection and active disease • A blood test is required • Insufficient data on sensitivity and specificity in HIV infection

The next 4 months are referred to as the *continuation phase*. In uncomplicated disease patients remain on rifampicin and isoniazid for a further 4 months (*Table 5.7*).

At baseline *all* patients should have the following investigations:
- CD4 count (and percentage).
- Full blood count.
- Liver function tests (LFTs).
- Urea and electrolytes; estimated glomerular filtration rate (eGFR).
- Hepatitis B and C serology.
- Testing of visual acuity with Snellen charts and colour vision with Ishihara plates.

Once on treatment, patients should have their LFTs repeated at 1–2 weeks post treatment initiation. If underlying liver disease is present, LFTs should be regularly monitored throughout the initial phase of treatment.

Table 5.7 Adjuncts to TB treatment

Pyridoxine
- Should be administered daily while the patient is on isoniazid to prevent the development of peripheral neuropathy

Corticosteroids
BHIVA recommends the co-administration of corticosteroids for:
- TB meningitis
- Spinal cord TB
- Pericardial TB

Prolonged continuation phase (in drug sensitive disease)
BHIVA recommends 7 months in patients with:
- Sensitive isolates who did not receive pyrazinamide in the initial phase
- Cavitating disease who remain sputum culture positive after the initial phase

BHIVA recommends 7–10 months in:
- TB meningitis
- CNS tuberculoma

When to start HAART

This remains the subject of great debate. If an individual's CD4 count is above treatment indication levels, HAART can be deferred until completion of TB therapy. Challenges arise when an individual with confirmed/suspected TB has a CD4 count that is at a level that requires HAART. In this situation, there is a fine balance between HIV disease progression and the complications of co-administered antiretroviral and antituberculous medication, i.e. drug interactions, drug toxicity, and IRIS.

The SAPIT (**S**tarting **A**ntiretroviral therapy in three **P**oints **I**n **T**uberculosis therapy) trial was an open-label study conducted in South Africa[13] that sought to determine the optimum time for commencing antiretroviral therapy (ART) by randomizing patients with CD4 counts less than 500 cells/mm^3 to three study arms:
- Early integrated treatment: Patients started ART within first 2 months of TB treatment.
- Late integrated treatment: Patients started ART after first 2 months of TB treatment.
- Sequential treatment: Patients started ART after completing TB treatment (*Table 5.8*, **5.14**).

The sequential arm was discontinued 3 years into the trial when it became apparent that patients in this arm had a 55% higher mortality rate in comparison to the other two arms.

The results so far provide compelling evidence that the treatment of TB infection in the context of HIV should be integrated in patients with CD4 counts above and below 200 cells/mm^3 (*Table 5.9*). Based on preliminary results from the above trial, BHIVA now recommends that HAART should be started as soon as practical if the blood CD4 count is <100 cells/mm^3; though HAART can wait until continuation Px phase if the CD4 count is 100–350 cells/mm^3; >350 cells/mm^3, it is at the phsician's discretion.

What antiretroviral agents to use: British HIV Association

As both antituberculous and antiretroviral agents include potent inducers of the cytochrome P450 system, it is important that co-administered drugs are selected carefully (*Table 5.10*).

Therapeutic drug monitoring (TDM) of non-nucleoside reverse transcriptase inhibitors (NNRTIs) and protease inhibitors (PIs) is recommended in the context of complex regimens. The Liverpool HIV Pharmacology website provides comprehensive, up-to-date information on potential drug–drug interactions and advice regarding dosing adjustments:

http://www.hiv-druginteractions.org/

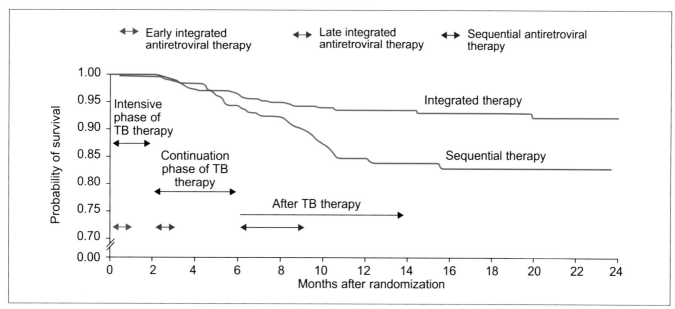

5.14 Timing of initiation of antiretroviral drugs during tuberculosis therapy. (Adapted from Karim SSA, et al., 2010[13].)

Table 5.8 Effect of timing of initiation of antiretroviral drugs during tuberculosis therapy (SAPIT)[13]

	Integrated therapy				Sequential therapy			
	No of patients	No of person-yr	No of deaths	Death rate/100 person-yr (95% CI)	No of patients	No of person-yr	No of deaths	Death rate/100 person-yr (95% CI)
All patients	429	467	25	5.4 (3.5–7.9)	213	223	27	12.1 (8.0–17.7)
≤200 cells/mm³	273	281	23	8.2 (5.2–12.3)	138	137	21	15.3 (9.6–23.5)
>200 cells/mm³	156	186	2	1.1 (0.1–3.9)	75	86	6	7.0 (2.6–15.3)

Table 5.9 BHIV recommendation: to start CART

Blood CD4 count (cells/mm³)	Recommendation
<100	As soon as practical after starting TB therapy
100–200	As soon as practical, but can wait until after 2 months' TB treatment (if drug interactions, adherence, or toxicity is a problem)
>200, <350	At physician's discretion; can wait until TB treatment complete

Table 5.10 Interactions between antiretroviral and antituberculous therapy

Drug	Co-administration with rifampicin	Co-administration with rifabutin
NRTI	No dose adjustment is required	No dose adjustment
NNRTI	*Efavirenz:* • Significant drop in efavirenz plasma concentrations which is determined by body weight and CYP2B6 genetic variation • Efavirenz may be prescribed at 800 mg od in individuals >50 kg • This should be guided by TDM to avoid the development of efavirenz toxicity *Nevirapine, etravirine, and rilpivirine:* • Rifampicin is generally not recommended	*Efavirenz:* • Rifabutin should be increased to 450 mg od *Etravirine:* • No dose adjustment *Rilpivirine:* • Rilpivirine dose should be doubled *Nevirapine:* • Generally not recommended
PI	• Not recommended	• Rifabutin 150 mg ×3/week with boosted PI • Rifabutin 150 mg od with unboosted PI
T20	• No dose adjustment	• No dose adjustment
Integrase	*Raltegravir:* • May need to increase raltegravir dose as drug exposure (area under curve) reduced by up to 40% *Elvitegravir:* • Do not use	• No data
CCR5	• Generally not recommended but if needed, double maraviroc dose	No dose adjustment required

Complications of treatment
Adverse events
The most common side-effects of first-line antituberculous therapy are shown in *Table 5.11*.

Patients on concurrent antiretroviral and antituberculous medication experience a higher frequency of severe (grade III or IV) adverse events during TB treatment in comparison to HIV-negative individuals. However, the discontinutation rates of antituberculous medication in both groups as a result of these adverse events is not thought to be that dissimilar[14].

Immune reconstitution inflammatory syndrome (IRIS)
Following the initiation of anti-TB therapy, both HIV-negative and HIV-positive individuals may experience paradoxical clinical or radiographical worsening of disease. HIV-positive patients are at an increased risk of developing these paradoxical reactions. A clinical working definition has been described[15] though there is no laboratory test to confirm this. Hence in practice it is often a diagnosis of exclusion. It is important that treatment failure (including drug resistance), re-infection and co-infection with another opportunistic disease are excluded. The most common presentations are fever and worsening or new lymphadenopathy[16] (**5.15**).

Drug resistance
Individuals with drug-resistant isolates acquire these strains from infected patients or from the evolution of endogenous strains during suboptimal therapy or periods of poor

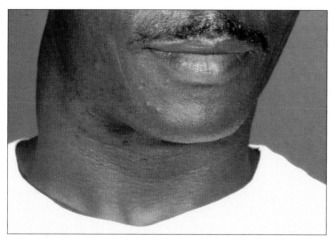

5.15 New lymphadenopathy following initiation of anti-TB therapy.

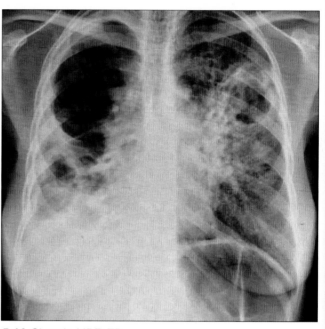

5.16 Chronic MDR TB.

Table 5.11 Side-effects of first-line antituberculous therapy

Isoniazid
- Peripheral neuropathy
- Hepatotoxicity
- CNS disturbance

Rifampicin
- Hepatotoxicity
- Gasrointestinal disturbance
- Thrombocytopenia
- Discoloration of body fluids orange/brown

Rifabutin
- Hepatotoxicity
- Gastrointestinal disturbance
- Thrombocytopenia
- Discoloration of body fluids orange/brown

Pyrazinamide
- Hepatotoxicity
- Hyperuricaemia
- Gastrointestinal disturbance
- Rash

Ethambutol
- Optic neuritis
- Hyperuricaemia

adherence. Resistance to isoniazid is predominantly through mutations in the *katG* and *inhA* genes[17] while resistance to rifampicin is through mutations in the *rpoB* gene[18].

Multidrug-resistant TB (MDR TB) is defined as resistance to at least isoniazid and rifampicin (**5.16**). In 2008, the WHO estimated that there were approximately half a million cases of MDR TB worldwide. Figure **5.17** illustrates the geographical distribution of MDR TB between 1994 and 2009.

The WHO recently endorsed a novel, automated (nucleic acid amplification test), rapid test for *M. tuberculosis* and rifampicin resistance – *Xpert MTB/Rif* [19]. It is hoped that even in resource poor environments its use will significantly facilitate the early diagnosis of MTB, the diagnosis of MDR TB, and diagnosis of TB in HIV-infected individuals.

Extensively drug-resistant TB (XDR TB) is defined by the WHO as resistance to:

isoniazid and rifampicin +

any fluouroquinolone +

at least one of the three injectable drugs used in second-line therapy (i.e. capreomycin, kanamycin, and amikacin).

It has not been possible to estimate the number of patients harbouring XDR TB isolates worldwide. However, by March 2010, 58 countries (in three distinct geographical regions) had reported at least one case (**5.18**).

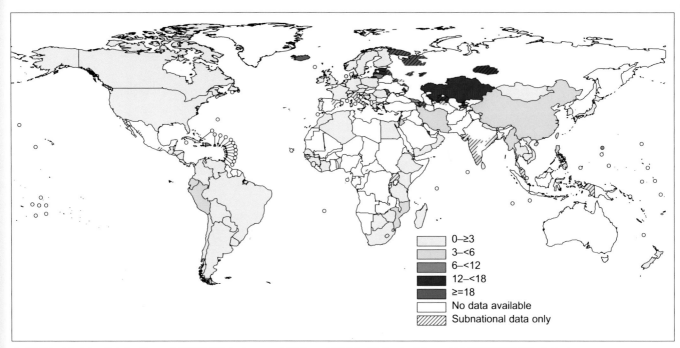

5.17 Worldwide distribution of MDR TB between 1994 and 2009. (Adapted from WHO/STOP TB data.)

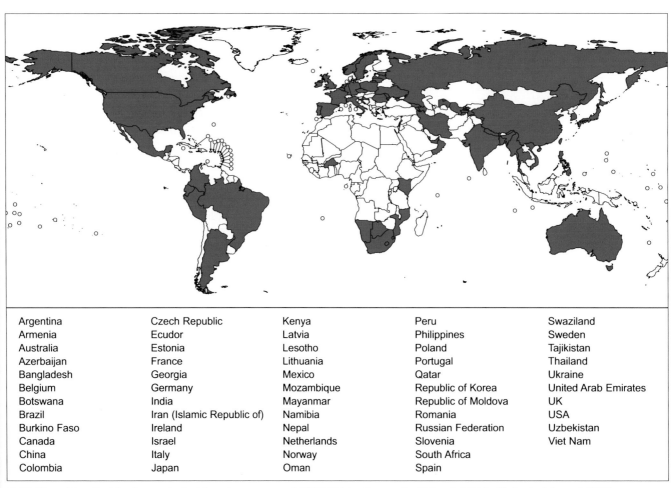

Argentina	Czech Republic	Kenya	Peru	Swaziland
Armenia	Ecudor	Latvia	Philippines	Sweden
Australia	Estonia	Lesotho	Poland	Tajikistan
Azerbaijan	France	Lithuania	Portugal	Thailand
Bangladesh	Georgia	Mexico	Qatar	Ukraine
Belgium	Germany	Mozambique	Republic of Korea	United Arab Emirates
Botswana	India	Mayanmar	Republic of Moldova	UK
Brazil	Iran (Islamic Republic of)	Namibia	Romania	USA
Burkino Faso	Ireland	Nepal	Russian Federation	Uzbekistan
Canada	Israel	Netherlands	Slovenia	Viet Nam
China	Italy	Norway	South Africa	
Colombia	Japan	Oman	Spain	

5.18 Countries that had reported at least one case of XDR TB by the end of March 2010. (Adapted from STOP TB/WHO data.)

Table 5.12 Risk of developing active TB from LTBI[19]

Risk factor		Estimated risk of active TB
High	AIDS	110–170
	HIV infection	50–110
	Transplantation	20–74
	Silicosis	30
	Chronic renal failure on haemodialysis	10–25
	Carcinoma (head and neck)	16
	TB infection within past 2 years	15
	Abnormal CXR	6–19
Increased	Glucocorticosteroids	4.9
	TNF-α inhibitors	1.5–4
	Diabetes	2.0–3.6
	BMI ≤20	2–3
	0–4 years of age	2.2–5
	Smoker	2–3
Low	Infected person, no known risk factor, normal CXR	1

Treatment of latent TB infection (LTBI)

LTBI is defined as evidence of exposure to MTB (a positive TST or IGRA) in the absence of active clinical or radiological disease. Active and subclinical TB should be excluded before this diagnosis is made. The risk of developing active TB from LTBI in HIV infection in comparison to other immunosuppressive illnesses or interventions is illustrated in *Table 5.12*[20].

BHIVA does NOT recommend routine chemo-prophylaxis for all HIV-positive patients. However, if patients have a positive TST or IGRA, chemoprophylaxis MAY be considered. The following regimens are recommended:

- A 6 month course of isoniazid.
  Or:
- Dual therapy with isoniazid and rifampicin for 3 months.

References

1 Zumla A, Malon P, Henderson J, Grange JM. Impact of HIV infection on tuberculosis. *Postgrad Med J* 2000;**76**(895):259–68.

2 Harries AD, Hargreaves NJ, Kemp J, et al. Deaths from tuberculosis in sub-Saharan African countries with a high prevalence of HIV-1. *Lancet* 2001;**357**(9267):1519–23.

3 Collins KR, Quinones-Mateu ME, Toossi Z, Arts EJ. Impact of tuberculosis on HIV-1 replication, diversity, and disease progression. *AIDS Rev* 2002;**4**(3):165–76.

4 Jones BE, Young SM, Antoniskis D, et al. Relationship of the manifestations of tuberculosis to CD4 cell counts in patients with human immunodeficiency virus infection. *Am Rev Respir Dis* 1993;**148**(5):1292–7.

5 Brown M, Varia H, Bassett P, et al. Prospective study of sputum induction, gastric washing, and bronchoalveolar lavage for the diagnosis of pulmonary tuberculosis in patients who are unable to expectorate. *Clin Infect Dis* 2007;**44**(11):1415–20.

6 Steingart KR, Ng V, Henry M, et al. Sputum processing methods to improve the sensitivity of smear microscopy for tuberculosis: a systematic review. *Lancet Infect Dis* 2006;**6**(10):664–74.

7 Getahun H, Harrington M, O'Brien R, Nunn P. Diagnosis of smear-negative pulmonary tuberculosis in people with HIV infection or AIDS in resource-constrained settings: informing urgent policy changes. *Lancet* 2007;**369**(9578):2042–9.

8 Perlman DC, el-Sadr WM, Nelson ET, *et al*. Variation of chest radiographic patterns in pulmonary tuberculosis by degree of human immunodeficiency virus-related immunosuppression. The Terry Beirn Community Programs for Clinical Research on AIDS (CPCRA). The AIDS Clinical Trials Group (ACTG). *Clin Infect Dis* 1997;**25**(2):242–6.

9 Huebner RE, Schein MF, Bass JB, Jr. The tuberculin skin test. *Clin Infect Dis* 1993;**17**(6):968–75.

10 Pai M, Riley LW, Colford JM, Jr. Interferon-gamma assays in the immunodiagnosis of tuberculosis: a systematic review. *Lancet Infect Dis* 2004;**4**(12):761–76.

11 Huebner RE, Schein MF, Hall CA, Barnes SA. Delayed-type hypersensitivity anergy in human immunodeficiency virus-infected persons screened for infection with *Mycobacterium tuberculosis*. *Clin Infect Dis* 1994;**19**(1):26–32.

12 British HIV Association guidelines for the treatment of TB/HIV co-infection 2009.

13 Karim SSA, *et al*. Timing of initiation of antiretroviral drugs during tuberculosis therapy. *N Engl J Med* 2010;**362**:697–705.

14 Breen RA, Miller RF, Gorsuch T, *et al*. Adverse events and treatment interruption in tuberculosis patients with and without HIV co-infection. *Thorax* 2006;**61**(9):791–4.

15 Meintjes G, Lawn SD, Scano F, *et al*. Tuberculosis-associated immune reconstitution inflammatory syndrome: case definitions for use in resource-limited settings. *Lancet Infect Dis* 2008;**8**(8):516–23.

16 Breen RA, Smith CJ, Bettinson H, Dart S, Bannister B, Johnson MA, *et al*. Paradoxical reactions during tuberculosis treatment in patients with and without HIV co-infection. *Thorax* 2004;**59**(8):704–7.

17 Hazbon MH, Brimacombe M, Bobadilla de Valle M, *et al*. Population genetics study of isoniazid resistance mutations and evolution of multidrug-resistant *Mycobacterium tuberculosis*. *Antimicrob Agents Chemother* 2006;**50**(8):2640–9.

18 Prammananan T, Cheunoy W, Taechamahapun D, *et al*. Distribution of rpoB mutations among multidrug-resistant *Mycobacterium tuberculosis* (MDRTB) strains from Thailand and development of a rapid method for mutation detection. *Clin Microbiol Infect* 2008;**14**(5):446–53.

19 Boehme CC, Nabeta P, *et al*. Rapid molecular detection of tuberculosis and rifampicin resistance. *N Engl J Med* 2010;**363**(11):1005–15.

20 Landry J, Menzies D. Preventive chemotherapy. Where has it got us? Where to go next? *Int J Tuberc Lung Dis* 2008;**12**(12):1352–64.

Further reading

World Health Organization Report 2010. Global Tuberculosis Control.

Multidrug and extensively drug resistant TB (M/XDR-TB). 2010 Global report on surveillance and response. WHO.

Health Protection Agency. Tuberculosis in the UK. Annual report on tuberculosis surveillance and control in the UK 2010.

Atypical mycobacteria

Aetiology

In the immunocompromised host, the most common cause of nontuberculous, mycobacterial disease is *Mycobacterium avium* complex (MAC).

MAC consists of *Mycobacterium avium* and *Mycobacterium intracellulare*. These free-living bacteria are found ubiquitously in the environment and are thought to be acquired through ingestion and inhalation.

Person-to-person spread does not occur and only patients with CD4 counts below 50 cells/mm^3 develop disseminated disease. Colonization of either the GI tract or the lungs often precedes dissemination (*Table 5.13*).

Incidence and survival

The advent of HAART as well as the use of effective chemoprophylaxis has resulted in a marked reduction in the number of cases. The use of effective therapies in the minority who develop disseminated disease has significantly improved patient survival (**5.19**).

Clinical presentation

Patients present with either disseminated disease or localized disease in the context of IRIS. Patients with disseminated disease often present with constitutional symptoms (fevers, night sweats, weight loss) accompanied by abdominal pain and diarrhoea. Localized disease/IRIS occurs in patients on HAART and can involve any site and can be accompanied by constitutional symptoms (**5.20**).

Diagnosis

Diagnosis is often difficult and protracted. Patients present with anaemia and elevated serum alkaline phosphatase and lactate dehydrogenase levels. Detection of the organism from blood culture is the gold standard though culture of sterile bone marrow and lymph node specimens may also aid diagnosis. Isolates should be tested for susceptibility to macrolides. Detection of MAC in stool and sputum may indicate colonization rather than infection.

Table 5.13 Factors associated with the development of MAC infection

HIV positive

- CD4 count <50 cells/mm^3
- HIV viral load >100,000 copies/ml[1,2]
- Previous colonization with MAC

HIV negative

- Underlying lung disease
- Blunted expression or function of immune responses e.g. interferon gamma

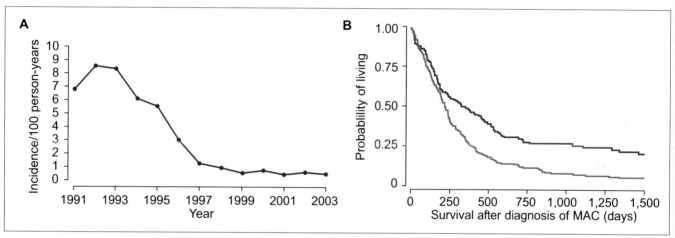

5.19A: Incidence of MAC infection in patients with a CD4 count <200 cells/mm^3 in the Johns Hopkins HIV Clinic Cohort; **B:** survival after a diagnosis of MAC in patients in the Johns Hopkins HIV Clinic Cohort. (Adapted from Karakousis PC, *et al.*, 2004[3].)

Treatment

The combination of a macrolide (clarithromycin or azithromycin) and ethambutol plus or minus rifabutin is often used. Though no significant differences in patient outcomes have been demonstrated, clarithromycin appears to be associated with faster clearance of MAC bacteraemia. The addition of rifabutin to the regimen is recommended by the CDC in:

- Patients with advanced immunosuppression.
- Patients with high mycobacterial loads (>2 log$_{10}$ colony forming units/ml of blood).
- Situations where the emergence of drug resistance is likely.

Treatment duration is guided by CD4 count, resolution of MAC bacteraemia, and the absence of symptoms. According to the CDC, treatment may be discontinued after a 12-month course if:

- Patients are asymptomatic.
- Patients have no MAC bacteraemia.
- Patients maintain a CD4 count >100 cells/mm^3 for at least 6 months while on HAART.

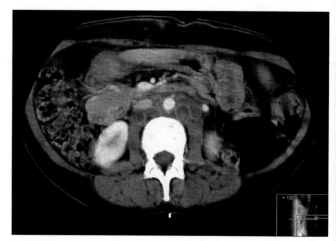

5.20 Mesenteric lymphadenopathy in a patient with MAC.

Table 5.14 Treatment and primary prophylaxis of MAC

Treatment regimens		Primary prophylaxis regimens	
Clarithromycin	500 mg bd	Azithromycin	1250 mg weekly
Ethambutol	15 mg/kg od	OR	
+/- Rifabutin	300 mg od	Clarithromycin	500 mg bd
OR		OR	
Azithromycin	500 mg od	Rifabutin	300 mg od
Ethambutol	15 mg/kg od		
+/- Rifabutin	300 mg od		

Primary prophylaxis

In the USA, this is generally recommended in patients with CD4 counts below 50 cells/mm^3. In the UK, as the background rates of MAC are much lower, primary prophylaxis is not recommended. Weekly azithromycin is the preferred regimen. However, daily clarithromycin or rifabutin is as effective (*Table 5.14*).

Prophylaxis may be discontinued once patients maintain a CD4 count >100 cells/mm^3 for at least 3 months while on HAART.

References

1 Kaplan JE, Hanson DL, Jones JL, Dworkin MS. Viral load as an independent risk factor for opportunistic infections in HIV-infected adults and adolescents. *AIDS* 2001;**15**(14):1831–6.

2 Williams PL, Currier JS, Swindells S. Joint effects of HIV-1 RNA levels and CD4 lymphocyte cells on the risk of specific opportunistic infections. *AIDS* 1999;**13**(9):1035–44.

2 Karakousis PC, Moore RD, Chaisson RE. *Mycobacterium avium* complex in patients with HIV infection in the era of highly active antiretroviral therapy. *Lancet Infect Dis* 2004;**4**(9):557–65.

Further reading

Gordin FM, Cohn DL, Sullam PM, *et al*. Early manifestations of disseminated *Mycobacterium avium* complex disease: a prospective evaluation. *J Infect Dis* 1997;**176**(1):126–32.

Griffith DE, *et al*. An Official ATS/IDSA Statement: Diagnosis, treatment and prevention of nontuberculous mycobacterial diseases. *Am J Respir Critical Care Med* 2007; **175**:367–416.

Horsburgh CR, Jr., Havlik JA, Ellis DA, *et al*. Survival of patients with acquired immune deficiency syndrome and disseminated *Mycobacterium avium* complex infection with and without antimycobacterial chemotherapy. *Am Rev Respir Dis* 1991;**144**(3 Pt 1):557–9.

Horsburgh CR, Jr. The pathophysiology of disseminated *Mycobacterium avium* complex disease in AIDS. *J Infect Dis* 1999;**179**(Suppl 3):S461–S465.

Jacobson MA, Hopewell PC, Yajko DM, *et al*. Natural history of disseminated *Mycobacterium avium* complex infection in AIDS. *J Infect Dis* 1991;**164**(5):994–8.

Kaplan JE, Benson C, Holmes KH, *et al*. Guidelines for prevention and treatment of opportunistic infections in HIV-infected adults and adolescents: recommendations from CDC, the National Institutes of Health, and the HIV Medicine Association of the Infectious Diseases Society of America. *MMWR Recomm Rep* 2009;**58**(RR-4):1–207.

Ward TT, Rimland D, Kauffman C, *et al*. Randomized, open-label trial of azithromycin plus ethambutol vs. clarithromycin plus ethambutol as therapy for *Mycobacterium avium* complex bacteremia in patients with human immunodeficiency virus infection. Veterans Affairs HIV Research Consortium. *Clin Infect Dis* 1998;**27**(5):1278–85.

Varicella-zoster virus

Aetiology

Varicella-zoster virus (VZV) is a neurotropic herpes virus and causes both varicella (chicken pox) and zoster (shingles). HIV-positive patients can present with severe disseminated disease with multiorgan involvement. Vaccination against VZV is recommended in HIV-positive patients with negative VZV serology.

HIV-positive patients who have been previously exposed to VZV can present with zoster. The mechanism involved in latency in the dorsal root ganglia is poorly understood, but in nonimmunosuppressed adults the incidence of reactivation of zoster is higher after the age of 50. In HIV-infected individuals herpes zoster can occur at any stage of HIV-induced immunosuppression. The distribution can be multidermatomal, but usually involves the thoracic or fifth cranial nerves.

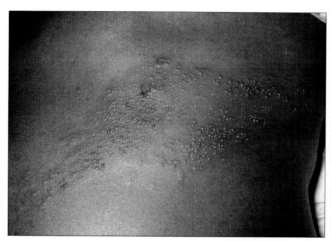

5.21 Herpes zoster virus (shingles): vesicular rash predominantly in dermatomal distribution.

Clinical presentation

Adults who develop chicken pox are at risk of pneumonitis and this can be particularly severe in HIV-positive adults. VZV encephalitis is a rare complication of VZV infection and can occur after chicken pox or zoster. VZV can also be associated with cerebral vasculitis and with retinitis and progressive outer retinal necrosis (PORN). PORN can be rapidly progressive leading to visual loss and often responds poorly to treatment.

Herpes zoster tends to present with a burning or tingling sensation which usually predate the appearance of the rash. Initially the rash is maculopapular and then evolves over 1–2 days to form vesicles which may coalesce to form bullae (**5.21**). In HIV-infected patients, the lesion may become haemorrhagic and necrotic. These usually heal in 2–3 weeks although in severe cases they can last considerably longer and heal with scarring. Zoster of the ophthalmic division of the trigeminal nerve can result in permanent visual loss.

Diagnosis

PCR techniques can identify VZV DNA in samples of CSF or vitreal fluid. Diagnosis of herpes zoster is usually clinical except in severe or atypical cases when skin scrapings to confirm the presence of viral antigens may be required. Figure **5.22** presents the sensory dermatome distribution.

Treatment

Treatment of varicella zoster (shingles) is with high-dose acyclovir, which should be started immediately to try to reduce the risk of dissemination and to shorten the clinical course of disease. Treatment is usually given for 7–10 days till the lesions crust over. Treatment is with IV acyclovir (10 mg/kg tds) for those with severe or disseminated infection, CNS or ophthalmic disease, or advanced HIV. Oral acyclovir (800 mg five times/day) or oral valaciclovir (1 g tds) may be given to those with less severe disease. Famciclovir is a further treatment option. Ophthalmologists must be involved in a patient with zoster ophthalmicus or retinal necrosis which may require intra-vitreal treatment. VZV cerebral vasculitis may require concurrent steroid therapy.

Post herpetic neuralgia can be disabling and treatment options include carbamazepine, amitriptyline, or gabapentin. Topical application of capsaicin is not thought to be of benefit.

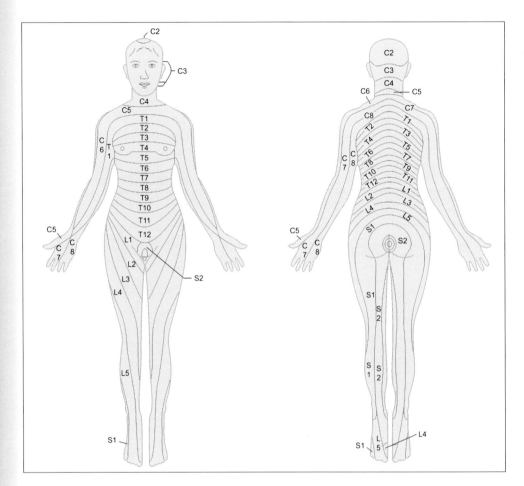

5.22 Sensory dermatomal distribution of VZV.

Cytomegalovirus

Aetiology

CMV is an important pathogen in immunocompromised individuals. It was a major cause of morbidity and mortality in the early stages of the HIV epidemic, in particular causing retinitis, but also GI and CNS disease. However, the advent of effective ARV has seen a dramatic reduction in occurrence of CMV end-organ disease to approximately 5% of that seen in the pre HAART era and CMV retinitis is now rarely seen in countries with access to ART.

Clinical presentation

CMV disease tends to present only at very low CD4 counts (<100 cells/mm^3). Common symptoms of CMV retinitis are reduced visual acuity or visual field loss and the appearance of 'floaters'. It is not painful, but can progress rapidly to blindness. Retinitis often is unilateral at the outset, but can commonly become bilateral (**5.23**). Ophthalmological screening for CMV retinitis in patients with advanced HIV (CD4 <100 cells/mm^3) is recommended. CMV quantitative polymerase chain

reaction (PCR) should be used to monitor likelihood of development of CMV end-organ disease and response to treatment.

CMV can also cause disease of the GI tract and is a differential diagnosis in painful dysphagia, with large often solitary ulcers seen on OGD. Colitis tends to present with abdominal pain, weight loss, diarrhoea, and fever and the differential diagnosis includes other opportunistic GI pathogens (**5.24**).

CMV pneumonitis is uncommon in HIV, unlike in other immunosuppressed groups such as haematology patients where it is a major cause of morbidity and mortality. The clinical picture is that of an interstitial pneumonitis and the chest X-ray shows diffuse interstitial shadowing. CMV can cause a polyradiculopathy affecting the lower spinal cord, which presents with lower limb weakness and spasticity, areflexia, and urinary sphincter disturbance often leading to urinary retention. CMV can also cause a subacute encephalitis which may have an indolent presentation in the severely immunocompromised.

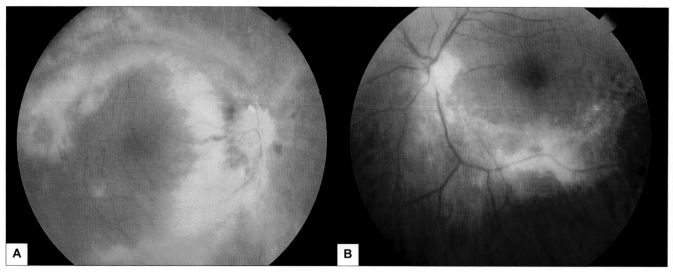

5.23 CMV retinitis. **A:** Late disease; **B:** inactive disease.

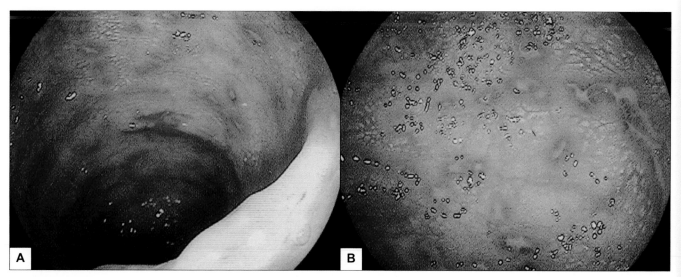

5.24A, B: CMV colitis.

Diagnosis

Diagnosis of CMV end-organ disease may be clinical and based on characteristic appearances, i.e. retinitis. In the GI tract biopsy may be required to show the characteristic histological evidence of viral inclusions (**5.25**). PCR-based techniques have become more commonly used but may only indicate reactivation of infection rather than true end-organ disease.

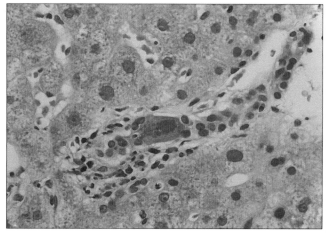

5.25 Disseminated CM.

Treatment

Patients with suspected CMV neurological or ophthalmic disease should be treated promptly. Ganciclovir forms the mainstay of treatment (*Table 5.15*). Prophylaxis regimens are presented in *Table 5.16*.

Table 5.15 Treatment of cytomegalovirus

	Choice of therapy
First line	*CMV retinitis* (after discussion with ophthalmology) 21 days (until 2+ CMV titre <200 copies/ml): • Ganciclovir 5 mg/kg IV bd for 21 days then secondary prophylaxis • Ganciclovir or foscarnet intraocular implants for immediate sight-threatening lesions (ophthalmology review) *CMV colitis/oesophagitis:* 21 days (or 2 CMV titre <200 copies/ml) till resolution of signs/symptoms: • Ganciclovir 5 mg/kg IV bd *CMV pneumonitis:* • As for colitis if suspected *CMV encephalitis:* • Consider ganciclovir +/- foscarnet (after discussion with virology, increased side-effects) *CMV viraemia:* • As for colitis after discussion with virology (a 'watch and wait approach' may be undertaken, with CMV VL >3,000 copies/ml as threshold for treatment)
Alternative	• Valganciclovir 900 mg PO bd may be substituted for IV if outpatient or no IV access
Alternative	Bone marrow suppression/possible ganciclovir resistance: • Foscarnet 90 mg/kg IV bd • Fluids 500 ml IV with each dose
Alternative	• Cidofovir 5 mg/kg once weekly for 2 weeks, then 5 mg/kg IV every 2 weeks • Probenecid 2 g PO 2 hours before the dose, then 1 g PO 3 hours and 8 hours post dose • Saline hydration

Comments

CMV viral load: Monitor twice weekly in those with detectable levels

Ophthalmology review: refer all patients for ophthalmology review

Immune recovery uveitis (IRU) may occur within 4–12 weeks from initiation of HAART. Discuss with ophthalmology regarding use of corticosteroids

Table 5.16 Secondary prophylaxis for CMV disease

Indication	*Choice of therapy*
Retinitis	• Valganciclovir 900 mg PO od +/- ganciclovir implant every 6–8 months if CD4 <100 cells/mm^3
Colitis/oesophagitis	• Valganciclovir 900 mg PO od
Pneumonitis	• Not usually indicated
Encephalitis	• Not usually indicated if HAART initiated although DHHS guidelines suggest use of valganciclovir
Viraemia	• Not usually indicated

Comment
Continue prophylaxis until CD4 >100 cells/mm^3 for at least 3–6 months

Herpes simplex

Aetiology

Herpes simplex virus type 1 (HSV-1) and type 2 (HSV-2) are double-stranded DNA viruses of the *Herpesviridae* family[1]. Traditionally HSV-1 tended to be acquired in childhood and causes oral ulcers, and HSV-2 tended to be transmitted sexually causing anogenital ulcers. However, oral infections with HSV-2 and genital infection, with HSV-1 are increasingly common, probably due to oral–genital sexual practices[1]. Infection with HSV is common in both HIV-positive and negative populations although prevalence is higher in the HIV-positive population, i.e. prevalence of HSV-2 ranges from 10–60% in the general population and from 50–90% in the HIV-positive population[1,2]. Infection with HSV is life long and is characterized by latency with periods of symptomatic reactivation and asymptomatic viral shedding. Individuals with HIV tend to have more frequent and more severe HSV reactivations that may take several weeks to heal.

Clinical presentation

HSV tends to present as ulcerative disease of the oral or genital areas. Classic presentation of primary HSV infection is with clusters of vesicles that will ulcerate, crust, and heal within 2–3 weeks (**5.26, 5.27**). Patients with primary HSV may also have systemic symptoms such as fever, headache, malaise, and myalgia. Genital HSV may cause aseptic meningitis, extragenital lesions, and autonomic dysfunction causing urinary retention[1]. Recurrence of HSV tends to

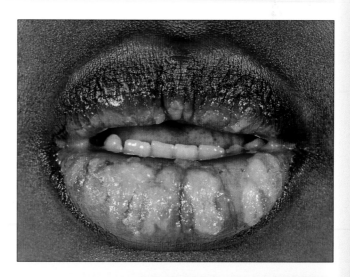

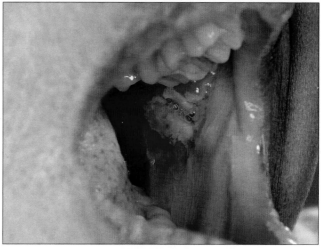

5.26, 5.27 Herpes simplex lesions.

have an initial prodrome of burning or tingling in the affected area prior to development of vesicles. Intervention with antiviral drugs at this stage may prevent progression. Genital HSV is more likely to have atypical presentation and both types can cause severe, persistent, and disabling disease in HIV-positive patients. More serious and disseminated HSV disease including meningo-encephalitis, hepatitis, pneumonitis, or retinal necrosis are rare even in HIV-positive patients. Rates of ocular keratitis are similar in both groups.

Treatment

The usual treatment course is acyclovir 400 mg five times a day for 7 days. Severe or recurrent disease may require maintenance therapy long term (acyclovir 400 mg twice a day). Treatment options include IV acyclovir (10 mg/kg tds) for those with severe or disseminated infection. Famciclovir, valaciclovir, and valganciclovir are other treatment options.

References

1 Gupta R, Warren T, Wald A. Genital herpes. *Lancet* 2007;**370**(9605):2127–37.
2 Strick LB, Wald A, Celum C. Management of herpes simplex virus type 2 infection in HIV type 1-infected persons. *Clin Infect Dis* 2006;**43**(3):347–56.

Further reading

Jacobson MA, O'Donnell JJ, Porteous D, Brodie HR, Feigal D, Mills J. Retinal and gastrointestinal disease due to cytomegalovirus in patients with the acquired immune deficiency syndrome: prevalence, natural history, and response to ganciclovir therapy. *Q J Med* 1988;**67**(254):473–86.

Chapter 6

HIV and malignancies

Kaposi's sarcoma

M Kronfli and C Collis

Introduction

Kaposi's sarcoma (KS) is a spindle cell tumour of endothelial cell lineage which affects the skin, mucosal surfaces, viscera, and lymphatic system. It is classified into four categories based on clinical presentation and disease course. All four categories are associated with human herpesvirus-8 (HHV-8) (*Table 6.1*).

HIV-associated KS

KS became a hallmark of AIDS at the start of the epidemic over three decades ago. In Europe during this period, KS was the presenting illness in more than 20% of patients diagnosed with HIV infection[1]. In the early years of the AIDS epidemic, patients with AIDS-related KS had high tumour burdens and rapidly progressive disease resulting in a life expectancy of less than 6 months. The advent of

Table 6.1 Categories of Kaposi's sarcoma

Category	Features
Classic–sporadic	• First described by Moritz Kaposi in 1872 • Occurs in elderly Mediterranean and Eastern European men • Predominantly involves the lower limbs • Indolent disease course
Endemic–African	• Occurs in equatorial Africa • Male preponderance • Affects individuals between their third and fourth decades but there is a rare pre-pubertal form • Manifestation varies from the chronic 'classic–sporadic' to the rare more aggressive visceral presentation. In children presentation is predominantly lymphatic
Immunosuppression-related	• Occurs post organ transplant or in patients treated with long-term immunosuppressive therapy
HIV-associated	• Most common neoplasm occurring in patients infected with HIV • AIDS-defining illness • May present in the context of an immune reconstitution inflammatory syndrome (IRIS)

highly active antiretroviral therapy (HAART) has considerably changed the incidence and clinical course of KS. In patients receiving HAART, the incidence of KS is lower and the disease takes a more indolent course. EuroSIDA, a large observational cohort study of HIV-1 infected patients in Europe, found that the incidence of KS in 2003 (1.8 per 1000 person-years of follow-up) was less than 10% of the incidence reported in 1994 (25.1 per 1000 person-years of follow-up)[2]. These findings are consistent with the results of several other studies. Unfortunately in sub-Saharan Africa where HAART is not universally available, the incidence and natural history of KS remain unchanged.

Risk factors for the development of KS in HIV infection include:

- Homosexual HIV transmission in men who have sex with men (MSM).
- Advanced immunosuppression.
- Geographic location.

In the EuroSIDA study, European patients with KS were more likely to be from Northern Europe. The Swiss HIV cohort study, on the other hand, demonstrated that birth in Africa or the Middle East was associated with an increased risk of KS[3].

In HIV infection, the presentation and morbidity of KS vary greatly amongst infected individuals. Symptoms usually occur when patients have extensive skin disease, or mucosal or visceral involvement. It can be potentially life threatening, for example due to haemorrhage from gastrointestinal tract (GI) lesions, airway obstruction from oropharyngeal lesions, or respiratory failure from pulmonary lesions. However, mild cutaneous KS is common and some patients are relatively asymptomatic with just one or two skin lesions. The psychological and social effects of these characteristic lesions can be profound, especially if they occur in a prominent area such as the face and in this context mild skin disease is often the sole indication for therapy.

Aetiology

KS is associated with HHV-8 (also called Kaposi's sarcoma-associated herpesvirus, KSHV), a γ-herpesvirus discovered in 1994 which is now known to be necessary for the development of KS[4]. This virus is also associated with the development of primary effusion lymphoma and multicentric Castleman's disease. The mode of transmission of HHV-8 is not clear, but it appears to be

mainly transmitted sexually. Several studies have also correlated behaviour involving exchange of saliva with risk of HHV-8 infection[5].

HHV-8-seropositive HIV-infected patients are 20,000 times more likely to develop KS than non-HIV infected patients as the risk of KS in the HHV-8-positive population is increased by HIV co-infection[6]. The presence of HHV-8 does not always result in KS, however, although the replication of HIV and HHV-8 is thought to be enhanced by each others' presence.

KS lesions are composed of endothelial cells, spindle cells, extravasated erythrocytes, and infiltrating inflammatory cells (6.1–6.3). In early lesions, vascular slit angiogenesis occurs in the superficial dermis, surrounding normal blood vessels. The abnormal vascularity expands throughout the dermis in later lesions, and clusters and fascicles of spindle cells arrange themselves around the vascular spaces. Extravasated erythrocytes are contained in these vascular spaces. The later, nodular lesions contain the characteristic spindle-shaped cells, forming distinct aggregates and fascicles[7]. These spindle cells are thought to be the tumour cells of KS, although it is not clear whether they represent true malignant proliferation or a reactive process.

The exact mechanism by which HHV-8 induces the above characteristic pathological changes has not been identified but several factors are known to be important. The HIV *Tat* gene, one of the regulatory genes of the HIV virus, enhances the activity of pro-angiogenic HHV-8 gene products[8]. HIV *Tat* is synergistic with a number of the inflammatory cytokines involved in the endothelial cell changes associated with KS and it is thought that HIV *Tat* and its interaction with these cytokines may explain the more aggressive nature of HIV-associated KS compared to other forms of KS. It should be observed, however, that although HIV-associated KS carried a poor prognosis in the first years of the HIV epidemic, KS lesions often regress in response to the initiation of HAART and therefore sometimes require no further treatment, unlike non-HIV-associated KS.

Much clinical evidence suggests that immuno-suppression and T-cell dysfunction are important in the pathogenesis of KS. This is supported by findings of impaired T-cell proliferation in HIV-positive, HHV-8-positive men and low quantities of HHV-8-specific T-cells in KS patients.

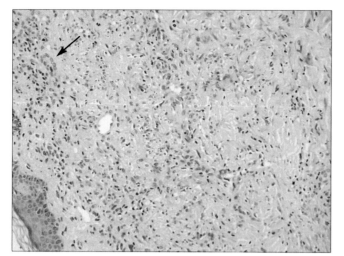

6.1 Hematoxylin and eosin stain of Kaposi's sarcoma lesion. Cross section of spindle cell fascicle (arrow).

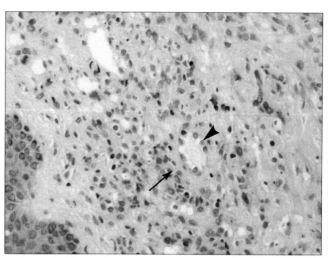

6.2 Hematoxylin and eosin stain of Kaposi's sarcoma lesion. Prominent vascular channels lined by spindle cells (arrowhead); extravasated erythrocytes (arrow).

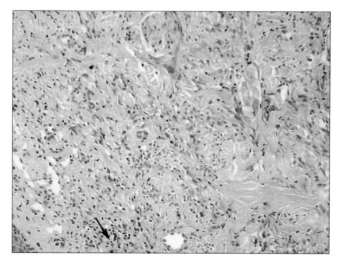

6.3 Hematoxylin and eosin stain of Kaposi's sarcoma lesion. Infiltrates of mononuclear cells (arrow) with spindle cell proliferation.

Diagnosis

Signs

Mild KS is common and can occur in patients who are newly diagnosed with HIV infection and in patients already stable on antiretroviral treatment. Patients usually present with skin lesions which usually precede visceral or lymph node involvement. In the early stages a macule or a papule may appear (**6.4–6.6**). These papules can progress to larger nodules eventually resulting in KS plaques in later stages. Complications of skin disease include ulcerating tumours (occurring in the nodular stage) and fungating lesions (unusual).

The face and lower extremities are the most common sites of KS, with plaque-like KS occurring on the soles of the feet (**6.7**). KS can also affect the genitalia, upper extremities, conjunctivae, and eyelids. Nodular KS can progress to cause widespread oedema (**6.8**). Although lymphadenopathy is thought to be an important factor, the mechanism underlying KS-associated oedema remains poorly understood.

All patients with a new diagnosis of HIV should undergo thorough cutaneous examination for KS lesions. Oral KS, which occurs in about one-third of patients[9], should raise the suspicion of KS in the GI or bronchopulmonary tract.

It is therefore important that all patients presenting with cutaneous disease are examined for KS lesions in the mouth and hard palate (**6.9**).

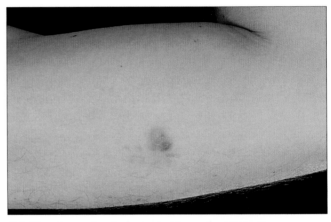

6.4 Macule on the forearm in Kaposi's sarcoma.

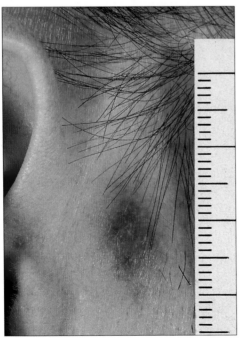

6.5 Typical cutaneous lesion on the face in Kaposi's sarcoma: a purple nodule with surrounding oedema and green-yellow discoloration on the tumour edge corresponding to haemorrhage.

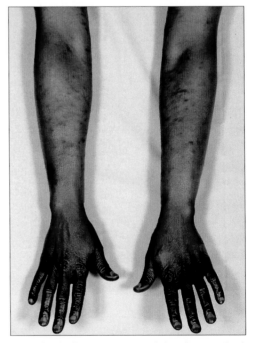

6.6 Multiple Kaposi's sarcoma nodules in a typical distribution throughout the forearms. Some lesions are older and have faded and become flatter.

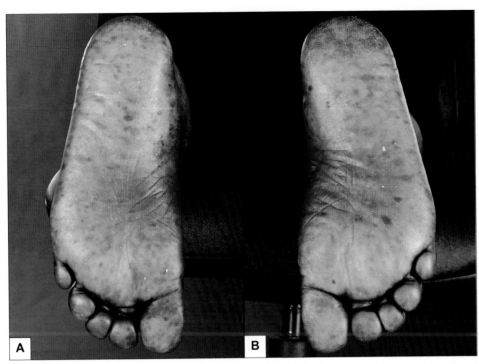

6.7A, B: Typical Karposi's sarcoma patch lesions on the sole of the foot. At the posterior aspect the lesions have coalesced.

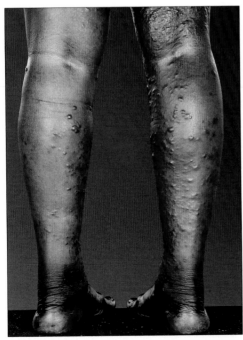

6.8 Severe Kaposi's sarcoma with multiple nodules throughout the lower legs. The distribution of the lesions is asymmetrical, and significant skin oedema is noted on the right thigh.

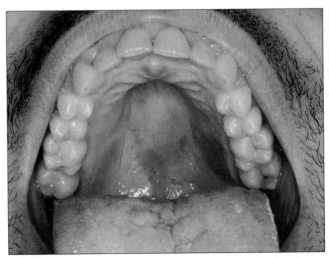

6.9 Kaposi's sarcoma of the hard palate. This lesion is flat and dark purple in colour. Lesions can become nodular and protrude, occasionally interfering with speech or eating.

Symptoms

Symptoms of GI KS include nausea, vomiting, abdominal pain, melaena, bleeding per rectum, dysphagia, and odynophagia. Bulky oral disease can be problematic and cause difficulty with eating or speaking. Full examination of the GI system should be performed, including lymph nodes. Symptoms of pulmonary KS include dyspnoea, cough, haemoptysis, fever, and chest pain. KS can also cause disease in other organs such as the heart, the liver, salivary glands, larynx, and the kidney.

Diagnosis

- Skin biopsy: As most patients have evidence of cutaneous disease, this is usually the preferred method for obtaining a tissue diagnosis. Immunohistochemistry for HHV-8 is performed on biopsy samples to confirm the diagnosis, as tumour cells of KS are strongly reactive for the HHV-8 marker. HHV-8 positivity is extremely rare in other tumours. (See **6.10**.)
- Chest X-ray (**6.11**).
- Blood tests: Full blood count, liver and renal function and electrolyte testing, and a clotting screen. Occult blood testing can be performed to screen for GI lesions.

If visceral disease is suspected the following investigations should also be performed:
- GI endoscopy if gastrointestinal disease is suspected (**6.12**).
- Bronchoscopy if there is clinical suspicion of respiratory involvement, i.e. symptoms of pulmonary disease or an abnormal chest X-ray.
- Computed tomography (CT) scanning of the chest, abdomen, and pelvis can be performed to assess the extent of disease. Thoracic high-resolution CT findings characteristic of KS include tumour masses (53%), multiple nodules (79%), bronchovascular thickening (66%), and pleural effusions (55%) (**6.13**). Other signs such as ground-glass opacities are not as common, and should prompt a search for another opportunistic infection[10].

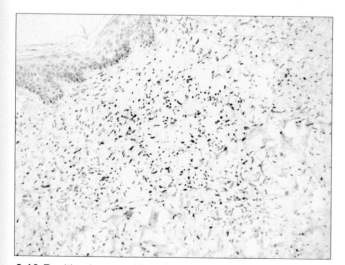

6.10 Positive immunohistochemistry for human herpesvirus-8 on a biopsy.

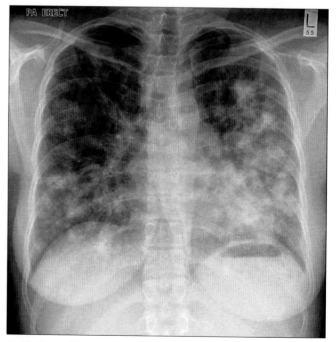

6.11 Chest X-ray findings in Kaposi's sarcoma. Poorly defined round opacities throughout both lung fields. In this case a pleural effusion is not present.

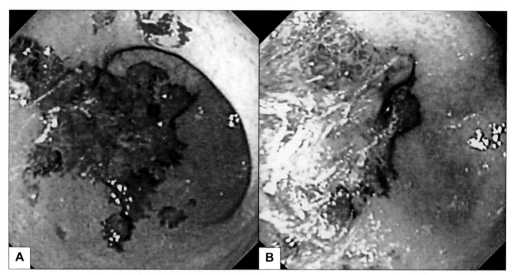

6.12A, B: Kaposi's sarcoma lesion in the stomach taken during an OGD.

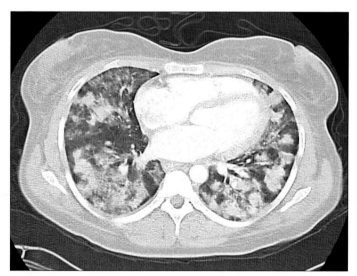

6.13 Kaposi's sarcoma on a CT scan of the thorax. Widespread, diffuse infiltrates can be seen with focal areas of consolidation and nodularity as well as areas of ground-glass opacification. In this case the patient had super-added infection at the time of the CT scan.

Table 6.2 Prognostic factors in Kaposi's sarcoma

Good	Points	Bad	Points
CD4 count	-1 for each 100 cells/mm^3	Age 50 years or over	+2
KS is the sole AIDS-defining illness	-3	Simultaneous presence of 2nd AIDS-defining illness	+3

The scale starts at 10, and gives scores ranging from 0–15. A low score indicates a good prognosis and a high score a bad prognosis. For example a patient with a CD4 count of 430 cells/mm^3 (-4), KS as their AIDS-defining illness (-3), aged 52 (+2) and with no other AIDS-associated illness would achieve a score of 5

Table 6.3 Percentage probability of survival from time of diagnosis by prognostic score

Score	6 months	1 year	2 years	5 years
0	99.8	99.3	99.0	98.4
5	98.7	96.7	94.6	91.8
10	93.3	83.4	74.1	63.1
15	69.2	37.8	19.9	08.4

(Adapted from Stebbing J, Sanitt A, Nelson M, *et al.* A prognostic index for AIDS-associated Kaposi's sarcoma in the era of highly active antiretroviral therapy. *Lancet* 2006;**367**:1495–502)

Prognostic score

Since the advent of HAART, a validated prognostic score consisting of four factors has been defined[11]. Good prognostic factors include high CD4 counts and the diagnosis of KS as the sole AIDS-defining illness. Advanced age (50 years or older) and the presence of another AIDS-defining illness confer a worse prognosis. The score can then be used to predict a patient's 6 month to 5 year prognosis (*Tables 6.2, 6.3*).

Management

The prognostic score can also be used to guide management decisions. It has been suggested that patients with a prognostic score of <12 should be commenced on systemic therapy while those with a score of <5 should be treated with HAART. Interestingly, the presence of visceral disease does not have a bearing on the overall prognosis in this index, and the suggestion is that those in the good prognosis group (score <5) should not receive systemic therapy even in the presence of visceral disease[12].

HAART

All patients with AIDS-related KS should receive HAART. Several studies demonstrate the benefit of HAART both in terms of decreased incidence of KS in patients receiving HAART[13] and the response of KS to HAART. The response to HAART usually takes from 3–6 months, although it can be more rapid. As well as causing regression in size and number of KS lesions and histological regression of existing lesions, HAART has also been shown to prolong time to treatment failure in patients receiving systemic chemotherapy[14].

It has been suggested that due to the antiangiogenic effects of protease inhibitors (PIs), a PI-containing regimen is superior. However, both PI-based and non-nucleoside reverse transcriptase (-NNRTI) -based regimes have been shown to be equally effective in protecting against KS. Decisions regarding HAART regimens should therefore be made on the basis of the individual requirements of the patient.

As well as the recognized side-effects of HAART, IRIS has been recognized with paradoxical worsening of a stable neoplasm in the context of HAART-induced recovery of the immune system[16].

Chemotherapy

Indications for systemic therapy:

- Consider in patients with widespread cutaneous involvement if there has been no improvement with HAART or if a prompt response is desirable.
- Patients with symptomatic local disease such as bulky oral disease, pedal or scrotal oedema, or symptomatic visceral disease (in particular lung disease) and those with IRIS.
- In patients with advanced or rapidly progressive disease, systemic therapy may be initiated in advance of HAART, as HAART can take up to 6 months to achieve its full effect.
- Organ dysfunction, especially hepatic impairment, and performance status should also be considered.

Liposomal doxorubicin

Liposomal doxorubicin is the most effective first-line treatment for HIV-associated Kaposi's sarcoma[17,18]. It is an anthracycline chemotherapy agent, which acts by inhibiting DNA synthesis. The liposome encapsulated formulation enhances delivery of the drug to tumours. This gives a longer plasma half-life and less toxicity compared with conventional anthracyclines. The relatively low dose (20 mg/m^2 every 3 weeks) used to treat KS results in minimal toxicity. Two phase III trials have demonstrated the superior overall response to liposomal doxorubicin compared to the previous standard chemotherapy regime (bleomycin and vincristine, with or without doxorubicin). These studies were conducted before the advent of HAART, and studies have since demonstrated both the safety and tolerability of liposomal doxorubicin in combination with HAART in terms of toxicity and maintenance of CD4 count as well as its efficacy[19]. Standard prophylaxis against opportunistic infections can be continued during the treatment with liposomal doxorubicin. Liposomal doxorubicin is still widely regarded as the gold standard for first-line treatment of AIDS-related KS. The cardiotoxicity seen with conventional anthracyclines has not been reported, and neuropathies and significant alopecia are rare, but myelosuppression and emesis are still recognized toxicities[20].

Paclitaxel

Paclitaxel is a chemotherapeutic agent of the taxane group, which works by inhibiting angiogenesis and interfering with the function of microtubules, thus impairing mitosis and many other cell functions. It is approved for second-line use, and two studies have demonstrated its efficacy as a second-line chemotherapy agent at a dose of 100 mg/m^2 2-weekly[21]. All patients in the second study were stabilized on HAART prior to receiving chemotherapy. No change in plasma HIV-1 viral load occurred during or after treatment, suggesting that concomitant treatment is safe. Toxicities of paclitaxel are significant and include alopecia, myalgia, and myelosuppression (although neutropenia was noted to have resolved before the subsequent cycle), and the infusion time is longer (3 hours compared to 1 hour for liposomal doxorubicin). There is also a concern that the corticosteroids required to prevent emesis may exacerbate or induce KS lesions. It is therefore a less attractive option than liposomal doxorubicin, and reserved for second-line use in patients with disease refractory to anthracycline treatment.

Local therapies

There are several local therapies available, and while these are useful for the treatment of localized disease which may cause cosmetic problems or local symptoms, they do not address new lesions appearing elsewhere.

Radiotherapy

AIDS-related KS is radiosensitive. Although radiotherapy was previously important in the treatment of KS, the introduction of HAART and better tolerated systemic treatments means it now has a limited role. It still has a role in certain specialized areas such as strontium-90 therapy for eyelid and conjunctival lesions[22] and remains useful in patients with symptomatic or refractory areas of cutaneous disease (e.g. peripheral lesions with significant oedema) and for cosmesis. Mucositis is a problem for patients with mucosal lesions even at low doses and the soles of the feet are also susceptible to significant toxicity.

Early studies demonstrated the superiority of fractionated radiotherapy over a single 8 Gy fraction, but this resulted in increased toxicity. Other studies have not demonstrated an advantage of fractionated regimes (e.g. 16 Gy in four fractions). Modified fractionated schedules are in use, for example 21 Gy in six fractions, three times per week. Electron therapy can also be used for superficial lesions, usually given once weekly in 4 Gy fractions.

Toxicities include skin discomfort, which usually resolves within 2 weeks of starting therapy, but skin ulceration and infection can also occur. These can be minimized with advice to minimize friction and sparing use of moisturizers.

Intra-lesional chemotherapy

Vinblastine is useful for small localized lesions, and is known to induce tumour regression in 80% of treated lesions. Disadvantages include the need for repeated injections and slow onset of action. Side-effects include blistering, ulceration, and changes in pigmentation.

Retinoic acid

Gel can be applied topically and is well tolerated. It has a 27–38% response rate (higher in patients receiving PIs) but it has a high relapse rate[25].

Cryotherapy

Cryotherapy is also used for small, superficial facial lesions. Side-effects include minimal discomfort and changes in pigmentation.

Interferon-α

Although interferon-α for KS was the first licensed indication for biological cancer therapy, it has a high toxicity rate (fever, chills, neutropenia, fatigue, hepatotoxicity, and cognitive impairment) and 6 months or more continued treatment is needed. It is therefore seldom used these days, although it is occasionally useful for patients stabilized on HAART with slowly progressive cutaneous disease. Caution should be exercised, however, as toxicity and response rates are worse in patients with CD4 counts less than 200 cells/ml[3].

Antivirals

These agents are of limited use, as there is little evidence that they are effective in KS, possibly due to the fact that KS tumour cells contain HHV-8 in the latent stage. However, there is now some anecdotal evidence that ganciclovir and foscarnet cause clinical regression of KS, and that they may reduce the risk of KS.

Newer agents

Recent insights into the role of intracellular signalling pathways in KS have resulted in the identification of several molecular agents that may be effective against KS. Although these agents are already in existence and approved for indications other than Kaposi's sarcoma, they are yet to be licensed for use in KS. They include:

- Inhibitors of vascular endothelial growth factor (VEGF): anti-VEGF agents include bevacizumab, a monoclonal antibody currently used in bowel cancer; sunitinib, which is used in renal cell carcinoma and gastrointestinal stromal carcinoma (GIST), and sorafenib, used in hepatocellular carcinoma and renal cell carcinoma. These agents are currently being investigated in clinical trials.
- Mammalian target of rapamycin (MTOR) inhibitors, e.g. temsirolimus, which is used for the treatment of renal cell carcinoma and bortezomib, a proteosome inhibitor currently used for the treatment of multiple myeloma[26].
- Tyrosine kinase inhibitors, e.g. imatinib, which acts against type III tyrosine kinase receptors and is currently used to treat chronic myeloid leukaemia (CML) and GIST. Treatment with oral imatinib has been shown in one small trial to reduce the size of KS skin lesions and cause histological tumour regression after 4 weeks of treatment, and larger trials are needed.
- Thalidomide, which acts as an antiangiogenesis agent, has been shown to be of benefit in early trials in KS.

References

1 Hermans P, Lundgren J, Sommereijns B, Pedersen C, Vella S, Katlama C, et al. Epidemiology of AIDS-related Kaposi's sarcoma in Europe over 10 years. AIDS in Europe Study Group. *AIDS* 1996 Jul;10(8):911–17.

2 Mocroft A, Kirk O, Clumeck N, Gargalianos-Kakolyris P, Trocha H, Chentsova N, et al. The changing pattern of Kaposi sarcoma in patients with HIV, 1994–2003: the EuroSIDA Study. *Cancer* 2004 Jun 15;100(12):2644–54.

3 Franceschi S, Maso LD, Rickenbach M, Polesel J, Hirschel B, Cavassini M, et al. Kaposi sarcoma incidence in the Swiss HIV Cohort Study before and after highly active antiretroviral therapy. *Br J Cancer* 2008 Sep 2;99(5):800–4.

4 Chang Y, Cesarman E, Pessin MS, Lee F, Culpepper J, Knowles DM, et al. Identification of herpesvirus-like DNA sequences in AIDS-associated Kaposi's sarcoma. *Science* 1994 Dec 16;266(5192):1865–9.

5 Casper C, Wald A, Pauk J, Tabet SR, Corey L, Celum CL. Correlates of prevalent and incident Kaposi's sarcoma-associated herpesvirus infection in men who have sex with men. *J Infect Dis* 2002 Apr 1;185(7):990–3.

6 Beral V, Peterman TA, Berkelman RL, Jaffe HW. Kaposi's sarcoma among persons with AIDS: a sexually transmitted infection? *Lancet* 1990 Jan 20;**335**(8682):123–8.

7 Gessain A, Duprez R. Spindle cells and their role in Kaposi's sarcoma. *Int J Biochem Cell Biol* 2005 Dec;**37**(12):2457–65.

8 Dezube BJ. The role of human immunodeficiency virus-I in the pathogenesis of acquired immunodeficiency syndrome-related Kaposi's sarcoma: the importance of an inflammatory and angiogenic milieu. *Semin Oncol* 2000 Aug;**27**(4):420–3.

9 Nichols CM, Flaitz CM, Hicks MJ. Treating Kaposi's lesions in the HIV-infected patient. *J Am Dent Assoc* 1993 Nov;**124**(11):78–84.

10 Khalil AM, Carette MF, Cadranel JL, Mayaud CM, Bigot JM. Intrathoracic Kaposi's sarcoma. CT findings. *Chest* 1995 Dec;**108**(6):1622–6.

11 Stebbing J, Sanitt A, Nelson M, Powles T, Gazzard B, Bower M. A prognostic index for AIDS-associated Kaposi's sarcoma in the era of highly active antiretroviral therapy. *Lancet* 2006 May 6;**367**(9521):1495–502.

12 Bower M, Collins S, Cottrill C, Cwynarski K, Montoto S, Nelson M, *et al.* British HIV Association guidelines for HIV-associated malignancies 2008. *HIV Med* 2008 Jul;**9**(6):336–88.

13 Ledergerber B, Telenti A, Egger M. Risk of HIV related Kaposi's sarcoma and non-Hodgkin's lymphoma with potent antiretroviral therapy: prospective cohort study. Swiss HIV Cohort Study. *BMJ* 1999 Jul 3;**319**(7201):23–4.

14 Bower M, Fox P, Fife K, Gill J, Nelson M, Gazzard B. Highly active anti-retroviral therapy (HAART) prolongs time to treatment failure in Kaposi's sarcoma. *AIDS* 1999 Oct 22;**13**(15):2105–11.

15 Grabar S, Abraham B, Mahamat A, Del GP, Rosenthal E, Costagliola D. Differential impact of combination antiretroviral therapy in preventing Kaposi's sarcoma with and without visceral involvement. *J Clin Oncol* 2006 Jul 20;**24**(21):3408–14.

16 Di LG, Konstantinopoulos PA, Pantanowitz L, Di TR, De PS, Dezube BJ. Management of AIDS-related Kaposi's sarcoma. *Lancet Oncol* 2007 Feb;**8**(2):167–76.

17 Stewart S, Jablonowski H, Goebel FD, Arasteh K, Spittle M, Rios A, *et al.* Randomized comparative trial of pegylated liposomal doxorubicin versus bleomycin and vincristine in the treatment of AIDS-related Kaposi's sarcoma. International Pegylated Liposomal Doxorubicin Study Group. *J Clin Oncol* 1998 Feb;**16**(2):683–91.

18 Northfelt DW, Dezube BJ, Thommes JA, Miller BJ, Fischl MA, Friedman-Kien A, *et al.* Pegylated-liposomal doxorubicin versus doxorubicin, bleomycin, and vincristine in the treatment of AIDS-related Kaposi's sarcoma: results of a randomized phase III clinical trial. *J Clin Oncol* 1998 Jul;**16**(7):2445–51.

19 Lichterfeld M, Qurishi N, Hoffmann C, Hochdorfer B, Brockmeyer NH, Arasteh K, *et al.* Treatment of HIV-1-associated Kaposi's sarcoma with pegylated liposomal doxorubicin and HAART simultaneously induces effective tumor remission and CD4+ T cell recovery. *Infection* 2005 Jun;**33**(3):140–7.

20 Krown SE, Northfelt DW, Osoba D, Stewart JS. Use of liposomal anthracyclines in Kaposi's sarcoma. *Semin Oncol* 2004 Dec;**31**(6 Suppl 13):36–52.

21 Tulpule A, Groopman J, Saville MW, Harrington W, Jr., Friedman-Kien A, Espina BM, *et al.* Multicenter trial of low-dose paclitaxel in patients with advanced AIDS-related Kaposi sarcoma. *Cancer* 2002 Jul 1;**95**(1):147–54.

22 Evans MD, Yassa M, Podgorsak EB, Roman TN, Schreiner LJ, Souhami L. Surface applicators for high dose rate brachytherapy in AIDS-related Kaposi's sarcoma. *Int J Radiat Oncol Biol Phys* 1997 Oct 1;**39**(3):769–74.

23 Lukawska J, Cottrill C, Bower M. The changing role of radiotherapy in AIDS-related malignancies. *Clin Oncol* (R Coll Radiol) 2003 Feb;**15**(1):2–6.

24 Boudreaux AA, Smith LL, Cosby CD, Bason MM, Tappero JW, Berger TG. Intralesional vinblastine for cutaneous Kaposi's sarcoma associated with acquired immunodeficiency syndrome. A clinical trial to evaluate efficacy and discomfort associated with infection. *J Am Acad Dermatol* 1993 Jan;**28**(1):61–5.

25 Duvic M, Friedman-Kien AE, Looney DJ, Miles SA, Myskowski PL, Scadden DT, *et al.* Topical treatment of cutaneous lesions of acquired immunodeficiency syndrome-related Kaposi sarcoma using alitretinoin gel: results of phase 1 and 2 trials. *Arch Dermatol* 2000 Dec;**136**(12):1461–9.

26 Sullivan RJ, Pantanowitz L, Casper C, Stebbing J, Dezube BJ. HIV/AIDS: epidemiology, pathophysiology, and treatment of Kaposi sarcoma-associated herpesvirus disease: Kaposi sarcoma, primary effusion lymphoma, and multicentric Castleman disease. *Clin Infect Dis* 2008 Nov 1;**47**(9):1209–15.

Haematological malignancies and HIV

M Heller and K Cwynarski

AIDS-related lymphoma (ARL)

HIV-infected patients have a 50–60-fold increased risk of developing non-Hodgkin's lymphoma (NHL) in comparison to noninfected individuals. ARL is an AIDS-defining illness (ADI) and related to the degree of immune suppression, and it is the second most common tumour in individuals with HIV infection (up to 10% incidence) (*Table 6.4*).

A decline in incidence of primary CNS lymphoma (PCNSL) has occurred through better immune reconstitution in the HAART era.

Table 6.4 Most common types of ARL (WHO classification)

Non-Hodgkin's lymphoma

- Diffuse large B-cell lymphoma (DLBCL) (**6.14**)
- Burkitt's lymphoma (40% lymphoma tissue Epstein–Barr virus [EBV] DNA-positive) (**6.15**)
- Primary cerebral lymphoma (100% lymphoma tissue EBV DNA-positive) (**6.16**)
- Primary effusion lymphoma (lymphoma tissue HHV-8 DNA-positive) (**6.17**)

Hodgkin's lymphoma

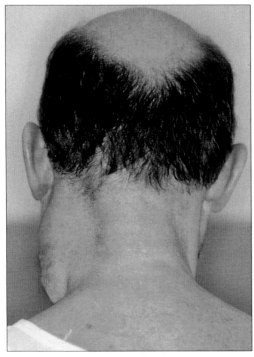

6.14 Extensive cervical lymphadenopathy in DLBCL.

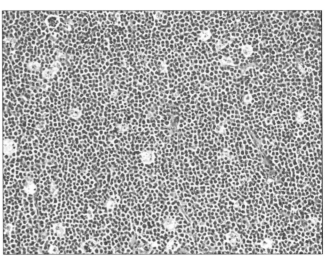

6.15 Burkitt's lymphoma. Diffuse infiltration of a lymph node with a 'starry sky' appearance. H&E ×100. (Courtesy of Professor AV Hoffbrand.)

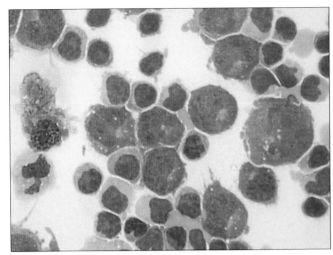

6.16 High-grade non-Hodgkin lymphoma (NHL) CSF. Large basophilic blasts containing several nucleoli interspersed with smaller more mature lymphoid cells. CytoSpin H&E ×600.

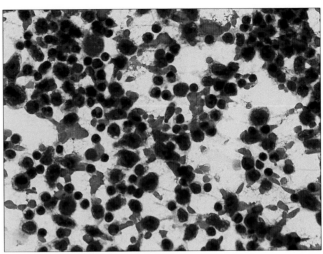

6.17 Primary effusion lymphoma. Large neoplastic cells in a pleural effusion. CytoSpin pleural fluid Papanicolau stain ×400. (Courtesy of Professor AV Hoffbrand.)

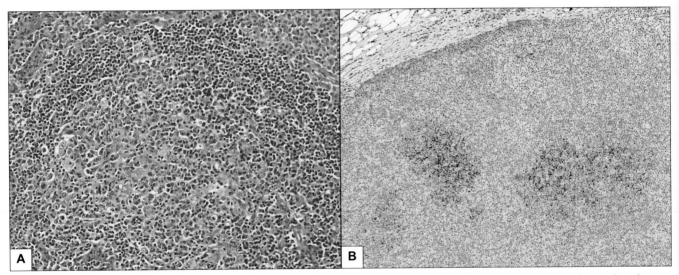

6.18A: Hyperplastic germinal centre. Lymph node of HIV-infected patient. H&E ×100. **B**: P24 immunostaining showing positivity in follicular dendritic cells. Lymph node of HIV-infected patient ×100. (Courtesy of Professor AV Hoffbrand.)

Patients tend to present with advanced stage disease, B symptoms, extra nodal sites of disease, and bone marrow involvement. The diagnosis of ARL should be based on a tissue sample rather than a cytological (fine-needle aspirate [FNA]) sample to rule out reactive lymphadenopathy (**6.18A, B**). The haemato-oncologist should be involved for appropriate staging investigations (bone marrow biopsy, CSF sampling **6.16**), CT scan, CT-positron emission tomography [PET] scan [**6.19**]) and treatment.

The histological diagnosis in the majority of such patients is DLBCL (60%) or Burkitt's lymphoma (30%). Hodgkin lymphoma is increasingly diagnosed in the post-HAART era.

Prior to the introduction of HAART, treatment with standard dose chemotherapy induced high levels of toxicity and a high incidence of opportunistic infections. Immunological function and haematopoietic reserve have improved dramatically with HAART (with the exception of

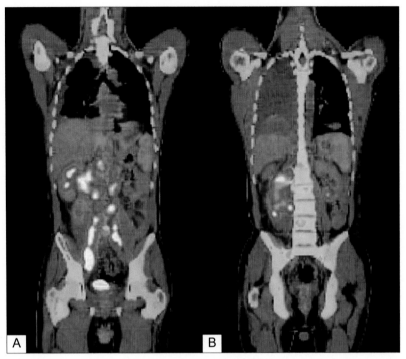

6.19A, B Coronal fluorodeoxyglucose (FDG) PET showing abnormal FDG uptake in lymph nodes above and below the diaphragm as well as a focus within the spleen and bone marrow involvement (lumbar spine and right pelvis). A right pleural effusion is also noted on the CT component. (Courtesy of Professor AV Hoffbrand.)

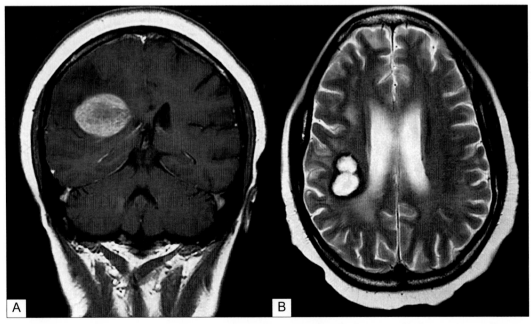

6.20 A: Primary CNS lymphoma in an HIV-positive patient. Coronal MRI. **B**: Primary CNS lymphoma R temporal lobe. Transverse MRI (gadolinium enhanced). (Courtesy of Professor AV Hoffbrand.)

zidovudine), which is associated with a reduction in opportunistic infections, and an outcome similar to that of HIV-negative patients. Increasingly, treatment strategies adopted from regimes for HIV-negative patients (e.g. CHOP, CODOX–M/IVAC, ABVD), with or without rituximab, are being used for ARL.

Primary CNS lymphoma (PCNSL)

PCNSL (**6.20A, B**) is with toxoplasmosis the commonest cause of a CNS lesion in HIV-infected persons, and they are often clinically indistinguishable. Both occur in severe immune deficiency (CD4 count <50/mm³) and present radiologically as solitary or multiple ring-enhancing lesions. The presence of Epstein–Barr virus (EBV) DNA in the cerebrospinal fluid (CSF), and uptake in a single photon emission computed tomography (SPECT) scan is highly suggestive of PCNSL. Similarly to DLBCL, regimes used in the HIV-negative patient have been adopted in combination with HAART with some success (e.g. high dose methotrexate-containing regimes).

Hodgkin's lymphoma

Similarly to NHL, the incidence of Hodgkin's lymphoma (**6.21**) is increased in HIV-infected persons in comparison to HIV-negative individuals. Again, EBV appears to be involved in the pathogenesis, and EBV DNA can be detected in lymphoma tissue. Treatment regimes are adapted from those used in the HIV-negative individual.

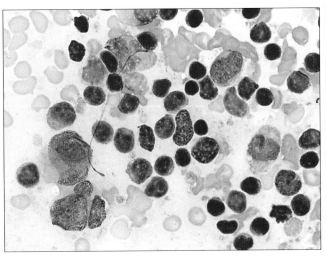

6.21 Hodgkin's Reed–Sternberg cell. BMA H&E ×600.

Stem cell transplantation

Improvements in the immune function and haematological reserves of patients treated with HAART (*Table 6.5*), and better supportive care, have resulted in the feasibility of high-dose chemotherapy and subsequent haematopoietic stem cell transplantation (HSCT). In a recently published large retrospective study, results of HSCT as treatment for relapsed lymphoma in HIV-positive patients were similar to those achieved in the HIV-negative patient.

Table 6.5 Impact of HAART therapy: improved outcome of HIV-associated lymphoma

- Higher CD4 count at presentation

- Decrease in extranodal disease

- Improved bone marrow reserve

Leads to:

- Reduction in opportunistic infections

- Reduction in lymphoma-related deaths

- Fewer HIV-related complications

Multicentric Castleman's disease

Multicentric Castleman's disease (MCD) is a rare lymphoproliferative disorder of plasmablastic cells arising from B-cell follicles (**6.22A**). Their progressive expansion marks the transformation into lymphoma. Human herpesvirus-8 (HHV-8) has been identified in all cases of HIV-associated MCD (**6.22B**) and many of the clinical features can be explained by its presence. HHV-8 encodes a viral homologue of interleukin-6 (vIL-6) and it is hypothesized that activation of the IL-6 signalling pathway by HHV-8 vIL-6 may transform naïve B-cells into plasmablasts and lead to lymphoproliferative diseases such as MCD.

Patients with MCD often present with generalized malaise, night sweats, rigors, fever, anorexia, and weight loss. Typical features include cytopenias, polylymphadenopathy, and multiorgan involvement (*Table 6.6*). An aggressive clinical course is not unusual and not only is MCD itself potentially fatal due to organ failure but it is also associated with an increased incidence of high-grade NHL. The haemato-oncologist should be involved for appropriate staging investigations (bone marrow biopsy, CSF sampling, CT scan, CT-PET scan) and treatment.

MCD is a relapsing and remitting disease. As MCD is rare, the prognosis is not well established. The effect of HAART on incidence and prognosis is also unclear. There are no standard treatments for MCD. Randomized trials have not been conducted on account of the infrequency of the diagnosis, and often only case reports exist.

Potential treatment options are outlined in *Table 6.7*. As recurrence is commonly observed on cessation of therapy, maintenance treatment with a number of agents has been advocated. Recently, the monocloncal antibody rituximab has been shown to induce an impressive clinical, biochemical, and radiological response in case reports and cohorts of patients with HIV-related MCD. Its main adverse event is reactivation of Kaposi's sarcoma.

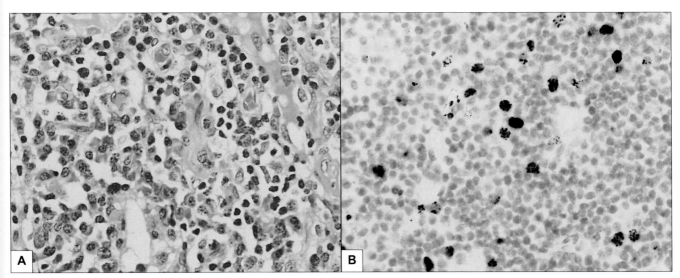

6.22 A: Castleman's disease. H&E ×400 LN. **B**: Castleman's disease. HHV-8 immunostaining ×400 lymph node.

Table 6.6 Clinical suspicion and diagnosis of MCD

Clinical features	
Systemic symptoms:	Fevers, night sweats, malaise, weight loss
Clinical examination:	Multifocal lymphadenopathy
	Hepatosplenomegaly, ascites, oedema, effusions
	Polyneuropathies, leptomeningeal and CNS infiltration
	POEMS syndrome (polyneuropathy, organomegaly, endocrinopathy, monoclonal gammopathy, and skin changes)
Laboratory investigations	
Cytopenias	Anaemia, autoimmune haemolytic anaemia, thrombocytopenia
Biochemistry	Hypoalbuminaemia
	Raised serum C-reactive protein
	Polyclonal hypergammaglobulinaemia
Virology	Raised plasma HHV-8 DNA level
Definitive diagnosis	
Histology:	Lymph node biopsy (or splenectomy)
	Typically plasma cell variant
	Interfollicular plasmablasts (express HHV-8 latent nuclear antigen)
	λ-light-chain restricted IgM (but polyclonal)
Staging	CT scan of neck, chest, abdomen, and pelvis
	Bone marrow aspirate and trephine (if indicated)
	FDG-PET scan (role not established)

Table 6.7 Treatment schedules in MCD

Immunotherapy	
Rituximab	Effective as 1st-line, salvage, and as re-induction treatment
Interferon alpha (IFN-α)	Alone, or in combination with other agents
Chemotherapy	
Single agent	Vinblastine, etoposide
Combination chemotherapy	CHOP (cyclophosphamide, doxorubicin, vincristine, prednisolone)
Thalidomide	
HAART	Usually in combination with cytotoxic chemotherapy
Antiviral	Ganciclovir, foscarnet, cidofovir
Monoclonal anti-IL-6	Produces temporary resolution of symptoms and signs
Surgical	Splenectomy (disease debulking, usually temporary resolution)

Further reading

Bower M, Powles T, *et al.* Brief communication: rituximab in HIV-associated multicentric Castleman disease. *Ann Intern Med* 2007;**147**(12):836–9.

Diez-Martin JL, Balsalobre P, *et al.* Comparable survival between HIV positive and HIV negative non-Hodgkin and Hodgkin lymphoma patients undergoing autologous peripheral blood stem cell transplantation. *Blood* 2009;**113**(23):6011–14.

Kaplan L, Lee DJY, *et al.* Rituximab does not improve clinical outcome in a randomized phase 3 trial of CHOP with or without rituximab in patients with HIV-associated non-Hodgkin lymphoma: AIDS-Malignancies Consortium Trial 010. *Blood* 2005;**106**(5):1538–43.

Matthews GV, Bower M, *et al.* Changes in acquired immunodeficiency syndrome-related lymphoma since the introduction of highly active antiretroviral therapy. *Blood* 2000;**96**(8):2730–4.

Oksenhendler E, Boulanger E, *et al.* High incidence of Kaposi sarcoma-associated herpesvirus-related non-Hodgkin lymphoma in patients with HIV infection and multicentric Castleman disease. *Blood* 2002;**99**(7):2331–6.

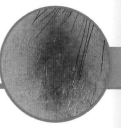

Chapter 7

Reproduction and prevention

HIV and pregnancy

R Shah and TW Mahungu

Introduction

Women now make up the fastest growing group of HIV-infected patients globally. They account for nearly 50% of people living with HIV worldwide and up to 60% of people living with HIV in sub-Saharan Africa. The reasons for this growing tide of infection are multifactorial. Gender inequality remains the key driver of the epidemic. This is further confounded by socioeconomic factors, such as poverty and a lack of adequate education. It was thought that women were also biologically more susceptible to HIV infection as vaginal mucosa was more readily exposed to infected seminal fluid[1,2], but more recent data have suggested that there may now be less increased risk of HIV transmission from man to women than initially thought. A meta-analysis of studies of the risk of HIV transmission during heterosexual sex have found that, in high-income countries prior to the introduction of combination therapy, the risk per sexual act was 0.04% if the female partner was HIV-positive, and 0.08% when the male partner was HIV-positive[3]. However, these rates were considerably higher in lower-income countries, if the HIV-positive partner was in either very early or late stage of HIV infection or had genital ulcer disease[4]. Recent data also suggest that genital viral load is independently associated with the risk of transmission. The Partner study and others, has suggested that there may now be less increased risk of HIV transmission from man to women than initially thought[5].

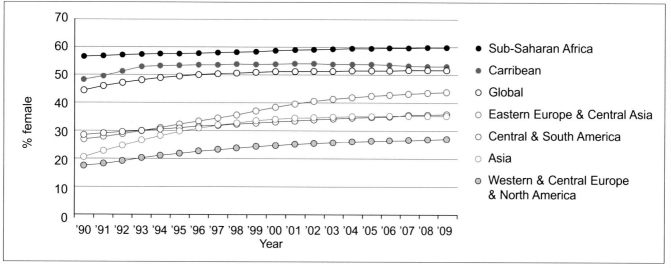

7.1 Percentage of HIV infected adults (15 years and above) who are female. (Adapted from UNAIDS data, 2010.)

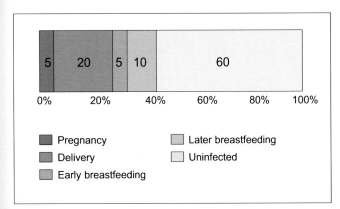

7.2 Mother-to-child transmission of HIV in the absence of intervention. (Adapted from Stringer J, *et al., CROI* 2009.)

Mother-to-child transmission of HIV

The risk of mother-to-child transmission without any intervention is 15–25% in nonbreastfeeding women and 25–40% in breastfeeding mothers. Transmission can occur at all three stages of pregnancy as is illustrated in Figure **7.**2.

Transmission is also increased by a number of other factors (*Table 7.1*).

Early intervention significantly reduces the risk of mother-to-child transmission from 25–35% to less than 1% if the pregnancy is managed in an expert setting (*Table 7.2*).

In the UK, data from the HPA shows a decrease in the proportion of HIV infection in exposed infants from 12% in 1999 to less than 3% in 2008 (**7.3**).

Reducing the risk of mother-to-child transmission
Antenatal screening
All women should be offered an HIV test at time of presentation to antenatal care. If women opt out of HIV testing, those who are considered at risk of HIV seroconversion or from communities with high prevalence rates should be re-offered testing in the third trimester. The regulations, laws, and policies of HIV screening of pregnant women vary worldwide.

The advantages of antenatal screening include:
- Early treatment of mother.
- Decreased risk of onward transmission to child and sexual partner.
- An opportunity to discuss future family planning issues.

The difference in prevalence rates by gender is particularly disproportionate in 15–24-year-olds in sub-Saharan Africa, where there is a growing epidemic among young women of childbearing age (**7.1**). Naturally, many of these women proceed to become mothers. Globally, of the estimated 370,000 children infected with HIV in 2007, a significant proportion acquired their infection through mother-to-child transmission.

Unlinked anonymous sero-surveillance revealed a 0.21% prevalence of HIV infection in pregnant women in the UK in 2008. The highest prevalence rates were in London and in women from sub-Saharan Africa. Although an increase in HIV prevalence in UK-born women giving birth has been observed over the last 10 years, prevalence in the last 5 years has remained stable; between 0.04% and 0.05%.

Table 7.1 Risk factors for mother-to-child transmission of HIV infection

Antepartum	*Intrapartum*	*Postpartum*
High maternal HIV viral load	Cervicovaginal HIV viral load	Breastfeeding
Low maternal CD4 count	Mode of delivery	Premature delivery
AIDS-defining illness	Prolonged rupture of membranes	
Maternal intravenous drug use		
Co-infection with:	Invasive procedures:	
Hepatitis C	Amniocentesis	
CMV	Foetal monitoring	
Bacterial vaginosis	Instrumental delivery	

- If negative an opportunity to discuss risk prevention strategies, including partner testing.

In the UK, universal antenatal testing has resulted in a higher uptake of HIV testing in women. Most antenatal clinics report uptake of >90%. After testing HIV positive, it is essential that a multidisciplinary approach is taken in the management of the pregnant woman. At the first visit to the antenatal HIV clinic, the following should be performed:
- HIV viral load and genotype, CD4 count.
- Serology for syphilis, hepatitis B, hepatitis C.
- Sexually transmitted infection (STI) screen.
- Discussion about disclosure to partner and testing of partner and other children.
- Discussion of personal wishes regarding mode of delivery.
- Discussion about measures to prevent transmission to the child.

All mothers should be given a *Birth Care Plan* denoting the mode of delivery, antiretroviral treatment (ART), baby's treatment, and full contact details for emergency admissions. This should be updated at each antenatal visit and finalized at 36 weeks. Managing HIV infection in pregnancy requires coordination and effective communication between all members of a multidisciplinary team, which should consist of an obstetrician with a special interest in HIV, a paediatrician, an HIV physician, and a specialist midwife.

Table 7.2 Interventions reducing the risk of mother-to-child transmission of HIV

Intervention	Risk reduction
Antenatal testing	25–30%
Antenatal antiretrovirals	
Elective caesarean section (ECS), or Spontaneous vaginal delivery (if on HAART and HIV viral load <50 copies/ml)	
Neonatal antiretrovirals	
Avoidance of breastfeeding	<1%

Antiretrovirals in pregnancy

Antiretrovirals (ARVs) have an important role in reducing mother-to-child transmission of HIV. The PACTG 076 study was a randomized, double blind, placebo-controlled trial where ARV-naïve, HIV-infected, pregnant women of between 14 and 34 week's gestation received zidovudine (AZT). AZT was administered to the mother antepartum (100 mg five times daily) and intrapartum (intravenous AZT during delivery) and the newborn received AZT

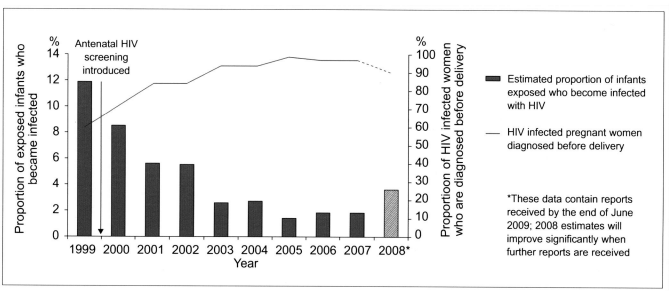

7.3 Estimated proportion of HIV-infected mothers diagnosed before delivery and of exposed infants becoming infected with HIV (in England and Scotland). (Adapted from HPA data 2010.)

monotherapy for 6 weeks. Mothers in the AZT arm had a 67% reduction in mother-to-child transmission when compared to the placebo arm (*7*.*4*, *Table 7.3*). Transmission was highest in mothers with higher HIV viral loads. This marked reduction in transmission is thought to be as a result of the combined effect of:

- Decreasing the maternal HIV viral load.
- Pre-exposure prophylaxis of infant.
- Post-exposure prophylaxis of infant.

The British HIV Association Guidelines for the management of HIV in pregnancy are presented in *Table 7.4*.

What to give when

HAART can be prescribed between 20 and 24/40 if the:

- Mother requires treatment for herself.
- Maternal HIV viral load is greater than 100,000 copies/ml.

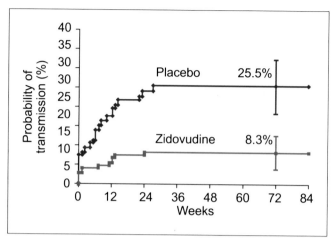

7.4 Probability of mother-to-child transmission in PACTG 076 study. (Adapted from Connor EM, *et al. New Engl J Med* 1994;**331**:1173–80.)

Table 7.3 Mother-to-child transmission by maternal HIV viral load (PACTG 076)

Maternal HIV RNA (copies/ml)	Mother-to-child transmission rate (%)	
	AZT arm	Placebo arm
≤1,730	2.5	7.1
1,731–5,660	7.5	26.2
5,661–15,700	5.9	17.8
>15,700	13.3	41.7

Table 7.4 British HIV Association Guidelines for the management of HIV in pregnancy

CD4 count <250–300 cells/mm³	CD4 count >250–350 cells/mm³	
Commence HAART after first trimester (earlier if mother needs it)	If NVD desired +/- HIV viral load >10,000 copies/ml	If HIV viral load <10,000 copies/ml
AZT + 3TC + boosted PI	HAART (with boosted PI & AZT) by 26/40 (but can be considered earlier)	AZT before 30/40 + ECS
Nevirapine + NRTIs may be be considered if CD4 <250 cells/mm³	If HIV viral load >100,000 copies/ml start HAART between 20 and 24/40	

- Maternal HIV genotype/phenotype is suggestive of drug resistance.
- Mother wishes to have a normal vaginal delivery.

Zidovudine (AZT) monotherapy at a dose of 250 mg bid can be prescribed before 30/40 if the:
- Mother does not require ART for her own health.
- Maternal HIV viral load is consistently below 10,000 copies/ml.
- Mother has wild type HIV virus.
- Mother consents to an elective caesarean section (ECS).

Short term HAART (START) can be prescribed if the mother does not require treatment for herself but wishes to have a normal vaginal delivery. If possible, AZT should be included in the regimen and started between 20 and 28 weeks (20–24 weeks if HIV viral load [VL] is >100,000 copies/ml). Commencing START prior to foetal viability (24 weeks) may be prudent. Treatment is discontinued after delivery, ideally when HIV VL is less than 50 copies/ml. Discontinuation of the constituent ARVs may need to be staggered if non-nucleoside reverse transcriptase inhibitors (NNRTIs) are included. Recent data also suggest the following:

- Women with HIV VL >10,000 should commence START by 24 weeks.
- Women with HIV VL >100,000 should commence START without delay.
- If HIV VL <10,000 START may be deferred to 26 weeks.
- If HIV VL >10,000 NNRTI-based HAART where appropriate may be successful.

HAART commenced preconception should normally be continued throughout the pregnancy, although changes may need to be considered on a case by case basis.

USA recommended ARVs are presented in *Table 7.5*.

Table 7.5 Recommended antiretrovirals (United States Department of Health and Human Services)

	PIs	NNRTIs	NRTIs	New agents
Recommended	Lopinavir/r[6] (C)	Nevirapine[4] (B)	Lamivudine (C)	Zidovudine[2] (C)
Alternative	Atazanavir/r (B) Indinavir/r (C) Nelfinavir (B) Saquinavir/r (B)		Abacavir (C) Didanosine[1] (B) Emtricitabine (B) Stavudine[1,2] (C) Tenofovir[3] (B)	
Insufficient data	Darunavir/r (C) Fosamprenavir/r (C) Tirpanavir/r (C)	Etravirine (B)	Enfuvirtide (B)	Maraviroc (B) Raltegravir (C)
Not recommended		Efavirenz[5] (D)		

1 DDI should not be used with stavudine unless no other alternatives are available.
2 Stavudine should not be used with zidovudine due to potential antagonism.
3 Tenofovir has limited data in pregnancy and so should only be used after careful consideration of other alternatives.
4 Nevirapine should be initiated in pregnant women with CD4 counts >250 cells/mm^3 only if benefit clearly outweighs risk, due to the increased risk of potentially life-threatening hepatotoxicity in women with high CD4 counts. Women who enter pregnancy on nevirapine regimens and are tolerating them well may continue therapy, regardless of CD4 count.
5 Use of efavirenz should be avoided in the first trimester. Use after the first trimester can be considered if, after consideration of other alternatives, this is the best choice for a specific woman. If efavirenz is to be continued postpartum, adequate contraception must be assured.
6 Low lopinavir levels have been noted during the third trimester, consider TDM. Avoid once-daily dosing.
Food and Drug Administration Pregnancy Categories:
A: Adequate and well-controlled studies of pregnant women fail to demonstrate a risk to the foetus during the first trimester of pregnancy (and no evidence exists of risk during later trimesters).
B: Animal reproduction studies fail to demonstrate a risk to the foetus, and adequate but well-controlled studies of pregnant women have not been conducted.
C: Safety in human pregnancy has not been determined; animal studies are either positive for foetal risk or have not been conducted, and the drug should not be used unless the potential benefit outweighs the potential risk to the foetus.
D: Positive evidence of human foetal risk that is based on adverse reaction data from investigational or marketing experiences, but the potential benefits from the use of the drug among pregnant women might be acceptable despite its potential risks.

Antiretroviral toxicity

Foetal toxicity

All pregnancies should be recorded prospectively in The Antiretroviral Pregnancy Registry (www.apregnancy.com). The purpose of this global, voluntary registry is to provide early signals of major teratogenicity involving ARVs to which pregnant women are exposed. Estimates are compared to the background rate of birth defects in the general population, which is approximately 3%. The registry supplements its database with data from animal, clinical, and epidemiological studies. The success of this registry is highly dependent on the participation of health professionals involved in the care of pregnant HIV-infected mothers and their offspring.

Efavirenz is classed as an FDA category D drug in view of potential neural birth defects based on anecdotal, retrospective data in humans and neural tube defects in pre-clinical primate studies. In view of this, efavirenz is not recommended as a first-line choice in pregnant women. However it should be noted that current APR data do not indicate any increase in congenital malformations in humans with first-trimester exposure to most ARVs including efavirenz.

Maternal toxicity

It is important to monitor all pregnant women regularly for signs and symptoms suggestive of potential toxicity[5] (Table 7.6). This should include regular monitoring of their glucose levels and liver function tests. There are conflicting data on the impact of ART on adverse pregnancy outcomes such as stillbirth, spontaneous abortion, intrauterine growth retardation, and an increased risk of premature delivery. Concerns about the clinical consequences of premature births and other adverse outcomes must be balanced against the considerable benefits of HAART in reducing mother-to-child transmission (MTCT).

Drug resistance is uncommon in pregnant women with low HIV viral loads taking zidovudine monotherapy.

Pharmacokinetics of antiretroviral drugs during pregnancy

Physiological changes during pregnancy may affect the absorption, distribution, metabolism, and elimination of ARVs. A number of studies have shown that drug levels may be affected during pregnancy. The current recommendation in the BHIVA Guidelines is for pregnant women to receive recommended adult doses. Therapeutic drug monitoring (TDM) is recommended for protease inhibitors and all new agents once patients reach steady state and are in the third trimester.

Obstetric management of pregnancy

Monitoring women during pregnancy is important:
- To provide regular HIV VL estimations (at least every 3 months and at week 36, if stable).
- To perform resistance tests in women with suboptimal suppression or virological rebound.
- To monitor regularly for ARV adverse events and obstetric complications.
- Ultrasound scans are recommended in the:
- *First trimester* to confirm gestational age and estimate timing of ECS.
- *Second trimester* to assess foetal anomaly.
- Folic acid should be continued for the duration of pregnancy (NB especially if on co-tramazole prophylaxis).

Table 7.6 Maternal toxicity of antiretroviral therapy

Drugs	Toxicity
NRTIs	Zidovudine may result in anaemia D4T and DDI may result in lactic acidosis
NNRTIs	Potential risk of hepatotoxicity in women with CD4 counts greater than 250 cells/mm^3 (especially after dose escalation)
PIs	Possible increased risk of gestational diabetes in the third trimester Possible increased risk of pre-eclampsia Possible increased risk of hepatotoxicity

- All obstetric procedures should ideally be avoided. If amniocentesis is required, it should be done under ARV cover. If available, nuchal translucency scans can replace invasive pre-natal screening for Down's syndrome.

Mode of delivery

Modes of delivery should be discussed with the obstetrician, HIV physician, and the mother-to-be. An informed decision must take into account the maternal HIV VL, data on mode of delivery, future pregnancy plans, the efficacy of ARVs, and the wishes of the mother.

The European Mode of Delivery Trial showed that ECS before rupture of membranes was consistently associated with a decrease in mother-to-child transmission. The combination of ARVs and an ECS further reduced the risk 12-fold. However, increasingly, *vaginal delivery* is an option for a woman on HAART and with an HIV VL of <50 copies/ml at the time of delivery.

ECS

An ECS is indicated in late-presenting mothers not on ARVs at the time of delivery or mothers who remain viraemic despite therapy at the time of delivery. It is also indicated in all women on ARV monotherapy and should be considered in mothers co-infected with hepatitis C. If mothers are on AZT monotherapy and their HIV VL is <50 copies/ml, the ECS should be at 38/40. If they are on HAART and their HIV VL is <50 copies/ml, the ECS should be at 39/40.

Spontaneous vaginal delivery

Spontaneous vaginal delivery (SVD) is an option for women on HAART with an HIV VL of <50 copies/ml. Vaginal delivery can also be considered after previous ECS, if there are no other obstetric contraindications.

- Avoid obstetric interventions such as amniocentesis pre delivery or procedures during the delivery, e.g. forceps/vacuum extractions, scalp electrodes as there is risk of foetal exposure to infected maternal blood – unless obstetrically indicated and duration is expected to be short.
- Induction of labour is also ideally to be avoided. However, if the woman is very keen for SVD and her HIV VL is <50 copies/ml, is on optimum treatment, and has a favourable cervix, induction may be considered. Women who have not delivered by 41 weeks should be booked for an ECS.

Intravenous AZT should be administered to the mother during delivery if the:

- Mother is on AZT monotherapy.
- Maternal HIV viral load remains detectable despite HAART.
- Mother presents late or has a premature delivery.

The recommended dose is 2 mg/kg over the first hour then 1 mg/hr every hour until the cord is cut.

Postpartum management of the neonate and the mother

Effective communication and coordination between members of all three specialities (HIV physicians, obstetricians, and paediatricians) and the HIV specialist pharmacist are essential once the baby is delivered.

Neonatal care

A further 4 weeks of treatment is given to the infant after birth in order to reduce the risk of mother-to-child transmission further. Most infants are given AZT syrup (2 mg/kg qds) for 4 weeks. This should be started within 4 hours of birth. Alternate regimens can be considered if the mother is resistant to AZT. This should be discussed with the HIV physician, paediatrician, and pharmacist.

HAART should be given as post-exposure prophylaxis (PEP) to babies if:

- They are born to untreated or late-presenting women.
- Mothers have detectable viraemia despite treatment.
- There is an unplanned delivery, e.g. prior to starting ARVs.

Premature delivery

Infants born before 30–32 weeks will not be able to feed orally for the first few days of life, therefore where possible, it is important to load the infant's ART via the mother. Options include a stat dose of nevirapine given 2 hours before delivery. Tenofovir may also have a role. Once the baby is born, intravenous AZT should be administered until oral feeding is established.

Breastfeeding

Breastfeeding is an important route of HIV transmission globally. Mothers should be advised that, although ARVs are likely to reduce free virus in the plasma and cell-associated virus in breast milk, the presence of HIV-1 DNA remains unaffected and may therefore constitute a transmission risk.

There are randomized controlled trials of breastfeeding in HIV-positive mothers on combination ARV currently under way in a number of African countries. Based on the growing body of data, the WHO recently reviewed its guidelines and now recommends that HIV-positive mothers or their infants take ARVs while breastfeeding to prevent HIV transmission. The WHO also recommends breastfeeding until 12 months of age, provided the HIV-positive mother or baby is taking ARVs during that period.

Breastfeeding is currently not recommended in HIV-positive mothers in the UK and USA. In the UK both BHIVA and CHIVA are re-evaluating their guidance but currently recommend that: 'HIV-positive mothers should refrain from breast-feeding from birth regardless of maternal HIV viral load or antiretroviral therapy'.

Post-partum management of the mother

Before discharge the following should be considered:

- Carbergoline 1 mg stat within 24 hrs of birth should be prescribed to suppress lactation.
- The importance of avoiding breastfeeding should be re-emphasized.
- Contraceptive methods should be discussed prior to discharge and at subsequent visits.
- Pre-discharge the mother should have enough HAART provided, if continuing her medications.

Follow-up appointments with her HIV specialist and paediatrics should also be made.

Psychosocial support

It is important to consider and be sensitive to the psychosocial issues surrounding pregnancy and HIV throughout and after the pregnancy. While mothers should be encouraged to disclose their status to their partners, it is important to remember that this often takes time and that disclosure can lead to adverse outcomes for some women, e.g. violence or being made homeless. It is also important for the clinician to be mindful of the fact that women diagnosed in the antenatal period often have to go through an intense period of adjustment in a comparatively short space of time, so support networks both in and out of the hospital setting should be available where possible.

Infant testing

Babies will be HIV antibody positive at birth as they carry maternal antibodies in their circulation. An HIV-positive diagnosis is therefore made on the basis of a positive HIV RNA polymerase chain reaction (PCR) test. Primers known to amplify maternal virus must be used so a sample of maternal blood must accompany the first infant sample. HIV viral RNA PCR testing is performed at:

- *Birth*: A negative HIV test at birth may be misleading if the mother is on treatment.
- *At 6 weeks*: The sensitivity of HIV DNA/RNA PCR tests increases once the baby is off therapy.
- *At 3 months*: The VL at 3 months is highly predictive of infection status (if not breastfeeding).
- The final test should be an HIV antibody test at 18 months.

Special considerations
HIV-2

- If HIV-2 VL is <50 copies/ml, intervention may be unnecessary and vaginal delivery may be an option.
- If HIV-2 VL is detectable, PI-based HAART is recommended.
- Do not prescribe AZT monotherapy.
- Avoid breastfeeding.

Hepatitis B virus (HBV)

- Transmission rates range from 40% (in mothers who are HBeAg negative) to 90% (in mothers who are HBeAg positive).
- Infants born to HBsAg- and HBeAg-positive mothers should receive HBV vaccination as well as hepatitis B immunoglobulin.
- ART for pregnant women with HBV co-infection should include drugs with activity against HBV.

Hepatitis C virus (HCV)

- Transmission rates are 15% (higher in mothers who are HCV viraemic).
- Mothers should be treated with HAART and an ECS considered.

Conclusion

HIV in pregnancy can be challenging with complex issues to deal with in a comparatively short space of time. It is therefore important that all involved in the care of the mother and baby do their utmost to ensure that the pregnancy is a normal, happy, and rewarding experience with the ultimate goal of a healthy HIV-negative baby.

References

1 Gray RH, Wawer MJ, Brookmeyer R. Probability of HIV-1 transmission per coital act in monogamous heterosexual, HIV-1 discordant couples in Rakai, Uganda. *Lancet* 2001;**357**:1149-53.

2 Nicolosi A, Leite MLC, Musicco M, *et al.* The efficacy of male-to-female and female-to-male transmission of the human immunodeficiency virus: a study of 730 stable couples. *Epidemiology* 1994;**5**(6).

3 Boily MC, Baggaley RF, Wang L, *et al.* Heterosexual risk of HIV-1 infection per sexual act: A systematic review and meta-analysis of observational studies. *Lancet Infect Dis* 2009;**9**:118–29.

4 Baeten J, *et al. Genital HIV-1 RNA Levels Predict Risk of Heterosexual HIV-1 Transmission.* Eighteenth Conference on Retroviruses and Opportunistic Infections, Boston, 2011, abstract 154.

5 Lorenzi P, Spicher VM, Laubereau B, *et al.* Antiretroviral therapies in pregnancy: maternal, fetal and neonatal effects. Swiss HIV Cohort Study, the Swiss Collaborative HIV and Pregnancy Study, and the Swiss Neonatal HIV Study. *AIDS* 1998 Dec 24;**12**(18):F241–F247.

Further reading

Report on the global AIDS epidemic 2008. UNAIDS.

Guidelines on HIV and infant feeding 2010. Principles and recommendations for infant feeding in the context of HIV and a summary of evidence (WHO, UNAIDS, UNFPA, UNICEF). Available at: http://www.who.int/

HIV in the United Kingdom: 2010 report. Health Protection Agency. Available at: http://www.hpa.org.uk/

Centers for Disease Control and Prevention (CDC). Revised Recommendations for HIV testing of adults, adolescents, and pregnant women in health-care settings. *MMWR Morb Mortal Wkly Rep* 2006;55(RR14):1–17. Available at: http://www.cdc.gov/mmwr/preview/mmwrhtml/rr5514a1.htm

Panel on Treatment of HIV-Infected Pregnant Women and Prevention of Perinatal Transmission. Recommendations for Use of Antiretroviral Drugs in Pregnant HIV-1-Infected Women for Maternal Health and Interventions to Reduce Perinatal HIV Transmission in the United States. May 24, 2010; pp 1-117. Available at http://aidsinfo.nih.gov/ContentFiles/PerinatalGL.pdf.

National Study of HIV in Pregnancy and Childhood (NSHPC) (www.nshpc.ucl.ac.uk).

The Antiretroviral Pregnancy Registry (www.apregistry.com).

Joint United Nations Programme on HIV/AIDS (UNAIDS). 2010 report on the global AIDS epidemic. Available at: http://www.unaids.org/

Connor EM, Sperling RS, Gelber R, *et al.* Reduction of maternal-infant transmission of human immunodeficiency virus type 1 with zidovudine treatment. Pediatric AIDS Clinical Trials Group Protocol 076 Study Group. *N Engl J Med* 1994 Nov 3;**331**(18):1173–80.

De Ruiter A, Mercey D, Anderson J, *et al.* British HIV Association and Children's HIV Association guidelines for the management of HIV infection in pregnant women. *HIV Medicine* 2008;**9**:452–502.

The European Mode of Delivery Collaboration. Elective caesarean-section versus vaginal delivery in prevention of vertical HIV-1 transmission: a randomised clinical trial. *Lancet* 1999 Mar 27;**353**(9158):1035–9.

Larbalestier N, Mullen J, O'Shea S, *et al.* Drug resistance is uncommon in pregnant women with low viral loads taking zidovudine monotherapy to prevent perinatal HIV transmission. *AIDS* 2003 Dec 5;**17**(18):2665–7.

Read P, Costelloe S, Mullen J, *et al.* New mutations associated with resistance not detected following zidovudine monotherapy in pregnancy when used in accordance with British HIV Association guidelines. *HIV Med* 2008 Aug;**9**(7):448–51.

Roustit M, Jlaiel M, Leclercq P, Stanke-Labesque F. Pharmacokinetics and therapeutic drug monitoring of antiretrovirals in pregnant women. *Br J Clin Pharmacol* 2008 Aug;**66**(2):179–95.

Townsend CL, Cortina-Borja M, Peckham CS, Tookey PA. Antiretroviral therapy and premature delivery in diagnosed HIV-infected women in the United Kingdom and Ireland. *AIDS* 2007 May 11;**21**(8):1019–26.

Townsend CL, Cortina-Borja M, Peckham CS, de Ruiter A, Lyall H, Tookey PA. Low rates of mother-to-child transmission of HIV following effective pregnancy interventions in the United Kingdom and Ireland, 2000–2006. *AIDS* 2008 May 11;**22**(8):973–81.

Tuomala RE, Shapiro DE, Mofenson LM, *et al.* Antiretroviral therapy during pregnancy and the risk of an adverse outcome. *N Engl J Med* 2002 Jun 13;**346**(24):1863–70.

Conception in HIV serodiscordant couples

TW Mahungu and R Shah

Horizontal transmission

The probability of horizontal transmission per sexual act:
- Increases with higher HIV VLs.
- Is facilitated by the presence of STIs.
- There is conflicting evidence on whether male to female transmission is higher than female to male transmission.

The risk of horizontal transmission is summarized in *Table 7.7*.

Table 7.7 Risk of horizontal transmission in serodiscordant couples

	Horizontal risk transmission (without intervention)	Options	Horizontal transmission risk (with intervention)
HIV-positive woman + HIV-negative man	0.1–2.0 %* (per sexual act)	Self insemination (If unsuccessful after 6–12 months, consider fertility assessment +/- referral for assisted conception) • Consider timed natural conception if HIV + woman: – Is adherent to antiretroviral therapy – Has had HIV VL <40 copies/ml for at least 6 months** – Is free of STIs	None
HIV-positive man + HIV-negative woman	0.1–2.0 %* (per sexual act)	• Sperm washing followed by either: – Intrauterine insemination – *In-vitro* fertilization – Intracytoplasmic sperm injection • Consider timed natural conception if HIV + man: – Is adherent to antiretroviral therapy – Has had HIV VL <40 copies/ml for at least 6 months** – Is free of STIs	Zero transmission (in published studies)

*Estimates based on studies on monogamous heterosexual couples
**Patients with undetectable HIV VLs in the serum may have detectable HIV RNA in their genital secretions

HIV serodiscordant couples contemplating conception:

- Should receive general as well as comprehensive HIV-related pre-conception counselling (see also HIV and pregnancy). This should include detailed information about all potential methods of conception and the associated risks of horizontal transmission with each option (*Table 7.7*).
- Should undergo regular sexual health screening.
- If the couple are attempting natural conception through timed unprotected sexual intercourse, the HIV-positive partner who is taking HAART should have regular HIV VL estimations.
- Should be advised to have fertility screening if:
- The serodiscordant couple are planning to attempt timed natural conception, or they are requesting referral for sperm washing.
- Their reproductive health history is suggestive of potential sub-fertility (e.g. anovulation, previous pelvic inflammatory disease, or male factor infertility).
- The female partner is over 35 years.
- Self insemination of an HIV-positive female has proved unsuccessful for 6–12 months.

Further reading

Barreiro, *et al.* Reproductive options for HIV-serodiscordant couples. *AIDS Rev* **8**:150–70.

British HIV Association and Children's HIV Association Guidelines for the management of HIV infection in pregnant women. 2008.

Gray, *et al.* Probability of HIV-1 transmission per coital act in monogamous, heterosexual, HIV-1-discordant couples in Rakai, Uganda. *Lancet* **357**:1149–53.

Royce, *et al.* Sexual transmission of HIV. *NEJM* **336**(15):1072–8.

Vernazza, *et al.* Les personnes seropositives ne souff rant d'aucune autre MST et suivant un traitement antiretroviral effi cie ne transmettent pas le VIH par voie sexuelle. *Bull Med Suisses* **89**:165–9.

Post-exposure prophylaxis of HIV infection following sexual and occupational exposure

TW Mahungu and R Shah

Post-exposure prophylaxis

There is great interest in the use of ARVs in the context of post-exposure prophylaxis. The risk of HIV transmission is determined by the *type of exposure* and the *risk that the source is HIV positive*. Transmission can happen in any one of these situations:

- Occupational:
- Needlestick injury.
- Accidental exposure to broken skin or damaged mucosal membranes.
- Sexual:
- Unprotected sexual intercourse.

- Recreational:
- Sharing needles for intravenous drug abuse.
- Iatrogenic:
- Transfusion of contaminated blood or blood products.

Type of exposure

In general, the risk of HIV transmission is higher with direct inoculation of contaminated blood compared to the breach of mucosal membranes. The risk of exposure is further modulated by the amount of virus transferred with the exposure. It is worth noting that HIV is at least 50–100 times less infectious than HBV and at least 10 times less infectious than HCV. The estimated risk of HIV transmission by exposure route is summarized in *Table 7.8*.

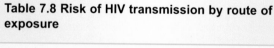

Table 7.8 Risk of HIV transmission by route of exposure

Exposure	Estimated risk of transmission per exposure (%)
Blood transfusion	90–100
Mother to child	30
Anal intercourse	
Receptive	0.1–3.0
Insertive	0.06
Vaginal intercourse	
Receptive	0.1–0.2
Insertive	0.03–0.09
Receptive oral sex (fellatio)	0–0.04
Sharing injecting equipment	0.67
Occupational	
Mucous membrane exposure	0.09
Needlestick injury	0.3

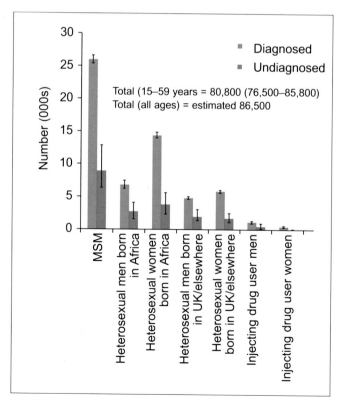

7.5 Estimated number of adults living with HIV infection in the UK in 2010. (Adapted from HPA data.)

Risk that the source is positive

This depends on local HIV prevalence rates by risk groups. HIV prevalence rates by risk groups in the UK are illustrated in Figure 7.5.

Rationale for post-exposure prophylaxis

There is a paucity of robust data on the optimum timing of initiation of post-exposure prophylaxis (PEP). Current guidelines are therefore based on a combination of data from animal models (macaques), mother-to-child transmission studies, and knowledge of the natural history of HIV infection. Pooled together these data suggest that there is a brief period between exposure to HIV and systemic infection during which HIV seroconversion can be interrupted. This period is thought to range between 48 and 72 hours. Data from animal studies suggest that PEP is most efficacious if commenced *within hours* of exposure.

Assessing individuals exposed to HIV infection
Initial assessment of exposure

A detailed history of the exposure should be taken to ascertain how the incident occurred. *Table 7.9* presents the data that need to be established.

Table 7.9 History of exposure

Sexual exposure	Occupational exposure
Date and time of exposure	*Date and time of exposure*
Protection used • Condoms • Gloves	*Protection used* • Gloves • Goggles
Route • Receptive/insertive anal • Receptive/insertive vaginal • Fellatio with/without ejaculation • Cunnilingus	*Route* • Percutaneous injury • Mucous membrane exposure • Contact with nonintact skin • Bite
Agent • Genital secretions • Blood • Saliva	*Agent (including volume and depth of exposure)* • Blood • Blood-stained fluids • Specific fluid (e.g. genital, CSF)
Health of source • HIV status/risk category – If HIV positive: recent CD4 and HIV VL, treatment, resistance tests • Hepatitis B status • Hepatitis C status	*Health of source* • HIV status/risk category – If HIV positive: recent CD4 and HIV VL, treatment, resistance tests • Hepatitis B status • Hepatitis C status
Health of 'exposed' individual • HIV status and risk category – and if on ARVs • Previous history of PEPSE • Hepatitis B and C status	*Health of 'exposed' individual* • HIV status and risk category – and if on ARVs • Previous history of PEP • Hepatitis B and C status

This initial assessment should also include a detailed discussion with the exposed individual explaining the indications, benefits, side-effects, and potential failure of PEP/PEPSE. Hepatitis B vaccination and a sexual health screen should also be considered. If the HIV status of the source individual is unknown, efforts must be made to clarify this as soon as possible.

Following exposure, the exposed site should be washed with soap and water, puncture wounds should be allowed to flow freely, and mucous membranes should be irrigated with water.

BHIVA recommendations for PEPSE after sexual exposure are listed in *Table 7.10*.

Department of Health (UK) recommendations for PEP in healthcare workers and others following occupational exposure are listed in *Table 7.11*.

Recommendations for drug regimens

It is generally accepted that PEP should be initiated as soon as possible (within 72 hours of exposure) and *administered for a duration of 4 weeks*. The evidence supporting timing of initiation and duration of prophylaxis is somewhat sparse.

As combination therapy with three drugs is more effective than mono- or dual-therapy in established infection, the recommendation in most guidelines is to use *two nucleosides* and a PI. As AZT is the only drug that has been studied and shown to reduce post-exposure infection (occupational), Combivir tends to be the most frequently prescribed nucleoside backbone. However, as AZT is poorly tolerated, the recommended regimen for PEP starter packs is:

Truvada (245 mg tenofovir/200 mg emtricitabine) one tablet once a day.

Kaletra (200 mg lopinavir/50 mg ritonavir) two tablets twice a day.

Table 7.10 BHIVA recommendations for PEPSE following sexual exposure

Source patient is HIV positive

PEPSE recommended after	Consider PEPSE after	PEPSE not recommended after
Insertive vaginal sex	Fellatio with ejaculation	Fellatio (no ejaculation)
Receptive vaginal sex	Semen splash to eye	Cunnilingus
Insertive anal sex		
Receptive anal sex		

Source patient is from a high-risk group or area of high HIV prevalence

PEPSE recommended after	Consider PEPSE after
Receptive anal sex	Insertive vaginal sex
	Receptive vaginal sex
	Insertive anal sex
	Fellatio with ejaculation

Source patient NOT from a high-risk group or area of high HIV prevalence

	Consider PEPSE after	PEPSE not recommended after
	Receptive anal sex	Insertive vaginal sex
		Receptive vaginal sex
		Insertive anal sex
		Fellatio with ejaculation

Abacavir, nevirapine, and efavirenz should be avoided as their toxicity profiles would potentially affect adherence. Individuals receiving PEP/PEPSE should be informed of the possible side-effects of the administered ARVs and be monitored closely, as HIV-negative individuals receiving PEP/PEPSE tend to be less tolerant of the medication in comparison to patients with established HIV infection.

Follow-up

Individuals on PEP/PEPSE should be reviewed at 72 hours as more information on the HIV status of the source and the risk of exposure may be available. The HIV status of the exposed individual may also be available at this point. Over the next 4 weeks, continued follow-up is recommended in order to monitor the tolerability and toxicity of the prescribed ARVs. A follow-up HIV antibody test is recommended 12 weeks after the exposure.

The transmission of HIV is not always prevented. PEP/PEPSE is more likely to fail if it is initiated late and taken over less than 4 weeks. Underlying transmitted drug resistance may also affect the success rates.

Other prevention strategies

Over the past couple of years significant resources have been utilized in the search for both ART and non-ART-based prevention strategies. There is increasing interest in the use of ARVs for *pre-exposure prophylaxis* (PrEP) following promising results from primate studies where tenofovir and emtricitabine were shown to have a protective effect. Results from the CAPRISA 004, a randomized, controlled trial conducted in South Africa, showed that the use of 1% tenofovir vaginal gel (as PrEP/microbicide) reduced the acquisition of HIV by 39%. More recently, the use of oral tenofovir disoproxil fumarate and emtricitabine as PrEP in men who have sex with men was shown to be associated with a 44% reduction in the incidence of HIV infection. Though promising, these findings need to be replicated in different cohorts. Other prevention strategies include:

- **In unexposed individuals:**
- Modification of sexual behaviour.
- Condoms.
- Treatment of STIs.
- Male circumcision.
- Vaccines.
- **In exposed individuals:**
- PrEP.
- Topical microbicides.
- PEP.
- **In infected individuals:**
- Treatment of chronic HIV infection to reduce transmission.

Table 7.11 Department of Health (UK) recommendations for PEP following occupatonal exposure

HIV-positive source

PEP recommended after	Consider PEP after	PEP not recommended after
Percutaneous needlestick injury		Contact with intact skin
Mucous membrane exposure		Contact with urine, saliva
Non-intact skin exposure		

HIV status of source unknown OR source of exposure unknown

PEP recommended after	Consider PEP after*	PEP not recommended after
	Percutaneous needlestick injury	Contact with intact skin
	Mucous membrane exposure	Contact with urine, saliva
	Nonintact skin exposure	

*Consider if source has high risk factors for HIV infection

Further reading

Fisher M, Benn P, Evans B, Pozniak A, Jones M, Maclean S, *et al.* UK Guideline for the use of post-exposure prophylaxis for HIV following sexual exposure. *Int J STD AIDS* 2006 Feb;**17**(2):81–92.

Fox J, Fiddler S. Sexual transmission of HIV-1. *Antiviral Res* 2010 Jan;**85**(1):276–85.

Grant RM. Antiretroviral agents used by HIV-uninfected persons for prevention: pr-e and post-exposure prophylaxis. *Clin Infec Dis* 2010 May 15;**50**(supplement 3):569–101.

Grant RM, *et al.* Pre-exposure chemoprophylaxis for HIV prevention in men who have sex with men. *N Engl J Med* 2010 Dec 30;**363**(27):2587–99.

HIV post-exposure prophylaxis. Guidance from the UK Chief Medical Officers' Expert Advisory Group on AIDS. Department of Health, 2008.

Karim QA, *et al.* Effectiveness and safety of tenofovir gel, an antiretroviral microbicide for the prevention of HIV infection in women. *Science* 2010;**329**(5996):1168–74.

Nicol MR, Kashuba ADM. Pharmacologic opportunities for HIV prevention. *Clin Pharmaco Ther* 2010;**88**(5):598–609.

Paxton LA, Hope T, Jaffe HW. Pre-exposure prophylaxis for HIV infection: what if it works? *Lancet* 2007 Jul 7;**370**(9581):89–93.

Updated US Public Health Service Guidelines for the Management of Occupational Exposures to HBV, HCV, and HIV and Recommendations for Postexposure Prophylaxis. *MMWR Recomm Rep* 2001 Jun 29;**50**(RR-11):1–52.

Index